The Professor

By

Charlotte Brontë

CHAPTER I. INTRODUCTORY.

The other day, in looking over my papers, I found in my desk the following copy of a letter, sent by me a year since to an old school acquaintance:—

"DEAR CHARLES,

"I think when you and I were at Eton together, we were neither of us what could be called popular characters: you were a sarcastic, observant, shrewd, cold-blooded creature; my own portrait I will not attempt to draw, but I cannot recollect that it was a strikingly attractive one—can you? What animal magnetism drew thee and me together I know not; certainly I never experienced anything of the Pylades and Orestes sentiment for you, and I have reason to believe that you, on your part, were equally free from all romantic regard to me. Still, out of school hours we walked and talked continually together; when the theme of conversation was our companions or our masters we understood each other, and when I recurred to some sentiment of affection, some vague love of an excellent or beautiful object, whether in animate or inanimate nature, your sardonic coldness did not move me. I felt myself superior to that check THEN as I do NOW.

"It is a long time since I wrote to you, and a still longer time since I saw you. Chancing to take up a newspaper of your county the other day, my eye fell upon your name. I began to think of old times; to run over the events which have transpired since we separated; and I sat down and commenced this letter. What you have been doing I know not; but you shall hear, if you choose to listen, how the world has wagged with me.

"First, after leaving Eton, I had an interview with my maternal uncles, Lord Tynedale and the Hon. John Seacombe. They asked me if I would enter the Church, and my uncle the nobleman offered me the living of Seacombe, which is in his gift, if I would; then my other uncle, Mr. Seacombe, hinted that when I became rector of Seacombe-cum-Scaife, I might perhaps be allowed to take, as mistress of my house and head of my parish, one of my six cousins, his daughters, all of whom I greatly dislike.

"I declined both the Church and matrimony. A good clergyman is a good thing, but I should have made a very bad one. As to the wife—oh how like a night-mare is the thought of being bound for life to one of my cousins! No doubt they are accomplished and pretty; but not an accomplishment, not a charm of theirs, touches a chord in my bosom. To think of passing the winter evenings by the parlour fire-side of Seacombe Rectory alone with one of them —for instance, the large and well-modelled statue, Sarah—no; I should be a bad husband, under such circumstances, as well as a bad clergyman.

"When I had declined my uncles' offers they asked me 'what I intended to do?' I said I should reflect. They reminded me that I had no fortune, and no expectation of any, and, after a considerable pause, Lord Tynedale demanded sternly, 'Whether I had thoughts of following my father's steps and engaging in trade?' Now, I had had no thoughts of the sort. I do not think that my turn of mind qualifies me to make a good tradesman; my taste, my ambition does not lie in that way; but such was the scorn expressed in Lord Tynedale's countenance as he pronounced the word TRADE—such the contemptuous sarcasm of his tone—that I was instantly decided. My father was but a name to me, yet that name I did not like to hear mentioned with a sneer to my very face. I answered then, with haste and warmth, 'I cannot do better than follow in my father's steps; yes, I will be a tradesman.' My uncles did not remonstrate; they and I parted with mutual disgust. In reviewing this transaction, I find that I was quite right to shake off the burden of Tynedale's patronage, but a fool to offer my shoulders instantly for the reception of another burden—one which might be more intolerable, and which certainly was yet untried.

"I wrote instantly to Edward—you know Edward—my only brother, ten years my senior, married to a rich mill-owner's daughter, and now possessor of the mill and business which was my father's before he failed. You are aware that my father—once reckoned a Croesus of wealth—became bankrupt a short time previous to his death, and that my mother lived in destitution for some six months after him, unhelped by her aristocratical brothers, whom she had mortally offended by her union with Crimsworth, the——shire manufacturer. At the end of the six months she brought me into the world, and then herself left it without, I should think, much regret, as it contained little hope or comfort for her.

"My father's relations took charge of Edward, as they did of me, till I was nine years old. At that period it chanced that the representation of an important borough in our county fell vacant; Mr. Seacombe stood for it. My uncle Crimsworth, an astute mercantile man, took the opportunity of writing a fierce letter to the candidate, stating that if he and Lord Tynedale did not consent to do something towards the support of their sister's orphan children, he would expose their relentless and malignant conduct towards that sister, and do his best to turn the circumstances against Mr. Seacombe's election. That gentleman and Lord T. knew well enough that the Crimsworths were an unscrupulous and determined race; they knew also that they had influence in the borough of X——; and, making a virtue of necessity, they consented to defray the expenses of my education. I was sent to Eton, where I remained ten years, during which space of time Edward and I never met. He, when he grew up, entered into trade, and pursued his calling with such diligence, ability, and success, that now, in his thirtieth year, he was fast making a fortune. Of this I was apprised by the occasional short letters I received from him, some three or four times a year; which said letters never concluded without some expression of determined enmity against the house of Seacombe, and some reproach to me for living, as he said, on the bounty of that house. At first, while still in boyhood, I could not understand why, as I had no parents, I should not be indebted to my uncles Tynedale and Seacombe for my education; but as I grew up, and heard by degrees of the persevering hostility, the hatred till death evinced by them against my father—of the sufferings of my mother—of all the wrongs, in short, of our house—then did I conceive shame of the dependence in which I lived, and form a resolution no more to take bread from hands which had refused to minister to the necessities of my dying mother. It was by these feelings I was influenced when I refused the Rectory of Seacombe, and the union with one of my patrician cousins.

"An irreparable breach thus being effected between my uncles and myself, I wrote to Edward; told him what had occurred, and informed him of my intention to follow his steps and be a tradesman. I asked, moreover, if he could give me employment. His answer expressed no approbation of my conduct, but he said I might come down to ——shire, if I liked, and he would 'see what could be done in the way of furnishing me with work.' I repressed all—even mental comment on his note—packed my trunk and carpet-bag, and started for the North directly.

"After two days' travelling (railroads were not then in existence) I arrived, one wet October afternoon, in the town of X——. I had always understood that Edward lived in this town, but on inquiry I found that it was only Mr. Crimsworth's mill and warehouse which were situated in the smoky atmosphere of Bigben Close; his RESIDENCE lay four miles out, in the country.

"It was late in the evening when I alighted at the gates of the habitation designated to me as my brother's. As I advanced up the avenue, I could see through the shades of twilight, and the dark gloomy mists which deepened those shades, that the house was large, and the grounds surrounding it sufficiently spacious. I paused a moment on the lawn in front, and leaning my back against a tall tree which rose in the centre, I gazed with interest on the exterior of Crimsworth Hall.

"Edward is rich," thought I to myself. 'I believed him to be doing well—but I did not know he was master of a mansion like this.' Cutting short all marvelling; speculation, conjecture, &c., I advanced to the front door and rang. A man-servant opened it—I announced myself—he relieved me of my wet cloak and carpet-bag, and ushered me into a room furnished as a library, where there was a bright fire and candles burning on the table; he informed me that his master was not yet returned from X——market, but that he would certainly be at home in the course of half an hour.

"Being left to myself, I took the stuffed easy chair, covered with red morocco, which stood by the fireside, and while my eyes watched the flames dart from the glowing coals, and the cinders fall at intervals on the hearth, my mind busied itself in conjectures concerning the meeting about to take place. Amidst much that was doubtful in the subject of these conjectures, there was one thing tolerably certain—I was in no danger of encountering severe disappointment; from this, the moderation of my expectations guaranteed me. I anticipated no overflowings of fraternal tenderness; Edward's letters had always been such as to prevent the engendering or harbouring of delusions of this sort. Still, as I sat awaiting his arrival, I felt eager—very eager—I cannot tell you why; my hand, so utterly a stranger to the grasp of a kindred hand, clenched itself to repress the tremor with which impatience would fain have shaken it.

"I thought of my uncles; and as I was engaged in wondering whether Edward's indifference would equal the cold disdain I had always experienced from them, I heard the avenue gates open: wheels approached the house; Mr. Crimsworth was arrived; and after the lapse of some minutes, and a brief dialogue between himself and his servant in the hall, his tread drew near the library door—that tread alone announced the master of the house.

"I still retained some confused recollection of Edward as he was ten years ago—a tall, wiry, raw youth; NOW, as I rose from my seat and turned towards the library door, I saw a fine-looking and powerful man, light-complexioned, well-made, and of athletic proportions; the first glance made me aware of an air of promptitude and sharpness, shown as well in his movements as in his port, his eye, and the general expression of his face. He greeted me with brevity, and, in the moment of shaking hands, scanned me from head to foot; he took his seat in the morocco covered arm-chair, and motioned me to another seat.

"'I expected you would have called at the counting-house in the Close,' said he; and his voice, I noticed, had an abrupt accent, probably habitual to him; he spoke also with a guttural northern tone, which sounded harsh in my ears, accustomed to the silvery utterance of the South.

"'The landlord of the inn, where the coach stopped, directed me here,' said I. 'I doubted at first the accuracy of his information, not being aware that you had such a residence as this.'

"'Oh, it is all right!' he replied, 'only I was kept half an hour behind time, waiting for you—that is all. I thought you must be coming by the eight o'clock coach.'

"I expressed regret that he had had to wait; he made no answer, but stirred the fire, as if to cover a movement of impatience; then he scanned me again.

"I felt an inward satisfaction that I had not, in the first moment of meeting, betrayed any warmth, any enthusiasm; that I had saluted this man with a quiet and steady phlegm.

"'Have you quite broken with Tynedale and Seacombe?' he asked hastily.

"'I do not think I shall have any further communication with them; my refusal of their proposals will, I fancy, operate as a barrier against all future intercourse.'

"'Why,' said he, 'I may as well remind you at the very outset of our connection, that "no man can serve two masters." Acquaintance with Lord Tynedale will be incompatible with assistance from me.' There was a kind of gratuitous menace in his eye as he looked at me in finishing this observation.

"Feeling no disposition to reply to him, I contented myself with an inward speculation on the differences which exist in the constitution of men's minds. I do not know what inference Mr. Crimsworth drew from my silence—whether he considered it a symptom of contumacity or an evidence of my being cowed by his peremptory manner. After a long and hard stare at me, he rose sharply from his seat.

"'To-morrow,' said he, 'I shall call your attention to some other points; but now it is supper time, and Mrs. Crimsworth is probably waiting; will you come?'

"He strode from the room, and I followed. In crossing the hall, I wondered what Mrs. Crimsworth might be. 'Is she,' thought I, 'as alien to what I like as Tynedale, Seacombe, the Misses Seacombe—as the affectionate relative now striding before me? or is she better than these? Shall I, in conversing with her, feel free to show something of my real nature; or—' Further conjectures were arrested by my entrance into the dining-room.

"A lamp, burning under a shade of ground-glass, showed a handsome apartment, wainscoted with oak; supper was laid on the table; by the fire-place, standing as if waiting our entrance, appeared a lady; she was young, tall, and well shaped; her dress was handsome and fashionable: so much my first glance sufficed to ascertain. A gay salutation passed between her and Mr. Crimsworth; she chid him, half playfully, half poutingly, for being late; her voice (I always take voices into the account in judging of character) was lively —it indicated, I thought, good animal spirits. Mr. Crimsworth soon checked her animated scolding with a kiss—a kiss that still told of the bridegroom (they had not yet been married a year); she took her seat at the supper-table in first-rate spirits. Perceiving me, she begged my pardon for not noticing me before, and then shook hands with me, as ladies do when a flow of good-humour disposes them to be cheerful to all, even the most indifferent of their acquaintance. It was now further obvious to me that she had a good complexion, and features sufficiently marked but agreeable; her hair was red—quite red. She and Edward talked much, always in a vein of playful contention; she was vexed, or pretended to be vexed, that he had that day driven a vicious horse in the gig, and he made light of her fears. Sometimes she appealed to me.

"'Now, Mr. William, isn't it absurd in Edward to talk so? He says he will drive Jack, and no other horse, and the brute has thrown him twice already.

"She spoke with a kind of lisp, not disagreeable, but childish. I soon saw also that there was more than girlish—a somewhat infantine expression in her by no means small features; this lisp and expression were, I have no doubt, a charm in Edward's eyes, and would be so to those of most men, but they were not to mine. I sought her eye, desirous to read there the intelligence which I could not discern in her face or hear in her conversation; it was merry, rather small; by turns I saw vivacity, vanity, coquetry, look out through its irid, but I watched in vain for a glimpse of soul. I am no Oriental; white necks, carmine lips and cheeks, clusters of bright curls, do not suffice for me without that Promethean spark which will live after the roses and lilies are faded, the burnished hair grown grey. In sunshine, in prosperity, the flowers are very well; but how many wet days are there in life—November seasons of disaster, when a man's hearth and home would be cold indeed, without the clear, cheering gleam of intellect.

"Having perused the fair page of Mrs. Crimsworth's face, a deep, involuntary sigh announced my disappointment; she took it as a homage to her beauty, and Edward, who was evidently proud of his rich and handsome young wife, threw on me a glance—half ridicule, half ire.

"I turned from them both, and gazing wearily round the room, I saw two pictures set in the oak panelling—one on each side the mantel-piece. Ceasing to take part in the bantering conversation that flowed on between Mr. and Mrs. Crimsworth, I bent my thoughts to the examination of these pictures. They were portraits—a lady and a gentleman, both costumed in the fashion of twenty years ago. The gentleman was in the shade. I could not see him well. The lady had the benefit of a full beam from the softly shaded lamp. I presently recognised her; I had seen this picture before in childhood; it was my mother; that and the companion picture being the only heir-looms saved out of the sale of my father's property.

"The face, I remembered, had pleased me as a boy, but then I did not understand it; now I knew how rare that class of face is in the world, and I appreciated keenly its thoughtful, yet gentle expression. The serious grey eye possessed for me a strong charm, as did certain lines in the features indicative of most true and tender feeling. I was sorry it was only a picture.

"I soon left Mr. and Mrs. Crimsworth to themselves; a servant conducted me to my bed-room; in closing my chamber-door, I shut out all intruders—you, Charles, as well as the rest.

"Good-bye for the present,

"WILLIAM CRIMSWORTH."

To this letter I never got an answer; before my old friend received it, he had accepted a Government appointment in one of the colonies, and was already on his way to the scene of his official labours. What has become of him since, I know not.

The leisure time I have at command, and which I intended to employ for his private benefit, I shall now dedicate to that of the public at large. My narrative is not exciting, and above all, not marvellous; but it may interest some individuals, who, having toiled in the same vocation as myself, will find in my experience frequent reflections of their own. The above letter will serve as an introduction. I now proceed.

CHAPTER II.

A fine October morning succeeded to the foggy evening that had witnessed my first introduction to Crimsworth Hall. I was early up and walking in the large park-like meadow surrounding the house. The autumn sun, rising over the ——shire hills, disclosed a pleasant country; woods brown and mellow varied the fields from which the harvest had been lately carried; a river, gliding between the woods, caught on its surface the somewhat cold gleam of the October sun and sky; at frequent intervals along the banks of the river, tall, cylindrical chimneys, almost like slender round towers, indicated the factories which the trees half concealed; here and there mansions, similar to Crimsworth Hall, occupied agreeable sites on the hill-side; the country wore, on the whole, a cheerful, active, fertile look. Steam, trade, machinery had long banished from it all romance and seclusion. At a distance of five miles, a valley, opening between the low hills, held in its cups the great town of X ——. A dense, permanent vapour brooded over this locality—there lay Edward's "Concern."

I forced my eye to scrutinize this prospect, I forced my mind to dwell on it for a time, and when I found that it communicated no pleasurable emotion to my heart—that it stirred in me none of the hopes a man ought to feel, when he sees laid before him the scene of his life's career—I said to myself, "William, you are a rebel against circumstances; you are a fool, and know not what you want; you have chosen trade and you shall be a tradesman. Look!" I continued mentally—"Look at the sooty smoke in that hollow, and know that there is your post! There you cannot dream, you cannot speculate and theorize—there you shall out and work!"

Thus self-schooled, I returned to the house. My brother was in the breakfast-room. I met him collectedly—I could not meet him cheerfully; he was standing on the rug, his back to the fire—how much did I read in the expression of his eye as my glance encountered his, when I advanced to bid him good morning; how much that was contradictory to my nature! He said "Good morning" abruptly and nodded, and then he snatched, rather than took, a newspaper from the table, and began to read it with the air of a master who seizes a pretext to escape the bore of conversing with an underling. It was well I had taken a resolution to endure for a time, or his manner would have gone far to render insupportable the disgust I had just been endeavouring to subdue. I looked at him: I measured his robust frame and powerful proportions; I saw my own reflection in the mirror over the mantel-piece; I amused myself with comparing the two pictures. In face I resembled him, though I was not so handsome; my features were less regular; I had a darker eye, and a broader brow—in form I was greatly inferior—thinner, slighter, not so tall. As an animal, Edward excelled me far; should he prove as paramount in mind as in person I must be a slave—for I must expect from him no lion-like generosity to one weaker than himself; his cold, avaricious eye, his stern, forbidding manner told me he would not spare. Had I then force of mind to cope with him? I did not know; I had never been tried.

Mrs. Crimsworth's entrance diverted my thoughts for a moment. She looked well, dressed in white, her face and her attire shining in morning and bridal freshness. I addressed her with the degree of ease her last night's careless gaiety seemed to warrant, but she replied with coolness and restraint: her husband had tutored her; she was not to be too familiar with his clerk.

As soon as breakfast was over Mr. Crimsworth intimated to me that they were bringing the gig round to the door, and that in five minutes he should expect me to be ready to go down with him to X——. I did not keep him waiting; we were soon dashing at a rapid rate along the road. The horse he drove was the same vicious animal about which Mrs. Crimsworth had expressed her fears the night before. Once or twice Jack seemed disposed to turn restive, but a vigorous and determined application of the whip from the ruthless hand of his master soon compelled him to submission, and Edward's dilated nostril expressed his triumph in the result of the contest; he scarcely spoke to me during the whole of the brief drive, only opening his lips at intervals to damn his horse.

X—— was all stir and bustle when we entered it; we left the clean streets where there were dwelling-houses and shops, churches, and public buildings; we left all these, and turned down to a region of mills and warehouses; thence we passed through two massive gates into a great paved yard, and we were in Bigben Close, and the mill was before us, vomiting soot from its long chimney, and quivering through its thick brick walls with the commotion of its iron bowels. Workpeople were passing to and fro; a waggon was being laden with pieces. Mr. Crimsworth looked from side to side, and seemed at one glance to comprehend all that was going on; he alighted, and leaving his horse and gig to the care of a man who hastened to take the reins from his hand, he bid me follow him to the counting-house. We entered it; a very different place from the parlours of Crimsworth Hall—a place for business, with a bare, planked floor, a safe, two high desks and stools, and some chairs. A person was seated at one of the desks, who took off his square cap when Mr. Crimsworth entered, and in an instant was again absorbed in his occupation of writing or calculating—I know not which.

Mr. Crimsworth, having removed his mackintosh, sat down by the fire. I remained standing near the hearth; he said presently—

"Steighton, you may leave the room; I have some business to transact with this gentleman. Come back when you hear the bell."

The individual at the desk rose and departed, closing the door as he went out. Mr. Crimsworth stirred the fire, then folded his arms, and sat a moment thinking, his lips compressed, his brow knit. I had nothing to do but to watch him—how well his features were cut! what a handsome man he was! Whence, then, came that air of contraction—that narrow and hard aspect on his forehead, in all his lineaments?

Turning to me he began abruptly:

"You are come down to ——shire to learn to be a tradesman?"

"Yes, I am."

"Have you made up your mind on the point? Let me know that at once."

"Yes."

"Well, I am not bound to help you, but I have a place here vacant, if you are qualified for it. I will take you on trial. What can you do? Do you know anything besides that useless trash of college learning—Greek, Latin, and so forth?"

"I have studied mathematics."

"Stuff! I dare say you have."

"I can read and write French and German."

"Hum!" He reflected a moment, then opening a drawer in a desk near him took out a letter, and gave it to me.

"Can you read that?" he asked.

It was a German commercial letter; I translated it; I could not tell whether he was gratified or not—his countenance remained fixed.

"It is well," he said, after a pause, "that you are acquainted with something useful, something that may enable you to earn your board and lodging: since you know French and German, I will take you as second clerk to manage the foreign correspondence of the house. I shall give you a good salary—90l. a year—and now," he continued, raising his voice, "hear once for all what I have to say about our relationship, and all that sort of humbug! I must have no nonsense on that point; it would never suit me. I shall excuse you nothing on the plea of being my brother; if I find you stupid, negligent, dissipated, idle, or possessed of any faults detrimental to the interests of the house, I shall dismiss you as I would any other clerk. Ninety pounds a year are good wages, and I expect to have the full value of my money out of you; remember, too, that things are on a practical footing in my establishment—business-like habits, feelings, and ideas, suit me best. Do you understand?"

"Partly," I replied. "I suppose you mean that I am to do my work for my wages; not to expect favour from you, and not to depend on you for any help but what I earn; that suits me exactly, and on these terms I will consent to be your clerk."

I turned on my heel, and walked to the window; this time I did not consult his face to learn his opinion: what it was I do not know, nor did I then care. After a silence of some minutes he recommenced:—

"You perhaps expect to be accommodated with apartments at Crimsworth Hall, and to go and come with me in the gig. I wish you, however, to be aware that such an arrangement would be quite inconvenient to me. I like to have the seat in my gig at liberty for any gentleman whom for business reasons I may wish to take down to the hall for a night or so. You will seek out lodgings in X———."

Quitting the window, I walked back to the hearth.

"Of course I shall seek out lodgings in X———," I answered. "It would not suit me either to lodge at Crimsworth Hall."

My tone was quiet. I always speak quietly. Yet Mr. Crimsworth's blue eye became incensed; he took his revenge rather oddly. Turning to me he said bluntly—

"You are poor enough, I suppose; how do you expect to live till your quarter's salary becomes due?"

"I shall get on," said I.

"How do you expect to live?" he repeated in a louder voice.

"As I can, Mr. Crimsworth."

"Get into debt at your peril! that's all," he answered. "For aught I know you may have extravagant aristocratic habits: if you have, drop them; I tolerate nothing of the sort here, and I will never give you a shilling extra, whatever liabilities you may incur—mind that."

"Yes, Mr. Crimsworth, you will find I have a good memory."

I said no more. I did not think the time was come for much parley. I had an instinctive feeling that it would be folly to let one's temper effervesce often with such a man as Edward. I said to myself, "I will place my cup under this continual dropping; it shall stand there still and steady; when full, it will run over of itself—meantime patience. Two things are certain. I am capable of performing the work Mr. Crimsworth has set me; I can earn my wages conscientiously, and those wages are sufficient to enable me to live. As to the fact of my brother assuming towards me the bearing of a proud, harsh master, the fault is his, not mine; and shall his injustice, his bad feeling, turn me at once aside from the path I have chosen? No; at least, ere I deviate, I will advance far enough to see whither my career tends. As yet I am only pressing in at the entrance—a strait gate enough; it ought to have a good terminus." While I thus reasoned, Mr. Crimsworth rang a bell; his first clerk, the individual dismissed previously to our conference, re-entered.

"Mr. Steighton," said he, "show Mr. William the letters from Voss, Brothers, and give him English copies of the answers; he will translate them."

Mr. Steighton, a man of about thirty-five, with a face at once sly and heavy, hastened to execute this order; he laid the letters on the desk, and I was soon seated at it, and engaged in rendering the English answers into German. A sentiment of keen pleasure accompanied this first effort to earn my own living—a sentiment neither poisoned nor weakened by the presence of the taskmaster, who stood and watched me for some time as I wrote. I thought he was trying to read my character, but I felt as secure against his scrutiny as if I had had on a casque with the visor down—or rather I showed him my countenance with the confidence that one would show an unlearned man a letter written in Greek; he might see lines, and trace characters, but he could make nothing of them; my nature was not his nature, and its signs were to him like the words of an unknown tongue. Ere long he turned away abruptly, as if baffled, and left the counting-house; he returned to it but twice in the course of that day; each time he mixed and swallowed a glass of brandy-and-water, the materials for making which he extracted from a cupboard on one side of the fireplace; having glanced at my translations—he could read both French and German—he went out again in silence.

CHAPTER III.

I served Edward as his second clerk faithfully, punctually, diligently. What was given me to do I had the power and the determination to do well. Mr. Crimsworth watched sharply for defects, but found none; he set Timothy Steighton, his favourite and head man, to watch also. Tim was baffled; I was as exact as himself, and quicker. Mr. Crimsworth made inquiries as to how I lived, whether I got into debt—no, my accounts with my landlady were always straight. I had hired small lodgings, which I contrived to pay for out of a slender fund—the accumulated savings of my Eton pocket-money; for as it had ever been abhorrent to my nature to ask pecuniary assistance, I had early acquired habits of self-denying economy; husbanding my monthly allowance with anxious care, in order to obviate the danger of being forced, in some moment of future exigency, to beg additional aid. I remember many called me miser at the time, and I used to couple the reproach with this consolation—better to be misunderstood now than repulsed hereafter. At this day I had my reward; I had had it before, when on parting with my irritated uncles one of them threw down on the table before me a 5l. note, which I was able to leave there, saying that my travelling expenses were already provided for. Mr. Crimsworth employed Tim to find out whether my landlady had any complaint to make on the score of my morals; she answered that she believed I was a very religious man, and asked Tim, in her turn, if he thought I had any intention of going into the Church some day; for, she said, she had had young curates to lodge in her house who were nothing equal to me for steadiness and quietness. Tim was "a religious man" himself; indeed, he was "a joined Methodist," which did not (be it understood) prevent him from being at the same time an engrained rascal, and he came away much posed at hearing this account of my piety. Having imparted it to Mr. Crimsworth, that gentleman, who himself frequented no place of worship, and owned no God but Mammon, turned the information into a weapon of attack against the equability of my temper. He commenced a series of covert sneers, of which I did not at first perceive the drift, till my landlady happened to relate the conversation she had had with Mr. Steighton; this enlightened me; afterwards I came to the counting-house prepared, and managed to receive the millowner's blasphemous sarcasms, when next levelled at me, on a buckler of impenetrable indifference. Ere long he tired of wasting his ammunition on a statue, but he did not throw away the shafts—he only kept them quiet in his quiver.

Once during my clerkship I had an invitation to Crimsworth Hall; it was on the occasion of a large party given in honour of the master's birthday; he had always been accustomed to invite his clerks on similar anniversaries, and could not well pass me over; I was, however, kept strictly in the background. Mrs. Crimsworth, elegantly dressed in satin and lace, blooming in youth and health, vouchsafed me no more notice than was expressed by a distant move; Crimsworth, of course, never spoke to me; I was introduced to none of the band of young ladies, who, enveloped in silvery clouds of white gauze and muslin, sat in array against me on the opposite side of a long and large room; in fact, I was fairly isolated, and could but contemplate the shining ones from afar, and when weary of such a dazzling scene, turn for a change to the consideration of the carpet pattern. Mr. Crimsworth, standing on the rug, his elbow supported by the marble mantelpiece, and about him a group of very pretty girls, with whom he conversed gaily—Mr. Crimsworth, thus placed, glanced at me; I looked weary, solitary, kept down like some desolate tutor or governess; he was satisfied.

Dancing began; I should have liked well enough to be introduced to some pleasing and intelligent girl, and to have freedom and opportunity to show that I could both feel and communicate the pleasure of social intercourse—that I was not, in short, a block, or a piece of furniture, but an acting, thinking, sentient man. Many smiling faces and graceful figures glided past me, but the smiles were lavished on other eyes, the figures sustained by other hands than mine. I turned away tantalized, left the dancers, and wandered into the oak-panelled dining-room. No fibre of sympathy united me to any living thing in this house; I looked for and found my mother's picture. I took a wax taper from a stand, and held it up. I gazed long, earnestly; my heart grew to the image. My mother, I perceived, had bequeathed to me much of her features and countenance—her forehead, her eyes, her complexion. No regular beauty pleases egotistical human beings so much as a softened and refined likeness of themselves; for this reason, fathers regard with complacency the lineaments of their daughters' faces, where frequently their own similitude is found flatteringly associated with softness of hue and delicacy of outline. I was just wondering how that picture, to me so interesting, would strike an impartial spectator, when a voice close behind me pronounced the words—

"Humph! there's some sense in that face."

I turned; at my elbow stood a tall man, young, though probably five or six years older than I—in other respects of an appearance the opposite to common place; though just now, as I am not disposed to paint his portrait in detail, the reader must be content with the silhouette I have just thrown off; it was all I myself saw of him for the moment: I did not investigate the colour of his eyebrows, nor of his eyes either; I saw his stature, and the outline of his shape; I saw, too, his fastidious-looking RETROUSSE nose; these observations, few in number, and general in character (the last excepted), sufficed, for they enabled me to recognize him.

"Good evening, Mr. Hunsden," muttered I with a bow, and then, like a shy noodle as I was, I began moving away—and why? Simply because Mr. Hunsden was a manufacturer and a millowner, and I was only a clerk, and my instinct propelled me from my superior. I had frequently seen Hunsden in Bigben Close, where he came almost weekly to transact business with Mr. Crimsworth, but I had never spoken to him, nor he to me, and I owed him a sort of involuntary grudge, because he had more than once been the tacit witness of insults offered by Edward to me. I had the conviction that he could only regard me as a poor-spirited slave, wherefore I now went about to shun his presence and eschew his conversation.

"Where are you going?" asked he, as I edged off sideways. I had already noticed that Mr. Hunsden indulged in abrupt forms of speech, and I perversely said to myself—

"He thinks he may speak as he likes to a poor clerk; but my mood is not, perhaps, so supple as he deems it, and his rough freedom pleases me not at all."

I made some slight reply, rather indifferent than courteous, and continued to move away. He coolly planted himself in my path.

"Stay here awhile," said he: "it is so hot in the dancing-room; besides, you don't dance; you have not had a partner to-night."

He was right, and as he spoke neither his look, tone, nor manner displeased me; my AMOUR-PROPRE was propitiated; he had not addressed me out of condescension, but because, having repaired to the cool dining-room for refreshment, he now wanted some one to talk to, by way of temporary amusement. I hate to be condescended to, but I like well enough to oblige; I stayed.

"That is a good picture," he continued, recurring to the portrait.

"Do you consider the face pretty?" I asked.

"Pretty! no—how can it be pretty, with sunk eyes and hollow cheeks? but it is peculiar; it seems to think. You could have a talk with that woman, if she were alive, on other subjects than dress, visiting, and compliments."

I agreed with him, but did not say so. He went on.

"Not that I admire a head of that sort; it wants character and force; there's too much of the sen-si-tive (so he articulated it, curling his lip at the same time) in that mouth; besides, there is Aristocrat written on the brow and defined in the figure; I hate your aristocrats."

"You think, then, Mr. Hunsden, that patrician descent may be read in a distinctive cast of form and features?"

"Patrician descent be hanged! Who doubts that your lordlings may have their 'distinctive cast of form and features' as much as we——shire tradesmen have ours? But which is the best? Not theirs assuredly. As to their women, it is a little different: they cultivate beauty from childhood upwards, and may by care and training attain to a certain degree of excellence in that point, just like the oriental odalisques. Yet even this superiority is doubtful. Compare the figure in that frame with Mrs. Edward Crimsworth—which is the finer animal?"

I replied quietly: "Compare yourself and Mr. Edward Crimsworth, Mr Hunsden."

"Oh, Crimsworth is better filled up than I am, I know besides he has a straight nose, arched eyebrows, and all that; but these advantages—if they are advantages—he did not inherit from his mother, the patrician, but from his father, old Crimsworth, who, MY father says, was as veritable a ——shire blue-dyer as ever put indigo in a vat yet withal the handsomest man in the three Ridings. It is you, William, who are the aristocrat of your family, and you are not as fine a fellow as your plebeian brother by long chalk."

There was something in Mr. Hunsden's point-blank mode of speech which rather pleased me than otherwise because it set me at my ease. I continued the conversation with a degree of interest.

"How do you happen to know that I am Mr. Crimsworth's brother? I thought you and everybody else looked upon me only in the light of a poor clerk."

"Well, and so we do; and what are you but a poor clerk? You do Crimsworth's work, and he gives you wages—shabby wages they are, too."

I was silent. Hunsden's language now bordered on the impertinent, still his manner did not offend me in the least—it only piqued my curiosity; I wanted him to go on, which he did in a little while.

"This world is an absurd one," said he.

"Why so, Mr. Hunsden?"

"I wonder you should ask: you are yourself a strong proof of the absurdity I allude to."

I was determined he should explain himself of his own accord, without my pressing him so to do—so I resumed my silence.

"Is it your intention to become a tradesman?" he inquired presently.

"It was my serious intention three months ago."

"Humph! the more fool you—you look like a tradesman! What a practical business-like face you have!"

"My face is as the Lord made it, Mr. Hunsden."

"The Lord never made either your face or head for X—— What good can your bumps of ideality, comparison, self-esteem, conscientiousness, do you here? But if you like Bigben Close, stay there; it's your own affair, not mine."

"Perhaps I have no choice."

"Well, I care nought about it—it will make little difference to me what you do or where you go; but I'm cool now—I want to dance again; and I see such a fine girl sitting in the corner of the sofa there by her mamma; see if I don't get her for a partner in a jiffy! There's Waddy—Sam Waddy making up to her; won't I cut him out?"

And Mr. Hunsden strode away. I watched him through the open folding-doors; he outstripped Waddy, applied for the hand of the fine girl, and led her off triumphant. She was a tall, well-made, full-formed, dashingly-dressed young woman, much in the style of Mrs. E. Crimsworth; Hunsden whirled her through the waltz with spirit; he kept at her side during the remainder of the evening, and I read in her animated and gratified countenance that he succeeded in making himself perfectly agreeable. The mamma too (a stout person in a turban—Mrs. Lupton by name) looked well pleased; prophetic visions probably flattered her inward eye. The Hunsdens were of an old stem; and scornful as Yorke (such was my late interlocutor's name) professed to be of the advantages of birth, in his secret heart he well knew and fully appreciated the distinction his ancient, if not high lineage conferred on him in a mushroom-place like X——, concerning whose inhabitants it was proverbially said, that not one in a thousand knew his own grandfather. Moreover the Hunsdens, once rich, were still independent; and report affirmed that Yorke bade fair, by his success in business, to restore to pristine prosperity the partially decayed fortunes of his house. These circumstances considered, Mrs. Lupton's broad face might well wear a smile of complacency as she contemplated the heir of Hunsden Wood occupied in paying assiduous court to her darling Sarah Martha. I, however, whose observations being less anxious, were likely to be more accurate, soon saw that the grounds for maternal self-congratulation were slight indeed; the gentleman appeared to me much more desirous of making, than susceptible of receiving an impression. I know not what it was in Mr. Hunsden that, as I watched him (I had nothing better to do), suggested to me, every now and then, the idea of a foreigner. In form and features he might be pronounced English, though even there one caught a dash of something Gallic; but he had no English shyness: he had learnt somewhere, somehow, the art of setting himself quite at his ease, and of allowing no insular timidity to intervene as a barrier between him and his convenience or pleasure. Refinement he did not affect, yet vulgar he could not be called; he was not odd—no quiz—yet he resembled no one else I had ever seen before; his general bearing intimated complete, sovereign satisfaction with himself; yet, at times, an indescribable shade passed like an eclipse over his countenance, and seemed to me like the sign of a sudden and strong inward doubt of himself, his words and actions an energetic discontent at his life or his social position, his future prospects or his mental attainments—I know not which; perhaps after all it might only be a bilious caprice.

CHAPTER IV.

No man likes to acknowledge that he has made a mistake in the choice of his profession, and every man, worthy of the name, will row long against wind and tide before he allows himself to cry out, "I am baffled!" and submits to be floated passively back to land. From the first week of my residence in X—— I felt my occupation irksome. The thing itself—the work of copying and translating business-letters—was a dry and tedious task enough, but had that been all, I should long have borne with the nuisance; I am not of an impatient nature, and influenced by the double desire of getting my living and justifying to myself and others the resolution I had taken to become a tradesman, I should have endured in silence the rust and cramp of my best faculties; I should not have whispered, even inwardly, that I longed for liberty; I should have pent in every sigh by which my heart might have ventured to intimate its distress under the closeness, smoke, monotony and joyless tumult of Bigben Close, and its panting desire for freer and fresher scenes; I should have set up the image of Duty, the fetish of Perseverance, in my small bedroom at Mrs. King's lodgings, and they two should have been my household gods, from which my darling, my cherished-in-secret, Imagination, the tender and the mighty, should never, either by softness or strength, have severed me. But this was not all; the antipathy which had sprung up between myself and my employer striking deeper root and spreading denser shade daily, excluded me from every glimpse of the sunshine of life; and I began to feel like a plant growing in humid darkness out of the slimy walls of a well.

Antipathy is the only word which can express the feeling Edward Crimsworth had for me—a feeling, in a great measure, involuntary, and which was liable to be excited by every, the most trifling movement, look, or word of mine. My southern accent annoyed him; the degree of education evinced in my language irritated him; my punctuality, industry, and accuracy, fixed his dislike, and gave it the high flavour and poignant relish of envy; he feared that I too should one day make a successful tradesman. Had I been in anything inferior to him, he would not have hated me so thoroughly, but I knew all that he knew, and, what was worse, he suspected that I kept the padlock of silence on mental wealth in which he was no sharer. If he could have once placed me in a ridiculous or mortifying position, he would have forgiven me much, but I was guarded by three faculties—Caution, Tact, Observation; and prowling and prying as was Edward's malignity, it could never baffle the lynx-eyes of these, my natural sentinels. Day by day did his malice watch my tact, hoping it would sleep, and prepared to steal snake-like on its slumber; but tact, if it be genuine, never sleeps.

I had received my first quarter's wages, and was returning to my lodgings, possessed heart and soul with the pleasant feeling that the master who had paid me grudged every penny of that hard-earned pittance—(I had long ceased to regard Mr. Crimsworth as my brother—he was a hard, grinding master; he wished to be an inexorable tyrant: that was all). Thoughts, not varied but strong, occupied my mind; two voices spoke within me; again and again they uttered the same monotonous phrases. One said: "William, your life is intolerable." The other: "What can you do to alter it?" I walked fast, for it was a cold, frosty night in January; as I approached my lodgings, I turned from a general view of my affairs to the particular speculation as to whether my fire would be out; looking towards the window of my sitting-room, I saw no cheering red gleam.

"That slut of a servant has neglected it as usual," said I, "and I shall see nothing but pale ashes if I go in; it is a fine starlight night—I will walk a little farther."

It WAS a fine night, and the streets were dry and even clean for X——; there was a crescent curve of moonlight to be seen by the parish church tower, and hundreds of stars shone keenly bright in all quarters of the sky.

Unconsciously I steered my course towards the country; I had got into Grove-street, and began to feel the pleasure of seeing dim trees at the extremity, round a suburban house, when a person leaning over the iron gate of one of the small gardens which front the neat dwelling-houses in this street, addressed me as I was hurrying with quick stride past.

"What the deuce is the hurry? Just so must Lot have left Sodom, when he expected fire to pour down upon it, out of burning brass clouds."

I stopped short, and looked towards the speaker. I smelt the fragrance, and saw the red spark of a cigar; the dusk outline of a man, too, bent towards me over the wicket.

"You see I am meditating in the field at eventide," continued this shade. "God knows it's cool work! especially as instead of Rebecca on a camel's hump, with bracelets on her arms and a ring in her nose, Fate sends me only a counting-house clerk, in a grey tweed wrapper." The voice was familiar to me —its second utterance enabled me to seize the speaker's identity.

"Mr. Hunsden! good evening."

"Good evening, indeed! yes, but you would have passed me without recognition if I had not been so civil as to speak first."

"I did not know you."

"A famous excuse! You ought to have known me; I knew you, though you were going ahead like a steam-engine. Are the police after you?"

"It wouldn't be worth their while; I'm not of consequence enough to attract them."

"Alas, poor shepherd! Alack and well-a-day! What a theme for regret, and how down in the mouth you must be, judging from the sound of your voice! But since you're not running from the police, from whom are you running? the devil?"

"On the contrary, I am going post to him."

"That is well—you're just in luck: this is Tuesday evening; there are scores of market gigs and carts returning to Dinneford to-night; and he, or some of his, have a seat in all regularly; so, if you'll step in and sit half-an-hour in my bachelor's parlour, you may catch him as he passes without much trouble. I think though you'd better let him alone to-night, he'll have so many customers to serve; Tuesday is his busy day in X—— and Dinneford; come in at all events."

He swung the wicket open as he spoke.

"Do you really wish me to go in?" I asked.

"As you please—I'm alone; your company for an hour or two would be agreeable to me; but, if you don't choose to favour me so far, I'll not press the point. I hate to bore any one."

It suited me to accept the invitation as it suited Hunsden to give it. I passed through the gate, and followed him to the front door, which he opened; thence we traversed a passage, and entered his parlour; the door being shut, he pointed me to an arm-chair by the hearth; I sat down, and glanced round me.

It was a comfortable room, at once snug and handsome; the bright grate was filled with a genuine ——shire fire, red, clear, and generous, no penurious South-of-England embers heaped in the corner of a grate. On the table a shaded lamp diffused around a soft, pleasant, and equal light; the furniture was almost luxurious for a young bachelor, comprising a couch and two very easy chairs; bookshelves filled the recesses on each side of the mantelpiece; they were well-furnished, and arranged with perfect order. The neatness of the room suited my taste; I hate irregular and slovenly habits. From what I saw I concluded that Hunsden's ideas on that point corresponded with my own. While he removed from the centre-table to the side-board a few pamphlets and periodicals, I ran my eye along the shelves of the book-case nearest me. French and German works predominated, the old French dramatists, sundry modern authors, Thiers, Villemain, Paul de Kock, George Sand, Eugene Sue; in German—Goethe, Schiller, Zschokke, Jean Paul Richter; in English there were works on Political Economy. I examined no further, for Mr. Hunsden himself recalled my attention.

"You shall have something," said he, "for you ought to feel disposed for refreshment after walking nobody knows how far on such a Canadian night as this; but it shall not be brandy-and-water, and it shall not be a bottle of port, nor ditto of sherry. I keep no such poison. I have Rhein-wein for my own drinking, and you may choose between that and coffee."

Here again Hunsden suited me: if there was one generally received practice I abhorred more than another, it was the habitual imbibing of spirits and strong wines. I had, however, no fancy for his acid German nectar, but I liked coffee, so I responded—

"Give me some coffee, Mr. Hunsden."

I perceived my answer pleased him; he had doubtless expected to see a chilling effect produced by his steady announcement that he would give me neither wine nor spirits; he just shot one searching glance at my face to ascertain whether my cordiality was genuine or a mere feint of politeness. I smiled, because I quite understood him; and, while I honoured his conscientious firmness, I was amused at his mistrust; he seemed satisfied, rang the bell, and ordered coffee, which was presently brought; for himself, a bunch of grapes and half a pint of something sour sufficed. My coffee was excellent; I told him so, and expressed the shuddering pity with which his anchorite fare inspired me. He did not answer, and I scarcely think heard my remark. At that moment one of those momentary eclipses I before alluded to had come over his face, extinguishing his smile, and replacing, by an abstracted and alienated look, the customarily shrewd, bantering glance of his eye. I employed the interval of silence in a rapid scrutiny of his physiognomy. I had never observed him closely before; and, as my sight is very short, I had gathered only a vague, general idea of his appearance; I was surprised now, on examination, to perceive how small, and even feminine, were his lineaments; his tall figure, long and dark locks, his voice and general bearing, had impressed me with the notion of something powerful and massive; not at all: —my own features were cast in a harsher and squarer mould than his. I discerned that there would be contrasts between his inward and outward man; contentions, too; for I suspected his soul had more of will and ambition than his body had of fibre and muscle. Perhaps, in these incompatibilities of the "physique" with the "morale," lay the secret of that fitful gloom; he WOULD but COULD not, and the athletic mind scowled scorn on its more fragile companion. As to his good looks, I should have liked to have a woman's opinion on that subject; it seemed to me that his face might produce the same effect on a lady that a very piquant and interesting, though scarcely pretty, female face would on a man. I have mentioned his dark locks—they were brushed sideways above a white and sufficiently expansive forehead; his cheek had a rather hectic freshness; his features might have done well on canvas, but indifferently in marble: they were plastic; character had set a stamp upon each; expression re-cast them at her pleasure, and strange metamorphoses she wrought, giving him now the mien of a morose bull, and anon that of an arch and mischievous girl; more frequently, the two semblances were blent, and a queer, composite countenance they made.

Starting from his silent fit, he began:—

"William! what a fool you are to live in those dismal lodgings of Mrs. King's, when you might take rooms here in Grove Street, and have a garden like me!"

"I should be too far from the mill."

"What of that? It would do you good to walk there and back two or three times a day; besides, are you such a fossil that you never wish to see a flower or a green leaf?"

"I am no fossil."

"What are you then? You sit at that desk in Crimsworth's counting-house day by day and week by week, scraping with a pen on paper, just like an automaton; you never get up; you never say you are tired; you never ask for a holiday; you never take change or relaxation; you give way to no excess of an evening; you neither keep wild company, nor indulge in strong drink."

"Do you, Mr. Hunsden?"

"Don't think to pose me with short questions; your case and mine are diametrically different, and it is nonsense attempting to draw a parallel. I say, that when a man endures patiently what ought to be unendurable, he is a fossil."

"Whence do you acquire the knowledge of my patience?"

"Why, man, do you suppose you are a mystery? The other night you seemed surprised at my knowing to what family you belonged; now you find subject for wonderment in my calling you patient. What do you think I do with my eyes and ears? I've been in your counting-house more than once when Crimsworth has treated you like a dog; called for a book, for instance, and when you gave him the wrong one, or what he chose to consider the wrong one, flung it back almost in your face; desired you to shut or open the door as if you had been his flunkey; to say nothing of your position at the party about a month ago, where you had neither place nor partner, but hovered about like a poor, shabby hanger-on; and how patient you were under each and all of these circumstances!"

"Well, Mr. Hunsden, what then?"

"I can hardly tell you what then; the conclusion to be drawn as to your character depends upon the nature of the motives which guide your conduct; if you are patient because you expect to make something eventually out of Crimsworth, notwithstanding his tyranny, or perhaps by means of it, you are what the world calls an interested and mercenary, but may be a very wise fellow; if you are patient because you think it a duty to meet insult with submission, you are an essential sap, and in no shape the man for my money; if you are patient because your nature is phlegmatic, flat, inexcitable, and that you cannot get up to the pitch of resistance, why, God made you to be crushed; and lie down by all means, and lie flat, and let Juggernaut ride well over you."

Mr. Hunsden's eloquence was not, it will be perceived, of the smooth and oily order. As he spoke, he pleased me ill. I seem to recognize in him one of those characters who, sensitive enough themselves, are selfishly relentless towards the sensitiveness of others. Moreover, though he was neither like Crimsworth nor Lord Tynedale, yet he was acrid, and, I suspected, overbearing in his way: there was a tone of despotism in the urgency of the very reproaches by which he aimed at goading the oppressed into rebellion against the oppressor. Looking at him still more fixedly than I had yet done, I saw written in his eye and mien a resolution to arrogate to himself a freedom so unlimited that it might often trench on the just liberty of his neighbours. I rapidly ran over these thoughts, and then I laughed a low and involuntary laugh, moved thereto by a slight inward revelation of the inconsistency of man. It was as I thought: Hunsden had expected me to take with calm his incorrect and offensive surmises, his bitter and haughty taunts; and himself was chafed by a laugh, scarce louder than a whisper.

His brow darkened, his thin nostril dilated a little.

"Yes," he began, "I told you that you were an aristocrat, and who but an aristocrat would laugh such a laugh as that, and look such a look? A laugh frigidly jeering; a look lazily mutinous; gentlemanlike irony, patrician resentment. What a nobleman you would have made, William Crimsworth! You are cut out for one; pity Fortune has baulked Nature! Look at the features, figure, even to the hands—distinction all over—ugly distinction! Now, if you'd only an estate and a mansion, and a park, and a title, how you could play the exclusive, maintain the rights of your class, train your tenantry in habits of respect to the peerage, oppose at every step the advancing power of the people, support your rotten order, and be ready for its sake to wade knee-deep in churls' blood; as it is, you've no power; you can do nothing; you're wrecked and stranded on the shores of commerce; forced into collision with practical men, with whom you cannot cope, for YOU'LL NEVER BE A TRADESMAN."

The first part of Hunsden's speech moved me not at all, or, if it did, it was only to wonder at the perversion into which prejudice had twisted his judgment of my character; the concluding sentence, however, not only moved, but shook me; the blow it gave was a severe one, because Truth wielded the weapon. If I smiled now, it, was only in disdain of myself.

Hunsden saw his advantage; he followed it up.

"You'll make nothing by trade," continued he; "nothing more than the crust of dry bread and the draught of fair water on which you now live; your only chance of getting a competency lies in marrying a rich widow, or running away with an heiress."

"I leave such shifts to be put in practice by those who devise them," said I, rising.

"And even that is hopeless," he went on coolly. "What widow would have you? Much less, what heiress? You're not bold and venturesome enough for the one, nor handsome and fascinating enough for the other. You think perhaps you look intelligent and polished; carry your intellect and refinement to market, and tell me in a private note what price is bid for them."

Mr. Hunsden had taken his tone for the night; the string he struck was out of tune, he would finger no other. Averse to discord, of which I had enough every day and all day long, I concluded, at last, that silence and solitude were preferable to jarring converse; I bade him good-night.

"What! Are you going, lad? Well, good-night: you'll find the door." And he sat still in front of the fire, while I left the room and the house. I had got a good way on my return to my lodgings before I found out that I was walking very fast, and breathing very hard, and that my nails were almost stuck into the palms of my clenched hands, and that my teeth were set fast; on making this discovery, I relaxed both my pace, fists, and jaws, but I could not so soon cause the regrets rushing rapidly through my mind to slacken their tide. Why did I make myself a tradesman? Why did I enter Hunsden's house this evening? Why, at dawn to-morrow, must I repair to Crimsworth's mill? All that night did I ask myself these questions, and all that night fiercely demanded of my soul an answer. I got no sleep; my head burned, my feet froze; at last the factory bells rang, and I sprang from my bed with other slaves.

CHAPTER V.

There is a climax to everything, to every state of feeling as well as to every position in life. I turned this truism over in my mind as, in the frosty dawn of a January morning, I hurried down the steep and now icy street which descended from Mrs. King's to the Close. The factory workpeople had preceded me by nearly an hour, and the mill was all lighted up and in full operation when I reached it. I repaired to my post in the counting-house as usual; the fire there, but just lit, as yet only smoked; Steighton had not yet arrived. I shut the door and sat down at the desk; my hands, recently washed in half-frozen water, were still numb; I could not write till they had regained vitality, so I went on thinking, and still the theme of my thoughts was the "climax." Self-dissatisfaction troubled exceedingly the current of my meditations.

"Come, William Crimsworth," said my conscience, or whatever it is that within ourselves takes ourselves to task—"come, get a clear notion of what you would have, or what you would not have. You talk of a climax; pray has your endurance reached its climax? It is not four months old. What a fine resolute fellow you imagined yourself to be when you told Tynedale you would tread in your father's steps, and a pretty treading you are likely to make of it! How well you like X——! Just at this moment how redolent of pleasant associations are its streets, its shops, its warehouses, its factories! How the prospect of this day cheers you! Letter-copying till noon, solitary dinner at your lodgings, letter-copying till evening, solitude; for you neither find pleasure in Brown's, nor Smith's, nor Nicholl's, nor Eccle's company; and as to Hunsden, you fancied there was pleasure to be derived from his society—

he! he! how did you like the taste you had of him last night? was it sweet? Yet he is a talented, an original-minded man, and even he does not like you; your self-respect defies you to like him; he has always seen you to disadvantage; he always will see you to disadvantage; your positions are unequal, and were they on the same level your minds could not assimilate; never hope, then, to gather the honey of friendship out of that thorn-guarded plant. Hello, Crimsworth! where are your thoughts tending? You leave the recollection of Hunsden as a bee would a rock, as a bird a desert; and your aspirations spread eager wings towards a land of visions where, now in advancing daylight—in X—— daylight—you dare to dream of congeniality, repose, union. Those three you will never meet in this world; they are angels. The souls of just men made perfect may encounter them in heaven, but your soul will never be made perfect. Eight o'clock strikes! your hands are thawed, get to work!"

"Work? why should I work?" said I sullenly: "I cannot please though I toil like a slave." "Work, work!" reiterated the inward voice. "I may work, it will do no good," I growled; but nevertheless I drew out a packet of letters and commenced my task—task thankless and bitter as that of the Israelite crawling over the sun-baked fields of Egypt in search of straw and stubble wherewith to accomplish his tale of bricks.

About ten o'clock I heard Mr. Crimsworth's gig turn into the yard, and in a minute or two he entered the counting-house. It was his custom to glance his eye at Steighton and myself, to hang up his mackintosh, stand a minute with his back to the fire, and then walk out. Today he did not deviate from his usual habits; the only difference was that when he looked at me, his brow, instead of being merely hard, was surly; his eye, instead of being cold, was fierce. He studied me a minute or two longer than usual, but went out in silence.

Twelve o'clock arrived; the bell rang for a suspension of labour; the workpeople went off to their dinners; Steighton, too, departed, desiring me to lock the counting-house door, and take the key with me. I was tying up a bundle of papers, and putting them in their place, preparatory to closing my desk, when Crimsworth reappeared at the door, and entering closed it behind him.

"You'll stay here a minute," said he, in a deep, brutal voice, while his nostrils distended and his eye shot a spark of sinister fire.

Alone with Edward I remembered our relationship, and remembering that forgot the difference of position; I put away deference and careful forms of speech; I answered with simple brevity.

"It is time to go home," I said, turning the key in my desk.

"You'll stay here!" he reiterated. "And take your hand off that key! leave it in the lock!"

"Why?" asked I. "What cause is there for changing my usual plans?"

"Do as I order," was the answer, "and no questions! You are my servant, obey me! What have you been about—?" He was going on in the same breath, when an abrupt pause announced that rage had for the moment got the better of articulation.

"You may look, if you wish to know," I replied. "There is the open desk, there are the papers."

"Confound your insolence! What have you been about?"

"Your work, and have done it well."

"Hypocrite and twaddler! Smooth-faced, snivelling greasehorn!" (This last term is, I believe, purely ——shire, and alludes to the horn of black, rancid whale-oil, usually to be seen suspended to cart-wheels, and employed for greasing the same.)

"Come, Edward Crimsworth, enough of this. It is time you and I wound up accounts. I have now given your service three months' trial, and I find it the most nauseous slavery under the sun. Seek another clerk. I stay no longer."

"What! do you dare to give me notice? Stop at least for your wages." He took down the heavy gig whip hanging beside his mackintosh.

I permitted myself to laugh with a degree of scorn I took no pains to temper or hide. His fury boiled up, and when he had sworn half-a-dozen vulgar, impious oaths, without, however, venturing to lift the whip, he continued:

"I've found you out and know you thoroughly, you mean, whining lickspittle! What have you been saying all over X—— about me? answer me that!"

"You? I have neither inclination nor temptation to talk about you."

"You lie! It is your practice to talk about me; it is your constant habit to make public complaint of the treatment you receive at my hands. You have gone and told it far and near that I give you low wages and knock you about like a dog. I wish you were a dog! I'd set-to this minute, and never stir from the spot till I'd cut every strip of flesh from your bones with this whip."

He flourished his tool. The end of the lash just touched my forehead. A warm excited thrill ran through my veins, my blood seemed to give a bound, and then raced fast and hot along its channels. I got up nimbly, came round to where he stood, and faced him.

"Down with your whip!" said I, "and explain this instant what you mean."

"Sirrah! to whom are you speaking?"

"To you. There is no one else present, I think. You say I have been calumniating you—complaining of your low wages and bad treatment. Give your grounds for these assertions."

Crimsworth had no dignity, and when I sternly demanded an explanation, he gave one in a loud, scolding voice.

"Grounds! you shall have them; and turn to the light that I may see your brazen face blush black, when you hear yourself proved to be a liar and a hypocrite. At a public meeting in the Town-hall yesterday, I had the pleasure of hearing myself insulted by the speaker opposed to me in the question under discussion, by allusions to my private affairs; by cant about monsters without natural affection, family despots, and such trash; and when I rose to answer, I was met by a shout from the filthy mob, where the mention of your name enabled me at once to detect the quarter in which this base attack had originated. When I looked round, I saw that treacherous villain, Hunsden acting as fugleman. I detected you in close conversation with Hunsden at my house a month ago, and I know that you were at Hunsden's rooms last night. Deny it if you dare."

"Oh, I shall not deny it! And if Hunsden hounded on the people to hiss you, he did quite right. You deserve popular execration; for a worse man, a harder master, a more brutal brother than you are has seldom existed."

"Sirrah! sirrah!" reiterated Crimsworth; and to complete his apostrophe, he cracked the whip straight over my head.

A minute sufficed to wrest it from him, break it in two pieces, and throw it under the grate. He made a headlong rush at me, which I evaded, and said—

"Touch me, and I'll have you up before the nearest magistrate."

Men like Crimsworth, if firmly and calmly resisted, always abate something of their exorbitant insolence; he had no mind to be brought before a magistrate, and I suppose he saw I meant what I said. After an odd and long stare at me, at once bull-like and amazed, he seemed to bethink himself that, after all, his money gave him sufficient superiority over a beggar like me, and that he had in his hands a surer and more dignified mode of revenge than the somewhat hazardous one of personal chastisement.

"Take your hat," said he. "Take what belongs to you, and go out at that door; get away to your parish, you pauper: beg, steal, starve, get transported, do what you like; but at your peril venture again into my sight! If ever I hear of your setting foot on an inch of ground belonging to me, I'll hire a man to cane you."

"It is not likely you'll have the chance; once off your premises, what temptation can I have to return to them? I leave a prison, I leave a tyrant; I leave what is worse than the worst that can lie before me, so no fear of my coming back."

"Go, or I'll make you!" exclaimed Crimsworth.

I walked deliberately to my desk, took out such of its contents as were my own property, put them in my pocket, locked the desk, and placed the key on the top.

"What are you abstracting from that desk?" demanded the millowner. "Leave all behind in its place, or I'll send for a policeman to search you."

"Look sharp about it, then," said I, and I took down my hat, drew on my gloves, and walked leisurely out of the counting-house—walked out of it to enter it no more.

I recollect that when the mill-bell rang the dinner hour, before Mr. Crimsworth entered, and the scene above related took place, I had had rather a sharp appetite, and had been waiting somewhat impatiently to hear the signal of feeding time. I forgot it now, however; the images of potatoes and roast mutton were effaced from my mind by the stir and tumult which the transaction of the last half-hour had there excited. I only thought of walking, that the action of my muscles might harmonize with the action of my nerves; and walk I did, fast and far. How could I do otherwise? A load was lifted off my heart; I felt light and liberated. I had got away from Bigben Close without a breach of resolution; without injury to my self-respect. I had not forced circumstances; circumstances had freed me. Life was again open to me; no longer was its horizon limited by the high black wall surrounding Crimsworth's mill. Two hours had elapsed before my sensations had so far subsided as to leave me calm enough to remark for what wider and clearer boundaries I had exchanged that sooty girdle. When I did look up, lo! straight before me lay Grovetown, a village of villas about five miles out of X——. The short winter day, as I perceived from the far-declined sun, was already approaching its close; a chill frost-mist was rising from the river on which X —— stands, and along whose banks the road I had taken lay; it dimmed the earth, but did not obscure the clear icy blue of the January sky. There was a great stillness near and far; the time of the day favoured tranquillity, as the people were all employed within-doors, the hour of evening release from the factories not being yet arrived; a sound of full-flowing water alone pervaded the air, for the river was deep and abundant, swelled by the melting of a late snow. I stood awhile, leaning over a wall; and looking down at the current: I watched the rapid rush of its waves. I desired memory to take a clear and permanent impression of the scene, and treasure it for future years. Grovetown church clock struck four; looking up, I beheld the last of that day's sun, glinting red through the leafless boughs of some very old oak trees surrounding the church—its light coloured and characterized the picture as I wished. I paused yet a moment, till the sweet, slow sound of the bell had quite died out of the air; then ear, eye and feeling satisfied, I quitted the wall and once more turned my face towards X——.

CHAPTER VI.

I re-entered the town a hungry man; the dinner I had forgotten recurred seductively to my recollection; and it was with a quick step and sharp appetite I ascended the narrow street leading to my lodgings. It was dark when I opened the front door and walked into the house. I wondered how my fire would be; the night was cold, and I shuddered at the prospect of a grate full of sparkless cinders. To my joyful surprise, I found, on entering my sitting-room, a good fire and a clean hearth. I had hardly noticed this phenomenon, when I became aware of another subject for wonderment; the chair I usually occupied near the hearth was already filled; a person sat there with his arms folded on his chest, and his legs stretched out on the rug. Short-sighted as I am, doubtful as was the gleam of the firelight, a moment's examination enabled me to recognize in this person my acquaintance, Mr. Hunsden. I could not of course be much pleased to see him, considering the manner in which I had parted from him the night before, and as I walked to the hearth, stirred the fire, and said coolly, "Good evening," my demeanour evinced as little cordiality as I felt; yet I wondered in my own mind what had brought him there; and I wondered, also, what motives had induced him to interfere so actively between me and Edward; it was to him, it appeared, that I owed my welcome dismissal; still I could not bring myself to ask him questions, to show any eagerness of curiosity; if he chose to explain, he might, but the explanation should be a perfectly voluntary one on his part; I thought he was entering upon it.

"You owe me a debt of gratitude," were his first words.

"Do I?" said I; "I hope it is not a large one, for I am much too poor to charge myself with heavy liabilities of any kind."

"Then declare yourself bankrupt at once, for this liability is a ton weight at least. When I came in I found your fire out, and I had it lit again, and made that sulky drab of a servant stay and blow at it with the bellows till it had burnt up properly; now, say 'Thank you!'"

"Not till I have had something to eat; I can thank nobody while I am so famished."

I rang the bell and ordered tea and some cold meat.

"Cold meat!" exclaimed Hunsden, as the servant closed the door, "what a glutton you are; man! Meat with tea! you'll die of eating too much."

"No, Mr. Hunsden, I shall not." I felt a necessity for contradicting him; I was irritated with hunger, and irritated at seeing him there, and irritated at the continued roughness of his manner.

"It is over-eating that makes you so ill-tempered," said he.

"How do you know?" I demanded. "It is like you to give a pragmatical opinion without being acquainted with any of the circumstances of the case; I have had no dinner."

What I said was petulant and snappish enough, and Hunsden only replied by looking in my face and laughing.

"Poor thing!" he whined, after a pause. "It has had no dinner, has it? What! I suppose its master would not let it come home. Did Crimsworth order you to fast by way of punishment, William!"

"No, Mr. Hunsden." Fortunately at this sulky juncture, tea, was brought in, and I fell to upon some bread and butter and cold beef directly. Having cleared a plateful, I became so far humanized as to intimate to Mr. Hunsden that he need not sit there staring, but might come to the table and do as I did, if he liked.

"But I don't like in the least," said he, and therewith he summoned the servant by a fresh pull of the bell-rope, and intimated a desire to have a glass of toast-and-water. "And some more coal," he added; "Mr. Crimsworth shall keep a good fire while I stay."

His orders being executed, he wheeled his chair round to the table, so as to be opposite me.

"Well," he proceeded. "You are out of work, I suppose."

"Yes," said I; and not disposed to show the satisfaction I felt on this point, I, yielding to the whim of the moment, took up the subject as though I considered myself aggrieved rather than benefited by what had been done. "Yes—thanks to you, I am. Crimsworth turned me off at a minute's notice, owing to some interference of yours at a public meeting, I understand."

"Ah! what! he mentioned that? He observed me signalling the lads, did he? What had he to say about his friend Hunsden—anything sweet?"

"He called you a treacherous villain."

"Oh, he hardly knows me yet! I'm one of those shy people who don't come out all at once, and he is only just beginning to make my acquaintance, but he'll find I've some good qualities—excellent ones! The Hunsdens were always unrivalled at tracking a rascal; a downright, dishonourable villain is their natural prey—they could not keep off him wherever they met him; you used the word pragmatical just now—that word is the property of our family; it has been applied to us from generation to generation; we have fine noses for abuses; we scent a scoundrel a mile off; we are reformers born, radical reformers; and it was impossible for me to live in the same town with Crimsworth, to come into weekly contact with him, to witness some of his conduct to you (for whom personally I care nothing; I only consider the brutal injustice with which he violated your natural claim to equality)—I say it was impossible for me to be thus situated and not feel the angel or the demon of my race at work within me. I followed my instinct, opposed a tyrant, and broke a chain."

Now this speech interested me much, both because it brought out Hunsden's character, and because it explained his motives; it interested me so much that I forgot to reply to it, and sat silent, pondering over a throng of ideas it had suggested.

"Are you grateful to me?" he asked, presently.

In fact I was grateful, or almost so, and I believe I half liked him at the moment, notwithstanding his proviso that what he had done was not out of regard for me. But human nature is perverse. Impossible to answer his blunt question in the affirmative, so I disclaimed all tendency to gratitude, and advised him if he expected any reward for his championship, to look for it in a better world, as he was not likely to meet with it here. In reply he termed me "a dry-hearted aristocratic scamp," whereupon I again charged him with having taken the bread out of my mouth.

"Your bread was dirty, man!" cried Hunsden—"dirty and unwholesome! It came through the hands of a tyrant, for I tell you Crimsworth is a tyrant,—a tyrant to his workpeople, a tyrant to his clerks, and will some day be a tyrant to his wife."

"Nonsense! bread is bread, and a salary is a salary. I've lost mine, and through your means."

"There's sense in what you say, after all," rejoined Hunsden. "I must say I am rather agreeably surprised to hear you make so practical an observation as that last. I had imagined now, from my previous observation of your character, that the sentimental delight you would have taken in your newly regained liberty would, for a while at least, have effaced all ideas of forethought and prudence. I think better of you for looking steadily to the needful."

"Looking steadily to the needful! How can I do otherwise? I must live, and to live I must have what you call 'the needful,' which I can only get by working. I repeat it, you have taken my work from me."

"What do you mean to do?" pursued Hunsden coolly. "You have influential relations; I suppose they'll soon provide you with another place."

"Influential relations? Who? I should like to know their names."

"The Seacombes."

"Stuff! I have cut them."

Hunsden looked at me incredulously.

"I have," said I, "and that definitively."

"You must mean they have cut you, William."

"As you please. They offered me their patronage on condition of my entering the Church; I declined both the terms and the recompence; I withdrew from my cold uncles, and preferred throwing myself into my elder brother's arms, from whose affectionate embrace I am now torn by the cruel intermeddling of a stranger—of yourself, in short."

I could not repress a half-smile as I said this; a similar demi-manifestation of feeling appeared at the same moment on Hunsden's lips.

"Oh, I see!" said he, looking into my eyes, and it was evident he did see right down into my heart. Having sat a minute or two with his chin resting on his hand, diligently occupied in the continued perusal of my countenance, he went on:

"Seriously, have you then nothing to expect from the Seacombes?"

"Yes, rejection and repulsion. Why do you ask me twice? How can hands stained with the ink of a counting-house, soiled with the grease of a wool-warehouse, ever again be permitted to come into contact with aristocratic palms?"

"There would be a difficulty, no doubt; still you are such a complete Seacombe in appearance, feature, language, almost manner, I wonder they should disown you."

"They have disowned me; so talk no more about it."

"Do you regret it, William?"

"No."

"Why not, lad?"

"Because they are not people with whom I could ever have had any sympathy."

"I say you are one of them."

"That merely proves that you know nothing at all about it; I am my mother's son, but not my uncles' nephew."

"Still—one of your uncles is a lord, though rather an obscure and not a very wealthy one, and the other a right honourable: you should consider worldly interest."

"Nonsense, Mr. Hunsden. You know or may know that even had I desired to be submissive to my uncles, I could not have stooped with a good enough grace ever to have won their favour. I should have sacrificed my own comfort and not have gained their patronage in return."

"Very likely—so you calculated your wisest plan was to follow your own devices at once?"

"Exactly. I must follow my own devices—I must, till the day of my death; because I can neither comprehend, adopt, nor work out those of other people."

Hunsden yawned. "Well," said he, "in all this, I see but one thing clearly-that is, that the whole affair is no business of mine." He stretched himself and again yawned. "I wonder what time it is," he went on: "I have an appointment for seven o'clock."

"Three quarters past six by my watch."

"Well, then I'll go." He got up. "You'll not meddle with trade again?" said he, leaning his elbow on the mantelpiece.

"No; I think not."

"You would be a fool if you did. Probably, after all, you'll think better of your uncles' proposal and go into the Church."

"A singular regeneration must take place in my whole inner and outer man before I do that. A good clergyman is one of the best of men."

"Indeed! Do you think so?" interrupted Hunsden, scoffingly.

"I do, and no mistake. But I have not the peculiar points which go to make a good clergyman; and rather than adopt a profession for which I have no vocation, I would endure extremities of hardship from poverty."

"You're a mighty difficult customer to suit. You won't be a tradesman or a parson; you can't be a lawyer, or a doctor, or a gentleman, because you've no money. I'd recommend you to travel."

"What! without money?"

"You must travel in search of money, man. You can speak French—with a vile English accent, no doubt—still, you can speak it. Go on to the Continent, and see what will turn up for you there."

"God knows I should like to go!" exclaimed I with involuntary ardour.

"Go: what the deuce hinders you? You may get to Brussels, for instance, for five or six pounds, if you know how to manage with economy."

"Necessity would teach me if I didn't."

"Go, then, and let your wits make a way for you when you get there. I know Brussels almost as well as I know X——, and I am sure it would suit such a one as you better than London."

"But occupation, Mr. Hunsden! I must go where occupation is to be had; and how could I get recommendation, or introduction, or employment at Brussels?"

"There speaks the organ of caution. You hate to advance a step before you know every inch of the way. You haven't a sheet of paper and a pen-and-ink?"

"I hope so," and I produced writing materials with alacrity; for I guessed what he was going to do. He sat down, wrote a few lines, folded, sealed, and addressed a letter, and held it out to me.

"There, Prudence, there's a pioneer to hew down the first rough difficulties of your path. I know well enough, lad, you are not one of those who will run their neck into a noose without seeing how they are to get it out again, and you're right there. A reckless man is my aversion, and nothing should ever persuade me to meddle with the concerns of such a one. Those who are reckless for themselves are generally ten times more so for their friends."

"This is a letter of introduction, I suppose?" said I, taking the epistle.

"Yes. With that in your pocket you will run no risk of finding yourself in a state of absolute destitution, which, I know, you will regard as a degradation—so should I, for that matter. The person to whom you will present it generally has two or three respectable places depending upon his recommendation."

"That will just suit me," said I.

"Well, and where's your gratitude?" demanded Mr. Hunsden; "don't you know how to say 'Thank you?'"

"I've fifteen pounds and a watch, which my godmother, whom I never saw, gave me eighteen years ago," was my rather irrelevant answer; and I further avowed myself a happy man, and professed that I did not envy any being in Christendom.

"But your gratitude?"

"I shall be off presently, Mr. Hunsden—to-morrow, if all be well: I'll not stay a day longer in X—— than I'm obliged."

"Very good—but it will be decent to make due acknowledgment for the assistance you have received; be quick! It is just going to strike seven: I'm waiting to be thanked."

"Just stand out of the way, will you, Mr. Hunsden: I want a key there is on the corner of the mantelpiece. I'll pack my portmanteau before I go to bed."

The house clock struck seven.

"The lad is a heathen," said Hunsden, and taking his hat from a sideboard, he left the room, laughing to himself. I had half an inclination to follow him: I really intended to leave X—— the next morning, and should certainly not have another opportunity of bidding him good-bye. The front door banged to.

"Let him go," said I, "we shall meet again some day."

CHAPTER VII.

Reader, perhaps you were never in Belgium? Haply you don't know the physiognomy of the country? You have not its lineaments defined upon your memory, as I have them on mine?

Three—nay four—pictures line the four-walled cell where are stored for me the records of the past. First, Eton. All in that picture is in far perspective, receding, diminutive; but freshly coloured, green, dewy, with a spring sky, piled with glittering yet showery clouds; for my childhood was not all sunshine—it had its overcast, its cold, its stormy hours. Second, X——, huge, dingy; the canvas cracked and smoked; a yellow sky, sooty clouds; no sun, no azure; the verdure of the suburbs blighted and sullied—a very dreary scene.

Third, Belgium; and I will pause before this landscape. As to the fourth, a curtain covers it, which I may hereafter withdraw, or may not, as suits my convenience and capacity. At any rate, for the present it must hang undisturbed. Belgium! name unromantic and unpoetic, yet name that whenever uttered has in my ear a sound, in my heart an echo, such as no other assemblage of syllables, however sweet or classic, can produce. Belgium! I repeat the word, now as I sit alone near midnight. It stirs my world of the past like a summons to resurrection; the graves unclose, the dead are raised; thoughts, feelings, memories that slept, are seen by me ascending from the clouds—haloed most of them—but while I gaze on their vapoury forms, and strive to ascertain definitely their outline, the sound which wakened them dies, and they sink, each and all, like a light wreath of mist, absorbed in the mould, recalled to urns, resealed in monuments. Farewell, luminous phantoms!

This is Belgium, reader. Look! don't call the picture a flat or a dull one—it was neither flat nor dull to me when I first beheld it. When I left Ostend on a mild February morning, and found myself on the road to Brussels, nothing could look vapid to me. My sense of enjoyment possessed an edge whetted to the finest, untouched, keen, exquisite. I was young; I had good health; pleasure and I had never met; no indulgence of hers had enervated or sated one faculty of my nature. Liberty I clasped in my arms for the first time, and the influence of her smile and embrace revived my life like the sun and the west wind. Yes, at that epoch I felt like a morning traveller who doubts not that from the hill he is ascending he shall behold a glorious sunrise; what if the track be strait, steep, and stony? he sees it not; his eyes are fixed on that summit, flushed already, flushed and gilded, and having gained it he is certain of the scene beyond. He knows that the sun will face him, that his chariot is even now coming over the eastern horizon, and that the herald breeze he feels on his cheek is opening for the god's career a clear, vast path of azure, amidst clouds soft as pearl and warm as flame. Difficulty and toil were to be my lot, but sustained by energy, drawn on by hopes as bright as vague, I deemed such a lot no hardship. I mounted now the hill in shade; there were pebbles, inequalities, briars in my path, but my eyes were fixed on the crimson peak above; my imagination was with the refulgent firmament beyond, and I thought nothing of the stones turning under my feet, or of the thorns scratching my face and hands.

I gazed often, and always with delight, from the window of the diligence (these, be it remembered, were not the days of trains and railroads). Well! and what did I see? I will tell you faithfully. Green, reedy swamps; fields fertile but flat, cultivated in patches that made them look like magnified kitchen-gardens; belts of cut trees, formal as pollard willows, skirting the horizon; narrow canals, gliding slow by the road-side; painted Flemish farmhouses; some very dirty hovels; a gray, dead sky; wet road, wet fields, wet house-tops: not a beautiful, scarcely a picturesque object met my eye along the whole route; yet to me, all was beautiful, all was more than picturesque. It continued fair so long as daylight lasted, though the moisture of many preceding damp days had sodden the whole country; as it grew dark, however, the rain recommenced, and it was through streaming and starless darkness my eye caught the first gleam of the lights of Brussels. I saw little of the city but its lights that night. Having alighted from the diligence, a fiacre conveyed me to the Hotel de ——, where I had been advised by a fellow-traveller to put up; having eaten a traveller's supper, I retired to bed, and slept a traveller's sleep.

Next morning I awoke from prolonged and sound repose with the impression that I was yet in X——, and perceiving it to be broad daylight I started up, imagining that I had overslept myself and should be behind time at the counting-house. The momentary and painful sense of restraint vanished before the revived and reviving consciousness of freedom, as, throwing back the white curtains of my bed, I looked forth into a wide, lofty foreign chamber; how different from the small and dingy, though not uncomfortable, apartment I had occupied for a night or two at a respectable inn in London while waiting for the sailing of the packet! Yet far be it from me to profane the memory of that little dingy room! It, too, is dear to my soul; for there, as I lay in quiet and darkness, I first heard the great bell of St. Paul's telling London it was midnight, and well do I recall the deep, deliberate tones, so full charged with colossal phlegm and force. From the small, narrow window of that room, I first saw THE dome, looming through a London mist. I suppose the sensations, stirred by those first sounds, first sights, are felt but once; treasure them, Memory; seal them in urns, and keep them in safe niches! Well—I rose. Travellers talk of the apartments in foreign dwellings being bare and uncomfortable; I thought my chamber looked stately and cheerful. It had such large windows—CROISEES that opened like doors, with such broad, clear panes of glass; such a great looking-glass stood on my dressing-table—such a fine mirror glittered over the mantelpiece—the painted floor looked so clean and glossy; when I had dressed and was descending the stairs, the broad marble steps almost awed me, and so did the lofty hall into which they conducted. On the first landing I met a Flemish housemaid: she had wooden shoes, a short red petticoat, a printed cotton bedgown, her face was broad, her physiognomy eminently stupid; when I spoke to her in French, she answered me in Flemish, with an air the reverse of civil; yet I thought her charming; if she was not pretty or polite, she was, I conceived, very picturesque; she reminded me of the female figures in certain Dutch paintings I had seen in other years at Seacombe Hall.

I repaired to the public room; that, too, was very large and very lofty, and warmed by a stove; the floor was black, and the stove was black, and most of the furniture was black: yet I never experienced a freer sense of exhilaration than when I sat down at a very long, black table (covered, however, in part by a white cloth), and, having ordered breakfast, began to pour out my coffee from a little black coffee-pot. The stove might be dismal-looking to some eyes, not to mine, but it was indisputably very warm, and there were two gentlemen seated by it talking in French; impossible to follow their rapid utterance, or comprehend much of the purport of what they said—yet French, in the mouths of Frenchmen, or Belgians (I was not then sensible of the horrors of the Belgian accent) was as music to my ears. One of these gentlemen presently discerned me to be an Englishman—no doubt from the fashion in which I addressed the waiter; for I would persist in speaking French in my execrable South-of-England style, though the man understood English. The gentleman, after looking towards me once or twice, politely accosted me in very good English; I remember I wished to God that I could speak French as well; his fluency and correct pronunciation impressed me for the first time with a due notion of the cosmopolitan character of the capital I was in; it was my first experience of that skill in living languages I afterwards found to be so general in Brussels.

I lingered over my breakfast as long as I could; while it was there on the table, and while that stranger continued talking to me, I was a free, independent traveller; but at last the things were removed, the two gentlemen left the room; suddenly the illusion ceased, reality and business came back. I, a bondsman just released from the yoke, freed for one week from twenty-one years of constraint, must, of necessity, resume the fetters of dependency. Hardly had I tasted the delight of being without a master when duty issued her stern mandate: "Go forth and seek another service." I never linger over a painful and necessary task; I never take pleasure before business, it is not in my nature to do so; impossible to enjoy a leisurely walk over the city, though I perceived the morning was very fine, until I had first presented Mr. Hunsden's letter of introduction, and got fairly on to the track of a new situation. Wrenching my mind from liberty and delight, I seized my hat, and forced my reluctant body out of the Hotel de —— into the foreign street.

It was a fine day, but I would not look at the blue sky or at the stately houses round me; my mind was bent on one thing, finding out "Mr. Brown, Numero ——, Rue Royale," for so my letter was addressed. By dint of inquiry I succeeded; I stood at last at the desired door, knocked, asked for Mr. Brown, and was admitted.

Being shown into a small breakfast-room, I found myself in the presence of an elderly gentleman—very grave, business-like, and respectable-looking. I presented Mr. Hunsden's letter; he received me very civilly. After a little desultory conversation he asked me if there was anything in which his advice or experience could be of use. I said, "Yes," and then proceeded to tell him that I was not a gentleman of fortune, travelling for pleasure, but an ex-counting-house clerk, who wanted employment of some kind, and that immediately too. He replied that as a friend of Mr. Hunsden's he would be willing to assist me as well as he could. After some meditation he named a place in a mercantile house at Liege, and another in a bookseller's shop at Louvain.

"Clerk and shopman!" murmured I to myself. "No." I shook my head. I had tried the high stool; I hated it; I believed there were other occupations that would suit me better; besides I did not wish to leave Brussels.

"I know of no place in Brussels," answered Mr. Brown, "unless indeed you were disposed to turn your attention to teaching. I am acquainted with the director of a large establishment who is in want of a professor of English and Latin."

I thought two minutes, then I seized the idea eagerly.

"The very thing, sir!" said I.

"But," asked he, "do you understand French well enough to teach Belgian boys English?"

Fortunately I could answer this question in the affirmative; having studied French under a Frenchman, I could speak the language intelligibly though not fluently. I could also read it well, and write it decently.

"Then," pursued Mr. Brown, "I think I can promise you the place, for Monsieur Pelet will not refuse a professor recommended by me; but come here again at five o'clock this afternoon, and I will introduce you to him."

The word "professor" struck me. "I am not a professor," said I.

"Oh," returned Mr. Brown, "professor, here in Belgium, means a teacher, that is all."

My conscience thus quieted, I thanked Mr. Brown, and, for the present, withdrew. This time I stepped out into the street with a relieved heart; the task I had imposed on myself for that day was executed. I might now take some hours of holiday. I felt free to look up. For the first time I remarked the sparkling clearness of the air, the deep blue of the sky, the gay clean aspect of the white-washed or painted houses; I saw what a fine street was the Rue Royale, and, walking leisurely along its broad pavement, I continued to survey its stately hotels, till the palisades, the gates, and trees of the park appearing in sight, offered to my eye a new attraction. I remember, before entering the park, I stood awhile to contemplate the statue of General Belliard, and then I advanced to the top of the great staircase just beyond, and I looked down into a narrow back street, which I afterwards learnt was called the Rue d'Isabelle. I well recollect that my eye rested on the green door of a rather large house opposite, where, on a brass plate, was inscribed, "Pensionnat de Demoiselles." Pensionnat! The word excited an uneasy sensation in my mind; it seemed to speak of restraint. Some of the demoiselles, externats no doubt, were at that moment issuing from the door—I looked for a pretty face amongst them, but their close, little French bonnets hid their features; in a moment they were gone.

I had traversed a good deal of Brussels before five o'clock arrived, but punctually as that hour struck I was again in the Rue Royale. Re-admitted to Mr. Brown's breakfast-room, I found him, as before, seated at the table, and he was not alone—a gentleman stood by the hearth. Two words of introduction designated him as my future master. "M. Pelet, Mr. Crimsworth; Mr. Crimsworth, M. Pelet," a bow on each side finished the ceremony. I don't know what sort of a bow I made; an ordinary one, I suppose, for I was in a tranquil, commonplace frame of mind; I felt none of the agitation which had troubled my first interview with Edward Crimsworth. M. Pelet's bow was extremely polite, yet not theatrical, scarcely French; he and I were presently seated opposite to each other. In a pleasing voice, low, and, out of consideration to my foreign ears, very distinct and deliberate, M. Pelet intimated that he had just been receiving from "le respectable M. Brown," an account of my attainments and character, which relieved him from all scruple as to the propriety of engaging me as professor of English and Latin in his establishment; nevertheless, for form's sake, he would put a few questions to test my powers. He did, and expressed in flattering terms his satisfaction at my answers. The subject of salary next came on; it was fixed at one thousand francs per annum, besides board and lodging. "And in addition," suggested M. Pelet, "as there will be some hours in each day during which your services will not be required in my establishment, you may, in time, obtain employment in other seminaries, and thus turn your vacant moments to profitable account."

I thought this very kind, and indeed I found afterwards that the terms on which M. Pelet had engaged me were really liberal for Brussels; instruction being extremely cheap there on account of the number of teachers. It was further arranged that I should be installed in my new post the very next day, after which M. Pelet and I parted.

Well, and what was he like? and what were my impressions concerning him? He was a man of about forty years of age, of middle size, and rather emaciated figure; his face was pale, his cheeks were sunk, and his eyes hollow; his features were pleasing and regular, they had a French turn (for M. Pelet was no Fleming, but a Frenchman both by birth and parentage), yet the degree of harshness inseparable from Gallic lineaments was, in his case, softened by a mild blue eye, and a melancholy, almost suffering, expression of countenance; his physiognomy was "fine et spirituelle." I use two French words because they define better than any English terms the species of intelligence with which his features were imbued. He was altogether an interesting and prepossessing personage. I wondered only at the utter absence of all the ordinary characteristics of his profession, and almost feared he could not be stern and resolute enough for a schoolmaster. Externally at least M. Pelet presented an absolute contrast to my late master, Edward Crimsworth.

Influenced by the impression I had received of his gentleness, I was a good deal surprised when, on arriving the next day at my new employer's house, and being admitted to a first view of what was to be the sphere of my future labours, namely the large, lofty, and well-lighted schoolrooms, I beheld a numerous assemblage of pupils, boys of course, whose collective appearance showed all the signs of a full, flourishing, and well-disciplined seminary. As I traversed the classes in company with M. Pelet, a profound silence reigned on all sides, and if by chance a murmur or a whisper arose, one glance from the pensive eye of this most gentle pedagogue stilled it instantly. It was astonishing, I thought, how so mild a check could prove so effectual. When I had perambulated the length and breadth of the classes, M. Pelet turned and said to me—

"Would you object to taking the boys as they are, and testing their proficiency in English?"

The proposal was unexpected. I had thought I should have been allowed at least three days to prepare; but it is a bad omen to commence any career by hesitation, so I just stepped to the professor's desk near which we stood, and faced the circle of my pupils. I took a moment to collect my thoughts, and likewise to frame in French the sentence by which I proposed to open business. I made it as short as possible:—

"Messieurs, prenez vos livres de lecture."

"Anglais ou Francais, monsieur?" demanded a thickset, moon-faced young Flamand in a blouse. The answer was fortunately easy:—

"Anglais."

I determined to give myself as little trouble as possible in this lesson; it would not do yet to trust my unpractised tongue with the delivery of explanations; my accent and idiom would be too open to the criticisms of the young gentlemen before me, relative to whom I felt already it would be necessary at once to take up an advantageous position, and I proceeded to employ means accordingly.

"Commencez!" cried I, when they had all produced their books. The moon-faced youth (by name Jules Vanderkelkov, as I afterwards learnt) took the first sentence. The "livre de lecture" was the "Vicar of Wakefield," much used in foreign schools because it is supposed to contain prime samples of conversational English; it might, however, have been a Runic scroll for any resemblance the words, as enunciated by Jules, bore to the language in ordinary use amongst the natives of Great Britain. My God! how he did snuffle, snort, and wheeze! All he said was said in his throat and nose, for it is thus the Flamands speak, but I heard him to the end of his paragraph without proffering a word of correction, whereat he looked vastly self-complacent, convinced, no doubt, that he had acquitted himself like a real born and bred "Anglais." In the same unmoved silence I listened to a dozen in rotation, and when the twelfth had concluded with splutter, hiss, and mumble, I solemnly laid down the book.

"Arretez!" said I. There was a pause, during which I regarded them all with a steady and somewhat stern gaze; a dog, if stared at hard enough and long enough, will show symptoms of embarrassment, and so at length did my bench of Belgians. Perceiving that some of the faces before me were beginning to look sullen, and others ashamed, I slowly joined my hands, and ejaculated in a deep "voix de poitrine"—

"Comme c'est affreux!"

They looked at each other, pouted, coloured, swung their heels; they were not pleased, I saw, but they were impressed, and in the way I wished them to be. Having thus taken them down a peg in their self-conceit, the next step was to raise myself in their estimation; not a very easy thing, considering that I hardly dared to speak for fear of betraying my own deficiencies.

"Ecoutez, messieurs!" said I, and I endeavoured to throw into my accents the compassionate tone of a superior being, who, touched by the extremity of the helplessness, which at first only excited his scorn, deigns at length to bestow aid. I then began at the very beginning of the "Vicar of Wakefield," and read, in a slow, distinct voice, some twenty pages, they all the while sitting mute and listening with fixed attention; by the time I had done nearly an hour had elapsed. I then rose and said:—

"C'est assez pour aujourd'hui, messieurs; demain nous recommencerons, et j'espere que tout ira bien."

With this oracular sentence I bowed, and in company with M. Pelet quitted the school-room.

"C'est bien! c'est tres bien!" said my principal as we entered his parlour. "Je vois que monsieur a de l'adresse; cela, me plait, car, dans l'instruction, l'adresse fait tout autant que le savoir."

From the parlour M. Pelet conducted me to my apartment, my "chambre," as Monsieur said with a certain air of complacency. It was a very small room, with an excessively small bed, but M. Pelet gave me to understand that I was to occupy it quite alone, which was of course a great comfort. Yet, though so limited in dimensions, it had two windows. Light not being taxed in Belgium, the people never grudge its admission into their houses; just here, however, this observation is not very APROPOS, for one of these windows was boarded up; the open windows looked into the boys' playground. I glanced at the other, as wondering what aspect it would present if disencumbered of the boards. M. Pelet read, I suppose, the expression of my eye; he explained:—

"La fenetre fermee donne sur un jardin appartenant a un pensionnat de demoiselles," said he, "et les convenances exigent—enfin, vous comprenez—n'est-ce pas, monsieur?"

"Oui, oui," was my reply, and I looked of course quite satisfied; but when M. Pelet had retired and closed the door after him, the first thing I did was to scrutinize closely the nailed boards, hoping to find some chink or crevice which I might enlarge, and so get a peep at the consecrated ground. My researches were vain, for the boards were well joined and strongly nailed. It is astonishing how disappointed I felt. I thought it would have been so pleasant to have looked out upon a garden planted with flowers and trees, so amusing to have watched the demoiselles at their play; to have studied female character in a variety of phases, myself the while sheltered from view by a modest muslin curtain, whereas, owing doubtless to the absurd scruples of some old duenna of a directress, I had now only the option of looking at a bare gravelled court, with an enormous "pas de geant" in the middle, and the monotonous walls and windows of a boys' school-house round. Not only then, but many a time after, especially in moments of weariness and low spirits, did I look with dissatisfied eyes on that most tantalizing board, longing to tear it away and get a glimpse of the green region which I imagined to lie beyond. I knew a tree grew close up to the window, for though there were as yet no leaves to rustle, I often heard at night the tapping of branches against the panes. In the daytime, when I listened attentively, I could hear, even through the boards, the voices of the demoiselles in their hours of recreation, and, to speak the honest truth, my sentimental reflections were occasionally a trifle disarranged by the not quite silvery, in fact the too often brazen sounds, which, rising from the unseen paradise below, penetrated clamorously into my solitude. Not to mince matters, it really seemed to me a doubtful case whether the lungs of Mdlle. Reuter's girls or those of M. Pelet's boys were the strongest, and when it came to shrieking the girls indisputably beat the boys hollow. I forgot to say, by-the-by, that Reuter was the name of the old lady who had had my window bearded up. I say old, for such I, of course, concluded her to be, judging from her cautious, chaperon-like proceedings; besides, nobody ever spoke of her as young. I remember I was very much amused when I first heard her Christian name; it was Zoraide—Mademoiselle Zoraide Reuter. But the continental nations do allow themselves vagaries in the choice of names, such as we sober English never run into. I think, indeed, we have too limited a list to choose from.

Meantime my path was gradually growing smooth before me. I, in a few weeks, conquered the teasing difficulties inseparable from the commencement of almost every career. Ere long I had acquired as much facility in speaking French as set me at my ease with my pupils; and as I had encountered them on a right footing at the very beginning, and continued tenaciously to retain the advantage I had early gained, they never attempted mutiny, which circumstance, all who are in any degree acquainted with the ongoings of Belgian schools, and who know the relation in which professors and pupils too frequently stand towards each other in those establishments, will consider an important and uncommon one. Before concluding this chapter I will say a word on the system I pursued with regard to my classes: my experience may possibly be of use to others.

It did not require very keen observation to detect the character of the youth of Brabant, but it needed a certain degree of tact to adopt one's measures to their capacity. Their intellectual faculties were generally weak, their animal propensities strong; thus there was at once an impotence and a kind of inert force in their natures; they were dull, but they were also singularly stubborn, heavy as lead and, like lead, most difficult to move. Such being the case, it would have been truly absurd to exact from them much in the way of mental exertion; having short memories, dense intelligence, feeble reflective powers, they recoiled with repugnance from any occupation that demanded close study or deep thought. Had the abhorred effort been extorted from them by injudicious and arbitrary measures on the part of the Professor, they would have resisted as obstinately, as clamorously, as desperate swine; and though not brave singly, they were relentless acting EN MASSE.

I understood that before my arrival in M. Pelet's establishment, the combined insubordination of the pupils had effected the dismissal of more than one English master. It was necessary then to exact only the most moderate application from natures so little qualified to apply—to assist, in every practicable way, understandings so opaque and contracted—to be ever gentle, considerate, yielding even, to a certain point, with dispositions so irrationally perverse; but, having reached that culminating point of indulgence, you must fix your foot, plant it, root it in rock—become immutable as the towers of Ste. Gudule; for a step—but half a step farther, and you would plunge headlong into the gulf of imbecility; there lodged, you would speedily receive proofs of Flemish gratitude and magnanimity in showers of Brabant saliva and handfuls of Low Country mud. You might smooth to the utmost the path of learning, remove every pebble from the track; but then you must finally insist with decision on the pupil taking your arm and allowing himself to be led quietly along the prepared road. When I had brought down my lesson to the lowest level of my dullest pupil's capacity—when I had shown myself the mildest, the most tolerant of masters—a word of impertinence, a movement of disobedience, changed me at once into a despot. I offered then but one alternative—submission and acknowledgment of error, or ignominious expulsion. This system answered, and my influence, by degrees, became established on a firm basis. "The boy is father to the man," it is said; and so I often thought when looked at my boys and remembered the political history of their ancestors. Pelet's school was merely an epitome of the Belgian nation.

CHAPTER VIII.

And Pelet himself? How did I continue to like him? Oh, extremely well! Nothing could be more smooth, gentlemanlike, and even friendly, than his demeanour to me. I had to endure from him neither cold neglect, irritating interference, nor pretentious assumption of superiority. I fear, however, two poor, hard-worked Belgian ushers in the establishment could not have said as much; to them the director's manner was invariably dry, stern, and cool. I believe he perceived once or twice that I was a little shocked at the difference he made between them and me, and accounted for it by saying, with a quiet sarcastic smile—

"Ce ne sont que des Flamands—allez!"

And then he took his cigar gently from his lips and spat on the painted floor of the room in which we were sitting. Flamands certainly they were, and both had the true Flamand physiognomy, where intellectual inferiority is marked in lines none can mistake; still they were men, and, in the main, honest men; and I could not see why their being aboriginals of the flat, dull soil should serve as a pretext for treating them with perpetual severity and contempt. This idea, of injustice somewhat poisoned the pleasure I might otherwise have derived from Pelet's soft affable manner to myself. Certainly it was agreeable, when the day's work was over, to find one's employer an intelligent and cheerful companion; and if he was sometimes a little sarcastic and sometimes a little too insinuating, and if I did discover that his mildness was more a matter of appearance than of reality—if I did occasionally suspect the existence of flint or steel under an external covering of velvet—still we are none of us perfect; and weary as I was of the atmosphere of brutality and insolence in which I had constantly lived at X——, I had no inclination now, on casting anchor in calmer regions, to institute at once a prying search after defects that were scrupulously withdrawn and carefully veiled from my view. I was willing to take Pelet for what he seemed—to believe him benevolent and friendly until some untoward event should prove him otherwise. He was not married, and I soon perceived he had all a Frenchman's, all a Parisian's notions about matrimony and women. I suspected a degree of laxity in his code of morals, there was something so cold and BLASE in his tone whenever he alluded to what he called "le beau sexe;" but he was too gentlemanlike to intrude topics I did not invite, and as he was really intelligent and really fond of intellectual subjects of discourse, he and I always found enough to talk about, without seeking themes in the mire. I hated his fashion of mentioning love; I abhorred, from my soul, mere licentiousness. He felt the difference of our notions, and, by mutual consent, we kept off ground debateable.

Pelet's house was kept and his kitchen managed by his mother, a real old Frenchwoman; she had been handsome—at least she told me so, and I strove to believe her; she was now ugly, as only continental old women can be; perhaps, though, her style of dress made her look uglier than she really was. Indoors she would go about without cap, her grey hair strangely dishevelled; then, when at home, she seldom wore a gown—only a shabby cotton camisole; shoes, too, were strangers to her feet, and in lieu of them she sported roomy slippers, trodden down at the heels. On the other hand, whenever it was her pleasure to appear abroad, as on Sundays and fete-days, she would put on some very brilliant-coloured dress, usually of thin texture, a silk bonnet with a wreath of flowers, and a very fine shawl. She was not, in the main, an ill-natured old woman, but an incessant and most indiscreet talker; she kept chiefly in and about the kitchen, and seemed rather to avoid her son's august presence; of him, indeed, she evidently stood in awe. When he reproved her, his reproofs were bitter and unsparing; but he seldom gave himself that trouble.

Madame Pelet had her own society, her own circle of chosen visitors, whom, however, I seldom saw, as she generally entertained them in what she called her "cabinet," a small den of a place adjoining the kitchen, and descending into it by one or two steps. On these steps, by-the-by, I have not unfrequently seen Madame Pelet seated with a trencher on her knee, engaged in the threefold employment of eating her dinner, gossiping with her favourite servant, the housemaid, and scolding her antagonist, the cook; she never dined, and seldom indeed took any meal with her son; and as to showing her face at the boys' table, that was quite out of the question. These details will sound very odd in English ears, but Belgium is not England, and its ways are not our ways.

Madame Pelet's habits of life, then, being taken into consideration, I was a good deal surprised when, one Thursday evening (Thursday was always a half-holiday), as I was sitting all alone in my apartment, correcting a huge pile of English and Latin exercises, a servant tapped at the door, and, on its being opened, presented Madame Pelet's compliments, and she would be happy to see me to take my "gouter" (a meal which answers to our English "tea") with her in the dining-room.

"Plait-il?" said I, for I thought I must have misunderstood, the message and invitation were so unusual; the same words were repeated. I accepted, of course, and as I descended the stairs, I wondered what whim had entered the old lady's brain; her son was out—gone to pass the evening at the Salle of the Grande Harmonie or some other club of which he was a member. Just as I laid my hand on the handle of the dining-room door, a queer idea glanced across my mind.

"Surely she's not going to make love to me," said I. "I've heard of old Frenchwomen doing odd things in that line; and the gouter? They generally begin such affairs with eating and drinking, I believe."

There was a fearful dismay in this suggestion of my excited imagination, and if I had allowed myself time to dwell upon it, I should no doubt have cut there and then, rushed back to my chamber, and bolted myself in; but whenever a danger or a horror is veiled with uncertainty, the primary wish of the mind is to ascertain first the naked truth, reserving the expedient of flight for the moment when its dread anticipation shall be realized. I turned the door-handle, and in an instant had crossed the fatal threshold, closed the door behind me, and stood in the presence of Madame Pelet.

Gracious heavens! The first view of her seemed to confirm my worst apprehensions. There she sat, dressed out in a light green muslin gown, on her head a lace cap with flourishing red roses in the frill; her table was carefully spread; there were fruit, cakes, and coffee, with a bottle of something—I did not know what. Already the cold sweat started on my brow, already I glanced back over my shoulder at the closed door, when, to my unspeakable relief, my eye, wandering mildly in the direction of the stove, rested upon a second figure, seated in a large fauteuil beside it. This was a woman, too, and, moreover, an old woman, and as fat and as rubicund as Madame Pelet was meagre and yellow; her attire was likewise very fine, and spring flowers of different hues circled in a bright wreath the crown of her violet-coloured velvet bonnet.

I had only time to make these general observations when Madame Pelet, coming forward with what she intended should be a graceful and elastic step, thus accosted me:

"Monsieur is indeed most obliging to quit his books, his studies, at the request of an insignificant person like me—will Monsieur complete his kindness by allowing me to present him to my dear friend Madame Reuter, who resides in the neighbouring house—the young ladies' school."

"Ah!" thought I, "I knew she was old," and I bowed and took my seat. Madame Reuter placed herself at the table opposite to me.

"How do you like Belgium, Monsieur?" asked she, in an accent of the broadest Bruxellois. I could now well distinguish the difference between the fine and pure Parisian utterance of M. Pelet, for instance, and the guttural enunciation of the Flamands. I answered politely, and then wondered how so coarse and clumsy an old woman as the one before me should be at the head of a ladies' seminary, which I had always heard spoken of in terms of high commendation. In truth there was something to wonder at. Madame Reuter looked more like a joyous, free-living old Flemish fermiere, or even a maitresse d'auberge, than a staid, grave, rigid directrice de pensionnat. In general the continental, or at least the Belgian old women permit themselves a licence of manners, speech, and aspect, such as our venerable granddames would recoil from as absolutely disreputable, and Madame Reuter's jolly face bore evidence that she was no exception to the rule of her country; there was a twinkle and leer in her left eye; her right she kept habitually half shut, which I thought very odd indeed. After several vain attempts to comprehend the motives of these two droll old creatures for inviting me to join them at their gouter, I at last fairly gave it up, and resigning myself to inevitable mystification, I sat and looked first at one, then at the other, taking care meantime to do justice to the confitures, cakes, and coffee, with which they amply supplied me. They, too, ate, and that with no delicate appetite, and having demolished a large portion of the solids, they proposed a "petit verre." I declined. Not so Mesdames Pelet and Reuter; each mixed herself what I thought rather a stiff tumbler of punch, and placing it on a stand near the stove, they drew up their chairs to that convenience, and invited me to do the same. I obeyed; and being seated fairly between them, I was thus addressed first by Madame Pelet, then by Madame Reuter.

"We will now speak of business," said Madame Pelet, and she went on to make an elaborate speech, which, being interpreted, was to the effect that she had asked for the pleasure of my company that evening in order to give her friend Madame Reuter an opportunity of broaching an important proposal, which might turn out greatly to my advantage.

"Pourvu que vous soyez sage," said Madame Reuter, "et a vrai dire, vous en avez bien l'air. Take one drop of the punch" (or ponche, as she pronounced it); "it is an agreeable and wholesome beverage after a full meal."

I bowed, but again declined it. She went on:

"I feel," said she, after a solemn sip—"I feel profoundly the importance of the commission with which my dear daughter has entrusted me, for you are aware, Monsieur, that it is my daughter who directs the establishment in the next house?"

"Ah! I thought it was yourself, madame." Though, indeed, at that moment I recollected that it was called Mademoiselle, not Madame Reuter's pensionnat.

"I! Oh, no! I manage the house and look after the servants, as my friend Madame Pelet does for Monsieur her son—nothing more. Ah! you thought I gave lessons in class—did you?"

And she laughed loud and long, as though the idea tickled her fancy amazingly.

"Madame is in the wrong to laugh," I observed; "if she does not give lessons, I am sure it is not because she cannot;" and I whipped out a white pocket-handkerchief and wafted it, with a French grace, past my nose, bowing at the same time.

"Quel charmant jeune homme!" murmured Madame Pelet in a low voice. Madame Reuter, being less sentimental, as she was Flamand and not French, only laughed again.

"You are a dangerous person, I fear," said she; "if you can forge compliments at that rate, Zoraide will positively be afraid of you; but if you are good, I will keep your secret, and not tell her how well you can flatter. Now, listen what sort of a proposal she makes to you. She has heard that you are an excellent professor, and as she wishes to get the very best masters for her school (car Zoraide fait tout comme une reine, c'est une veritable maitresse-femme), she has commissioned me to step over this afternoon, and sound Madame Pelet as to the possibility of engaging you. Zoraide is a wary general; she never advances without first examining well her ground. I don't think she would be pleased if she knew I had already disclosed her intentions to you; she did not order me to go so far, but I thought there would be no harm in letting you into the secret, and Madame Pelet was of the same opinion. Take care, however, you don't betray either of us to Zoraide—to my daughter, I mean; she is so discreet and circumspect herself, she cannot understand that one should find a pleasure in gossiping a little—"

"C'est absolument comme mon fils!" cried Madame Pelet.

"All the world is so changed since our girlhood!" rejoined the other: "young people have such old heads now. But to return, Monsieur. Madame Pelet will mention the subject of your giving lessons in my daughter's establishment to her son, and he will speak to you; and then to-morrow, you will step over to our house, and ask to see my daughter, and you will introduce the subject as if the first intimation of it had reached you from M. Pelet himself, and be sure you never mention my name, for I would not displease Zoraide on any account."

"Bien! bien!" interrupted I—for all this chatter and circumlocution began to bore me very much; "I will consult M. Pelet, and the thing shall be settled as you desire. Good evening, mesdames—I am infinitely obliged to you."

"Comment! vous vous en allez deja?" exclaimed Madame Pelet.

"Prenez encore quelquechose, monsieur; une pomme cuite, des biscuits, encore une tasse de cafe?"

"Merci, merci, madame—au revoir." And I backed at last out of the apartment.

Having regained my own room, I set myself to turn over in my mind the incident of the evening. It seemed a queer affair altogether, and queerly managed; the two old women had made quite a little intricate mess of it; still I found that the uppermost feeling in my mind on the subject was one of satisfaction. In the first place it would be a change to give lessons in another seminary, and then to teach young ladies would be an occupation so interesting—to be admitted at all into a ladies' boarding-school would be an incident so new in my life. Besides, thought I, as I glanced at the boarded window, "I shall now at last see the mysterious garden: I shall gaze both on the angels and their Eden."

CHAPTER IX.

M. Pelet could not of course object to the proposal made by Mdlle. Reuter; permission to accept such additional employment, should it offer, having formed an article of the terms on which he had engaged me. It was, therefore, arranged in the course of next day that I should be at liberty to give lessons in Mdlle. Reuter's establishment four afternoons in every week.

When evening came I prepared to step over in order to seek a conference with Mademoiselle herself on the subject; I had not had time to pay the visit before, having been all day closely occupied in class. I remember very well that before quitting my chamber, I held a brief debate with myself as to whether I should change my ordinary attire for something smarter. At last I concluded it would be a waste of labour. "Doubtless," thought I, "she is some stiff old maid; for though the daughter of Madame Reuter, she may well number upwards of forty winters; besides, if it were otherwise, if she be both young and pretty, I am not handsome, and no dressing can make me so, therefore I'll go as I am." And off I started, cursorily glancing sideways as I passed the toilet-table, surmounted by a looking-glass: a thin irregular face I saw, with sunk, dark eyes under a large, square forehead, complexion destitute of bloom or attraction; something young, but not youthful, no object to win a lady's love, no butt for the shafts of Cupid.

I was soon at the entrance of the pensionnat, in a moment I had pulled the bell; in another moment the door was opened, and within appeared a passage paved alternately with black and white marble; the walls were painted in imitation of marble also; and at the far end opened a glass door, through which I saw shrubs and a grass-plat, looking pleasant in the sunshine of the mild spring evening—for it was now the middle of April.

This, then, was my first glimpse of the garden; but I had not time to look long, the portress, after having answered in the affirmative my question as to whether her mistress was at home, opened the folding-doors of a room to the left, and having ushered me in, closed them behind me. I found myself in a salon with a very well-painted, highly varnished floor; chairs and sofas covered with white draperies, a green porcelain stove, walls hung with pictures in gilt frames, a gilt pendule and other ornaments on the mantelpiece, a large lustre pendent from the centre of the ceiling, mirrors, consoles, muslin curtains, and a handsome centre table completed the inventory of furniture. All looked extremely clean and glittering, but the general effect would have been somewhat chilling had not a second large pair of folding-doors, standing wide open, and disclosing another and smaller salon, more snugly furnished, offered some relief to the eye. This room was carpeted, and therein was a piano, a couch, a chiffonniere—above all, it contained a lofty window with a crimson curtain, which, being undrawn, afforded another glimpse of the garden, through the large, clear panes, round which some leaves of ivy, some tendrils of vine were trained.

"Monsieur Creemsvort, n'est ce pas?" said a voice behind me; and, starting involuntarily, I turned. I had been so taken up with the contemplation of the pretty little salon that I had not noticed the entrance of a person into the larger room. It was, however, Mdlle. Reuter who now addressed me, and stood close beside me; and when I had bowed with instantaneously recovered sang-froid —for I am not easily embarrassed—I commenced the conversation by remarking on the pleasant aspect of her little cabinet, and the advantage she had over M. Pelet in possessing a garden.

"Yes," she said, "she often thought so;" and added, "it is my garden, monsieur, which makes me retain this house, otherwise I should probably have removed to larger and more commodious premises long since; but you see I could not take my garden with me, and I should scarcely find one so large and pleasant anywhere else in town."

I approved her judgment.

"But you have not seen it yet," said she, rising; "come to the window and take a better view." I followed her; she opened the sash, and leaning out I saw in full the enclosed demesne which had hitherto been to me an unknown region. It was a long, not very broad strip of cultured ground, with an alley bordered by enormous old fruit trees down the middle; there was a sort of lawn, a parterre of rose-trees, some flower-borders, and, on the far side, a thickly planted copse of lilacs, laburnums, and acacias. It looked pleasant, to me—very pleasant, so long a time had elapsed since I had seen a garden of any sort. But it was not only on Mdlle. Reuter's garden that my eyes dwelt; when I had taken a view of her well-trimmed beds and budding shrubberies, I allowed my glance to come back to herself, nor did I hastily withdraw it.

I had thought to see a tall, meagre, yellow, conventual image in black, with a close white cap, bandaged under the chin like a nun's head-gear; whereas, there stood by me a little and roundly formed woman, who might indeed be older than I, but was still young; she could not, I thought, be more than six or seven and twenty; she was as fair as a fair Englishwoman; she had no cap; her hair was nut-brown, and she wore it in curls; pretty her features were not, nor very soft, nor very regular, but neither were they in any degree plain, and I already saw cause to deem them expressive. What was their predominant cast? Was it sagacity?—sense? Yes, I thought so; but I could scarcely as yet be sure. I discovered, however, that there was a certain serenity of eye, and freshness of complexion, most pleasing to behold. The colour on her cheek was like the bloom on a good apple, which is as sound at the core as it is red on the rind.

Mdlle. Reuter and I entered upon business. She said she was not absolutely certain of the wisdom of the step she was about to take, because I was so young, and parents might possibly object to a professor like me for their daughters: "But it is often well to act on one's own judgment," said she, "and to lead parents, rather than be led by them. The fitness of a professor is not a matter of age; and, from what I have heard, and from what I observe myself, I would much rather trust you than M. Ledru, the music-master, who is a married man of near fifty."

I remarked that I hoped she would find me worthy of her good opinion; that if I knew myself, I was incapable of betraying any confidence reposed in me. "Du reste," said she, "the surveillance will be strictly attended to." And then she proceeded to discuss the subject of terms. She was very cautious, quite on her guard; she did not absolutely bargain, but she warily sounded me to find out what my expectations might be; and when she could not get me to name a sum, she reasoned and reasoned with a fluent yet quiet circumlocution of speech, and at last nailed me down to five hundred francs per annum—not too much, but I agreed. Before the negotiation was completed, it began to grow a little dusk. I did not hasten it, for I liked well enough to sit and hear her talk; I was amused with the sort of business talent she displayed. Edward could not have shown himself more practical, though he might have evinced more coarseness and urgency; and then she had so many reasons, so many explanations; and, after all, she succeeded in proving herself quite disinterested and even liberal. At last she concluded, she could say no more, because, as I acquiesced in all things, there was no further ground for the exercise of her parts of speech. I was obliged to rise. I would rather have sat a little longer; what had I to return to but my small empty room? And my eyes had a pleasure in looking at Mdlle. Reuter, especially now, when the twilight softened her features a little, and, in the doubtful dusk, I could fancy her forehead as open as it was really elevated, her mouth touched with turns of sweetness as well as defined in lines of sense. When I rose to go, I held out my hand, on purpose, though I knew it was contrary to the etiquette of foreign habits; she smiled, and said—

"Ah! c'est comme tous les Anglais," but gave me her hand very kindly.

"It is the privilege of my country, Mademoiselle," said I; "and, remember, I shall always claim it."

She laughed a little, quite good-naturedly, and with the sort of tranquillity obvious in all she did—a tranquillity which soothed and suited me singularly, at least I thought so that evening. Brussels seemed a very pleasant place to me when I got out again into the street, and it appeared as if some cheerful, eventful, upward-tending career were even then opening to me, on that selfsame mild, still April night. So impressionable a being is man, or at least such a man as I was in those days.

CHAPTER X.

Next day the morning hours seemed to pass very slowly at M. Pelet's; I wanted the afternoon to come that I might go again to the neighbouring pensionnat and give my first lesson within its pleasant precincts; for pleasant they appeared to me. At noon the hour of recreation arrived; at one o'clock we had lunch; this got on the time, and at last St. Gudule's deep bell, tolling slowly two, marked the moment for which I had been waiting.

At the foot of the narrow back-stairs that descended from my room, I met M. Pelet.

"Comme vous avez l'air rayonnant!" said he. "Je ne vous ai jamais vu aussi gai. Que s'est-il donc passe?"

"Apparemment que j'aime les changements," replied I.

"Ah! je comprends—c'est cela—soyez sage seulement. Vous etes bien jeune—trop jeune pour le role que vous allez jouer; il faut prendre garde—

savez-vous?"

"Mais quel danger y a-t-il?"

"Je n'en sais rien—ne vous laissez pas aller a de vives impressions—voila tout."

I laughed: a sentiment of exquisite pleasure played over my nerves at the thought that "vives impressions" were likely to be created; it was the deadness, the sameness of life's daily ongoings that had hitherto been my bane; my blouse-clad "eleves" in the boys' seminary never stirred in me any "vives impressions" except it might be occasionally some of anger. I broke from M. Pelet, and as I strode down the passage he followed me with one of his laughs—a very French, rakish, mocking sound.

Again I stood at the neighbouring door, and soon was re-admitted into the cheerful passage with its clear dove-colour imitation marble walls. I followed the portress, and descending a step, and making a turn, I found myself in a sort of corridor; a side-door opened, Mdlle. Reuter's little figure, as graceful as it was plump, appeared. I could now see her dress in full daylight; a neat, simple mousseline-laine gown fitted her compact round shape to perfection—delicate little collar and manchettes of lace, trim Parisian brodequins showed her neck, wrists, and feet, to complete advantage; but how grave was her face as she came suddenly upon me! Solicitude and business were in her eye—on her forehead; she looked almost stern. Her "Bon jour, monsieur," was quite polite, but so orderly, so commonplace, it spread directly a cool, damp towel over my "vives impressions." The servant turned back when her mistress appeared, and I walked slowly along the corridor, side by side with Mdlle. Reuter.

"Monsieur will give a lesson in the first class to-day," said she; "dictation or reading will perhaps be the best thing to begin with, for those are the easiest forms of communicating instruction in a foreign language; and, at the first, a master naturally feels a little unsettled."

She was quite right, as I had found from experience; it only remained for me to acquiesce. We proceeded now in silence. The corridor terminated in a hall, large, lofty, and square; a glass door on one side showed within a long narrow refectory, with tables, an armoire, and two lamps; it was empty; large glass doors, in front, opened on the playground and garden; a broad staircase ascended spirally on the opposite side; the remaining wall showed a pair of great folding-doors, now closed, and admitting, doubtless, to the classes.

Mdlle. Reuter turned her eye laterally on me, to ascertain, probably, whether I was collected enough to be ushered into her sanctum sanctorum. I suppose she judged me to be in a tolerable state of self-government, for she opened the door, and I followed her through. A rustling sound of uprising greeted our entrance; without looking to the right or left, I walked straight up the lane between two sets of benches and desks, and took possession of the empty chair and isolated desk raised on an estrade, of one step high, so as to command one division; the other division being under the surveillance of a maitresse similarly elevated. At the back of the estrade, and attached to a moveable partition dividing this schoolroom from another beyond, was a large tableau of wood painted black and varnished; a thick crayon of white chalk lay on my desk for the convenience of elucidating any grammatical or verbal obscurity which might occur in my lessons by writing it upon the tableau; a wet sponge appeared beside the chalk, to enable me to efface the marks when they had served the purpose intended.

I carefully and deliberately made these observations before allowing myself to take one glance at the benches before me; having handled the crayon, looked back at the tableau, fingered the sponge in order to ascertain that it was in a right state of moisture, I found myself cool enough to admit of looking calmly up and gazing deliberately round me.

And first I observed that Mdlle. Reuter had already glided away, she was nowhere visible; a maitresse or teacher, the one who occupied the corresponding estrade to my own, alone remained to keep guard over me; she was a little in the shade, and, with my short sight, I could only see that she was of a thin bony figure and rather tallowy complexion, and that her attitude, as she sat, partook equally of listlessness and affectation. More obvious, more prominent, shone on by the full light of the large window, were the occupants of the benches just before me, of whom some were girls of fourteen, fifteen, sixteen, some young women from eighteen (as it appeared to me) up to twenty; the most modest attire, the simplest fashion of wearing the hair, were apparent in all; and good features, ruddy, blooming complexions, large and brilliant eyes, forms full, even to solidity, seemed to abound. I did not bear the first view like a stoic; I was dazzled, my eyes fell, and in a voice somewhat too low I murmured—

"Prenez vos cahiers de dictee, mesdemoiselles."

Not so had I bid the boys at Pelet's take their reading-books. A rustle followed, and an opening of desks; behind the lifted lids which momentarily screened the heads bent down to search for exercise-books, I heard tittering and whispers.

"Eulalie, je suis prete a pleuer de rire," observed one.

"Comme il a rougi en parlant!"

"Oui, c'est un veritable blanc-bec."

"Tais-toi, Hortense—il nous ecoute."

And now the lids sank and the heads reappeared; I had marked three, the whisperers, and I did not scruple to take a very steady look at them as they emerged from their temporary eclipse. It is astonishing what ease and courage their little phrases of flippancy had given me; the idea by which I had been awed was that the youthful beings before me, with their dark nun-like robes and softly braided hair, were a kind of half-angels. The light titter, the giddy whisper, had already in some measure relieved my mind of that fond and oppressive fancy.

The three I allude to were just in front, within half a yard of my estrade, and were among the most womanly-looking present. Their names I knew afterwards, and may as well mention now; they were Eulalie, Hortense, Caroline. Eulalie was tall, and very finely shaped: she was fair, and her features were those of a Low Country Madonna; many a "figure de Vierge" have I seen in Dutch pictures exactly resembling hers; there were no angles in her shape or in her face, all was curve and roundness—neither thought, sentiment, nor passion disturbed by line or flush the equality of her pale, clear skin; her noble bust heaved with her regular breathing, her eyes moved a little —by these evidences of life alone could I have distinguished her from some large handsome figure moulded in wax. Hortense was of middle size and stout, her form was ungraceful, her face striking, more alive and brilliant than Eulalie's, her hair was dark brown, her complexion richly coloured; there were frolic and mischief in her eye: consistency and good sense she might possess, but none of her features betokened those qualities.

Caroline was little, though evidently full grown; raven-black hair, very dark eyes, absolutely regular features, with a colourless olive complexion, clear as to the face and sallow about the neck, formed in her that assemblage of points whose union many persons regard as the perfection of beauty. How, with the tintless pallor of her skin and the classic straightness of her lineaments, she managed to look sensual, I don't know. I think her lips and eyes contrived the affair between them, and the result left no uncertainty on the beholder's mind. She was sensual now, and in ten years' time she would be coarse—promise plain was written in her face of much future folly.

If I looked at these girls with little scruple, they looked at me with still less. Eulalie raised her unmoved eye to mine, and seemed to expect, passively but securely, an impromptu tribute to her majestic charms. Hortense regarded me boldly, and giggled at the same time, while she said, with an air of impudent freedom—

"Dictez-nous quelquechose de facile pour commencer, monsieur."

Caroline shook her loose ringlets of abundant but somewhat coarse hair over her rolling black eyes; parting her lips, as full as those of a hot-blooded

Maroon, she showed her well-set teeth sparkling between them, and treated me at the same time to a smile "de sa facon." Beautiful as Pauline Borghese, she looked at the moment scarcely purer than Lucrece de Borgia. Caroline was of noble family. I heard her lady-mother's character afterwards, and then I ceased to wonder at the precocious accomplishments of the daughter. These three, I at once saw, deemed themselves the queens of the school, and conceived that by their splendour they threw all the rest into the shade. In less than five minutes they had thus revealed to me their characters, and in less than five minutes I had buckled on a breast-plate of steely indifference, and let down a visor of impassible austerity.

"Take your pens and commence writing," said I, in as dry and trite a voice as if I had been addressing only Jules Vanderkelkov and Co.

The dictee now commenced. My three belles interrupted me perpetually with little silly questions and uncalled-for remarks, to some of which I made no answer, and to others replied very quietly and briefly. "Comment dit-on point et virgule en Anglais, monsieur?"

"Semi-colon, mademoiselle."

"Semi-collong? Ah, comme c'est drole!" (giggle.)

"J'ai une si mauvaise plume—impossible d'ecrire!"

"Mais, monsieur—je ne sais pas suivre—vous allez si vite."

"Je n'ai rien compris, moi!"

Here a general murmur arose, and the teacher, opening her lips for the first time, ejaculated—

"Silence, mesdemoiselles!"

No silence followed—on the contrary, the three ladies in front began to talk more loudly.

"C'est si difficile, l'Anglais!"

"Je deteste la dictee."

"Quel ennui d'ecrire quelquechose que l'on ne comprend pas!"

Some of those behind laughed: a degree of confusion began to pervade the class; it was necessary to take prompt measures.

"Donnez-moi votre cahier," said I to Eulalie in an abrupt tone; and bending over, I took it before she had time to give it.

"Et vous, mademoiselle—donnez-moi le votre," continued I, more mildly, addressing a little pale, plain looking girl who sat in the first row of the other division, and whom I had remarked as being at once the ugliest and the most attentive in the room; she rose up, walked over to me, and delivered her book with a grave, modest curtsey. I glanced over the two dictations; Eulalie's was slurred, blotted, and full of silly mistakes—Sylvie's (such was the name of the ugly little girl) was clearly written, it contained no error against sense, and but few faults of orthography. I coolly read aloud both exercises, marking the faults—then I looked at Eulalie:

"C'est honteux!" said I, and I deliberately tore her dictation in four parts, and presented her with the fragments. I returned Sylvie her book with a smile, saying—

"C'est bien—je suis content de vous."

Sylvie looked calmly pleased, Eulalie swelled like an incensed turkey, but the mutiny was quelled: the conceited coquetry and futile flirtation of the first bench were exchanged for a taciturn sullenness, much more convenient to me, and the rest of my lesson passed without interruption.

A bell clanging out in the yard announced the moment for the cessation of school labours. I heard our own bell at the same time, and that of a certain public college immediately after. Order dissolved instantly; up started every pupil, I hastened to seize my hat, bow to the maitresse, and quit the room before the tide of externats should pour from the inner class, where I knew near a hundred were prisoned, and whose rising tumult I already heard.

I had scarcely crossed the hall and gained the corridor, when Mdlle. Reuter came again upon me.

"Step in here a moment," said she, and she held open the door of the side room from whence she had issued on my arrival; it was a SALLE-A-MANGER, as appeared from the beaufet and the armoire vitree, filled with glass and china, which formed part of its furniture. Ere she had closed the door on me and herself, the corridor was already filled with day-pupils, tearing down their cloaks, bonnets, and cabas from the wooden pegs on which they were suspended; the shrill voice of a maitresse was heard at intervals vainly endeavouring to enforce some sort of order; vainly, I say: discipline there was none in these rough ranks, and yet this was considered one of the best-conducted schools in Brussels.

"Well, you have given your first lesson," began Mdlle. Reuter in the most calm, equable voice, as though quite unconscious of the chaos from which we were separated only by a single wall.

"Were you satisfied with your pupils, or did any circumstance in their conduct give you cause for complaint? Conceal nothing from me, repose in me entire confidence."

Happily, I felt in myself complete power to manage my pupils without aid; the enchantment, the golden haze which had dazzled my perspicuity at first, had been a good deal dissipated. I cannot say I was chagrined or downcast by the contrast which the reality of a pensionnat de demoiselles presented to my vague ideal of the same community; I was only enlightened and amused; consequently, I felt in no disposition to complain to Mdlle. Reuter, and I received her considerate invitation to confidence with a smile.

"A thousand thanks, mademoiselle, all has gone very smoothly."

She looked more than doubtful.

"Et les trois demoiselles du premier banc?" said she.

"Ah! tout va au mieux!" was my answer, and Mdlle. Reuter ceased to question me; but her eye—not large, not brilliant, not melting, or kindling, but astute, penetrating, practical, showed she was even with me; it let out a momentary gleam, which said plainly, "Be as close as you like, I am not dependent on your candour; what you would conceal I already know."

By a transition so quiet as to be scarcely perceptible, the directress's manner changed; the anxious business-air passed from her face, and she began chatting about the weather and the town, and asking in neighbourly wise after M. and Madame Pelet. I answered all her little questions; she prolonged her talk, I went on following its many little windings; she sat so long, said so much, varied so often the topics of discourse, that it was not difficult to perceive she had a particular aim in thus detaining me. Her mere words could have afforded no clue to this aim, but her countenance aided; while her lips uttered only affable commonplaces, her eyes reverted continually to my face. Her glances were not given in full, but out of the corners, so quietly, so stealthily, yet I think I lost not one. I watched her as keenly as she watched me; I perceived soon that she was feeling after my real character; she was searching for salient points, and weak points, and eccentric points; she was applying now this test, now that, hoping in the end to find some chink, some niche, where she could put in her little firm foot and stand upon my neck— mistress of my nature. Do not mistake me, reader, it was no amorous influence she wished to gain—at that time it was only the power of the politician to which she aspired; I was now installed as a professor in her establishment, and she wanted to know where her mind was superior to mine—by what feeling or opinion she could lead me.

I enjoyed the game much, and did not hasten its conclusion; sometimes I gave her hopes, beginning a sentence rather weakly, when her shrewd eye would light up—she thought she had me; having led her a little way, I delighted to turn round and finish with sound, hard sense, whereat her countenance would fall. At last a servant entered to announce dinner; the conflict being thus necessarily terminated, we parted without having gained any advantage on either side: Mdlle. Reuter had not even given me an opportunity of attacking her with feeling, and I had managed to baffle her little schemes of craft. It was a regular drawn battle. I again held out my hand when I left the room, she gave me hers; it was a small and white hand, but how cool! I met her eye too in full—obliging her to give me a straightforward look; this last test went against me: it left her as it found her—moderate, temperate, tranquil; me it disappointed.

"I am growing wiser," thought I, as I walked back to M. Pelet's. "Look at this little woman; is she like the women of novelists and romancers? To read of female character as depicted in Poetry and Fiction, one would think it was made up of sentiment, either for good or bad—here is a specimen, and a most sensible and respectable specimen, too, whose staple ingredient is abstract reason. No Talleyrand was ever more passionless than Zoraide Reuter!" So I thought then; I found afterwards that blunt susceptibilities are very consistent with strong propensities.

CHAPTER XI.

I had indeed had a very long talk with the crafty little politician, and on regaining my quarters, I found that dinner was half over. To be late at meals was against a standing rule of the establishment, and had it been one of the Flemish ushers who thus entered after the removal of the soup and the commencement of the first course, M. Pelet would probably have greeted him with a public rebuke, and would certainly have mulcted him both of soup and fish; as it was, that polite though partial gentleman only shook his head, and as I took my place, unrolled my napkin, and said my heretical grace to myself, he civilly despatched a servant to the kitchen, to bring me a plate of "puree aux carottes" (for this was a maigre-day), and before sending away the first course, reserved for me a portion of the stock-fish of which it consisted. Dinner being over, the boys rushed out for their evening play; Kint and Vandam (the two ushers) of course followed them. Poor fellows! if they had not looked so very heavy, so very soulless, so very indifferent to all things in heaven above or in the earth beneath, I could have pitied them greatly for the obligation they were under to trail after those rough lads everywhere and at all times; even as it was, I felt disposed to scout myself as a privileged prig when I turned to ascend to my chamber, sure to find there, if not enjoyment, at least liberty; but this evening (as had often happened before) I was to be still farther distinguished.

"Eh bien, mauvais sujet!" said the voice of M. Pelet behind me, as I set my foot on the first step of the stair, "ou allez-vous? Venez a la salle-a-manger, que je vous gronde un peu."

"I beg pardon, monsieur," said I, as I followed him to his private sitting-room, "for having returned so late—it was not my fault."

"That is just what I want to know," rejoined M. Pelet, as he ushered me into the comfortable parlour with a good wood-fire—for the stove had now been removed for the season. Having rung the bell he ordered "Coffee for two," and presently he and I were seated, almost in English comfort, one on each side of the hearth, a little round table between us, with a coffee-pot, a sugar-basin, and two large white china cups. While M. Pelet employed himself in choosing a cigar from a box, my thoughts reverted to the two outcast ushers, whose voices I could hear even now crying hoarsely for order in the playground.

"C'est une grande responsabilite, que la surveillance," observed I.

"Plait-il?" dit M. Pelet.

I remarked that I thought Messieurs Vandam and Kint must sometimes be a little fatigued with their labours.

"Des betes de somme,—des betes de somme," murmured scornfully the director. Meantime I offered him his cup of coffee.

"Servez-vous mon garcon," said he blandly, when I had put a couple of huge lumps of continental sugar into his cup. "And now tell me why you stayed so long at Mdlle. Reuter's. I know that lessons conclude, in her establishment as in mine, at four o'clock, and when you returned it was past five."

"Mdlle. wished to speak with me, monsieur."

"Indeed! on what subject? if one may ask."

"Mademoiselle talked about nothing, monsieur."

"A fertile topic! and did she discourse thereon in the schoolroom, before the pupils?"

"No; like you, monsieur, she asked me to walk into her parlour."

"And Madame Reuter—the old duenna—my mother's gossip, was there, of course?"

"No, monsieur; I had the honour of being quite alone with mademoiselle."

"C'est joli—cela," observed M. Pelet, and he smiled and looked into the fire.

"Honi soit qui mal y pense," murmured I, significantly.

"Je connais un peu ma petite voisine—voyez-vous."

"In that case, monsieur will be able to aid me in finding out what was mademoiselle's reason for making me sit before her sofa one mortal hour, listening to the most copious and fluent dissertation on the merest frivolities."

"She was sounding your character."

"I thought so, monsieur."

"Did she find out your weak point?"

"What is my weak point?"

"Why, the sentimental. Any woman sinking her shaft deep enough, will at last reach a fathomless spring of sensibility in thy breast, Crimsworth."

I felt the blood stir about my heart and rise warm to my cheek.

"Some women might, monsieur."

"Is Mdlle. Reuter of the number? Come, speak frankly, mon fils; elle est encore jeune, plus agee que toi peut-etre, mais juste assey pour unir la tendresse d'une petite maman a l'amour d'une epouse devouee; n'est-ce pas que cela t'irait superieurement?"

"No, monsieur; I should like my wife to be my wife, and not half my mother."

"She is then a little too old for you?"

"No, monsieur, not a day too old if she suited me in other things."

"In what does she not suit you, William? She is personally agreeable, is she not?"

"Very; her hair and complexion are just what I admire; and her turn of form, though quite Belgian, is full of grace."

"Bravo! and her face? her features? How do you like them?"

"A little harsh, especially her mouth."

"Ah, yes! her mouth," said M. Pelet, and he chuckled inwardly. "There is character about her mouth—firmness—but she has a very pleasant smile; don't you think so?"

"Rather crafty."

"True, but that expression of craft is owing to her eyebrows; have you remarked her eyebrows?"

I answered that I had not.

"You have not seen her looking down then?" said he.

"No."

"It is a treat, notwithstanding. Observe her when she has some knitting, or some other woman's work in hand, and sits the image of peace, calmly intent on her needles and her silk, some discussion meantime going on around her, in the course of which peculiarities of character are being developed, or important interests canvassed; she takes no part in it; her humble, feminine mind is wholly with her knitting; none of her features move; she neither presumes to smile approval, nor frown disapprobation; her little hands assiduously ply their unpretending task; if she can only get this purse finished, or this bonnet-grec completed, it is enough for her. If gentlemen approach her chair, a deeper quiescence, a meeker modesty settles on her features, and clothes her general mien; observe then her eyebrows, et dites-moi s'il n'y a pas du chat dans l'un et du renard dans l'autre."

"I will take careful notice the first opportunity," said I.

"And then," continued M. Pelet, "the eyelid will flicker, the light-coloured lashes be lifted a second, and a blue eye, glancing out from under the screen, will take its brief, sly, searching survey, and retreat again."

I smiled, and so did Pelet, and after a few minutes' silence, I asked:

"Will she ever marry, do you think?"

"Marry! Will birds pair? Of course it is both her intention and resolution to marry when she finds a suitable match, and no one is better aware than herself of the sort of impression she is capable of producing; no one likes better to captivate in a quiet way. I am mistaken if she will not yet leave the print of her stealing steps on thy heart, Crimsworth."

"Of her steps? Confound it, no! My heart is not a plank to be walked on."

"But the soft touch of a patte de velours will do it no harm."

"She offers me no patte de velours; she is all form and reserve with me."

"That to begin with; let respect be the foundation, affection the first floor, love the superstructure; Mdlle. Reuter is a skilful architect."

"And interest, M. Pelet—interest. Will not mademoiselle consider that point?"

"Yes, yes, no doubt; it will be the cement between every stone. And now we have discussed the directress, what of the pupils? N'y a-t-il pas de belles etudes parmi ces jeunes tetes?"

"Studies of character? Yes; curious ones, at least, I imagine; but one cannot divine much from a first interview."

"Ah, you affect discretion; but tell me now, were you not a little abashed before these blooming young creatures?"

"At first, yes; but I rallied and got through with all due sang-froid."

"I don't believe you."

"It is true, notwithstanding. At first I thought them angels, but they did not leave me long under that delusion; three of the eldest and handsomest undertook the task of setting me right, and they managed so cleverly that in five minutes I knew them, at least, for what they were—three arrant coquettes."

"Je les connais!" exclaimed M. Pelet. "Elles sont toujours au premier rang a l'eglise et a la promenade; une blonde superbe, une jolie espiegle, une belle brune."

"Exactly."

"Lovely creatures all of them—heads for artists; what a group they would make, taken together! Eulalie (I know their names), with her smooth braided hair and calm ivory brow. Hortense, with her rich chesnut locks so luxuriantly knotted, plaited, twisted, as if she did not know how to dispose of all their abundance, with her vermilion lips, damask cheek, and roguish laughing eye. And Caroline de Blemont! Ah, there is beauty! beauty in perfection. What a cloud of sable curls about the face of a houri! What fascinating lips! What glorious black eyes! Your Byron would have worshipped her, and you—you cold, frigid islander!—you played the austere, the insensible in the presence of an Aphrodite so exquisite?"

I might have laughed at the director's enthusiasm had I believed it real, but there was something in his tone which indicated got-up raptures. I felt he was only affecting fervour in order to put me off my guard, to induce me to come out in return, so I scarcely even smiled. He went on:

"Confess, William, do not the mere good looks of Zoraide Reuter appear dowdyish and commonplace compared with the splendid charms of some of her pupils?"

The question discomposed me, but I now felt plainly that my principal was endeavouring (for reasons best known to himself—at that time I could not fathom them) to excite ideas and wishes in my mind alien to what was right and honourable. The iniquity of the instigation proved its antidote, and when he further added:—

"Each of those three beautiful girls will have a handsome fortune; and with a little address, a gentlemanlike, intelligent young fellow like you might make himself master of the hand, heart, and purse of any one of the trio."

I replied by a look and an interrogative "Monsieur?" which startled him.

He laughed a forced laugh, affirmed that he had only been joking, and demanded whether I could possibly have thought him in earnest. Just then the bell rang; the play-hour was over; it was an evening on which M. Pelet was accustomed to read passages from the drama and the belles lettres to his pupils. He did not wait for my answer, but rising, left the room, humming as he went some gay strain of Beranger's.

CHAPTER XII.

Daily, as I continued my attendance at the seminary of Mdlle. Reuter, did I find fresh occasions to compare the ideal with the real. What had I known of female character previously to my arrival at Brussels? Precious little. And what was my notion of it? Something vague, slight, gauzy, glittering; now when I came in contact with it I found it to be a palpable substance enough; very hard too sometimes, and often heavy; there was metal in it, both lead and iron.

Let the idealists, the dreamers about earthly angel and human flowers, just look here while I open my portfolio and show them a sketch or two, pencilled after nature. I took these sketches in the second-class schoolroom of Mdlle. Reuter's establishment, where about a hundred specimens of the genus "jeune fille" collected together offered a fertile variety of subject. A miscellaneous assortment they were, differing both in caste and country; as I sat on my estrade and glanced over the long range of desks, I had under my eye French, English, Belgians, Austrians, and Prussians. The majority belonged to the class bourgeois; but there were many countesses, there were the daughters of two generals and of several colonels, captains, and government EMPLOYES; these ladies sat side by side with young females destined to be demoiselles de magasins, and with some Flamandes, genuine aborigines of the country. In dress all were nearly similar, and in manners there was small difference; exceptions there were to the general rule, but the majority gave the tone to the establishment, and that tone was rough, boisterous, masked by a point-blank disregard of all forbearance towards each other or their teachers; an eager pursuit by each individual of her own interest and convenience; and a coarse indifference to the interest and convenience of every one else. Most of them could lie with audacity when it appeared advantageous to do so. All understood the art of speaking fair when a point was to be gained, and could with consummate skill and at a moment's notice turn the cold shoulder the instant civility ceased to be profitable. Very little open quarrelling ever took place amongst them; but backbiting and talebearing were universal. Close friendships were forbidden by the rules of the school, and no one girl seemed to cultivate more regard for another than was just necessary to secure a companion when solitude would have been irksome. They were each and all supposed to have been reared in utter unconsciousness of vice. The precautions used to keep them ignorant, if not innocent, were innumerable. How was it, then, that scarcely one of those girls having attained the age of fourteen could look a man in the face with modesty and propriety? An air of bold, impudent flirtation, or a loose, silly leer, was sure to answer the most ordinary glance from a masculine eye. I know nothing of the arcana of the Roman Catholic religion, and I am not a bigot in matters of theology, but I suspect the root of this precocious impurity, so obvious, so general in Popish countries, is to be found in the discipline, if not the doctrines of the Church of Rome. I record what I have seen: these girls belonged to what are called the respectable ranks of society; they had all been carefully brought up, yet was the mass of them mentally depraved. So much for the general view: now for one or two selected specimens.

The first picture is a full length of Aurelia Koslow, a German fraulein, or rather a half-breed between German and Russian. She is eighteen years of age, and has been sent to Brussels to finish her education; she is of middle size, stiffly made, body long, legs short, bust much developed but not compactly moulded, waist disproportionately compressed by an inhumanly braced corset, dress carefully arranged, large feet tortured into small bottines, head small, hair smoothed, braided, oiled, and gummed to perfection; very low forehead, very diminutive and vindictive grey eyes, somewhat Tartar features, rather flat nose, rather high-cheek bones, yet the ensemble not positively ugly; tolerably good complexion. So much for person. As to mind, deplorably ignorant and ill-informed: incapable of writing or speaking correctly even German, her native tongue, a dunce in French, and her attempts at learning English a mere farce, yet she has been at school twelve years; but as she invariably gets her exercises, of every description, done by a fellow pupil, and reads her lessons off a book concealed in her lap, it is not wonderful that her progress has been so snail-like. I do not know what Aurelia's daily habits of life are, because I have not the opportunity of observing her at all times; but from what I see of the state of her desk, books, and papers, I should say she is slovenly and even dirty; her outward dress, as I have said, is well attended to, but in passing behind her bench, I have remarked that her neck is gray for want of washing, and her hair, so glossy with gum and grease, is not such as one feels tempted to pass the hand over, much less to run the fingers through. Aurelia's conduct in class, at least when I am present, is something extraordinary, considered as an index of girlish innocence. The moment I enter the room, she nudges her next neighbour and indulges in a half-suppressed laugh. As I take my seat on the estrade, she fixes her eye on me; she seems resolved to attract, and, if possible, monopolize my notice: to this end she launches at me all sorts of looks, languishing, provoking, leering, laughing. As I am found quite proof against this sort of artillery—for we scorn what, unasked, is lavishly offered—she has recourse to the expedient of making noises; sometimes she sighs, sometimes groans, sometimes utters inarticulate sounds, for which language has no name. If, in walking up the schoolroom, I pass near her, she puts out her foot that it may touch mine; if I do not happen to observe the manoeuvre, and my boot comes in contact with her brodequin, she affects to fall into convulsions of suppressed laughter; if I notice the snare and avoid it, she expresses her mortification in sullen muttering, where I hear myself abused in bad French, pronounced with an intolerable Low German accent.

Not far from Mdlle. Koslow sits another young lady by name Adele Dronsart: this is a Belgian, rather low of stature, in form heavy, with broad waist, short neck and limbs, good red and white complexion, features well chiselled and regular, well-cut eyes of a clear brown colour, light brown hair, good teeth, age not much above fifteen, but as full-grown as a stout young Englishwoman of twenty. This portrait gives the idea of a somewhat dumpy but good-looking damsel, does it not? Well, when I looked along the row of young heads, my eye generally stopped at this of Adele's; her gaze was ever waiting for mine, and it frequently succeeded in arresting it. She was an unnatural-looking being—so young, fresh, blooming, yet so Gorgon-like. Suspicion, sullen ill-temper were on her forehead, vicious propensities in her eye, envy and panther-like deceit about her mouth. In general she sat very still; her massive shape looked as if it could not bend much, nor did her large head —so broad at the base, so narrow towards the top—seem made to turn readily on her short neck. She had but two varieties of expression; the prevalent one a forbidding, dissatisfied scowl, varied sometimes by a most pernicious and perfidious smile. She was shunned by her fellow-pupils, for, bad as many of them were, few were as bad as she.

Aurelia and Adele were in the first division of the second class; the second division was headed by a pensionnaire named Juanna Trista. This girl was of mixed Belgian and Spanish origin; her Flemish mother was dead, her Catalonian father was a merchant residing in the —— Isles, where Juanna had been born and whence she was sent to Europe to be educated. I wonder that any one, looking at that girl's head and countenance, would have received her under their roof. She had precisely the same shape of skull as Pope Alexander the Sixth; her organs of benevolence, veneration, conscientiousness, adhesiveness, were singularly small, those of self-esteem, firmness, destructiveness, combativeness, preposterously large; her head sloped up in the penthouse shape, was contracted about the forehead, and prominent behind; she had rather good, though large and marked features; her temperament was fibrous and bilious, her complexion pale and dark, hair and eyes black, form angular and rigid but proportionate, age fifteen.

Juanna was not very thin, but she had a gaunt visage, and her "regard" was fierce and hungry; narrow as was her brow, it presented space enough for the legible graving of two words, Mutiny and Hate; in some one of her other lineaments I think the eye—cowardice had also its distinct cipher. Mdlle. Trista thought fit to trouble my first lessons with a coarse work-day sort of turbulence; she made noises with her mouth like a horse, she ejected her saliva, she uttered brutal expressions; behind and below her were seated a band of very vulgar, inferior-looking Flamandes, including two or three examples of that deformity of person and imbecility of intellect whose frequency in the Low Countries would seem to furnish proof that the climate is such as to induce degeneracy of the human mind and body; these, I soon found, were completely under her influence, and with their aid she got up and sustained a swinish tumult, which I was constrained at last to quell by ordering her and two of her tools to rise from their seats, and, having kept them standing five minutes, turning them bodily out of the schoolroom: the accomplices into a large place adjoining called the grands salle; the principal into a cabinet, of which I closed the door and pocketed the key. This judgment I executed in the presence of Mdlle. Reuter, who looked much aghast at beholding so decided a proceeding—the most severe that had ever been ventured on in her establishment. Her look of affright I answered with one of composure, and finally with a smile, which perhaps flattered, and certainly soothed her. Juanna Trista remained in Europe long enough to repay, by malevolence and ingratitude, all who had ever done her a good turn; and she then went to join her father in the—— Isles, exulting in the thought that she should there have slaves, whom, as she said, she could kick and strike at will.

These three pictures are from the life. I possess others, as marked and as little agreeable, but I will spare my reader the exhibition of them.

Doubtless it will be thought that I ought now, by way of contrast, to show something charming; some gentle virgin head, circled with a halo, some sweet personification of innocence, clasping the dove of peace to her bosom. No: I saw nothing of the sort, and therefore cannot portray it. The pupil in the school possessing the happiest disposition was a young girl from the country, Louise Path; she was sufficiently benevolent and obliging, but not well taught nor well mannered; moreover, the plague-spot of dissimulation was in her also; honour and principle were unknown to her, she had scarcely heard their names. The least exceptionable pupil was the poor little Sylvie I have mentioned once before. Sylvie was gentle in manners, intelligent in mind; she was even sincere, as far as her religion would permit her to be so, but her physical organization was defective; weak health stunted her growth and chilled her spirits, and then, destined as she was for the cloister, her whole soul was warped to a conventual bias, and in the tame, trained subjection of her manner, one read that she had already prepared herself for her future course of life, by giving up her independence of thought and action into the hands of some despotic confessor. She permitted herself no original opinion, no preference of companion or employment; in everything she was guided by another. With a pale, passive, automaton air, she went about all day long doing what she was bid; never what she liked, or what, from innate conviction, she thought it right to do. The poor little future religieuse had been early taught to make the dictates of her own reason and conscience quite subordinate to the will of her spiritual director. She was the model pupil of Mdlle. Reuter's establishment; pale, blighted image, where life lingered feebly, but whence the soul had been conjured by Romish wizard-craft!

A few English pupils there were in this school, and these might be divided into two classes. 1st. The continental English—the daughters chiefly of broken adventurers, whom debt or dishonour had driven from their own country. These poor girls had never known the advantages of settled homes, decorous example, or honest Protestant education; resident a few months now in one Catholic school, now in another, as their parents wandered from land to land— from France to Germany, from Germany to Belgium—they had picked up some scanty instruction, many bad habits, losing every notion even of the first elements of religion and morals, and acquiring an imbecile indifference to every sentiment that can elevate humanity; they were distinguishable by an habitual look of sullen dejection, the result of crushed self-respect and constant browbeating from their Popish fellow-pupils, who hated them as English, and scorned them as heretics.

The second class were British English. Of these I did not encounter half a dozen during the whole time of my attendance at the seminary; their characteristics were clean but careless dress, ill-arranged hair (compared with the tight and trim foreigners), erect carriage, flexible figures, white and taper hands, features more irregular, but also more intellectual than those of the Belgians, grave and modest countenances, a general air of native propriety and decency; by this last circumstance alone I could at a glance distinguish the daughter of Albion and nursling of Protestantism from the foster-child of Rome, the PROTEGEE of Jesuistry: proud, too, was the aspect of these British girls; at once envied and ridiculed by their continental associates, they warded off insult with austere civility, and met hate with mute disdain; they eschewed company-keeping, and in the midst of numbers seemed to dwell isolated.

The teachers presiding over this mixed multitude were three in number, all

French—their names Mdlles. Zephyrine, Pelagie, and Suzette; the two last were commonplace personages enough; their look was ordinary, their manner was ordinary, their temper was ordinary, their thoughts, feelings, and views were all ordinary—were I to write a chapter on the subject I could not elucidate it further. Zephyrine was somewhat more distinguished in appearance and deportment than Pelagie and Suzette, but in character genuine Parisian coquette, perfidious, mercenary, and dry-hearted. A fourth maitresse I sometimes saw who seemed to come daily to teach needlework, or netting, or lace-mending, or some such flimsy art; but of her I never had more than a passing glimpse, as she sat in the CARRE, with her frames and some dozen of the elder pupils about her, consequently I had no opportunity of studying her character, or even of observing her person much; the latter, I remarked, had a very English air for a maitresse, otherwise it was not striking; of character I should think she possessed but little, as her pupils seemed constantly "en revolte" against her authority. She did not reside in the house; her name, I think, was Mdlle. Henri.

Amidst this assemblage of all that was insignificant and defective, much that was vicious and repulsive (by that last epithet many would have described the two or three stiff, silent, decently behaved, ill-dressed British girls), the sensible, sagacious, affable directress shone like a steady star over a marsh full of Jack-o'-lanthorns; profoundly aware of her superiority, she derived an inward bliss from that consciousness which sustained her under all the care and responsibility inseparable from her position; it kept her temper calm, her brow smooth, her manner tranquil. She liked—as who would not?—on entering the school-room, to feel that her sole presence sufficed to diffuse that order and quiet which all the remonstrances, and even commands, of her underlings frequently failed to enforce; she liked to stand in comparison, or rather—contrast, with those who surrounded her, and to know that in personal as well as mental advantages, she bore away the undisputed palm of preference—(the three teachers were all plain.) Her pupils she managed with such indulgence and address, taking always on herself the office of recompenser and eulogist, and abandoning to her subalterns every invidious task of blame and punishment, that they all regarded her with deference, if not with affection; her teachers did not love her, but they submitted because they were her inferiors in everything; the various masters who attended her school were each and all in some way or other under her influence; over one she had acquired power by her skilful management of his bad temper; over another by little attentions to his petty caprices; a third she had subdued by flattery; a fourth—a timid man—she kept in awe by a sort of austere decision of mien; me, she still watched, still tried by the most ingenious tests—she roved round me, baffled, yet persevering; I believe she thought I was like a smooth and bare precipice, which offered neither jutting stone nor tree-root, nor tuft of grass to aid the climber. Now she flattered with exquisite tact, now she moralized, now she tried how far I was accessible to mercenary motives, then she disported on the brink of affection—knowing that some men are won by weakness—anon, she talked excellent sense, aware that others have the folly to admire judgment. I found it at once pleasant and easy to evade all these efforts; it was sweet, when she thought me nearly won, to turn round and to smile in her very eyes, half scornfully, and then to witness her scarcely veiled, though mute mortification. Still she persevered, and at last, I am bound to confess it, her finger, essaying, proving every atom of the casket, touched its secret spring, and for a moment the lid sprung open; she laid her hand on the jewel within; whether she stole and broke it, or whether the lid shut again with a snap on her fingers, read on, and you shall know.

It happened that I came one day to give a lesson when I was indisposed; I had a bad cold and a cough; two hours' incessant talking left me very hoarse and tired; as I quitted the schoolroom, and was passing along the corridor, I met Mdlle. Reuter; she remarked, with an anxious air, that I looked very pale and tired. "Yes," I said, "I was fatigued;" and then, with increased interest, she rejoined, "You shall not go away till you have had some refreshment." She persuaded me to step into the parlour, and was very kind and gentle while I stayed. The next day she was kinder still; she came herself into the class to see that the windows were closed, and that there was no draught; she exhorted me with friendly earnestness not to over-exert myself; when I went away, she gave me her hand unasked, and I could not but mark, by a respectful and gentle pressure, that I was sensible of the favour, and grateful for it. My modest demonstration kindled a little merry smile on her countenance; I thought her almost charming. During the remainder of the evening, my mind was full of impatience for the afternoon of the next day to arrive, that I might see her again.

I was not disappointed, for she sat in the class during the whole of my subsequent lesson, and often looked at me almost with affection. At four o'clock she accompanied me out of the schoolroom, asking with solicitude after my health, then scolding me sweetly because I spoke too loud and gave myself too much trouble; I stopped at the glass-door which led into the garden, to hear her lecture to the end; the door was open, it was a very fine day, and while I listened to the soothing reprimand, I looked at the sunshine and flowers, and felt very happy. The day-scholars began to pour from the schoolrooms into the passage.

"Will you go into the garden a minute or two," asked she, "till they are gone?"

I descended the steps without answering, but I looked back as much as to say—

"You will come with me?"

In another minute I and the directress were walking side by side down the alley bordered with fruit-trees, whose white blossoms were then in full blow as well as their tender green leaves. The sky was blue, the air still, the May afternoon was full of brightness and fragrance. Released from the stifling class, surrounded with flowers and foliage, with a pleasing, smiling, affable woman at my side—how did I feel? Why, very enviably. It seemed as if the romantic visions my imagination had suggested of this garden, while it was yet hidden from me by the jealous boards, were more than realized; and, when a turn in the alley shut out the view of the house, and some tall shrubs excluded M. Pelet's mansion, and screened us momentarily from the other houses, rising amphitheatre-like round this green spot, I gave my arm to Mdlle. Reuter, and led her to a garden-chair, nestled under some lilacs near. She sat down; I took my place at her side. She went on talking to me with that ease which communicates ease, and, as I listened, a revelation dawned in my mind that I was on the brink of falling in love. The dinner-bell rang, both at her house and M. Pelet's; we were obliged to part; I detained her a moment as she was moving away.

"I want something," said I.

"What?" asked Zoraide naively.

"Only a flower."

"Gather it then—or two, or twenty, if you like."

"No—one will do--but you must gather it, and give it to me."

"What a caprice!" she exclaimed, but she raised herself on her tip-toes, and, plucking a beautiful branch of lilac, offered it to me with grace. I took it, and went away, satisfied for the present, and hopeful for the future.

Certainly that May day was a lovely one, and it closed in moonlight night of summer warmth and serenity. I remember this well; for, having sat up late that evening, correcting devoirs, and feeling weary and a little oppressed with the closeness of my small room, I opened the often-mentioned boarded window, whose boards, however, I had persuaded old Madame Pelet to have removed since I had filled the post of professor in the pensionnat de demoiselles, as, from that time, it was no longer "inconvenient" for me to overlook my own pupils at their sports. I sat down in the window-seat, rested my arm on the sill, and leaned out: above me was the clear-obscure of a cloudless night sky—splendid moonlight subdued the tremulous sparkle of the stars—below lay the garden, varied with silvery lustre and deep shade, and all fresh with dew—a grateful perfume exhaled from the closed blossoms of the fruit-trees—not a leaf stirred, the night was breezeless. My window looked directly down upon a certain walk of Mdlle. Reuter's garden, called "l'allee defendue," so named because the pupils were forbidden to enter it on account of its proximity to the boys' school. It was here that the lilacs and laburnums grew especially thick; this was the most sheltered nook in the enclosure, its shrubs screened the garden-chair where that afternoon I had sat with the young directress. I need not say that my thoughts were chiefly with her as I leaned from the lattice, and let my eye roam, now over the walks and borders of the garden, now along the many-windowed front of the house which rose white beyond the masses of foliage. I wondered in what part of the building was situated her apartment; and a single light, shining through the persiennes of one croisee, seemed to direct me to it.

"She watches late," thought I, "for it must be now near midnight. She is a fascinating little woman," I continued in voiceless soliloquy; "her image forms a pleasant picture in memory; I know she is not what the world calls pretty— no matter, there is harmony in her aspect, and I like it; her brown hair, her blue eye, the freshness of her cheek, the whiteness of her neck, all suit my taste. Then I respect her talent; the idea of marrying a doll or a fool was always abhorrent to me: I know that a pretty doll, a fair fool, might do well enough for the honeymoon; but when passion cooled, how dreadful to find a lump of wax and wood laid in my bosom, a half idiot clasped in my arms, and to remember that I had made of this my equal—nay, my idol—to know that I must pass the rest of my dreary life with a creature incapable of understanding what I said, of appreciating what I thought, or of sympathizing with what I felt! "Now, Zoraide Reuter," thought I, "has tact, CARACTERE, judgment, discretion; has she heart? What a good, simple little smile played about her lips when she gave me the branch of lilacs! I have thought her crafty, dissembling, interested sometimes, it is true; but may not much that looks like cunning and dissimulation in her conduct be only the efforts made by a bland temper to traverse quietly perplexing difficulties? And as to interest, she wishes to make her way in the world, no doubt, and who can blame her? Even if she be truly deficient in sound principle, is it not rather her misfortune than her fault? She has been brought up a Catholic: had she been born an Englishwoman, and reared a Protestant, might she not have added straight integrity to all her other excellences? Supposing she were to marry an English and Protestant husband, would she not, rational, sensible as she is, quickly acknowledge the superiority of right over expediency, honesty over policy? It would be worth a man's while to try the experiment; to-morrow I will renew my observations. She knows that I watch her: how calm she is under scrutiny! it seems rather to gratify than annoy her." Here a strain of music stole in upon my monologue, and suspended it; it was a bugle, very skilfully played, in the neighbourhood of the park, I thought, or on the Place Royale. So sweet were the tones, so subduing their effect at that hour, in the midst of silence and under the quiet reign of moonlight, I ceased to think, that I might listen more intently. The strain retreated, its sound waxed fainter and was soon gone; my ear prepared to repose on the absolute hush of midnight once more. No. What murmur was that which, low, and yet near and approaching nearer, frustrated the expectation of total silence? It was some one conversing—yes, evidently, an audible, though subdued voice spoke in the garden immediately below me. Another answered; the first voice was that of a man, the second that of a woman; and a man and a woman I saw coming slowly down the alley. Their forms were at first in shade, I could but discern a dusk outline of each, but a ray of moonlight met them at the termination of the walk, when they were under my very nose, and revealed very plainly, very unequivocally, Mdlle. Zoraide Reuter, arm-in-arm, or hand-in-hand (I forget which) with my principal, confidant, and counsellor, M. Francois Pelet. And M. Pelet was saying—

"A quand donc le jour des noces, ma bien-aimee?"

And Mdlle. Reuter answered—

"Mais, Francois, tu sais bien qu'il me serait impossible de me marier avant les vacances."

"June, July, August, a whole quarter!" exclaimed the director. "How can I wait so long?—I who am ready, even now, to expire at your feet with impatience!"

"Ah! if you die, the whole affair will be settled without any trouble about notaries and contracts; I shall only have to order a slight mourning dress, which will be much sooner prepared than the nuptial trousseau."

"Cruel Zoraide! you laugh at the distress of one who loves you so devotedly as I do: my torment is your sport; you scruple not to stretch my soul on the rack of jealousy; for, deny it as you will, I am certain you have cast encouraging glances on that school-boy, Crimsworth; he has presumed to fall in love, which he dared not have done unless you had given him room to hope."

"What do you say, Francois? Do you say Crimsworth is in love with me?"

"Over head and ears."

"Has he told you so?"

"No—but I see it in his face: he blushes whenever your name is mentioned." A little laugh of exulting coquetry announced Mdlle. Reuter's gratification at this piece of intelligence (which was a lie, by-the-by—I had never been so far gone as that, after all). M. Pelet proceeded to ask what she intended to do with me, intimating pretty plainly, and not very gallantly, that it was nonsense for her to think of taking such a "blanc-bec" as a husband, since she must be at least ten years older than I (was she then thirty-two? I should not have thought it). I heard her disclaim any intentions on the subject—the director, however, still pressed her to give a definite answer.

"Francois," said she, "you are jealous," and still she laughed; then, as if suddenly recollecting that this coquetry was not consistent with the character for modest dignity she wished to establish, she proceeded, in a demure voice: "Truly, my dear Francois, I will not deny that this young Englishman may have made some attempts to ingratiate himself with me; but, so far from giving him any encouragement, I have always treated him with as much reserve as it was possible to combine with civility; affianced as I am to you, I would give no man false hopes; believe me, dear friend." Still Pelet uttered murmurs of distrust—so I judged, at least, from her reply.

"What folly! How could I prefer an unknown foreigner to you? And then —not to flatter your vanity—Crimsworth could not bear comparison with you either physically or mentally; he is not a handsome man at all; some may call him gentleman-like and intelligent-looking, but for my part—"

The rest of the sentence was lost in the distance, as the pair, rising from the chair in which they had been seated, moved away. I waited their return, but soon the opening and shutting of a door informed me that they had re-entered the house; I listened a little longer, all was perfectly still; I listened more than an hour—at last I heard M. Pelet come in and ascend to his chamber. Glancing once more towards the long front of the garden-house, I perceived that its solitary light was at length extinguished; so, for a time, was my faith in love and friendship. I went to bed, but something feverish and fiery had got into my veins which prevented me from sleeping much that night.

CHAPTER XIII.

Next morning I rose with the dawn, and having dressed myself and stood half-an-hour, my elbow leaning on the chest of drawers, considering what means I should adopt to restore my spirits, fagged with sleeplessness, to their ordinary tone—for I had no intention of getting up a scene with M. Pelet, reproaching him with perfidy, sending him a challenge, or performing other gambadoes of the sort—I hit at last on the expedient of walking out in the cool of the morning to a neighbouring establishment of baths, and treating myself to a bracing plunge. The remedy produced the desired effect. I came back at seven o'clock steadied and invigorated, and was able to greet M. Pelet, when he entered to breakfast, with an unchanged and tranquil countenance; even a cordial offering of the hand and the flattering appellation of "mon fils," pronounced in that caressing tone with which Monsieur had, of late days especially, been accustomed to address me, did not elicit any external sign of the feeling which, though subdued, still glowed at my heart. Not that I nursed vengeance—no; but the sense of insult and treachery lived in me like a kindling, though as yet smothered coal. God knows I am not by nature vindictive; I would not hurt a man because I can no longer trust or like him; but neither my reason nor feelings are of the vacillating order—they are not of that sand-like sort where impressions, if soon made, are as soon effaced. Once convinced that my friend's disposition is incompatible with my own, once assured that he is indelibly stained with certain defects obnoxious to my principles, and I dissolve the connection. I did so with Edward. As to Pelet, the discovery was yet new; should I act thus with him? It was the question I placed before my mind as I stirred my cup of coffee with a half-pistolet (we never had spoons), Pelet meantime being seated opposite, his pallid face looking as knowing and more haggard than usual, his blue eye turned, now sternly on his boys and ushers, and now graciously on me.

"Circumstances must guide me," said I; and meeting Pelet's false glance and insinuating smile, I thanked heaven that I had last night opened my window and read by the light of a full moon the true meaning of that guileful countenance. I felt half his master, because the reality of his nature was now known to me; smile and flatter as he would, I saw his soul lurk behind his smile, and heard in every one of his smooth phrases a voice interpreting their treacherous import.

But Zoraide Reuter? Of course her defection had cut me to the quick? That stint must have gone too deep for any consolations of philosophy to be available in curing its smart? Not at all. The night fever over, I looked about for balm to that wound also, and found some nearer home than at Gilead. Reason was my physician; she began by proving that the prize I had missed was of little value: she admitted that, physically, Zoraide might have suited me, but affirmed that our souls were not in harmony, and that discord must have resulted from the union of her mind with mine. She then insisted on the suppression of all repining, and commanded me rather to rejoice that I had escaped a snare. Her medicament did me good. I felt its strengthening effect when I met the directress the next day; its stringent operation on the nerves suffered no trembling, no faltering; it enabled me to face her with firmness, to pass her with ease. She had held out her hand to me—that I did not choose to see. She had greeted me with a charming smile—it fell on my heart like light on stone. I passed on to the estrade, she followed me; her eye, fastened on my face, demanded of every feature the meaning of my changed and careless manner. "I will give her an answer," thought I; and, meeting her gaze full, arresting, fixing her glance, I shot into her eyes, from my own, a look, where there was no respect, no love, no tenderness, no gallantry; where the strictest analysis could detect nothing but scorn, hardihood, irony. I made her bear it, and feel it; her steady countenance did not change, but her colour rose, and she approached me as if fascinated. She stepped on to the estrade, and stood close by my side; she had nothing to say. I would not relieve her embarrassment, and negligently turned over the leaves of a book.

"I hope you feel quite recovered to-day," at last she said, in a low tone.

"And I, mademoiselle, hope that you took no cold last night in consequence of your late walk in the garden."

Quick enough of comprehension, she understood me directly; her face became a little blanched—a very little—but no muscle in her rather marked features moved; and, calm and self-possessed, she retired from the estrade, taking her seat quietly at a little distance, and occupying herself with netting a purse. I proceeded to give my lesson; it was a "Composition," i.e., I dictated certain general questions, of which the pupils were to compose the answers from memory, access to books being forbidden. While Mdlle. Eulalie, Hortense, Caroline, &c., were pondering over the string of rather abstruse grammatical interrogatories I had propounded, I was at liberty to employ the vacant half hour in further observing the directress herself. The green silk purse was progressing fast in her hands; her eyes were bent upon it; her attitude, as she sat netting within two yards of me, was still yet guarded; in her whole person were expressed at once, and with equal clearness, vigilance and repose—a rare union! Looking at her, I was forced, as I had often been before, to offer her good sense, her wondrous self-control, the tribute of involuntary admiration. She had felt that I had withdrawn from her my esteem; she had seen contempt and coldness in my eye, and to her, who coveted the approbation of all around her, who thirsted after universal good opinion, such discovery must have been an acute wound. I had witnessed its effect in the momentary pallor of her cheek--cheek unused to vary; yet how quickly, by dint of self-control, had she recovered her composure! With what quiet dignity she now sat, almost at my side, sustained by her sound and vigorous sense; no trembling in her somewhat lengthened, though shrewd upper lip, no coward shame on her austere forehead!

"There is metal there," I said, as I gazed. "Would that there were fire also, living ardour to make the steel glow—then I could love her."

Presently I discovered that she knew I was watching her, for she stirred not, she lifted not her crafty eyelid; she had glanced down from her netting to her small foot, peeping from the soft folds of her purple merino gown; thence her eye reverted to her hand, ivory white, with a bright garnet ring on the forefinger, and a light frill of lace round the wrist; with a scarcely perceptible movement she turned her head, causing her nut-brown curls to wave gracefully. In these slight signs I read that the wish of her heart, the design of her brain, was to lure back the game she had scared. A little incident gave her the opportunity of addressing me again.

While all was silence in the class—silence, but for the rustling of copy-books and the travelling of pens over their pages—a leaf of the large folding-door, opening from the hall, unclosed, admitting a pupil who, after making a hasty obeisance, ensconced herself with some appearance of trepidation, probably occasioned by her entering so late, in a vacant seat at the desk nearest the door. Being seated, she proceeded, still with an air of hurry and embarrassment, to open her cabas, to take out her books; and, while I was waiting for her to look up, in order to make out her identity—for, shortsighted as I was, I had not recognized her at her entrance—Mdlle. Reuter, leaving her chair, approached the estrade.

"Monsieur Creemsvort," said she, in a whisper: for when the schoolrooms were silent, the directress always moved with velvet tread, and spoke in the most subdued key, enforcing order and stillness fully as much by example as precept: "Monsieur Creemsvort, that young person, who has just entered, wishes to have the advantage of taking lessons with you in English; she is not a pupil of the house; she is, indeed, in one sense, a teacher, for she gives instruction in lace-mending, and in little varieties of ornamental needle-work. She very properly proposes to qualify herself for a higher department of education, and has asked permission to attend your lessons, in order to perfect her knowledge of English, in which language she has, I believe, already made some progress; of course it is my wish to aid her in an effort so praiseworthy; you will permit her then to benefit by your instruction—n'est ce pas, monsieur?" And Mdlle. Reuter's eyes were raised to mine with a look at once naive, benign, and beseeching.

I replied, "Of course," very laconically, almost abruptly.

"Another word," she said, with softness: "Mdlle. Henri has not received a regular education; perhaps her natural talents are not of the highest order: but I can assure you of the excellence of her intentions, and even of the amiability of her disposition. Monsieur will then, I am sure, have the goodness to be considerate with her at first, and not expose her backwardness, her inevitable deficiencies, before the young ladies, who, in a sense, are her pupils. Will Monsieur Creemsvort favour me by attending to this hint?" I nodded. She continued with subdued earnestness—

"Pardon me, monsieur, if I venture to add that what I have just said is of importance to the poor girl; she already experiences great difficulty in impressing these giddy young things with a due degree of deference for her authority, and should that difficulty be increased by new discoveries of her incapacity, she might find her position in my establishment too painful to be retained; a circumstance I should much regret for her sake, as she can ill afford to lose the profits of her occupation here."

Mdlle. Reuter possessed marvellous tact; but tact the most exclusive, unsupported by sincerity, will sometimes fail of its effect; thus, on this occasion, the longer she preached about the necessity of being indulgent to the governess pupil, the more impatient I felt as I listened. I discerned so clearly that while her professed motive was a wish to aid the dull, though well-meaning Mdlle. Henri, her real one was no other than a design to impress me with an idea of her own exalted goodness and tender considerateness; so having again hastily nodded assent to her remarks, I obviated their renewal by suddenly demanding the compositions, in a sharp accent, and stepping from the estrade, I proceeded to collect them. As I passed the governess-pupil, I said to her—

"You have come in too late to receive a lesson to-day; try to be more punctual next time."

I was behind her, and could not read in her face the effect of my not very civil speech. Probably I should not have troubled myself to do so, had I been full in front; but I observed that she immediately began to slip her books into her cabas again; and, presently, after I had returned to the estrade, while I was arranging the mass of compositions, I heard the folding-door again open and close; and, on looking up, I perceived her place vacant. I thought to myself, "She will consider her first attempt at taking a lesson in English something of a failure;" and I wondered whether she had departed in the sulks, or whether stupidity had induced her to take my words too literally, or, finally, whether my irritable tone had wounded her feelings. The last notion I dismissed almost as soon as I had conceived it, for not having seen any appearance of sensitiveness in any human face since my arrival in Belgium, I had begun to regard it almost as a fabulous quality. Whether her physiognomy announced it I could not tell, for her speedy exit had allowed me no time to ascertain the circumstance. I had, indeed, on two or three previous occasions, caught a passing view of her (as I believe has been mentioned before); but I had never stopped to scrutinize either her face or person, and had but the most vague idea of her general appearance. Just as I had finished rolling up the compositions, the four o'clock bell rang; with my accustomed alertness in obeying that signal, I grasped my hat and evacuated the premises.

CHAPTER XIV.

If I was punctual in quitting Mdlle. Reuter's domicile, I was at least equally punctual in arriving there; I came the next day at five minutes before two, and on reaching the schoolroom door, before I opened it, I heard a rapid, gabbling sound, which warned me that the "priere du midi" was not yet concluded. I waited the termination thereof; it would have been impious to intrude my heretical presence during its progress. How the repeater of the prayer did cackle and splutter! I never before or since heard language enounced with such steam-engine haste. "Notre Pere qui etes au ciel" went off like a shot; then followed an address to Marie "vierge celeste, reine des anges, maison d'or, tour d'ivoire!" and then an invocation to the saint of the day; and then down they all sat, and the solemn (?) rite was over; and I entered, flinging the door wide and striding in fast, as it was my wont to do now; for I had found that in entering with aplomb, and mounting the estrade with emphasis, consisted the grand secret of ensuring immediate silence. The folding-doors between the two classes, opened for the prayer, were instantly closed; a maitresse, work-box in hand, took her seat at her appropriate desk; the pupils sat still with their pens and books before them; my three beauties in the van, now well humbled by a demeanour of consistent coolness, sat erect with their hands folded quietly on their knees; they had given up giggling and whispering to each other, and no longer ventured to utter pert speeches in my presence; they now only talked to me occasionally with their eyes, by means of which organs they could still, however, say very audacious and coquettish things. Had affection, goodness, modesty, real talent, ever employed those bright orbs as interpreters, I do not think I could have refrained from giving a kind and encouraging, perhaps an ardent reply now and then; but as it was, I found pleasure in answering the glance of vanity with the gaze of stoicism. Youthful, fair, brilliant, as were many of my pupils, I can truly say that in me they never saw any other bearing than such as an austere, though just guardian, might have observed towards them. If any doubt the accuracy of this assertion, as inferring more conscientious self-denial or Scipio-like self-control than they feel disposed to give me credit for, let them take into consideration the following circumstances, which, while detracting from my merit, justify my veracity.

Know, O incredulous reader! that a master stands in a somewhat different relation towards a pretty, light-headed, probably ignorant girl, to that occupied by a partner at a ball, or a gallant on the promenade. A professor does not meet his pupil to see her dressed in satin and muslin, with hair perfumed and curled, neck scarcely shaded by aerial lace, round white arms circled with bracelets, feet dressed for the gliding dance. It is not his business to whirl her through the waltz, to feed her with compliments, to heighten her beauty by the flush of gratified vanity. Neither does he encounter her on the smooth-rolled, tree shaded Boulevard, in the green and sunny park, whither she repairs clad in her becoming walking dress, her scarf thrown with grace over her shoulders, her little bonnet scarcely screening her curls, the red rose under its brim adding a new tint to the softer rose on her cheek; her face and eyes, too, illumined with smiles, perhaps as transient as the sunshine of the gala-day, but also quite as brilliant; it is not his office to walk by her side, to listen to her lively chat, to carry her parasol, scarcely larger than a broad green leaf, to lead in a ribbon her Blenheim spaniel or Italian greyhound. No: he finds her in the schoolroom, plainly dressed, with books before her. Owing to her education or her nature books are to her a nuisance, and she opens them with aversion, yet her teacher must instil into her mind the contents of these books; that mind resists the admission of grave information, it recoils, it grows restive, sullen tempers are shown, disfiguring frowns spoil the symmetry of the face, sometimes coarse gestures banish grace from the deportment, while muttered expressions, redolent of native and ineradicable vulgarity, desecrate the sweetness of the voice. Where the temperament is serene though the intellect be sluggish, an unconquerable dullness opposes every effort to instruct. Where there is cunning but not energy, dissimulation, falsehood, a thousand schemes and tricks are put in play to evade the necessity of application; in short, to the tutor, female youth, female charms are like tapestry hangings, of which the wrong side is continually turned towards him; and even when he sees the smooth, neat external surface he so well knows what knots, long stitches, and jagged ends are behind that he has scarce a temptation to admire too fondly the seemly forms and bright colours exposed to general view.

Our likings are regulated by our circumstances. The artist prefers a hilly country because it is picturesque; the engineer a flat one because it is convenient; the man of pleasure likes what he calls "a fine woman"—she suits him; the fashionable young gentleman admires the fashionable young lady— she is of his kind; the toil-worn, fagged, probably irritable tutor, blind almost to beauty, insensible to airs and graces, glories chiefly in certain mental qualities: application, love of knowledge, natural capacity, docility, truthfulness, gratefulness, are the charms that attract his notice and win his regard. These he seeks, but seldom meets; these, if by chance he finds, he would fain retain for ever, and when separation deprives him of them he feels as if some ruthless hand had snatched from him his only ewe-lamb. Such being the case, and the case it is, my readers will agree with me that there was nothing either very meritorious or very marvellous in the integrity and moderation of my conduct at Mdlle. Reuter's pensionnat de demoiselles.

My first business this afternoon consisted in reading the list of places for the month, determined by the relative correctness of the compositions given the preceding day. The list was headed, as usual, by the name of Sylvie, that plain, quiet little girl I have described before as being at once the best and ugliest pupil in the establishment; the second place had fallen to the lot of a certain Leonie Ledru, a diminutive, sharp-featured, and parchment-skinned creature of quick wits, frail conscience, and indurated feelings; a lawyer-like thing, of whom I used to say that, had she been a boy, she would have made a model of an unprincipled, clever attorney. Then came Eulalie, the proud beauty, the Juno of the school, whom six long years of drilling in the simple grammar of the English language had compelled, despite the stiff phlegm of her intellect, to acquire a mechanical acquaintance with most of its rules. No smile, no trace of pleasure or satisfaction appeared in Sylvie's nun-like and passive face as she heard her name read first. I always felt saddened by the sight of that poor girl's absolute quiescence on all occasions, and it was my custom to look at her, to address her, as seldom as possible; her extreme docility, her assiduous perseverance, would have recommended her warmly to my good opinion; her modesty, her intelligence, would have induced me to feel most kindly—most affectionately towards her, notwithstanding the almost ghastly plainness of her features, the disproportion of her form, the corpse-like lack of animation in her countenance, had I not been aware that every friendly word, every kindly action, would be reported by her to her confessor, and by him misinterpreted and poisoned. Once I laid my hand on her head, in token of approbation; I thought Sylvie was going to smile, her dim eye almost kindled; but, presently, she shrank from me; I was a man and a heretic; she, poor child! a destined nun and devoted Catholic: thus a four-fold wall of separation divided her mind from mine. A pert smirk, and a hard glance of triumph, was Leonie's method of testifying her gratification; Eulalie looked sullen and envious—she had hoped to be first. Hortense and Caroline exchanged a reckless grimace on hearing their names read out somewhere near the bottom of the list; the brand of mental inferiority was considered by them as no disgrace, their hopes for the future being based solely on their personal attractions.

This affair arranged, the regular lesson followed. During a brief interval, employed by the pupils in ruling their books, my eye, ranging carelessly over the benches, observed, for the first time, that the farthest seat in the farthest row—a seat usually vacant—was again filled by the new scholar, the Mdlle. Henri so ostentatiously recommended to me by the directress. To-day I had on my spectacles; her appearance, therefore, was clear to me at the first glance; I had not to puzzle over it. She looked young; yet, had I been required to name her exact age, I should have been somewhat nonplussed; the slightness of her figure might have suited seventeen; a certain anxious and pre-occupied expression of face seemed the indication of riper years. She was dressed, like all the rest, in a dark stuff gown and a white collar; her features were dissimilar to any there, not so rounded, more defined, yet scarcely regular. The shape of her head too was different, the superior part more developed, the base considerably less. I felt assured, at first sight, that she was not a Belgian; her complexion, her countenance, her lineaments, her figure, were all distinct from theirs, and, evidently, the type of another race—of a race less gifted with fullness of flesh and plenitude of blood; less jocund, material, unthinking. When I first cast my eyes on her, she sat looking fixedly down, her chin resting on her hand, and she did not change her attitude till I commenced the lesson. None of the Belgian girls would have retained one position, and that a reflective one, for the same length of time. Yet, having intimated that her appearance was peculiar, as being unlike that of her Flemish companions, I have little more to say respecting it; I can pronounce no encomiums on her beauty, for she was not beautiful; nor offer condolence on her plainness, for neither was she plain; a careworn character of forehead, and a corresponding moulding of the mouth, struck me with a sentiment resembling surprise, but these traits would probably have passed unnoticed by any less crotchety observer.

Now, reader, though I have spent more than a page in describing Mdlle. Henri, I know well enough that I have left on your mind's eye no distinct picture of her; I have not painted her complexion, nor her eyes, nor her hair, nor even drawn the outline of her shape. You cannot tell whether her nose was aquiline or retrousse, whether her chin was long or short, her face square or oval; nor could I the first day, and it is not my intention to communicate to you at once a knowledge I myself gained by little and little.

I gave a short exercise: which they all wrote down. I saw the new pupil was puzzled at first with the novelty of the form and language; once or twice she looked at me with a sort of painful solicitude, as not comprehending at all what I meant; then she was not ready when the others were, she could not write her phrases so fast as they did; I would not help her, I went on relentless. She looked at me; her eye said most plainly, "I cannot follow you." I disregarded the appeal, and, carelessly leaning back in my chair, glancing from time to time with a NONCHALANT air out of the window, I dictated a little faster. On looking towards her again, I perceived her face clouded with embarrassment, but she was still writing on most diligently; I paused a few seconds; she employed the interval in hurriedly re-perusing what she had written, and shame and discomfiture were apparent in her countenance; she evidently found she had made great nonsense of it. In ten minutes more the dictation was complete, and, having allowed a brief space in which to correct it, I took their books; it was with a reluctant hand Mdlle. Henri gave up hers, but, having once yielded it to my possession, she composed her anxious face, as if, for the present she had resolved to dismiss regret, and had made up her mind to be thought unprecedentedly stupid. Glancing over her exercise, I found that several lines had been omitted, but what was written contained very few faults; I instantly inscribed "Bon" at the bottom of the page, and returned it to her; she smiled, at first incredulously, then as if reassured, but did not lift her eyes; she could look at me, it seemed, when perplexed and bewildered, but not when gratified; I thought that scarcely fair.

CHAPTER XV.

Some time elapsed before I again gave a lesson in the first class; the holiday of Whitsuntide occupied three days, and on the fourth it was the turn of the second division to receive my instructions. As I made the transit of the CARRE, I observed, as usual, the band of sewers surrounding Mdlle. Henri; there were only about a dozen of them, but they made as much noise as might have sufficed for fifty; they seemed very little under her control; three or four at once assailed her with importunate requirements; she looked harassed, she demanded silence, but in vain. She saw me, and I read in her eye pain that a stranger should witness the insubordination of her pupils; she seemed to entreat order—her prayers were useless; then I remarked that she compressed her lips and contracted her brow; and her countenance, if I read it correctly, said—"I have done my best; I seem to merit blame notwithstanding; blame me then who will." I passed on; as I closed the school-room door, I heard her say, suddenly and sharply, addressing one of the eldest and most turbulent of the lot—

"Amelie Mullenberg, ask me no question, and request of me no assistance, for a week to come; during that space of time I will neither speak to you nor help you."

The words were uttered with emphasis—nay, with vehemence—and a comparative silence followed; whether the calm was permanent, I know not; two doors now closed between me and the CARRE.

Next day was appropriated to the first class; on my arrival, I found the directress seated, as usual, in a chair between the two estrades, and before her was standing Mdlle. Henri, in an attitude (as it seemed to me) of somewhat reluctant attention. The directress was knitting and talking at the same time. Amidst the hum of a large school-room, it was easy so to speak in the ear of one person, as to be heard by that person alone, and it was thus Mdlle. Reuter parleyed with her teacher. The face of the latter was a little flushed, not a little troubled; there was vexation in it, whence resulting I know not, for the directress looked very placid indeed; she could not be scolding in such gentle whispers, and with so equable a mien; no, it was presently proved that her discourse had been of the most friendly tendency, for I heard the closing words
—

"C'est assez, ma bonne amie; a present je ne veux pas vous retenir davantage."

Without reply, Mdlle. Henri turned away; dissatisfaction was plainly evinced in her face, and a smile, slight and brief, but bitter, distrustful, and, I thought, scornful, curled her lip as she took her place in the class; it was a secret, involuntary smile, which lasted but a second; an air of depression succeeded, chased away presently by one of attention and interest, when I gave the word for all the pupils to take their reading-books. In general I hated the reading-lesson, it was such a torture to the ear to listen to their uncouth mouthing of my native tongue, and no effort of example or precept on my part ever seemed to effect the slightest improvement in their accent. To-day, each in her appropriate key, lisped, stuttered, mumbled, and jabbered as usual; about fifteen had racked me in turn, and my auricular nerve was expecting with resignation the discords of the sixteenth, when a full, though low voice, read out, in clear correct English.

"On his way to Perth, the king was met by a Highland woman, calling herself a prophetess; she stood at the side of the ferry by which he was about to travel to the north, and cried with a loud voice, 'My lord the king, if you pass this water you will never return again alive!'"—(VIDE the HISTORY OF SCOTLAND).

I looked up in amazement; the voice was a voice of Albion; the accent was pure and silvery; it only wanted firmness, and assurance, to be the counterpart of what any well-educated lady in Essex or Middlesex might have enounced, yet the speaker or reader was no other than Mdlle. Henri, in whose grave, joyless face I saw no mark of consciousness that she had performed any extraordinary feat. No one else evinced surprise either. Mdlle. Reuter knitted away assiduously; I was aware, however, that at the conclusion of the paragraph, she had lifted her eyelid and honoured me with a glance sideways; she did not know the full excellency of the teacher's style of reading, but she perceived that her accent was not that of the others, and wanted to discover what I thought; I masked my visage with indifference, and ordered the next girl to proceed.

When the lesson was over, I took advantage of the confusion caused by breaking up, to approach Mdlle. Henri; she was standing near the window and retired as I advanced; she thought I wanted to look out, and did not imagine that I could have anything to say to her. I took her exercise-book out of her hand; as I turned over the leaves I addressed her:—

"You have had lessons in English before?" I asked.

"No, sir."

"No! you read it well; you have been in England?"

"Oh, no!" with some animation.

"You have been in English families?"

Still the answer was "No." Here my eye, resting on the flyleaf of the book, saw written, "Frances Evan Henri."

"Your name?" I asked

"Yes, sir."

My interrogations were cut short; I heard a little rustling behind me, and close at my back was the directress, professing to be examining the interior of a desk.

"Mademoiselle," said she, looking up and addressing the teacher, "Will you have the goodness to go and stand in the corridor, while the young ladies are putting on their things, and try to keep some order?"

Mdlle. Henri obeyed.

"What splendid weather!" observed the directress cheerfully, glancing at the same time from the window. I assented and was withdrawing. "What of your new pupil, monsieur?" continued she, following my retreating steps. "Is she likely to make progress in English?"

"Indeed I can hardly judge. She possesses a pretty good accent; of her real knowledge of the language I have as yet had no opportunity of forming an opinion."

"And her natural capacity, monsieur? I have had my fears about that: can you relieve me by an assurance at least of its average power?"

"I see no reason to doubt its average power, mademoiselle, but really I scarcely know her, and have not had time to study the calibre of her capacity. I wish you a very good afternoon."

She still pursued me. "You will observe, monsieur, and tell me what you think; I could so much better rely on your opinion than on my own; women cannot judge of these things as men can, and, excuse my pertinacity, monsieur, but it is natural I should feel interested about this poor little girl (pauvre petite); she has scarcely any relations, her own efforts are all she has to look to, her acquirements must be her sole fortune; her present position has once been mine, or nearly so; it is then but natural I should sympathize with her; and sometimes when I see the difficulty she has in managing pupils, I feel quite chagrined. I doubt not she does her best, her intentions are excellent; but, monsieur, she wants tact and firmness. I have talked to her on the subject, but I am not fluent, and probably did not express myself with clearness; she never appears to comprehend me. Now, would you occasionally, when you see an opportunity, slip in a word of advice to her on the subject; men have so much more influence than women have—they argue so much more logically than we do; and you, monsieur, in particular, have so paramount a power of making yourself obeyed; a word of advice from you could not but do her good; even if she were sullen and headstrong (which I hope she is not), she would scarcely refuse to listen to you; for my own part, I can truly say that I never attend one of your lessons without deriving benefit from witnessing your management of the pupils. The other masters are a constant source of anxiety to me; they cannot impress the young ladies with sentiments of respect, nor restrain the levity natural to youth: in you, monsieur, I feel the most absolute confidence; try then to put this poor child into the way of controlling our giddy, high-spirited Brabantoises. But, monsieur, I would add one word more; don't alarm her AMOUR PROPRE; beware of inflicting a wound there. I reluctantly admit that in that particular she is blameably—some would say ridiculously—susceptible. I fear I have touched this sore point inadvertently, and she cannot get over it."

During the greater part of this harangue my hand was on the lock of the outer door; I now turned it.

"Au revoir, mademoiselle," said I, and I escaped. I saw the directress's stock of words was yet far from exhausted. She looked after me, she would fain have detained me longer. Her manner towards me had been altered ever since I had begun to treat her with hardness and indifference: she almost cringed to me on every occasion; she consulted my countenance incessantly, and beset me with innumerable little officious attentions. Servility creates despotism. This slavish homage, instead of softening my heart, only pampered whatever was stern and exacting in its mood. The very circumstance of her hovering round me like a fascinated bird, seemed to transform me into a rigid pillar of stone; her flatteries irritated my scorn, her blandishments confirmed my reserve. At times I wondered what she meant by giving herself such trouble to win me, when the more profitable Pelet was already in her nets, and when, too, she was aware that I possessed her secret, for I had not scrupled to tell her as much: but the fact is that as it was her nature to doubt the reality and under-value the worth of modesty, affection, disinterestedness—to regard these qualities as foibles of character—so it was equally her tendency to consider pride, hardness, selfishness, as proofs of strength. She would trample on the neck of humility, she would kneel at the feet of disdain; she would meet tenderness with secret contempt, indifference she would woo with ceaseless assiduities. Benevolence, devotedness, enthusiasm, were her antipathies; for dissimulation and self-interest she had a preference—they were real wisdom in her eyes; moral and physical degradation, mental and bodily inferiority, she regarded with indulgence; they were foils capable of being turned to good account as set-offs for her own endowments. To violence, injustice, tyranny, she succumbed—they were her natural masters; she had no propensity to hate, no impulse to resist them; the indignation their behests awake in some hearts was unknown in hers. From all this it resulted that the false and selfish called her wise, the vulgar and debased termed her charitable, the insolent and unjust dubbed her amiable, the conscientious and benevolent generally at first accepted as valid her claim to be considered one of themselves; but ere long the plating of pretension wore off, the real material appeared below, and they laid her aside as a deception.

CHAPTER XVI.

In the course of another fortnight I had seen sufficient of Frances Evans Henri, to enable me to form a more definite opinion of her character. I found her possessed in a somewhat remarkable degree of at least two good points, viz., perseverance and a sense of duty; I found she was really capable of applying to study, of contending with difficulties. At first I offered her the same help which I had always found it necessary to confer on the others; I began with unloosing for her each knotty point, but I soon discovered that such help was regarded by my new pupil as degrading; she recoiled from it with a certain proud impatience. Hereupon I appointed her long lessons, and left her to solve alone any perplexities they might present. She set to the task with serious ardour, and having quickly accomplished one labour, eagerly demanded more. So much for her perseverance; as to her sense of duty, it evinced itself thus: she liked to learn, but hated to teach; her progress as a pupil depended upon herself, and I saw that on herself she could calculate with certainty; her success as a teacher rested partly, perhaps chiefly, upon the will of others; it cost her a most painful effort to enter into conflict with this foreign will, to endeavour to bend it into subjection to her own; for in what regarded people in general the action of her will was impeded by many scruples; it was as unembarrassed as strong where her own affairs were concerned, and to it she could at any time subject her inclination, if that inclination went counter to her convictions of right; yet when called upon to wrestle with the propensities, the habits, the faults of others, of children especially, who are deaf to reason, and, for the most part, insensate to persuasion, her will sometimes almost refused to act; then came in the sense of duty, and forced the reluctant will into operation. A wasteful expense of energy and labour was frequently the consequence; Frances toiled for and with her pupils like a drudge, but it was long ere her conscientious exertions were rewarded by anything like docility on their part, because they saw that they had power over her, inasmuch as by resisting her painful attempts to convince, persuade, control—by forcing her to the employment of coercive measures—they could inflict upon her exquisite suffering. Human beings—human children especially—seldom deny themselves the pleasure of exercising a power which they are conscious of possessing, even though that power consist only in a capacity to make others wretched; a pupil whose sensations are duller than those of his instructor, while his nerves are tougher and his bodily strength perhaps greater, has an immense advantage over that instructor, and he will generally use it relentlessly, because the very young, very healthy, very thoughtless, know neither how to sympathize nor how to spare. Frances, I fear, suffered much; a continual weight seemed to oppress her spirits; I have said she did not live in the house, and whether in her own abode, wherever that might be, she wore the same preoccupied, unsmiling, sorrowfully resolved air that always shaded her features under the roof of Mdlle. Reuter, I could not tell.

One day I gave, as a devoir, the trite little anecdote of Alfred tending cakes in the herdsman's hut, to be related with amplifications. A singular affair most of the pupils made of it; brevity was what they had chiefly studied; the majority of the narratives were perfectly unintelligible; those of Sylvie and Leonie Ledru alone pretended to anything like sense and connection. Eulalie, indeed, had hit, upon a clever expedient for at once ensuring accuracy and saving trouble; she had obtained access somehow to an abridged history of England, and had copied the anecdote out fair. I wrote on the margin of her production "Stupid and deceitful," and then tore it down the middle.

Last in the pile of single-leaved devoirs, I found one of several sheets, neatly written out and stitched together; I knew the hand, and scarcely needed the evidence of the signature "Frances Evans Henri" to confirm my conjecture as to the writer's identity.

Night was my usual time for correcting devoirs, and my own room the usual scene of such task—task most onerous hitherto; and it seemed strange to me to feel rising within me an incipient sense of interest, as I snuffed the candle and addressed myself to the perusal of the poor teacher's manuscript.

"Now," thought I, "I shall see a glimpse of what she really is; I shall get an idea of the nature and extent of her powers; not that she can be expected to express herself well in a foreign tongue, but still, if she has any mind, here will be a reflection of it."

The narrative commenced by a description of a Saxon peasant's hut, situated within the confines of a great, leafless, winter forest; it represented an evening in December; flakes of snow were falling, and the herdsman foretold a heavy storm; he summoned his wife to aid him in collecting their flock, roaming far away on the pastoral banks of the Thone; he warns her that it will be late ere they return. The good woman is reluctant to quit her occupation of baking cakes for the evening meal; but acknowledging the primary importance of securing the herds and flocks, she puts on her sheep-skin mantle; and, addressing a stranger who rests half reclined on a bed of rushes near the hearth, bids him mind the bread till her return.

"Take care, young man," she continues, "that you fasten the door well after us; and, above all, open to none in our absence; whatever sound you hear, stir not, and look not out. The night will soon fall; this forest is most wild and lonely; strange noises are often heard therein after sunset; wolves haunt these glades, and Danish warriors infest the country; worse things are talked of; you might chance to hear, as it were, a child cry, and on opening the door to afford it succour, a great black bull, or a shadowy goblin dog, might rush over the threshold; or, more awful still, if something flapped, as with wings, against the lattice, and then a raven or a white dove flew in and settled on the hearth, such a visitor would be a sure sign of misfortune to the house; therefore, heed my advice, and lift the latchet for nothing."

Her husband calls her away, both depart. The stranger, left alone, listens awhile to the muffled snow-wind, the remote, swollen sound of the river, and then he speaks.

"It is Christmas Eve," says he, "I mark the date; here I sit alone on a rude couch of rushes, sheltered by the thatch of a herdsman's hut; I, whose inheritance was a kingdom, owe my night's harbourage to a poor serf; my throne is usurped, my crown presses the brow of an invader; I have no friends; my troops wander broken in the hills of Wales; reckless robbers spoil my country; my subjects lie prostrate, their breasts crushed by the heel of the brutal Dane. Fate! thou hast done thy worst, and now thou standest before me resting thy hand on thy blunted blade. Ay; I see thine eye confront mine and demand why I still live, why I still hope. Pagan demon, I credit not thine omnipotence, and so cannot succumb to thy power. My God, whose Son, as on this night, took on Him the form of man, and for man vouchsafed to suffer and bleed, controls thy hand, and without His behest thou canst not strike a stroke. My God is sinless, eternal, all-wise—in Him is my trust; and though stripped and crushed by thee—though naked, desolate, void of resource—I do not despair, I cannot despair: were the lance of Guthrum now wet with my blood, I should not despair. I watch, I toil, I hope, I pray; Jehovah, in his own time, will aid."

I need not continue the quotation; the whole devoir was in the same strain. There were errors of orthography, there were foreign idioms, there were some faults of construction, there were verbs irregular transformed into verbs regular; it was mostly made up, as the above example shows, of short and somewhat rude sentences, and the style stood in great need of polish and sustained dignity; yet such as it was, I had hitherto seen nothing like it in the course of my professorial experience. The girl's mind had conceived a picture of the hut, of the two peasants, of the crownless king; she had imagined the wintry forest, she had recalled the old Saxon ghost-legends, she had appreciated Alfred's courage under calamity, she had remembered his Christian education, and had shown him, with the rooted confidence of those primitive days, relying on the scriptural Jehovah for aid against the mythological Destiny. This she had done without a hint from me: I had given the subject, but not said a word about the manner of treating it.

"I will find, or make, an opportunity of speaking to her," I said to myself as I rolled the devoir up; "I will learn what she has of English in her besides the name of Frances Evans; she is no novice in the language, that is evident, yet she told me she had neither been in England, nor taken lessons in English, nor lived in English families."

In the course of my next lesson, I made a report of the other devoirs, dealing out praise and blame in very small retail parcels, according to my custom, for there was no use in blaming severely, and high encomiums were rarely merited. I said nothing of Mdlle. Henri's exercise, and, spectacles on nose, I endeavoured to decipher in her countenance her sentiments at the omission. I wanted to find out whether in her existed a consciousness of her own talents. "If she thinks she did a clever thing in composing that devoir, she will now look mortified," thought I. Grave as usual, almost sombre, was her face; as usual, her eyes were fastened on the cahier open before her; there was something, I thought, of expectation in her attitude, as I concluded a brief review of the last devoir, and when, casting it from me and rubbing my hands, I bade them take their grammars, some slight change did pass over her air and mien, as though she now relinquished a faint prospect of pleasant excitement; she had been waiting for something to be discussed in which she had a degree of interest; the discussion was not to come on, so expectation sank back, shrunk and sad, but attention, promptly filling up the void, repaired in a moment the transient collapse of feature; still, I felt, rather than saw, during the whole course of the lesson, that a hope had been wrenched from her, and that if she did not show distress, it was because she would not.

At four o'clock, when the bell rang and the room was in immediate tumult, instead of taking my hat and starting from the estrade, I sat still a moment. I looked at Frances, she was putting her books into her cabas; having fastened the button, she raised her head; encountering my eye, she made a quiet, respectful obeisance, as bidding good afternoon, and was turning to depart:—

"Come here," said I, lifting my finger at the same time. She hesitated; she could not hear the words amidst the uproar now pervading both school-rooms;

I repeated the sign; she approached; again she paused within half a yard of the estrade, and looked shy, and still doubtful whether she had mistaken my meaning.

"Step up," I said, speaking with decision. It is the only way of dealing with diffident, easily embarrassed characters, and with some slight manual aid I presently got her placed just where I wanted her to be, that is, between my desk and the window, where she was screened from the rush of the second division, and where no one could sneak behind her to listen.

"Take a seat," I said, placing a tabouret; and I made her sit down. I knew what I was doing would be considered a very strange thing, and, what was more, I did not care. Frances knew it also, and, I fear, by an appearance of agitation and trembling, that she cared much. I drew from my pocket the rolled-up devoir.

"This is yours, I suppose?" said I, addressing her in English, for I now felt sure she could speak English.

"Yes," she answered distinctly; and as I unrolled it and laid it out flat on the desk before her with my hand upon it, and a pencil in that hand, I saw her moved, and, as it were, kindled; her depression beamed as a cloud might behind which the sun is burning.

"This devoir has numerous faults," said I. "It will take you some years of careful study before you are in a condition to write English with absolute correctness. Attend: I will point out some principal defects." And I went through it carefully, noting every error, and demonstrating why they were errors, and how the words or phrases ought to have been written. In the course of this sobering process she became calm. I now went on:

"As to the substance of your devoir, Mdlle. Henri, it has surprised me; I perused it with pleasure, because I saw in it some proofs of taste and fancy. Taste and fancy are not the highest gifts of the human mind, but such as they are you possess them—not probably in a paramount degree, but in a degree beyond what the majority can boast. You may then take courage; cultivate the faculties that God and nature have bestowed on you, and do not fear in any crisis of suffering, under any pressure of injustice, to derive free and full consolation from the consciousness of their strength and rarity."

"Strength and rarity!" I repeated to myself; "ay, the words are probably true," for on looking up, I saw the sun had dissevered its screening cloud, her countenance was transfigured, a smile shone in her eyes—a smile almost triumphant; it seemed to say—

"I am glad you have been forced to discover so much of my nature; you need not so carefully moderate your language. Do you think I am myself a stranger to myself? What you tell me in terms so qualified, I have known fully from a child."

She did say this as plainly as a frank and flashing glance could, but in a moment the glow of her complexion, the radiance of her aspect, had subsided; if strongly conscious of her talents, she was equally conscious of her harassing defects, and the remembrance of these obliterated for a single second, now reviving with sudden force, at once subdued the too vivid characters in which her sense of her powers had been expressed. So quick was the revulsion of feeling, I had not time to check her triumph by reproof; ere I could contract my brows to a frown she had become serious and almost mournful-looking.

"Thank you, sir," said she, rising. There was gratitude both in her voice and in the look with which she accompanied it. It was time, indeed, for our conference to terminate; for, when I glanced around, behold all the boarders (the day-scholars had departed) were congregated within a yard or two of my desk, and stood staring with eyes and mouths wide open; the three maitresses formed a whispering knot in one corner, and, close at my elbow, was the directress, sitting on a low chair, calmly clipping the tassels of her finished purse.

CHAPTER XVII.

After all I had profited but imperfectly by the opportunity I had so boldly achieved of speaking to Mdlle. Henri; it was my intention to ask her how she came to be possessed of two English baptismal names, Frances and Evans, in addition to her French surname, also whence she derived her good accent. I had forgotten both points, or, rather, our colloquy had been so brief that I had not had time to bring them forward; moreover, I had not half tested her powers of speaking English; all I had drawn from her in that language were the words "Yes," and "Thank you, sir." "No matter," I reflected. "What has been left incomplete now, shall be finished another day." Nor did I fail to keep the promise thus made to myself. It was difficult to get even a few words of particular conversation with one pupil among so many; but, according to the old proverb, "Where there is a will, there is a way;" and again and again I managed to find an opportunity for exchanging a few words with Mdlle. Henri, regardless that envy stared and detraction whispered whenever I approached her.

"Your book an instant." Such was the mode in which I often began these brief dialogues; the time was always just at the conclusion of the lesson; and motioning to her to rise, I installed myself in her place, allowing her to stand deferentially at my side; for I esteemed it wise and right in her case to enforce strictly all forms ordinarily in use between master and pupil; the rather because I perceived that in proportion as my manner grew austere and magisterial, hers became easy and self-possessed—an odd contradiction, doubtless, to the ordinary effect in such cases; but so it was.

"A pencil," said I, holding out my hand without looking at her. (I am now about to sketch a brief report of the first of these conferences.) She gave me one, and while I underlined some errors in a grammatical exercise she had written, I observed—

"You are not a native of Belgium?"

"No."

"Nor of France?"

"No."

"Where, then, is your birthplace?"

"I was born at Geneva."

"You don't call Frances and Evans Swiss names, I presume?"

"No, sir; they are English names."

"Just so; and is it the custom of the Genevese to give their children English appellatives?"

"Non, Monsieur; mais—"

"Speak English, if you please."

"Mais—"

"English—"

"But" (slowly and with embarrassment) "my parents were not all the two Genevese."

"Say BOTH, instead of 'all the two,' mademoiselle."

"Not BOTH Swiss: my mother was English."

"Ah! and of English extraction?"

"Yes—her ancestors were all English."

"And your father?"

"He was Swiss."

"What besides? What was his profession?"

"Ecclesiastic—pastor—he had a church."

"Since your mother is an Englishwoman, why do you not speak English with more facility?"

"Maman est morte, il y a dix ans."

"And you do homage to her memory by forgetting her language. Have the goodness to put French out of your mind so long as I converse with you—keep to English."

"C'est si difficile, monsieur, quand on n'en a plus l'habitude."

"You had the habitude formerly, I suppose? Now answer me in your mother tongue."

"Yes, sir, I spoke the English more than the French when I was a child."

"Why do you not speak it now?"

"Because I have no English friends."

"You live with your father, I suppose?"

"My father is dead."

"You have brothers and sisters?"

"Not one."

"Do you live alone?"

"No—I have an aunt—ma tante Julienne."

"Your father's sister?"

"Justement, monsieur."

"Is that English?"

"No—but I forget—"

"For which, mademoiselle, if you were a child I should certainly devise some slight punishment; at your age—you must be two or three and twenty, I should think?"

"Pas encore, monsieur—en un mois j'aurai dix-neuf ans."

"Well, nineteen is a mature age, and, having attained it, you ought to be so solicitous for your own improvement, that it should not be needful for a master to remind you twice of the expediency of your speaking English whenever practicable."

To this wise speech I received no answer; and, when I looked up, my pupil was smiling to herself a much-meaning, though not very gay smile; it seemed to say, "He talks of he knows not what:" it said this so plainly, that I determined to request information on the point concerning which my ignorance seemed to be thus tacitly affirmed.

"Are you solicitous for your own improvement?"

"Rather."

"How do you prove it, mademoiselle?"

An odd question, and bluntly put; it excited a second smile.

"Why, monsieur, I am not inattentive—am I? I learn my lessons well—"

"Oh, a child can do that! and what more do you do?"

"What more can I do?"

"Oh, certainly, not much; but you are a teacher, are you not, as well as a pupil?"

"Yes."

"You teach lace-mending?"

"Yes."

"A dull, stupid occupation; do you like it?"

"No—it is tedious."

"Why do you pursue it? Why do you not rather teach history, geography, grammar, even arithmetic?"

"Is monsieur certain that I am myself thoroughly acquainted with these studies?"

"I don't know; you ought to be at your age."

"But I never was at school, monsieur—"

"Indeed! What then were your friends—what was your aunt about? She is very much to blame."

"No monsieur, no—my aunt is good—she is not to blame—she does what she can; she lodges and nourishes me" (I report Mdlle. Henri's phrases literally, and it was thus she translated from the French). "She is not rich; she has only an annuity of twelve hundred francs, and it would be impossible for her to send me to school."

"Rather," thought I to myself on hearing this, but I continued, in the dogmatical tone I had adopted:—

"It is sad, however, that you should be brought up in ignorance of the most ordinary branches of education; had you known something of history and grammar you might, by degrees, have relinquished your lace-mending drudgery, and risen in the world."

"It is what I mean to do."

"How? By a knowledge of English alone? That will not suffice; no respectable family will receive a governess whose whole stock of knowledge consists in a familiarity with one foreign language."

"Monsieur, I know other things."

"Yes, yes, you can work with Berlin wools, and embroider handkerchiefs and collars—that will do little for you."

Mdlle. Henri's lips were unclosed to answer, but she checked herself, as thinking the discussion had been sufficiently pursued, and remained silent.

"Speak," I continued, impatiently; "I never like the appearance of acquiescence when the reality is not there; and you had a contradiction at your tongue's end."

"Monsieur, I have had many lessons both in grammar, history, geography, and arithmetic. I have gone through a course of each study."

"Bravo! but how did you manage it, since your aunt could not afford to send you to school?"

"By lace-mending; by the thing monsieur despises so much."

"Truly! And now, mademoiselle, it will be a good exercise for you to explain to me in English how such a result was produced by such means."

"Monsieur, I begged my aunt to have me taught lace-mending soon after we came to Brussels, because I knew it was a METIER, a trade which was easily learnt, and by which I could earn some money very soon. I learnt it in a few days, and I quickly got work, for all the Brussels ladies have old lace—very precious—which must be mended all the times it is washed. I earned money a little, and this money I gave for lessons in the studies I have mentioned; some of it I spent in buying books, English books especially; soon I shall try to find a place of governess, or school-teacher, when I can write and speak English well; but it will be difficult, because those who know I have been a lace-mender will despise me, as the pupils here despise me. Pourtant j'ai mon projet," she added in a lower tone.

"What is it?"

"I will go and live in England; I will teach French there."

The words were pronounced emphatically. She said "England" as you might suppose an Israelite of Moses' days would have said Canaan.

"Have you a wish to see England?"

"Yes, and an intention."

And here a voice, the voice of the directress, interposed:

"Mademoiselle Henri, je crois qu'il va pleuvoir; vous feriez bien, ma bonne amie, de retourner chez vous tout de suite."

In silence, without a word of thanks for this officious warning, Mdlle. Henri collected her books; she moved to me respectfully, endeavoured to move to her superior, though the endeavour was almost a failure, for her head seemed as if it would not bend, and thus departed.

Where there is one grain of perseverance or wilfulness in the composition, trifling obstacles are ever known rather to stimulate than discourage. Mdlle. Reuter might as well have spared herself the trouble of giving that intimation about the weather (by-the-by her prediction was falsified by the event—it did not rain that evening). At the close of the next lesson I was again at Mdlle. Henri's desk. Thus did I accost her:—

"What is your idea of England, mademoiselle? Why do you wish to go there?"

Accustomed by this time to the calculated abruptness of my manner, it no longer discomposed or surprised her, and she answered with only so much of hesitation as was rendered inevitable by the difficulty she experienced in improvising the translation of her thoughts from French to English.

"England is something unique, as I have heard and read; my idea of it is vague, and I want to go there to render my idea clear, definite."

"Hum! How much of England do you suppose you could see if you went there in the capacity of a teacher? A strange notion you must have of getting a clear and definite idea of a country! All you could see of Great Britain would be the interior of a school, or at most of one or two private dwellings."

"It would be an English school; they would be English dwellings."

"Indisputably; but what then? What would be the value of observations made on a scale so narrow?"

"Monsieur, might not one learn something by analogy? An—echantillon—a—a sample often serves to give an idea of the whole; besides, narrow and wide are words comparative, are they not? All my life would perhaps seem narrow in your eyes—all the life of a—that little animal subterranean—une taupe—comment dit-on?"

"Mole."

"Yes—a mole, which lives underground would seem narrow even to me."

"Well, mademoiselle—what then? Proceed."

"Mais, monsieur, vous me comprenez."

"Not in the least; have the goodness to explain."

"Why, monsieur, it is just so. In Switzerland I have done but little, learnt but little, and seen but little; my life there was in a circle; I walked the same round every day; I could not get out of it; had I rested—remained there even till my death, I should never have enlarged it, because I am poor and not skilful, I have not great acquirements; when I was quite tired of this round, I begged my aunt to go to Brussels; my existence is no larger here, because I am no richer or higher; I walk in as narrow a limit, but the scene is changed; it would change again if I went to England. I knew something of the bourgeois of Geneva, now I know something of the bourgeois of Brussels; if I went to London, I would know something of the bourgeois of London. Can you make any sense out of what I say, monsieur, or is it all obscure?"

"I see, I see—now let us advert to another subject; you propose to devote your life to teaching, and you are a most unsuccessful teacher; you cannot keep your pupils in order."

A flush of painful confusion was the result of this harsh remark; she bent her head to the desk, but soon raising it replied—

"Monsieur, I am not a skilful teacher, it is true, but practice improves; besides, I work under difficulties; here I only teach sewing, I can show no power in sewing, no superiority—it is a subordinate art; then I have no associates in this house, I am isolated; I am too a heretic, which deprives me of influence."

"And in England you would be a foreigner; that too would deprive you of influence, and would effectually separate you from all round you; in England you would have as few connections, as little importance as you have here."

"But I should be learning something; for the rest, there are probably difficulties for such as I everywhere, and if I must contend, and perhaps be conquered, I would rather submit to English pride than to Flemish coarseness; besides, monsieur—"

She stopped—not evidently from any difficulty in finding words to express herself, but because discretion seemed to say, "You have said enough."

"Finish your phrase," I urged.

"Besides, monsieur, I long to live once more among Protestants; they are more honest than Catholics; a Romish school is a building with porous walls, a hollow floor, a false ceiling; every room in this house, monsieur, has eyeholes and ear-holes, and what the house is, the inhabitants are, very treacherous; they all think it lawful to tell lies; they all call it politeness to profess friendship where they feel hatred."

"All?" said I; "you mean the pupils—the mere children—inexperienced, giddy things, who have not learnt to distinguish the difference between right and wrong?"

"On the contrary, monsieur—the children are the most sincere; they have not yet had time to become accomplished in duplicity; they will tell lies, but they do it inartificially, and you know they are lying; but the grown-up people are very false; they deceive strangers, they deceive each other—"

A servant here entered:—

"Mdlle. Henri—Mdlle. Reuter vous prie de vouloir bien conduire la petite de Dorlodot chez elle, elle vous attend dans le cabinet de Rosalie la portiere—c'est que sa bonne n'est pas venue la chercher—voyez-vous."

"Eh bien! est-ce que je suis sa bonne—moi?" demanded Mdlle. Henri; then smiling, with that same bitter, derisive smile I had seen on her lips once before, she hastily rose and made her exit.

CHAPTER XVIII.

The young Anglo-Swiss evidently derived both pleasure and profit from the study of her mother-tongue. In teaching her I did not, of course, confine myself to the ordinary school routine; I made instruction in English a channel for instruction in literature. I prescribed to her a course of reading; she had a little selection of English classics, a few of which had been left her by her mother, and the others she had purchased with her own penny-fee. I lent her some more modern works; all these she read with avidity, giving me, in writing, a clear summary of each work when she had perused it. Composition, too, she delighted in. Such occupation seemed the very breath of her nostrils, and soon her improved productions wrung from me the avowal that those qualities in her I had termed taste and fancy ought rather to have been denominated judgment and imagination. When I intimated so much, which I did as usual in dry and stinted phrase, I looked for the radiant and exulting smile my one word of eulogy had elicited before; but Frances coloured. If she did smile, it was very softly and shyly; and instead of looking up to me with a conquering glance, her eyes rested on my hand, which, stretched over her shoulder, was writing some directions with a pencil on the margin of her book.

"Well, are you pleased that I am satisfied with your progress?" I asked.

"Yes," said she slowly, gently, the blush that had half subsided returning.

"But I do not say enough, I suppose?" I continued. "My praises are too cool?"

She made no answer, and, I thought, looked a little sad. I divined her thoughts, and should much have liked to have responded to them, had it been expedient so to do. She was not now very ambitious of my admiration—not eagerly desirous of dazzling me; a little affection—ever so little—pleased her better than all the panegyrics in the world. Feeling this, I stood a good while behind her, writing on the margin of her book. I could hardly quit my station or relinquish my occupation; something retained me bending there, my head very near hers, and my hand near hers too; but the margin of a copy-book is not an illimitable space—so, doubtless, the directress thought; and she took occasion to walk past in order to ascertain by what art I prolonged so disproportionately the period necessary for filling it. I was obliged to go. Distasteful effort—to leave what we most prefer!

Frances did not become pale or feeble in consequence of her sedentary employment; perhaps the stimulus it communicated to her mind counterbalanced the inaction it imposed on her body. She changed, indeed, changed obviously and rapidly; but it was for the better. When I first saw her, her countenance was sunless, her complexion colourless; she looked like one who had no source of enjoyment, no store of bliss anywhere in the world; now the cloud had passed from her mien, leaving space for the dawn of hope and interest, and those feelings rose like a clear morning, animating what had been depressed, tinting what had been pale. Her eyes, whose colour I had not at first known, so dim were they with repressed tears, so shadowed with ceaseless dejection, now, lit by a ray of the sunshine that cheered her heart, revealed irids of bright hazel—irids large and full, screened with long lashes; and pupils instinct with fire. That look of wan emaciation which anxiety or low spirits often communicates to a thoughtful, thin face, rather long than round, having vanished from hers, a clearness of skin almost bloom, and a plumpness almost embonpoint, softened the decided lines of her features. Her figure shared in this beneficial change; it became rounder, and as the harmony of her form was complete and her stature of the graceful middle height, one did not regret (or at least I did not regret) the absence of confirmed fulness, in contours, still slight, though compact, elegant, flexible—the exquisite turning of waist, wrist, hand, foot, and ankle satisfied completely my notions of symmetry, and allowed a lightness and freedom of movement which corresponded with my ideas of grace.

Thus improved, thus wakened to life, Mdlle. Henri began to take a new footing in the school; her mental power, manifested gradually but steadily, ere long extorted recognition even from the envious; and when the young and healthy saw that she could smile brightly, converse gaily, move with vivacity and alertness, they acknowledged in her a sisterhood of youth and health, and tolerated her as of their kind accordingly.

To speak truth, I watched this change much as a gardener watches the growth of a precious plant, and I contributed to it too, even as the said gardener contributes to the development of his favourite. To me it was not difficult to discover how I could best foster my pupil, cherish her starved feelings, and induce the outward manifestation of that inward vigour which sunless drought and blighting blast had hitherto forbidden to expand. Constancy of attention—a kindness as mute as watchful, always standing by her, cloaked in the rough garb of austerity, and making its real nature known only by a rare glance of interest, or a cordial and gentle word; real respect masked with seeming imperiousness, directing, urging her actions, yet helping her too, and that with devoted care: these were the means I used, for these means best suited Frances' feelings, as susceptible as deep vibrating—her nature at once proud and shy.

The benefits of my system became apparent also in her altered demeanour as a teacher; she now took her place amongst her pupils with an air of spirit and firmness which assured them at once that she meant to be obeyed—and obeyed she was. They felt they had lost their power over her. If any girl had rebelled, she would no longer have taken her rebellion to heart; she possessed a source of comfort they could not drain, a pillar of support they could not overthrow: formerly, when insulted, she wept; now, she smiled.

The public reading of one of her devoirs achieved the revelation of her talents to all and sundry; I remember the subject—it was an emigrant's letter to his friends at home. It opened with simplicity; some natural and graphic touches disclosed to the reader the scene of virgin forest and great, New-World river—barren of sail and flag—amidst which the epistle was supposed to be indited. The difficulties and dangers that attend a settler's life, were hinted at; and in the few words said on that subject, Mdlle. Henri failed not to render audible the voice of resolve, patience, endeavour. The disasters which had driven him from his native country were alluded to; stainless honour, inflexible independence, indestructible self-respect there took the word. Past days were spoken of; the grief of parting, the regrets of absence, were touched upon; feeling, forcible and fine, breathed eloquent in every period. At the close, consolation was suggested; religious faith became there the speaker, and she spoke well.

The devoir was powerfully written in language at once chaste and choice, in a style nerved with vigour and graced with harmony.

Mdlle. Reuter was quite sufficiently acquainted with English to understand it when read or spoken in her presence, though she could neither speak nor write it herself. During the perusal of this devoir, she sat placidly busy, her eyes and fingers occupied with the formation of a "riviere" or open-work hem round a cambric handkerchief; she said nothing, and her face and forehead, clothed with a mask of purely negative expression, were as blank of comment as her lips. As neither surprise, pleasure, approbation, nor interest were evinced in her countenance, so no more were disdain, envy, annoyance, weariness; if that inscrutable mien said anything, it was simply this—

"The matter is too trite to excite an emotion, or call forth an opinion."

As soon as I had done, a hum rose; several of the pupils, pressing round Mdlle. Henri, began to beset her with compliments; the composed voice of the directress was now heard:—

"Young ladies, such of you as have cloaks and umbrellas will hasten to return home before the shower becomes heavier" (it was raining a little), "the remainder will wait till their respective servants arrive to fetch them." And the school dispersed, for it was four o'clock.

"Monsieur, a word," said Mdlle. Reuter, stepping on to the estrade, and signifying, by a movement of the hand, that she wished me to relinquish, for an instant, the castor I had clutched.

"Mademoiselle, I am at your service."

"Monsieur, it is of course an excellent plan to encourage effort in young people by making conspicuous the progress of any particularly industrious pupil; but do you not think that in the present instance, Mdlle. Henri can hardly be considered as a concurrent with the other pupils? She is older than most of them, and has had advantages of an exclusive nature for acquiring a knowledge of English; on the other hand, her sphere of life is somewhat beneath theirs; under these circumstances, a public distinction, conferred upon Mdlle. Henri, may be the means of suggesting comparisons, and exciting feelings such as would be far from advantageous to the individual forming their object. The interest I take in Mdlle. Henri's real welfare makes me desirous of screening her from annoyances of this sort; besides, monsieur, as I have before hinted to you, the sentiment of AMOUR-PROPRE has a somewhat marked preponderance in her character; celebrity has a tendency to foster this sentiment, and in her it should be rather repressed—she rather needs keeping down than bringing forward; and then I think, monsieur—it appears to me that ambition, LITERARY ambition especially, is not a feeling to be cherished in the mind of a woman: would not Mdlle. Henri be much safer and happier if taught to believe that in the quiet discharge of social duties consists her real vocation, than if stimulated to aspire after applause and publicity? She may never marry; scanty as are her resources, obscure as are her connections, uncertain as is her health (for I think her consumptive, her mother died of that complaint), it is more than probable she never will. I do not see how she can rise to a position, whence such a step would be possible; but even in celibacy it would be better for her to retain the character and habits of a respectable decorous female."

"Indisputably, mademoiselle," was my answer. "Your opinion admits of no doubt;" and, fearful of the harangue being renewed, I retreated under cover of that cordial sentence of assent.

At the date of a fortnight after the little incident noted above, I find it recorded in my diary that a hiatus occurred in Mdlle. Henri's usually regular attendance in class. The first day or two I wondered at her absence, but did not like to ask an explanation of it; I thought indeed some chance word might be dropped which would afford me the information I wished to obtain, without my running the risk of exciting silly smiles and gossiping whispers by demanding it. But when a week passed and the seat at the desk near the door still remained vacant, and when no allusion was made to the circumstance by any individual of the class—when, on the contrary, I found that all observed a marked silence on the point—I determined, COUTE QUI COUTE, to break the ice of this silly reserve. I selected Sylvie as my informant, because from her I knew that I should at least get a sensible answer, unaccompanied by wriggle, titter, or other flourish of folly.

"Ou donc est Mdlle. Henri?" I said one day as I returned an exercise-book I had been examining.

"Elle est partie, monsieur."

"Partie? et pour combien de temps? Quand reviendra-t-elle?"

"Elle est partie pour toujours, monsieur; elle ne reviendra plus."

"Ah!" was my involuntary exclamation; then after a pause:—

"En etes-vous bien sure, Sylvie?"

"Oui, oui, monsieur, mademoiselle la directrice nous l'a dit elle-meme il y a deux ou trois jours."

And I could pursue my inquiries no further; time, place, and circumstances forbade my adding another word. I could neither comment on what had been said, nor demand further particulars. A question as to the reason of the teacher's departure, as to whether it had been voluntary or otherwise, was indeed on my lips, but I suppressed it—there were listeners all round. An hour after, in passing Sylvie in the corridor as she was putting on her bonnet, I stopped short and asked:—

"Sylvie, do you know Mdlle. Henri's address? I have some books of hers," I added carelessly, "and I should wish to send them to her."

"No, monsieur," replied Sylvie; "but perhaps Rosalie, the portress, will be able to give it you."

Rosalie's cabinet was just at hand; I stepped in and repeated the inquiry. Rosalie—a smart French grisette—looked up from her work with a knowing smile, precisely the sort of smile I had been so desirous to avoid exciting. Her answer was prepared; she knew nothing whatever of Mdlle. Henri's address—had never known it. Turning from her with impatience—for I believed she lied and was hired to lie—I almost knocked down some one who had been standing at my back; it was the directress. My abrupt movement made her recoil two or three steps. I was obliged to apologize, which I did more concisely than politely. No man likes to be dogged, and in the very irritable mood in which I then was the sight of Mdlle. Reuter thoroughly incensed me. At the moment I turned her countenance looked hard, dark, and inquisitive; her eyes were bent upon me with an expression of almost hungry curiosity. I had scarcely caught this phase of physiognomy ere it had vanished; a bland smile played on her features; my harsh apology was received with good-humoured facility.

"Oh, don't mention it, monsieur; you only touched my hair with your elbow; it is no worse, only a little dishevelled." She shook it back, and passing her fingers through her curls, loosened them into more numerous and flowing ringlets. Then she went on with vivacity:

"Rosalie, I was coming to tell you to go instantly and close the windows of the salon; the wind is rising, and the muslin curtains will be covered with dust."

Rosalie departed. "Now," thought I, "this will not do; Mdlle. Reuter thinks her meanness in eaves-dropping is screened by her art in devising a pretext, whereas the muslin curtains she speaks of are not more transparent than this same pretext." An impulse came over me to thrust the flimsy screen aside, and confront her craft boldly with a word or two of plain truth. "The rough-shod foot treads most firmly on slippery ground," thought I; so I began:

"Mademoiselle Henri has left your establishment—been dismissed, I presume?"

"Ah, I wished to have a little conversation with you, monsieur," replied the directress with the most natural and affable air in the world; "but we cannot talk quietly here; will Monsieur step into the garden a minute?" And she preceded me, stepping out through the glass-door I have before mentioned.

"There," said she, when we had reached the centre of the middle alley, and when the foliage of shrubs and trees, now in their summer pride, closing behind and around us, shut out the view of the house, and thus imparted a sense of seclusion even to this little plot of ground in the very core of a capital.

"There, one feels quiet and free when there are only pear-trees and rose-bushes about one; I dare say you, like me, monsieur, are sometimes tired of being eternally in the midst of life; of having human faces always round you, human eyes always upon you, human voices always in your ear. I am sure I often wish intensely for liberty to spend a whole month in the country at some little farm-house, bien gentille, bien propre, tout entouree de champs et de bois; quelle vie charmante que la vie champetre! N'est-ce pas, monsieur?"

"Cela depend, mademoiselle."

"Que le vent est bon et frais!" continued the directress; and she was right there, for it was a south wind, soft and sweet. I carried my hat in my hand, and this gentle breeze, passing through my hair, soothed my temples like balm. Its refreshing effect, however, penetrated no deeper than the mere surface of the frame; for as I walked by the side of Mdlle. Reuter, my heart was still hot within me, and while I was musing the fire burned; then spake I with my tongue:—

"I understand Mdlle. Henri is gone from hence, and will not return?"

"Ah, true! I meant to have named the subject to you some days ago, but my time is so completely taken up, I cannot do half the things I wish: have you never experienced what it is, monsieur, to find the day too short by twelve hours for your numerous duties?"

"Not often. Mdlle. Henri's departure was not voluntary, I presume? If it had been, she would certainly have given me some intimation of it, being my pupil."

"Oh, did she not tell you? that was strange; for my part, I never thought of adverting to the subject; when one has so many things to attend to, one is apt to forget little incidents that are not of primary importance."

"You consider Mdlle. Henri's dismission, then, as a very insignificant event?"

"Dismission? Ah! she was not dismissed; I can say with truth, monsieur, that since I became the head of this establishment no master or teacher has ever been dismissed from it."

"Yet some have left it, mademoiselle?"

"Many; I have found it necessary to change frequently—a change of instructors is often beneficial to the interests of a school; it gives life and variety to the proceedings; it amuses the pupils, and suggests to the parents the idea of exertion and progress."

"Yet when you are tired of a professor or maitresse, you scruple to dismiss them?"

"No need to have recourse to such extreme measures, I assure you. Allons, monsieur le professeur—asseyons-nous; je vais vous donner une petite lecon dans votre etat d'instituteur." (I wish I might write all she said to me in French —it loses sadly by being translated into English.) We had now reached THE garden-chair; the directress sat down, and signed to me to sit by her, but I only rested my knee on the seat, and stood leaning my head and arm against the embowering branch of a huge laburnum, whose golden flowers, blent with the dusky green leaves of a lilac-bush, formed a mixed arch of shade and sunshine over the retreat. Mdlle. Reuter sat silent a moment; some novel movements were evidently working in her mind, and they showed their nature on her astute brow; she was meditating some CHEF D'OEUVRE of policy. Convinced by several months' experience that the affectation of virtues she did not possess was unavailing to ensnare me—aware that I had read her real nature, and would believe nothing of the character she gave out as being hers —she had determined, at last, to try a new key, and see if the lock of my heart would yield to that; a little audacity, a word of truth, a glimpse of the real. "Yes, I will try," was her inward resolve; and then her blue eye glittered upon me—it did not flash—nothing of flame ever kindled in its temperate gleam.

"Monsieur fears to sit by me?" she inquired playfully.

"I have no wish to usurp Pelet's place," I answered, for I had got the habit of speaking to her bluntly—a habit begun in anger, but continued because I saw that, instead of offending, it fascinated her. She cast down her eyes, and drooped her eyelids; she sighed uneasily; she turned with an anxious gesture, as if she would give me the idea of a bird that flutters in its cage, and would fain fly from its jail and jailer, and seek its natural mate and pleasant nest.

"Well—and your lesson?" I demanded briefly.

"Ah!" she exclaimed, recovering herself, "you are so young, so frank and fearless, so talented, so impatient of imbecility, so disdainful of vulgarity, you need a lesson; here it is then: far more is to be done in this world by dexterity than by strength; but, perhaps, you knew that before, for there is delicacy as well as power in your character—policy, as well as pride?"

"Go on," said I; and I could hardly help smiling, the flattery was so piquant, so finely seasoned. She caught the prohibited smile, though I passed my hand over my month to conceal it; and again she made room for me to sit beside her. I shook my head, though temptation penetrated to my senses at the moment, and once more I told her to go on.

"Well, then, if ever you are at the head of a large establishment, dismiss nobody. To speak truth, monsieur (and to you I will speak truth), I despise people who are always making rows, blustering, sending off one to the right, and another to the left, urging and hurrying circumstances. I'll tell you what I like best to do, monsieur, shall I?" She looked up again; she had compounded her glance well this time—much archness, more deference, a spicy dash of coquetry, an unveiled consciousness of capacity. I nodded; she treated me like the great Mogul; so I became the great Mogul as far as she was concerned.

"I like, monsieur, to take my knitting in my hands, and to sit quietly down in my chair; circumstances defile past me; I watch their march; so long as they follow the course I wish, I say nothing, and do nothing; I don't clap my hands, and cry out 'Bravo! How lucky I am!' to attract the attention and envy of my neighbours—I am merely passive; but when events fall out ill—when circumstances become adverse—I watch very vigilantly; I knit on still, and still I hold my tongue; but every now and then, monsieur, I just put my toe out —so—and give the rebellious circumstance a little secret push, without noise, which sends it the way I wish, and I am successful after all, and nobody has seen my expedient. So, when teachers or masters become troublesome and inefficient—when, in short, the interests of the school would suffer from their retaining their places—I mind my knitting, events progress, circumstances glide past; I see one which, if pushed ever so little awry, will render untenable the post I wish to have vacated—the deed is done—the stumbling-block removed—and no one saw me: I have not made an enemy, I am rid of an incumbrance."

A moment since, and I thought her alluring; this speech concluded, I looked on her with distaste. "Just like you," was my cold answer. "And in this way you have ousted Mdlle. Henri? You wanted her office, therefore you rendered it intolerable to her?"

"Not at all, monsieur, I was merely anxious about Mdlle. Henri's health; no, your moral sight is clear and piercing, but there you have failed to discover the truth. I took—I have always taken a real interest in Mdlle. Henri's welfare; I did not like her going out in all weathers; I thought it would be more advantageous for her to obtain a permanent situation; besides, I considered her now qualified to do something more than teach sewing. I reasoned with her; left the decision to herself; she saw the correctness of my views, and adopted them."

"Excellent! and now, mademoiselle, you will have the goodness to give me her address."

"Her address!" and a sombre and stony change came over the mien of the directress. "Her address? Ah?—well—I wish I could oblige you, monsieur, but I cannot, and I will tell you why; whenever I myself asked her for her address, she always evaded the inquiry. I thought—I may be wrong—but I THOUGHT her motive for doing so, was a natural, though mistaken reluctance to introduce me to some, probably, very poor abode; her means were narrow, her origin obscure; she lives somewhere, doubtless, in the 'basse ville.'"

"I'll not lose sight of my best pupil yet," said I, "though she were born of beggars and lodged in a cellar; for the rest, it is absurd to make a bugbear of her origin to me—I happen to know that she was a Swiss pastor's daughter, neither more nor less; and, as to her narrow means, I care nothing for the poverty of her purse so long as her heart overflows with affluence."

"Your sentiments are perfectly noble, monsieur," said the directress, affecting to suppress a yawn; her sprightliness was now extinct, her temporary candour shut up; the little, red-coloured, piratical-looking pennon of audacity she had allowed to float a minute in the air, was furled, and the broad, sober-hued flag of dissimulation again hung low over the citadel. I did not like her thus, so I cut short the TETE-A-TETE and departed.

CHAPTER XIX.

Novelists should never allow themselves to weary of the study of real life. If they observed this duty conscientiously, they would give us fewer pictures chequered with vivid contrasts of light and shade; they would seldom elevate their heroes and heroines to the heights of rapture—still seldomer sink them to the depths of despair; for if we rarely taste the fulness of joy in this life, we yet more rarely savour the acrid bitterness of hopeless anguish; unless, indeed, we have plunged like beasts into sensual indulgence, abused, strained, stimulated, again overstrained, and, at last, destroyed our faculties for enjoyment; then, truly, we may find ourselves without support, robbed of hope. Our agony is great, and how can it end? We have broken the spring of our powers; life must be all suffering—too feeble to conceive faith—death must be darkness—God, spirits, religion can have no place in our collapsed minds, where linger only hideous and polluting recollections of vice; and time brings us on to the brink of the grave, and dissolution flings us in—a rag eaten through and through with disease, wrung together with pain, stamped into the churchyard sod by the inexorable heel of despair.

But the man of regular life and rational mind never despairs. He loses his property—it is a blow—he staggers a moment; then, his energies, roused by the smart, are at work to seek a remedy; activity soon mitigates regret. Sickness affects him; he takes patience—endures what he cannot cure. Acute pain racks him; his writhing limbs know not where to find rest; he leans on Hope's anchors. Death takes from him what he loves; roots up, and tears violently away the stem round which his affections were twined—a dark, dismal time, a frightful wrench—but some morning Religion looks into his desolate house with sunrise, and says, that in another world, another life, he shall meet his kindred again. She speaks of that world as a place unsullied by sin—of that life, as an era unembittered by suffering; she mightily strengthens her consolation by connecting with it two ideas—which mortals cannot comprehend, but on which they love to repose—Eternity, Immortality; and the mind of the mourner, being filled with an image, faint yet glorious, of heavenly hills all light and peace—of a spirit resting there in bliss—of a day when his spirit shall also alight there, free and disembodied—of a reunion perfected by love, purified from fear—he takes courage—goes out to encounter the necessities and discharge the duties of life; and, though sadness may never lift her burden from his mind, Hope will enable him to support it.

Well—and what suggested all this? and what is the inference to be drawn therefrom? What suggested it, is the circumstance of my best pupil—my treasure—being snatched from my hands, and put away out of my reach; the inference to be drawn from it is—that, being a steady, reasonable man, I did not allow the resentment, disappointment, and grief, engendered in my mind by this evil chance, to grow there to any monstrous size; nor did I allow them to monopolize the whole space of my heart; I pent them, on the contrary, in one strait and secret nook. In the daytime, too, when I was about my duties, I put them on the silent system; and it was only after I had closed the door of my chamber at night that I somewhat relaxed my severity towards these morose nurslings, and allowed vent to their language of murmurs; then, in revenge, they sat on my pillow, haunted my bed, and kept me awake with their long, midnight cry.

A week passed. I had said nothing more to Mdlle. Reuter. I had been calm in my demeanour to her, though stony cold and hard. When I looked at her, it was with the glance fitting to be bestowed on one who I knew had consulted jealousy as an adviser, and employed treachery as an instrument—the glance of quiet disdain and rooted distrust. On Saturday evening, ere I left the house, I stept into the SALLE-A-MANGER, where she was sitting alone, and, placing myself before her, I asked, with the same tranquil tone and manner that I should have used had I put the question for the first time—

"Mademoiselle, will you have the goodness to give me the address of

Frances Evans Henri?"

A little surprised, but not disconcerted, she smilingly disclaimed any knowledge of that address, adding, "Monsieur has perhaps forgotten that I explained all about that circumstance before—a week ago?"

"Mademoiselle," I continued, "you would greatly oblige me by directing me to that young person's abode."

She seemed somewhat puzzled; and, at last, looking up with an admirably counterfeited air of naivete, she demanded, "Does Monsieur think I am telling an untruth?"

Still avoiding to give her a direct answer, I said, "It is not then your intention, mademoiselle, to oblige me in this particular?"

"But, monsieur, how can I tell you what I do not know?"

"Very well; I understand you perfectly, mademoiselle, and now I have only two or three words to say. This is the last week in July; in another month the vacation will commence, have the goodness to avail yourself of the leisure it will afford you to look out for another English master—at the close of August, I shall be under the necessity of resigning my post in your establishment."

I did not wait for her comments on this announcement, but bowed and immediately withdrew.

That same evening, soon after dinner, a servant brought me a small packet; it was directed in a hand I knew, but had not hoped so soon to see again; being in my own apartment and alone, there was nothing to prevent my immediately opening it; it contained four five-franc pieces, and a note in English.

"MONSIEUR,

"I came to Mdlle. Reuter's house yesterday, at the time when I knew you would be just about finishing your lesson, and I asked if I might go into the schoolroom and speak to you. Mdlle. Reuter came out and said you were already gone; it had not yet struck four, so I thought she must be mistaken, but concluded it would be vain to call another day on the same errand. In one sense a note will do as well—it will wrap up the 20 francs, the price of the lessons I have received from you; and if it will not fully express the thanks I owe you in addition—if it will not bid you good-bye as I could wish to have done—if it will not tell you, as I long to do, how sorry I am that I shall probably never see you more—why, spoken words would hardly be more adequate to the task. Had I seen you, I should probably have stammered out something feeble and unsatisfactory—something belying my feelings rather than explaining them; so it is perhaps as well that I was denied admission to your presence. You often remarked, monsieur, that my devoirs dwelt a great deal on fortitude in bearing grief—you said I introduced that theme too often: I find indeed that it is much easier to write about a severe duty than to perform it, for I am oppressed when I see and feel to what a reverse fate has condemned me; you were kind to me, monsieur—very kind; I am afflicted—I am heart-broken to be quite separated from you; soon I shall have no friend on earth. But it is useless troubling you with my distresses. What claim have I on your sympathy? None; I will then say no more.

"Farewell, Monsieur.

"F. E. HENRI."

I put up the note in my pocket-book. I slipped the five-franc pieces into my purse—then I took a turn through my narrow chamber.

"Mdlle. Reuter talked about her poverty," said I, "and she is poor; yet she pays her debts and more. I have not yet given her a quarter's lessons, and she has sent me a quarter's due. I wonder of what she deprived herself to scrape together the twenty francs—I wonder what sort of a place she has to live in, and what sort of a woman her aunt is, and whether she is likely to get employment to supply the place she has lost. No doubt she will have to trudge about long enough from school to school, to inquire here, and apply there—be rejected in this place, disappointed in that. Many an evening she'll go to her bed tired and unsuccessful. And the directress would not let her in to bid me good-bye? I might not have the chance of standing with her for a few minutes at a window in the schoolroom and exchanging some half-dozen of sentences—getting to know where she lived—putting matters in train for having all things arranged to my mind? No address on the note"—I continued, drawing it again from the pocket-book and examining it on each side of the two leaves: "women are women, that is certain, and always do business like women; men mechanically put a date and address to their communications. And these five-franc pieces?"—(I hauled them forth from my purse)—"if she had offered me them herself instead of tying them up with a thread of green silk in a kind of Lilliputian packet, I could have thrust them back into her little hand, and shut up the small, taper fingers over them—so—and compelled her shame, her pride, her shyness, all to yield to a little bit of determined Will—now where is she? How can I get at her?"

Opening my chamber door I walked down into the kitchen.

"Who brought the packet?" I asked of the servant who had delivered it to me.

"Un petit commissionaire, monsieur."

"Did he say anything?"

"Rien."

And I wended my way up the back-stairs, wondrously the wiser for my inquiries.

"No matter," said I to myself, as I again closed the door. "No matter—I'll seek her through Brussels."

And I did. I sought her day by day whenever I had a moment's leisure, for four weeks; I sought her on Sundays all day long; I sought her on the Boulevards, in the Allee Verte, in the Park; I sought her in Ste. Gudule and St. Jacques; I sought her in the two Protestant chapels; I attended these latter at the German, French, and English services, not doubting that I should meet her at one of them. All my researches were absolutely fruitless; my security on the last point was proved by the event to be equally groundless with my other calculations. I stood at the door of each chapel after the service, and waited till every individual had come out, scrutinizing every gown draping a slender form, peering under every bonnet covering a young head. In vain; I saw girlish figures pass me, drawing their black scarfs over their sloping shoulders, but none of them had the exact turn and air of Mdlle. Henri's; I saw pale and thoughtful faces "encadrees" in bands of brown hair, but I never found her forehead, her eyes, her eyebrows. All the features of all the faces I met seemed frittered away, because my eye failed to recognize the peculiarities it was bent upon; an ample space of brow and a large, dark, and serious eye, with a fine but decided line of eyebrow traced above.

"She has probably left Brussels—perhaps is gone to England, as she said she would," muttered I inwardly, as on the afternoon of the fourth Sunday, I turned from the door of the chapel-royal which the door-keeper had just closed and locked, and followed in the wake of the last of the congregation, now dispersed and dispersing over the square. I had soon outwalked the couples of English gentlemen and ladies. (Gracious goodness! why don't they dress better? My eye is yet filled with visions of the high-flounced, slovenly, and tumbled dresses in costly silk and satin, of the large unbecoming collars in expensive lace; of the ill-cut coats and strangely fashioned pantaloons which every Sunday, at the English service, filled the choirs of the chapel-royal, and after it, issuing forth into the square, came into disadvantageous contrast with freshly and trimly attired foreign figures, hastening to attend salut at the church of Coburg.) I had passed these pairs of Britons, and the groups of pretty British children, and the British footmen and waiting-maids; I had crossed the Place Royale, and got into the Rue Royale, thence I had diverged into the Rue de Louvain—an old and quiet street. I remember that, feeling a little hungry, and not desiring to go back and take my share of the "gouter," now on the refectory-table at Pelet's—to wit, pistolets and water—I stepped into a baker's and refreshed myself on a COUC(?)—it is a Flemish word, I don't know how to spell it—A CORINTHE-ANGLICE, a currant bun—and a cup of coffee; and then I strolled on towards the Porte de Louvain. Very soon I was out of the city, and slowly mounting the hill, which ascends from the gate, I took my time; for the afternoon, though cloudy, was very sultry, and not a breeze stirred to refresh the atmosphere. No inhabitant of Brussels need wander far to search for solitude; let him but move half a league from his own city and he will find her brooding still and blank over the wide fields, so drear though so fertile, spread out treeless and trackless round the capital of Brabant. Having gained the summit of the hill, and having stood and looked long over the cultured but lifeless campaign, I felt a wish to quit the high road, which I had hitherto followed, and get in among those tilled grounds—fertile as the beds of a Brobdignagian kitchen-garden—spreading far and wide even to the boundaries of the horizon, where, from a dusk green, distance changed them to a sullen blue, and confused their tints with those of the livid and thunderous-looking sky. Accordingly I turned up a by-path to the right; I had not followed it far ere it brought me, as I expected, into the fields, amidst which, just before me, stretched a long and lofty white wall enclosing, as it seemed from the foliage showing above, some thickly planted nursery of yew and cypress, for of that species were the branches resting on the pale parapets, and crowding gloomily about a massive cross, planted doubtless on a central eminence and extending its arms, which seemed of black marble, over the summits of those sinister trees. I approached, wondering to what house this well-protected garden appertained; I turned the angle of the wall, thinking to see some stately residence; I was close upon great iron gates; there was a hut serving for a lodge near, but I had no occasion to apply for the key—the gates were open; I pushed one leaf back—rain had rusted its hinges, for it groaned dolefully as they revolved. Thick planting embowered the entrance. Passing up the avenue, I saw objects on each hand which, in their own mute language of inscription and sign, explained clearly to what abode I had made my way. This was the house appointed for all living; crosses, monuments, and garlands of everlastings announced, "The Protestant Cemetery, outside the gate of Louvain."

The place was large enough to afford half an hour's strolling without the monotony of treading continually the same path; and, for those who love to peruse the annals of graveyards, here was variety of inscription enough to occupy the attention for double or treble that space of time. Hither people of many kindreds, tongues, and nations, had brought their dead for interment; and here, on pages of stone, of marble, and of brass, were written names, dates, last tributes of pomp or love, in English, in French, in German, and Latin. Here the Englishman had erected a marble monument over the remains of his Mary Smith or Jane Brown, and inscribed it only with her name. There the French widower had shaded the grave of his Elmire or Celestine with a brilliant thicket of roses, amidst which a little tablet rising, bore an equally bright testimony to her countless virtues. Every nation, tribe, and kindred, mourned after its own fashion; and how soundless was the mourning of all! My own tread, though slow and upon smooth-rolled paths, seemed to startle, because it formed the sole break to a silence otherwise total. Not only the winds, but the very fitful, wandering airs, were that afternoon, as by common consent, all fallen asleep in their various quarters; the north was hushed, the south silent, the east sobbed not, nor did the west whisper. The clouds in heaven were condensed and dull, but apparently quite motionless. Under the trees of this cemetery nestled a warm breathless gloom, out of which the cypresses stood up straight and mute, above which the willows hung low and still; where the flowers, as languid as fair, waited listless for night dew or thunder-shower; where the tombs, and those they hid, lay impassible to sun or shadow, to rain or drought.

Importuned by the sound of my own footsteps, I turned off upon the turf, and slowly advanced to a grove of yews; I saw something stir among the stems; I thought it might be a broken branch swinging, my short-sighted vision had caught no form, only a sense of motion; but the dusky shade passed on, appearing and disappearing at the openings in the avenue. I soon discerned it was a living thing, and a human thing; and, drawing nearer, I perceived it was a woman, pacing slowly to and fro, and evidently deeming herself alone as I had deemed myself alone, and meditating as I had been meditating. Ere long she returned to a seat which I fancy she had but just quitted, or I should have caught sight of her before. It was in a nook, screened by a clump of trees; there was the white wall before her, and a little stone set up against the wall, and, at the foot of the stone, was an allotment of turf freshly turned up, a new-made grave. I put on my spectacles, and passed softly close behind her; glancing at the inscription on the stone, I read, "Julienne Henri, died at Brussels, aged sixty. August 10th, 18—." Having perused the inscription, I looked down at the form sitting bent and thoughtful just under my eyes, unconscious of the vicinity of any living thing; it was a slim, youthful figure in mourning apparel of the plainest black stuff, with a little simple, black crape bonnet; I felt, as well as saw, who it was; and, moving neither hand nor foot, I stood some moments enjoying the security of conviction. I had sought her for a month, and had never discovered one of her traces—never met a hope, or seized a chance of encountering her anywhere. I had been forced to loosen my grasp on expectation; and, but an hour ago, had sunk slackly under the discouraging thought that the current of life, and the impulse of destiny, had swept her for ever from my reach; and, behold, while bending suddenly earthward beneath the pressure of despondency—while following with my eyes the track of sorrow on the turf of a graveyard—here was my lost jewel dropped on the tear-fed herbage, nestling in the messy and mouldy roots of yew-trees.

Frances sat very quiet, her elbow on her knee, and her head on her hand. I knew she could retain a thinking attitude a long time without change; at last, a tear fell; she had been looking at the name on the stone before her, and her heart had no doubt endured one of those constrictions with which the desolate living, regretting the dead, are, at times, so sorely oppressed. Many tears rolled down, which she wiped away, again and again, with her handkerchief; some distressed sobs escaped her, and then, the paroxysm over, she sat quiet as before. I put my hand gently on her shoulder; no need further to prepare her, for she was neither hysterical nor liable to fainting-fits; a sudden push, indeed, might have startled her, but the contact of my quiet touch merely woke attention as I wished; and, though she turned quickly, yet so lightning-swift is thought—in some minds especially—I believe the wonder of what—the consciousness of who it was that thus stole unawares on her solitude, had passed through her brain, and flashed into her heart, even before she had effected that hasty movement; at least, Amazement had hardly opened her eyes and raised them to mine, ere Recognition informed their irids with most speaking brightness. Nervous surprise had hardly discomposed her features ere a sentiment of most vivid joy shone clear and warm on her whole countenance. I had hardly time to observe that she was wasted and pale, ere called to feel a responsive inward pleasure by the sense of most full and exquisite pleasure glowing in the animated flush, and shining in the expansive light, now diffused over my pupil's face. It was the summer sun flashing out after the heavy summer shower; and what fertilizes more rapidly than that beam, burning almost like fire in its ardour?

I hate boldness—that boldness which is of the brassy brow and insensate nerves; but I love the courage of the strong heart, the fervour of the generous blood; I loved with passion the light of Frances Evans' clear hazel eye when it did not fear to look straight into mine; I loved the tones with which she uttered the words—

"Mon maitre! mon maitre!"

I loved the movement with which she confided her hand to my hand; I loved her as she stood there, penniless and parentless; for a sensualist charmless, for me a treasure—my best object of sympathy on earth, thinking such thoughts as I thought, feeling such feelings as I felt; my ideal of the shrine in which to seal my stores of love; personification of discretion and forethought, of diligence and perseverance, of self-denial and self-control— those guardians, those trusty keepers of the gift I longed to confer on her—the gift of all my affections; model of truth and honour, of independence and conscientiousness—those refiners and sustainers of an honest life; silent possessor of a well of tenderness, of a flame, as genial as still, as pure as quenchless, of natural feeling, natural passion—those sources of refreshment and comfort to the sanctuary of home. I knew how quietly and how deeply the well bubbled in her heart; I knew how the more dangerous flame burned safely under the eye of reason; I had seen when the fire shot up a moment high and vivid, when the accelerated heat troubled life's current in its channels; I had seen reason reduce the rebel, and humble its blaze to embers. I had confidence in Frances Evans; I had respect for her, and as I drew her arm through mine, and led her out of the cemetery, I felt I had another sentiment, as strong as confidence, as firm as respect, more fervid than either—that of love.

"Well, my pupil," said I, as the ominous sounding gate swung to behind us —"Well, I have found you again: a month's search has seemed long, and I little thought to have discovered my lost sheep straying amongst graves."

Never had I addressed her but as "Mademoiselle" before, and to speak thus was to take up a tone new to both her and me. Her answer suprised me that this language ruffled none of her feelings, woke no discord in her heart:

"Mon maitre," she said, "have you troubled yourself to seek me? I little imagined you would think much of my absence, but I grieved bitterly to be taken away from you. I was sorry for that circumstance when heavier troubles ought to have made me forget it."

"Your aunt is dead?"

"Yes, a fortnight since, and she died full of regret, which I could not chase from her mind; she kept repeating, even during the last night of her existence, 'Frances, you will be so lonely when I am gone, so friendless:' she wished too that she could have been buried in Switzerland, and it was I who persuaded her in her old age to leave the banks of Lake Leman, and to come, only as it seems to die, in this flat region of Flanders. Willingly would I have observed her last wish, and taken her remains back to our own country, but that was impossible; I was forced to lay her here."

"She was ill but a short time, I presume?"

"But three weeks. When she began to sink I asked Mdlle. Reuter's leave to stay with her and wait on her; I readily got leave."

"Do you return to the pensionnat!" I demanded hastily.

"Monsieur, when I had been at home a week Mdlle. Reuter called one evening, just after I had got my aunt to bed; she went into her room to speak to her, and was extremely civil and affable, as she always is; afterwards she came and sat with me a long time, and just as she rose to go away, she said: "Mademoiselle, I shall not soon cease to regret your departure from my establishment, though indeed it is true that you have taught your class of pupils so well that they are all quite accomplished in the little works you manage so skilfully, and have not the slightest need of further instruction; my second teacher must in future supply your place, with regard to the younger pupils, as well as she can, though she is indeed an inferior artiste to you, and doubtless it will be your part now to assume a higher position in your calling; I am sure you will everywhere find schools and families willing to profit by your talents.' And then she paid me my last quarter's salary. I asked, as mademoiselle would no doubt think, very bluntly, if she designed to discharge me from the establishment. She smiled at my inelegance of speech, and answered that 'our connection as employer and employed was certainly dissolved, but that she hoped still to retain the pleasure of my acquaintance; she should always be happy to see me as a friend;' and then she said something about the excellent condition of the streets, and the long continuance of fine weather, and went away quite cheerful."

I laughed inwardly; all this was so like the directress—so like what I had expected and guessed of her conduct; and then the exposure and proof of her lie, unconsciously afforded by Frances:—"She had frequently applied for Mdlle. Henri's address," forsooth; "Mdlle. Henri had always evaded giving it," &c., &c., and here I found her a visitor at the very house of whose locality she had professed absolute ignorance!

Any comments I might have intended to make on my pupil's communication, were checked by the plashing of large rain-drops on our faces and on the path, and by the muttering of a distant but coming storm. The warning obvious in stagnant air and leaden sky had already induced me to take the road leading back to Brussels, and now I hastened my own steps and those of my companion, and, as our way lay downhill, we got on rapidly. There was an interval after the fall of the first broad drops before heavy rain came on; in the meantime we had passed through the Porte de Louvain, and were again in the city.

"Where do you live?" I asked; "I will see you safe home."

"Rue Notre Dame aux Neiges," answered Frances.

It was not far from the Rue de Louvain, and we stood on the doorsteps of the house we sought ere the clouds, severing with loud peal and shattered cataract of lightning, emptied their livid folds in a torrent, heavy, prone, and broad.

"Come in! come in!" said Frances, as, after putting her into the house, I paused ere I followed: the word decided me; I stepped across the threshold, shut the door on the rushing, flashing, whitening storm, and followed her upstairs to her apartments. Neither she nor I were wet; a projection over the door had warded off the straight-descending flood; none but the first, large drops had touched our garments; one minute more and we should not have had a dry thread on us.

Stepping over a little mat of green wool, I found myself in a small room with a painted floor and a square of green carpet in the middle; the articles of furniture were few, but all bright and exquisitely clean; order reigned through its narrow limits—such order as it soothed my punctilious soul to behold. And I had hesitated to enter the abode, because I apprehended after all that Mdlle. Reuter's hint about its extreme poverty might be too well-founded, and I feared to embarrass the lace-mender by entering her lodgings unawares! Poor the place might be; poor truly it was; but its neatness was better than elegance, and had but a bright little fire shone on that clean hearth, I should have deemed it more attractive than a palace. No fire was there, however, and no fuel laid ready to light; the lace-mender was unable to allow herself that indulgence, especially now when, deprived by death of her sole relative, she had only her own unaided exertions to rely on. Frances went into an inner room to take off her bonnet, and she came out a model of frugal neatness, with her well-fitting black stuff dress, so accurately defining her elegant bust and taper waist, with her spotless white collar turned back from a fair and shapely neck, with her plenteous brown hair arranged in smooth bands on her temples, and in a large Grecian plait behind: ornaments she had none—neither brooch, ring, nor ribbon; she did well enough without them—perfection of fit, proportion of form, grace of carriage, agreeably supplied their place. Her eye, as she re-entered the small sitting-room, instantly sought mine, which was just then lingering on the hearth; I knew she read at once the sort of inward ruth and pitying pain which the chill vacancy of that hearth stirred in my soul: quick to penetrate, quick to determine, and quicker to put in practice, she had in a moment tied a holland apron round her waist; then she disappeared, and reappeared with a basket; it had a cover; she opened it, and produced wood and coal; deftly and compactly she arranged them in the grate.

"It is her whole stock, and she will exhaust it out of hospitality," thought I.

"What are you going to do?" I asked: "not surely to light a fire this hot evening? I shall be smothered."

"Indeed, monsieur, I feel it very chilly since the rain began; besides, I must boil the water for my tea, for I take tea on Sundays; you will be obliged to try and bear the heat."

She had struck a light; the wood was already in a blaze; and truly, when contrasted with the darkness, the wild tumult of the tempest without, that peaceful glow which began to beam on the now animated hearth, seemed very cheering. A low, purring sound, from some quarter, announced that another being, besides myself, was pleased with the change; a black cat, roused by the light from its sleep on a little cushioned foot-stool, came and rubbed its head against Frances' gown as she knelt; she caressed it, saying it had been a favourite with her "pauvre tante Julienne."

The fire being lit, the hearth swept, and a small kettle of a very antique pattern, such as I thought I remembered to have seen in old farmhouses in England, placed over the now ruddy flame, Frances' hands were washed, and her apron removed in an instant; then she opened a cupboard, and took out a tea-tray, on which she had soon arranged a china tea-equipage, whose pattern, shape, and size, denoted a remote antiquity; a little, old-fashioned silver spoon was deposited in each saucer; and a pair of silver tongs, equally old-fashioned, were laid on the sugar-basin; from the cupboard, too, was produced a tidy silver cream-ewer, not larger then an egg-shell. While making these preparations, she chanced to look up, and, reading curiosity in my eyes, she smiled and asked—

"Is this like England, monsieur?"

"Like the England of a hundred years ago," I replied.

"Is it truly? Well, everything on this tray is at least a hundred years old: these cups, these spoons, this ewer, are all heirlooms; my great-grandmother left them to my grandmother, she to my mother, and my mother brought them with her from England to Switzerland, and left them to me; and, ever since I was a little girl, I have thought I should like to carry them back to England, whence they came."

She put some pistolets on the table; she made the tea, as foreigners do make tea—i.e., at the rate of a teaspoonful to half-a-dozen cups; she placed me a chair, and, as I took it, she asked, with a sort of exaltation—

"Will it make you think yourself at home for a moment?"

"If I had a home in England, I believe it would recall it," I answered; and, in truth, there was a sort of illusion in seeing the fair-complexioned English-looking girl presiding at the English meal, and speaking in the English language.

"You have then no home?" was her remark.

"None, nor ever have had. If ever I possess a home, it must be of my own making, and the task is yet to begin." And, as I spoke, a pang, new to me, shot across my heart: it was a pang of mortification at the humility of my position, and the inadequacy of my means; while with that pang was born a strong desire to do more, earn more, be more, possess more; and in the increased possessions, my roused and eager spirit panted to include the home I had never had, the wife I inwardly vowed to win.

Frances' tea was little better than hot water, sugar, and milk; and her pistolets, with which she could not offer me butter, were sweet to my palate as manna.

The repast over, and the treasured plate and porcelain being washed and put by, the bright table rubbed still brighter, "le chat de ma tante Julienne" also being fed with provisions brought forth on a plate for its special use, a few stray cinders, and a scattering of ashes too, being swept from the hearth, Frances at last sat down; and then, as she took a chair opposite to me, she betrayed, for the first time, a little embarrassment; and no wonder, for indeed I had unconsciously watched her rather too closely, followed all her steps and all her movements a little too perseveringly with my eyes, for she mesmerized me by the grace and alertness of her action—by the deft, cleanly, and even decorative effect resulting from each touch of her slight and fine fingers; and when, at last, she subsided to stillness, the intelligence of her face seemed beauty to me, and I dwelt on it accordingly. Her colour, however, rising, rather than settling with repose, and her eyes remaining downcast, though I kept waiting for the lids to be raised that I might drink a ray of the light I loved—a light where fire dissolved in softness, where affection tempered penetration, where, just now at least, pleasure played with thought—this expectation not being gratified, I began at last to suspect that I had probably myself to blame for the disappointment; I must cease gazing, and begin talking, if I wished to break the spell under which she now sat motionless; so recollecting the composing effect which an authoritative tone and manner had ever been wont to produce on her, I said—

"Get one of your English books, mademoiselle, for the rain yet falls heavily, and will probably detain me half an hour longer."

Released, and set at ease, up she rose, got her book, and accepted at once the chair I placed for her at my side. She had selected "Paradise Lost" from her shelf of classics, thinking, I suppose, the religious character of the book best adapted it to Sunday; I told her to begin at the beginning, and while she read Milton's invocation to that heavenly muse, who on the "secret top of Oreb or Sinai" had taught the Hebrew shepherd how in the womb of chaos, the conception of a world had originated and ripened, I enjoyed, undisturbed, the treble pleasure of having her near me, hearing the sound of her voice—a sound sweet and satisfying in my ear—and looking, by intervals, at her face: of this last privilege, I chiefly availed myself when I found fault with an intonation, a pause, or an emphasis; as long as I dogmatized, I might also gaze, without exciting too warm a flush.

"Enough," said I, when she had gone through some half dozen pages (a work of time with her, for she read slowly and paused often to ask and receive information)—"enough; and now the rain is ceasing, and I must soon go." For indeed, at that moment, looking towards the window, I saw it all blue; the thunder-clouds were broken and scattered, and the setting August sun sent a gleam like the reflection of rubies through the lattice. I got up; I drew on my gloves.

"You have not yet found another situation to supply the place of that from which you were dismissed by Mdlle. Reuter?"

"No, monsieur; I have made inquiries everywhere, but they all ask me for references; and to speak truth, I do not like to apply to the directress, because I consider she acted neither justly nor honourably towards me; she used underhand means to set my pupils against me, and thereby render me unhappy while I held my place in her establishment, and she eventually deprived me of it by a masked and hypocritical manoeuvre, pretending that she was acting for my good, but really snatching from me my chief means of subsistence, at a crisis when not only my own life, but that of another, depended on my exertions: of her I will never more ask a favour."

"How, then, do you propose to get on? How do you live now?"

"I have still my lace-mending trade; with care it will keep me from starvation, and I doubt not by dint of exertion to get better employment yet; it is only a fortnight since I began to try; my courage or hopes are by no means worn out yet."

"And if you get what you wish, what then? what are your ultimate views?"

"To save enough to cross the Channel: I always look to England as my Canaan."

"Well, well—ere long I shall pay you another visit; good evening now," and I left her rather abruptly; I had much ado to resist a strong inward impulse, urging me to take a warmer, more expressive leave: what so natural as to fold her for a moment in a close embrace, to imprint one kiss on her cheek or forehead? I was not unreasonable—that was all I wanted; satisfied in that point, I could go away content; and Reason denied me even this; she ordered me to turn my eyes from her face, and my steps from her apartment—to quit her as dryly and coldly as I would have quitted old Madame Pelet. I obeyed, but I swore rancorously to be avenged one day. "I'll earn a right to do as I please in this matter, or I'll die in the contest. I have one object before me now —to get that Genevese girl for my wife; and my wife she shall be—that is, provided she has as much, or half as much regard for her master as he has for her. And would she be so docile, so smiling, so happy under my instructions if she had not? would she sit at my side when I dictate or correct, with such a still, contented, halcyon mien?" for I had ever remarked, that however sad or harassed her countenance might be when I entered a room, yet after I had been near her, spoken to her a few words, given her some directions, uttered perhaps some reproofs, she would, all at once, nestle into a nook of happiness, and look up serene and revived. The reproofs suited her best of all: while I scolded she would chip away with her pen-knife at a pencil or a pen; fidgetting a little, pouting a little, defending herself by monosyllables, and when I deprived her of the pen or pencil, fearing it would be all cut away, and when I interdicted even the monosyllabic defence, for the purpose of working up the subdued excitement a little higher, she would at last raise her eyes and give me a certain glance, sweetened with gaiety, and pointed with defiance, which, to speak truth, thrilled me as nothing had ever done, and made me, in a fashion (though happily she did not know it), her subject, if not her slave. After such little scenes her spirits would maintain their flow, often for some hours, and, as I remarked before, her health therefrom took a sustenance and vigour which, previously to the event of her aunt's death and her dismissal, had almost recreated her whole frame.

It has taken me several minutes to write these last sentences; but I had thought all their purport during the brief interval of descending the stairs from Frances' room. Just as I was opening the outer door, I remembered the twenty francs which I had not restored; I paused: impossible to carry them away with me; difficult to force them back on their original owner; I had now seen her in her own humble abode, witnessed the dignity of her poverty, the pride of order, the fastidious care of conservatism, obvious in the arrangement and economy of her little home; I was sure she would not suffer herself to be excused paying her debts; I was certain the favour of indemnity would be accepted from no hand, perhaps least of all from mine: yet these four five-franc pieces were a burden to my self-respect, and I must get rid of them. An expedient—a clumsy one no doubt, but the best I could devise-suggested itself to me. I darted up the stairs, knocked, re-entered the room as if in haste:—

"Mademoiselle, I have forgotten one of my gloves; I must have left it here."

She instantly rose to seek it; as she turned her back, I—being now at the hearth—noiselessly lifted a little vase, one of a set of china ornaments, as old-fashioned as the tea-cups—slipped the money under it, then saying—"Oh here is my glove! I had dropped it within the fender; good evening, mademoiselle," I made my second exit.

Brief as my impromptu return had been, it had afforded me time to pick up a heart-ache; I remarked that Frances had already removed the red embers of her cheerful little fire from the grate: forced to calculate every item, to save in every detail, she had instantly on my departure retrenched a luxury too expensive to be enjoyed alone.

"I am glad it is not yet winter," thought I; "but in two months more come the winds and rains of November; would to God that before then I could earn the right, and the power, to shovel coals into that grate AD LIBITUM!"

Already the pavement was drying; a balmy and fresh breeze stirred the air, purified by lightning; I felt the West behind me, where spread a sky like opal; azure immingled with crimson: the enlarged sun, glorious in Tyrian tints, dipped his brim already; stepping, as I was, eastward, I faced a vast bank of clouds, but also I had before me the arch of an evening rainbow; a perfect rainbow—high, wide, vivid. I looked long; my eye drank in the scene, and I suppose my brain must have absorbed it; for that night, after lying awake in pleasant fever a long time, watching the silent sheet-lightning, which still played among the retreating clouds, and flashed silvery over the stars, I at last fell asleep; and then in a dream were reproduced the setting sun, the bank of clouds, the mighty rainbow. I stood, methought, on a terrace; I leaned over a parapeted wall; there was space below me, depth I could not fathom, but hearing an endless dash of waves, I believed it to be the sea; sea spread to the horizon; sea of changeful green and intense blue: all was soft in the distance; all vapour-veiled. A spark of gold glistened on the line between water and air, floated up, approached, enlarged, changed; the object hung midway between heaven and earth, under the arch of the rainbow; the soft but dusk clouds diffused behind. It hovered as on wings; pearly, fleecy, gleaming air streamed like raiment round it; light, tinted with carnation, coloured what seemed face and limbs; a large star shone with still lustre on an angel's forehead; an upraised arm and hand, glancing like a ray, pointed to the bow overhead, and a voice in my heart whispered—

"Hope smiles on Effort!"

CHAPTER XX.

A competency was what I wanted; a competency it was now my aim and resolve to secure; but never had I been farther from the mark. With August the school-year (l'annee scolaire) closed, the examinations concluded, the prizes were adjudged, the schools dispersed, the gates of all colleges, the doors of all pensionnats shut, not to be reopened till the beginning or middle of October. The last day of August was at hand, and what was my position? Had I advanced a step since the commencement of the past quarter? On the contrary, I had receded one. By renouncing my engagement as English master in Mdlle. Reuter's establishment, I had voluntarily cut off 20l. from my yearly income; I had diminished my 60l. per annum to 40l., and even that sum I now held by a very precarious tenure.

It is some time since I made any reference to M. Pelet. The moonlight walk is, I think, the last incident recorded in this narrative where that gentleman cuts any conspicuous figure: the fact is, since that event, a change had come over the spirit of our intercourse. He, indeed, ignorant that the still hour, a cloudless moon, and an open lattice, had revealed to me the secret of his selfish love and false friendship, would have continued smooth and complaisant as ever; but I grew spiny as a porcupine, and inflexible as a blackthorn cudgel; I never had a smile for his raillery, never a moment for his society; his invitations to take coffee with him in his parlour were invariably rejected, and very stiffly and sternly rejected too; his jesting allusions to the directress (which he still continued) were heard with a grim calm very different from the petulant pleasure they were formerly wont to excite. For a long time Pelet bore with my frigid demeanour very patiently; he even increased his attentions; but finding that even a cringing politeness failed to thaw or move me, he at last altered too; in his turn he cooled; his invitations ceased; his countenance became suspicious and overcast, and I read in the perplexed yet brooding aspect of his brow, a constant examination and comparison of premises, and an anxious endeavour to draw thence some explanatory inference. Ere long, I fancy, he succeeded, for he was not without penetration; perhaps, too, Mdlle. Zoraide might have aided him in the solution of the enigma; at any rate I soon found that the uncertainty of doubt had vanished from his manner; renouncing all pretence of friendship and cordiality, he adopted a reserved, formal, but still scrupulously polite deportment. This was the point to which I had wished to bring him, and I was now again comparatively at my ease. I did not, it is true, like my position in his house; but being freed from the annoyance of false professions and double-dealing I could endure it, especially as no heroic sentiment of hatred or jealousy of the director distracted my philosophical soul; he had not, I found, wounded me in a very tender point, the wound was so soon and so radically healed, leaving only a sense of contempt for the treacherous fashion in which it had been inflicted, and a lasting mistrust of the hand which I had detected attempting to stab in the dark.

This state of things continued till about the middle of July, and then there was a little change; Pelet came home one night, an hour after his usual time, in a state of unequivocal intoxication, a thing anomalous with him; for if he had some of the worst faults of his countrymen, he had also one at least of their virtues, i.e. sobriety. So drunk, however, was he upon this occasion, that after having roused the whole establishment (except the pupils, whose dormitory being over the classes in a building apart from the dwelling-house, was consequently out of the reach of disturbance) by violently ringing the hall-bell and ordering lunch to be brought in immediately, for he imagined it was noon, whereas the city bells had just tolled midnight; after having furiously rated the servants for their want of punctuality, and gone near to chastise his poor old mother, who advised him to go to bed, he began raving dreadfully about "le maudit Anglais, Creemsvort." I had not yet retired; some German books I had got hold of had kept me up late; I heard the uproar below, and could distinguish the director's voice exalted in a manner as appalling as it was unusual. Opening my door a little, I became aware of a demand on his part for "Creemsvort" to be brought down to him that he might cut his throat on the hall-table and wash his honour, which he affirmed to be in a dirty condition, in infernal British blood. "He is either mad or drunk," thought I, "and in either case the old woman and the servants will be the better of a man's assistance," so I descended straight to the hall. I found him staggering about, his eyes in a fine frenzy rolling—a pretty sight he was, a just medium between the fool and the lunatic.

"Come, M. Pelet," said I, "you had better go to bed," and I took hold of his arm. His excitement, of course, increased greatly at sight and touch of the individual for whose blood he had been making application: he struggled and struck with fury—but a drunken man is no match for a sober one; and, even in his normal state, Pelet's worn out frame could not have stood against my sound one. I got him up-stairs, and, in process of time, to bed. During the operation he did not fail to utter comminations which, though broken, had a sense in them; while stigmatizing me as the treacherous spawn of a perfidious country, he, in the same breath, anathematized Zoraide Reuter; he termed her "femme sotte et vicieuse," who, in a fit of lewd caprice, had thrown herself away on an unprincipled adventurer; directing the point of the last appellation by a furious blow, obliquely aimed at me. I left him in the act of bounding elastically out of the bed into which I had tucked him; but, as I took the precaution of turning the key in the door behind me, I retired to my own room, assured of his safe custody till the morning, and free to draw undisturbed conclusions from the scene I had just witnessed.

Now, it was precisely about this time that the directress, stung by my coldness, bewitched by my scorn, and excited by the preference she suspected me of cherishing for another, had fallen into a snare of her own laying—was herself caught in the meshes of the very passion with which she wished to entangle me. Conscious of the state of things in that quarter, I gathered, from the condition in which I saw my employer, that his lady-love had betrayed the alienation of her affections—inclinations, rather, I would say; affection is a word at once too warm and too pure for the subject—had let him see that the cavity of her hollow heart, emptied of his image, was now occupied by that of his usher. It was not without some surprise that I found myself obliged to entertain this view of the case; Pelet, with his old-established school, was so convenient, so profitable a match—Zoraide was so calculating, so interested a woman—I wondered mere personal preference could, in her mind, have prevailed for a moment over worldly advantage: yet, it was evident, from what Pelet said, that, not only had she repulsed him, but had even let slip expressions of partiality for me. One of his drunken exclamations was, "And the jade doats on your youth, you raw blockhead! and talks of your noble deportment, as she calls your accursed English formality—and your pure morals, forsooth! des moeurs de Caton a-t-elle dit—sotte!" Hers, I thought, must be a curious soul, where in spite of a strong, natural tendency to estimate unduly advantages of wealth and station, the sardonic disdain of a fortuneless subordinate had wrought a deeper impression than could be imprinted by the most flattering assiduities of a prosperous CHEF D'INSTITUTION. I smiled inwardly; and strange to say, though my AMOUR PROPRE was excited not disagreeably by the conquest, my better feelings remained untouched. Next day, when I saw the directress, and when she made an excuse to meet me in the corridor, and besought my notice by a demeanour and look subdued to Helot humility, I could not love, I could scarcely pity her. To answer briefly and dryly some interesting inquiry about my health—to pass her by with a stern bow—was all I could; her presence and manner had then, and for some time previously and consequently, a singular effect upon me: they sealed up all that was good, elicited all that was noxious in my nature; sometimes they enervated my senses, but they always hardened my heart. I was aware of the detriment done, and quarrelled with myself for the change. I had ever hated a tyrant; and, behold, the possession of a slave, self-given, went near to transform me into what I abhorred! There was at once a sort of low gratification in receiving this luscious incense from an attractive and still young worshipper; and an irritating sense of degradation in the very experience of the pleasure. When she stole about me with the soft step of a slave, I felt at once barbarous and sensual as a pasha. I endured her homage sometimes; sometimes I rebuked it. My indifference or harshness served equally to increase the evil I desired to check.

"Que le dedain lui sied bien!" I once overheard her say to her mother: "il est beau comme Apollon quand il sourit de son air hautain."

And the jolly old dame laughed, and said she thought her daughter was bewitched, for I had no point of a handsome man about me, except being straight and without deformity. "Pour moi," she continued, "il me fait tout l'effet d'un chat-huant, avec ses besicles."

Worthy old girl! I could have gone and kissed her had she not been a little too old, too fat, and too red-faced; her sensible, truthful words seemed so wholesome, contrasted with the morbid illusions of her daughter.

When Pelet awoke on the morning after his frenzy fit, he retained no recollection of what had happened the previous night, and his mother fortunately had the discretion to refrain from informing him that I had been a witness of his degradation. He did not again have recourse to wine for curing his griefs, but even in his sober mood he soon showed that the iron of jealousy had entered into his soul. A thorough Frenchman, the national characteristic of ferocity had not been omitted by nature in compounding the ingredients of his character; it had appeared first in his access of drunken wrath, when some of his demonstrations of hatred to my person were of a truly fiendish character, and now it was more covertly betrayed by momentary contractions of the features, and flashes of fierceness in his light blue eyes, when their glance chanced to encounter mine. He absolutely avoided speaking to me; I was now spared even the falsehood of his politeness. In this state of our mutual relations, my soul rebelled sometimes almost ungovernably, against living in the house and discharging the service of such a man; but who is free from the constraint of circumstances? At that time, I was not: I used to rise each morning eager to shake off his yoke, and go out with my portmanteau under my arm, if a beggar, at least a freeman; and in the evening, when I came back from the pensionnat de demoiselles, a certain pleasant voice in my ear; a certain face, so intelligent, yet so docile, so reflective, yet so soft, in my eyes; a certain cast of character, at once proud and pliant, sensitive and sagacious, serious and ardent, in my head; a certain tone of feeling, fervid and modest, refined and practical, pure and powerful, delighting and troubling my memory —visions of new ties I longed to contract, of new duties I longed to undertake, had taken the rover and the rebel out of me, and had shown endurance of my hated lot in the light of a Spartan virtue.

But Pelet's fury subsided; a fortnight sufficed for its rise, progress, and extinction: in that space of time the dismissal of the obnoxious teacher had been effected in the neighbouring house, and in the same interval I had declared my resolution to follow and find out my pupil, and upon my application for her address being refused, I had summarily resigned my own post. This last act seemed at once to restore Mdlle. Reuter to her senses; her sagacity, her judgment, so long misled by a fascinating delusion, struck again into the right track the moment that delusion vanished. By the right track, I do not mean the steep and difficult path of principle—in that path she never trod; but the plain highway of common sense, from which she had of late widely diverged. When there she carefully sought, and having found, industriously pursued the trail of her old suitor, M. Pelet. She soon overtook him. What arts she employed to soothe and blind him I know not, but she succeeded both in allaying his wrath, and hoodwinking his discernment, as was soon proved by the alteration in his mien and manner; she must have managed to convince him that I neither was, nor ever had been, a rival of his, for the fortnight of fury against me terminated in a fit of exceeding graciousness and amenity, not unmixed with a dash of exulting self-complacency, more ludicrous than irritating. Pelet's bachelor's life had been passed in proper French style with due disregard to moral restraint, and I thought his married life promised to be very French also. He often boasted to me what a terror he had been to certain husbands of his acquaintance; I perceived it would not now be difficult to pay him back in his own coin.

The crisis drew on. No sooner had the holidays commenced than note of preparation for some momentous event sounded all through the premises of Pelet: painters, polishers, and upholsterers were immediately set to work, and there was talk of "la chambre de Madame," "le salon de Madame." Not deeming it probable that the old duenna at present graced with that title in our house, had inspired her son with such enthusiasm of filial piety, as to induce him to fit up apartments expressly for her use, I concluded, in common with the cook, the two housemaids, and the kitchen-scullion, that a new and more juvenile Madame was destined to be the tenant of these gay chambers.

Presently official announcement of the coming event was put forth. In another week's time M. Francois Pelet, directeur, and Mdlle. Zoraide Reuter, directrice, were to be joined together in the bands of matrimony. Monsieur, in person, heralded the fact to me; terminating his communication by an obliging expression of his desire that I should continue, as heretofore, his ablest assistant and most trusted friend; and a proposition to raise my salary by an additional two hundred francs per annum. I thanked him, gave no conclusive answer at the time, and, when he had left me, threw off my blouse, put on my coat, and set out on a long walk outside the Porte de Flandre, in order, as I thought, to cool my blood, calm my nerves, and shake my disarranged ideas into some order. In fact, I had just received what was virtually my dismissal. I could not conceal, I did not desire to conceal from myself the conviction that, being now certain that Mdlle. Reuter was destined to become Madame Pelet it would not do for me to remain a dependent dweller in the house which was soon to be hers. Her present demeanour towards me was deficient neither in dignity nor propriety; but I knew her former feeling was unchanged. Decorum now repressed, and Policy masked it, but Opportunity would be too strong for either of these—Temptation would shiver their restraints.

I was no pope—I could not boast infallibility: in short, if I stayed, the probability was that, in three months' time, a practical modern French novel would be in full process of concoction under the roof of the unsuspecting Pelet. Now, modern French novels are not to my taste, either practically or theoretically. Limited as had yet been my experience of life, I had once had the opportunity of contemplating, near at hand, an example of the results produced by a course of interesting and romantic domestic treachery. No golden halo of fiction was about this example, I saw it bare and real, and it was very loathsome. I saw a mind degraded by the practice of mean subterfuge, by the habit of perfidious deception, and a body depraved by the infectious influence of the vice-polluted soul. I had suffered much from the forced and prolonged view of this spectacle; those sufferings I did not now regret, for their simple recollection acted as a most wholesome antidote to temptation. They had inscribed on my reason the conviction that unlawful pleasure, trenching on another's rights, is delusive and envenomed pleasure—its hollowness disappoints at the time, its poison cruelly tortures afterwards, its effects deprave for ever.

From all this resulted the conclusion that I must leave Pelet's, and that instantly; "but," said Prudence, "you know not where to go, nor how to live;" and then the dream of true love came over me: Frances Henri seemed to stand at my side; her slender waist to invite my arm; her hand to court my hand; I felt it was made to nestle in mine; I could not relinquish my right to it, nor could I withdraw my eyes for ever from hers, where I saw so much happiness, such a correspondence of heart with heart; over whose expression I had such influence; where I could kindle bliss, infuse awe, stir deep delight, rouse sparkling spirit, and sometimes waken pleasurable dread. My hopes to will and possess, my resolutions to merit and rise, rose in array against me; and here I was about to plunge into the gulf of absolute destitution; "and all this," suggested an inward voice, "because you fear an evil which may never happen!" "It will happen; you KNOW it will," answered that stubborn monitor, Conscience. "Do what you feel is right; obey me, and even in the sloughs of want I will plant for you firm footing." And then, as I walked fast along the road, there rose upon me a strange, inly-felt idea of some Great Being, unseen, but all present, who in His beneficence desired only my welfare, and now watched the struggle of good and evil in my heart, and waited to see whether I should obey His voice, heard in the whispers of my conscience, or lend an ear to the sophisms by which His enemy and mine—the Spirit of Evil—sought to lead me astray. Rough and steep was the path indicated by divine suggestion; mossy and declining the green way along which Temptation strewed flowers; but whereas, methought, the Deity of Love, the Friend of all that exists, would smile well-pleased were I to gird up my loins and address myself to the rude ascent; so, on the other hand, each inclination to the velvet declivity seemed to kindle a gleam of triumph on the brow of the man-hating, God-defying demon. Sharp and short I turned round; fast I retraced my steps; in half an hour I was again at M. Pelet's: I sought him in his study; brief parley, concise explanation sufficed; my manner proved that I was resolved; he, perhaps, at heart approved my decision. After twenty minutes' conversation, I re-entered my own room, self-deprived of the means of living, self-sentenced to leave my present home, with the short notice of a week in which to provide another.

CHAPTER XXI.

Directly as I closed the door, I saw laid on the table two letters; my thought was, that they were notes of invitation from the friends of some of my pupils; I had received such marks of attention occasionally, and with me, who had no friends, correspondence of more interest was out of the question; the postman's arrival had never yet been an event of interest to me since I came to Brussels. I laid my hand carelessly on the documents, and coldly and slowly glancing at them, I prepared to break the seals; my eye was arrested and my hand too; I saw what excited me, as if I had found a vivid picture where I expected only to discover a blank page: on one cover was an English postmark; on the other, a lady's clear, fine autograph; the last I opened first:—

"MONSIEUR,

"I FOUND out what you had done the very morning after your visit to me; you might be sure I should dust the china, every day; and, as no one but you had been in my room for a week, and as fairy-money is not current in Brussels, I could not doubt who left the twenty francs on the chimney-piece. I thought I heard you stir the vase when I was stooping to look for your glove under the table, and I wondered you should imagine it had got into such a little cup. Now, monsieur, the money is not mine, and I shall not keep it; I will not send it in this note because it might be lost—besides, it is heavy; but I will restore it to you the first time I see you, and you must make no difficulties about taking it; because, in the first place, I am sure, monsieur, you can understand that one likes to pay one's debts; that it is satisfactory to owe no man anything; and, in the second place, I can now very well afford to be honest, as I am provided with a situation. This last circumstance is, indeed, the reason of my writing to you, for it is pleasant to communicate good news; and, in these days, I have only my master to whom I can tell anything.

"A week ago, monsieur, I was sent for by a Mrs. Wharton, an English lady; her eldest daughter was going to be married, and some rich relation having made her a present of a veil and dress in costly old lace, as precious, they said, almost as jewels, but a little damaged by time, I was commissioned to put them in repair. I had to do it at the house; they gave me, besides, some embroidery to complete, and nearly a week elapsed before I had finished everything. While I worked, Miss Wharton often came into the room and sat with me, and so did Mrs. Wharton; they made me talk English; asked how I had learned to speak it so well; then they inquired what I knew besides—what books I had read; soon they seemed to make a sort of wonder of me, considering me no doubt as a learned grisette. One afternoon, Mrs. Wharton brought in a Parisian lady to test the accuracy of my knowledge of French; the result of it was that, owing probably in a great degree to the mother's and daughter's good humour about the marriage, which inclined them to do beneficent deeds, and partly, I think, because they are naturally benevolent people, they decided that the wish I had expressed to do something more than mend lace was a very legitimate one; and the same day they took me in their carriage to Mrs. D.'s, who is the directress of the first English school at Brussels. It seems she happened to be in want of a French lady to give lessons in geography, history, grammar, and composition, in the French language. Mrs. Wharton recommended me very warmly; and, as two of her younger daughters are pupils in the house, her patronage availed to get me the place. It was settled that I am to attend six hours daily (for, happily, it was not required that I should live in the house; I should have been sorry to leave my lodgings), and, for this, Mrs. D. will give me twelve hundred francs per annum.

"You see, therefore, monsieur, that I am now rich; richer almost than I ever hoped to be: I feel thankful for it, especially as my sight was beginning to be injured by constant working at fine lace; and I was getting, too, very weary of sitting up late at nights, and yet not being able to find time for reading or study. I began to fear that I should fall ill, and be unable to pay my way; this fear is now, in a great measure, removed; and, in truth, monsieur, I am very grateful to God for the relief; and I feel it necessary, almost, to speak of my happiness to some one who is kind-hearted enough to derive joy from seeing others joyful. I could not, therefore, resist the temptation of writing to you; I argued with myself it is very pleasant for me to write, and it will not be exactly painful, though it may be tiresome to monsieur to read. Do not be too angry with my circumlocution and inelegancies of expression, and, believe me

"Your attached pupil,

"F. E. HENRI."

Having read this letter, I mused on its contents for a few moments—whether with sentiments pleasurable or otherwise I will hereafter note—and then took up the other. It was directed in a hand to me unknown—small, and rather neat; neither masculine nor exactly feminine; the seal bore a coat of arms, concerning which I could only decipher that it was not that of the Seacombe family, consequently the epistle could be from none of my almost forgotten, and certainly quite forgetting patrician relations. From whom, then, was it? I removed the envelope; the note folded within ran as follows:

"I have no doubt in the world that you are doing well in that greasy Flanders; living probably on the fat of the unctuous land; sitting like a black-haired, tawny-skinned, long-nosed Israelite by the flesh-pots of Egypt; or like a rascally son of Levi near the brass cauldrons of the sanctuary, and every now and then plunging in a consecrated hook, and drawing out of the sea of broth the fattest of heave-shoulders and the fleshiest of wave-breasts. I know this, because you never write to any one in England. Thankless dog that you are! I, by the sovereign efficacy of my recommendation, got you the place where you are now living in clover, and yet not a word of gratitude, or even acknowledgment, have you ever offered in return; but I am coming to see you, and small conception can you, with your addled aristocratic brains, form of the sort of moral kicking I have, ready packed in my carpet-bag, destined to be presented to you immediately on my arrival.

"Meantime I know all about your affairs, and have just got information, by Brown's last letter, that you are said to be on the point of forming an advantageous match with a pursy, little Belgian schoolmistress—a Mdlle. Zenobie, or some such name. Won't I have a look at her when I come over! And this you may rely on: if she pleases my taste, or if I think it worth while in a pecuniary point of view, I'll pounce on your prize and bear her away triumphant in spite of your teeth. Yet I don't like dumpies either, and Brown says she is little and stout—the better fitted for a wiry, starved-looking chap like you. "Be on the look-out, for you know neither the day nor hour when your ——" (I don't wish to blaspheme, so I'll leave a blank)—cometh.

"Yours truly,

"HUNSDEN YORKE HUNSDEN."

"Humph!" said I; and ere I laid the letter down, I again glanced at the small, neat handwriting, not a bit like that of a mercantile man, nor, indeed, of any man except Hunsden himself. They talk of affinities between the autograph and the character: what affinity was there here? I recalled the writer's peculiar face and certain traits I suspected, rather than knew, to appertain to his nature, and I answered, "A great deal."

Hunsden, then, was coming to Brussels, and coming I knew not when; coming charged with the expectation of finding me on the summit of prosperity, about to be married, to step into a warm nest, to lie comfortably down by the side of a snug, well-fed little mate.

"I wish him joy of the fidelity of the picture he has painted," thought I. "What will he say when, instead of a pair of plump turtle doves, billing and cooing in a bower of roses, he finds a single lean cormorant, standing mateless and shelterless on poverty's bleak cliff? Oh, confound him! Let him come, and let him laugh at the contrast between rumour and fact. Were he the devil himself, instead of being merely very like him, I'd not condescend to get out of his way, or to forge a smile or a cheerful word wherewith to avert his sarcasm."

Then I recurred to the other letter: that struck a chord whose sound I could not deaden by thrusting my fingers into my ears, for it vibrated within; and though its swell might be exquisite music, its cadence was a groan.

That Frances was relieved from the pressure of want, that the curse of excessive labour was taken off her, filled me with happiness; that her first thought in prosperity should be to augment her joy by sharing it with me, met and satisfied the wish of my heart. Two results of her letter were then pleasant, sweet as two draughts of nectar; but applying my lips for the third time to the cup, and they were excoriated as with vinegar and gall.

Two persons whose desires are moderate may live well enough in Brussels on an income which would scarcely afford a respectable maintenance for one in London: and that, not because the necessaries of life are so much dearer in the latter capital, or taxes so much higher than in the former, but because the English surpass in folly all the nations on God's earth, and are more abject slaves to custom, to opinion, to the desire to keep up a certain appearance, than the Italians are to priestcraft, the French to vain-glory, the Russians to their Czar, or the Germans to black beer. I have seen a degree of sense in the modest arrangement of one homely Belgian household, that might put to shame the elegance, the superfluities, the luxuries, the strained refinements of a hundred genteel English mansions. In Belgium, provided you can make money, you may save it; this is scarcely possible in England; ostentation there lavishes in a month what industry has earned in a year. More shame to all classes in that most bountiful and beggarly country for their servile following of Fashion; I could write a chapter or two on this subject, but must forbear, at least for the present. Had I retained my 60l. per annum I could, now that Frances was in possession of 50l., have gone straight to her this very evening, and spoken out the words which, repressed, kept fretting my heart with fever; our united income would, as we should have managed it, have sufficed well for our mutual support; since we lived in a country where economy was not confounded with meanness, where frugality in dress, food, and furniture, was not synonymous with vulgarity in these various points. But the placeless usher, bare of resource, and unsupported by connections, must not think of this; such a sentiment as love, such a word as marriage, were misplaced in his heart, and on his lips. Now for the first time did I truly feel what it was to be poor; now did the sacrifice I had made in casting from me the means of living put on a new aspect; instead of a correct, just, honourable act, it seemed a deed at once light and fanatical; I took several turns in my room, under the goading influence of most poignant remorse; I walked a quarter of an hour from the wall to the window; and at the window, self-reproach seemed to face me; at the wall, self-disdain: all at once out spoke Conscience:—

"Down, stupid tormenters!" cried she; "the man has done his duty; you shall not bait him thus by thoughts of what might have been; he relinquished a temporary and contingent good to avoid a permanent and certain evil he did well. Let him reflect now, and when your blinding dust and deafening hum subside, he will discover a path."

I sat down; I propped my forehead on both my hands; I thought and thought an hour—two hours; vainly. I seemed like one sealed in a subterranean vault, who gazes at utter blackness; at blackness ensured by yard-thick stone walls around, and by piles of building above, expecting light to penetrate through granite, and through cement firm as granite. But there are chinks, or there may be chinks, in the best adjusted masonry; there was a chink in my cavernous cell; for, eventually, I saw, or seemed to see, a ray—pallid, indeed, and cold, and doubtful, but still a ray, for it showed that narrow path which conscience had promised after two, three hours' torturing research in brain and memory, I disinterred certain remains of circumstances, and conceived a hope that by putting them together an expedient might be framed, and a resource discovered. The circumstances were briefly these:

Some three months ago M. Pelet had, on the occasion of his fete, given the boys a treat, which treat consisted in a party of pleasure to a certain place of public resort in the outskirts of Brussels, of which I do not at this moment remember the name, but near it were several of those lakelets called etangs; and there was one etang, larger than the rest, where on holidays people were accustomed to amuse themselves by rowing round it in little boats. The boys having eaten an unlimited quantity of "gaufres," and drank several bottles of Louvain beer, amid the shades of a garden made and provided for such crams, petitioned the director for leave to take a row on the etang. Half a dozen of the eldest succeeded in obtaining leave, and I was commissioned to accompany them as surveillant. Among the half dozen happened to be a certain Jean Baptiste Vandenhuten, a most ponderous young Flamand, not tall, but even now, at the early age of sixteen, possessing a breadth and depth of personal development truly national. It chanced that Jean was the first lad to step into the boat; he stumbled, rolled to one side, the boat revolted at his weight and capsized. Vandenhuten sank like lead, rose, sank again. My coat and waistcoat were off in an instant; I had not been brought up at Eton and boated and bathed and swam there ten long years for nothing; it was a natural and easy act for me to leap to the rescue. The lads and the boatmen yelled; they thought there would be two deaths by drowning instead of one; but as Jean rose the third time, I clutched him by one leg and the collar, and in three minutes more both he and I were safe landed. To speak heaven's truth, my merit in the action was small indeed, for I had run no risk, and subsequently did not even catch cold from the wetting; but when M. and Madame Vandenhuten, of whom Jean Baptiste was the sole hope, came to hear of the exploit, they seemed to think I had evinced a bravery and devotion which no thanks could sufficiently repay. Madame, in particular, was "certain I must have dearly loved their sweet son, or I would not thus have hazarded my own life to save his." Monsieur, an honest-looking, though phlegmatic man, said very little, but he would not suffer me to leave the room, till I had promised that in case I ever stood in need of help I would, by applying to him, give him a chance of discharging the obligation under which he affirmed I had laid him. These words, then, were my glimmer of light; it was here I found my sole outlet; and in truth, though the cold light roused, it did not cheer me; nor did the outlet seem such as I should like to pass through. Right I had none to M. Vandenhuten's good offices; it was not on the ground of merit I could apply to him; no, I must stand on that of necessity: I had no work; I wanted work; my best chance of obtaining it lay in securing his recommendation. This I knew could be had by asking for it; not to ask, because the request revolted my pride and contradicted my habits, would, I felt, be an indulgence of false and indolent fastidiousness. I might repent the omission all my life; I would not then be guilty of it.

That evening I went to M. Vandenhuten's; but I had bent the bow and adjusted the shaft in vain; the string broke. I rang the bell at the great door (it was a large, handsome house in an expensive part of the town); a manservant opened; I asked for M. Vandenhuten; M. Vandenhuten and family were all out of town—gone to Ostend—did not know when they would be back. I left my card, and retraced my steps.

CHAPTER XXII

A week is gone; LE JOUR DES NOCES arrived; the marriage was solemnized at St. Jacques; Mdlle. Zoraide became Madame Pelet, NEE Reuter; and, in about an hour after this transformation, "the happy pair," as newspapers phrase it, were on their way to Paris; where, according to previous arrangement, the honeymoon was to be spent. The next day I quitted the pensionnat. Myself and my chattels (some books and clothes) were soon transferred to a modest lodging I had hired in a street not far off. In half an hour my clothes were arranged in a commode, my books on a shelf, and the "flitting" was effected. I should not have been unhappy that day had not one pang tortured me—a longing to go to the Rue Notre Dame aux Neiges, resisted, yet irritated by an inward resolve to avoid that street till such time as the mist of doubt should clear from my prospects.

It was a sweet September evening—very mild, very still; I had nothing to do; at that hour I knew Frances would be equally released from occupation; I thought she might possibly be wishing for her master, I knew I wished for my pupil. Imagination began with her low whispers, infusing into my soul the soft tale of pleasures that might be.

"You will find her reading or writing," said she; "you can take your seat at her side; you need not startle her peace by undue excitement; you need not embarrass her manner by unusual action or language. Be as you always are; look over what she has written; listen while she reads; chide her, or quietly approve; you know the effect of either system; you know her smile when pleased, you know the play of her looks when roused; you have the secret of awakening what expression you will, and you can choose amongst that pleasant variety. With you she will sit silent as long as it suits you to talk alone; you can hold her under a potent spell: intelligent as she is, eloquent as she can be, you can seal her lips, and veil her bright countenance with diffidence; yet, you know, she is not all monotonous mildness; you have seen, with a sort of strange pleasure, revolt, scorn, austerity, bitterness, lay energetic claim to a place in her feelings and physiognomy; you know that few could rule her as you do; you know she might break, but never bend under the hand of Tyranny and Injustice, but Reason and Affection can guide her by a sign. Try their influence now. Go—they are not passions; you may handle them safely."

"I will NOT go was my answer to the sweet temptress. A man is master of himself to a certain point, but not beyond it. Could I seek Frances to-night, could I sit with her alone in a quiet room, and address her only in the language of Reason and Affection?"

"No," was the brief, fervent reply of that Love which had conquered and now controlled me.

Time seemed to stagnate; the sun would not go down; my watch ticked, but I thought the hands were paralyzed.

"What a hot evening!" I cried, throwing open the lattice; for, indeed, I had seldom felt so feverish. Hearing a step ascending the common stair, I wondered whether the "locataire," now mounting to his apartments, were as unsettled in mind and condition as I was, or whether he lived in the calm of certain resources, and in the freedom of unfettered feelings. What! was he coming in person to solve the problem hardly proposed in inaudible thought? He had actually knocked at the door—at MY door; a smart, prompt rap; and, almost before I could invite him in, he was over the threshold, and had closed the door behind him.

"And how are you?" asked an indifferent, quiet voice, in the English language; while my visitor, without any sort of bustle or introduction, put his hat on the table, and his gloves into his hat, and drawing the only armchair the room afforded a little forward, seated himself tranquilly therein.

"Can't you speak?" he inquired in a few moments, in a tone whose nonchalance seemed to intimate that it was much the same thing whether I answered or not. The fact is, I found it desirable to have recourse to my good friends "les besicles;" not exactly to ascertain the identity of my visitor—for I already knew him, confound his impudence! but to see how he looked—to get a clear notion of his mien and countenance. I wiped the glasses very deliberately, and put them on quite as deliberately; adjusting them so as not to hurt the bridge of my nose or get entangled in my short tufts of dun hair. I was sitting in the window-seat, with my back to the light, and I had him VIS-A-VIS; a position he would much rather have had reversed; for, at any time, he preferred scrutinizing to being scrutinized. Yes, it was HE, and no mistake, with his six feet of length arranged in a sitting attitude; with his dark travelling surtout with its velvet collar, his gray pantaloons, his black stock, and his face, the most original one Nature ever modelled, yet the least obtrusively so; not one feature that could be termed marked or odd, yet the effect of the whole unique. There is no use in attempting to describe what is indescribable. Being in no hurry to address him, I sat and stared at my ease.

"Oh, that's your game—is it?" said he at last. "Well, we'll see which is soonest tired." And he slowly drew out a fine cigar-case, picked one to his taste, lit it, took a book from the shelf convenient to his hand, then leaning back, proceeded to smoke and read as tranquilly as if he had been in his own room, in Grove-street, X——shire, England. I knew he was capable of continuing in that attitude till midnight, if he conceived the whim, so I rose, and taking the book from his hand, I said,—

"You did not ask for it, and you shall not have it."

"It is silly and dull," he observed, "so I have not lost much;" then the spell being broken, he went on: "I thought you lived at Pelet's; I went there this afternoon expecting to be starved to death by sitting in a boarding-school drawing-room, and they told me you were gone, had departed this morning; you had left your address behind you though, which I wondered at; it was a more practical and sensible precaution than I should have imagined you capable of. Why did you leave?"

"Because M. Pelet has just married the lady whom you and Mr. Brown assigned to me as my wife."

"Oh, indeed!" replied Hunsden with a short laugh; "so you've lost both your wife and your place?"

"Precisely so."

I saw him give a quick, covert glance all round my room; he marked its narrow limits, its scanty furniture: in an instant he had comprehended the state of matters—had absolved me from the crime of prosperity. A curious effect this discovery wrought in his strange mind; I am morally certain that if he had found me installed in a handsome parlour, lounging on a soft couch, with a pretty, wealthy wife at my side, he would have hated me; a brief, cold, haughty visit, would in such a case have been the extreme limit of his civilities, and never would he have come near me more, so long as the tide of fortune bore me smoothly on its surface; but the painted furniture, the bare walls, the cheerless solitude of my room relaxed his rigid pride, and I know not what softening change had taken place both in his voice and look ere he spoke again.

"You have got another place?"

"No."

"You are in the way of getting one?"

"No."

"That is bad; have you applied to Brown?"

"No, indeed."

"You had better; he often has it in his power to give useful information in such matters."

"He served me once very well; I have no claim on him, and am not in the humour to bother him again."

"Oh, if you're bashful, and dread being intrusive, you need only commission me. I shall see him to-night; I can put in a word."

"I beg you will not, Mr. Hunsden; I am in your debt already; you did me an important service when I was at X——; got me out of a den where I was dying: that service I have never repaid, and at present I decline positively adding another item to the account."

"If the wind sits that way, I'm satisfied. I thought my unexampled generosity in turning you out of that accursed counting-house would be duly appreciated some day: 'Cast your bread on the waters, and it shall be found after many days,' say the Scriptures. Yes, that's right, lad—make much of me —I'm a nonpareil: there's nothing like me in the common herd. In the meantime, to put all humbug aside and talk sense for a few moments, you would be greatly the better of a situation, and what is more, you are a fool if you refuse to take one from any hand that offers it."

"Very well, Mr. Hunsden; now you have settled that point, talk of something else. What news from X——?"

"I have not settled that point, or at least there is another to settle before we get to X——. Is this Miss Zenobie" (Zoraide, interposed I)—"well, Zoraide—is she really married to Pelet?"

"I tell you yes—and if you don't believe me, go and ask the cure of St. Jacques."

"And your heart is broken?"

"I am not aware that it is; it feels all right—beats as usual."

"Then your feelings are less superfine than I took them to be; you must be a coarse, callous character, to bear such a thwack without staggering under it."

"Staggering under it? What the deuce is there to stagger under in the circumstance of a Belgian schoolmistress marrying a French schoolmaster? The progeny will doubtless be a strange hybrid race; but that's their look-out —not mine."

"He indulges in scurrilous jests, and the bride was his affianced one!"

"Who said so?"

"Brown."

"I'll tell you what, Hunsden—Brown is an old gossip."

"He is; but in the meantime, if his gossip be founded on less than fact—if you took no particular interest in Miss Zoraide—why, O youthful pedagogue! did you leave your place in consequence of her becoming Madame Pelet?"

"Because—" I felt my face grow a little hot; "because—in short, Mr. Hunsden, I decline answering any more questions," and I plunged my hands deep in my breeches pocket.

Hunsden triumphed: his eyes—his laugh announced victory.

"What the deuce are you laughing at, Mr. Hunsden?"

"At your exemplary composure. Well, lad, I'll not bore you; I see how it is: Zoraide has jilted you—married some one richer, as any sensible woman would have done if she had had the chance."

I made no reply—I let him think so, not feeling inclined to enter into an explanation of the real state of things, and as little to forge a false account; but it was not easy to blind Hunsden; my very silence, instead of convincing him that he had hit the truth, seemed to render him doubtful about it; he went on:—

"I suppose the affair has been conducted as such affairs always are amongst rational people: you offered her your youth and your talents—such as they are—in exchange for her position and money: I don't suppose you took appearance, or what is called LOVE, into the account—for I understand she is older than you, and Brown says, rather sensible-looking than beautiful. She, having then no chance of making a better bargain, was at first inclined to come to terms with you, but Pelet—the head of a flourishing school—stepped in with a higher bid; she accepted, and he has got her: a correct transaction—perfectly so—business-like and legitimate. And now we'll talk of something else."

"Do," said I, very glad to dismiss the topic, and especially glad to have baffled the sagacity of my cross-questioner—if, indeed, I had baffled it; for though his words now led away from the dangerous point, his eyes, keen and watchful, seemed still preoccupied with the former idea.

"You want to hear news from X——? And what interest can you have in X——? You left no friends there, for you made none. Nobody ever asks after you—neither man nor woman; and if I mention your name in company, the men look as if I had spoken of Prester John; and the women sneer covertly. Our X—— belles must have disliked you. How did you excite their displeasure?"

"I don't know. I seldom spoke to them—they were nothing to me. I considered them only as something to be glanced at from a distance; their dresses and faces were often pleasing enough to the eye: but I could not understand their conversation, nor even read their countenances. When I caught snatches of what they said, I could never make much of it; and the play of their lips and eyes did not help me at all."

"That was your fault, not theirs. There are sensible, as well as handsome women in X——; women it is worth any man's while to talk to, and with whom I can talk with pleasure: but you had and have no pleasant address; there is nothing in you to induce a woman to be affable. I have remarked you sitting near the door in a room full of company, bent on hearing, not on speaking; on observing, not on entertaining; looking frigidly shy at the commencement of a party, confusingly vigilant about the middle, and insultingly weary towards the end. Is that the way, do you think, ever to communicate pleasure or excite interest? No; and if you are generally unpopular, it is because you deserve to be so."

"Content!" I ejaculated.

"No, you are not content; you see beauty always turning its back on you; you are mortified and then you sneer. I verily believe all that is desirable on earth—wealth, reputation, love—will for ever to you be the ripe grapes on the high trellis: you'll look up at them; they will tantalize in you the lust of the eye; but they are out of reach: you have not the address to fetch a ladder, and you'll go away calling them sour."

Cutting as these words might have been under some circumstances, they drew no blood now. My life was changed; my experience had been varied since I left X——, but Hunsden could not know this; he had seen me only in the character of Mr. Crimsworth's clerk—a dependant amongst wealthy strangers, meeting disdain with a hard front, conscious of an unsocial and unattractive exterior, refusing to sue for notice which I was sure would be withheld, declining to evince an admiration which I knew would be scorned as worthless. He could not be aware that since then youth and loveliness had been to me everyday objects; that I had studied them at leisure and closely, and had seen the plain texture of truth under the embroidery of appearance; nor could he, keen-sighted as he was, penetrate into my heart, search my brain, and read my peculiar sympathies and antipathies; he had not known me long enough, or well enough, to perceive how low my feelings would ebb under some influences, powerful over most minds; how high, how fast they would flow under other influences, that perhaps acted with the more intense force on me, because they acted on me alone. Neither could he suspect for an instant the history of my communications with Mdlle. Reuter; secret to him and to all others was the tale of her strange infatuation; her blandishments, her wiles had been seen but by me, and to me only were they known; but they had changed me, for they had proved that I COULD impress. A sweeter secret nestled deeper in my heart; one full of tenderness and as full of strength: it took the sting out of Hunsden's sarcasm; it kept me unbent by shame, and unstirred by wrath. But of all this I could say nothing—nothing decisive at least; uncertainty sealed my lips, and during the interval of silence by which alone I replied to Mr. Hunsden, I made up my mind to be for the present wholly misjudged by him, and misjudged I was; he thought he had been rather too hard upon me, and that I was crushed by the weight of his upbraidings; so to re-assure me he said, doubtless I should mend some day; I was only at the beginning of life yet; and since happily I was not quite without sense, every false step I made would be a good lesson.

Just then I turned my face a little to the light; the approach of twilight, and my position in the window-seat, had, for the last ten minutes, prevented him from studying my countenance; as I moved, however, he caught an expression which he thus interpreted:—

"Confound it! How doggedly self-approving the lad looks! I thought he was fit to die with shame, and there he sits grinning smiles, as good as to say, 'Let the world wag as it will, I've the philosopher's stone in my waist-coat pocket, and the elixir of life in my cupboard; I'm independent of both Fate and Fortune.'"

"Hunsden—you spoke of grapes; I was thinking of a fruit I like better than your X—— hot-house grapes—an unique fruit, growing wild, which I have marked as my own, and hope one day to gather and taste. It is of no use your offering me the draught of bitterness, or threatening me with death by thirst: I have the anticipation of sweetness on my palate; the hope of freshness on my lips; I can reject the unsavoury, and endure the exhausting."

"For how long?"

"Till the next opportunity for effort; and as the prize of success will be a treasure after my own heart, I'll bring a bull's strength to the struggle."

"Bad luck crushes bulls as easily as bullaces; and, I believe, the fury dogs you: you were born with a wooden spoon in your mouth, depend on it."

"I believe you; and I mean to make my wooden spoon do the work of some people's silver ladles: grasped firmly, and handled nimbly, even a wooden spoon will shovel up broth."

Hunsden rose: "I see," said he; "I suppose you're one of those who develop best unwatched, and act best unaided—work your own way. Now, I'll go." And, without another word, he was going; at the door he turned:—

"Crimsworth Hall is sold," said he.

"Sold!" was my echo.

"Yes; you know, of course, that your brother failed three months ago?"

"What! Edward Crimsworth?"

"Precisely; and his wife went home to her father's; when affairs went awry, his temper sympathized with them; he used her ill; I told you he would be a tyrant to her some day; as to him—"

"Ay, as to him—what is become of him?"

"Nothing extraordinary—don't be alarmed; he put himself under the protection of the court, compounded with his creditors—tenpence in the pound; in six weeks set up again, coaxed back his wife, and is flourishing like a green bay-tree."

"And Crimsworth Hall—was the furniture sold too?"

"Everything—from the grand piano down to the rolling-pin."

"And the contents of the oak dining-room—were they sold?"

"Of course; why should the sofas and chairs of that room be held more sacred than those of any other?"

"And the pictures?"

"What pictures? Crimsworth had no special collection that I know of—he did not profess to be an amateur."

"There were two portraits, one on each side the mantelpiece; you cannot have forgotten them, Mr. Hunsden; you once noticed that of the lady—"

"Oh, I know! the thin-faced gentlewoman with a shawl put on like drapery. —Why, as a matter of course, it would be sold among the other things. If you had been rich, you might have bought it, for I remember you said it represented your mother: you see what it is to be without a sou."

I did. "But surely," I thought to myself, "I shall not always be so poverty-stricken; I may one day buy it back yet.—Who purchased it? do you know?" I asked.

"How is it likely? I never inquired who purchased anything; there spoke the unpractical man—to imagine all the world is interested in what interests himself! Now, good night—I'm off for Germany to-morrow morning; I shall be back here in six weeks, and possibly I may call and see you again; I wonder whether you'll be still out of place!" he laughed, as mockingly, as heartlessly as Mephistopheles, and so laughing, vanished.

Some people, however indifferent they may become after a considerable space of absence, always contrive to leave a pleasant impression just at parting; not so Hunsden, a conference with him affected one like a draught of Peruvian bark; it seemed a concentration of the specially harsh, stringent, bitter; whether, like bark, it invigorated, I scarcely knew.

A ruffled mind makes a restless pillow; I slept little on the night after this interview; towards morning I began to doze, but hardly had my slumber become sleep, when I was roused from it by hearing a noise in my sitting room, to which my bed-room adjoined—a step, and a shoving of furniture; the movement lasted barely two minutes; with the closing of the door it ceased. I listened; not a mouse stirred; perhaps I had dreamt it; perhaps a locataire had made a mistake, and entered my apartment instead of his own. It was yet but five o'clock; neither I nor the day were wide awake; I turned, and was soon unconscious. When I did rise, about two hours later, I had forgotten the circumstance; the first thing I saw, however, on quitting my chamber, recalled it; just pushed in at the door of my sitting-room, and still standing on end, was a wooden packing-case—a rough deal affair, wide but shallow; a porter had doubtless shoved it forward, but seeing no occupant of the room, had left it at the entrance.

"That is none of mine," thought I, approaching; "it must be meant for somebody else." I stooped to examine the address:—

"Wm. Crimsworth, Esq., No —, — St., Brussels."

I was puzzled, but concluding that the best way to obtain information was to ask within, I cut the cords and opened the case. Green baize enveloped its contents, sewn carefully at the sides; I ripped the pack-thread with my pen-knife, and still, as the seam gave way, glimpses of gilding appeared through the widening interstices. Boards and baize being at length removed, I lifted from the case a large picture, in a magnificent frame; leaning it against a chair, in a position where the light from the window fell favourably upon it, I stepped back—already I had mounted my spectacles. A portrait-painter's sky (the most sombre and threatening of welkins), and distant trees of a conventional depth of hue, raised in full relief a pale, pensive-looking female face, shadowed with soft dark hair, almost blending with the equally dark clouds; large, solemn eyes looked reflectively into mine; a thin cheek rested on a delicate little hand; a shawl, artistically draped, half hid, half showed a slight figure. A listener (had there been one) might have heard me, after ten minutes' silent gazing, utter the word "Mother!" I might have said more—but with me, the first word uttered aloud in soliloquy rouses consciousness; it reminds me that only crazy people talk to themselves, and then I think out my monologue, instead of speaking it. I had thought a long while, and a long while had contemplated the intelligence, the sweetness, and—alas! the sadness also of those fine, grey eyes, the mental power of that forehead, and the rare sensibility of that serious mouth, when my glance, travelling downwards, fell on a narrow billet, stuck in the corner of the picture, between the frame and the canvas. Then I first asked, "Who sent this picture? Who thought of me, saved it out of the wreck of Crimsworth Hall, and now commits it to the care of its natural keeper?" I took the note from its niche; thus it spoke:—

"There is a sort of stupid pleasure in giving a child sweets, a fool his bells, a dog a bone. You are repaid by seeing the child besmear his face with sugar; by witnessing how the fool's ecstasy makes a greater fool of him than ever; by watching the dog's nature come out over his bone. In giving William Crimsworth his mother's picture, I give him sweets, bells, and bone all in one; what grieves me is, that I cannot behold the result; I would have added five shillings more to my bid if the auctioneer could only have promised me that pleasure.

"H. Y. H.

"P.S.—You said last night you positively declined adding another item to your account with me; don't you think I've saved you that trouble?"

I muffled the picture in its green baize covering, restored it to the case, and having transported the whole concern to my bed-room, put it out of sight under my bed. My pleasure was now poisoned by pungent pain; I determined to look no more till I could look at my ease. If Hunsden had come in at that moment, I should have said to him, "I owe you nothing, Hunsden—not a fraction of a farthing: you have paid yourself in taunts!"

Too anxious to remain any longer quiescent, I had no sooner breakfasted, than I repaired once more to M. Vandenhuten's, scarcely hoping to find him at home; for a week had barely elapsed since my first call: but fancying I might be able to glean information as to the time when his return was expected. A better result awaited me than I had anticipated, for though the family were yet at Ostend, M. Vandenhuten had come over to Brussels on business for the day. He received me with the quiet kindness of a sincere though not excitable man. I had not sat five minutes alone with him in his bureau, before I became aware of a sense of ease in his presence, such as I rarely experienced with strangers. I was surprised at my own composure, for, after all, I had come on business to me exceedingly painful—that of soliciting a favour. I asked on what basis the calm rested—I feared it might be deceptive. Ere long I caught a glimpse of the ground, and at once I felt assured of its solidity; I knew where it was.

M. Vandenhuten was rich, respected, and influential; I, poor, despised and powerless; so we stood to the world at large as members of the world's society; but to each other, as a pair of human beings, our positions were reversed. The Dutchman (he was not Flamand, but pure Hollandais) was slow, cool, of rather dense intelligence, though sound and accurate judgment; the Englishman far more nervous, active, quicker both to plan and to practise, to conceive and to realize. The Dutchman was benevolent, the Englishman susceptible; in short our characters dovetailed, but my mind having more fire and action than his, instinctively assumed and kept the predominance.

This point settled, and my position well ascertained, I addressed him on the subject of my affairs with that genuine frankness which full confidence can alone inspire. It was a pleasure to him to be so appealed to; he thanked me for giving him this opportunity of using a little exertion in my behalf. I went on to explain to him that my wish was not so much to be helped, as to be put into the way of helping myself; of him I did not want exertion—that was to be my part—but only information and recommendation. Soon after I rose to go. He held out his hand at parting—an action of greater significance with foreigners than with Englishmen. As I exchanged a smile with him, I thought the benevolence of his truthful face was better than the intelligence of my own. Characters of my order experience a balm-like solace in the contact of such souls as animated the honest breast of Victor Vandenhuten.

The next fortnight was a period of many alternations; my existence during its lapse resembled a sky of one of those autumnal nights which are specially haunted by meteors and falling stars. Hopes and fears, expectations and disappointments, descended in glancing showers from zenith to horizon; but all were transient, and darkness followed swift each vanishing apparition. M. Vandenhuten aided me faithfully; he set me on the track of several places, and himself made efforts to secure them for me; but for a long time solicitation and recommendation were vain—the door either shut in my face when I was about to walk in, or another candidate, entering before me, rendered my further advance useless. Feverish and roused, no disappointment arrested me; defeat following fast on defeat served as stimulants to will. I forgot fastidiousness, conquered reserve, thrust pride from me: I asked, I persevered, I remonstrated, I dunned. It is so that openings are forced into the guarded circle where Fortune sits dealing favours round. My perseverance made me known; my importunity made me remarked. I was inquired about; my former pupils' parents, gathering the reports of their children, heard me spoken of as talented, and they echoed the word: the sound, bandied about at random, came at last to ears which, but for its universality, it might never have reached; and at the very crisis when I had tried my last effort and knew not what to do, Fortune looked in at me one morning, as I sat in drear and almost desperate deliberation on my bedstead, nodded with the familiarity of an old acquaintance—though God knows I had never met her before—and threw a prize into my lap.

In the second week of October, 18—, I got the appointment of English professor to all the classes of —— College, Brussels, with a salary of three thousand francs per annum; and the certainty of being able, by dint of the reputation and publicity accompanying the position, to make as much more by private means. The official notice, which communicated this information, mentioned also that it was the strong recommendation of M. Vandenhuten, negociant, which had turned the scale of choice in my favour.

No sooner had I read the announcement than I hurried to M. Vandenhuten's bureau, pushed the document under his nose, and when he had perused it, took both his hands, and thanked him with unrestrained vivacity. My vivid words and emphatic gesture moved his Dutch calm to unwonted sensation. He said he was happy—glad to have served me; but he had done nothing meriting such thanks. He had not laid out a centime—only scratched a few words on a sheet of paper.

Again I repeated to him—

"You have made me quite happy, and in a way that suits me; I do not feel an obligation irksome, conferred by your kind hand; I do not feel disposed to shun you because you have done me a favour; from this day you must consent to admit me to your intimate acquaintance, for I shall hereafter recur again and again to the pleasure of your society."

"Ainsi soit-il," was the reply, accompanied by a smile of benignant content. I went away with its sunshine in my heart.

CHAPTER XXIII

It was two o'clock when I returned to my lodgings; my dinner, just brought in from a neighbouring hotel, smoked on the table; I sat down thinking to eat —had the plate been heaped with potsherds and broken glass, instead of boiled beef and haricots, I could not have made a more signal failure: appetite had forsaken me. Impatient of seeing food which I could not taste, I put it all aside into a cupboard, and then demanded, "What shall I do till evening?" for before six P.M. it would be vain to seek the Rue Notre Dame aux Neiges; its inhabitant (for me it had but one) was detained by her vocation elsewhere. I walked in the streets of Brussels, and I walked in my own room from two o'clock till six; never once in that space of time did I sit down. I was in my chamber when the last-named hour struck; I had just bathed my face and feverish hands, and was standing near the glass; my cheek was crimson, my eye was flame, still all my features looked quite settled and calm. Descending swiftly the stair and stepping out, I was glad to see Twilight drawing on in clouds; such shade was to me like a grateful screen, and the chill of latter Autumn, breathing in a fitful wind from the north-west, met me as a refreshing coolness. Still I saw it was cold to others, for the women I passed were wrapped in shawls, and the men had their coats buttoned close.

When are we quite happy? Was I so then? No; an urgent and growing dread worried my nerves, and had worried them since the first moment good tidings had reached me. How was Frances? It was ten weeks since I had seen her, six since I had heard from her, or of her. I had answered her letter by a brief note, friendly but calm, in which no mention of continued correspondence or further visits was made. At that hour my bark hung on the topmost curl of a wave of fate, and I knew not on what shoal the onward rush of the billow might hurl it; I would not then attach her destiny to mine by the slightest thread; if doomed to split on the rock, or run aground on the sand-bank, I was resolved no other vessel should share my disaster: but six weeks was a long time; and could it be that she was still well and doing well? Were not all sages agreed in declaring that happiness finds no climax on earth? Dared I think that but half a street now divided me from the full cup of contentment—the draught drawn from waters said to flow only in heaven?

I was at the door; I entered the quiet house; I mounted the stairs; the lobby was void and still, all the doors closed; I looked for the neat green mat; it lay duly in its place.

"Signal of hope!" I said, and advanced. "But I will be a little calmer; I am not going to rush in, and get up a scene directly." Forcibly staying my eager step, I paused on the mat.

"What an absolute hush! Is she in? Is anybody in?" I demanded to myself. A little tinkle, as of cinders falling from a grate, replied; a movement—a fire was gently stirred; and the slight rustle of life continuing, a step paced equably backwards and forwards, backwards and forwards, in the apartment. Fascinated, I stood, more fixedly fascinated when a voice rewarded the attention of my strained ear—so low, so self-addressed, I never fancied the speaker otherwise than alone; solitude might speak thus in a desert, or in the hall of a forsaken house.

"'And ne'er but once, my son,' he said,

'Was yon dark cavern trod;

In persecution's iron days,

When the land was left by God.

From Bewley's bog, with slaughter red,

A wanderer hither drew;

And oft he stopp'd and turn'd his head,

As by fits the night-winds blew.

For trampling round by Cheviot-edge

Were heard the troopers keen;

And frequent from the Whitelaw ridge

The death-shot flash'd between.'" &c. &c.

The old Scotch ballad was partly recited, then dropt; a pause ensued; then another strain followed, in French, of which the purport, translated, ran as follows:—

I gave, at first, attention close;

Then interest warm ensued;

From interest, as improvement rose,

Succeeded gratitude.

Obedience was no effort soon,

And labour was no pain;

If tired, a word, a glance alone

Would give me strength again.

From others of the studious band,

  Ere long he singled me;

But only by more close demand,

  And sterner urgency.

The task he from another took,

  From me he did reject;

He would no slight omission brook,

  And suffer no defect.

If my companions went astray,

  He scarce their wanderings blam'd;

If I but falter'd in the way,

  His anger fiercely flam'd.

Something stirred in an adjoining chamber; it would not do to be surprised eaves-dropping; I tapped hastily, and as hastily entered. Frances was just before me; she had been walking slowly in her room, and her step was checked by my advent: Twilight only was with her, and tranquil, ruddy Firelight; to these sisters, the Bright and the Dark, she had been speaking, ere I entered, in poetry. Sir Walter Scott's voice, to her a foreign, far-off sound, a mountain echo, had uttered itself in the first stanzas; the second, I thought, from the style and the substance, was the language of her own heart. Her face was grave, its expression concentrated; she bent on me an unsmiling eye—an eye just returning from abstraction, just awaking from dreams: well-arranged was her simple attire, smooth her dark hair, orderly her tranquil room; but what—with her thoughtful look, her serious self-reliance, her bent to meditation and haply inspiration—what had she to do with love? "Nothing," was the answer of her own sad, though gentle countenance; it seemed to say, "I must cultivate fortitude and cling to poetry; one is to be my support and the other my solace through life. Human affections do not bloom, nor do human passions glow for me." Other women have such thoughts. Frances, had she been as desolate as she deemed, would not have been worse off than thousands of her sex. Look at the rigid and formal race of old maids—the race whom all despise; they have fed themselves, from youth upwards, on maxims of resignation and endurance. Many of them get ossified with the dry diet; self-control is so continually their thought, so perpetually their object, that at last it absorbs the softer and more agreeable qualities of their nature; and they die mere models of austerity, fashioned out of a little parchment and much bone. Anatomists will tell you that there is a heart in the withered old maid's carcass

—the same as in that of any cherished wife or proud mother in the land. Can this be so? I really don't know; but feel inclined to doubt it.

I came forward, bade Frances "good evening," and took my seat. The chair I had chosen was one she had probably just left; it stood by a little table where were her open desk and papers. I know not whether she had fully recognized me at first, but she did so now; and in a voice, soft but quiet, she returned my greeting. I had shown no eagerness; she took her cue from me, and evinced no surprise. We met as we had always met, as master and pupil—nothing more. I proceeded to handle the papers; Frances, observant and serviceable, stepped into an inner room, brought a candle, lit it, placed it by me; then drew the curtain over the lattice, and having added a little fresh fuel to the already bright fire, she drew a second chair to the table and sat down at my right hand, a little removed. The paper on the top was a translation of some grave French author into English, but underneath lay a sheet with stanzas; on this I laid hands. Frances half rose, made a movement to recover the captured spoil, saying, that was nothing—a mere copy of verses. I put by resistance with the decision I knew she never long opposed; but on this occasion her fingers had fastened on the paper. I had quietly to unloose them; their hold dissolved to my touch; her hand shrunk away; my own would fain have followed it, but for the present I forbade such impulse. The first page of the sheet was occupied with the lines I had overheard; the sequel was not exactly the writer's own experience, but a composition by portions of that experience suggested. Thus while egotism was avoided, the fancy was exercised, and the heart satisfied. I translate as before, and my translation is nearly literal; it continued thus:—

When sickness stay'd awhile my course,

 He seem'd impatient still,

Because his pupil's flagging force

 Could not obey his will.

One day when summoned to the bed

 Where pain and I did strive,

I heard him, as he bent his head,

 Say, "God, she must revive!"

I felt his hand, with gentle stress,

 A moment laid on mine,

And wished to mark my consciousness

 By some responsive sign.

But pow'rless then to speak or move,
 I only felt, within,
The sense of Hope, the strength of Love,
 Their healing work begin.

And as he from the room withdrew,
 My heart his steps pursued;
I long'd to prove, by efforts new;
 My speechless gratitude.

When once again I took my place,
 Long vacant, in the class,
Th' unfrequent smile across his face
 Did for one moment pass.

The lessons done; the signal made
 Of glad release and play,
He, as he passed, an instant stay'd,
 One kindly word to say.

"Jane, till to-morrow you are free
 From tedious task and rule;
This afternoon I must not see
 That yet pale face in school.

"Seek in the garden-shades a seat,
 Far from the play-ground din;
The sun is warm, the air is sweet:
 Stay till I call you in."

A long and pleasant afternoon
 I passed in those green bowers;
All silent, tranquil, and alone
 With birds, and bees, and flowers.

Yet, when my master's voice I heard
 Call, from the window, "Jane!"

I entered, joyful, at the word,
 The busy house again.
He, in the hall, paced up and down;
 He paused as I passed by;
His forehead stern relaxed its frown:
 He raised his deep-set eye.

"Not quite so pale," he murmured low.
 "Now Jane, go rest awhile."
And as I smiled, his smoothened brow
 Returned as glad a smile.

My perfect health restored, he took
 His mien austere again;
And, as before, he would not brook
 The slightest fault from Jane.

The longest task, the hardest theme
 Fell to my share as erst,
And still I toiled to place my name
 In every study first.

He yet begrudged and stinted praise,
 But I had learnt to read
The secret meaning of his face,
 And that was my best meed.

Even when his hasty temper spoke
 In tones that sorrow stirred,
My grief was lulled as soon as woke
 By some relenting word.

And when he lent some precious book,
 Or gave some fragrant flower,
I did not quail to Envy's look,
 Upheld by Pleasure's power.

At last our school ranks took their ground,
 The hard-fought field I won;
The prize, a laurel-wreath, was bound
 My throbbing forehead on.
Low at my master's knee I bent,
 The offered crown to meet;
Its green leaves through my temples sent
 A thrill as wild as sweet.
The strong pulse of Ambition struck
 In every vein I owned;
At the same instant, bleeding broke
 A secret, inward wound.
The hour of triumph was to me
 The hour of sorrow sore;
A day hence I must cross the sea,
 Ne'er to recross it more.
An hour hence, in my master's room
 I with him sat alone,
And told him what a dreary gloom
 O'er joy had parting thrown.
He little said; the time was brief,
 The ship was soon to sail,
And while I sobbed in bitter grief,
 My master but looked pale.
They called in haste; he bade me go,
 Then snatched me back again;
He held me fast and murmured low,
 "Why will they part us, Jane?"
"Were you not happy in my care?
 Did I not faithful prove?

> Will others to my darling bear
>
> As true, as deep a love?
>
> "O God, watch o'er my foster child!
>
> O guard her gentle head!
>
> When minds are high and tempests wild
>
> Protection round her spread!
>
> "They call again; leave then my breast;
>
> Quit thy true shelter, Jane;
>
> But when deceived, repulsed, opprest,
>
> Come home to me again!"

I read—then dreamily made marks on the margin with my pencil; thinking all the while of other things; thinking that "Jane" was now at my side; no child, but a girl of nineteen; and she might be mine, so my heart affirmed; Poverty's curse was taken off me; Envy and Jealousy were far away, and unapprized of this our quiet meeting; the frost of the Master's manner might melt; I felt the thaw coming fast, whether I would or not; no further need for the eye to practise a hard look, for the brow to compress its expanse into a stern fold: it was now permitted to suffer the outward revelation of the inward glow—to seek, demand, elicit an answering ardour. While musing thus, I thought that the grass on Hermon never drank the fresh dews of sunset more gratefully than my feelings drank the bliss of this hour.

Frances rose, as if restless; she passed before me to stir the fire, which did not want stirring; she lifted and put down the little ornaments on the mantelpiece; her dress waved within a yard of me; slight, straight, and elegant, she stood erect on the hearth.

There are impulses we can control; but there are others which control us, because they attain us with a tiger-leap, and are our masters ere we have seen them. Perhaps, though, such impulses are seldom altogether bad; perhaps Reason, by a process as brief as quiet, a process that is finished ere felt, has ascertained the sanity of the deed. Instinct meditates, and feels justified in remaining passive while it is performed. I know I did not reason, I did not plan or intend, yet, whereas one moment I was sitting solus on the chair near the table, the next, I held Frances on my knee, placed there with sharpness and decision, and retained with exceeding tenacity.

"Monsieur!" cried Frances, and was still: not another word escaped her lips; sorely confounded she seemed during the lapse of the first few moments; but the amazement soon subsided; terror did not succeed, nor fury: after all, she was only a little nearer than she had ever been before, to one she habitually respected and trusted; embarrassment might have impelled her to contend, but self-respect checked resistance where resistance was useless.

"Frances, how much regard have you for me?" was my demand. No answer; the situation was yet too new and surprising to permit speech. On this consideration, I compelled myself for some seconds to tolerate her silence, though impatient of it: presently, I repeated the same question—probably, not in the calmest of tones; she looked at me; my face, doubtless, was no model of composure, my eyes no still wells of tranquillity.

"Do speak," I urged; and a very low, hurried, yet still arch voice said—

"Monsieur, vous me faites mal; de grace lachez un peu ma main droite."

In truth I became aware that I was holding the said "main droite" in a somewhat ruthless grasp: I did as desired; and, for the third time, asked more gently—

"Frances, how much regard have you for me?"

"Mon maitre, j'en ai beaucoup," was the truthful rejoinder.

"Frances, have you enough to give yourself to me as my wife?—to accept me as your husband?"

I felt the agitation of the heart, I saw "the purple light of love" cast its glowing reflection on cheeks, temples, neck; I desired to consult the eye, but sheltering lash and lid forbade.

"Monsieur," said the soft voice at last,—"Monsieur desire savoir si je consens—si—enfin, si je veux me marier avec lui?"

"Justement."

"Monsieur sera-t-il aussi bon mari qu'il a ete bon maitre?"

"I will try, Frances."

A pause; then with a new, yet still subdued inflexion of the voice—an inflexion which provoked while it pleased me—accompanied, too, by a "sourire a la fois fin et timide" in perfect harmony with the tone:—

"C'est a dire, monsieur sera toujours un peu entete exigeant, volontaire—?"

"Have I been so, Frances?"

"Mais oui; vous le savez bien."

"Have I been nothing else?"

"Mais oui; vous avez ete mon meilleur ami."

"And what, Frances, are you to me?"

"Votre devouee eleve, qui vous aime de tout son coeur."

"Will my pupil consent to pass her life with me? Speak English now, Frances."

Some moments were taken for reflection; the answer, pronounced slowly, ran thus:—

"You have always made me happy; I like to hear you speak; I like to see you; I like to be near you; I believe you are very good, and very superior; I know you are stern to those who are careless and idle, but you are kind, very kind to the attentive and industrious, even if they are not clever. Master, I should be GLAD to live with you always;" and she made a sort of movement, as if she would have clung to me, but restraining herself she only added with earnest emphasis—"Master, I consent to pass my life with you."

"Very well, Frances."

I drew her a little nearer to my heart; I took a first kiss from her lips, thereby sealing the compact, now framed between us; afterwards she and I were silent, nor was our silence brief. Frances' thoughts, during this interval, I know not, nor did I attempt to guess them; I was not occupied in searching her countenance, nor in otherwise troubling her composure. The peace I felt, I wished her to feel; my arm, it is true, still detained her; but with a restraint that was gentle enough, so long as no opposition tightened it. My gaze was on the red fire; my heart was measuring its own content; it sounded and sounded, and found the depth fathomless.

"Monsieur," at last said my quiet companion, as stirless in her happiness as a mouse in its terror. Even now in speaking she scarcely lifted her head.

"Well, Frances?" I like unexaggerated intercourse; it is not my way to overpower with amorous epithets, any more than to worry with selfishly importunate caresses.

"Monsieur est raisonnable, n'est-ce pas?"

"Yes; especially when I am requested to be so in English: but why do you ask me? You see nothing vehement or obtrusive in my manner; am I not tranquil enough?"

"Ce n'est pas cela—" began Frances.

"English!" I reminded her.

"Well, monsieur, I wished merely to say, that I should like, of course, to retain my employment of teaching. You will teach still, I suppose, monsieur?"

"Oh, yes! It is all I have to depend on."

"Bon!—I mean good. Thus we shall have both the same profession. I like that; and my efforts to get on will be as unrestrained as yours—will they not, monsieur?"

"You are laying plans to be independent of me," said I.

"Yes, monsieur; I must be no incumbrance to you—no burden in any way."

"But, Frances, I have not yet told you what my prospects are. I have left M. Pelet's; and after nearly a month's seeking, I have got another place, with a salary of three thousand francs a year, which I can easily double by a little additional exertion. Thus you see it would be useless for you to fag yourself by going out to give lessons; on six thousand francs you and I can live, and live well."

Frances seemed to consider. There is something flattering to man's strength, something consonant to his honourable pride, in the idea of becoming the providence of what he loves—feeding and clothing it, as God does the lilies of the field. So, to decide her resolution, I went on:—

"Life has been painful and laborious enough to you so far, Frances; you require complete rest; your twelve hundred francs would not form a very important addition to our income, and what sacrifice of comfort to earn it! Relinquish your labours: you must be weary, and let me have the happiness of giving you rest."

I am not sure whether Frances had accorded due attention to my harangue; instead of answering me with her usual respectful promptitude, she only sighed and said,—

"How rich you are, monsieur!" and then she stirred uneasy in my arms. "Three thousand francs!" she murmured, "While I get only twelve hundred!" She went on faster. "However, it must be so for the present; and, monsieur, were you not saying something about my giving up my place? Oh no! I shall hold it fast;" and her little fingers emphatically tightened on mine.

"Think of my marrying you to be kept by you, monsieur! I could not do it; and how dull my days would be! You would be away teaching in close, noisy school-rooms, from morning till evening, and I should be lingering at home, unemployed and solitary; I should get depressed and sullen, and you would soon tire of me."

"Frances, you could read and study—two things you like so well."

"Monsieur, I could not; I like a contemplative life, but I like an active life better; I must act in some way, and act with you. I have taken notice, monsieur, that people who are only in each other's company for amusement, never really like each other so well, or esteem each other so highly, as those who work together, and perhaps suffer together."

"You speak God's truth," said I at last, "and you shall have your own way, for it is the best way. Now, as a reward for such ready consent, give me a voluntary kiss."

After some hesitation, natural to a novice in the art of kissing, she brought her lips into very shy and gentle contact with my forehead; I took the small gift as a loan, and repaid it promptly, and with generous interest.

I know not whether Frances was really much altered since the time I first saw her; but, as I looked at her now, I felt that she was singularly changed for me; the sad eye, the pale cheek, the dejected and joyless countenance I remembered as her early attributes, were quite gone, and now I saw a face dressed in graces; smile, dimple, and rosy tint rounded its contours and brightened its hues. I had been accustomed to nurse a flattering idea that my strong attachment to her proved some particular perspicacity in my nature; she was not handsome, she was not rich, she was not even accomplished, yet was she my life's treasure; I must then be a man of peculiar discernment. To-night my eyes opened on the mistake I had made; I began to suspect that it was only my tastes which were unique, not my power of discovering and appreciating the superiority of moral worth over physical charms. For me Frances had physical charms: in her there was no deformity to get over; none of those prominent defects of eyes, teeth, complexion, shape, which hold at bay the admiration of the boldest male champions of intellect (for women can love a downright ugly man if he be but talented); had she been either "edentee, myope, rugueuse, ou bossue," my feelings towards her might still have been kindly, but they could never have been impassioned; I had affection for the poor little misshapen Sylvie, but for her I could never have had love. It is true Frances' mental points had been the first to interest me, and they still retained the strongest hold on my preference; but I liked the graces of her person too. I derived a pleasure, purely material, from contemplating the clearness of her brown eyes, the fairness of her fine skin, the purity of her well-set teeth, the proportion of her delicate form; and that pleasure I could ill have dispensed with. It appeared, then, that I too was a sensualist, in my temperate and fastidious way.

Now, reader, during the last two pages I have been giving you honey fresh from flowers, but you must not live entirely on food so luscious; taste then a little gall—just a drop, by way of change.

At a somewhat late hour I returned to my lodgings: having temporarily forgotten that man had any such coarse cares as those of eating and drinking, I went to bed fasting. I had been excited and in action all day, and had tasted no food since eight that morning; besides, for a fortnight past, I had known no rest either of body or mind; the last few hours had been a sweet delirium, it would not subside now, and till long after midnight, broke with troubled ecstacy the rest I so much needed. At last I dozed, but not for long; it was yet quite dark when I awoke, and my waking was like that of Job when a spirit passed before his face, and like him, "the hair of my flesh stood up." I might continue the parallel, for in truth, though I saw nothing, yet "a thing was secretly brought unto me, and mine ear received a little thereof; there was silence, and I heard a voice," saying—"In the midst of life we are in death."

That sound, and the sensation of chill anguish accompanying it, many would have regarded as supernatural; but I recognized it at once as the effect of reaction. Man is ever clogged with his mortality, and it was my mortal nature which now faltered and plained; my nerves, which jarred and gave a false sound, because the soul, of late rushing headlong to an aim, had overstrained the body's comparative weakness. A horror of great darkness fell upon me; I felt my chamber invaded by one I had known formerly, but had thought for ever departed. I was temporarily a prey to hypochondria.

She had been my acquaintance, nay, my guest, once before in boyhood; I had entertained her at bed and board for a year; for that space of time I had her to myself in secret; she lay with me, she ate with me, she walked out with me, showing me nooks in woods, hollows in hills, where we could sit together, and where she could drop her drear veil over me, and so hide sky and sun, grass and green tree; taking me entirely to her death-cold bosom, and holding me with arms of bone. What tales she would tell me at such hours! What songs she would recite in my ears! How she would discourse to me of her own country—the grave—and again and again promise to conduct me there ere long; and, drawing me to the very brink of a black, sullen river, show me, on the other side, shores unequal with mound, monument, and tablet, standing up in a glimmer more hoary than moonlight. "Necropolis!" she would whisper, pointing to the pale piles, and add, "It contains a mansion prepared for you."

But my boyhood was lonely, parentless; uncheered by brother or sister; and there was no marvel that, just as I rose to youth, a sorceress, finding me lost in vague mental wanderings, with many affections and few objects, glowing aspirations and gloomy prospects, strong desires and slender hopes, should lift up her illusive lamp to me in the distance, and lure me to her vaulted home of horrors. No wonder her spells THEN had power; but NOW, when my course was widening, my prospect brightening; when my affections had found a rest; when my desires, folding wings, weary with long flight, had just alighted on the very lap of fruition, and nestled there warm, content, under the caress of a soft hand—why did hypochondria accost me now?

I repulsed her as one would a dreaded and ghastly concubine coming to embitter a husband's heart toward his young bride; in vain; she kept her sway over me for that night and the next day, and eight succeeding days. Afterwards, my spirits began slowly to recover their tone; my appetite returned, and in a fortnight I was well. I had gone about as usual all the time, and had said nothing to anybody of what I felt; but I was glad when the evil spirit departed from me, and I could again seek Frances, and sit at her side, freed from the dreadful tyranny of my demon.

CHAPTER XXIV.

One fine, frosty Sunday in November, Frances and I took a long walk; we made the tour of the city by the Boulevards; and, afterwards, Frances being a little tired, we sat down on one of those wayside seats placed under the trees, at intervals, for the accommodation of the weary. Frances was telling me about Switzerland; the subject animated her; and I was just thinking that her eyes spoke full as eloquently as her tongue, when she stopped and remarked—

"Monsieur, there is a gentleman who knows you."

I looked up; three fashionably dressed men were just then passing—Englishmen, I knew by their air and gait as well as by their features; in the tallest of the trio I at once recognized Mr. Hunsden; he was in the act of lifting his hat to Frances; afterwards, he made a grimace at me, and passed on.

"Who is he?"

"A person I knew in England."

"Why did he bow to me? He does not know me."

"Yes, he does know you, in his way."

"How, monsieur?" (She still called me "monsieur"; I could not persuade her to adopt any more familiar term.)

"Did you not read the expression of his eyes?"

"Of his eyes? No. What did they say?"

"To you they said, 'How do you do, Wilhelmina Crimsworth?' To me, 'So you have found your counterpart at last; there she sits, the female of your kind!'"

"Monsieur, you could not read all that in his eyes; he was so soon gone."

"I read that and more, Frances; I read that he will probably call on me this evening, or on some future occasion shortly; and I have no doubt he will insist on being introduced to you; shall I bring him to your rooms?"

"If you please, monsieur—I have no objection; I think, indeed, I should rather like to see him nearer; he looks so original."

As I had anticipated, Mr. Hunsden came that evening. The first thing he said was:—

"You need not begin boasting, Monsieur le Professeur; I know about your appointment to —— College, and all that; Brown has told me." Then he intimated that he had returned from Germany but a day or two since; afterwards, he abruptly demanded whether that was Madame Pelet-Reuter with whom he had seen me on the Boulevards. I was going to utter a rather emphatic negative, but on second thoughts I checked myself, and, seeming to assent, asked what he thought of her?

"As to her, I'll come to that directly; but first I've a word for you. I see you are a scoundrel; you've no business to be promenading about with another man's wife. I thought you had sounder sense than to get mixed up in foreign hodge-podge of this sort."

"But the lady?"

"She's too good for you evidently; she is like you, but something better than you—no beauty, though; yet when she rose (for I looked back to see you both walk away) I thought her figure and carriage good. These foreigners understand grace. What the devil has she done with Pelet? She has not been married to him three months—he must be a spoon!"

I would not let the mistake go too far; I did not like it much.

"Pelet? How your head runs on Mons. and Madame Pelet! You are always talking about them. I wish to the gods you had wed Mdlle. Zoraide yourself!"

"Was that young gentlewoman not Mdlle. Zoraide?"

"No; nor Madame Zoraide either."

"Why did you tell a lie, then?"

"I told no lie; but you are is such a hurry. She is a pupil of mine—a Swiss girl."

"And of course you are going to be married to her? Don't deny that."

"Married! I think I shall—if Fate spares us both ten weeks longer. That is my little wild strawberry, Hunsden, whose sweetness made me careless of your hothouse grapes."

"Stop! No boasting—no heroics; I won't hear them. What is she? To what caste does she belong?"

I smiled. Hunsden unconsciously laid stress on the word caste, and, in fact, republican, lord-hater as he was, Hunsden was as proud of his old ——shire blood, of his descent and family standing, respectable and respected through long generations back, as any peer in the realm of his Norman race and Conquest-dated title. Hunsden would as little have thought of taking a wife from a caste inferior to his own, as a Stanley would think of mating with a Cobden. I enjoyed the surprise I should give; I enjoyed the triumph of my practice over his theory; and leaning over the table, and uttering the words slowly but with repressed glee, I said concisely—

"She is a lace-mender."

Hunsden examined me. He did not SAY he was surprised, but surprised he was; he had his own notions of good breeding. I saw he suspected I was going to take some very rash step; but repressing declamation or remonstrance, he only answered—

"Well, you are the best judge of your own affairs. A lace-mender may make a good wife as well as a lady; but of course you have taken care to ascertain thoroughly that since she has not education, fortune or station, she is well furnished with such natural qualities as you think most likely to conduce to your happiness. Has she many relations?"

"None in Brussels."

"That is better. Relations are often the real evil in such cases. I cannot but think that a train of inferior connections would have been a bore to you to your life's end."

After sitting in silence a little while longer, Hunsden rose, and was quietly bidding me good evening; the polite, considerate manner in which he offered me his hand (a thing he had never done before), convinced me that he thought I had made a terrible fool of myself; and that, ruined and thrown away as I was, it was no time for sarcasm or cynicism, or indeed for anything but indulgence and forbearance.

"Good night, William," he said, in a really soft voice, while his face looked benevolently compassionate. "Good night, lad. I wish you and your future wife much prosperity; and I hope she will satisfy your fastidious soul."

I had much ado to refrain from laughing as I beheld the magnanimous pity of his mien; maintaining, however, a grave air, I said:—

"I thought you would have liked to have seen Mdlle. Henri?"

"Oh, that is the name! Yes—if it would be convenient, I should like to see her—but——." He hesitated.

"Well?"

"I should on no account wish to intrude."

"Come, then," said I. We set out. Hunsden no doubt regarded me as a rash, imprudent man, thus to show my poor little grisette sweetheart, in her poor little unfurnished grenier; but he prepared to act the real gentleman, having, in fact, the kernel of that character, under the harsh husk it pleased him to wear by way of mental mackintosh. He talked affably, and even gently, as we went along the street; he had never been so civil to me in his life. We reached the house, entered, ascended the stair; on gaining the lobby, Hunsden turned to mount a narrower stair which led to a higher story; I saw his mind was bent on the attics.

"Here, Mr. Hunsden," said I quietly, tapping at Frances' door. He turned; in his genuine politeness he was a little disconcerted at having made the mistake; his eye reverted to the green mat, but he said nothing.

We walked in, and Frances rose from her seat near the table to receive us; her mourning attire gave her a recluse, rather conventual, but withal very distinguished look; its grave simplicity added nothing to beauty, but much to dignity; the finish of the white collar and manchettes sufficed for a relief to the merino gown of solemn black; ornament was forsworn. Frances curtsied with sedate grace, looking, as she always did, when one first accosted her, more a woman to respect than to love; I introduced Mr. Hunsden, and she expressed her happiness at making his acquaintance in French. The pure and polished accent, the low yet sweet and rather full voice, produced their effect immediately; Hunsden spoke French in reply; I had not heard him speak that language before; he managed it very well. I retired to the window-seat; Mr. Hunsden, at his hostess's invitation, occupied a chair near the hearth; from my position I could see them both, and the room too, at a glance. The room was so clean and bright, it looked like a little polished cabinet; a glass filled with flowers in the centre of the table, a fresh rose in each china cup on the mantelpiece gave it an air of FETE. Frances was serious, and Mr. Hunsden subdued, but both mutually polite; they got on at the French swimmingly: ordinary topics were discussed with great state and decorum; I thought I had never seen two such models of propriety, for Hunsden (thanks to the constraint of the foreign tongue) was obliged to shape his phrases, and measure his sentences, with a care that forbade any eccentricity. At last England was mentioned, and Frances proceeded to ask questions. Animated by degrees, she began to change, just as a grave night-sky changes at the approach of sunrise: first it seemed as if her forehead cleared, then her eyes glittered, her features relaxed, and became quite mobile; her subdued complexion grew warm and transparent; to me, she now looked pretty; before, she had only looked ladylike.

She had many things to say to the Englishman just fresh from his island-country, and she urged him with an enthusiasm of curiosity, which ere long thawed Hunsden's reserve as fire thaws a congealed viper. I use this not very flattering comparison because he vividly reminded me of a snake waking from torpor, as he erected his tall form, reared his head, before a little declined, and putting back his hair from his broad Saxon forehead, showed unshaded the gleam of almost savage satire which his interlocutor's tone of eagerness and look of ardour had sufficed at once to kindle in his soul and elicit from his eyes: he was himself; as Frances was herself, and in none but his own language would he now address her.

"You understand English?" was the prefatory question.

"A little."

"Well, then, you shall have plenty of it; and first, I see you've not much more sense than some others of my acquaintance" (indicating me with his thumb), "or else you'd never turn rabid about that dirty little country called England; for rabid, I see you are; I read Anglophobia in your looks, and hear it in your words. Why, mademoiselle, is it possible that anybody with a grain of rationality should feel enthusiasm about a mere name, and that name England? I thought you were a lady-abbess five minutes ago, and respected you accordingly; and now I see you are a sort of Swiss sibyl, with high Tory and high Church principles!"

"England is your country?" asked Frances.

"Yes."

"And you don't like it?"

"I'd be sorry to like it! A little corrupt, venal, lord-and-king-cursed nation, full of mucky pride (as they say in ——shire), and helpless pauperism; rotten with abuses, worm-eaten with prejudices!"

"You might say so of almost every state; there are abuses and prejudices everywhere, and I thought fewer in England than in other countries."

"Come to England and see. Come to Birmingham and Manchester; come to St. Giles' in London, and get a practical notion of how our system works. Examine the footprints of our august aristocracy; see how they walk in blood, crushing hearts as they go. Just put your head in at English cottage doors; get a glimpse of Famine crouched torpid on black hearthstones; of Disease lying bare on beds without coverlets, of Infamy wantoning viciously with Ignorance, though indeed Luxury is her favourite paramour, and princely halls are dearer to her than thatched hovels——"

"I was not thinking of the wretchedness and vice in England; I was thinking of the good side—of what is elevated in your character as a nation."

"There is no good side—none at least of which you can have any knowledge; for you cannot appreciate the efforts of industry, the achievements of enterprise, or the discoveries of science: narrowness of education and obscurity of position quite incapacitate you from understanding these points; and as to historical and poetical associations, I will not insult you, mademoiselle, by supposing that you alluded to such humbug."

"But I did partly."

Hunsden laughed—his laugh of unmitigated scorn.

"I did, Mr. Hunsden. Are you of the number of those to whom such associations give no pleasure?"

"Mademoiselle, what is an association? I never saw one. What is its length, breadth, weight, value—ay, VALUE? What price will it bring in the market?"

"Your portrait, to any one who loved you, would, for the sake of association, be without price."

That inscrutable Hunsden heard this remark and felt it rather acutely, too, somewhere; for he coloured—a thing not unusual with him, when hit unawares on a tender point. A sort of trouble momentarily darkened his eye, and I believe he filled up the transient pause succeeding his antagonist's home-thrust, by a wish that some one did love him as he would like to be loved—some one whose love he could unreservedly return.

The lady pursued her temporary advantage.

"If your world is a world without associations, Mr. Hunsden, I no longer wonder that you hate England so. I don't clearly know what Paradise is, and what angels are; yet taking it to be the most glorious region I can conceive, and angels the most elevated existences—if one of them—if Abdiel the Faithful himself" (she was thinking of Milton) "were suddenly stripped of the faculty of association, I think he would soon rush forth from 'the ever-during gates,' leave heaven, and seek what he had lost in hell. Yes, in the very hell from which he turned 'with retorted scorn.'"

Frances' tone in saying this was as marked as her language, and it was when the word "hell" twanged off from her lips, with a somewhat startling emphasis, that Hunsden deigned to bestow one slight glance of admiration. He liked something strong, whether in man or woman; he liked whatever dared to clear conventional limits. He had never before heard a lady say "hell" with that uncompromising sort of accent, and the sound pleased him from a lady's lips; he would fain have had Frances to strike the string again, but it was not in her way. The display of eccentric vigour never gave her pleasure, and it only sounded in her voice or flashed in her countenance when extraordinary circumstances—and those generally painful—forced it out of the depths where it burned latent. To me, once or twice, she had in intimate conversation, uttered venturous thoughts in nervous language; but when the hour of such manifestation was past, I could not recall it; it came of itself and of itself departed. Hunsden's excitations she put by soon with a smile, and recurring to the theme of disputation, said—

"Since England is nothing, why do the continental nations respect her so?"

"I should have thought no child would have asked that question," replied Hunsden, who never at any time gave information without reproving for stupidity those who asked it of him. "If you had been my pupil, as I suppose you once had the misfortune to be that of a deplorable character not a hundred miles off, I would have put you in the corner for such a confession of ignorance. Why, mademoiselle, can't you see that it is our GOLD which buys us French politeness, German good-will, and Swiss servility?" And he sneered diabolically.

"Swiss?" said Frances, catching the word "servility." "Do you call my countrymen servile?" and she started up. I could not suppress a low laugh; there was ire in her glance and defiance in her attitude. "Do you abuse Switzerland to me, Mr. Hunsden? Do you think I have no associations? Do you calculate that I am prepared to dwell only on what vice and degradation may be found in Alpine villages, and to leave quite out of my heart the social greatness of my countrymen, and our blood-earned freedom, and the natural glories of our mountains? You're mistaken—you're mistaken."

"Social greatness? Call it what you will, your countrymen are sensible fellows; they make a marketable article of what to you is an abstract idea; they have, ere this, sold their social greatness and also their blood-earned freedom to be the servants of foreign kings."

"You never were in Switzerland?"

"Yes—I have been there twice."

"You know nothing of it."

"I do."

"And you say the Swiss are mercenary, as a parrot says 'Poor Poll,' or as the Belgians here say the English are not brave, or as the French accuse them of being perfidious: there is no justice in your dictums."

"There is truth."

"I tell you, Mr. Hunsden, you are a more unpractical man than I am an unpractical woman, for you don't acknowledge what really exists; you want to annihilate individual patriotism and national greatness as an atheist would annihilate God and his own soul, by denying their existence."

"Where are you flying to? You are off at a tangent—I thought we were talking about the mercenary nature of the Swiss."

"We were—and if you proved to me that the Swiss are mercenary to-morrow (which you cannot do) I should love Switzerland still."

"You would be mad, then—mad as a March hare—to indulge in a passion for millions of shiploads of soil, timber, snow, and ice."

"Not so mad as you who love nothing."

"There's a method in my madness; there's none in yours."

"Your method is to squeeze the sap out of creation and make manure of the refuse, by way of turning it to what you call use."

"You cannot reason at all," said Hunsden; "there is no logic in you."

"Better to be without logic than without feeling," retorted Frances, who was now passing backwards and forwards from her cupboard to the table, intent, if not on hospitable thoughts, at least on hospitable deeds, for she was laying the cloth, and putting plates, knives and forks thereon.

"Is that a hit at me, mademoiselle? Do you suppose I am without feeling?"

"I suppose you are always interfering with your own feelings, and those of other people, and dogmatizing about the irrationality of this, that, and the other sentiment, and then ordering it to be suppressed because you imagine it to be inconsistent with logic."

"I do right."

Frances had stepped out of sight into a sort of little pantry; she soon reappeared.

"You do right? Indeed, no! You are much mistaken if you think so. Just be so good as to let me get to the fire, Mr. Hunsden; I have something to cook." (An interval occupied in settling a casserole on the fire; then, while she stirred its contents:) "Right! as if it were right to crush any pleasurable sentiment that God has given to man, especially any sentiment that, like patriotism, spreads man's selfishness in wider circles" (fire stirred, dish put down before it).

"Were you born in Switzerland?"

"I should think so, or else why should I call it my country?"

"And where did you get your English features and figure?"

"I am English, too; half the blood in my veins is English; thus I have a right to a double power of patriotism, possessing an interest in two noble, free, and fortunate countries."

"You had an English mother?"

"Yes, yes; and you, I suppose, had a mother from the moon or from Utopia, since not a nation in Europe has a claim on your interest?"

"On the contrary, I'm a universal patriot, if you could understand me rightly: my country is the world."

"Sympathies so widely diffused must be very shallow: will you have the goodness to come to table. Monsieur" (to me who appeared to be now absorbed in reading by moonlight)—"Monsieur, supper is served."

This was said in quite a different voice to that in which she had been bandying phrases with Mr. Hunsden—not so short, graver and softer.

"Frances, what do you mean by preparing, supper? we had no intention of staying."

"Ah, monsieur, but you have stayed, and supper is prepared; you have only the alternative of eating it."

The meal was a foreign one, of course; it consisted in two small but tasty dishes of meat prepared with skill and served with nicety; a salad and "fromage francais," completed it. The business of eating interposed a brief truce between the belligerents, but no sooner was supper disposed of than they were at it again. The fresh subject of dispute ran on the spirit of religious intolerance which Mr. Hunsden affirmed to exist strongly in Switzerland, notwithstanding the professed attachment of the Swiss to freedom. Here Frances had greatly the worst of it, not only because she was unskilled to argue, but because her own real opinions on the point in question happened to coincide pretty nearly with Mr. Hunsden's, and she only contradicted him out of opposition. At last she gave in, confessing that she thought as he thought, but bidding him take notice that she did not consider herself beaten.

"No more did the French at Waterloo," said Hunsden.

"There is no comparison between the cases," rejoined Frances; "mine was a sham fight."

"Sham or real, it's up with you."

"No; though I have neither logic nor wealth of words, yet in a case where my opinion really differed from yours, I would adhere to it when I had not another word to say in its defence; you should be baffled by dumb determination. You speak of Waterloo; your Wellington ought to have been conquered there, according to Napoleon; but he persevered in spite of the laws of war, and was victorious in defiance of military tactics. I would do as he did."

"I'll be bound for it you would; probably you have some of the same sort of stubborn stuff in you."

"I should be sorry if I had not; he and Tell were brothers, and I'd scorn the Swiss, man or woman, who had none of the much-enduring nature of our heroic William in his soul."

"If Tell was like Wellington, he was an ass."

"Does not ASS mean BAUDET?" asked Frances, turning to me.

"No, no," replied I, "it means an ESPRIT-FORT; and now," I continued, as I saw that fresh occasion of strife was brewing between these two, "it is high time to go."

Hunsden rose. "Good bye," said he to Frances; "I shall be off for this glorious England to-morrow, and it may be twelve months or more before I come to Brussels again; whenever I do come I'll seek you out, and you shall see if I don't find means to make you fiercer than a dragon. You've done pretty well this evening, but next interview you shall challenge me outright. Meantime you're doomed to become Mrs. William Crimsworth, I suppose; poor young lady? but you have a spark of spirit; cherish it, and give the Professor the full benefit thereof."

"Are you married. Mr. Hunsden?" asked Frances, suddenly.

"No. I should have thought you might have guessed I was a Benedict by my look."

"Well, whenever you marry don't take a wife out of Switzerland; for if you begin blaspheming Helvetia, and cursing the cantons—above all, if you mention the word ASS in the same breath with the name Tell (for ass IS baudet, I know; though Monsieur is pleased to translate it ESPRIT-FORT) your mountain maid will some night smother her Breton-bretonnant, even as your own Shakspeare's Othello smothered Desdemona."

"I am warned," said Hunsden; "and so are you, lad," (nodding to me). "I hope yet to hear of a travesty of the Moor and his gentle lady, in which the parts shall be reversed according to the plan just sketched—you, however, being in my nightcap. Farewell, mademoiselle!" He bowed on her hand, absolutely like Sir Charles Grandison on that of Harriet Byron; adding —"Death from such fingers would not be without charms."

"Mon Dieu!" murmured Frances, opening her large eyes and lifting her distinctly arched brows; "c'est qu'il fait des compliments! je ne m'y suis pas attendu." She smiled, half in ire, half in mirth, curtsied with foreign grace, and so they parted.

No sooner had we got into the street than Hunsden collared me.

"And that is your lace-mender?" said he; "and you reckon you have done a fine, magnanimous thing in offering to marry her? You, a scion of Seacombe, have proved your disdain of social distinctions by taking up with an ouvriere! And I pitied the fellow, thinking his feelings had misled him, and that he had hurt himself by contracting a low match!"

"Just let go my collar, Hunsden."

On the contrary, he swayed me to and fro; so I grappled him round the waist. It was dark; the street lonely and lampless. We had then a tug for it; and after we had both rolled on the pavement, and with difficulty picked ourselves up, we agreed to walk on more soberly.

"Yes, that's my lace-mender," said I; "and she is to be mine for life—God willing."

"God is not willing—you can't suppose it; what business have you to be suited so well with a partner? And she treats you with a sort of respect, too, and says, 'Monsieur' and modulates her tone in addressing you, actually, as if you were something superior! She could not evince more deference to such a one as I, were she favoured by fortune to the supreme extent of being my choice instead of yours."

"Hunsden, you're a puppy. But you've only seen the title-page of my happiness; you don't know the tale that follows; you cannot conceive the interest and sweet variety and thrilling excitement of the narrative."

Hunsden—speaking low and deep, for we had now entered a busier street —desired me to hold my peace, threatening to do something dreadful if I stimulated his wrath further by boasting. I laughed till my sides ached. We soon reached his hotel; before he entered it, he said—

"Don't be vainglorious. Your lace-mender is too good for you, but not good enough for me; neither physically nor morally does she come up to my ideal of a woman. No; I dream of something far beyond that pale-faced, excitable little Helvetian (by-the-by she has infinitely more of the nervous, mobile Parisienne in her than of the the robust 'jungfrau'). Your Mdlle. Henri is in person "chetive", in mind "sans caractere", compared with the queen of my visions. You, indeed, may put up with that "minois chiffone"; but when I marry I must have straighter and more harmonious features, to say nothing of a nobler and better developed shape than that perverse, ill-thriven child can boast."

"Bribe a seraph to fetch you a coal of fire from heaven, if you will," said I, "and with it kindle life in the tallest, fattest, most boneless, fullest-blooded of Ruben's painted women—leave me only my Alpine peri, and I'll not envy you."

With a simultaneous movement, each turned his back on the other. Neither said "God bless you;" yet on the morrow the sea was to roll between us.

CHAPTER XXV.

In two months more Frances had fulfilled the time of mourning for her aunt. One January morning—the first of the new year holidays—I went in a fiacre, accompanied only by M. Vandenhuten, to the Rue Notre Dame aux Neiges, and having alighted alone and walked upstairs, I found Frances apparently waiting for me, dressed in a style scarcely appropriate to that cold, bright, frosty day. Never till now had I seen her attired in any other than black or sad-coloured stuff; and there she stood by the window, clad all in white, and white of a most diaphanous texture; her array was very simple, to be sure, but it looked imposing and festal because it was so clear, full, and floating; a veil shadowed her head, and hung below her knee; a little wreath of pink flowers fastened it to her thickly tressed Grecian plait, and thence it fell softly on each side of her face. Singular to state, she was, or had been crying; when I asked her if she were ready, she said "Yes, monsieur," with something very like a checked sob; and when I took a shawl, which lay on the table, and folded it round her, not only did tear after tear course unbidden down her cheek, but she shook to my ministration like a reed. I said I was sorry to see her in such low spirits, and requested to be allowed an insight into the origin thereof. She only said, "It was impossible to help it," and then voluntarily, though hurriedly, putting her hand into mine, accompanied me out of the room, and ran downstairs with a quick, uncertain step, like one who was eager to get some formidable piece of business over. I put her into the fiacre. M. Vandenhuten received her, and seated her beside himself; we drove all together to the Protestant chapel, went through a certain service in the Common Prayer Book, and she and I came out married. M. Vandenhuten had given the bride away.

We took no bridal trip; our modesty, screened by the peaceful obscurity of our station, and the pleasant isolation of our circumstances, did not exact that additional precaution. We repaired at once to a small house I had taken in the faubourg nearest to that part of the city where the scene of our avocations lay.

Three or four hours after the wedding ceremony, Frances, divested of her bridal snow, and attired in a pretty lilac gown of warmer materials, a piquant black silk apron, and a lace collar with some finishing decoration of lilac ribbon, was kneeling on the carpet of a neatly furnished though not spacious parlour, arranging on the shelves of a chiffoniere some books, which I handed to her from the table. It was snowing fast out of doors; the afternoon had turned out wild and cold; the leaden sky seemed full of drifts, and the street was already ankle-deep in the white downfall. Our fire burned bright, our new habitation looked brilliantly clean and fresh, the furniture was all arranged, and there were but some articles of glass, china, books, &c., to put in order. Frances found in this business occupation till tea-time, and then, after I had distinctly instructed her how to make a cup of tea in rational English style, and after she had got over the dismay occasioned by seeing such an extravagant amount of material put into the pot, she administered to me a proper British repast, at which there wanted neither candles nor urn, firelight nor comfort.

Our week's holiday glided by, and we readdressed ourselves to labour. Both my wife and I began in good earnest with the notion that we were working people, destined to earn our bread by exertion, and that of the most assiduous kind. Our days were thoroughly occupied; we used to part every morning at eight o'clock, and not meet again till five P.M.; but into what sweet rest did the turmoil of each busy day decline! Looking down the vista of memory, I see the evenings passed in that little parlour like a long string of rubies circling the dusky brow of the past. Unvaried were they as each cut gem, and like each gem brilliant and burning.

A year and a half passed. One morning (it was a FETE, and we had the day to ourselves) Frances said to me, with a suddenness peculiar to her when she had been thinking long on a subject, and at last, having come to a conclusion, wished to test its soundness by the touchstone of my judgment:—

"I don't work enough."

"What now?" demanded I, looking up from my coffee, which I had been deliberately stirring while enjoying, in anticipation, a walk I proposed to take with Frances, that fine summer day (it was June), to a certain farmhouse in the country, where we were to dine. "What now?" and I saw at once, in the serious ardour of her face, a project of vital importance.

"I am not satisfied," returned she; "you are now earning eight thousand francs a year" (it was true; my efforts, punctuality, the fame of my pupils' progress, the publicity of my station, had so far helped me on), "while I am still at my miserable twelve hundred francs. I CAN do better, and I WILL."

"You work as long and as diligently as I do, Frances."

"Yes, monsieur, but I am not working in the right way, and I am convinced of it."

"You wish to change—you have a plan for progress in your mind; go and put on your bonnet; and, while we take our walk, you shall tell me of it."

"Yes, monsieur."

She went—as docile as a well-trained child; she was a curious mixture of tractability and firmness: I sat thinking about her, and wondering what her plan could be, when she re-entered.

"Monsieur, I have given Minnie" (our bonne) "leave to go out too, as it is so very fine; so will you be kind enough to lock the door, and take the key with you?"

"Kiss me, Mrs. Crimsworth," was my not very apposite reply; but she looked so engaging in her light summer dress and little cottage bonnet, and her manner in speaking to me was then, as always, so unaffectedly and suavely respectful, that my heart expanded at the sight of her, and a kiss seemed necessary to content its importunity.

"There, monsieur."

"Why do you always call me 'Monsieur'? Say, 'William.'"

"I cannot pronounce your W; besides, 'Monsieur' belongs to you; I like it best."

Minnie having departed in clean cap and smart shawl, we, too, set out, leaving the house solitary and silent—silent, at least, but for the ticking of the clock. We were soon clear of Brussels; the fields received us, and then the lanes, remote from carriage-resounding CHAUSSEES. Ere long we came upon a nook, so rural, green, and secluded, it might have been a spot in some pastoral English province; a bank of short and mossy grass, under a hawthorn, offered a seat too tempting to be declined; we took it, and when we had admired and examined some English-looking wild-flowers growing at our feet, I recalled Frances' attention and my own to the topic touched on at breakfast.

"What was her plan?" A natural one—the next step to be mounted by us, or, at least, by her, if she wanted to rise in her profession. She proposed to begin a school. We already had the means for commencing on a careful scale, having lived greatly within our income. We possessed, too, by this time, an extensive and eligible connection, in the sense advantageous to our business; for, though our circle of visiting acquaintance continued as limited as ever, we were now widely known in schools and families as teachers. When Frances had developed her plan, she intimated, in some closing sentences, her hopes for the future. If we only had good health and tolerable success, me might, she was sure, in time realize an independency; and that, perhaps, before we were too old to enjoy it; then both she and I would rest; and what was to hinder us from going to live in England? England was still her Promised Land.

I put no obstacle in her way; raised no objection; I knew she was not one who could live quiescent and inactive, or even comparatively inactive. Duties she must have to fulfil, and important duties; work to do—and exciting, absorbing, profitable work; strong faculties stirred in her frame, and they demanded full nourishment, free exercise: mine was not the hand ever to starve or cramp them; no, I delighted in offering them sustenance, and in clearing them wider space for action.

"You have conceived a plan, Frances," said I, "and a good plan; execute it; you have my free consent, and wherever and whenever my assistance is wanted, ask and you shall have."

Frances' eyes thanked me almost with tears; just a sparkle or two, soon brushed away; she possessed herself of my hand too, and held it for some time very close clasped in both her own, but she said no more than "Thank you, monsieur."

We passed a divine day, and came home late, lighted by a full summer moon.

Ten years rushed now upon me with dusty, vibrating, unresting wings; years of bustle, action, unslacked endeavour; years in which I and my wife, having launched ourselves in the full career of progress, as progress whirls on in European capitals, scarcely knew repose, were strangers to amusement, never thought of indulgence, and yet, as our course ran side by side, as we marched hand in hand, we neither murmured, repented, nor faltered. Hope indeed cheered us; health kept us up; harmony of thought and deed smoothed many difficulties, and finally, success bestowed every now and then encouraging reward on diligence. Our school became one of the most popular in Brussels, and as by degrees we raised our terms and elevated our system of education, our choice of pupils grew more select, and at length included the children of the best families in Belgium. We had too an excellent connection in England, first opened by the unsolicited recommendation of Mr. Hunsden, who having been over, and having abused me for my prosperity in set terms, went back, and soon after sent a leash of young ——shire heiresses—his cousins; as he said "to be polished off by Mrs. Crimsworth."

As to this same Mrs. Crimsworth, in one sense she was become another woman, though in another she remained unchanged. So different was she under different circumstances. I seemed to possess two wives. The faculties of her nature, already disclosed when I married her, remained fresh and fair; but other faculties shot up strong, branched out broad, and quite altered the external character of the plant. Firmness, activity, and enterprise, covered with grave foliage, poetic feeling and fervour; but these flowers were still there, preserved pure and dewy under the umbrage of later growth and hardier nature: perhaps I only in the world knew the secret of their existence, but to me they were ever ready to yield an exquisite fragrance and present a beauty as chaste as radiant.

In the daytime my house and establishment were conducted by Madame the directress, a stately and elegant woman, bearing much anxious thought on her large brow; much calculated dignity in her serious mien: immediately after breakfast I used to part with this lady; I went to my college, she to her schoolroom; returning for an hour in the course of the day, I found her always in class, intently occupied; silence, industry, observance, attending on her presence. When not actually teaching, she was overlooking and guiding by eye and gesture; she then appeared vigilant and solicitous. When communicating instruction, her aspect was more animated; she seemed to feel a certain enjoyment in the occupation. The language in which she addressed her pupils, though simple and unpretending, was never trite or dry; she did not speak from routine formulas—she made her own phrases as she went on, and very nervous and impressive phrases they frequently were; often, when elucidating favourite points of history, or geography, she would wax genuinely eloquent in her earnestness. Her pupils, or at least the elder and more intelligent amongst them, recognized well the language of a superior mind; they felt too, and some of them received the impression of elevated sentiments; there was little fondling between mistress and girls, but some of Frances' pupils in time learnt to love her sincerely, all of them beheld her with respect; her general demeanour towards them was serious; sometimes benignant when they pleased her with their progress and attention, always scrupulously refined and considerate. In cases where reproof or punishment was called for she was usually forbearing enough; but if any took advantage of that forbearance, which sometimes happened, a sharp, sudden and lightning-like severity taught the culprit the extent of the mistake committed. Sometimes a gleam of tenderness softened her eyes and manner, but this was rare; only when a pupil was sick, or when it pined after home, or in the case of some little motherless child, or of one much poorer than its companions, whose scanty wardrobe and mean appointments brought on it the contempt of the jewelled young countesses and silk-clad misses. Over such feeble fledglings the directress spread a wing of kindliest protection: it was to their bedside she came at night to tuck them warmly in; it was after them she looked in winter to see that they always had a comfortable seat by the stove; it was they who by turns were summoned to the salon to receive some little dole of cake or fruit—to sit on a footstool at the fireside—to enjoy home comforts, and almost home liberty, for an evening together—to be spoken to gently and softly, comforted, encouraged, cherished—and when bedtime came, dismissed with a kiss of true tenderness. As to Julia and Georgiana G——, daughters of an English baronet, as to Mdlle. Mathilde de ——, heiress of a Belgian count, and sundry other children of patrician race, the directress was careful of them as of the others, anxious for their progress, as for that of the rest—but it never seemed to enter her head to distinguish them by a mark of preference; one girl of noble blood she loved dearly—a young Irish baroness—lady Catherine ——; but it was for her enthusiastic heart and clever head, for her generosity and her genius, the title and rank went for nothing.

My afternoons were spent also in college, with the exception of an hour that my wife daily exacted of me for her establishment, and with which she would not dispense. She said that I must spend that time amongst her pupils to learn their characters, to be AU COURANT with everything that was passing in the house, to become interested in what interested her, to be able to give her my opinion on knotty points when she required it, and this she did constantly, never allowing my interest in the pupils to fall asleep, and never making any change of importance without my cognizance and consent. She delighted to sit by me when I gave my lessons (lessons in literature), her hands folded on her knee, the most fixedly attentive of any present. She rarely addressed me in class; when she did it was with an air of marked deference; it was her pleasure, her joy to make me still the master in all things.

At six o'clock P.M. my daily labours ceased. I then came home, for my home was my heaven; ever at that hour, as I entered our private sitting-room, the lady-directress vanished from before my eyes, and Frances Henri, my own little lace-mender, was magically restored to my arms; much disappointed she would have been if her master had not been as constant to the tryst as herself, and if his truthfull kiss had not been prompt to answer her soft, "Bon soir, monsieur."

Talk French to me she would, and many a punishment she has had for her wilfulness. I fear the choice of chastisement must have been injudicious, for instead of correcting the fault, it seemed to encourage its renewal. Our evenings were our own; that recreation was necessary to refresh our strength for the due discharge of our duties; sometimes we spent them all in conversation, and my young Genevese, now that she was thoroughly accustomed to her English professor, now that she loved him too absolutely to fear him much, reposed in him a confidence so unlimited that topics of conversation could no more be wanting with him than subjects for communion with her own heart. In those moments, happy as a bird with its mate, she would show me what she had of vivacity, of mirth, of originality in her well-dowered nature. She would show, too, some stores of raillery, of "malice," and would vex, tease, pique me sometimes about what she called my "bizarreries anglaises," my "caprices insulaires," with a wild and witty wickedness that made a perfect white demon of her while it lasted. This was rare, however, and the elfish freak was always short: sometimes when driven a little hard in the war of words—for her tongue did ample justice to the pith, the point, the delicacy of her native French, in which language she always attacked me—I used to turn upon her with my old decision, and arrest bodily the sprite that teased me. Vain idea! no sooner had I grasped hand or arm than the elf was gone; the provocative smile quenched in the expressive brown eyes, and a ray of gentle homage shone under the lids in its place. I had seized a mere vexing fairy, and found a submissive and supplicating little mortal woman in my arms. Then I made her get a book, and read English to me for an hour by way of penance. I frequently dosed her with Wordsworth in this way, and Wordsworth steadied her soon; she had a difficulty in comprehending his deep, serene, and sober mind; his language, too, was not facile to her; she had to ask questions, to sue for explanations, to be like a child and a novice, and to acknowledge me as her senior and director. Her instinct instantly penetrated and possessed the meaning of more ardent and imaginative writers. Byron excited her; Scott she loved; Wordsworth only she puzzled at, wondered over, and hesitated to pronounce an opinion upon.

But whether she read to me, or talked with me; whether she teased me in French, or entreated me in English; whether she jested with wit, or inquired with deference; narrated with interest, or listened with attention; whether she smiled at me or on me, always at nine o'clock I was left abandoned. She would extricate herself from my arms, quit my side, take her lamp, and be gone. Her mission was upstairs; I have followed her sometimes and watched her. First she opened the door of the dortoir (the pupils' chamber), noiselessly she glided up the long room between the two rows of white beds, surveyed all the sleepers; if any were wakeful, especially if any were sad, spoke to them and soothed them; stood some minutes to ascertain that all was safe and tranquil; trimmed the watch-light which burned in the apartment all night, then withdrew, closing the door behind her without sound. Thence she glided to our own chamber; it had a little cabinet within; this she sought; there, too, appeared a bed, but one, and that a very small one; her face (the night I followed and observed her) changed as she approached this tiny couch; from grave it warmed to earnest; she shaded with one hand the lamp she held in the other; she bent above the pillow and hung over a child asleep; its slumber (that evening at least, and usually, I believe) was sound and calm; no tear wet its dark eyelashes; no fever heated its round cheek; no ill dream discomposed its budding features. Frances gazed, she did not smile, and yet the deepest delight filled, flushed her face; feeling pleasurable, powerful, worked in her whole frame, which still was motionless. I saw, indeed, her heart heave, her lips were a little apart, her breathing grew somewhat hurried; the child smiled; then at last the mother smiled too, and said in low soliloquy, "God bless my little son!" She stooped closer over him, breathed the softest of kisses on his brow, covered his minute hand with hers, and at last started up and came away. I regained the parlour before her. Entering it two minutes later she said quietly as she put down her extinguished lamp—

"Victor rests well: he smiled in his sleep; he has your smile, monsieur."

The said Victor was of course her own boy, born in the third year of our marriage: his Christian name had been given him in honour of M. Vandenhuten, who continued always our trusty and well-beloved friend.

Frances was then a good and dear wife to me, because I was to her a good, just, and faithful husband. What she would have been had she married a harsh, envious, careless man—a profligate, a prodigal, a drunkard, or a tyrant—is another question, and one which I once propounded to her. Her answer, given after some reflection, was—

"I should have tried to endure the evil or cure it for awhile; and when I found it intolerable and incurable, I should have left my torturer suddenly and silently."

"And if law or might had forced you back again?"

"What, to a drunkard, a profligate, a selfish spendthrift, an unjust fool?"

"Yes."

"I would have gone back; again assured myself whether or not his vice and my misery were capable of remedy; and if not, have left him again."

"And if again forced to return, and compelled to abide?"

"I don't know," she said, hastily. "Why do you ask me, monsieur?"

I would have an answer, because I saw a strange kind of spirit in her eye, whose voice I determined to waken.

"Monsieur, if a wife's nature loathes that of the man she is wedded to, marriage must be slavery. Against slavery all right thinkers revolt, and though torture be the price of resistance, torture must be dared: though the only road to freedom lie through the gates of death, those gates must be passed; for freedom is indispensable. Then, monsieur, I would resist as far as my strength permitted; when that strength failed I should be sure of a refuge. Death would certainly screen me both from bad laws and their consequences."

"Voluntary death, Frances?"

"No, monsieur. I'd have courage to live out every throe of anguish fate assigned me, and principle to contend for justice and liberty to the last."

"I see you would have made no patient Grizzle. And now, supposing fate had merely assigned you the lot of an old maid, what then? How would you have liked celibacy?"

"Not much, certainly. An old maid's life must doubtless be void and vapid —her heart strained and empty. Had I been an old maid I should have spent existence in efforts to fill the void and ease the aching. I should have probably failed, and died weary and disappointed, despised and of no account, like other single women. But I'm not an old maid," she added quickly. "I should have been, though, but for my master. I should never have suited any man but Professor Crimsworth—no other gentleman, French, English, or Belgian, would have thought me amiable or handsome; and I doubt whether I should have cared for the approbation of many others, if I could have obtained it. Now, I have been Professor Crimsworth's wife eight years, and what is he in my eyes? Is he honourable, beloved ——?" She stopped, her voice was cut off, her eyes suddenly suffused. She and I were standing side by side; she threw her arms round me, and strained me to her heart with passionate earnestness: the energy of her whole being glowed in her dark and then dilated eye, and crimsoned her animated cheek; her look and movement were like inspiration; in one there was such a flash, in the other such a power. Half an hour afterwards, when she had become calm, I asked where all that wild vigour was gone which had transformed her ere-while and made her glance so thrilling and ardent—her action so rapid and strong. She looked down, smiling softly and passively:—

"I cannot tell where it is gone, monsieur," said she, "but I know that, whenever it is wanted, it will come back again."

Behold us now at the close of the ten years, and we have realized an independency. The rapidity with which we attained this end had its origin in three reasons:— Firstly, we worked so hard for it; secondly, we had no incumbrances to delay success; thirdly, as soon as we had capital to invest, two well-skilled counsellors, one in Belgium, one in England, viz. Vandenhuten and Hunsden, gave us each a word of advice as to the sort of investment to be chosen. The suggestion made was judicious; and, being promptly acted on, the result proved gainful—I need not say how gainful; I communicated details to Messrs. Vandenhuten and Hunsden; nobody else can be interested in hearing them.

Accounts being wound up, and our professional connection disposed of, we both agreed that, as mammon was not our master, nor his service that in which we desired to spend our lives; as our desires were temperate, and our habits unostentatious, we had now abundance to live on—abundance to leave our boy; and should besides always have a balance on hand, which, properly managed by right sympathy and unselfish activity, might help philanthropy in her enterprises, and put solace into the hand of charity.

To England we now resolved to take wing; we arrived there safely; Frances realized the dream of her lifetime. We spent a whole summer and autumn in travelling from end to end of the British islands, and afterwards passed a winter in London. Then we thought it high time to fix our residence. My heart yearned towards my native county of ——shire; and it is in ——shire I now live; it is in the library of my own home I am now writing. That home lies amid a sequestered and rather hilly region, thirty miles removed from X——; a region whose verdure the smoke of mills has not yet sullied, whose waters still run pure, whose swells of moorland preserve in some ferny glens that lie between them the very primal wildness of nature, her moss, her bracken, her blue-bells, her scents of reed and heather, her free and fresh breezes. My house is a picturesque and not too spacious dwelling, with low and long windows, a trellised and leaf-veiled porch over the front door, just now, on this summer evening, looking like an arch of roses and ivy. The garden is chiefly laid out in lawn, formed of the sod of the hills, with herbage short and soft as moss, full of its own peculiar flowers, tiny and starlike, imbedded in the minute embroidery of their fine foliage. At the bottom of the sloping garden there is a wicket, which opens upon a lane as green as the lawn, very long, shady, and little frequented; on the turf of this lane generally appear the first daisies of spring—whence its name—Daisy Lane; serving also as a distinction to the house.

It terminates (the lane I mean) in a valley full of wood; which wood—chiefly oak and beech—spreads shadowy about the vicinage of a very old mansion, one of the Elizabethan structures, much larger, as well as more antique than Daisy Lane, the property and residence of an individual familiar both to me and to the reader. Yes, in Hunsden Wood—for so are those glades and that grey building, with many gables and more chimneys, named—abides Yorke Hunsden, still unmarried; never, I suppose, having yet found his ideal, though I know at least a score of young ladies within a circuit of forty miles, who would be willing to assist him in the search.

The estate fell to him by the death of his father, five years since; he has given up trade, after having made by it sufficient to pay off some incumbrances by which the family heritage was burdened. I say he abides here, but I do not think he is resident above five months out of the twelve; he wanders from land to land, and spends some part of each winter in town: he frequently brings visitors with him when he comes to ——shire, and these visitors are often foreigners; sometimes he has a German metaphysician, sometimes a French savant; he had once a dissatisfied and savage-looking

Italian, who neither sang nor played, and of whom Frances affirmed that he had "tout l'air d'un conspirateur."

What English guests Hunsden invites, are all either men of Birmingham or Manchester—hard men, seemingly knit up in one thought, whose talk is of free trade. The foreign visitors, too, are politicians; they take a wider theme—European progress—the spread of liberal sentiments over the Continent; on their mental tablets, the names of Russia, Austria, and the Pope, are inscribed in red ink. I have heard some of them talk vigorous sense—yea, I have been present at polyglot discussions in the old, oak-lined dining-room at Hunsden Wood, where a singular insight was given of the sentiments entertained by resolute minds respecting old northern despotisms, and old southern superstitions: also, I have heard much twaddle, enounced chiefly in French and Deutsch, but let that pass. Hunsden himself tolerated the drivelling theorists; with the practical men he seemed leagued hand and heart.

When Hunsden is staying alone at the Wood (which seldom happens) he generally finds his way two or three times a week to Daisy Lane. He has a philanthropic motive for coming to smoke his cigar in our porch on summer evenings; he says he does it to kill the earwigs amongst the roses, with which insects, but for his benevolent fumigations, he intimates we should certainly be overrun. On wet days, too, we are almost sure to see him; according to him, it gets on time to work me into lunacy by treading on my mental corns, or to force from Mrs. Crimsworth revelations of the dragon within her, by insulting the memory of Hofer and Tell.

We also go frequently to Hunsden Wood, and both I and Frances relish a visit there highly. If there are other guests, their characters are an interesting study; their conversation is exciting and strange; the absence of all local narrowness both in the host and his chosen society gives a metropolitan, almost a cosmopolitan freedom and largeness to the talk. Hunsden himself is a polite man in his own house: he has, when he chooses to employ it, an inexhaustible power of entertaining guests; his very mansion too is interesting, the rooms look storied, the passages legendary, the low-ceiled chambers, with their long rows of diamond-paned lattices, have an old-world, haunted air: in his travels he has collected stores of articles of VERTU, which are well and tastefully disposed in his panelled or tapestried rooms: I have seen there one or two pictures, and one or two pieces of statuary which many an aristocratic connoisseur might have envied.

When I and Frances have dined and spent an evening with Hunsden, he often walks home with us. His wood is large, and some of the timber is old and of huge growth. There are winding ways in it which, pursued through glade and brake, make the walk back to Daisy Lane a somewhat long one. Many a time, when we have had the benefit of a full moon, and when the night has been mild and balmy, when, moreover, a certain nightingale has been singing, and a certain stream, hid in alders, has lent the song a soft accompaniment, the remote church-bell of the one hamlet in a district of ten miles, has tolled midnight ere the lord of the wood left us at our porch. Free-flowing was his talk at such hours, and far more quiet and gentle than in the day-time and before numbers. He would then forget politics and discussion, and would dwell on the past times of his house, on his family history, on himself and his own feelings—subjects each and all invested with a peculiar zest, for they were each and all unique. One glorious night in June, after I had been taunting him about his ideal bride and asking him when she would come and graft her foreign beauty on the old Hunsden oak, he answered suddenly—

"You call her ideal; but see, here is her shadow; and there cannot be a shadow without a substance."

He had led us from the depth of the "winding way" into a glade from whence the beeches withdrew, leaving it open to the sky; an unclouded moon poured her light into this glade, and Hunsden held out under her beam an ivory miniature.

Frances, with eagerness, examined it first; then she gave it to me—still, however, pushing her little face close to mine, and seeking in my eyes what I thought of the portrait. I thought it represented a very handsome and very individual-looking female face, with, as he had once said, "straight and harmonious features." It was dark; the hair, raven-black, swept not only from the brow, but from the temples—seemed thrust away carelessly, as if such beauty dispensed with, nay, despised arrangement. The Italian eye looked straight into you, and an independent, determined eye it was; the mouth was as firm as fine; the chin ditto. On the back of the miniature was gilded "Lucia."

"That is a real head," was my conclusion.

Hunsden smiled.

"I think so," he replied. "All was real in Lucia."

"And she was somebody you would have liked to marry—but could not?"

"I should certainly have liked to marry her, and that I HAVE not done so is a proof that I COULD not."

He repossessed himself of the miniature, now again in Frances' hand, and put it away.

"What do YOU think of it?" he asked of my wife, as he buttoned his coat over it.

"I am sure Lucia once wore chains and broke them," was the strange answer. "I do not mean matrimonial chains," she added, correcting herself, as if she feared mis-interpretation, "but social chains of some sort. The face is that of one who has made an effort, and a successful and triumphant effort, to wrest some vigorous and valued faculty from insupportable constraint; and when Lucia's faculty got free, I am certain it spread wide pinions and carried her higher than—" she hesitated.

"Than what?" demanded Hunsden.

"Than 'les convenances' permitted you to follow."

"I think you grow spiteful—impertinent."

"Lucia has trodden the stage," continued Frances. "You never seriously thought of marrying her; you admired her originality, her fearlessness, her energy of body and mind; you delighted in her talent, whatever that was, whether song, dance, or dramatic representation; you worshipped her beauty, which was of the sort after your own heart: but I am sure she filled a sphere from whence you would never have thought of taking a wife."

"Ingenious," remarked Hunsden; "whether true or not is another question. Meantime, don't you feel your little lamp of a spirit wax very pale, beside such a girandole as Lucia's?"

"Yes."

"Candid, at least; and the Professor will soon be dissatisfied with the dim light you give?"

"Will you, monsieur?"

"My sight was always too weak to endure a blaze, Frances," and we had now reached the wicket.

I said, a few pages back, that this is a sweet summer evening; it is—there has been a series of lovely days, and this is the loveliest; the hay is just carried from my fields, its perfume still lingers in the air. Frances proposed to me, an hour or two since, to take tea out on the lawn; I see the round table, loaded with china, placed under a certain beech; Hunsden is expected—nay, I hear he is come—there is his voice, laying down the law on some point with authority; that of Frances replies; she opposes him of course. They are disputing about Victor, of whom Hunsden affirms that his mother is making a milksop. Mrs. Crimsworth retaliates:—

"Better a thousand times he should be a milksop than what he, Hunsden, calls 'a fine lad;' and moreover she says that if Hunsden were to become a fixture in the neighbourhood, and were not a mere comet, coming and going, no one knows how, when, where, or why, she should be quite uneasy till she had got Victor away to a school at least a hundred miles off; for that with his mutinous maxims and unpractical dogmas, he would ruin a score of children."

I have a word to say of Victor ere I shut this manuscript in my desk—but it must be a brief one, for I hear the tinkle of silver on porcelain.

Victor is as little of a pretty child as I am of a handsome man, or his mother of a fine woman; he is pale and spare, with large eyes, as dark as those of Frances, and as deeply set as mine. His shape is symmetrical enough, but slight; his health is good. I never saw a child smile less than he does, nor one who knits such a formidable brow when sitting over a book that interests him, or while listening to tales of adventure, peril, or wonder, narrated by his mother, Hunsden, or myself. But though still, he is not unhappy—though serious, not morose; he has a susceptibility to pleasurable sensations almost too keen, for it amounts to enthusiasm. He learned to read in the old-fashioned way out of a spelling-book at his mother's knee, and as he got on without driving by that method, she thought it unnecessary to buy him ivory letters, or to try any of the other inducements to learning now deemed indispensable. When he could read, he became a glutton of books, and is so still. His toys have been few, and he has never wanted more. For those he possesses, he seems to have contracted a partiality amounting to affection; this feeling, directed towards one or two living animals of the house, strengthens almost to a passion.

Mr. Hunsden gave him a mastiff cub, which he called Yorke, after the donor; it grew to a superb dog, whose fierceness, however, was much modified by the companionship and caresses of its young master. He would go nowhere, do nothing without Yorke; Yorke lay at his feet while he learned his lessons, played with him in the garden, walked with him in the lane and wood, sat near his chair at meals, was fed always by his own hand, was the first thing he sought in the morning, the last he left at night. Yorke accompanied Mr. Hunsden one day to X——, and was bitten in the street by a dog in a rabid state. As soon as Hunsden had brought him home, and had informed me of the circumstance, I went into the yard and shot him where he lay licking his wound: he was dead in an instant; he had not seen me level the gun; I stood behind him. I had scarcely been ten minutes in the house, when my ear was struck with sounds of anguish: I repaired to the yard once more, for they proceeded thence. Victor was kneeling beside his dead mastiff, bent over it, embracing its bull-like neck, and lost in a passion of the wildest woe: he saw me.

"Oh, papa, I'll never forgive you! I'll never forgive you!" was his exclamation. "You shot Yorke—I saw it from the window. I never believed you could be so cruel—I can love you no more!"

I had much ado to explain to him, with a steady voice, the stern necessity of the deed; he still, with that inconsolable and bitter accent which I cannot render, but which pierced my heart, repeated—

"He might have been cured—you should have tried—you should have burnt the wound with a hot iron, or covered it with caustic. You gave no time; and now it is too late—he is dead!"

He sank fairly down on the senseless carcase; I waited patiently a long while, till his grief had somewhat exhausted him; and then I lifted him in my arms and carried him to his mother, sure that she would comfort him best. She had witnessed the whole scene from a window; she would not come out for fear of increasing my difficulties by her emotion, but she was ready now to receive him. She took him to her kind heart, and on to her gentle lap; consoled him but with her lips, her eyes, her soft embrace, for some time; and then, when his sobs diminished, told him that Yorke had felt no pain in dying, and that if he had been left to expire naturally, his end would have been most horrible; above all, she told him that I was not cruel (for that idea seemed to give exquisite pain to poor Victor), that it was my affection for Yorke and him which had made me act so, and that I was now almost heart-broken to see him weep thus bitterly.

Victor would have been no true son of his father, had these considerations, these reasons, breathed in so low, so sweet a tone—married to caresses so benign, so tender—to looks so inspired with pitying sympathy—produced no effect on him. They did produce an effect: he grew calmer, rested his face on her shoulder, and lay still in her arms. Looking up, shortly, he asked his mother to tell him over again what she had said about Yorke having suffered no pain, and my not being cruel; the balmy words being repeated, he again pillowed his cheek on her breast, and was again tranquil.

Some hours after, he came to me in my library, asked if I forgave him, and desired to be reconciled. I drew the lad to my side, and there I kept him a good while, and had much talk with him, in the course of which he disclosed many points of feeling and thought I approved of in my son. I found, it is true, few elements of the "good fellow" or the "fine fellow" in him; scant sparkles of the spirit which loves to flash over the wine cup, or which kindles the passions to a destroying fire; but I saw in the soil of his heart healthy and swelling germs of compassion, affection, fidelity. I discovered in the garden of his intellect a rich growth of wholesome principles—reason, justice, moral courage, promised, if not blighted, a fertile bearing. So I bestowed on his large forehead, and on his cheek—still pale with tears—a proud and contented kiss, and sent him away comforted. Yet I saw him the next day laid on the mound under which Yorke had been buried, his face covered with his hands; he was melancholy for some weeks, and more than a year elapsed before he would listen to any proposal of having another dog.

Victor learns fast. He must soon go to Eton, where, I suspect, his first year or two will be utter wretchedness: to leave me, his mother, and his home, will give his heart an agonized wrench; then, the fagging will not suit him—but emulation, thirst after knowledge, the glory of success, will stir and reward him in time. Meantime, I feel in myself a strong repugnance to fix the hour which will uproot my sole olive branch, and transplant it far from me; and, when I speak to Frances on the subject, I am heard with a kind of patient pain, as though I alluded to some fearful operation, at which her nature shudders, but from which her fortitude will not permit her to recoil. The step must, however, be taken, and it shall be; for, though Frances will not make a milksop of her son, she will accustom him to a style of treatment, a forbearance, a congenial tenderness, he will meet with from none else. She sees, as I also see, a something in Victor's temper—a kind of electrical ardour and power—which emits, now and then, ominous sparks; Hunsden calls it his spirit, and says it should not be curbed. I call it the leaven of the offending Adam, and consider that it should be, if not WHIPPED out of him, at least soundly disciplined; and that he will be cheap of any amount of either bodily or mental suffering which will ground him radically in the art of self-control. Frances gives this something in her son's marked character no name; but when it appears in the grinding of his teeth, in the glittering of his eye, in the fierce revolt of feeling against disappointment, mischance, sudden sorrow, or supposed injustice, she folds him to her breast, or takes him to walk with her alone in the wood; then she reasons with him like any philosopher, and to reason Victor is ever accessible; then she looks at him with eyes of love, and by love Victor can be infallibly subjugated; but will reason or love be the weapons with which in future the world will meet his violence? Oh, no! for that flash in his black eye —for that cloud on his bony brow—for that compression of his statuesque lips, the lad will some day get blows instead of blandishments—kicks instead of kisses; then for the fit of mute fury which will sicken his body and madden his soul; then for the ordeal of merited and salutary suffering, out of which he will come (I trust) a wiser and a better man.

I see him now; he stands by Hunsden, who is seated on the lawn under the beech; Hunsden's hand rests on the boy's collar, and he is instilling God knows what principles into his ear. Victor looks well just now, for he listens with a sort of smiling interest; he never looks so like his mother as when he smiles—pity the sunshine breaks out so rarely! Victor has a preference for Hunsden, full as strong as I deem desirable, being considerably more potent, decided, and indiscriminating, than any I ever entertained for that personage myself. Frances, too, regards it with a sort of unexpressed anxiety; while her son leans on Hunsden's knee, or rests against his shoulder, she roves with restless movement round, like a dove guarding its young from a hovering hawk; she says she wishes Hunsden had children of his own, for then he would better know the danger of inciting their pride end indulging their foibles.

Frances approaches my library window; puts aside the honeysuckle which half covers it, and tells me tea is ready; seeing that I continue busy she enters the room, comes near me quietly, and puts her hand on my shoulder.

"Monsieur est trop applique."

"I shall soon have done."

She draws a chair near, and sits down to wait till I have finished; her presence is as pleasant to my mind as the perfume of the fresh hay and spicy flowers, as the glow of the westering sun, as the repose of the midsummer eve are to my senses.

But Hunsden comes; I hear his step, and there he is, bending through the lattice, from which he has thrust away the woodbine with unsparing hand, disturbing two bees and a butterfly.

"Crimsworth! I say, Crimsworth! take that pen out of his hand, mistress, and make him lift up his head."

"Well, Hunsden? I hear you—"

"I was at X—— yesterday! your brother Ned is getting richer than Croesus by railway speculations; they call him in the Piece Hall a stag of ten; and I have heard from Brown. M. and Madame Vandenhuten and Jean Baptiste talk of coming to see you next month. He mentions the Pelets too; he says their domestic harmony is not the finest in the world, but in business they are doing 'on ne peut mieux,' which circumstance he concludes will be a sufficient consolation to both for any little crosses in the affections. Why don't you invite the Pelets to ——shire, Crimsworth? I should so like to see your first flame, Zoraide. Mistress, don't be jealous, but he loved that lady to distraction; I know it for a fact. Brown says she weighs twelve stones now; you see what you've lost, Mr. Professor. Now, Monsieur and Madame, if you don't come to tea, Victor and I will begin without you."

"Papa, come!"

Milton Keynes UK
Ingram Content Group UK Ltd.
UKHW051620020624
443378UK00024B/566

The Way to (o) Weard

A Musical Memoir of (not) growing up in the Sixties (or since)

ROY WEARD

Typeset by Jonathan Downes, Jessica Taylor
Nosferatu cover image by Tony Bowall
Live cover image by Maureen Essex
Cover and Layout by SPiderKaT for CFZ Communications
Using Microsoft Word 2000, Microsoft Publisher 2000, Adobe Photoshop CS.

First published in Great Britain by Gonzo Multimedia

c/o Brooks City,
6th Floor New Baltic House
65 Fenchurch Street,
London EC3M 4BE
Fax: +44 (0)191 5121104
Tel: +44 (0) 191 5849144
International Numbers:
Germany: Freephone 08000 825 699

© Gonzo Multimedia MMXV

ISBN: 978-1-908728-45-6

Dedication

Dedicated to all the people I have known, played music with and loved/been loved by through all these years but especially to:

My children, Jemima Harrison and Tim Wood,
Julia Wesnigk-Wood and Barbara Wesnigk-Wood
Their mothers, Valerie Graves (who sadly died just
as I was finishing this) and Saskia Wesnigk-Wood
My brothers Norman and Rick Wood, and the memory of my
wonderful mother.

And some other very important people:

Andrea Bach, Steve Wollington, Mous, Tony Morley, John
Trelawney, Alan Essex, and the cast and crew of my life...roll on
the movie!

Preface

I would not have even started to write this had it not been for the pestering of my friend Darren Brannagh with whom I shared many alcoholic beverages on my visits to Ireland and who was on the receiving end of far too many rock and roll tales. The idea lodged in my head and gradually pushed me towards writing it down.

When I started I was encouraged by my wife Saskia, and by my long time friend Andrea Bach. I think I might have stalled a few times had it not been for them. I was further assisted by my equally long term friend Steve Wollington, who was a stalwart roadie through many years of *Wooden Lion/Dogwatch/Last Post* and finally *That Legendary Wooden Lion* again, and who came out on the road with me on many tours. I needed his powers of recall to help straighten out a few kinks in my own memory.

I have tried, in writing this, to be as truthful as my mind will let me. I have also tried not to offend anyone (well not many anyway). Some of it deals with my early attempts at rock and roll immortality but most of this concerns the crews I worked with rather than the famous bands – there are enough people writing about them anyway. Road crews are a special bunch of people in almost every stretch of the word. Many of the people I shared hotels, stages, cars, minibuses and sleeper coaches with were great fun to be with and I can recall only a couple of tours when I would not miss their company after we parted. My thanks to you all.

Finally, I would like to say, my decision to push through this and write it all down is to leave something for my children. My own father spoke little of his childhood or of his life before becoming my Dad. He communicated very little of himself and that aspect of him, in turn, passed to his children. I have in no way been an angel in this life and, I hope, I fully admit my own selfishness and weaknesses in these pages too. In the end most people's lives are a series of errors held together with love.

Tres Amigos - me, Ricky and Norman back in the 50s,
I was even dressing up back then too.

CHAPTER 1

And so it starts...

I blame my aunt and uncle and the epidemic of polio that swept through England in the early 50s. Had it not been for these people and things I may have grown up to have a normal life, working in an office or in a chemical laboratory. As it was, I didn't. So I blame those three factors for deviating me from the course of normality – and I thank them for that deviation, from the depths of my existence.

My mother and father were of normal East End stock. My mother was born Dorothy May Boden in Poplar, in the heart of 'Cockneyland' in 1920. She worked as a secretary for Johnson Matthey, dealers in gold and jewellery in the city, and she married my father, Frederick William James Wood during the height of the war. She said to me much later in her life that she married him because she did not expect him to come back from the war. To me, someone whose entire life has been lived in relative peace time (at least the wars were on someone else's land and so anonymous and removed from my childhood.), that seems an odd decision but those were special times and death and destruction lurked everywhere.

I was born in 1948. The eldest of three brothers, Norman was born in 1950 and Eric in 1952. By that time the family have moved out of the ruins of the East End of London and been re-housed in Essex. My earliest recollections were a flat in Green Lanes, Dagenham and then moving onto the vast sprawling Dagenham council estate that sat, like a brick desert between the 'nice' houses of Barking (at the time a gentle and rather genteel, suburban town and not the home of National Front style right wing extremism it is today) and the marshes of Rainham.

My father worked at Fords after he left the Navy – practically everyone on that estate did, and those that didn't were in the service industries that clustered around it like so many sucker fish. We moved to Becontree at first and then to a three bedroom house, in a roadless cul-de-sac that the locals called a 'banjo'. It is still there, only now its ruthless, almost Eastern bloc conformity, has been broken by Thatcher's sell off of the council estates. Back in those days armies of painters would sweep through the streets at intervals painting front doors in alternating red / green / black sequences, painting window frames white, small crooked rollup behind one ear and a pencil behind the other. Now that uniformity has been replaced by stone cladding, fake leaded windows and all manner of architectural excess.

Everyone smoked in those days. My childhood was spent in a fog of cigarette smoke in the house and a smog of coal fired 'Gor blimey guv it's a real pea souper' outside. But that was the 50s. I was the eldest of three children, all two years apart. I was born in Upney Hospital, but the other two were born at home. My father was on endless shift work and on the weeks when he 'worked nights' we had to creep around the house after school so as not to wake him. Not that that was hard. We had no radio in our house and TV did not start till after 6pm when he would wake and have food with us before leaving for work.

So, there we were, a fairly typical working class family. My aunt and uncle lived in the same 'banjo' as us – in a ground floor flat at the far end and my grandfather lived above them so we had this tight family group. In and out of each other's houses all the time, and this is where my three factors came into play.

When I was six and my brother, Norman, was four, he went into hospital for a routine removal of a cyst. The boy in the next bed died of polio while he was in there and my brother contracted the disease. They sent him home and said he had a cold and was a bit drowsy. My mother did not like this and called our family physician, a loud Irish doctor called Murphy. I can remember hearing him pronounce that 'this child has to be taken back to hospital', and all chaos ensued. I don't recall too much more of this but somehow Norman was whisked off to hospital when he quickly deteriorated. Polio is a vicious disease that causes carnage in the muscles and, if untreated, paralyses the lung muscles, causing death. Norman fought it back, with the aid of the doctors but was very ill. Eric, my youngest brother was barely two at the time so my mother took him everywhere with her. I was six, as I said, and I went to stay with my aunt – all the way over the banjo.

My aunt was my mother's sister and had married another naval man. My Uncle George, had been an engineer in the Merchant Navy. They were childless, I never found out if it was choice or not, and they adopted me as a part-time son. Their house was a revelation when I first went there, before all the drama happened, and now I was living in it for a few weeks. She had a radiogram! A giant piece of furniture that housed a radio and a record player, and she had a piano, which she played on occasion. They also had books. Story books, picture books about the Great Exhibition, encyclopaedias, all sorts. There were few books in my house.

I devoured all this and especially the music. Her record collection was small but varied. 'Living Doll', 'Seven Little Girls, Sitting in the Back Seat', 'Mack the Knife', on the one side and Grieg's Piano Concerto, Beethoven, Tchaikovsky and all manner of other classical music on the other with a sprinkling of 'My Fair Lady' and 'The King and I'. I listened to it all. When we played 'Istanbul, not Constantinople' by Frankie Vaughan, I used to put on my uncle's old coat and trilby hat and he and I would walk around the sofa in time with the music.

I cannot, for the life of me, recall why after all these years, but I think it set some sort of seal on what followed.

Apart from the records, we listened to the Home Service and all those comedy shows. 'The Goons', 'Life of Bliss', 'The Navy Lark', Hancock's Half Hour', Round The Horne' - all that wonderful comedy. I think this also set some sort of cast on my young mind. My mother was pretty tied up dealing with Norman and toting a two year old around with her. We did not have a car in those days and my mother was never allowed to learn to drive. My father was pretty authoritarian and I think that he resented my spending so much time with my aunt and uncle, filling my head with all this arty stuff. They took me to the theatre, to classical concerts, all over the place. I was mad keen on Spaceflight so they took me to a lecture on Space Travel at the Royal Academy.

Norman had, by this time, been moved from the hospital to a 'home' in Barnet. These were harsher times, you must remember. There was no P.C. 'mobility challenged', 'disabled' vocabulary to cover this situation. The country was awash with people back from the war, with missing limbs, damaged lungs, and ruined minds. They were just crippled. The polio virus had done its work. My mother was told, 'This is it. He will never walk again. You may as well leave him here with us.' Cue big red flapping thing to a female bull. She was having none of this. 'He is coming home', she said, 'and he will walk again', and home he came. Of course this was not an overnight thing and so I got to spend many weekends with my Aunt and Uncle absorbing all that other culture. Even when my brother came home I spent weekends with them. My mother had a lot to cope with. Norman was in a wheel chair at first but she was determined he would walk. She got them to provide callipers to fit to his legs to give him back some sort of rigidity, and she rigged a line that ran the length of the garden so he could hold onto something. Then she tempted him into walking, luring him on with small chipolata sausages, which were his favourite food then. Step by painful step he began to walk. Her belief and his determination conquered the weakness of his legs and he began to walk.

My mother had a bit of education, and was determined that her three sons would have a chance at that too. Primary school and Junior schools came and went and then I hit the 11-plus exam. Crossroads on the educational roadmap of the time. I failed, but only just, and my mother fought tooth and nail to get me into a better school than the 'oiks academy' down the road; the aptly named Erkewald Senior School. In the end she got me into Park Modern Secondary School and I had a daily trip through Mayesbrook Park, to and from school. In the winter it was pretty much the 'pea souper' described above. A phalanx of children coughing their way through the smog like an image of some WW1 infantry. Marching off to get an education... or not.

Park Modern Secondary School was where it began to change for me. I arrived, a small, skinny child with hair Brylcreemed into a quiff, just like my father's, in 1960. Pop music was beginning to become a 'big thing' but I was steeped in deeper stuff. Right from the start I was listening to symphonies, going to the theatre with my aunt and uncle, and I had acquired a huge radio of my own. A radio, with great big, glowing, valves inside, and that musty smell of cooked dust and static electricity. It had all those exotic names on the dial. Hilversum,

Athlone, Luxembourg, and Lille are the ones that spring to mind. That radio opened my mind to the world. I listened to science fiction, to Dylan Thomas, to comedy, to the spoken word. Between my aunt and uncle, the polio virus and the BBC Home Service I was awash with the world.

Sports were a problem for me. I could see no point in being the fastest to run round a track, no point in carrying a ball to a touchline (we played rugby there – in later life I met a fanatical Welsh rugby supporter and I had to say, 'I don't see the point in this. When my children fight over a ball I take it away from them.' – he was bemused). My father tried to introduce me to football and took me to a match. I was cold and bored and never went again. I found all those people roaring at someone kicking a ball incomprehensible. Why did it matter so much? I did enjoy cricket. I liked bowling, and cricket was the only sport I ever made any effort to be part of. I always saw it as chess with human beings and balls and it was so wonderfully English. My uncle used to listen to the Test Match commentary on the radio in the summer and I often listened with him, all those magical names - Truman, Cowdery, Boycott - some of whom you still hear on the Test Match Special today. Geoff Boycott always seems about to break into that Monty Python sketch, 'In my day we used to live in a box in't middle of road, get up three hours before we went to bed.......bloody marvellous'

I was really into the Englishness thing. While those around me deployed the glottal stop, missed the letter 'h' from the front of words and the letter 'g' from the ends I travelled in the opposite direction. I was trying to emulate the clipped pronunciation of the BBC announcers or the avuncular tones of Kenneth Horne. Apart from that, all that business of littering your sentences with swear words was also a bit of an anathema. You can image how all of this combined to make me the target of some ridicule at school but that pushed me more in that direction. I decided to use that ridicule and became the class clown. Always the one to get into trouble, messing about, pulling practical jokes. This rapidly turned into a concept of writing comedy sketches.

By 1963 everyone was well into the pop phenomena. I had become friends with another lad in my class called Brian Sanis, and we went off to concerts at the Festival Hall. Dressed in suits and ties we attended all manner of orchestral works but my tastes were leaning towards Shostakovich, Stravinsky, Mahler, Prokofiev, Khachaturian and other such composers. Most pop music bored me and, since we now had a radiogram at home, I would often come back from school and put on some of the classical records I had accumulated.

My other friend at school was Robert Milne and we used to get together and do little comedy shows – for our own consumption mostly, although we did invite a few people round to Rob's house and put a bit of a show on. One of us, Brian I think, had a tape recorder, a big reel to reel thing, and we recorded some of it on that. Rob's father played accordion in an Irish Showband at the time and when he found out about the tape recorder he insisted we recorded him playing. The family originated from Aberdeen and he was, certainly to me, an archetype. We set up the tape player in Rob's kitchen and he played 'A Thousand Pipers an o'er' – seemingly endlessly I recall. They told me that the singer in the band was a fanatical Jim Reeves fan and one night, a St Patrick's night dance in the local Irish Club, the compère walked on stage and said, 'And now, songs from six feet under. It's a Jim Reeves number'. At which point the singer stood up and knocked him out. A mass brawl ensued and the evening was broken up by the police.

I was the first of the bunch to pass the driving test, although we were all taking lessons. Shortly before Rob's test, we were going out for the night and I suggested that he drove while I was 'qualified driver'. We backed Rob's car out of his garage, I put my one in its place, and we went out. When we came back I was getting my car from the garage when Rob's father appeared, complete with long nightgown and hat, shouting at me, 'Do you think us Scots are stupid? You canna put yer car in our garage!'. A memory that has always stayed with me.

My two brothers were of a more normal bent and they would watch 'Top Of The Pops' and 'Ready, Steady, Go' but I just couldn't get into it. Norman decided to learn to play the guitar at this point and so my mother started to look for a guitar teacher. Pivotal point for me.

There was this girl..............well, there always is, isn't there? Sheila Harrigan was her name. She was small, dark haired and beautiful, and I had a complete crush on her. I was a young, naive 16 year old. I had no idea how to get a conversation started. I was writing poetry by this time. Shakespearean style sonnets which I transcribed, in Old English typefaces, by hand, using a calligraphic pen. I still have some of it here. I even wrote an acrostic, which is where you start each line with a letter which spells out a word when read downwards. Mine spelled out her name. God, I was gone. I was, in fact, so far gone that I even showed the poems to our Biology teacher, Miss Dove; telling that. She was the class head for the class that Sheila was in and was regarded as a fearful harridan by most of the school. An example of reverse nominative determinism.

Anyhow I knew that Sheila liked acoustic guitar music, classical and Spanish. So I decided I would learn to play guitar too. I bought a nylon strung guitar and headed off to the same teacher as my brother and that was where it all started.

Singing in a folk club with Sheila Harrigan

CHAPTER 2
Striking a Chord

The music teacher lived in Seven Kings, a small area just east of Ilford and my mother ferried us over there once a week. I soon learned that this was no great classical tutor I was going to. He gave me a couple of chords to learn, showed me some music and got me to pick out the notes from 'September In The Rain'. This was not going to be the great display of musical prowess that would have Sheila sighing and wanting to be by my side. Apart from that, it was *so* slow. Weeks dragged by and still my fingers refused to go where I wanted them to and I could barely play that bloody 'September' song - which is up on my list of most hated songs along with 'Free Bird' by *Lynyrd Skynyrd* (I will come back to that later).

Outside of the musical world things were changing, and so was I. My reading had led me to more radical stuff and I began thinking about politics. My mother was always a Conservative voter and my Father, holding true to his working class roots and union membership, staunch Labour. I began to read about Communism, Anarchy and all that. I was also being drawn toward the burgeoning folk music scene. Dylan was singing about war and my thoughts were leaning the same way. I also realised that I did not need to play 'September'. The few chords I had would do me for folk music.

So swift left turn, ditch the Brylcreem and start learning some folk songs then. Ditching the oil slick on my head had one, unfortunate, side effect. Our class teacher was called Mr Waterson and, like many of the teachers in the school, he used to walk around the class dishing out occasional physical attacks on the pupils. His favourite method was to come up behind you and clout you across the back of the head with a book. The first time he did it to me my head left a sizeable Torrey Canyon slick of Brylcreem on the tome. He did not repeat that process from then on – until I discontinued hair treatment, whereupon he launched back into it with gusto. 'You are a Nemesis, Wood', he used to say.

Many of the teachers were quite used to this casual violence as a means of keeping discipline. Our music teacher ran an after-school club that I attended and we played records and talked about music; mostly classical, but some jazz and some pop. When he caught us doing something wrong one day, I can't recall what it was, he lined us all up and went along the line delivering a sharp punch to the sternum, thus removing our breath. He was later dismissed for sexually assaulting one of the more precocious and developed girls in our class. I suspect she led him on because she did that a lot to some of the boys in our class. We were never told the details. Our metalwork teacher was also as mad as they come and was prone to hurling lumps of metal at pupils if he thought their work was shoddy, shouting, 'This is rubbish, boy'. At least once a week he would drive into the school playground and crash his car into one of the gates. He would look at it, go into the school and re-appear with a hammer so he could knock the dent out.

Anyhow, the change of hairstyle and folk guitar playing had given me more confidence and I took my chance and asked Sheila out – and it worked! I had a girlfriend. Not only did she come out with me but she also sang with me and we began to play at local folk clubs. I did a lot of standard folk tunes back then. Phil Ochs protest songs, Tom Paxton and all that stuff, both with Sheila and on my own. I started going on CND marches and embracing that whole left wing folk culture

My family did not want me to stay on at school, so I left at 16 and got a job in the laboratories at May and Baker's chemical factory in Dagenham East. When I went for the interview, straight from school, I was led into a room and confronted by three middle-aged men in blazers and ties. I was, of course, also wearing a suit and tie. After a round of questions about my academic qualifications and such like one of them asked, 'Is there any other job you had considered doing?' (Presumably to test my level of dedication to being a lab rat with a white coat on). 'Yes', I replied, 'I would have liked to have been a comedian'. The look of disgust and incredulity that crossed their faces was priceless. By this time I had passed my driving test and Sheila and I were driving out into the countryside for some sweaty groping. Never anything else. Breasts were fondled, lots of kissing happened but, apart from that, no direct sexual contact was made. There was that exciting area of flesh between the stockings and the forbidden area of the groin, but that was it. Still it was exciting in that seventeen year old way.

The factory sent me on Day-Release to Rush Green Technical College to study for, what we would these days call, a Non Vocational Qualification as a laboratory technician and analyst. Among the other pupils in that class was a guy called Roger who also played acoustic guitar. The pair of us decided we would try to put a folk club together in the college. Roger had a little duo and his musical partner was a guy called Richard Digance. Richard came along to play at one of these gigs and we became friends. He was moving up in the world, getting better gigs (which, in those days, meant actually being asked to come and play instead of just turning up, doe-eyed and trying to get in for free if you did a couple of songs). He had a great guitar style, complex but relaxed somehow, and he had a good line in between-songs patter. I was still awkward, trying to fit some of my songs in, but sort of knowing they were not good enough and falling back on more standard fare.

I went to a lot of gigs with Richard in those years and, once again, wound up as the qualified driver when he drove to a few shows before he passed his test. He had a battered Renault Dauphin in which we travelled to a gig in Reigate. Part of the way there it started to snow. 'Shit!', he said, 'The windscreen wipers don't work.' We stopped the car and I attached a piece of string to each wiper and then fed it through the quarterlights in the front doors. I then proceeded to pull the wipers back and forth while he drove to the gig.

Then John Martyn made an appearance. He knew Richard from a while ago and had been staying at the row of cottages owned by *The Incredible String Band*, up in Scotland. His album, 'London Conversations', had just been released so he was travelling around doing gigs. At the time he was pretty wild and wired. I knew little about drugs then, but folk music was slowly sliding into a new scene and people were drifting off to become hippies.

1965 had seen the release of Rubber Soul and the sitar had made an appearance on the scene. This fascinated many musicians because of its strange sound and alien note interval. Ravi Shankar, widely regarded as the Indian 'Sitar Hero', began to appear in folk venues. I remember seeing him at the Hermit Club in Brentwood, supported by Bert Jansch and John Renbourne who both sat, wide-eyed, at the side of the stage while he played.

Many of the folk musicians I knew then smoked dope but, since I did not even smoke cigarettes at the time, I had never partaken. John Martyn, however, went for everything in a big way. I was at one gig with him in Ilford. There was a pub there called *The General Havelock* and, once a month the upstairs room was the venue for 'The Toad Hall Folk Club'. I first started going to the club a year or so before, when it was held at the *Railway Arms* in West Ham, but they had to relocate to Ilford High Road. John took to the stage and began to play, and play and play. He didn't stop. Songs flowed into other songs for well over an hour. Suddenly he stopped playing and looked up in surprise as if seeing the audience for the first time. The hall broke into cheers and applause and he wandered off the stage. He came up to Richard and I and said, 'That was weird. I took a tab of acid before I went on and I was playing one song and I thought, oh, that bit sounds like..... so I played that and then that sounded like....' He shook his head, put his guitar down and went downstairs.

A few moments later there were shouts coming from downstairs. We went to investigate and found John in a full on fight with the barman. It seems that the barman, who was very overtly gay, had tried to 'pull' John, who objected violently. Still that was John. Always unpredictable and capable of going from spaced hippy to street fighting man at the drop of.....well anything really.

Years later when I was tour managing Donovan, we went up to Glasgow to do a gig at the festival. Don flew in from Ireland where he was living, and I flew up from London to meet him. There was a bit of confusion about what flights we were on, but we met up in the end. We were supposed to meet a journalist from the *Glasgow Herald* at the airport to give an interview but we could not find him and headed off to the hotel. When we arrived at the hotel the journalist was waiting there. Don sat down to do his interview in the foyer, and I checked us in. As I was doing this, a call came in from Don's agent, Steve Mather, who was also handling John Martyn. The receptionist spoke to him for a while and then said, 'yes, they are here, they have just arrived. I'll ask them'. She turned to us and said, 'Steve says that John Martyn is staying in the hotel too and was due to leave tomorrow after his show, but they want him to stay another night and do a TV show. We have no rooms available for tomorrow. Would either of you be willing to share a room with John?'. The reply from both Don and I, almost in unison, was an emphatic 'No!'.

The following day the Herald's interview with Don started with the lines, 'There was some confusion with flight information when I went to meet Donovan at the airport and we missed each other. Later, when we met at his hotel, one thing both he and his tour manager were sure about was that neither of them would share a room with John Martyn'.

More and more of the interesting performers were drifting off into electric bands, music got more interesting and I was moving further away from the classical stuff I started out listening to. I had been to see a few pop bands by then. *The Small Faces* performing at a local pub, *The Kinks* at Barking Assembly Hall, *The Rolling Stones* and Dave Berry in a cinema in East Ham, and *The Who* in a gig in Bournemouth when I was on holiday with my parents. Exciting stuff, but not really what I wanted. But then along came Frank Zappa. Freak Out came out in 1966 and that was something which triggered a whole new direction.

CHAPTER 3

Freak Out

After two years at May and Baker I was bored. This was a massive factory that stretched from Dagenham East tube line all the way to the Rainham Marshlands. I worked in a laboratory that ran analysis on intermediate chemicals; things we made, that were used to make other things. The place stank. A horrid chemical smell that wafted around and permeated everything. It did have a couple of good sides to it, though, one being the comical way some of the inhabitants of this malodorous factory took themselves so seriously.

The lab I was in had a commanding view of one of the roads that ran the length of the factory. We were situated opposite the furnace where they disposed of all the more combustible stuff. This was the '60s and recycling then meant going home on your bike. Everything was thrown away.

For some reason we seemed to use a lot of cyanide, I was never sure why. Every day a guy would come round with a trolley with three trays on it. Top tray was for stuff that could be poured down the sink, middle tray was for stuff that had to go to the incinerator and the bottom tray was all the hazardous waste which went to a special disposal centre – probably, in those days, a sink that no one could see that led to the Rainham Marshes. The company was given a sizeable grant to employ disabled people, and the man that wheeled the trolley was someone who had been in a serious road accident and been left with brain damage. Not exactly the ideal choice for that *particular* task as it turned out. He came to our lab and collected some concentrated hydrochloric acid. He then went on to the next lab and collected their waste, and continued doing the rounds until the trolley was full. He would then go down the road to the main lab when he would sort the waste and dispose of all of the harmless stuff before passing the rest on. While I stood at my bench, performing some mindless piece of analysis, I idly watched him go into the lab down the road. Five minutes later everyone left that lab in an extreme hurry. One brave soul raced back into the building and a few seconds later trolley man was dragged out and being resuscitated. Seems he had first poured the waste cyanide into the sink, and followed it with the hydrochloric acid. Instant gas bomb. He survived, but was not employed to do that job again.

May and Baker had its own little fire engine and Trumpton-style fire crew, complete with nice uniforms with rows of shiny buttons. Every week a truck would pull into the factory and back up under the big overhang of the incinerator. Two huge doors would swing open and a load of ash and debris would fall into the truck. One day, when this happened, the ashes were still on fire. Cue the May and Baker Trumpton service. They rattled round the corner on their tiny little antique fire engine and surveyed the burning ashes in the truck. One fireman, dressed in his splendid uniform, got out a step ladder and a large cylinder. A moment later and he was engulfed in white power, a bit like a party in Elton John's dressing room back in the '70s. When the powder died down the immaculate fireman was a statue in white, eyes blinking through the dust at the flames which still burned merrily round the back of the truck. A second fireman climbed the ladder and began to train a hose onto the truck. Lots of steam arose but the flames remained persistent. Sacks were brought and placed over the burning areas – they caught fire. More sacks were brought and doused in water and the rest of the fire crew climbed into the back of the truck and began trampling them down. They retreated when it all got a bit hot, and then gave up and drove the truck, now sporting burning sacks as well as hot ashes, out of the factory. It was that kind of place.

The final straw came when I rolled in one morning, walked round to side of the building and turned on the cylinders that fed the gas chromatograph. The two large cylinders contained hydrogen and oxygen respectively. As I walked up the stairs, I noticed my hands were black and that there was an ominous hissing noise. Then I noticed the wall was black, and the stairs - and that the building that normally stood beside ours was no longer there. It had blown up in the night damaging the pipes from the gas cylinders which were now leaking a dangerous mixture of hydrogen and oxygen into the air. I raced back down the stair and turned them off. 'Time for a new job', I thought. It was a shame to leave there in some ways, because I had a friend in the next lab who was teaching me more guitar chords and finger-picking, but I had to go.

I decided to run my own folk club in a pub at Romford Market. I put on all sorts of acts. *The Young Tradition* did OK there. A bit on the 'finger in the ear'/Widecombe Fair/traditional' side but people liked them. I booked a fledgling Al Stewart; I did not know who he was at the time, but the agency said he had just released an album and was going to be big. I was putting posters up and a young man walked in, clutching a guitar case. 'Are you a floor singer?' I asked. 'I'm Al Stewart' he replied, timidly. I also booked Roy Harper, someone I *did* know, and liked very much. He recounted all sorts of tales about feigning madness to get out of the RAF and almost being sectioned. A great guy and a superb act. There were some seeds of all the future promoting I did in this. The trouble is, I have always been drawn towards booking people I respected, and enjoyed, rather than those that would make money. In later years I would do the same when choosing which acts to tour with (when I got a choice). It did mean I heard and mixed some great music, but it also meant I did not get rich.

I moved on work at Guys Hospital, in a lab called 'The Interdepartmental Research Laboratory'. If you break this down into its component parts it is quite good.

- Inter – in the middle of.
- Depart – leaving.
- Mental – well that is obvious.

It was the laboratory for doing research on people in the middle of leaving their minds. And they were, all of them. It was a madhouse, and I fitted in quite well.

There was a doctor who was working on allergic reactions and who spoke with a sharp nasal twang – an acute case of over-Oxbridgeification, She was my direct superior. There was an Indian doctor from Delhi, who delighted in taking the students who signed on as interns with him to see his 'other' laboratory. He would march them rapidly through the corridors and fling open a set of double doors, beckoning them to follow. It was the dissecting room, and in it were corpses in various stages of dismemberment. He used to bet with the others on how many would faint and how many would throw up. His party trick was to kill the lab rats by letting them run up his arm, grabbing their tails and swinging them in a circle so their necks would break when the hit the table. Professor Nichols, who ran the lab, was a kindly old soul, on the verge of retirement. And then there was Keith, Terry, and the beautiful Jenny, and a few other people whose names I forget.

By this time I was going to the UFO club in the Tottenham Court Road. I knew no-one there but the music was stupendous. All sorts of fascinating bands played there. *Pink Floyd* with Syd Barrett, *Soft Machine*, *The Move*, all kinds of stuff. Lots of drugs going down, but I was still straight as far as that was concerned. Apart from that I was totally into it. I was growing my hair longer, and Sheila was getting fed up with me going out with her on a Friday night, taking her home and going on to UFO for an all-nighter session. I offered to take her too but she would not come. I would get home at 7 or 8 in the morning and sleep through Saturday until the afternoon. She also objected to the hair and clothes which were beginning to be odder. Finally she said, 'Get your hair cut or don't come back' – so I didn't come back. My first love, and it cut me up terribly; but I could sense something else calling to me.

I had made a few attempts at bands by then. The first couple were a bit straight, folky sort of things but I was moving towards an electric band. There was so much music trying to cram itself into my skull at the time. I was flitting between musicians trying to make up a band that would do something. My hair was now getting a bit longer and I was sporting a very wispy beard, dressing in kaftans most of the time. My father was becoming increasingly annoyed at my appearance and coming up with ever more bizarre stories about why I should have a haircut.

UFO had closed by then, thrown out by the Irish Club that had housed it, but a new club beckoned. Middle Earth opened in Covent Garden and I started going there. I must have made a strange figure at the time, dressed in a surgeon's gown decorated with all sorts of odd symbols. But everyone was wearing odd stuff by then. I hooked up with a few people there.

Pete Brown was a friend, although I had no idea at the time he was writing the lyrics for the *Cream* songs. I also knew a couple of American girls who had a flat in Gloucester Terrace, just off Earl's Court Road. Gradually my weekends began to end up there and I wound up sleeping with one of the girls, blundering through my first sexual experience in a room full of people. In the middle of it she shouted to her friend 'Hey, look what we are doing!' She used to get acid shipped over in eye dropper bottles from California and that was my first experience of drugs. She was also into 'skin popping' heroin. I saw the way it knocked her out and decided that was not for me. All sorts of people passed through that flat. Stefan was an effeminate young man who was into speed. He got strung out on it one day and stole a car, and, paranoid about being arrested and trying to get out of London, he raced through the Piccadilly road tunnel scraping the car along the side. He was arrested at the end of the tunnel and went to jail.

Another frequent visitor to the flat was Lemmy. He had just started working with Sam Gopal, playing guitar and doing vocals. He lived in a flat not far away with a guy called Liam. He often wound up at our place, and sometimes did a whole load of 'downers' and passed out on the floor. When this happened Stefan and I used to manhandle him into the car and take him home. One time we just propped him up against the door, rang the doorbell and left as Liam opened the door.

Around Christmas in 1967 I attended the 'Christmas on Earth Continued' all nighter at Earls Court. This featured *The Jimi Hendrix Experience*, Eric Burdon, *Pink Floyd*, *The Move*, *Soft Machine*, *Tomorrow*, *Traffic*, *Graham Bond Organisation*, Sam Gopal, the enigmatically named *Paper Blitz Tissue* and some other acts. I am sure Arthur Brown played there although he is not mentioned on the poster. I went there with two friends; Ian, a banjo player and John a trumpet player. At around 4am they decided they wanted to leave but I was pretty tired. I had not taken any drugs but I wanted to curl up in a corner and get an hour or two's sleep. They were insistent, so we got in my E93A Ford Popular and set off. As we approached South Kensington I nodded off, and I crashed into a lamppost at the point where the road goes around the one-way system. Ian was playing banjo in the back seat of the car. The lamp post fell down across the road. I bit through my lower lip. John crashed into the windscreen. We all got out of the car looking dazed. Ian took one look at me, with blood running down my lip and John with blood on his face and fainted. He was actually unhurt. An off-duty policeman arrived and took charge. First to arrive on the scene was the electricity board to deal with the lamp post. Next up was the police and then, finally, an ambulance to whisk us off to hospital. Ian came round and his first words were, 'Is my banjo OK?'. It was broken but I did not want to tell him. At the hospital they asked if anyone had been unconscious. We said Ian had and they took him off for tests leaving John and I dripping blood onto the floor. Later they took us in and fixed our wounds. It was a day or so before Christmas and there was evidence of a degree of partying going on at the hospital. They tried to stitch my mouth but my tongue got in the way and nearly got stitched to my lip. They took some of the glass from John's face but it was still coming out weeks later. My car was a write-off. They sent us home by train and I can still recall standing at the station waiting for the first train to arrive. I had concussion and was in bed over Christmas, listening to 'Supernatural Fairy Tale' by *Art* (who later became *Spooky Tooth*) and Strange Days by *The Doors*.

20

Stranger than Yesterday

My poetry folder from Middle Earth – decorated by a delightful young woman in the office who called herself 'Ice Cream'

Peta Watson

All this time I was still attending a day release course at the Rush Green College, but I had changed it to an English literature course instead of the Laboratory Technicians one I was supposed to be on. It was there I encountered another pivotal figure. John dealt acid and had an interesting attitude to life. We would take a tab and then go somewhere completely inappropriate.

One of the oddest places was a bar round the back of Park Lane which was packed full of fat German tourists smoking cigars. I remember that the woman behind the bar had boots on that went right up her thighs, and a very short skirt. We were sitting at the bar looking at her and debating if she had leather legs in that acid logic sort of way. We also attended the various free gigs that were going down at the time; the early blossoming of the free festivals. I was at Parliament Hill Fields for the series of free shows there as part of the Camden Festival. The first one, in 1968, was with *Jefferson Airplane* and *Fairport Convention*. They repeated this the following year with three shows. I was standing at the top of the hill having taken a tab of acid, looking down at the crowd; more people than were there for the show the year before. *Pink Floyd* headlined that show with *The Pretty Things*, Roy Harper, *Pete Brown's Battered Ornaments* and Jody Grind (featuring a young Tim Hinkley on keyboards) in support. At one point I thought I saw a park bench floating over the audience. 'Wow, I thought. 'This acid is strong'. Then I realised that it was indeed a park bench being passed hand to hand over the heads of the crowd because it was in the way. It made its way sedately over the assembled hippies and was deposited on the fringe where the people thinned out. The acid was kicking in though and I remember being drawn down into the spiralling light show the Floyd used that night – and someone coming up to me and asking if I had any sausages.

Two other events from those gigs spring to mind. The first was during the one daytime show they put on which featured *Soft Machine*, *The Third Ear Band*, *Yes* and *Blossom Toes*, with *Procol Harum* headlining. I was, once more, tripping, and dark storm clouds began to gather towards the end of the show as *Procol Harum* played. Just as they launched into 'Whiter Shade of Pale' a break in the cloud sent a straight beam of sunlight down to the earth. This made for a pretty dramatic lightshow. It didn't quite alight on the stage, but I recall it being so 'on cue' as to make a large number of people around me gasp. At the very end, just as they finished playing, the storm broke. We had worked our way to the edge of the crowd by then and the multitude made their way towards the small exit gates to the back drop of what was an exceptionally dramatic sky and the beginnings of a vicious hailstorm. I can still remember being reminded of the final scenes in the last of the Narnia books when Aslan is judging the people at the end of the world. All acid-enhanced, of course, it was probably only raining a bit.

When *Fleetwood Mac* played there for the last of the three shows, there was a near riot. All was going well until they launched into 'Albatross', their current hit. A bunch of militant hippies started shouting 'Sell outs!', 'Capitalists!' and throwing drinks cans. The band retreated and their roadie (bands only had one in those days, not a whole army of them – but then they had very little gear to move around anyway) came on and starting shouting over the PA, 'This is the number one band in the fucking country and you are booing them offstage! They are playing for you for free!' Of course this was met with a further hail of missiles and the gig was over.

I was fronting a band called *Stranger than Yesterday* by this time. We lurched between standard fare, versions of 'Summertime', Country Joe's 'Flyin' High', 'Mr Blue' (a Tom Paxton song that was covered by *Clear Light* and whose arrangement we used) and a smattering of self-written songs. We did a few interesting gigs and a lot of scudsy ones but that was the way of things in those days. We supported *The Pretty Things* at Rush Green Technical College and then, later on that year, played with *Pink Floyd* (8/11/1968) at *The Fishmonger's Arms*. All the best stuff eh? It is hard to imagine now, but a lot of the gigs that the bigger bands were doing were just the back rooms of pubs. The Floyd gig was complete chaos.

It did not start well because our drummer was exceptionally nervous. He took some acid, and then a 'downer' to calm down and then thought he was too out of it so did some speed to come back up. By the time we got to the gig he was all over the place. The Floyd had a mountain of equipment and the stage was none too big so we had to squeeze our stuff on wherever we could. This meant that Mick, our drummer, was right in the stage left corner. Not only was he out of it, he couldn't hear much either. At the end of the set Paul, our bass player, poured lighter fuel on his bass and set it on fire. The fuel ran down his arm as he held it aloft and flames began to spring from his bare arm. He threw the burning guitar onto the floor so he could put his arm out and there it set fire to someone's fur coat. Roger Waters came up to me after we had finished playing and said he had lost his guitar strap and could he borrow mine? I leant it to him - and never saw it again. That was pretty much the end of that band. Alan Gray, the other guitarist and singer, was fed up with the way it was going and quit, and after that we all went our separate ways.

Things at the hospital had taken a strange turn. One of the guys who worked there, who went by the name of Keith, became very interested in some of the hippy ideas I was talking about. Keith was very tall, six foot nine at least, and had to bend his head when he went through a door. He and I were asked to go over to the old pathology labs, which were, at the time, being demolished to make way for a new surgical block. The basic remit was to see if there was anything left there that we could use in our lab.

The old block was dark, dusty and deserted. Like many of the old laboratories it had big, lead-topped benches that stretched down the centre of the room. We began opening cupboards and checking to see what was there. There were several shelves and storage spaces under the benches and Keith screwed his massive frame up to crawl underneath to see what was there. Moments later there was a sharp cry, a thud and the bench lifted very slightly. Keith emerged rubbing his head. He then delved back into the gloom and emerged clutching a glass jar containing two severed hands! While he was under there he swung the torch around and the two hands were hanging inches from his face. We had no idea to whom they belonged - no labels or other identification - so he took them back to the lab and spent the next month dissolving the flesh from the bones and mounting the hands onto a wooden plaque – wiring the small bones together. The finished skeletal hands then sat proudly on his desk.

In the lab above us there were a couple more eccentric characters. Terry also had long blonde hair and the pair of us used to borrow stethoscopes and, in our white lab coats, wander aimlessly through the outpatients, much to the consternation of those waiting for treatment. They were worried they might be being treated by hippies. Terry worked for a doctor from the Far East (I have no idea where from or what his name was) and he invited us over to his place one evening. He lived opposite the *Swiss Cottage* pub at the end of the Finchley Road. His balcony looked directly at the pub. In the summer he would sit on the balcony with a small pipe of opium and a telescope, looking over at the pub. If he saw a woman he fancied he would go over there – if not it was a night in with a pipe.

Keith also got into the life of the band and we took to making a speaker cabinet during our lunch break, a process that was curtailed after protests from the other residents of the lab about the amount of sawdust we were generating. Keith was also using joss sticks in the lab and the consensus of opinion was that I should be asked to leave as a disturbing influence. The upshot of this was that I decided I would go back to college and do some 'A' levels with the idea that I should go to University.

By this time I had also taken to reading poetry at Middle Earth. I would get up between bands and read some of my stuff out. I usually did this at the DJ booth, standing on a crate. Jeff Dexter, resident DJ there, once remarked I was the only poet to get high on a milk crate. Middle Earth was probably my favourite venue of them all. UFO had moved to doing shows at the Roundhouse by then, but this was a less intimate space than the one in Covent Garden. Mind you, the Roundhouse was not the swanky, upmarket, place it is now. In those days it was still little more than the engine shed it had started life as. They had taken out the turntable and put in a stage, but it still had whole sections piled high with rails and sleepers, and it was still very dirty.

I was at Middle Earth when Captain Beefheart played there for the first time. It was, in fact, his first ever gig in the UK. He had been sponsored by John Peel who was also the DJ for the night. I had been looking forward to this show for a while. The place was pretty full but Captain Beefheart was not that well known and Middle Earth did not really need to do much advertising because the audience was mostly made up of people who came along each week anyway. Hippiedom was going mainstream though, and there was a lot of interest in 'Underground Music ' in the Press and elsewhere.

Billy Walker was a boxer who ran a nightclub in Forest Gate. This was called 'The Upper Cut' and had opened in Dec 1966 with *The Who*. They put on mostly 'mod' type bands and would send people out to go to other clubs to see what they are doing. Now Middle Earth did not have an alcohol licence – they did not need it because all the highs that went on there were not exactly of the kind you could get a licence for. They sold Coca Cola and milk and a few other soft drinks, but that was all. As a consequence, there was little or no trouble there.

On the night of the Beefheart show they *did* have a drunk in, and he was trying, in a very aggressive way, to chat up a girl I knew. She changed places a couple of times but still this oaf followed her. My chivalry gene kicked in and I said something along the lines of 'I don't think she wants to talk to you'. His response was to turn around and hit me. I reeled back from the punch but did not fall over. I recall him looking at me in amazement and taking a couple of steps back as I attempted to say, 'What did you do that for?' I say attempted because, for some reason, my jaw would not work. The guy was hustled out of the club and people gathered round to ask if I was OK. After a few minutes I decided I would be better off going to a hospital. University College Hospital had an Outpatients Department so I got in the car and drove there. I was told I would need an X-Ray and the radiologist would not be in for a few hours. It was 2am at the time. I decided to go back and see Beefheart's second set, which is what I did.

I then drove back to the hospital, got X-Rayed and discovered he had broken my jaw on one side and shattered it on the other (where the blow had landed) Turns out my assailant was one of Billy Walker's sparring partners. The hospital admitted me and operated on my jaw to rebuild it. This rebuilding took the form of getting two of those metal jaw-shaped trays that dentists use when they take an impression of your teeth. These ones, however, had hooks along the sides and, once the broken parts of my jaw were in the correct place, they glued the tray in place. They then fixed a similar plate to my upper teeth and clamped my jaw together with yellow elastic bands. All of this was done under general anaesthetic. When I woke from the anaesthetic I felt woozy and a bit sick. I sat up and threw up – but it had nowhere to go! My jaws were clamped shut. This has been an enduring memory. Sitting up in a hospital bed with a mouth full of vomit, wondering what to do next. Only one answer really – swallow it. While I was in hospital, Middle Earth was raided for the last time and then invaded by the people who worked at the market, falsely informed that 'The Hippies are burning a child at the stake down there'. That was the end of the club.

I was out of hospital in a few days with a mouthful of metal. My chances of attracting any female attention were greatly reduced by the fact that any attempt at a smile revealed a scrapyard held together with yellow elastic bands. During the six weeks I had to wear the things I did a couple of *Stranger than Yesterday* gigs and read some poetry – no mean feat with your jaws clamped together.

There was a thriving music scene in the East End of London. Just ten minutes walk from my parent's house there was a real 'geezers' pub called the *Roundhouse* whose back room was home to the Village Blues Club. That room saw most of the bands that were later to become the huge stadium bands of the later '70s. *Pink Floyd, Led Zeppelin, Free*, and loads of others all played there. There were also gigs at other pubs in the area like the *Greyhound* at Chadwell Heath. It was there that I met Peta and Judy. They lived in a bedsit in Seven Kings and I would often spend an evening there taking acid and smoking dope. These evenings rapidly turned into weekends and, one day, one of the girls said, 'You spend so much time here you may as well move in' – so I did.

I am not sure that they really meant it though. The bedsit was in a house which was supposed to be 'girls only' so I had to be a bit cautious, but we got on OK with the other girls there. Peta was a lovely woman and we were friends for many years. Soon after I moved in we met Dave Stocker. Dave was a complete 'stoner'; whatever there was to take he would take it. He did come up with some interesting dope. He was also far more of a sexual predator than I was and would wander round all the other girls seeing who would let him in. I was still quite naive at the time and missed out on a couple of sexual encounters. Dave, on the other hand found them all. One girl, who lived in the flat beneath us, was well into threesomes and I got invited down to take part. One day, however, she brought two men back from an evening out and left them in the flat when she went to work. They broke into many of the other flats and stole whatever they could find. This meant that the police were called and they went from flat to flat taking notes about what was lost. We had lost nothing because I was in at the time and they had left our flat alone.

I think that one of the officers took a fancy to one of the girls and came back on the Friday night to 'take more notes'. They were sitting at the kitchen table talking while we were in our room – tripping. Peta decided that she would make everyone hot chocolate and we went into the kitchen. She boiled a saucepan full of milk and put the chocolate powder into the cups on a tray, just beside the policeman. When the milk boiled she lifted it from the stove and carried it to the table. She stood there looking from the cups to the saucepan and back again. She then up ended the saucepan over the cups! Milk, chocolate powder and cups went everywhere causing the policeman to jump up and try to rescue his sodden notebook from a table full of hot milk and chocolate powder. Peta looked up and smiled. 'Seemed like the best way to do it' she said.

Just down the road from the flat was a small coffee bar called the 'Casa Mia'. This was a regular hang out for local 'heads'. There was a kind of segregation that went on in those days. Pubs were either places that put bands on in back rooms, or places where your dad went. Many of the young people of the time, especially the hippies, would not go into pubs much – possibly because of the hostility shown by the straighter members of the community towards people with long hair, beads and flamboyant clothing. I was excessively over the top in the clothing department, wearing all sorts of strange costumes. I had a long fur coat, from which I had removed the sleeves and collar, and some pretty wild tunics. My mother indulged me a bit in this, making some of these for me from materials I had been out and bought. Shame I have no pictures of any of this apart from the few of the bands. Cameras and film developing were expensive in those days.

The Casa was also the place where you could get a 'quid deal'. A small lump of dope which was passed to you under the table. Andy Clarke and Mick Hutchinson, of the band *Clarke Hutchinson*, were in there a lot as were some of the people from *The Deviants* who had a house near Ilford. Seven Kings was a mass of bed sitters in those days so there were a lot of musicians and students living there. It made for a very vibrant community.

Al Haines and I in 'Grope'

CHAPTER 4

Groping in the Dark

Two of the friends I made in Middle Earth were John Phillips and Tom Barrett. John worked at Roneo Vickers, another one of those sprawling factories, similar to May and Baker. They specialised in the manufacture of duplicating machines. Office document copying was, in those days, a purely mechanical affair. A secretary had to type up the document onto a master stencil and this was then fastened to a drum. The user would feed in paper and turn a handle and printed sheets would come out. The process was messy and prone to failure, but there was no alternative back then. The whole task of copying documents became known as 'Roneoing'.

When I left East Ham Tech I needed a summer job, and John said they were recruiting at Roneo so I went along. I emphasised my chemical knowledge, hoping for a job in the lab. I got, instead, a job in the case hardening shop. The case hardening shop was a long building. At the far end was the 'heat treatment furnace' – a large vat full of sodium cyanide which was heated to about 270 degrees Celsius. This made the cyanide liquid. Next to it was a tank of whale oil, and next to that two water tanks. The factory would machine gears and spindles out of normal steel, truck them down to the case hardening shop where it was my task to string them into long festoons which could be hung from a frame and dipped into the cyanide. They would stay there for a while. Cyanide is rich in nitrogen and some of that nitrogen would transfer to the steel, giving it a hard surface. They were then removed from the furnace and quenched in the whale oil. After that they were put through the water baths to remove any cyanide that might still remain, and I would break them off the festoons and put them into boxes ready to go off to be used in machines. I was just the assistant here so I had no real responsibility. The man who ran it all was a louché and rather lazy person who would often come in drunk from the night before. One day he did not come in at all – and I was promoted to being in charge, mostly because no one else wanted the job.

Health and Safety did not get much of a look in back then. I found it too hot to wear the overall I was given so I did the job stripped to the waist; I would often come home with bits of sodium cyanide in my skin when a hot spurt had flown out of the furnace and burnt its way into my flesh. I was, however much more efficient about it so, whereas the previous incumbent would often have a backlog, I would usually be ahead of the game. This left me time to sit down and read a bit. I was doing this when the Managing Director decided to visit.

The conversation went a bit like this:

'What are you doing?' he asked.

'I'm reading a book'.

'Why are you not working?'

'I have done it all. I am waiting for the next lot come round.'

'Couldn't you make yourself busy? Sweep up or something?'

'Does it need sweeping?', I gestured round the room. 'Look, I do the jobs when they come in, I clean up, keep the place tidy, but I am not going to pretend to work when there isn't any to do, just to satisfy you'.

He thought about that for a while.

'Maybe I'll get a bed put in for you and you can have a snooze', He said sarcastically

'That's no good, I would oversleep and not get anything done', I retorted, and went back to the book.

I knew I was arguing from a position of strength because I knew no one else would take the job. If they sacked me there would be no one to take my place so he shook his head and walked out.

The building next door to mine was the one in which the rubber rollers were moulded and fastened to the various spindles and parts that fed the paper through the machines. It was mostly staffed by women of various ages and presided over by a Sid James lookalike. The 70s were a haven for casual sexism and the kind of suggestive comment that would land a department head in court these days. He was not beyond touching up some of the female workers and, I have to say, many played up to that too. I used to go in there for tea breaks because I was working on my own at the time. Most of the women were a lot older than I was but we got on well and I suppose it was a bit of a relief to talk to a man without having your bottom felt. Ted, their boss, was always regaling me with stories about sex parties he was going to, or had been to. Pornography was rife in the factory but, at that time, was limited to the odd foreign magazine, purchased in Soho, or black and white photos passed furtively around. No digital media in that age.

Stranger than Yesterday had disbanded by this time and I was working on a new line up. This was a bit more hard edged that the previous band and featured a guy called Al Haines on vocals. Al was a punk before there were punks. He had all the attitude and was right there, in your face, going for it. He was a bit into speed (amphetamines – for the uninitiated) and that added to the edge. We had been looking for a name for the new band for a while and then along it came - right on cue.

At work one day Ted passed me a stack of grubby, dog-eared pictures. They showed a group of people indulging in various sexual acts. One stood out. It was probably the least pornographic of the lot. It showed a large woman's breast being squeezed and pulled upwards by a hand that came over her shoulder. I had the name for the new band! *Grope*! It fitted perfectly. I borrowed the picture and took it to a friend in the lab at Roneo. He made a large master copy and we scrawled the word 'Grope' in that blobby, hippy, script and added our house phone number below it. Of course I was naively stupid. That poster did not get us any gigs – but we did get a few phone calls.

Around about this time Idi Amin ejected the Asians from Uganda. Many of them came to the UK and Roneo took on one of these as my assistant. He was a nice chap, albeit a bit bewildered to find himself in the UK - a country whose customs and climate are wildly different to the ones he was used to. He came into the furnace room and I showed him around. Having explained about the vat of cyanide he backed away and would not go near it again. He was happy enough to wire up the parts though, so we got along OK.

One day he said to me,

'What you do for sex in this country?'

I was a bit puzzled by this, 'Same as in yours, I suppose.'

'No, where you go to have sex?'

'Home' I said, 'I have a girlfriend.'

He looked a bit exasperated. 'No, you don't understand. In my country you pay a woman one pound and you stay all night. Here, I give a woman ten pounds and she throw me out after half an hour. That is not long enough.'

I had not had experience of hookers by that time so I really did not know what to tell him.

'Get a girlfriend,' I suggested.

Roneo had its own Trumpton-style fire service, just like the one they had in May and Bakers. It was, in fact, just outside the door to my workplace. The firemen were all volunteers from other parts of the factory, and when the alarm went off they would all race to the garage, get into their uniforms, and drive their little fire engine out. They system was that every department had a fire alarm button. If a fire started in your department you hit the button and a light lit up on a map in the guardhouse at the gates. They would then sound the alarm and tell the firemen where the fire was.

I was off sick for a week and when I came back they told me what had happened. They needed some parts hardening urgently and persuaded my assistant to do it. He had lowered the parts into the cyanide (I can just imagine the look of terror on his face as he did this). At the allotted time he lifted the stuff from the cyanide and went to lower it into the whale oil. The whale oil was used back then because it was cheap and because it would not burn – easily. Just lowering red hot metal into it was OK. Put the metal in and pull it out again, however, produced flames and thick, black smoke as the whale oil burnt off the metal. My assistant did just that. He lowered the stack of metal and missed the hooks. He then pulled the rack of parts upwards to try a second time only to find there was smoke and flames everywhere. He then managed to get the whole contraption caught half in and half out of the oil. The place filled with smoke. He ran out of the building to the fire station and hit the button outside the station door. This was the general alarm for the whole factory. He then ran back into our workshop.

My friend, who ran the rubber workshop (how apt), said they all assembled outside their building when the alarm went off. The firemen ran to the fire station, got into uniform and climbed on the little fire engine which headed off to the gatehouse because no one knew where the fire was. As they watched it go down the road and turn right towards the gate a door opened behind them and, accompanied by a large plume of black smoke, my wild-eyed assistant ran out screaming. No damage was done, but he left and never came back.

Grope gigged for a while, going through various line-ups. At one point Mick Cole, our drummer, and Al Haines shared a flat in Ilford High Road with a black guy called 'Chas'. Chas was a wonderful character; I will quote Al's description of him:

> 'Chas tried to emulate Eddie Grant by firstly having bleached blond and then ginger hair.' He used to work at Fyffe's and used to say he was a banana bender. I think I was also in a car with him when another black guy cut him up and he sounded his horn, wound the window down and shouted 'Go back to your own country you black bastard'. The guy looked round and saw Chas grinning at him and could not work out who had shouted. Chas, he of the Eddie Grant complex was indeed an inverted racist. Way ahead of his time I would say. If he didn't like anything he would say, 'it's well out o forder'. The f being omitted from the 'of' and placed, with emphasis, in front of the 'order'. Mick and I pounced on this grammatical faux pas and it became our catch phrase. For us everything was 'well out o forder'.'

We decided to try to get some publicity for the band and told the guys who ran the Indian restaurant below Mick and Al's flat that we would set up in front of their shop and take some pictures of the band. We did this and then quickly dropped a power cable down from above and began playing. Not quite *The Beatles* playing on top of the Apple building, but we did stop the traffic and get moved on by the police.

Grope began to expire after a few more gigs and Johnny Lyons, bass player at the time, and I began to think about forming a new band. I got talking to John Phillips at Roneo one day and he said he wanted to form a band, so we recruited him and began to write and rehearse with John on vocals, Johnny Lyons on Bass, Gareth Kiddier on 12-string and six-string guitars, Wal Mansefield on drums and me on electric guitar and vocals. Again the question of a name came up. People who came to rehearsals often said, 'I saw Wood and Lyons new band last night'. *Wooden Lion* was born.

The first *Wooden Lion* Line up (from left) Gareth Kiddier, me, Wal Mansefield, Johnny Lyons, John Phillips

CHAPTER 5

A Wooden Lion

I can't quite remember *Wooden Lion's* first gig. John was not a natural singer by any means but we did have a bunch of full-on songs, all written by the band, and Gareth Kiddier and John Lyons were pretty good musicians, so we began to get more gigs. There were the inevitable line up changes – firstly when Gareth left the band, and later when John Lyons also left, to be replaced by Rob Dee. Shortly after this Alan Essex (later rechristened 'Cardinal Biggles'), a friend of Rob's, joined on synth. We played all over London at that time and had a regular spot at *The Cafe Des Artistes* in Chelsea. This was a bit of a disco haunt, given to renditions of the long version of 'Gimme Some Lovin' by *Traffic*, 'Haitian Divorce' by *Steely Dan* and 'Superstition' by Stevie Wonder. God knows what the patrons made of our brand of music, but we kept getting rebooked. We also played around the East End of London. *Havering College*, *The Growling Budgie* in Ilford (where the DJ said of the support act – 'Sounds like that guitarist got Bert Weedon's 'Play in a Day' book, and he only got it this afternoon.').

We also had a regular spot at *The Greyhound* in the Fulham Palace Road, West London. *Grope* had played there in its later days and we carried that forward, having developed a friendship with Duncan, the landlord. This was a cavern of a gig. At some point in its history someone had taken an enormous bite out of the first floor and that allowed people on that floor to look down onto the stage. The stage was a good size and there was a balcony that ran around the back so, not only could you look at the band from the front on ground and first floor levels, you could also look straight down on them from behind. The other interesting part was the two large sloping pillars that went from the side of the stage all the way up to the balcony. I would often climb these and jump up and surprise the punters up there. I had a poster – now sadly lost, which showed the gigs for one week. Thursday night they had *Roxy Music*, Friday was *Be-Bop Deluxe* (Bill Nelson's amazing band), Sunday was *Status Quo* and on the Saturday – *Wooden Lion*! I often wondered why we kept getting the Saturday night slot.

It was only later that I realised that the pub was always packed on a Saturday, no matter who played. Why book a band to pull when you can book one that was quite cheap?

This was all in the height of the early '70s and the place was heaving most weekends, lots of interesting women and odd punters. My old friend Lemmy, by then playing bass for *Hawkwind*, was often there, as were many other well known musicians.

Music still lived in small clubs at that time, as can be seen from *The Greyhound* poster, and many posters from other venues of the time. I used to go to *The Railway Tavern* in Stratford to see various bands like *Free* play to a small audience, all sitting on the floor of an upstairs function room in a dilapidated pub. *Sam Apple Pie* were the resident band and they seemed to run things. They were a great blues based band with a strong singer and a great guitarist in 'Snakehips' Johnson. It was there that I met Patsy.

I met Patricia Carr one night at a gig there and we stayed together for quite a while. She was a beautiful woman who had been born and raised in Canning Town and had a real East End down to earthiness about her. A great woman to be with - and she painted the original *Wooden Lion* logo which wound up emblazoned on the back of our van, a vehicle which, sadly, wound up as a hay store in a field in Sheerness. Patsy moved into the house in Romford Road with me for a while. It all got wilder and wilder there, and pretty soon we found we were being asked to move on.

One thing occurs to me as I write this. Back in the '70s there were very few young homeless people. Yes, there were squatters and sometimes there were people who needed a place to stay for a while but, on the whole, flats were cheap and the deposit was low. These days, if you find yourself with nowhere to live and little money, the chances of getting any kind of accommodation are slender. A lack of housing stock, and the way that we treat property as an investment, rather than a place to live, means that those at the bottom end of society don't get a look in.

Anyhow, I moved out of the rooms in Romford Road and into a small flat over a takeaway fast food outlet not far away. Patricia and I split up then and she moved back home with her parents in New Barn Street. I shared this new flat with Alan Grey, the *Stranger Than Yesterday* guitarist.

Wooden Lion were still playing lots of gigs. One of these was at the fledgling Asgard Club at *The Railway Tavern*, run by a college friend of mine, Paul Fenn. This club operated on Fridays and *Sam Apple Pie's* Blues club was there on Sundays. I remember walking out of there with an amplifier, carrying it to the van. Now, upstairs at *The Railway Tavern* there were swirling light shows, hippies, loud music and mayhem. Downstairs was a trip in time worthy of Dr Who. The downstairs bar was peopled by older guys in drab raincoats and hats nursing pints of Pale or Brown Ale. So, there I was, a slightly stoned hippie carrying an amp head. The cable hooked round a free standing fire extinguisher and it fell over. I stood it up again and turned away – but it was one of those old style units which, when turned over, broke a vial of acid (not the kind I was used to) and this mixed with a carbonate mixture which, when it met the acid, generated carbon dioxide and, in turn propelled the liquid from the extinguisher's nozzle. As I walked away the process began, with an arc of liquid shooting across the bar and soaking the clientele. I put the amp down and tried to do something with the extinguisher, but there was no way to stop it and all I succeeded in doing was to soak the landlord who had rushed over to try to direct the liquid out of the pub. It was all like a scene from a slapstick comedy – Carry On Tripping, maybe.

In the meantime, my old friend Jacko was continuing to hold wild parties in his family's rambling house. in Hornchurch. His father had decided that enough was enough and the whole family decamped to the US, leaving Jacko alone in the 8-bedroom house. He was no housekeeper, in fact he had no clue about almost anything practical. Even when his family were living there he managed to make disaster happen all around him – on his own, he was a one man Armageddon. He bought a car from an ad in the paper. This was a Mk 1 Ford Consul, one owner from new in very nice condition. Not a fast car by any means but he managed to write it off on the way back from buying it. I had my share of accidents, but most of my cars lasted longer than a few minutes. Luckily cars were slower then and more robust so he did not get hurt.

His family had finally decided to sell the house and he was soon to have to find somewhere to live; I would imagine the house must be worth the best part of a million pounds these days. Jacko decided to have one last party, a Guy Fawkes Night special. There was a big bonfire in the back garden, copious drugs and some alcohol. I arrived, along with my friends Mick Worwood, Peta Watson and Anna Sutton. The first thing that struck me was a line of milk bottles on the step – 15 or 20 of them. The last in the line were milk and as they travelled along the row, there was increasing decomposition and separation in the liquid so that the last one was almost clear with a brown sludge at the bottom. Like some sort of experiment.

Inside the house things were no better. We asked if there was any bread to make toast. Jacko said there was some in the chest freezer in the garage so Mick and I went there. The chest freezer was a solid block of ice with a few bits of frozen foodstuff embedded in it, like a section of glacier that had rolled its way through a corner shop. In the kitchen the sink was full to the brim with mould and there were a couple of dirty saucepans lying in the bottom – the source of the growth. On the table was a chopping board with a chunk of meat, piece of cheese and some bread which were likewise turning into a garden. Quite amazing really. How could anyone live like that, whatever state they were in?

The bonfire was lit, substances ingested, and fireworks produced. A friend of Jacko's had brought her children along and, at one point I saw Jacko run frantically down the garden to stop them putting some wood on the fire – it was the kitchen door!

By this time the band had gone through a bit of an upheaval and John Phillips had left. I was debating getting a new singer but decided to take the role on myself. Up till now I had been the guitarist and backing vocalist, but I decided to abandon the guitar and take on the front man role. I was pretty sure I was up to the showman bit but not too sure of the vocal side. My confidence was not boosted by Tom Barrett (our roadie) saying 'you can do all those funny

The *Wooden Lion* van after a bit of injudicious parking

Second *Wooden Lion* Line up ; Terry Morley, me, Wal, Tony Morley and just off shot,
The Cardinal Biggles

Patricia Carr

voices'. Anyhow we had to find a new guitarist and bass player.

At this point I also decided we needed more effects. I was already making flash bombs from a car battery, broken flash bulbs (back in the seventies there were no LEDs. Flash photography was achieved by small glass bulbs containing magnesium ribbon which was ignited by having an electric current passed through it. I would take these apart, put them in cut down bean cans, sprinkle with magnesium powder, and connect them to a car battery. Flash!) We then discovered 'The Theatre Scene Armoury' in Covent Garden. This was a small office just off the market square. Pretty nondescript, but crammed with explosives. They provided many of the explosions and special effects for the stage, TV and films.

One of their clients was a ventriloquist whose dummy had a hollow head filled with offal. Towards the end of the show he would say, 'I've got a bad headache', 'I feel ill', 'Me head is really hurting' etc. At that point the ventriloquist would press a button and a small maroon (stage explosion) would go off in the dummy's head spraying offal into the audience. Any idea why this act never became famous?

So we were all primed up. Explosions, smoke bombs, strobes, the Full Monty. Alan Essex, who played a variety of homemade synths, had been in a band a while before and called the bass player from that band to see if he was free. Terry Morley joined the band and brought his brother Tony with him. This was the new band and we began to do a whole load of gigs. They also brought with them a guy called Steve Wollington who was to become our roadie. Steve was there through all of the *Wooden Lion* gigs from then on.

We had been doing a number of shows with a street Theatre group called *East*. They were a fairly anarchic bunch of people who all lived in a house in East London. They would do various impromptu street theatre shows, as well as putting on children's shows for the local community. As our friendship developed we began to go along to some of these shows and then play on the stage after they had finished. There were often a load of kids still there, looking slightly baffled by the odd collection of hippies that would turn up to see us and the antics of the madmen on the stage. Alan's swooping and screeching synth noises, and the general air of mayhem added to it. East would also come along to our own shows in costume and act out all sorts of stuff in the audience.

One of the songs was called 'The Last Forest' and, for that, I dressed up in a cardboard tree, complete with branches and a mask I had made from *papier mâché*, which sported a few twigs. It was very hard to get this contraption on and off. At one gig in a pub in North London I was struggling to get the costume off on stage right. Steve, who was standing on stage left rushed round the back of the stage to help. On the way round he tripped over a cable that lead to some of the lights and knocked them down, smashing the 'Black Light' UV tube and a few more items in the process. From then on he was known as 'The Wrekka'. These costumes and the effects that went with them provoked some odd looks when we performed to these audiences, left over from a children's show, in the parks.

At one of these shows, on a damp spring evening, we found one of the flash pots did not go off. I sat on the stage tossing matches into it, but it still did not ignite. I then broke off a few match heads and threw then in. As I did this, the flash went off. My hand was black and everyone was looking at me in amazement. 'That was warm', I said and went to wash my hand. That was when I found it was not soot, it was the skin that was black, and that was when it began to hurt. I decided to go and sit in the van with the band's girlfriends. I had, apparently, turned a little green. They asked if I was OK and I replied, 'I think I need to go to a hospital'. I had fourth degree burns. Much fun was made of my request for them not to cut my rings off.

This was nothing compared to the 'Albemarle Incident'. We were friends with a band called *Storm* who used to end their set with a bit of the 1812 Overture. There was a brass cannon on the stage which would go off and launch sweets   into the audience – better than offal I suppose. They were playing an all day show at the Albemarle Youth Club in Harold Hill, Essex. Mick Worwood's band, *Castle Farm*, were playing that day too. The story I heard was that they were late and the roadie loaded the cannon in the van, and when they arrived the promoter said they could not play because they had rearranged the slots. They decided to let the cannon off in the car park and when it went off, it came apart – as did the roadie. He was killed instantly.

The explosion took the side off the van, blew the keyboard player's girlfriend into a wall and shattered her leg as well as taking out all of the windows in the building. God knows how many people would have been hurt if that had gone off in a packed youth club. Mick said his band had to go on and play straight after, just to keep the audience in the building while the police and ambulances arrived. Not only had they made the cannon, they also made the explosives using weed killer and sugar – a mixture later used by the IRA.

I have read a few reports of this incident later and they say that the main youth worker had asked to see the cannon working and that was why it was fired outside. Whatever the real reason was, that stopped all pyrotechnics at council venues. That did not stop us doing them in other places though. We got a gig at the Dagenham *Roundhouse*, supporting *The Sensational Alex Harvey Band*. Alan's friend, Steve, (later renamed Suicidal Stevie) used to do the explosions and stuff, but another friend of ours said that since it was a bigger gig we would need bigger smoke bombs. The end of our set was a number called 'Haunter of the Dark' (after an H.P. Lovecraft story). At the climax of this I shouted 'Let me out of this place!', the maroon went off, smoke bombs poured smoke, strobes fired and we went into the last section – the lyrically challenging 'Help, let me out' over and over again. At the *Roundhouse* we used the 'big smoke bombs' and the room filled with a choking acrid smoke. It seems he had got hold of a tank obscuring grenade from a friend in the T.A. They had to open all the doors and windows to get the smoke out, and SAHB went on nearly an hour late.

The Loft in Woodford Green 1972

CHAPTER 6
The Leafy Suburb of Woodford Green

The band at the time were all mostly living in different houses and some of us decided that we would try to get a house together. Alan found a small terraced house in Woodford Green, last outpost of London at the time, verging on Epping Forest. The house had a front room, dining room, kitchen, front bedroom, and a room in the middle of the house which connected to the bathroom and the converted loft. The toilet was one of those 'outside' ones, accessed by the garden door. I think it had been inhabited by someone who had lived there for years and never seen any point in modernising it. Not that we did either.

I took over the loft. I have always liked these small loft spaces and I am writing this in the loft in my current house, just outside Brighton. Our drummer, Wal Mansefield, took the front bedroom, Alan converted the front room into his bedroom, and Tom Barrett, our other long-time roadie, was content to live in the middle room. I was the first to move into the house. I got there early on Friday afternoon and moved my stuff in. As it got dark I realised that there was only one light bulb in the house. The previous tenant - or some interim estate agent - had removed all but the one in the front room. This was back in the early '70s and all shops shut at 5pm so I had no way to get any bulbs till the following day. There was a pub not far from the house that we went to on occasion, so I decided to go there and see if anyone was around. Almost the first person I met there was Jacko. After a couple of drinks we decided to go back to the house and have a couple of spliffs.

The only music system I owned was one of those old Phillips cassette players – the kind with the single knob that you pushed forward for play or from side to side for fast forward and rewind. I had made up a lead for this to plug it into one of our PA columns to improve the sound. Jacko and I sat in the front room chatting, listening to music and smoking some hash. At one point he asked me where the toilet was, I said, 'Outside' and then watched in amazement as he went out and pissed up the garden fence. When I asked him why he did that he said: 'When you said outside I thought you meant you did not have one.'

This kind of summed Jacko up really. I decided to retire to bed and said that Jacko could take one of the other rooms since the others were not arriving until the following day. We had been listening to 'Islands' by *King Crimson* – a beautiful album sung by Boz Burrell with whom I became friends much later on. When the last track finished I unplugged the cassette machine from the speaker, removed the solitary light bulb, and headed up the stairs, in the pitch black, in an unfamiliar house, a little stoned. A voice came out of the darkness, '...let's try it with the violins....' I almost fell down the stairs. There was an extra track on the cassette that I had never heard before. The thing about cassette tapes was that very often the music on one side was longer than the music on the other one. When the music finished I would run it forward to the end and turn it over so I never heard the hidden track which started one or two minutes after the main music finished.

It was quite a shock for the residents of that quiet street in Woodford Green. Suddenly there were four hippies (and associated - sometimes dissociated - women) living in their midst. One older woman, whose name was Wenzle and who lived up the street, complained a lot about us and became known at 'Wenzall them hippies gonna move out?'. Alan had the most hair. It hung down to his waist and it was accompanied by a bushy beard and round, John Lennon spectacles. Mine was fairly long too, as was my own beard, although this was pretty wispy at the time. Tom and Wal were fairly respectable compared to us. The problems were compounded by the fact that three of us had cars and Tom had an old school bus which was the band's transport at the time. One particularly stroppy individual came out one day as Tom and I pulled up in his bus. Bristling with rage he shouted, 'I am fed up with seeing your dirty van parked outside my house!' I said, 'Oh, hang on a minute', went inside and filled a bucket with soapy water, picked up a sponge and came back out. I placed the bucket on the floor in front of him. 'You can wash it if you like', I said. He was not impressed. He then took to leaving notes on the windscreen saying, 'Please move your van'. I responded by leaving notes on his door saying 'Please move your house.' I do not think this did anything for community relations, but I was young and a lot more inconsiderate in those days.

Over the period that we lived there we had a few different cars. Alan was a keen Morris Minor enthusiast and had a couple of those, winding up with a very nice split screen model. I think I got through the most cars. I had a Riley 1.5 and a Wolseley 1500. These were both identical bodies. They had been designed as the replacement for the Morris Minor, and were built on the same chassis, unfortunately they also had the same rust problems with the box chassis that supported the engine and the front of the car. I turned up in the Riley for a gig one day, saw the bus parked down an alley, and decided to park behind it. The thing I did not know was that the kerb was very high and they would put ramps in when vehicles had to drive up the alley – and then take them away. I drove forward and hit the kerb – and the whole front of the car dropped down! The jolt had separated the welded ends of the box section and, since the front of the body was supported by the traverse box section, the car began to resemble some kind of racer. I was stopped by police driving it like this and the guy who stopped me was talking about the car and how much he liked these old '60s vehicles. 'I do hate it when people lower the front suspension like this', he said. I was thinking that I did not want him to look underneath and see the rusted outriggers.

We made regular trips to *The Greyhound* in Fulham Palace Road at the weekend. It was the other side of London, but it was a good venue for music and a place to meet women. Since we played there a bit ourselves we had a bit of local celebrity value, which made it easier and it was always packed. One girl in particular offered to give Alan a copy of a *Pink Fairies* LP if he got me to sleep with her. It was no hardship on my part because she was pretty and rather nice so I was happy to oblige. We were together for a while until she became ill and went back up to Norwich to live. On another occasion I consumed a bit too much alcohol and got one of the others to drive me home. I was never a big fan of being drunk, I didn't like the feeling of being out of control, but on that night I tipped the balance. In the morning I woke up beside a beautiful black girl. I did not recall bringing her home or, sadly, any sex we had. I was hung over and confused. It got more confusing when she woke and said 'Good Morning' in a broad Glaswegian accent. She was lovely and, once I had sobered up and we had breakfast, I drove her home – back to Fulham. I was too embarrassed by my state the previous night to follow up the encounter.

Tom and I also met two Welsh women who had just come down to London from Wales. We took them back to where they were living, which proved to be a convent, and they smuggled us in for the night – and out again the following morning. They were both complaining about 'heat bumps' but it turned out that they had scabies (a parasite that burrowed into your skin and lays its eggs there). Tom and I completely failed to get infected – and you could not get any closer to them than we had!

The Greyhound was also the place where I had my first encounter with the long arm of the law. Alan Tom, Jacko, Wal and I were all there at around 10pm when the local Hammersmith Police decided to raid the place. They poured into the building and began to approach the punters asking them to turn out their pockets, looking for drugs. I knew Jacko had a bit of hash in his pocket so, when one young policeman came up to our group, I came forward to be searched. I did this so that Jacko would have a chance to dump the drugs or at least move them to a more secure location. In order to distract him further, and because I was pretty mischievous at the time, I said, 'You have lovely soft hands for a policeman, I bet you like this, feeling up all the men'. He blushed somewhat and, after a bout of further teasing from me, escorted me out of the venue - followed by my group of friends. Off the hook!

Things did not stop there, however. I still had a drink in my hand and another policeman came up to me and said, 'You can't drink that out here'.

'I can't drink it in there, he just threw me out', I replied, at which point he took it from me and threw it, glass and all, on the ground. 'Bloody hell', I said.

'Right, you're nicked' was the response, and he bundled me into a van. I found myself with about twenty other people in a big holding cell in Hammersmith Police Station. Most of the assembled miscreants had done little to deserve incarceration. A few minor swearing sessions, a couple of counts of possession of a little bit of hash, and one guy who hit one of the arresting officers on the head with a pint glass. We were taken out separately and charged, mostly with 'behaviour likely to cause a breach of the peace' and 'insulting words and behaviour'; two catch-all charges that would serve to be vague enough to be able to get a prosecution. The general consensus in the room was that they would all plead guilty, get fined a salutary sum and go free the next day. I was not playing. I had not done anything, as far as I could see, except have a little fun at the expense of a PC.

The next day I was in a magistrate's court mid-way through a queue of punters. I, alone, pleaded 'not guilty' and was released on bail to appear the following week to face trial. I arrived at court and stood in the dock, feeling fairly confident. I was under the mistaken belief, naive as I was, that the police would not lie. Wrong. The arresting officer got up, opened his notebook and read from it.

> *'I approached the defendant in The Greyhound Public House in Fulham Palace Road,'* he began, *'I said to him "Drink up son, it is past closing time"'*

(it wasn't, it was around 10pm as I said).

> *'He replied to me, " Fuck off flatfoot! You are a bunch of cunts and you're always come in here trying to fuck us over. Piss off and leave me alone". I said to him, "Come on Son, just drink up and move on" to which he replied, "Fuck off and leave me alone you fucking cunt". I was forced to arrest him"*

I was rather stunned by this. I had not expected such blatant lying, nor had I expected him to read the lies from his notebook. The magistrate asked me if I had anything to say. I looked at the bench, three older men dressed in grey suits and ties looking very seriously at me.

'Is he allowed to make it up like that?', I asked. Not the answer they expected either I suspect. 'You had better find me guilty and I will appeal the decision, give me a chance to bring some witnesses'. They duly found me guilty and fined me £10. I appealed.

So, next up, Southwark Crown Court. I went along with Alan and Wal as witnesses. Now, just for the record here, I should say that I don't really swear. I don't have any problem with the words themselves but I find no reason to litter my conversations with unnecessary verbs or nouns that have nothing to do with the content of the actual sentence. By the time we were presented to the court the charge had morphed into Offensive Words and Behaviour and the other charge of Behaviour Liable To Cause A Breach Of The Peace, had been dropped. OK, I was ready for this. I had no lawyer, I was going to do it myself. Alan and Wal went off to the witness area to wait to be called.

In court I was faced by a weasely little man in full gown and wig – barrister for the police. I stood in the dock as 'the accused'. Exciting stuff, just like on TV, I remember thinking, but Dixon of Dock Green it was not. The policeman stood up and read from his book again.

'I approached the defendant outside the Greyhound Pub in the Fulham Palace Road and asked him to put down his drink as he could not drink outside the pub's premises. He replied with a torrent of obscenities and two old ladies, who were passing at the time, were offended'

I was no lawyer. It had not occurred to me he would change his statement or that I should have got a transcript of the previous trial. The judge asked me if I had any questions. OK, I thought, go for it.

I started, 'Would you agree that there was a police raid going on at the pub at the time?'

'Yes,' he replied, 'we were conducting a drugs raid.'

'So, how many police vehicles were there on the raid when this happened?'

'I don't really know,' he said.

'If I said there were three or four police cars, at least four vans and several motorbikes would you agree with that?'

'Yes, I think so, sounds right.'

'Ok, where were these vehicles parked?'

'Um, well, I don't recall.'

He was looking puzzled as to where this was going and I was scenting blood and quite enjoying it.

'If I suggested that they were all parked on the pub's small forecourt and on the zigzag lines marking approaches to the zebra crossing would you agree?'

'Yes, well we were raiding the pub at the time.'

'No argument about that,' I said, closing in, 'My question is, where did these two old ladies walk? Between the cars, amongst the twenty or so people you arrested that night and were putting into vans, through the middle of the thirty or so police officers that were there? Or did they walk round the outside, in the road?'

He grabbed his opportunity, 'In the road,' he said, 'They walked round the outside.'

'Ah', I said. This was the answer I wanted. 'They were walking in the Fulham Palace Road at, according to you, 11pm at night. Have you ever tried to cross the Fulham Palace Road at that time on a Friday night? It is crammed full of traffic. If I had been one of these ladies I would have used the crossing to get to the other side and avoid the melee. Can you produce these ladies in court? Are they here as witnesses?'

At this point he could say nothing. He was blushing deeply and was lost for a reply. All he could manage was 'Er, I don't know. No they are not here.'

'I thought not', I said.

I called my witness. I had only one left because Wal had been thrown out of the court for not standing when the Judge walked in.   Alan stood in the witness box dressed in a denim jacket, hair down to his waist, full on Karl Marx beard, and round tinted glasses.

'Mr Essex,' I began, 'How long have we known each other?'

'About four years', he answered.

'And, in that time, would you agree that you have rarely heard me use offensive words or made scatological references or indeed used bad language?'

'I would agree with that', he said, 'Not something you do.'

'And where were you when the alleged offence took place?'

' I was following you out from the pub,' he said.

' No further questions,' I said. I felt quite confident at this point.

The weasel in the gown got up, voice nasal and sarcastic.

'Mr Essex,' he sneered, 'What do we do for a living, Mr. Essex?'

'I am an electronic design draughtsman,' Alan replied

'And when was the last time we worked?' whined the weasel, hands in that typical posture so beloved of TV barristers, clutching the breast area of his gown.

'About 11 o'clock this morning, when I left Plessey's to come here,' Alan replied.

I was convinced I had got this in the bag.

The Judge, in his summing up, said, 'I will give you the benefit of the doubt. Fined £25'.

I could not believe it. As we were leaving we met the young police guy coming out of the back room with an older sergeant. He was still red-faced and seemed a bit agitated. They came up to me.

'Quite the little Perry Mason on the quiet, aren't we?' he said. Then, turning to the constable, 'Some people have a lot to learn'.

'Where do you pay fines?' I asked.

'I don't know, I don't pay fines,' was the reply.

'Nor do I' – and I didn't. I got arrested for the non-payment of that fine years later when I came back into the country from abroad, but that is another story.

Alan told me that when he sat in the witness area he was flanked by police. Once said to him, 'are you undercover?'

'No, witness for the defence.'

And they all moved away.

Wooden Lion playing in Basingstoke; Colin, Rob Dee, me, Wal Mansefield, Tony Morley, The Cardinal Biggles

CHAPTER 7

Free Festivals

The band had been playing a number of gigs around London. Looking back, and listening to some of the stuff that got recorded on scratchy cassette tapes, I don't think we were all that competent, but we were busy. One thing that got us noticed a bit was the stage act – in which I played a large part. We wrote all our own tunes and some of it was fairly rudimentary but my early encounters with *The Crazy World of Arthur Brown* (and all that dressing up at my aunt's house) had struck a chord. I was never one to stand still on stage and, inspired by Arthur's mad genius, I began to adopt more and more elaborate stage personae.

Somehow or other we managed to get onto one of the Windsor Park Free Festivals. I think it was at the second one, held in 1973, that we did a short set and got in with some of the organisers. So much so, that we began to get invited to other gigs arranged around these events. We had a bigger presence in the 1974 one where we played on one of the larger stages. We had arrived at this festival on the Friday afternoon after several bouts of car trouble. This set the stamp for our involvement in Free Festivals for the coming year. These festivals were very much 'open' events. People who visit the open air gigs of today would not recognise the way they were run back then. There was no backstage area, no VIP suites, no catering of any kind. It was just a scaffolding stage, often with no roof, and a generator parked nearby. One of the stages was taking its power from an ice cream van. We didn't stay long for the first couple of festivals, but we were definitely going to be more involved for the next ones.

There was, in those days, something very amateurish in the way most gigs were run. There was still a network of agents and bookers but they seemed a bit bemused by the turn the music business had taken in the late '60s. They had been used to booking acts like *The Hollies*, Cliff Richard and that whole pantheon of 'pop stars' who arrived in the early days of the decade. People they could control and hand songs to. A lot had changed since then. Most bands wrote their own material and many of the real hippy bands eschewed management in favour of going out and doing free shows.

We were invited by a band that went under the name of *Thor* (later, or previously, called *The Nova Mob* - I cannot quite recall what order the name changed in) to appear in Memorial Park, Basingstoke. When we arrived there we found that the PA was provided by Ian, from the *Half Human Band*. He later went on to found the music company HHB which is still selling audio equipment to this day. We had always carried a small PA of our own and so we decided to use our PA to run The Cardinal's synthesisers as a quad system,

PA systems were pretty much in their infancy in those days. Back in the late '60s the free gigs in Hyde Park and Parliament Hill Fields were powered by WEM (Watkins Electric Music) speakers. These were columns with four 12" speakers mounted vertically. WEM also made a mixer amp, which would take four microphones and then went on to introduce 'slave' amps which would take the power up, in 100watt steps, to whatever size you could afford – or find the power for. This was known as 'The Watkins Wall of Sound'. From then on PA systems began to develop at an alarming rate. Most of the 'mixing' in the '60s and early '70s was done at the side of the stage until someone came up with the idea of putting a mixing desk out in the audience. People began to use 'crossovers' to divide sound of different frequencies and to send these sounds to speakers more suited to the frequency range.

Anyhow, we wired The Cardinal Biggles' synth outputs to the four WEM columns we had with us and set them up out in the field . We did not often put microphones on the instruments in those days, although, for this gig, the bass drum and snare drum had mics. The result was a lot of electronics whooshing its way around the field. The local councillors and officials all went mad at the noise and both bands were banned from playing there again. Banned from Basingstoke! Wonderful.

The following year the big free festival was moved to Watchfield. The end of the previous year's Windsor Festival had turned into an ugly pitched battle between police and hippies because no one had given permission for a gig to take place in the start and, although they had managed two previous shows there with little trouble, that time they had outstayed their welcome and the police wanted to move them on. There was a general feeling of antagonism towards hippies expressed by the establishment, and I have no doubt that some of the behaviour by the various people who attended the gigs was less than acceptable by many people.

As a placatory measure they gave us a disused airfield and said we could hold the festival there. Police were controlling this one much more forcefully and we were warned that there would be a lot of 'stop and search' activity on the way in so we did not have very many illegal substances on us. When *Wooden Lion* took to the stage, last but one act on the Friday night, I casually announced that we did not have much dope and anyone who had some to sell should come and see us later. During the show there was a constant stream of people walking to the stage and putting stuff down for us for free. Steve Wollington, our roadie, gathered all this up for later. During one of the guitar solos, about halfway through our set, I wandered over to him to see what we had; 'few bits of black resin, chunk of Moroccan, bag of grass some other assorted bits of resin and a pyramid of acid', he said. 'I'll have the acid now', I answered and popped it in my mouth.

Of course it came on before the show finished.

I liked acid back then. I never had a bad trip and I was always able function OK on it – even if I did make a few unconventional decisions. The end of the set was our mad finale 'Haunter of the Dark'; a multi-parted 15 minute epic full of spacey synths, mad rocking sections and culminating in a loud explosion (courtesy of the Theatre Scene armoury's largest maroon), smoke, strobe lighting and a rocking riff over which I sang 'Help, Let me out' and ad-libbed lyrics. I was dressed in a long black cloak, green leotard (I only realise now, as I look back at a selection of photos from those days, that it was a lot more anatomically revealing than I first thought) and a three headed mask.

The acid was in charge. As we launched into the final riff, I climbed the post at the side of the stage and did the last verses on top of it. At the end, of course, a little bit of logic crept in and I could see there was no graceful way of getting down from there, and the following day I saw I had bent the scaffolding at the top of the stage. It was never meant to take that kind of weight.

Years later, after I had posted this anecdote on a website dedicated to free festivals, someone wrote to me and said he was glad I posted that – he had always thought he dreamed it. When we arrived back at the house after Watchfield we opened the door to find the kitchen ceiling was now in the kitchen sink, having collapsed. The landlord of the place gave us some money to fix it, but I think we spent it on food and drugs instead.

The theatre group *East* had an amazing collection of odd characters in its complement although they were, on the whole, quite likeable. Two of these came along to the Watchfield gigs. Vince was a small thin man who seemed to have been prone at the time to some odd accidents. One day he turned up at a show with wood shavings stuck all up his arm and one side of his face.

'I slipped and fell into a puddle of Evo-Stick,' he said when I questioned his appearance.

'So where did the wood chips come from?'

'Oh, I fell into a pile of wood shavings straight after.'

He had made no discernible attempt to remove any of it.

Vince had a girlfriend called Eve. Eve was a large lady. We had fantasies of the two of them having sex. It must have been like a twig bouncing around on a waterbed. The pair turned up on Vince's Honda 50, with Eve riding pillion. It must have been an effort keeping the front wheel on the ground, I thought, and from behind it looked like a peach riding on a razor blade.

At some point during their stay Vince decided to teach her to ride the bike. He put her on it showed her the controls and then spun the accelerator and let go. She careened along shrieking for a few minutes before crashing into a tent.

After Watchfield we moved into the planning stage for the next festival. They decided to hold a meeting at a squat in Cornwall Terrace, off Regents Park. I believe the house was owned by The Royal Trust, but I never knew for sure. Of course there were bands playing and, of course we went to do a set. Things were all pretty chaotic and the timing for our set got shuffled around, so much so that I wound up arguing with the bassist, Rob Dee, guitarist, Tony Morley and drummer Wal 'Blimey-Yeah' Mansefield. They stormed off just as I was setting the PA up but came back to do the set. This led to Tony and Rob leaving the band and we needing two new members.

After a bit of advertising we picked a guitarist called Jimmy McGrother; he was due to come round the house for a chat. Our Drummer, Wal 'Blimey-Yeah', had been married to a woman called Patti (who had also been the girlfriend of our original bassist back in the *Stranger Than Yesterday* days). They had separated but Wal had been to see her and his child that day and found her in bed with two guys. A row ensued and one of the guys hit him over the head with a milk bottle. With blood streaming down his head he broke free and got in his car to drive home.

He was pretty wound-up, as you might expect, and the blood was getting in his eyes so his driving was erratic. He arrived back at the house and only Tom Barrett, our roadie, was in. Tom got him to lie on the living room floor and fetched a towel and a bowl to wash the blood away. At this moment there was a knock on the door. Tom answered it and it was Jimmy, looking a bit white-faced.

'I was just driving here', he said, 'and some madman with blood all over his head nearly ran me off the road........and there he is.' He had reached the living room to find said madman lying on the floor. 'That's Wal, our drummer,' said Tom, 'He played badly at the last gig.....' Amazingly enough Jimmy still joined the band.

CHAPTER 8

Jacko gets drunk and gets us Raided!

Jacko's father had finally sold the house, having had enough of his son living in a rambling mansion by himself. He turfed him out to fend for himself. His form of fending was to sleep on floors and sofas of friends who had flats. In this role he took over the front room. We were all working at the time so we would get up and go to work and then return to find him lying on the sofa surrounded by roaches (discarded ends of spliffs for the uninitiated) dirty cups and plates. He was prone to eating anything he found in the house, and very rarely replenished the cupboards. At night we would retire and leave him to sleep on the sofa; if Tom was late getting back he would assume he was staying at his girlfriend's flat and get into his bed. I was often woken to the sound of Tom prising Jacko out of his bed.

The back door to the house did not fit too well, and during the night slugs would come in from the back garden. In the morning you could see the silver trails on the carpet where they had come up to the sofa, where Jacko lay stoned and supine, and then return to the garden again. We decided it was a form of worship and that Jacko was 'King of the Slugs'.

During this period Jacko got caught drink driving and was summoned to appear for trial. He decided that the best way to deal with this was to go to America for a few months to visit his family. When he came back he returned to our sofa and the worshipful slugs. He brought me back a bottle of Southern Comfort and I managed to drink the entire contents during the following evening, leaving me feeling very ill. I had promised I would drive a couple of friends home after the party, but I was far too drunk so I slept on the floor and gave them my bed. In the morning I felt very unwell, and I have never touched Southern Comfort since. In fact I gave up drinking at that point.

Jacko had assumed that the police would give up looking for him, but they were visiting all his known addresses with a warrant for his arrest. Wal, too, saw a bit of police activity because he was not paying maintenance to his ex-wife, Patti and, on one occasion he climbed through the bathroom window and escaped over the gardens as the police came through the front door. All a bit disconcerting, given the amount of dope we smoked at the time.

One day, while I was out with a friend, Jacko borrowed my car to go and buy drugs. The woman he was buying them from lived in Brentwood and was a friend of ours, not really a big time dealer, but many dealers were like that, as I said before; buy a big block of dope and sell it in smaller pieces to make enough to be able to smoke for free. The police were watching the house and stopping people as they left. Jacko was stopped and had managed to stash the drugs beyond detection. When he came in he announced:

'I got stopped by the police tonight'

'How did you get away with that?' I said, 'There is a warrant out for your arrest.'

'It's OK. I gave them your name.'

Not a good idea really.

The house was one of those old terraced ones. Very narrow. As you came through the front door there was a passage with two doors. One led to Alan's bedroom and the other to the living room. Rather than leave the gear in the van overnight we used to load it all into the front room and pile it along the wall. It was so heavy that the joists began to give way after a while.

Alan was cleaning his car in the street when the raid happened. A phalanx of police officers marched past him and straight through the open door to our house. They had two warrants. One to arrest Jacko, and the other to search the house for drugs. They thought we were supplying the woman whose house they had been watching. Only Alan and Wal were at home. The police sat them down on the sofa and said, 'Alright lads. Where's the gear?'

Wal pointed to the pile of drums, speakers and amps.

'No, no. No,' said the policeman, 'You know what I mean, the GEAR, the drugs.'

'We haven't got any,' said Wal.

They proceeded to empty drawers, look in cupboards, take up carpets, and ransack the place.

Mind you, being hippies, it looked like it had already been ransacked. He found a box of stuff that belonged to Jacko.

'Do you know the whereabouts of Roy Jackson?' he demanded.

'He went to America', said Wal

'Without this?' said the policeman, holding up Jacko's driving licence and passport. 'Oh, he must have come back', was Wal's meek reply.

This was all going quite well for us. All they had found was a couple of roaches in my room and some cigarette papers. No big drugs raid, this........... and then Wal wanted to go to the toilet. He was accompanied by an officer who stood by the door to the outside loo. While he stood there he noticed a pot plant and saw it was a POT plant. He also noticed some glass window frames formed in the shape of a cloche with more plants underneath it.

He marched Wal back into the room, sat him down and said, 'What is this?'

'I dunno, tomato maybe,' said Wal.

The policeman produced a cigarette lighter from Jacko's box, bearing a picture of a dope leaf and the words '*Cannabis sativa*'.

He waved the two items at Wal.

'Don't you think it looks a lot like this?' he asked.

'Oh yeah,' he said, 'So it does.'

I came home a while later and got the whole story. The police had left the ultimatum that either one person owned up to growing the plants or the whole house would get done. Since I had been the chief instigator – and, indeed, propagator of the crop – I felt it was down to me to own up. They had left a phone number and, since we did not have a phone in the house, I walked to the local phone box. I had this conversation with Chelmsford CID:

'Hi, I got a message you needed to speak to me.'

'Yes, it is about the cannabis plants growing in your garden.'

'Yes, I know about them.'

'Do you know who grew them?'

Yes, it was me.'

''Ah, good. Can you come here and make a statement?'

'Where are you?'

'Chelmsford'

'No, can you come and pick me up?'

'No'

'We have a problem then. Why don't I walk down to my local police station and make a statement there?'

'OK, we will call them.'

No time like the present, I thought, and set off up the road to the police station. Now Woodford Green in the early 1970s was a bit like 'Heartbeat', still living in the early '60s, and the police station was a small affair. I pushed open the door and walked in. Behind the desk was a portly Sergeant, almost a stereotype.

'Can I help you?' he asked.

'I have come to make a statement.'

'What about?'

'Growing dope in my back garden.'

He looked amazed, paused for a moment and then said, 'Just step in here, please,' and opened a door. I stepped in, and heard him lock it behind me.

Five minutes later I was joined by a laughing CID man.

'He thought you had cracked up,' he said, 'Come to confess'.

I have only just had the call from Chelmsford CID. He looked at the notes. He shook his head, 'If I had been there I would just have ignored this. Complete waste of my time really, still I have to go through with it now.'

We spent half and hour going through the details and then he bailed me to appear at the local court. This time I pleaded guilty, 'bang to rights' as they say, and I got fined £150, which was a lot of money then. I left the court and went home.

Now I thought that I could treat this like a motoring fine, so I went back to court at the end of the period in which I had to pay the fine and said, 'I can't pay this in one sum, can I pay it off monthly?' To my astonishment the judge said, 'Alternative sentence is 3 months. Take him down', and I found myself being escorted into the cells. My car was outside the court on a parking meter. I managed to get the car keys to my girlfriend so she could drive it home and the next thing I knew I was in a van en route to Pentonville.

If Woodford Green Police were still in the 1960s, Pentonville was still in the 1860s; a big stone edifice with cells and barred doors. I was seriously wondering how I was going to get out of this one.

Jacko on the right – the crop at Woodford Green

There was a kind of induction meeting at the prison at the time – maybe there still is – a bit like a school assembly, but with showers. So we all took a shower and were issued with prison clothes. We were then led to a row of chairs and sat down to await our names being called. The question on everyone's lips was 'what are you in here for, then?' To my right sat two pleasant looking hippies, about my age, and to my left a rather bruised and battered guy, with a scar, broken nose and a bit missing from his ear. He spoke first, 'I didn't pay maintenance to me ex did I? Kept running from the police. I had tickets to the Cup Final and I wanted to go to that first. I would rather spend 2 months in here than give that bitch any money'.

I explained why I was there – they laughed and then the two hippies told me why they were in there. 'Possession of £10,000 pounds worth of amphetamines, evading arrest, hijacking a truck, attempted murder of two policemen by ramming a roadblock.....'

'Woah!' This was all said in a very matter of fact way.

There were two other people in the cell with me. One was a nicely spoken younger man, and the other a more middle-aged business man on his third drink driving charge, and facing 3 months inside. He was frantic, hated being there, didn't know how he would handle it at all and spent most of the first night sobbing. The other guy told me why he was in. He got a job when he left school and worked for a while. He got a credit card and then decided he did not like working and retired - at 24! He then decided to take all of his friends out for Chinese and Indian meals, on his credit cards, which he could not repay because he was not working. When the bank started to write him letters he took action. No computers in those days so banks would have a list of customers that they had to check before giving them money. Armed with a torch and a pair of binoculars he looked in through the bank's window and wrote down the top five names on that list. He then complained to the main branch that they were displaying the bad debtors list. Eventually the police were called. They came round to his house, but he was out. His mother invited them in and said, 'It's not his fault you know, he takes drugs', so they did him for that too. He ended this story with, 'I hope they don't find out about my Barclaycard'. Four months later I was in court again, this time for having a defective headlight on my car. He was there too.

'They found out about my Barclaycard,' he said.

I was released from my incarceration the following day when my friends got together and paid my fine. £150 less £1.67 for 'time served'.

A few months later a police car arrived at our house and I opened the door. I thought they said 'We have come to bring your grass back', but I was wrong, it was just the glass.

None of the above stopped us from growing dope in our back garden, and the next year we had a great crop.

Whilst not 'Britain's Most Wanted', Jacko was still the subject of police attention and they seemed to have decided that he had to be a lynchpin in some big drugs ring. A less likely 'Mr. Big' I have yet to meet. Be that as it may, they continued to call round to try to catch him and finally, months later, arrested him at an open air gig somewhere. Once in custody they obviously began asking questions about his drug dealing. They had him for the drink driving charge and evading arrest so they had no need to go easy and, when he was arrested, he had a little bit of dope on him, but not much as far as I could tell. That made what followed even odder because Jacko proceeded to give them chapter and verse about every illegal substance he had bought and passed on. I got to see his statement and it ran to 19 pages. Everything he did for almost the whole time I knew him. I was fairly surprised that he was able to recall it. The upshot was that he got 18 months in prison. He was originally placed in Wandsworth Prison but later moved to Ford Open Prison. Ford was one of the prisons where they say to you, 'The gates are over there. If you are going to abscond please go through the gates rather than over the wire fence. Remember, though, that when you are caught you will be sent to a closed prison'. That seemed to stop most escapes.

They would send the prisoners out into the local fields to work and we noticed a change in Jacko over the year when we visited him. The grey limp person that he was before was transformed into someone with a tan and muscles. When he came out he looked good – it lasted about a week. After that he was back to being a flaked out wastrel. Jill, Tom's girlfriend, came by one time and, as she was leaving she said, 'Prison has really affected him hasn't it?'

'Yes, but it has worn off now.' I replied.

A few days after he came out we saw that *Stackridge*, one of his favourite bands, was playing at *The Marquee*. We all piled into Tom's bus to go along to see them. Jacko got pretty wasted at the gig and when we came out we could see he was a bit worse for wear. We drove up Wardour Street behind a 3 tonne truck, which came to a halt because someone had parked a Luton Transit half on the kerb, so that the top of the van overhung the road. The truck driver did not think he could get through.

Now, one of the things Jacko had been doing to earn money was driving a truck.

'You could get a bus through there', he snorted, and jumped out of Tom's bus to tell the driver. We could hear him saying:

'Give me the keys and I'll drive it through'. The truck driver was understandably reluctant to pass control of his vehicle over to a drunken hippie.

He came back to the bus complaining, and Tom put the vehicle into reverse to get back to the nearest turn off. As we shot backwards a police van pulled out of the turning we were going for. We missed hitting it, but stopped. Once more Jacko disembarked and went over to them to remonstrate about the recalcitrant truck driver. As we watched, a door slid open and a hand emerged, grabbed his jacket and hauled him into the van. Another officer got out and strolled over to us.

'Is he your mate?' he asked.

'Yes.'

'He will be spending the night with us.'

'He has only just come out of prison,' I said.

'Well, he'll be used to it then, won't he?'

One other incident with him springs to mind. He came along to our gigs, ostensibly as a roadie. The usual course of events was that he would help us load in, be there for the gig and then we would load out, go off and try to find where he was and then, if we found him, load him into the bus to go home. We were trying to get a gig at *The Roundhouse* in Chalk Farm and, not knowing any of the agencies that were booking the bands for the gigs, we naively called the number on the adverts. After a preamble about wanting a gig, the guy on the phone asked, 'Do you mic up the drums?' Seemed an odd question, but I said we didn't and he offered a series of shows for the next month. We were elated until we found out that it was not *The Roundhouse* we were playing at, but a restaurant/club round the corner, and the stuff we were doing was not really what they had in mind. Jacko and Dee, Jimmy's girlfriend, had been arguing about who could drink the most, so they had a competition during the show. Jacko lost and Dee seemed unaffected. When we had finished the load out we went looking for him as usual. He was nowhere to be seen. I tried the toilets and the grounds of the place, but no trace. We were about to leave but I decided to check the toilets one more time. I had been calling his name and got no answer, but one cubicle was closed so I thought he may have passed out. I climbed on the toilet beside the locked one. There he was sitting on the closed seat, head in hands, but awake. Our conversation went like this:

'Come on, we are leaving.'

'I can't get out.'

'Why?'

'Door won't open', he said pushing at the section in front of him.

'That is a wall. The door is to your right.'

'Oh.'

He opened the door and we left. At the bus Tom refused to take him at first, convinced he was going to throw up. We convinced Tom he was not going to do that, and sat Jacko in the bus.

'If he starts to throw up I am going to push him out,' said Tom, so we followed them all the way home. Jacko did not get ejected, but when we arrived back at the house he was upside down, head under the seat, feet in the air. We helped him in and he lay on the sofa for a while. After a few minutes he stirred and turned the music up really loud.

'Can't hear it,' he slurred.

We turned it back down again, but the sudden movement involved in getting up stirred something in his stomach and he lurched to his feet and made for the back door, and with one hand over his mouth, he stood there tugging furiously at the handle. The door would not budge. It was bolted. I leaned over and withdrew the bolt and the door flew open, smashing into my forehead as he rushed by to throw up in the outside loo. He drifted off to stay with other people after this and we did not see him for a while.

Going back to the cars for a moment, the best vehicle I had in all that time was an old MG Magnette. It was a wonderful car - 1800cc engine with twin carburettors, leather seats, real walnut dashboard - and it was also a wreck. It cost me £18.00 from a car lot in Plaistow. The previous owner had jacked up the rear suspension and put big wheels on it but had failed to complete the cosmetic conversion of the wheel arches, and so the wheels stuck out from the cut back bodywork. The driver's side front headlight was mounted on a ring of rust which, when it finally went all the way round, meant that any kind of sharp stop would leave the lamp dangling by its wires. The suspension was soft as anything and there was a hole in the floor you could see the road through. In spite of that I loved it. It took me to loads of gigs and all over the place, great vehicle. Over the time I owned it the clutch began to go so I put it onto ramps and dropped the gearbox to replace the clutch. Alan and I did a lot of our own car repairs and he reminded me, when we talked on the phone recently, that we had a metal box which was full of odd parts, spark plugs, points etc. When any of the cars went wrong we would rake through this box to try to find a part which would get the vehicle going again.

It took me a while to get the clutch in place and then I had the mad task of lying on my back with the gearbox balanced between my knees trying to marry it back up to the engine housing, and then get a bolt or two in before it fell apart. The whole process of reassembling the car took two weeks, in which time it remained on the ramps. When I finally got it completed, I rolled it off the ramps to find the brakes didn't work! It rolled straight into Tom's van. The brakes would work if you pumped them, which led me to believe that the answer was to try to bleed them to get the air out. I had some success with this, but they were still a bit iffy.

It was in this condition when Alan and I climbed into the MG and set off to *The Marquee* in London. As we drove through Holborn we were stopped by the police – well two Fabulous Furry Freak Brother Look-alikes in battered car might as well have had a target painted on them. I was trying to nonchalantly pump the brakes as they stopped us but the headlight's drooping eye was unmissable. They decided to search the car, and in the process noticed some of the things that were wrong, including the hole in the floor. They called for a vehicle inspection. While we waited the police continued to lift the seats and carpets looking for a stash of drugs. Now, on the way to a gig a week or so before, we had eaten a large bar of Cadbury's Fruit and Nut. One of those huge great things. When we finished it we were in a traffic jam, and I neatly folded the silver paper over and over and then casually rubbed the resulting cube on the steering wheel. As the traffic moved off I tossed the cube into the glove box. It was this cube that the searching officer found – and his eyes lit up. He began to unravel it slowly, opening it up and just getting an ever-expanding piece of silver paper, and when he was approaching the end of the unravelling he said:

'Have you ever been in trouble with the police before?'

'I got done for growing dope in my back garden,' I replied casually.

At this point he realised there was nothing inside the cube, no white powder, no hash, no pills, nothing. He looked in his lap to see if anything had fallen out, looked on the floor, grunted in disappointment, screwed up the paper and threw it out of the window.

'I didn't get done for littering though,' I said.

That has always been my problem. I could never resist a quip or fly remark. Needless to say this did not endear me to the police, but we were clean. Nothing illegal on us at all. The vehicle inspector, however, found 25 faults with the car and presented me with a long list of things, most of which I had no idea were wrong. Amazingly, I never got a summons over it. I had to scrap the car though. I don't think I would have got away with it if I was caught driving it again, and I could not afford to repair it either.

CHAPTER 9

Flour Power

By this time I had changed jobs and began working for a flour mill in Ponders End, Enfield. Wrights Flour was the company, and the mill there had been in the same family for generations. There had, in fact, been a mill on these premises since the early 16th Century. It was a water mill, driven by an offshoot of the River Lea, until 1913, when the King George V Reservoir was built and the water no longer flowed after that it started to make the transformation into an electrically powered mill. It was an amazing place and, I believe, it still mills flour now. The oldest part of the building, a red brick and wooden slatted tower was the original mill and the water wheel and grinding stones could still be seen at the base. Even more amazing was the roof. Back in the days of the sailing ships there was a thriving business in Barking, building and repairing sea going vessels, right at the bottom of the River Lea. The owners of the mill would travel down the river and buy up second hand ship's timbers which had been damaged at sea and replaced, and the roof of this building comprised of these timbers – joined together with ancient carpentry skills. I spent some time up there marvelling at the history that was crammed into this small space.

I went there to work in the laboratory. I would test incoming grain for disease and grade the gluten content. I also had to go into the mill itself to take samples of the flour at various stages in its milling. It was a fascinating job, made even more engaging by the people who worked there. The guy in charge of the lab was 50ish with grey hair and a grey beard and he was always reading magazines about swinging and other sexual activities. And then there was Ted.

Ted was the miller and he ran the whole thing. A large rotund guy, and one of those 'old school', hands on, engineers. He had a workshop where he made parts for the mill by hand. He also drove a '60s Chevrolet, one of those wide motors with great flaring wings at the back. He always seemed to drive this very slowly and I later found out why. He had sold the great big 8 cylinder engine that the car came with and replaced it with a 4 cylinder engine from an Austin A40. He opened the bonnet and showed me one day. He had built long engine mounts to be able to hold the tiny engine in that vast arena of the engine compartment. He said all he wanted was the comfort and the air conditioning (unknown in UK cars at the time). He was also a bit of a rocker and that big Yankee car went well with his image.

After I had been there a year or so I was called to the office to be confronted by the owner and Ted. I wondered what I had done wrong, but I was completely surprised when the owner said, 'Ted will be retiring in 5 years time, and he has suggested that we train you to be our next miller.' I had not seen that coming. Still it was interesting, so I started a course in milling and they began to give me jobs in other departments, so I could get an overview of how the mill worked.

I had always had an interest in religions and mysticism. In some ways I really wanted to believe that there was something 'out there' that we could not quite grasp or understand. The main problem with this, for me, was that I could not see any real evidence for any of it. I read a lot of books, I tried tarot cards and various other approaches, but nothing convinced me. The other side of the coin was that I could see how so many addicts, drug and alcohol, fall straight into some kind of religion. Followers of gurus abound in this area, as do those who got sucked into the L. Ron Hubbard's world of Scientology, but some even drifted off into straight religions. It all did not inspire me to believe in anything.

I decided, however, to give Tai Chi a go. I was already doing yoga once a week, mostly for the physical mobility and flexibility, but I was drawn into the concept of Tai Chi. I went along to a seminar in Acton Park. We were treated to a demonstration of the first few stages on the Tai Chi movement and then we had lunch. I had already been a vegetarian for a few years by this time so the meal provided by the centre was a delight. Some of my fellow diners, however, did not find it to their taste and kept lifting vegetables and surveying the table to look for the meat. They were an interesting and very assorted bunch. There was a lady doctor, a lawyer, a monk, a builder, all sorts. We were discussing whether we would take the course, and the fact that the bulk of the movements are done with knees bent, at the crouch.

'I could not do this', the builder declared, 'messed up my hamstring playing football.'

'I damaged my ankle playing hockey', the lady doctor told us.

'I have no cartilage in my knee because I played rugby at university', and so on round the table with almost everyone coming up with some sporting injury. All except the monk and I. The monk summed it up.

'I can do this,' he said in hushed tones, 'I'm perfectly healthy. I refused to do sports when I was at school.'

'I'm with you,' I replied.

The Tai Chi and the yoga had led me down a path which made me decide to give up all drugs and alcohol. It just seemed like the right thing to do.

Around this time we were asked by the company that handled the rental of the house, if we would leave. Alan pointed out that we had an agreement and we would be happy to move if they found us another house or paid us to move. Negotiations about the situation flowed back and forth between the two parties. Finally we were called into the estate agent's office. He explained that the house belonged to one of Charlie Kray's henchmen (we never found out who it was) who had now been jailed. His property was being sold off so that house would have to be sold. We said he could sell it with us as sitting tenants, but he did not think that would work. After a lengthy discussion he sighed and offered us a joint mortgage. So it was that the four of us became house owners. Not only that, but the house was sold to us for around £6500 if I recall correctly.

Meanwhile, Mick Worwood, my old college friend and former singer of *Castle Farm* had been off to Cornwall with bass player Spyder Curphney. Spyder had been heavily involved in designing those iron-on T-shirt logos that became very popular around the mid-'70s. I am not sure if Spyder invented the process or not, but he and Mick spent the whole summer selling T-shirts on the beach. This led to the idea of doing the same sort of thing for bands. I do not think anyone had even tried this before, but they managed to get the contract to provide T-shirts for all sorts of gigs. While Spyder concentrated on building the business of making and selling the transfers, Mick was busy negotiating with rock bands for contracts to sell shirts. This led him forming a company called Brockum, which became one of the first and biggest players in this area.

So the band was playing and I was working at the flour mill and we all picked up the odd weekend's work manning the merchandise stands for Mick. Tom, our roadie, threw himself into this completely and wound up going off on tour with the *Mahavishnu Orchestra*. Gradually we were all getting sucked into doing some work for Brockum. I did the Bob Dylan Open Air show at Blackbushe Airport and the Elton John gigs at Earl's Court. The tour was named after an alleged conversation with Princess Margaret when she arrived backstage at a previous gig. According to the account I heard, and I emphasise I only heard this second hand, when Princess Margaret came backstage after an Elton John show, she walked in on people bent over a mirror. Her first words were, 'Ah cocaine, the prince of drugs'. Elton asked if she had enjoyed the show and she said 'You are louder than Concorde, but not as pretty.'

That is how the 'Louder than Concorde, but not as Pretty' tour got its name.

I'll digress from this to make a statement about how I feel about celebrities, and the way they tend to deny things and avoid the big pointy finger. There does tend to be a kind of received morality; sexually and narcotically. Leaving aside the sexual side of things, there is no doubt that we do have a drug problem in most of the world. Many countries try to put a lid on it with severe penalties for possession and even worse, sometimes lethal, penalties for importing and selling. All of these tactics do little to actually curb drug use. We use the term 'substance abuse' which is complete nonsense. It is not the inanimate substance that is suffering if you take that slant on it. If you assume that the drug user is using the substance in a way other than how it should be used you are on even shakier ground. Cannabis resin is formed on the leaves of the cannabis plant to protect them from the sun so you could say that this is true – it is being abused. However apple trees produce apples in order to propagate their species and grow new apple trees. Every time you eat an apple you are also guilty of substance abuse.

Coming back to the sexual side of things I would say that there was a time when announcing you are gay, or being exposed as gay, was certain career death if you were a celebrity. These days, movie stars, musicians and even politicians can openly announce their sexual preferences without too much of a fuss being made. I feel we need to develop that same openness with drug use. To a degree it *does* happen. George Michael was open about his penchant for 'the herb', but more people need to follow that example – especially those outside of the entertainment world.

It would be unusual, given the kind of lifestyle that Princess Margaret lived, to assume she had *not* come across cocaine. I also recall seeing a picture of Fergie (before she became *persona non grata*) in a tabloid newspaper entitled 'Fergie, the Princess who rolls her own'. There she was with a 'rollup' lying on the table. Large cigarette papers and a line of what is, so obviously, not rolling tobacco, nestling within. This is blatantly a spliff she is rolling, but no-one said a word. This was in the days before she became a tabloid punch-bag. It seems to me we do people a disservice by implying that *all* drug users are degenerate and will die early and suffer terribly, when the reality is so far from that.

I am not making the case here for universal drug use. In the many years I have been involved in music and the entertainment world I have seen many well-known people having the odd smoke, doing a line of coke and other stuff. I have seen people spend an entire life indulging in 'substances' to little or no detriment to their health, but I have equally seen others get drawn in and sucked down into the depths. As with alcohol, you can have a few drinks and say, 'that was nice', and not drink again for ages or you can have a few drinks and not stop for the rest of your life. If we could only understand what it was that made one person react one way and another react differently we would be able to help those who fall victim, allow those who don't to enjoy it and have a much more open and honest society. Of course, the other side of drugs, especially cocaine and heroin, is the suffering, death and violence that go with the illegal trade, and the amount of money that greases the wheels of the trade. Taking a different approach to addiction would be a bold but more courageous path. It is a shame that so few people seem strong, honest or motivated enough to take it.

So, having said all that, in the following pages I will mention drug and alcohol use when it forms part of the narrative and where I have actually seen it with my own eyes or, of course, indulged in.

The merchandising business was doing well for Mick and he was asking us to do more and more gigs and tours. John Brown, who drove the van for *Grope* and did some of the oil and food dye light shows for us, went to work for him permanently, as did Tom. We all went to work at the series of gigs that were happening at football grounds around the UK. At one of these, 'The Who Put The Boot In' in Charlton Football Ground, I encountered Jacko again.

I was walking through the crowd and this dervish descended on me. Hair matted, face plastered with dirt, off his head – of course - and with a whole arm streaked with blood where he had cut himself trying to open a beer can.

We also sold some merchandise at the *Yes* gig in Stoke Football Ground in May 1975. This was part of their 'Relayer' tour and Roger Dean had commissioned large white fibreglass clouds so the stage set resembled the cover of the album. *The Sensational Alex Harvey Band* were one of the support acts, and he had his own backdrop. There was a large set of 'flats', the scenery boards they use in theatre, depicting the side of a building. Against this there was scaffolding so Alex could go up there and do some of the songs from above the band. He used to spray 'Vambo Rools' on this wall during one of the songs but, on this occasion he went one further, climbed right to the top and sprayed 'Vambo Rools' on the nearest of *Yes*' pristine white clouds. They did not have time to do anything about it so it stayed there for the whole gig.

I always thought *Yes* were a bit of a pompous band, and Alex Harvey went up considerably in my estimation after this. I always liked his stuff but this was downright mischievous. I got to do his last ever tour as *The Sensational Alex Harvey Band* and it was a real experience. But I will come to that later. After a few more of these weekend and evening shows for Brockum, Mick asked me if I had any available holiday time where I worked. I said I had a couple of weeks and he offered me two weeks work in Europe with the *Rolling Stones*. There was originally a three man crew going over to do a few festivals in Holland, Germany and France but one of the crew was ill. I could take his place for a couple of weeks and get paid from my job as well as by him.

I had never been out of England before so I jumped at the chance. Of course I had no passport but, back in the '70s there was a European Travel Passport. It was just a sheet of cardboard, folded in three places with a photo and some details on it, but you could buy it over the counter at a Post Office. It would also only take you to Europe (France, Belgium, Holland, Spain and Germany) but I was only going there so it was OK. I was all set for a couple of weeks in Europe.

CHAPTER 10

Been There – Got the T-shirt

The plan was to join the other two and travel to the first show, which was in The Hague. We had a Ford Camper van – a transit with windows, beds and a set of sub-MFI kitchen units in it. We drove down to the ferry and emerged, a few hours later, in Belgium. At this point my two travelling companions said they were too tired to drive – so I had to do it. My first trip onto foreign soil, driving a vehicle I had never driven before - a lumbering shack on wheels - on the wrong side of the road. I had looked on the map and had a good idea where 'The Hague' was so, while they slept, I drove.

It all went very well until we were in Holland itself. The Hague is on the coast of Holland, just up from Rotterdam, and I had made a list of the towns I needed to head for on the way so it was not too bad. There does seem to be some sort of rule in Holland though. You cannot use a town name in more than one format. If it is on a signpost you cannot use it on a map. I was struggling, but getting there, and then all signs for 'The Hague' vanished. I was already off the motorway and heading in, towards the area of Rotterdam and that whole industrial / dockland complex. I stopped and asked directions, and was pleased to be told straight on. Still no signs for The Hague though. Finally, in a town in which I was completely lost, I stopped and asked someone. 'Here', they said, 'This is it.' I was puzzled. I was in a town called 'Den Haag' and then it dawned on me, Den Haag was The Hague in Dutch. How dumb!

We set up a couple of stalls and sold the merchandise on the football pitch they were holding the concert on and it all seemed to go OK. I had to spend a bit of time making the shirts – using a hot press to transfer the lip and tongue logo onto a pile of plain shirts. It was a good day, we could hear the music and the punters were friendly, and it seemed like a stupidly nice way to earn money. After Holland we set off for Dortmund for the next show.

This was held in the Westfallenhalle, a vast cavern of a building that was the venue for many of the larger gigs in that area. We were outside the main hall this time but that was not so bad because I had not thought much of the *Rolling Stones* performance at the first show. It seemed messy and a bit out of tune. *The Meters*, who were the support act, were no better really. I could not see why the audience applauded so much. It was only much later I realised that, for many people, especially the 'real fans', just being there is enough; seeing your heroes live on stage. These were the days before tuners of any kind and long before the kind of technology that would hold a guitar in tune.

I also began to appreciate the job for a different reason. We were out there with the punters, loads of impressionable women, all of whom wanted to know what it was like to be on tour with the Stones. One could not afford a T-shirt but wanted me to iron the transfer onto her own shirt. I agreed a price and she promptly took off her shirt and stood there, bare breasted until I had done the job. That night one of these women came back to the camper van and joined me. I had the bed over the driver's compartment, which was lucky because it was a bit bigger that the fold out ones on the sides of the vehicle. The drawback was that it was an enclosed space and we got very hot up there. In the morning, Bill, one of my companions said, 'If I had known the crossing was going to be so rough I would have taken a sea sickness pill'. I had not thought about what effect our night's exertions might have had on the soft suspension of the camper van.

From Dortmund we headed off to Cologne, and then to Paris. Paris, that city which evokes images of chic sophistication in many people's minds, chose to put the Stones in a disused abattoir, which they cunningly disguised by calling it *Pavillon de Paris* (Les Abattoirs). This was a cold building, even in the hot June weather of 1976. It still had the runnels down the floor that would have carried the blood. It was a pretty horrid place that I would come back to a few times in my career as merchandiser – some of which have their own story. It was also the place I met a dodgy Moroccan called Jean. Jean was also one of those loveable crooks. People you shouldn't really like but did anyway. He came along and manned one of the other stalls we set up to make sure we had all the exits covered. Paris was never a city I liked very much, but I did have a couple of adventures there with some interesting women over the years and tours. More of that later.

The Stones tour moved on to Lyon and then down to Barcelona. We had traded our camper van for a standard Transit now and it was just Bill and I doing the selling but, for the Barcelona gig, Bill headed off back to London for more stock and I took a train down to Spain alone. The mysterious 'ill person' had not returned yet, but I was enjoying the gig. Jean came down to meet me in Barcelona to help us out and brought his girlfriend. The gig was being held in a bullring, the *Plaza de Toros Monumental*. This was a classic bullring, like something off a picture postcard – in fact they were selling postcards of it. There was only one entrance to the outer building itself, which is via a smallish courtyard flanked by two towers. The public entered via a series of metal gates set in front of the building. We had set up our stand in the courtyard and were hanging around in the warm Spanish sun as the punters gathered outside. Suddenly there was chaos as a smoke bomb was thrown over the gates and the assembled crowd decided to force their way in. The police responded by closing the gates and standing against them and it looked, for all the world, like some ancient battle was about to take place. I went up into the tower so I could get a better view, and so that I did not choke on the smoke. By this time the police were firing their guns over the heads of the mob and lobbing the odd tear gas canister. They were fighting a small group of would-be freeloaders back along the streets, but the opposition were not giving in easily and, as I watched, I saw people with guns hiding behind cars and firing back at the police. It was all like some mad movie was taking place. Several hours passed before order was restored and the people with tickets were allowed in.

The following day we headed off towards Nice in Jean's car. His driving matched his personality completely. We hurtled round narrow roads at high speed with Jean arguing with his girlfriend in French the whole time. We had two days to make the journey in so we were able to stop in a small hotel along the way to rest. A welcome experience after Jean's driving and the constant jabber of argument, followed by sullen silences. Mind you, after a day of that, they still retired to their room and tried to reduce their bed to wreckage, just as noisily, that night.

Nice was hot and sunny. The Stones crew were mainly travelling in hire cars, most of which were demolished by the time that they had moved on to the next country. I was told, but I could not confirm it, that in Nice the tour manager picked up a new Mercedes from Hertz Car Rental, drove it out of the compound, turned into oncoming traffic and wound up racing up a grass verge. In the middle of the verge was a stone which neatly took off the car's sump. He walked back into the office before the clerk had finished dealing with the rest of the crew and said, 'Can I have another one? I have broken this one'.

The gig itself was in a football stadium, *Parc Des Sports De* L'Ouest, on 13th June 1976. European football stadiums at the time tended to have high fences around them so the fans could not invade the pitch or hurl objects at the players, and this was no exception. There was a 12ft high chain link fence with only a few small gates set into it to allow the players and officials onto the field. It took the audience a long time to get onto the pitch where the stage was set up along one of the long sides. We set up our stand almost opposite the band, and not far from one of these gates. We had managed to get some crash barriers around us, which was a very good precaution. The sun was out and the crowd were in. There was a space between us and the edge of the crowd which was filled with children playing games, and a few people lying there sunbathing. It was a fairly idyllic setting. I can only recall two of the support bands that were on. Robin Trower's band were directly under the *Meters* (tour support) on the bill and I remember *John Miles Band* playing. Apparently *Little Feat* and *Kokomo* also played. It was John Miles that got the first blow.

During his set, the audience became restive and things began to fly around a bit. Towards the end of the set he launched into his hit 'Music was my First Love'. It clearly was not the first love of the audience there who pelted him with bottles and sandwiches (don't ask me why sandwiches) until he left the stage. At some point during the day there were some screams and shouts, and we were aghast to see the entire audience running away from the stage – straight at us and the tiny door to get out! We gathered as many children as we could onto our side of the crash barrier. They did not quite reach us the first time, but they repeated the stampede a couple more times before things quietened down. We found out later that a woman was assaulted in front of the stage and the Hell's Angels marched in and started hitting people – anxious to do a re-run of Altmont. Scary stuff in anyone's book, and a baptism of fire for me.

Despite all of this I was enjoying that 'life on the on road' thing. In the many years I spent touring in various forms I have seen many people who cannot really handle it. People who need roots, who cannot live a life in hotel rooms. For me it was easy. I never once had a problem with it. I may have had problems while I was working, with the people I worked with and with the jobs themselves, but the whole business of being away, travelling from place to place and living from day to day never got to me.

I was coming to the end of the time I was allotted as a holiday from my flour mill job, and the other person who was supposed to take over from me on this tour had not materialised. Mick came out and joined us in Nice and I told him I would quit my job and finish the tour. He said that was good and he would give me some more work when this tour was over. That made my mind up, but I had another problem. My toy town passport would not get me into Yugoslavia which was the next but one country on the tour. We left France and headed up to Zurich. When I got there I spent a day at the British Embassy and got them, after a lot of lying about the 'major part' I played in the tour and how I had been a last minute replacement etc., to issue me with a full passport.

After the Zurich show we headed off to Zagreb in, what was then, the communist republic of Yugoslavia. This was another eye-opening moment for me. Yugoslavia was one of the most open, and probably most affluent of the communist countries, but some parts of it that we drove through were decidedly impoverished. The places where we stopped to eat were very run down and there were still horse drawn wagons hauling farm equipment and produce around.

Zagreb itself was, however, a much more cosmopolitan place. There were better restaurants and hotels and it had a much more western feel to it, although there was still an edginess to it; a feeling the some of those eastern bloc gangsters were watching you from every street corner. The gig was indoors in a vast sports hall, *The Dom Sportova*, and we were told that, when John Mayall had played there the month before he had decided to come back on stage for an encore – even though he was already over the curfew time. The crowd were all shouting for more so he and his band marched out of the dressing room to head for the stage – and the police set the dogs on them and chased them back to the room. We were warned that, no matter who you were, the curfew was strictly enforced.

Yugoslavian currency was called the dinar and was what was known as a 'soft' currency. You could change western money for dinar with no problem, but the other way around was not easy and you did not get a good deal from it. Mick went off on the day after the show with most of the local money we had made at the gig, and tried to buy things to sell back in England in order to get some return from the show. He settled on buying some wolf furs and some gold jewellery, which he parcelled up and we hid in the flight cases. The wolf skins were not cured properly and went off with a spectacularly bad smell a while later – before he got around to selling them.

After the gig we went back to the crew's hotel where there was a bit of a party in place. I did not see any of the band there, but there were a lot of guys from the tour and a lot of women. They were due to fly to the next show, which was in Vienna, but we had to drive and the only way we would get there on time was to set off overnight. Because the crew had no further use for their cars they decided to play bumper cars with them in the hotel car park. Bill and I left the party and drove out of the demolition derby that was going on outside the *Intercontinental Hotel*.

We were both tired so I said I would get in the back and sleep for a bit while Bill took the first driving stint. I told him to wake me when he felt drowsy and I made a bed from the T-shirts, climbed into my sleeping bag, and nodded off. A while later I began to wake up because we seemed to be weaving around a bit. I was just about to extract myself from the sleeping bag when the van left the road. There was an almighty crash and we rolled sideways and crashed into a tree.

I wriggled out of the sleeping bag and crawled forward. Bill had his head on the steering wheel and a large amount of tree was now protruding through the smashed side window of the van. The windscreen was unbroken but had popped out of the frame. Bill raised his head and cascades of glass fell from his hair. I could see he was not cut and was glad he had not smashed into the steering wheel or suffered some other damage.

'I really fucked it this time, didn't I?' he mumbled.

We both laughed and climbed out of the van. It was on its side and impaled on a tree. It was already getting light by this time and we had not been standing there long, trying to work out what to do next, when a small police car pulled up. The police got out and looked at us, then down at the van, then back at us again. One of them went down and had a look into the vehicle. He came back up and spoke to his companion, and looked back at us.

'Driver?' he said, looking at me.

'No, asleep', I replied, miming two hands beside my head.

He turned to Bill and repeated the question.

'Driver?'

'Asleep,' was Bill's response – because, he was after all, asleep when the van crashed.

The police guy looked at the van, looked at each of us in turn, noticed the glass in Bill's hair, and said, definitively, 'Driver!' and put the handcuffs on him.

While this was going on, a tow truck arrived and began the process of righting the van and pulling it back onto the road. The driver's door was caved in and the driver's side window was smashed, but there was little other damage apart from the windscreen. We could not put this back into the frame but, with the aid of a bit of gaffa tape, and by twisting the windscreen wipers into a vertical position we managed to get it to stay on. The police put Bill into their car and took him away and I followed in the tow truck.

Bill was arrested. I think they charged him with 'entering Yugoslavian territory without permission' or something similar because our visas were only valid for the main roads and the city of Zagreb. Since he was going to be held overnight I knew I had to go off to Vienna on my own and do the show that night. They had impounded the van so I took a train and set off for Austria. Once I was there I went to the venue and called Mick to tell him what had happened and where Bill was. We had a couple of flight cases full of stock on the truck so I was able to run the show, and as luck would have it, I also found a very nice Austrian woman who took me back to her flat for the night.

Mick arrived the following day and we both went down to the small town where Bill had been incarcerated. We found Bill and the van sitting on the street. The police had taken him to court, fined him all the money he had on him and then kicked him out, with no money. He hadn't eaten and had slept in the van during the day. We took him off for a meal, and then drove Mick back to Vienna so he could fly back to England.

Bill and I drove the battered van back to the UK. We went through part of the Alps on the way and on the route we came to one of those long winding mountain descents so beloved of *Top Gear* and *James Bond*. As I drove down this I realised, in that classic way that people in films suddenly do, that the brakes were not exactly 100% functional. In fact, they went straight down to the floor and had to be pumped up in order to work at all.

I turned to Bill, 'We don't have any brakes', I remarked casually.

'Yeah', he laughed.

All my years of driving vehicles that did not actually work properly came into play and I steered the van down to the bottom. At the bottom there was a small restaurant so I pulled in there and we had lunch. After lunch Bill got in the driver's seat of the van and we drove off. At the first corner he put his foot on the brakes and they did not work.

'Shit! You were not joking!' he shouted.

I thought he had taken it all a bit casually.

When we got back to the UK we parked the van at the Brockum office – beside another van from the same hire company whose back door had been ripped off and was lying on the floor of the van. The door got trashed by someone trying to break in and steal the merchandise while it was parked at a *Yes* festival. We could not hire any vans from that company any more.

I knew then that this was a great thing to do for a living, and I would have left that day on another tour if I could have.

CHAPTER 11

Rainbows and Vambos

I came back from the Stones tour and felt pretty good about the whole thing. I thought I had coped well with the new world I had found myself in and I was ready for the next challenge. I did a bit of work for Brockum at some festivals and the band had a few stabs at doing some gigs, but it seemed to have pretty much run its course and I was hungry to get back out on the road. During the course of the Stones tour I had slipped back into having a spliff every now and then. Having been away for a few weeks I had dropped behind the Tai Chi class although I was still doing yoga. I decided not to attend the Tai Chi classes anymore.

Mick had an office in London on the Finchley Road, and I would go up there a lot to help get tour merchandise together. Although we were still preparing T-shirts using the iron-on transfers, at times a lot of the shirts were being silkscreened instead. This was a good thing because during one of the Stones festivals I had been preparing some shirts when the trestle table, that had the press on, collapsed. I caught the press on the way down, but it was still switched on and very hot. By the time I had found a place to put it down I had two severe burns, one on each arm. The scars are still faintly visible now – 37 years later. I had no wish to repeat this. Silkscreen was much easier.

The next tour I was sent out on was with *Richie Blackmore's Rainbow* at the end of August 1976.. The first show was at the *Bristol Hippodrome* and I seem to recall that there was one of those 'something or other 'On Ice'' spectaculars on the day before our get in. They were melting down a huge block of ice, which was on a rink which covered the stage. Everything was wet and there were pipes and stuff all over the place. Richie's tour featured a large rainbow which needed to be set up on the stage. It was in several sections, all of which had to be flown in the air and bolted, then wired together. Back in the '70s the technology for this kind of thing was 'hammer and nail' primitive. The rainbow itself consumed so much power that there were times on the European leg when it drew the power from the stage and the guitar amps would falter.

This was also a much more hard core crew than others I had worked with previously, and I was to find out just how hard core a bit later. For the UK shows we travelled by van with the merchandise in the back. This was OK and no real problem, and it also gave us a chance to relax since we did not have to be at the shows until the middle of the afternoon.

For the crew it was much, much harder. The rainbow took a while to rig so, what with the trusses for the lighting, the get-ins became very early and the get-outs very late. No sound or backline could be rigged until all the lights and the rainbow were in, up and running.

The *Bristol Hippodrome* is a magnificent old building, all balustrades and boxes, plush but faded velvet seats and a marble edge that runs around the front of the stage. At the end of the set Richie Blackmore whipped off his guitar and began flailing away at the front of the stage. The Fender Strat obstinately refused to break. It took several blows before he managed to separate the neck from the body and throw the detritus into the crowd. He later got fined for breaking some lumps from the marble, and had to pay to have the stage repaired.

When the tour moved to Europe I realised how hard it was for the crew, and came a cropper. They had a very strict protocol. Lights in first and when they are rigged the sound goes in. After the gig the sound and backline come out and the respective crews get taken to the hotel. When the lighting is out the lighting crew go back to the hotel. One hour later everyone gets on the bus, and we head off to the next gig. The process for the crew was exhausting so they decided to cope with it sensibly, like all road crews did. They partied all night. This was an ordinary coach, not a modern tour sleeper bus. We slept upright in our seats – or didn't, if the party really went for it. It was OK for us and the sound guys because they got to go to the hotel when we arrived, but the lighting crew went straight to work. The guy who rigged the show was a superhuman. I saw him climb girders to put in the flying points for the rainbow and the trusses, and all of that after a night of partying. Two shows into the tour I made my first mistake. I packed down the merchandise and went to the bus to write up the evening's sales and count the money. I stood the two merchandise trunks by the back of the truck meaning to go out and load them in, and I fell asleep. I was woken by the sound crew complaining to me that they had to load my trunks and I should have been there. A few nights later I made a bigger error. I went back to the hotel with the crew having helped with all the loading as a penance. I had just about got back into their good books. I took a shower and fell asleep and was woken by a pounding on the door. They did not know what room I was in because I was booking my own hotel rooms, and had been waiting for me to come out. More penance and more loading, but I never quite got back in with that crew. On one journey, after a particularly hard load out they laced a bottle of water with several acid tabs and passed it around. Everyone on the coach was tripping for the whole journey. The rigger, whose name I forget, fell asleep with his head resting on his hand. When he awoke he found he could not feel or move his hand. After seeing a doctor he was told he had shut off the blood supply to the nerves and it would take a while to come back to life. So he carried on climbing the walls and rafters with one hand until it did come back. I think Mick finally lost that contract when

Richie grabbed Mick's sister's tit in a lift and he floored him. Oh well, Rock and Roll.

I came off that tour and went straight out with *The Sensational Alex Harvey Band.* I was quite happy about this. They were a great band and I was determined not to mess up on this one. I went out to meet the crew at the load out, after a rehearsal in London. They seemed a much easier bunch to get on with. The lighting designer was Bill Duffield and we got on immediately. Once we were out on the road it was clear there was some tension in Alex Harvey's band and management. Alex's long time manager Bill Fehilly had been killed in a plane crash just before the tour, and Alex was drinking a little more than usual. He was touring the same stage set he had when he did the *Yes* festivals in the summer. The backdrop of a house with the scaffolding in front of it was a big thing to put up each day (although not as bad as the rainbow had been). Every night Alex would walk through part of the wall, a section made of polystyrene bricks, and announce 'I was framed'. Every day, when it was put up, the guy who did it carefully replaced the bricks and repainted it back to being a wall.

In Hamburg, Alex came through the wall dressed, not in his usual striped jumper, but in a full Hitler outfit with a stick on moustache. This did not go down too well, but Alex was determined to carry on doing it at the next shows in Dortmund and Frankfurt. When we got to Berlin he did the same thing but was a bit the worse for wear with drink and crawled through the wall rather than walking. The promoter from Berlin was absolutely livid about it and was shouting, 'He will never work in Germany again'.

On many of those tours there were always several touts outside selling pirate T-shirts and other merchandise. We got on OK with guys and did not give them a hard time because they were trying very hard to make a living, and doing it in a very hard way. After the Berlin show they asked us where the next one was and I said 'Stockholm'. They were crestfallen. That would be an expensive trip for them. The PA they were using for this tour had some of those huge bass bins that were all the rage then, the size of a garden shed, in fact. While the crew were not looking, one of the touts slipped in between two of the bins on the back of the truck. What the guy did not know was that there were two days between the gigs and the truck, having driven all night and travelled on a ferry from Bremerhaven to Sweden, was then parked up in a sub zero Swedish winter. As the crew began to unload the truck they became aware of an increasingly bad smell. When they pulled apart the bass bins a soiled, dehydrated T-shirt pirate rolled out. He was taken off to hospital suffering from dehydration and exposure. All he had with him was a bottle of whiskey and some crisps - and he was trapped in pitch black for two days with nowhere to pee or anything. Must have seemed like a good idea at the time.

It was snowing in Stockholm, quite a lot in fact. I decided to go and buy a razor and shave off the beard I had worn for so long. It had been reduced from its full, wispy, lack of splendour to something like an extended stubble but, on stepping out of the coach to go into the gig, I certainly noticed that it was not there.

Alex collapsed onstage that night but managed, somehow, to finish the show. Back at the hotel he collapsed again and was diagnosed with exhaustion. We travelled overnight to Chateau Neuf in Oslo, only to find a note on the door reading:

'Dear Crew. The tour is over, go back to England.'

So we did. That was the last tour Alex ever did with the band, although he did recover and come back with a new band in 1979. The band tried to carry on without him but, good as they were, once you have been fronted by someone like him whatever else you do looks pretty tame.

Around this time we all began to drift away from the house in Woodford Green. Alan and Maureen were going to get married and we all decided to leave them in the house. Tom Barratt went off with his partner Jill, and they wound up living on the Isle of Skye. Jacko had made another one of his reappearances and told me that his father had bought a flat for his sister in South London while she was studying to be a nurse at Kings College Hospital. Now that she had graduated she was going over to the US to join her family, and the flat was now his. He suggested I move in with him. Since he owned the flat there would be no rent, all we had to do was to share the bills. Seemed fair after all the years he had sponged off us, so I moved in. I also bought myself a new car. This was a Sunbeam Alpine sports car, one of those perfect little sports cars that the UK used to make so well. Over the next few months I would drop the car into my friend's garage every time I went away and have some work done on it. The significance of this will become clear later.

CHAPTER 12

Flying Pigs

At the start of 1977 I was offered a tour of Europe with the *Pink Floyd*. The Floyd had long been one of my favourite bands, right from the early days at UFO, and I was really looking forward to doing this. I had two people travelling with me because it was quite a large tour. Trevor was a New Zealander with a wicked sense of humour and very upfront manner, and Mark was a reasonably straight up English guy. They were both in a band, the name of which escapes me. Trev sang and Mark played drums. We were travelling with the crew on a coach, but the gigs were pretty relaxed with a day off between each town. The stage crew would go in the evening before to start rigging the set and all of the flying stuff, but sound and backline got a day off. Most of the gigs were at least two days at each town too. They were a nice bunch of guys on that crew. Thoroughly professional and relaxed about it too.

We kicked off in the *Westfallenhalle* in Dortmund, Germany. I nipped in to see the show and I was a bit disappointed. The band sounded a bit under rehearsed, not the tight unit I had seen the year before, and some of the production seemed a bit loose too. Roger Waters thought the same and so, after the German dates, we went to the *Sportpaleis* in Antwerp and set the whole thing up for four days . The crew had some desk tapes of the show which they ran over the PA and got the production finely tuned. I believe that the band went back to England and did a few days rehearsal as well, and then they came and joined us for a day in Antwerp for a run through. After that it was all on track. And we carried on.

In Frankfurt we decided to go for a meal after the first show. We left the gig and took a taxi into town. It was all getting a bit late and many of the restaurants were closing down for the night. We walked into one Italian restaurant and the guy said he could do some cold stuff, but he had just turned off the ovens. I was OK with that but Trev was trying to persuade him to fire them back up for us. He still had a backstage pass hanging round his neck and the restaurant owner saw this.

'Oh, *Pink Floyd*', he said.

'That's us,' Trev replied without even a slight hesitation. The man in the restaurant took it all in without even thinking that maybe the members of *Pink Floyd* might have some big restaurant lined up to go to after their show.

'I have all your records,' he gushed and he turned on the ovens and started to prepare us pizzas. While they were warming up he went upstairs to his flat and came back down with LPs and pens and asked us to sign them. Once again there was no hesitation from Trev, although Mark and I were quite embarrassed by this subterfuge. The guy did not even question why one of the members of the quintessentially English band had a strong Australian accent. When we left he thanked us for coming to his restaurant and was really happy. I did not have much change so I only left a few coins as a tip but, strangely enough, Trev was quite indignant about that.

'He will think *Pink Floyd* are cheapskates,' he said, and left a 20 deutschemark note on the table.

Trev was an ex-Hare Krishna and something had gone down between him and them a while back. He was hazy about the details but he hinted that it involved him running a café in South America, and coming back to the UK with some money and then deciding to run away and not be part of it anymore. He was so afraid of them that, when we walked down a street in Sweden on another tour, he ducked into a shop as two of the shaven headed tribe approached.

'I was at the Temple with one of them,' he told me. 'If they see me they will try to take me back.'

I must admit the thought of a 'Hare Krishna heavy' amused me somewhat but he seemed to be genuinely afraid. We got talking about religions and being vegetarian. He asked me why I was a vegetarian and I said that I could not see any reason for anything to die so that I could live. If I can stay alive and healthy without having to eat any meat or fish then I was happy to do that. I asked him why he was a veggie.

'It's in The Book,' was the reply.

'What Book?'

'The Hare Krishna book. It says you have to take one re-incarnation for every hair on the head of the animal you eat.'

I remarked that I did not think the earth would last long enough for some people to manage that and thought no more of it until we got to Berlin. In Berlin, after the first show, we were all invited out to a Japanese restaurant for a meal. I looked at the menu and saw there was nothing on there for me to eat so I stayed behind, but Trev went. When he came back I asked him what he had to eat.

'I had squid', he said.

'But a squid is a cephalopod – it is an animal'.

'Ah, but it's got no hairs on it', was his answer. It's all in the fine print, this religious stuff.

We did go out for a meal after one of the other Floyd shows in Germany. This time we found a restaurant that was open and we sat down and had a relaxed meal. It was quite crowded in there, and when we left there were already people heading for our table. We got into a taxi and headed for the hotel. As I got out I reached for my briefcase – it was not there! I suddenly realised that I had put it right under the table. I jumped back in the taxi and luckily he knew what restaurant he had picked us up from. I marched into the restaurant up to the table and reached under, the briefcase was still there. The other diners looked a bit surprised, especially the ones eating at that table. Little did they know that the briefcase I retrieved contained the merchandise takings for all the German *Pink Floyd* shows. These amounted to several hundred thousand pounds! Heart-stopping moment that. I will come back to the money thing in a bit.

In Berlin, the sound guy came up to us and asked us if we would like to drive his car to Vienna. He had decided not to be in the crew coach and came in his own car, but he had friends in Vienna so wanted to fly there and spend the day off with them He said he would pay us to do it so we agreed. He handed over the car documents and the permit for his CB radio. Berlin was, at the time, an island of West Germany inside East Germany. You had to travel through checkpoints to get there and everything was tightly controlled. You could only travel on the designated roads and could not go into any of the towns along the way. The journey time was usually logged and, if you went over the time, there were often questions asked. I was told all of this before when we went through with Alex Harvey the year before, but I had only ever been in and out on coaches, and had never driven in the East.

The day after the show we set off. We went down to the checkpoint and passed through into East German territory. The first problem was unexpected. There were no road signs to anywhere in the west. The journey in had been less than an hour, I thought, so I expected to see a sign to a town I knew but there was nothing. We had no map, certainly not a map of East Germany, and nowhere to buy one. I continued to drive and then, to my relief, saw a sign for Frankfurt. That was the right direction, I thought, and headed that way. Two hours later we were still driving. Something was not right. This was confirmed when we saw a sign saying 'Poland 5km'. We had been travelling east. Mark had an airline map, one of those things you get stuffed in the seat of a plane so he pulled that out and then we found out there were two Frankfurts. Frankfurt am Main was on the River Main in West Germany, and Frankfurt am Oder was on the River Oder and the Polish Border!

We turned around and drove back. The fuel was running low and we had now been in East Germany too long. All those scare stories came back to haunt me. Luckily we managed to choose the right road, and, a few hours later pulled into a checkpoint to the west manned by stocky Russians in full 'fur hat, Kalashnikov and greatcoat' regalia seen in so many spy films. He gestured for us to park by the office and took our passports and visas. Ahead was a fortified barrier with guards and tank traps. I had a small piece of dope on me, which I had hidden in my socks in my suitcase. No easy way to get to that and throw it away if they decided to search us. Mark was getting very nervous.

'I have to have a cigarette,' he said and lit up.

The CB Radio was mounted on the dashboard and the speaker for it sat where the ashtray normally was. The guard had come out of the office and was walking towards us. Mark lifted the speaker, in search of the ash tray and there was a huge lump of black hash sitting there. He put the speaker back down. 'Shit!' was all he could say. The guard came to the window and gestured for me to wind it down. There was a pause.

'It's OK, you may go', he said in clipped English.

Trying not to breathe a sigh of relief I accepted the passports, wound up the window and drove through the barrier. As we passed the assembled guards Trev wound his window down and shouted back:

'We got away with it, you bastards!'

That was Trev. Always one to try to make a situation into an incident.

He had been walking around the German streets with a small tape recorder, interviewing people. The conversation would go like this:

'Hi, I'm from the New Zealand Broadcasting Company and I would like to ask you a few questions.'

Germans, being on the whole polite and willing to talk, would often agree to be interviewed by him.

'My dad was in the New Zealand Air Force in the war and he flew over Germany. You guys shot him down and he ruined his best pair of trousers. What I want to know is, what are you guys gonna do about it?'

Faced with such inane nonsense most people had no idea how to respond. Which pleased Trev a lot.

Anyhow, when we handed the car over in Vienna we mentioned the dope. He said he had put it there in the UK and forgotten all about it. We took a lump as compensation for the anxiety it had caused us.

The tour rolled on and we found ourselves doing three days at that horrid gig, *Les Abattoirs*, in Paris. They had dropped the abattoir reference from the name but the *Pavillion de Paris* was still the same ghastly gig. It was February and very cold, especially where the T-shirt stalls

Pink Floyd merchandising 1977

were. I was frozen standing there all evening and we took turns going into the gig to warm up. On the second evening a bunch of girls hung around the stall and came back to the hotel with us. I wound up with two of them, which, in the words of the Fast Show, was 'nice'. They both were quite 'up for it' although one was more into a threesome than the other one. She was saying to her friend, 'Come on. Just for the experience' or something similar in French. They left during the early hours of the morning but there was a knock on the door a few hours later and the more adventurous of the two had come back for more before she went to college. The situation with the hotel was the usual one with these tours. We were booked into the same hotel as the crew, but we paid our own bills. I had been receiving notes from the hotel reception to come and speak to them about it but I had not done anything about it yet. While I was engaged with this girl there was a knock on the door and the woman came in to deal with the mini bar. This was in the corridor of our room (we were staying in the *Paris Sheraton* at the time so the rooms were large and spacious). Shortly after this there was another knock on the door and a woman marched in. The young lady's head was under the covers as she arrived. 'It's about the hotel bill,' she started, 'We need to get some money from you.'

At this point, my companion's head emerged from under the covers and I said:

'Ok how much do you need?' and made to stand up.

The woman flushed bright red and said, 'Don't get out of bed!' and rushed off.

I went down to reception and paid the bill a while later.

This young lady was quite keen and came back to the show the next two nights as well. She also came to visit me in England with another eager female friend, but I was leaving that day on another tour so I did not get a chance to revisit those delights.

We flew down from Paris to Austria and I can't quite recall why we did not go directly to Munich, but we found ourselves in Austria having to drive up to Munich in a rental car. It started OK but as we approached the higher ground around the German border it began to snow. The snow got worse and our progress slowed. What had seemed like a nice simple afternoon drive through southern Germany was turning into a slow overnight slog. The road had become hard to pick out in the rapidly deepening snow. Then we reached a patch of road that had been cleared by the snowplough and were able to get a bit more speed up. As we sped through the night we began to relax and look forward to a hotel room in Munich. It was then that I saw the snowplough coming back towards us on the other side of the road. Once it had got close to us I realised it was travelling in its own private blizzard, sucking the snow from the road and blowing it to the side. It would be OK, but the wind was blowing it straight back onto the road. We entered the snowstorm and I instinctively touched the brakes. The car began to skid on the icy road and, although I fought it, I lost control and we found ourselves sliding off the road and into a snow filled ditch. We got out and looked at the car. There was no way we could drive it out of that. A moment later we heard another car coming down the road, this also entered the snowplough blizzard, and shortly after joined us in the bottom of the ditch.

We all stood there looking at the situation. From somewhere further up the road we heard the sound of another car approaching. We looked up onto the road but could see no lights. This was because the car was approaching us along the ditch. Wheels spinning in the snow, a little Fiat 500 came beetling along the ditch towards us. The driver of this vehicle was obviously following the ditch hoping to find a way to get back onto the road, but our two cars blocked his progress. A while later the snowplough pulled up on the road above us; a brief negotiation, money changed hands, and the snowplough pulled all three vehicles back onto the road. There was no real damage done to our car. There was a bit of mud and mess down the side, and maybe a couple of scratches, but nothing drastic. We headed off to Munich.

In Munich the promoters threw a party for the band and crew. We all went back to the hotel to change and get cleaned up, and then boarded the tour bus to go to a remote night club. We had been promised all sorts of things; food, drink, drugs, women. The bus driver, however, had no idea where the place was and after an hour or so attempted a U-turn in a field – and promptly sunk the bus to its axles in mud. Some people got out and tried to find taxis but most of us sat there until we were towed out again. By the time we arrived at the party, the party had already left the building.

When we returned the hire car at Munich Airport we were running a bit late for the plane. We dropped off the keys and said we had to rush to get the flight. As we climbed into a taxi to get to the terminal the guy from the rental place came running up saying:

'It is dirty, there is mud all over it'

'Well, it was in a ditch in the snow – I am sure it will wash off,' I replied, and we sped away leaving him looking distraught.

The Floyd tour moved to the UK. By this time it was a very finely honed show and everything was going perfectly. The special effects guy told me that, at one gig, they had replaced the wire that the aeroplane ran down during one of the songs. The plane would start at the top and hurtle down the wire crashing into the back of the stage with a large explosion. They put a new wire up because the old one was getting worn. After running a few tests and repeatedly re-tensioning the wire they decided it was OK and they would go for it. On the day of the show he decided to run it one last time to test it. The plane came down and took out the first three rows of seats. If he had not done that test there would have been some serious injuries.

After 5 nights at the *Empire Pool*, Wembley we moved on to the *New Bingley Hall* in Staffordshire. This was a cattle shed. No, really, it actually was a cattle shed. It was the place where they held the country show and was more often filled with sheep, pigs and cows than it was with rock bands. You could smell it too. We had a stall at the far end of the hall because, being just a large metal shed, there was no foyer or anything like that. We were running a bit low on shirts, and a few other things, so they decided to send someone up to give us some more. They sent the youngest of their employees who could not drive. This meant he had to get a train with four or five large boxes of merchandise. He set off in the morning and they dropped him at the station. When he had not arrived by late afternoon we called the office to find out what had happened to him.

He was told to 'go to the Bingley Hall' so he did. The *New Bingley Hall* is in Staffordshire, as I said, near Birmingham. He went to Bingley, in West Yorkshire, which is a village a way outside Bradford. He got a taxi and asked to go to the *Bingley Hall* and found himself, with his boxes of merchandise, standing outside a church hall in which a scout meeting was taking place. He didn't make it down to us until the following day.

It was at the *Bingley Hall* on that gig that I met Erica. She was a beautiful young hippy who came up to talk to us. She was, however, being followed around by someone she wanted to get rid of. Since we were being a bit silly - end of tour and all that - we had been out and bought water pistols and were secretly shooting people as they walked past the stall, catching them when they were not looking and leaving them wondering where the water had come from. We turned out full fire, or water, power on Erica's stalker forcing him to retreat soaked. Erica and I became close friends and we still write to each other today – some 35 years on.

After the Floyd shows were over I went out again. This time it was *Black Sabbath*'s 'Technical Ecstasy Tour'. This was a completely different kind of tour, but one with lasting consequences. Jacko had started working for Brockum by this time and we went out on tour together. I was thinking at the time that, given his 'previous', this could be a liability but we navigated the first shows in Paris and Colmar and it all seemed to be going very well. *AC/DC* were the support act for the tour and they were in serious danger of blowing *Black Sabbath* offstage every night; Bon Scott and Angus Young had a raw energy that Sabbath's bluster could not quite match. *AC/DC* were unknown at the time and they were a very sociable bunch of guys. They hung out with the crew a lot and that was always a good thing for a support act to do. Gets them a lot of co-operation and shows they don't think they are stars ....yet.

The first few shows in Germany were mini festivals, some of which had very odd bills. The first one, with *Ian Gillan's Band* and the *Doctors of Madness* added to the line up was OK, but for some odd reason they also put the *Commodores* on as well. A case of Once, Twice, Three Times a Whatever For? I recall them not going down too well with an audience of rockers. The next one, in Cologne, featured krautrock band *Jane* and that was OK but, in Nuremburg they added *Caravan* and *John Mclaughlin's Shakti*, along with the *Commodores* and *The Doctors of Madness*. Talk about throwing all the styles up in the air and seeing what falls out. *Caravan* got by on sheer whimsy and happy beats, but John Mclaughlin, sitting cross-legged on a riser with tabla and tambora players got canned off. They repeated the same bill in Ludwigshafen the next day with a similar result. German festivals did tend to do this kind of genre shifting thing.

When we got to Brussels the gig was in the *Cirque Royale* and back to being just the two bands. The Belgian promoter had a bit of a reputation for being a bit tricky with the rider. He would provide all sorts of good stuff and bill the production for it. As soon as the bands left the building he would lock the dressing rooms and take all the leftover goodies home with him later. At the end of this show we had packed the shirts down and come into the hall to lend the crew a hand packing up. Ozzy appeared onstage with his tour manager and a couple of others bearing boxes of stuff, drink, food fruit; all sorts. 'There you are boys, put this on your bus.' They had cleared the dressing rooms themselves and the promoter was furious.

Jacko on the merchandise stand

Then we came to Hamburg. We were staying in the hotel with was part of the *Congress Centrum Hamburg*. Unfortunately the gig was in the *Ernst Merck Halle* on the other side of the park. Since the T-shirts and other merchandise were on the truck, we left the van parked at the hotel and walked to the gig. As the load in and set up progressed we sorted out the shirts and began to get the stall together. Late in the afternoon a couple of young ladies arrived. Both of them looked pretty good and drew a bit of attention from those members of the crew that were not actively working. I took a great liking to one of the girls. She was dressed in a leather jacket and looked quite lovely. One of the guys from the lighting crew was also drawn towards this girl and we went into that kind of male competition area. This developed into a bit of rivalry and eventually into a 'beer fight'. A 'beer fight' an extension of a game called 'the beer hunter'. You get six cans of beer, shake one up and then face away as someone shuffles the cans. Each person takes turns in holding a can to his head and cracking the tab. If it does not explode all over him he puts it down. When the shaken can shoots its contents over one of the players, that player has to drink all of the opened cans and play is resumed. This is usually a short messy game. In a beer fight you arm yourself with two cans of beer and try to soak your opponent in a similar way. During the course of this exchange my adversary was a bit premature in spraying his cans and did not get me at all. As he ducked under a table, to get more beer, I jumped up on the table and soaked him with both cans. This had me winning the fight - and the lady.

Andrea was her name and, when she came back to the show that night, we got to know each other better - mostly in the course of a lot of kissing and cuddling on a pile of T-shirts. I did not notice it at the time, but that whole episode was illuminated by the follow spot operator – the one I had defeated in the beer fight. This was to be the start of a long, and often very intense, relationship. I did not realise it at the time, but this woman was to be at the centre of several pivotal moments in my life. At the end of the gig I started packing down and offered to take Andrea home. Jacko was nowhere to be seen. How unusual. After I had got everything done and wheeled the trunk onto the truck we went off to find Jacko. He had spent the entire gig up on the follow spot tower drinking and smoking hash, and was completely wasted. We walked him back to the hotel with him complaining all the time and asking why I had not got the van. I left Andrea in the van while I went to the foyer and took him up to the room. We got into the lift at the same time as a rotund American businessman. The CCH is a tall hotel and the first few floors are just the Congress Centre and halls so the lift took off – so did Jacko's stomach. He looked around for somewhere to throw up and spied a receptacle on the wall. He leaned on it and threw up, and the contents went straight through and onto his legs and feet. The receptacle was only a wire mesh waste paper basket. The American tried to blend himself into the wall.

Having got Jacko into the room, and his stinking jeans and shoes into a bag hanging out of the window, I returned and took Andrea back to her home. After a bit more embracing and such like I had to say goodnight. She was still living with her parents so we had to part. We exchanged addresses – no internet back then – and I had to find my way back across Hamburg to the hotel with the feel and smell of her still clouding my head. She told me that I ate a banana as I drove her home that night (strange, the things we remember) - and added, 'you might say that you met someone that night who was going to love you from then on until forever – now how many people can say that?'

Not many I suppose. We wrote to each other a lot and I saw her a few times when I was anywhere near Hamburg, but we lived too far apart to do much about it then. It was obvious though that there was something special between us and we were to meet again, and again. She told me later that all the guys from *AC/DC* had tried to chat her up too – but she wanted to come back with me.

After Hamburg we moved on to Copenhagen and a gig in the *Falkoner Teatret* (Falkoner Theatre). The gig has a hotel attached to it and we were staying the hotel that night. After the show Bon Scott and Angus came up to our room and we sat around having a smoke. *Slade* were playing the following night so we all decided to stay on and watch them. The support act was a Danish band who were teenage heartthrobs, and so there were a lot of young women hanging out waiting to catch a glimpse of them. Bon and the bassist, (called George I think), were up in our room and we were looking down at the crowd below. The lead singer of the Danish band also had long fair hair and, since we were a few floors up, the girls below mistook me for him and started screaming. Bon and George gathered up all the toilet rolls they could find and began pelting the crowd.

After this we went on to Gothenburg in Sweden, and the tour got pulled with the rest of the Scandinavian gigs cancelled including Helsinki, which has the distinction, for me at least, of being the most cancelled destination. I have never yet managed to get to Helsinki. It appeared on tour itineraries from that tour right through my touring career and I never ever went there. I developed a theory. The town Helsinki does not exist. It is a mistake made by early map makers and they were too embarrassed to correct it. The word Helsinki is another word for 'day off' in some obscure Scandinavian dialect and that is how it gets translated when we get the final tour list. The only way to disprove this theory is for the Finland Tourist Board to invite me there for a free week's holiday........hint, hint.

The premature cancellation of the tour meant we had to get on a ferry back to the UK. That night we decided we needed to smoke the rest of the dope that we had in order not to be bringing anything through customs. Bon and some of the band joined us and, when we ran out of cigarette papers, we resorted to smoking the stuff under glass. If you have never done this, the trick is to impale a lump of dope on a open pin or badge. You light the dope and place a glass over it. When the glass is full of smoke you lift the edge of the glass and draw in the smoke. This can be a bit harsh on the throat, but it works.

In the morning we met *AC/DC* and Bon could barely speak. We exchanged a few hoarse 'G'Day's and he told me they had a Radio 1 session the next day. I listened to the show when it went out, and he did not sound too bad so he must have recovered by then.

Maria – of the grass perfumed passport
Genesis 1977

CHAPTER 13

A Bit of Genesis and Santana in the Sun

In the spring of 1977 we went out to do some gigs with *Genesis*. In the gig in Frankfurt I met up again with some friends of mine from the earlier tours. Klaus and Jenny lived near to Frankfurt and were often involved with some of the merchandising stands. Klaus was also a lighting engineer in his own right but, as I later found out, it was not easy to get a good job on a tour unless you lived in the country that the tour starts in, or the artist comes from. There were some very good German acts touring, but the big shows were nearly all either English or American.

The show was the first time that I saw *Manfred Mann's Earthband* in action and I was pretty impressed. Some superb playing from this band. I had never realised what a good live act they were. The downside to the gig was that the heavens opened up and we all got drenched. We went back to Klaus' house that night and stayed there. That evening we all went out to an Italian restaurant for a meal. Almost everyone there was German, and I had no clue what they were all on about. At one point, during a long and rather intense sounding conversation the girl sitting beside me said 'remember you're a vomble......' and carried on in German. I burst into uncontrollable laughter. It just sounded so wrong. That night I learned my first words in German – 'fliegende Untertasse' the German for flying saucers – literally. Typical for the German language to be so literal. A saucer is an 'undercup' so it is 'flying undercups'. Wonderful.

I met up with Klaus and Jenny a few times in the course of my touring, and was sad to learn that Klaus had been killed in 1978 in an autobahn accident. He was in the lighting crew for Tina Turner and they stopped for a rest on the hard shoulder. A truck came off the road and crashed into them, killing them all. Given the nature of rock and roll, especially at that time, with all the drugs, long hours, overnight drives and the like, it was a miracle so many of us survived through it.

In Paris we met a lovely young lady called Maria who came with us down to the next few gigs in Southern Germany and Switzerland. We were heading back to the UK after the Zurich show, but I agreed to take her home on the way. She lived in a small town called La Cluses just over the French border with Switzerland.

I will divert myself from the story at this point to talk about money. One of the more interesting things about doing this, apart from the girls, the drugs, the travelling and the music was that it was all a bit illegal. The reason I had all that money in my briefcase was because I could not do much with it. We could not easily send it back to the UK. International banking was nowhere near as simple then as it is now and most countries would only let you take certain amounts of cash out with you. On a big tour, like the Floyd or *Genesis*, when you had several stands, we would wind up with thousands of pounds in cash and we had, somehow to get that back to England. Mick, or one of the others would fly over at times and take some back with them, but it was as risky for them as it was for us and none of us looked like we were pillars of society, so the chances of getting stopped and searched at customs were high. The upside was that it was usually going into a country that got you stopped, and taking money into a country was not illegal, so it was easier. It still gave me a little shiver when I went through carrying so much cash though.

On the last German gig of the *Genesis* tour another friend of mine, Hans Herman, who used to sell 'head supplies' (paraphernalia for the consumption of hash) gave me a wonderfully etched glass bubble pipe. It was brand new and I left it in its cardboard box. We drove through Switzerland and passed through the boarder to enter France. I passed over the passports. The French customs guy looked at them and then began to sniff them. Maria suddenly said:

'Oh, I put my passport in a bag of grass!'

'What?'

Now I could think of many things a passport could smell of innocently, but grass was not one of them. The customs officer waved us over to the shed at the side of the border post. He then sent my companions off to be searched. I stayed with the van as a couple of them began to look through it. In the back there were some T-shirts and a pile of posters and programmes. They ruffled through this lot and left them very messily strewn around the van. I asked if I could go back and tidy them up and, when I was allowed to do that, I quickly stashed a small packet with some dope and a little cocaine in it under the posters. Feeling a bit more relieved I went to the front of the van. They had found the bubble pipe.

'What is this?' he demanded.

'A present from a friend.'

'It is illegal in France,' he said and took it away.

My travelling companions had come back by now, searched and passed as 'clean'.

He was just about to let us go when he saw my briefcase in the wheel well of the van. His eye lit up. 'Aha!'

We took the briefcase into the office, and he opened it. Inside, along with the various staplers and office stuff, were several brown envelopes. His eyes lit up and he looked at his colleagues with a significant smile.

Triumphantly he ripped the first one open. It was full of high denomination German marks. He repeated this with all the other envelopes and more and more money, of various currencies, accumulated on his desk. I said nothing. When he had finished he looked up at me.

'Just a bit of money I had left over from my holidays,' I smiled.

This find, of course, now meant he had to fill in a large form to say how much money I had brought into France. When I left the country I had to present the form to French Customs to be stamped. They had, conveniently laundered the money for me.

After the *Genesis* gigs we went out with *Santana* to do a few shows in Italy. Italy, in 1977, was a hotbed of student unrest. There were lots of riots and strikes going on and much argument about the activities of the CIA. One of the other things that they had complained of was that the ticket prices for gigs like this were too high, and they were petitioning the government to rule that they should be lower. That was the background to us setting off to do a series of gigs in a few Italian cities. We flew down to the first show in Turin, and with all the merchandise loaded onto the trucks we could just travel with a bit of personal luggage. This tour looked as if it would be a doddle. We were quite wrong about that. The Turin show was in a velodrome – first one I had ever seen actually. The stage was set up against the opposite side of the arena to the main audience entrance, and we had a stand set up in the foyer. There was some trouble going on outside in the street, some of which I could see through the glass doors. At some point in this argument it turned ugly. The people outside the venue turned over a car and set fire to it. Police began to advance with riot shields raised. Things were being thrown. It was all reminiscent of the earlier Stones riot. The police began to use tear gas on the crowd, and it all began to get rather violent.

Like most sports stadiums, the velodrome in Turin had some pretty big extractor fans in the rook and they were going full tilt in the heat. This had the effect of drawing in air from the ground level of the building, and that air came complete with tear gas! Pretty soon the auditorium was beginning to look a little hazy and our eyes were smarting from the gas. I decided that I would abandon the foyer and go downstairs to the crew rooms to have a spliff. I opened my briefcase and took out the dope, papers and cigarettes. At that point a large hand came over my shoulder and closed on mine. I turned to be confronted by a member of the Carabinieri, one of the military style police. He spoke to me in Italian and gestured I should accompany him somewhere. I declined, in English, saying I had to do the show. He took my passport from my briefcase and went away. I realised I was in trouble here so I sought out the promoter. He told me not to worry, he would go and have a word with them. I was feeling a bit apprehensive about it all, but we carried on and did the show.

During the evening the promoter came back and said, 'It will be OK, I have spoken to him.' That made me feel a lot better but the Carabinieri did still have my passport. At the end of the show the officer approached me. He pointed at the T-shirts, held up two fingers and then pointed at himself. I decided to co-operate and handed over two shirts. He then gave me back my passport. Well, that was a big relief. A short time later he came back and repeated the process. I decided I would comply, but was not going to give him anything else. He accepted the two shirts and produced the dope and made to hand it back to me. He changed his mind, produced a knife and cut off a little piece, which he popped into his pocket. 'I smoke this later,' he said, and handed the rest to me. Well!

I put all the stock into the trunk and applied the padlock. At this point he came back again.

'Come,' he said.

Everything was safely locked up and the drugs were securely in the flight case so I followed him. We entered a room at the side of the foyer – which was packed with Carabinieri. He put his arm around my shoulders, 'Hey, this is my friend from England,' he cried to the assembled police. They gave me a cup of coffee and then they all shook my hand. This was not the outcome I was expecting at the start of all of this.

The tour moved on to Milan and the concert was held in a football pitch in blazing sunshine. The promoter came up to me and asked how it had all panned out the day before. I told him we had sorted it all out in the end, and thanked him for his help. He then said that he could not give me any dope to replace the stuff that was confiscated, but pressed a small packet of coke into my hand. He told me that he got it shipped over especially for him by some Mafia friends in Sicily.

'Do you know why people snort cocaine?', he asked me.

I assumed he meant the history of the drug and I said I knew that the native South Americans chewed the coca leaves with lime, and that the lime worked to convert the substance in the leaves to cocaine hydrochloride which was the active version of the drug.

'Ah', he said, 'the history is much more interesting. Back in the early 1900s there was a wine made from cocaine and ethyl alcohol known as the 'Peruvian Wine of Coca'. This drink was very popular in the US and Europe and especially favoured by Pope Leo XIII, who carried a hip flask full of it at all times. When the narcotic and addictive properties of cocaine were uncovered, the drink was banned but the Pope was hopelessly addicted to it. The Mafia, wishing to help the Pope, manufactured the white powder and supplied the Pope with it. The Pope used to have it in a small container and inhaled it from his thumbnail saying it was 'white snuff'.'

I have no idea how much truth there is in this story, but it was a fascinating tale.

We set out our stall in the field just behind the mixing desk riser and sat out in the sun,

Gary (FB) *Genesis* 1977

Dave of the Lighting crew.
Santana 77

Jean – Port Grimeau
Santana 1977

Merchandising stall in Bad Segeburg
Santana 1977

Santana setting up in Frejus 1977

enjoying the music and the substances. I started to talk to an Italian girl who, unfortunately, had very little English. Part way through the set the music stopped. I looked round and I could see the band running off the stage to the accompaniment of a hail of missiles. People were shouting and the whole event had gone from a gentle afternoon in the sun to a full on riot. As I watched, I saw a larger shape spin through the air, crash into the PA stack on stage left and burst into flames. This was followed by another and then a couple more. The stage was on fire by this time and the crew were rushing on and grabbing guitars and other instruments. The Carabinieri, who had been walking menacingly round the crowd with their rifles on their shoulders, had all vanished and an Italian announcer began talking on the PA. I turned to the girl I had been talking to and asked what he was saying.

'It's the shame of Milan. It's the shame of Milan', was all she could say.

The Carabinieri had closed all of the doors to the venue so no one could get out and the crowd were wandering around looking angry. We packed our stuff down, and the band's crew were also packing up as fast as they could. One whole side of the PA was burnt out and the tour was obviously over at this point. As we walked back across the field I found another bag of Molotov cocktails and took them backstage. When I got there I went to hand them over to one of the security staff, but this caught the eye of Bill Graham, the legendary promoter who was managing *Santana* at the time. He was arguing with the promoter, his 6 foot plus frame towering over the diminutive Italian. Bill Graham grabbed the bag of fire bombs and said:

'Give them to me. I will burn this fucking stadium to the ground.'

The Italian was jumping up and down trying to get the bag.

'No, no, no. I paid 200,000,000 lira deposit.'

'This tour is fucking over,' Bill Graham said and stormed off.

I turned to the promoter.

'Shame about that, I was looking forward to going to Rome. I have never been there before.'

'In Milan they have fire bombs – in Rome they have guns,' he said. The truck drivers announced that they were leaving for England that night and they would not stop until they were out of Italy and, back at the hotel, we were all told it was officially over until the other European dates started. Trev, Mark and I had Apex plane tickets which meant that we could not change the date or place of departure without buying a new ticket, so we were in Italy for a few days. Trev had an idea.

'Let's go to Venice, eh?'

So, the next morning, we got on a train and set off to Venice. I had been touring around Europe for a while now, but this was the first time I had travelled as a tourist. We checked into a cheapish hotel, and the next day went out to look around. Trev was on top form.

'Let's go on a gondola, eh?' he suggested, so we walked down to the main canal. There were several gondolas moored up and Trev scrutinised the various people who were running them.

'We've got to find one with a stripy jumper, eh?'

He was intent on the full cheesy tourist experience here. We found a gondola with a man attired in the full traditional regalia and climbed aboard. As soon as we had set off along the canal, Trev had another idea.

'Can you sing that song you guys sing, eh?'

So, there we were, three guys in a gondola, being serenaded by another guy, in almost stereotype cartoon boatman costume, whilst being ferried around the canals of Venice. Probably one of the most embarrassing moments I have had to endure.

After a few days there we took a train to the airport in Rome, and flew back to the UK to get ready for the next part of the tour. The *Santana* tour had another few adventures to play out yet though.

Brockum had been part owned by Harvey Goldsmith for a while, but there was an incident with one particularly dim person who was sent out on a *Jethro Tull* tour. The tour itself was in the UK and not very arduous. He was accompanied by two women, Nancy, a sparking young Canadian with a penchant for threesomes, and who had been in and out of my bed a bit, and Gillian, a rather hard-nosed person who was always dressing up to the nines and trying to get herself noticed. I went out on a few of the dates to get them started as it was their first tour, and then came back to resume the *Santana* outing. After I had left them, the office heard nothing for a week. Being a UK tour it was quite easy to bank the money, but nothing was being banked. When they finally got back in touch, the woman who ran the office, whose name escapes me right now, asked about the cash. He said he had it all so she said to put it in the bank, that was why they had a paying-in book. Three days later he called again to say he had run out of money in Manchester. Seems he had banked all of the money, and not kept any back for a float. From then till the end of the tour they again heard nothing from him. The two girls came in to get paid, but the guy was not around. Neither was the hire van, the rest of the merchandise or the money. Harvey and Mick were getting a little worked up about the situation and were fairly sure he had skipped with several thousand pounds. Just before we were about to go off with *Santana,* Mick called me up and asked if I could pop over to his house. Someone had dumped the missing hire van there and put the keys through the letterbox. He wanted me to drive to the office for him. I did this and then we opened up the back. There were piles of T-shirts, posters and other merchandise, and five of six full bin bags. We were about to discard these, thinking they were rubbish, when we heard the chinking of metal. I opened one and found it was full of money. Unsorted, crumpled notes and loose change. All of the bin bags were like this. We took them into the office and spent the next five hours flattening the money, sorting it and finally counting it. There were no accounts from any of the shows – just a note to the effect that he couldn't handle it. I think this may have decided Harvey to get rid of his part of Brockum, and he sold it on to a company called 'Ahead of Hair' who sold wigs in Selfridges. They called us all into their office and said we would all have to do some training. Naturally we all declined. They then tried to get us to watch some of the training films. These were made by John Cleese and were quite funny, but bore little relation to what went on when we were on tour. Paul Pike, Mick's right hand man, and a couple of us tried to explain, but they did not really get it. So they said they would send someone out on the road with us to see for himself. Welcome aboard Mick. He was to fly out and join us on the German leg of the tour. First we had a gig in France.

We loaded the van with all the merchandise and filled in the carnet. Back then, before the EU came into existence, any vehicle carrying goods to Europe had to have a carnet describing the contents and what was going to happen with them. This had to be stamped in and out at every country's border crossing. Our destination was Frejus in the South of France and we had given ourselves a comfortable couple of days to get there from England. We boarded the ferry to Le Havre in good spirits, looking forward to a nice drive down through France and a few days on the Riviera. Then it all went wrong.

When we disembarked in France, we proceeded to the customs post to get the carnet stamped. We were told it was a national holiday in France and we would have to wait until tomorrow morning. We tried to persuade them that it was important that we got the carnet processed and that we were up against it, time wise, to get to our destination, but we were met with that Gallic stone wall which the French are so good at. A shrug of the shoulders and 'Boh' translates as, 'You expect me to care?'

Gradually the customs enclosure emptied. What few trucks were there had been parked up and the drivers headed off into town, leaving only a few customs guys sitting in their offices smoking and looking bored. There was no barrier across the exit and hot-headed anarchy took over.

'Sod it', I said, 'Let's just piss off'

We started the engine, drove through the gates and headed off along the motorway. We might almost have got away with it had it not been for the system of French toll roads. The first toll we came to, the barriers went down and we were ushered into a slip road to await the police. Trev wandered down the slope to go for a pee as the little police car rolled up. Two of the police in the car rushed down the slope to look around and see what it was he had been doing down there and then they escorted us back to the port.

When we got there all the customs men were there, pulled in from their holiday to check out these mad English hippies who had tried to run the customs. They emptied the van and painstakingly counted all the merchandise. An hour later they had checked through the carnet and looked puzzled.

'This is all in order,' he said bemusedly. 'Why did you run off?'

'Of course,' I replied, 'I just wanted the damn thing stamped so I could head off to the gig. I told you we were on a tight schedule. If we do not get there by tomorrow afternoon there will be little point in going.'

The customs gathered in a huddle, fined us for running the customs, stamped the carnet – because they had to now that they had processed it - and let us go. We set off back through the same toll booth, waving at the same toll man who looked like he was wondering how these people who had just been arrested were off again so soon, and down to the South of France.

We were joined there by my friend from Paris, Jean, who helped out with the stands again. The gig was in the ruins of an old Roman amphitheatre. It was a beautiful setting and this time there were no riots to spoil the event. We had a few days to spare now, so Jean, Trev and I set off down the coast to Port Grimau for a day's relaxation on the beach before heading back up into Germany for the last few shows.

After this, Trev and I drove up to Germany and began the German shows. We picked the 'Ahead of Hair' stooge, Mick, up at the airport in Munster and did the first show there. He was clearly a bit bemused by it all and I am not sure he had ever been to a rock and roll gig before, let alone on tour in Germany. After the show we packed the stuff down and went off to check in to the hotel. We then went up the road for a drink. The bar was heaving; full of people drinking and chatting, so we joined in. I noticed Mick with a beer in his hand and mentioned to him that he should be careful and that some of these German beers were stronger than they tasted. He dismissed this and carried on drinking. Sure enough, a short time later, we found him passed out on a chair, head back, mouth open, dead to the world. His jacket was slightly open and I could see the corner of his traveller's cheques poking out. I decided I would give him a fright that might make him take a bit more care when drinking and went to remove them. Then I noticed his passport was there too, and a more wicked prank suggested itself.

We had a Polaroid camera with us and we were documenting the gigs as we went round, trying to help others who had not been out before. Trev went back to the van and fetched it, and my briefcase. We took his photo, supine on the seat, and carefully cut it down to passport size. Using the Sellotape in my briefcase we then stuck the picture over the one in his passport. Back in the '70s passports came with a separate section below the main one titled 'Spouse'. There was a space there for the man to include his wife on his passport, thus ensuring she would not run off with some 'Johnny Foreigner' or go off travelling without him. I was contemplating asking one of the young ladies in the group that had gathered around to watch this activity if they would drape themselves over him but, in the end, took off my T-shirt, mussed up my hair so you could not see my face and put my head down over his groin – simulating a blow job. This was duly photographed and put into his passport in the 'Spouse' section. We put the stuff back into his pocket to a big cheer from the assembled watchers. Mick stirred and we woke him up and took him back to the hotel.

The next day he announced he needed to go to a bank and change some traveller's cheques so we went with him. He went up to the counter and handed over a completed cheque and, without looking at it, his passport. The woman teller, opened the passport, laughed and showed it to the guy next to her. Pretty soon they were passing his document all round the bank and calling people in from other offices to look. Mick was getting embarrassed, but had no idea what they were laughing at – until they gave it back to him! Trev and I were cracking up inside but trying to keep a straight face. As we left the bank a rather red-faced Mick, said 'I suppose that will teach me a lesson about not getting too drunk.' It didn't!

One of the shows on the tour was an open air event in Bad Segeberg. This town boasts a large cowboy theme park where they stage elaborate wild west shows taken from the books of Karl May. He wrote many 'westerns' featuring 'Old Shatterhand' and 'Winnetou', books that were avidly consumed by many Germans from 1900 onwards. Quite an amazing character, Karl May. He had never been to the US but told everyone that he had. He also spent a bit of time in jail for theft and other minor offences, and did not publish his first book until 1893 – when he was 51 - and then went on to inspire generations of weekend German cowboys.

It was this complex of fake log cabins, landscaped to look like the western movies of the '60s, that was playing host to *Santana*. I was mightily confused by this when we arrived, but we found some places to set up stalls, the gates were opened and we started selling merchandise. I had told the lovely Andrea that I would be there, and she turned up with a friend during the afternoon. We had the van parked beside the stall and, pretty soon, we were in the back of that, rolling around on T-shirts again – this time without a follow spot on us. After the gig we drove back to Hamburg and Andrea invited us to stay at her house because her parents were away. Trev and Mick – who had by now been renamed 'The Easter Bunny' - slept in Andrea's parents' bed – causing a few questions when they got home – which I believe she never really answered. I slept with her in her room. Trev decided to take a bath and was much surprised when a naked Andrea came in and had a pee and sat there talking to him. As she said,'well, he was an Aussie wasn't he, and us continental Europeans don't give a toss about nudity anyway so that worked out alright…'

He was actually a lot more repressed than he let on, but it was funny anyway.

We left in the morning and that was the last time I would see her for a while. We wrote a lot but none of the later tours came near. Nevertheless the story does not end there by a long chalk.

At the next gig in Germany Mick announced that he would like to take charge of the accounts and that he had orders from his boss to do so.

'Ok by me,' I replied. 'Less work for me to do. Let's finish tonight's show and do a full inventory of the stock we have. Then tomorrow we can go through the accounts so far and I will get you to sign for them.'

I was not convinced by Mick at all, and if he was going to take over I decided I would make sure it was all signed off that I had done it correctly till then. So, that was what we did.

Towards the end of the tour we did a show in Nuremburg on the famous 'Zeppelinfeld'. This was the place that you often see in black and white newsreels when there is a mention of Nazi rallies. Great long ranks of German soldiers standing in regimented rows listening to their leader and repeating the famous 'Sieg Heil' salute. The whole area had been taken over by the US Army and the show we were attending was very much an all American affair. *Santana, Earth Wind and Fire* and *Chicago* were the main acts. At the start of the show I went up onto the podium, the one on which Hitler had stood all those years ago, and looked across the field. In my mind's eye I could see the rows of German soldiers but, with my real eyes, I could see a sprawling mass of people with cans of beer at their sides, lying on the grass, waiting for the show to start. A stark contrast to those earlier pictures.

We were setting up the stall and Mick was bustling around trying to sort the stock and get it all ready. He was, at the same time, having the odd swig of beer. Mick Worwood, who ran the company, had called the hotel that morning saying he was going to fly out that day and collect the money so we did not have so much to carry back. Mick, the 'Ahead of Hair' stooge was absurdly bothered by this. A lifetime of subservience to bosses had left him afraid of being castigated when they came out to see him working. He compensated by drinking a bit more and, pretty soon, the effects of the alcohol began to show. Trev suggested that he stopped drinking and maybe went and slept it off in the van, but he said he needed to get everything right for when Mick W arrived. Trev then suggested that he should maybe have a line of coke to straighten himself out a bit. He agreed, although, as far as I knew, he had never done it before. After the line he went back to sorting out the stall with a bit more gusto. A few minutes later Trev asked him what he thought of the cocaine.

'Didn't affect me, didn't affect me at all. Can't feel anything, no effect, nothing,' he replied in a very rapid way.

Hmmmm we thought.

At the end of the tour we went back to the UK and sorted all the stuff out. I handed in the accounts from the first part, and Mick did the rest. I did not really see what he had done so I had no idea of how he handled it. A week later we were called into the office. Paul Pike, who was Mick Worwood's main partner in running the office, was there as were a couple of people from 'Ahead of Hair'. They spoke first.

'We have checked the accounts and there is either some stock or some money missing,' they started, looking directly at me.

'Which part of the tour was this from?' I asked.

'At the end of the tour – the final accounts.'

'Ah, well, if you look at this paper here,' I said, producing the second copy of the accounts that I had got Mick the stooge to sign, 'You can see that, when I handed the money and stock over we did an inventory and he signed to say it was all correct. After that it was all down to him. I suggest you ask him what went wrong.'

'Why did you hand it over to him?' they asked me.

'He said you told him to do that,' was my answer. 'I'll leave you to work it out, eh?' and I stood up and left.

Paul came up to me later, laughing. He said they gave Mick the stooge a right grilling because they had not asked him to take over at all. During the course of the conversation he said that Trev and I were both on drugs, as if that explained everything. The two managers turned to Paul.

'Is this true?' they asked. 'Does Roy smoke cocaine?'

Paul said he replied 'No – he sticks it up his nose.'

This was a complete revelation to them. They did not last long as partners in the business.

Paul was a funny guy. Quite straight in most ways, but very relaxed and together in others. He was a little bit naive about drugs though. On my birthday that year, Jill, Tom Barrett's girlfriend, made me a chocolate hash cake. This was made with some quite potent dope. So potent, in fact, that she licked a little of the mixtures from a spoon after she had made it and then went to catch a bus. Apparently she passed out at the bus stop and came round to find two old ladies helping her.

'Must be something you ate,' one said.

'Sure ways,' Jill agreed.

I cut a couple of pieces of cake and took them in to the office. I dropped one off to Mick W and warned him that it was quite strong. Mick had a meeting that afternoon to discuss a forthcoming tour and so put the cake to one side. The meeting went on for some time and suddenly, out of the blue, Paul said:

'Actually, Mick, I don't give a fuck.'

Mick looked at him astonished, and then looked at the cake – which was half consumed.

'Did you eat the cake? Did I not tell you it was a hash cake?'

'Yes, I picked the lumps out,' he said.

'The lumps were chocolate. The hash is in the cake itself.'

Paul was clearly completely ripped and Mick suggested he went home. He did have one last thing to do before going home though. The company's secretary was an interesting woman. Judy was largish and, to me at least, it seemed to me she would put her make up on at the start of the week and then just layer over the cracks until the end of the week, when she would remove it, probably with a cold chisel, and prepare the surface for the next week's application. She always struck me as being a very tough person but, when I sliced a hole in my hand with a Stanley knife I saw a different side to her. I went to ask if we had a first aid kit and if she thought I should go to hospital for stitches. She took one brief look and said that we should go to hospital. I wrapped a handkerchief around my hand and we set off – with me driving. After a few moments she said she was feeling ill so I had to take her home first before driving myself to the hospital to get stitches in my hand.

I had put a water bed together for her a couple of weeks before, but left quickly when she seemed to be suggesting we tried it out. Paul's last errand, before going home, was going to be to call in to her flat and drop in some letters and notes from the less stoned part of the meeting with Mick.

Paul recounted the above story to me the next day. He was looking a little worried. He said he got to Judy's flat and sat down on her waterbed to sign something. A water bed is not the most stable surface to sit on and he said it made him feel very wobbly, and she suggested he lay down. He woke up in bed with her in the morning and he could not recall if anything had happened or not. Best not to know I feel.

My Sunbeam Alpine in *Starsky and Hutch* livery, 1978

CHAPTER 14

Thank Clapton!

When I got back from the *Santana* tour I found a new Jacko. Washed, spruced and – most astonishingly - with a girlfriend. He had taken up with Gillian from the Brockum office and she had set a path to get him sorted out. This was something of an odd thing. Having known him for quite a while it was hard to get used to this new Jacko. Even stranger was the concept that he was going to marry this woman. I was asked to move out so they could share this flat alone, and I wound up living with Dave and an American woman called Sue – both lighting engineers from Zenith Lighting - in a shared house in Muswell Hill. Sue was quite nice but had hands that were scarred and calloused from rigging so many trusses. She made a couple of slight overtures towards me, but I was not too keen.

During the *Santana* tour I had put my Sunbeam Alpine in for a re-spray and the car had come back with a very nice red paint job and a white swoop across the side and over the back. I was quite pleased with it. That year David Soul had stepped out from behind his persona as 'Hutch' in the 'Starsky and Hutch' TV series and was touring as a middle of the road style singer. I knew a bit about the series, but had never seen it. We had been out of the country a lot and neither of the flats I had lived in had TV sets. He was performing at the *Rainbow Theatre* in Finsbury Park and Brockum were doing the merchandising. Mick asked me if I would drop the crew and band jackets in to them so I shoved them in the boot of my car and drove over to the theatre. When I arrived I seemed to attract quite a bit of attention from the fans gathering outside as I parked the car, took out the box, and walked into the theatre. There was a big poster of 'Hutch' in his TV role, posing beside the car. It was then that I realised why I had attracted so many looks. The guy who had re-sprayed the car had copied the design of their vehicle! Of course the people in the Brockum office knew this and also knew that I had no idea about, and that was why they got me to go over and drop the stuff off.

In 1978 I went out on one of the last tours I was to do for Brockum and that was with 'God' himself, Eric Clapton. I was never overly enthusiastic about his work but the epithet came from some graffiti scrawled on a wall somewhere saying 'Clapton is God'. Most of this tour was uneventful except when we came to Glasgow. He played two nights at *The Apollo*, a venue with an absurdly high stage, around eighteen feet from the base of the orchestra pit. *The Apollo* was also renown for the hard time that Scots audiences gave to English performers. Glasgow itself was not really a very safe place in those days anyway. On the first day we had two shows, a matinee in the afternoon and a second show in the evening. So it was going to be a long day.

When the doors opened for the first show the audience poured in and began to buy stuff frantically. We were barely able to keep up, and had it not been for the crash barriers around the stall, we would have been crushed into the wall. All we could do was to stuff the money into bags and put it into the flight case for safety. There was a brief breather during the show, and the scrum was repeated on the way out. Straight after this we launched into the evening show which was a repeat of the same scrum – fuelled by a little more alcohol. By the end of the night we were exhausted. We counted up the products and I brought the van round to the front. All of the takings for the night were in a black bin bag, uncounted and crumpled. While I was waiting for my partner to come back from the toilet, a man was ejected from the fish shop beside the venue. He obviously did not like that so he went back inside. Moments later he flew backwards through the door sporting a bloody nose. Undeterred, he marched back in, there were shouts and the sound of a scuffle and he again flew back out of the door to land, on his back, in the road. He stood up and walked, unsteadily, but with a definite sense of purpose, to the door. As he got there an arm came out of the door and hit him straight in the face. Down he went again and, at this point two of his friends came over and helped him away. Glasgow!

We went back to the hotel. Not exactly a five star establishment. I cannot recall the name of it now but we did have to cross Sauchiehall Street, which in those days was renowned for its fighting and drunkenness. We got away with that, although my companion was asked by someone who he was 'lookin at pal' and then asked if he was in the CID. The hotel had once been a good one, but that was in the days of horse drawn carriages. Now it was faded, dark and damp. The night porter was the only person on duty, but he agreed to make us some coffee and sandwiches and bring them to our room. When we got there we emptied the three bags of crumpled money onto one of the beds and started sorting it out. There was a knock on the door and the night porter came in with the food and drink. When he saw the pile of money on the bed he stopped still and began to shake slightly. God knows what he thought we had been doing. Two scruffy hippies with a bed full of money in the early hours of the morning.

The following day we went back to *The Apollo* for the last show. While I was in the foyer setting up the stall, a police officer came in holding the arm of a young boy of about 12. He asked the manager if he could use his office. A short while later two more police arrived. One went into the office and the other stood outside.

'What happened?' I enquired.

'Caught him trying to set fire to the chip shop,' he replied. 'They beat his brother up there last night.'

I was coming to the end of all of this though. In the last couple of years I had done a lot of travelling, seen a lot of bands, and made some great friends. A lot of the time it had been absolutely enormous fun, but I wanted to perform again. I stood at the side of the stage in Lund, Sweden, and watched a band, who were not as good as some of my old bands had been, and I thought this is it. Go back to the UK and put a band together. When I got home again I began to look around and see what I could do. Starting from scratch is never easy, but I did hook up with one band out in Essex who needed a singer. I thought I would join them for a while at least and see if I could not do something else. They were all a bit fixated on *Hawkwind* and I was keen on opening their horizons a bit more.

The American lighting designer, Sue, asked me if I would drive a van for her. She was doing lighting for a show in London – a bunch of dancers doing a bash for a company party. I agreed and we went along to a club in London that had been hired for the evening. When we got there I helped get the rig into the building and set it up. I was holding the torch while Sue put the mains in and I just passed out. I remember saying, 'Hold the torch for a moment' and then I was on the floor. I recovered from that quite quickly though. No idea why it happened. I had not taken anything that day.

Only three of the dancers – all women – turned up. After a few frantic phone calls they found out that the others had contracted food poisoning from a gig they had done the day before and were all ill in bed. This led to a lot of discussion about what kind of a show they could put on with only three of them. They turned to me. Could I dance? Well the answer would have to be no – but maybe I could perform. They had a few routines they could do with just one of two participants and the final part was to be a piece set to the *Tubes* instrumental, 'A Special Ballet'. They dug out a white robe and a few wooden staves from their costume trunk, made a mask from tin foil and we worked up a routine between us. So I was performing again! Not quite as I had intended, but it was fun sitting in the dressing room with two half naked dancers, having a line or two of coke and then going out and doing a sort of dance routine. I had gone from van driver to performer that day – and then back to van driver to take it all back to the warehouse.

Mr Juan D'Erful, 1979

CHAPTER 15

Dogwatch, Sound Systems and the Last Post

The house in Muswell Hill was breaking up so I had to find another flat. This led me back to the East End of London and a ground floor flat in Leyton. I began to go along to a pub in Stratford to see a band called *Dogwatch*. They were a very interesting band with a strange line in music and a front man with a mad attitude, which echoed my own in some ways. At some point that year their lead singer Paul Balance, and keyboard player Bernie Clarke, left the band, and I went along to audition as vocalist. I never expected to get the job but I did, and I broke off with the band in Essex to join *Dogwatch*.

Dogwatch was an odd band. Nick Sack played some very tight and precise drums and Roger Glynn was a gifted and fluent guitarist – if a little hard on the brain cells at times. The bass was handled by Pete Murdoch who owned the small PA system which we used. Pete used to also hire this out to other bands and go out with it as engineer. The main force in the band was John Trelawney who played trumpet, flugelhorn, violin and euphonium – an interesting combination for a rock (ish) band. After I had joined, we auditioned keyboard players and took on a girl called Linda Shepherd.

We rehearsed in a studio in an old warehouse in south London, near the Elephant and Castle, run by a Spanish guy called Alberto. Alberto had one single charge whatever we asked for.

'Can we hire a guitar amp?'

'Ten queeed'

'Can we rehearse and extra hour?'

'Ten queeed,' and so on.

Upstairs from these rehearsal rooms was the *Elephant Recording Studio*, a little eight track unit run by a guy called Graham Sharpe.

Rehearsals for the band went quite well, but I came across one problem I had never encountered before as a vocalist. They wanted me to sing! Since all of my previous bands had played songs written by me I was able to bend the vocals in ways that suited my voice. This band had songs of their own and some of these had melody lines which they wanted me to sing, and which they wanted to harmonise around. Not something I was used to or really able to do that easily. Some songs worked well and other were really hard. The material was odd too. Some of it was almost straight rock, usually written by Roger Glynn, and some had tinges of vaudeville to them. The latter were mostly written by John Trelawney. And then there were the ballads - these were the hardest to sing. Some of it I never managed a convincing vocal line to. Still, we rehearsed a set and began looking for some gigs.

John and Nick were anxious to know what I was going to do for a stage act. Paul had been very much the front man when he had sung for them, dressing in a frock coat at times and adopting military garb for 'The Captain', a song about a World War 1 veteran. I was still fitting in with them, because it always takes a while for personalities to gel in a band. If they don't, the band will never work. I have never been in a band without tensions of some kind, but there does have to be a general agreement about where you are, and some kind of friendship when you start playing together. Of course friendships and working relationships often get strained as the band progresses. Egos rise rampant, people feel that they are being sidelined, laughed at, or all manner of other slights – real or imagined – often get in the way of group harmony. If you are famous and doing well you can put it to one side and get on with it, but smaller bands fall apart over it and cannot work together. The two brothers who fronted *The Kinks* famously fought their way through the sixties, and there are numerous other examples of similar fractiousness.

Anyhow I went for an Arthur Brownian sci-fi kind of persona with a bit of military uniform for 'The Captain' and an old raincoat and 'Old Man' mask for 'Moments', the closing number. Since they had only seen me standing in a studio singing they were very much surprised to see what being up on the stage did to me. Gradually we began to write new songs and I began to develop more and more bizarre costumes to go with them. We had a small lighting rig and a PA, and I threw some smoke and explosions, courtesy of *The Theatre Scene Armoury*, into the mix to go with it. The band was beginning to develop nicely.

One slight problem with this was that it was 1978 – the year that punk was in full swing. Just knowing which way round to hold a guitar was considered a hanging offence and there we were with a full on show and five accomplished musicians. We went down fine in London, but each time we travelled to places outside we were panned. Still we were not going to give up on it. The props and the act just got wilder. One of the acts that Pete Murdoch had been hiring his PA to was *Dire Straits* and they suddenly rocketed to fame with 'The Sultans of Swing'. Pete said he would quit the band, sold us the PA, and went off on tour with them. This left us without a bass player and facing a search for a replacement. I ran into Tony Morley, the man who had played guitar for 'Wooden Lion' a few years previously, and invited him along to see a show. When he turned up to see us he said he was playing bass these days so we invited him along to audition for us. No sooner had he joined the band than we started writing songs together again. Steve Wollington was back as roadie for us too. He lived in Basildon and would often stay over at my flat, or at some other people's flats depending on who was going back with whom. He had a wonderful sense of humour – very sharp and quick. There was a girl called Martine who had been doing the rounds of men that were in our social group. One evening I dropped Steve off with her because he was staying with another friend of ours. When I called Steve the next day and told him some unusual news his reply was, 'Well, fuck my old boots. Oh, talking of old boots I fucked Martine last night!'

Years later he had a job as stage manager at *The Festival Hall*.............Basildon. There was a gig there with Frankie Howard who was notoriously cranky. We spoke on the phone the next day.

'How was Frankie Howard then?'

'I saved his life.'

'How did you do that?'

'I didn't go backstage and kill the bastard.'

Typical of Steve really. Frankie Howard did an advert for Sony Televisions at the time. It was a close up of his face with the slogan, 'One reason you may not want the clear definition of a Sony Television'. I cut the advert from a magazine and removed all the lettering. I then wrote 'Thanks for saving my life, Frankie xxx' put it in a frame and sent it to Steve. He knew immediately who had done it.

The band went from strength to strength after that. A residency at the *Ruskin Arms* in East Ham (the place where so many bands cut their teeth – *Iron Maiden* to name but one) led to offers of gigs in all sorts of places. We regularly played *The Bridge House* in Canning Town, a venue that was widely regarded as one of the most prestigious in East London. Despite the predominance of punk in the media of the time there was still a thriving rock scene in many venues all round London. We found ourselves on a circuit with bands like *Marillion*, always appearing just before us, or just after. The band had a hard core following of fans many of whom would turn up to most gigs – even when we played two or three times in the same week.

I had, at this time, moved into a flat in Leytonstone, East London, with John Phillips, former *Wooden Lion* vocalist. *Dogwatch*'s increasing popularity on the local scene gave me an advantage in the sexual arena. These were free and easy times and AIDS had yet to raise its head, so there were many female visitors to the flat in those years and it was home to some fairly wild scenes. Steve Wollington was doing every gig with us as crew and pretty soon we also had a backline guy, Tony Whenman and a girl called Mous who ran the lights. Tony lent Roger his own 4 x 12 speaker cabinet which got gradually more battered. This led to an amusing exchange between him and John. Tony said:

'I think the band should buy me a new speaker.'

'Why?' John asked.

'Because the crew have trashed mine.'

'Tony, you are part of the crew.'

There was a long silence.

Steve also had a cracking argument with Tony, which I stood and watched. I have no idea if he planned it in advance but, just as the argument was reaching a climax Steve said:

'Tony, you are completely *banaal*.' (he mispronounced the word banal)

'It's not *baanal*,' Tony replied, 'It is banal.'

'No, it is *baanal* because *baanal* rhymes with anal and suits an arsehole like you.'

He has never told me if that was planned or if he genuinely mispronounced the word by mistake, but it was such a great line. If you look at the lyrics for 'Sweet Nothings' you will find a reference to it there and a credit for Steve for the 'banal joke'.

The stage act got wilder too. I was doing up to 10 costume changes during the set and I scoured the jumble sales looking for costumes to wear. I got a vicar's cassock from one which, together with the bald wig and Kohl eye makeup, gave rise to the Nosferatu character in 'On The Blink'. There was also the harem-trousered djinn for 'Queen of the Nile', and the dandy for 'Pocket Casanova'. One of the people who came along to see us was a German called Werner and his girlfriend, Julie. Werner ran a sex shop in Southend and was very intrigued by the stage show. One day he turned up and gave me a blow up sex doll to use in the stage act. I decided to use this in ''Pocket Casanova', a song about a serial lover (I suspect John based this on me) and, like many of these dolls it had a wide gaping mouth, which made an ideal mike stand. I would place the microphone in its mouth and sing straight into it. Of course I could never stop there and pretty soon the microphone migrated lower and I was singing the song with the dolls legs around my head. I went through a few of these dolls because they always seemed to spring a leak – leading to the comment, 'My blow up doll has gone down on me.' I wondered how long they lasted when used for the purpose for which they were intended. Werner came along to many of the shows and was not averse to sharing his girlfriend with Nick, our drummer.

Other parts of the stage act were equally bizarre. We used to close each gig with a song called 'Moments'. I had a long and very dirty raincoat and an 'old man' mask and I used to slip off to the back of the audience as the song started. During the intro I would make my way forward, through the crowd clutching a black and gold vibrator. I would set this going and brush it against people's cheeks from behind. I would then get on the stage and do the vocals, finally coming back down into the front of the crowd and inciting a mock fight with Steve – our roadie. He would hit me and I would go down spitting fake blood. At one gig in South London a friend of John's, who was seeing us for the first time, was about to lamp Steve with a bottle. John's wife, Marion, had to stop him and explain it was an act.

We also did a regular gig in Gravesend. This was a very small pub run by a young couple with two small girls. The only place to get changed was in their kitchen. In order to do the quick changes required I used to lay out all of the costumes, masks and wigs so it was ready when needed. I laid out the 'Moments' coat, mask and vibrator. We were chatting to the family as I was doing it. The little girl picked up the vibrator and said:

'Mummy has one of these under her pillow.'

You could make toast from the heat from her face right then.

Another place we played a lot was a gig called the *Double Six* in Basildon. The patrons of that establishment were very volatile. One evening, as we were playing, two rather large women started to fight. One of the two was actually trying to poke a cigarette into the others eyes! The fight was going on right in front of the stage and we were trying very hard to play through it. The bundle of fighting women gradually worked its way to the back of the hall and out of the building. On another gig Tony, who looked after the backline, was 'on a promise' with a girl he had brought along with him. During the show the microphone stand came apart and I was left with the top half in my hand. I looked at Tony and gestured that I would throw the half a stand to him so he could re-assemble it for me. I threw the stand – he caught it – or rather he caught the top part. The bottom part of the stand performed a small arc and connected neatly with his testicles. His smile of triumph in catching the stand turned into a grimace of pain and he slowly sunk, first to his knees and then flat on his face. John, who was about to take a trumpet solo, almost swallowed the instrument as he guffawed with laughter. I am not sure Tony got the joke.

The *Bridge House* started its own record label and began putting out vinyl albums and singles. John was trying to persuade Terry Murphy, the owner, to give us a go and put out something for us. Paul Ballance, *Dogwatch*'s former singer, had a band called *The Warm Jets* featuring Milton Reame-James on keyboards and Paul Jeffreys on bass (both from the original *Cockney Rebel*), Dave Cairns on drums and Maciej Hyrobowicz (known as 'Magic') on guitar (he went on to play guitar for Carole Grimes) and they put out a single on *Bridge House Records* called 'Sticky Jack'. To publicise this they put on a gig at the *Music Machine*, a large Victorian building in Camden, and we were second on the bill. The place was packed and we went down really well with a surprising number of our fans there. This, together with John's nagging at Terry, led to us being offered the chance to record a live album at the *Bridge House*.

The recording was made on 5th April 1979. Terry hired Ronnie Lane's mobile recording studio and parked it on the forecourt of the pub with the multicore running through the window. Any thought that we were now 'rock stars' was dispelled by the fact that, during the day, as we were doing the soundchecks, Roger and I had only enough money to share a bag of chips from the local chippie. The recording went well though – to a packed house of cheering fans. It was subsequently released on *Bridge House Records* later that year. Always the wheeler dealer, Terry was trying to shift some of his signings on to bigger companies and *Polydor* were interested in taking on our album. We began negotiations with them and they took the master tapes and remixed them. Terry tried to get other people interested in us as well. He invited Mickie Most, the record producer, down to see the band and after the show, took him up to the dressing room to meet us. They opened the door to find Tony and Bernie Clarke, the band's old keyboard player, fighting on the floor. Bernie had tried to chat up, or touch up, Linda and Tony took offence. That was the end of that chance at stardom.

Shortly after this I discovered my girlfriend, Val, was pregnant and my daughter, Jemima, was born in December 1979. Val and I were not living together at the time but I was staying with her a lot. We had not quite decided what we were going to do. John Phillips found out that his girlfriend, Sandy, was also pregnant, so I moved out of the Leytonstone flat into another flat in Greenwich.

I was in the rehearsal studio when Val thought she was about to give birth and she called there to tell me. I went over to her house, but it seemed to be a false alarm. We went to bed and, in the small hours of the morning, her waters broke and we were off to the hospital. She was living in Plaistow, East London, but she had elected to have the baby in Fulham, West London, so we got in an ambulance and drove all the way over to the hospital there. She was in labour all night and most of the next day. I had a problem. We had been hiring out the PA to various bands in order to make some money to buy new gear. I had a gig that day with *Rio and The Robots*, a band I did sound for on a regular basis. The gig was at 'The Greyhound' in Fulham, which was just around the corner from the hospital – the problem was that the van and equipment were in Greenwich. As the day wore on and the baby did not appear I began to make phone calls to try to get someone to pick up the van and do the gig for me. Steve Wollington could do the gig but no-one was able to drive the van. In the end I set off myself to get the van. I travelled across London to Greenwich and picked up the van. Everything was against me getting back to Fulham. Road works and diversions took me off course and the final straw was getting stuck behind a very slow moving dustbin lorry. I got to the gig, slung the keys to Steve and took a taxi to the hospital. I arrived twenty five minutes after the baby was born!

The producer assigned to the task of remixing the album had decided to release one of the tracks 'Oh Johanna' as a single. This was remixed and prepared for release just as Jemima was born and Terry kept saying I should call her Johanna and they would use that as publicity for the record. I was not really interested in using my child for that, and turned him down. Things were beginning to look interesting for us and then, out of the blue, *Polydor* were taken over by *Phonogram*. The A and R man that had been interested in us was sacked - and we were dropped. Back to the pubs I suppose.

John Trelawney and I had been talking about children's names. He said he wanted to call his daughter Xanthe (meaning 'blonde haired, possibly one of the Greek Muses) but his wife would not let him. Jemima's first name had been chosen by her mother, but I gave her Xanthe as a middle name. My son, who was born two years later, is called Timothy Trelawney, after John.

One of my possessions was a badge-making machine and we used to turn out all sorts of badges – many containing 'in-jokes' and confusing the punters. Roger was fond of proclaiming 'Come on my team' whenever he was leaving with a bunch of people and, when losing an argument once, faced with a final proof he was wrong came out with , 'Well, that is purely academic' and both of these wound up on badges. John once said we should be a 'Well oiled machine' so we made him a badge saying 'I'm a well oiled machine'. My one was a bit more painful. I was rigging the horns on the PA, standing on the bass cabs. When I finished I just jumped backwards but, what had been an empty space when I climbed up was now occupied by microphone stands. The stand I used to use was a Valan Atlas. Look them up on the net. They are dubbed the 'greatest mic stand in the world'. If you go to 'Purchase a stand' you will see a banner saying 'We sell these stands all over the world' and beneath it, 'Please select your country' and you get the offer of the USA or Canada. Small world! The main thing about this stand is that it has one long section made of a very study tube with a clutch mechanism in it so that the top half will slide up and down with no need to adjust anything. This was the stand I landed on – backwards – dead centre – bull's-eye. One leg each side of the stand with the main part of the stand right up the 'jacksie' as they say. Now my legs are not as long as the lower part of the stand so I kind of balanced there for a minute or so before toppling over. This made for a very sore backside for a week or so and a badge that read 'Mic Stands are a Pain in The Arse'.

Away from the world of music I was seeing more of Val and my daughter. Although we were not together at the time I was thinking more and more about what I should do. I had been seeing someone for a while and was quite attached to her but Jemima was beautiful and we were all three getting along very well so I decided I should try to give family life a go and asked Val if she and Jemima would like to move into the flat in Greenwich with me. It was not easy coming down from being a rock and roll rake, but I gave it a shot. In all the time of being in the band so far I had been involved with some wonderful women, some wild and rampant and some sweet and less willing to enjoy the passions of the flesh. One in particular remains in my memory. She had been the victim of some sexual violence and had been raped. Although we slept together for several months we never made love. She just found it too difficult. She was beautiful and good to be with and, although we got on very well, we drifted apart. A few weeks after we had decided to split up she called and asked if she could come over. She stayed the night and we made love. In the morning she said she was going to get married the next year. She said the time she had spent with me had made her more trusting of men again and the fact that I had never tried to talk, or force, her into sex, even though we were sharing a bed, had given her the chance to be close to someone without that pressure. This made me feel very special. I have always seen sex as something that has to be a mutual pleasure and that it should be the objective of each partner to give as much pleasure to the other one as possible. I could not force or even try to persuade anyone to have sex with me. When she had explained her problems I was content to let the relationship play out as it would. She said she had come back to say goodbye and sleep with me because she wanted me to be the first man she made love with since that incident. It was all very gentle and we parted as good friends.

So Val and Jemima moved into the shared flat over the health food shop and we applied for a council flat. During the year that we lived there we shared it with Tony Whenman, *Dogwatch*'s part time roadie, Dave Lear, the band's new guitarist and Mous, among others.

Cars continued to flow through my hands. My beautiful sports car had been wrecked in an accident a year or so before and I was driving around an ex-Co-op bread van. We were doing quite a few shows and hiring the PA out so having a van was essential. The van had an engine that was in the middle of the cab – between the driver's seat and the passenger seat. On one journey to Oxford to play the *Corn Dolly* there were three of us in the van – Steve, Mous and I. Mous was sitting on a cushion on the engine and began complaining it was getting hot. We opened the windows, but she still complained. It turned out that the engine was on fire and we had been slowly roasting her from underneath! We put the fire out but then found we had no electrics. Luckily it was diesel van so we were able to bump start it to get to the gig. We stayed in Oxford overnight and got someone to tow us to get it started again to get back to London. That was the end of that van. The PA went in the transit van we had bought from Pete Murdoch but, because we had added extra bins and monitors we could not fit the backline in too. I saw a 'Commer Walkthrough' up for sale. This was the same van that we had with *Wooden Lion* so we bought it. There was tons of room in that. The steering though was absolutely solid and really hard to turn. John said it was like some of the trucks he used to drive in the Army, but I was convinced there was something wrong with it. The heater didn't seem to work either. Soon after we got it we drove up to Nottingham in the freezing fog. Everyone in the van had overcoats, gloves and hats on and we all froze. When the time came for an MOT we put it into a garage and it failed on the steering. They fixed it and when John picked the van up he nearly drove into the garage wall because it was now so much easier to turn the wheel. When I put the van into a garage to get something else fixed a year later I asked about the heater and they told me that the big brass nut in the middle of the dashboard turned it on. It had worked all the time but there were no markings on the knob and it just looked like something which held the dashboard on. This was at a time of petrol shortage and everyone had cans of petrol stashed somewhere in case the rationing came into force. It was a foggy evening when I went to collect the van from the garage, and I found it locked up apart from the office. There were two Iranians in the office and I explained that I needed the van because we had a gig that night. He told me all the keys were locked up in the safe and the guy with the keys had gone home early, but he would drive me round to the guy's house. We piled into his estate car and set off, careering through the fog at high speed. Both the Iranians were smoking and I suddenly noticed that behind me there were two open vats of petrol. I was pretty glad to get out of that car.

The era of possible petrol rationing had another effect on us. We carried a five gallon can of fuel in the back of the van, strapped to the side. This can had a spout with a lid on it. At some point, someone must have put some fuel into the van from that can but, since we all drove it at various intervals, we never knew who it was. The van developed a fault which manifested itself by the vehicle suddenly losing power and stopping. It felt like it had run out of petrol but there was fuel in there. We would check the pipes, the fuel filter, everything, but find no fault and the van would start again after a few turns of the key. The worst place it ever broke down was in the middle of the Rotherhithe Tunnel. Since this was built in 1908, and never widened, you can imagine the chaos that caused.

We were on our way to a gig at the *Greyhound* in Fulham when it really began to mess up. We would manage a mile or so and it would stop. We tried everything – even bought a new fuel pump kit and dismantled and replaced the pump by the roadside but it just kept stopping. Finally I decided enough was enough. The engine on those vans protruded back into the vehicle so I took off the engine cover and attached some tubing to the carburettor feed. I then ran that back into the van and attached the other end to the spout from the 5 gallon can. We screwed this into another can from which I had removed the bottom. I taped the whole thing up with gaffa tape and insulating tape, and gaffa'd the can to the dashboard. We now had a gravity fed fuel system. We drove the van like this all the way to the gig. On the way home we stopped to buy a couple of cans of fuel. One of these we used to immediately top up the gravity system. I noticed that the Indian garage attendant was staring wide-eyed at us. I realised he could not see the can I was pouring the petrol into. It must have looked like we were pouring fuel all over the inside of our van!

I was hiring out the PA a lot at the time and began working with a guitarist who ran a music shop over in Highgate. Robert Greenfield was his name. He had an eight piece salsa jazz band. I can't recall how I got to meet him but I did their second gig which was in the nurses' social hall in the *Royal Free Hospital*. They were a funny bunch. Ron Carthy played trumpet, Paul Neiman on trombone, Bud Beadle on sax, and Roy Davies on keyboards, to name a few. When the band first got together it was because they were mostly patrons of Robert's music shop and all liked Latin-based salsa jazz music. Most of them had been involved with other bands, and they formed the band as a way of playing stuff they enjoyed a lot. Just before their first gig they were trying to decide on a name. Lots of names were banded about and one was *Robert Greenfield's Red Hot Peppers*. Ron Carthy, the trumpet player, had apparently left the rehearsal at this point but they carried on discussing it. Finally someone thought of a name. Not *Robert Greenfield's Red Hot Peppers*, but *Roberto Campoverde's Cayenne*. Translating it into another language to make it sound better worked a treat. The trouble was, that when Ron arrived at the gig , he saw that name up on the 'appearing tonight' board outside and decided he was at the wrong place and set off looking for a different gig!

They were great fun to work with. Lots of improvisation went on and the whole thing was held together with hook lines, leading them from solo to solo. There was not often a vocalist so it was mainly instrumental. On one occasion Paul the trombonist could not make it because he was part of a brass ensemble that was doing a high end concert somewhere. He called on a friend to stand in and this guy turned out to be Pete Thoms, who had played with lots of really classy bands. He turned up just before the soundcheck and asked if they had a tape of the gig he could listen to. He then put the headphones on and listened to a bit, picked up the trombone and played a few notes muttering 'in E Flat, yup' and things like that and then fast forwarding to the next bit. The rest of the band were watching him do this with interest. After the soundcheck they were all convinced he was just posing and could not have learnt all that so

John Trelawney and I - 1979

Roy Weard at the *Corn Dolly* 1979

Dogwatch in Oxford. From left; Nick Sack, John Trelawney, Linda Kelsey (seated), Roger Glynn, me, Tony Morley 1979

Linda Kelsey

Roberto Campoverde's Cayenne – with the mixing desk in front of the stage

Jemima and I at the Greenwich flat

Tim, Jemima and I

quickly. During the gig they all made mistakes because they were all watching him, waiting for him to slip up, but he did not put a foot wrong all night.

One of our friends had been in India for a few months and, before he left, he had sent some small statues back to England. When he came back he collected these and revealed that he had stuff the insides with Nepalese temple balls. This is a very potent form of hash. Quite gooey and oily in texture and the only way to roll a joint with it was to pinch of a small piece, roll it into a long thin string and place that in the papers and tobacco. He gave us all a couple each as Christmas presents and we found that, at first, it knocked us out totally. After a while we got used to it a bit. Tony and I had to go to do a New Year's Eve show with *Cayenne* in a disco in Dartford called 'Flicks' (I remembers this because one of the band's wives saw it written in his diary and, because of his bad handwriting, thought it read 'Fucks' and thought he was going to a sex party). When we arrived we were immediately collared by Roy Davies the keyboard player.

'Have you got anything to smoke?' he asked, knowing we usually had a bit of puff.

'Yes, but you don't want it before the show,' I answered. 'It is temple ball and it will wipe you out.'

He said he had been smoking for years and nothing wiped him out any more, but we put him off – for the moment at least. After the soundcheck was over, and we had been off to eat, we came back to the hall and he started again.

'Just a little one then, come on, I have not been able to get anything since Christmas.'

We had planned to have a little smoke ourselves so we rolled a very light spliff and shared it with him just before they went on stage.

The show usually started with a keyboard riff, which would usually end in some syncopated chords and the whole band would then launch into the first number. Roy sat down at the piano and began to play, and play and play. Head down he launched into a flurry of improvised riffs and arpeggios, and after a good five or six minutes he looked up. The band had all raised their instruments as he started but, by this time, they had lowered them again and were all looking at Roy. He played the intro chords and they made a rather ragged start. When the show was over he came to us and said.

'I see what you mean. I started to play and forgot I was at a gig. I thought I was at home just playing to myself. I was totally lost in it all. I can see why you said I should not have smoked it before the gig.'

We gave him a little bit as a New Year's present. *Cayenne* did a few gigs for the *Royal Free Hospital* including one with Ron Carthy's old band *Gonzalez*. I was on my way to that in my old Morris Minor when the wheel came off. This was a common problem with these old cars and I knew all about it so I jacked it up and started to dismantle the swivel bracket at the bottom of the steering leg. The torsion bar was held on by a single bolt but that was rusted solid. I took a hacksaw to it, and when it finally gave, the hacksaw went straight through into my left thumb. I could see the bone! I got out a handkerchief and wrapped it round the wound and then applied some gaffa tape. There was a breaker's yard just around the corner so I got a new swivel from them and reattached it to the car. I stopped off at home to clean the dirt and grease from my hand, but left the wounded thumb. I then drove to the gig and did the soundcheck, trying not to get the blood that was dripping from my hand, onto the desk. When I had finished I asked one of the nurses if she could slip me into A&E to get someone to look at my thumb. She took me through and let me jump the queue. When they took the gaffa and blood soaked bandage off they were shocked to see my thumb all black, but I explained it was from the car and not the onset of gangrene. They cleaned it up and dobbed a blob of swarfega into the wound to get it clean as well - now that hurt more than the injury had. Finally they gave me 4 stitches and I was able to go back and do the gig. Good job it was at a hospital.

John Trelawney had been a friend of Manfred Mann's for some time and knew many of the other local musicians who would hang out in *The Workhouse Studio* in the Old Kent Road. Manfred had just bought a big house just outside Lewisham and was having it redecorated.

This was being done by a guy called Thomas Smith who had taken up residence in the loft rooms while he did the job. It was a pretty big task because the house had been three floors of bed sits, each with several layers of white emulsion daubed over woodchip wallpaper, even more layers of white gloss paint on the woodwork, and sinks and cookers in every room. Manfred wanted it turned back into a family house. The task was to strip each room back to the bare wood and plaster, repair the surfaces and re-decorate. Manfred put the word out among all of the many unemployed musicians that there was some casual work going helping Thomas, and I took the opportunity to do this. There were not many takers because it was messy work, but one of the other guys who was there working was Steve 'Boltz' Bolton. Steve had been the guitarist who had taken over from John Du Cann in *Atomic Rooster* in 1971 and he had played with many local bands and sessions in *The Workhouse*. At the time he was fronting his own band, *The Vampire Bats From Lewisham*. We became good friends during that time. At one point we were both stripping a room down to the flaky distemper that had been put on the walls back in the '40s. The radio was playing as we were washing this down and they played the *Atomic Rooster* hit 'Devil's Answer'. The radio announcer launched into the standard cliché:

'Atomic Rooster there, from 1971, and I wonder where they all are now?'

'Covered in shit, washing a wall for Manfred Mann,' was Boltz's immediate response.

Work on the house continued for nearly two years, but by the time it was finished it looked beautiful.

Dogwatch was beginning to wobble a bit in late 1979. We had replaced our drummer, guitarist and keyboard player over the previous months, but we had not really moved forward in getting a record deal or any further than being local heroes. We were still getting good crowds at various venues around London, but seemed to be marking time in other ways. Our current keyboard player was also called Linda and, pretty soon she had moved in with Tony Morley in a flat in South London just round the corner from Tower Bridge. Tony and I were writing a lot of stuff together at this time and he had adopted the writing name of 'Mr Juan D'Erful' (actually I think I more or less forced it on him so the songs would be 'Weard and Juan D'Erful' compositions.) My favourite moment at the flat was while Tony and I were deep in writing a song and Linda walked in.

'Milkman's come again, five pints!' she announced, and could not understand why we fell about laughing.

Dogwatch decided to go into the studio and record some stuff off our own back and so we booked into the *Elephant Recording Studio* and put down four tracks. 'Mornington Crescent', 'Cutouts', 'Life on the Line' and 'Dangerous Game' (a song dedicated to a friend from *Zenith Lighting*, Bill Duffield, who had died on the Kate Bush tour that year). John contacted Laurie Latham who was working as a tape op at the time at *The Workhouse*. Laurie agreed to let us use Manfred's studio, *The Workhouse*, to mix and master two tracks and said he would produce them for us. We took 'Cutouts' and 'Mornington Crescent' in, and Laurie worked on them for us. He did a superb job and we later released them as a single on our own 'Half Tone' label. The studio was a favourite meeting place for a bunch of musicians who would hang out there in the hope of some session work. It was a very professional set up, and was used by many of the big acts of the time. Ian Drury recorded 'New Boots and Panties' there for instance, and all of the 'Earthband' albums were laid down in those rooms. Later on these session musicians would do a series of early hours of the morning sessions with *Q-Tips* singer Paul Young. These sessions, which were produced and recorded by Laurie, went on to be Paul's first big hit 'Wherever I Lay My Hat', and first album. It catapulted Laurie into the big league of record producers too.

Roger could be difficult though. When we were playing the *City Arms* in London he caused a major incident. I had been standing talking to some friends after the show, and a fight broke out on the other side of the room. I turned to look.

'Oh look, a brawl,' I remarked and then, seeing who it was, 'Shit its Roger.'

Roger had knocked over someone's drink and just airily waved at them, so they launched into him and he was on the floor getting a kicking. I went round and tried to pull the guys away from him so that he could stand up. One of his assailants picked up one of those big cut glass ashtrays and wacked me over the head with it. It shattered. I wobbled a bit, but stood my ground and turned to face him. He picked up a chair and held it in front of him as he backed through the door looking scared.

'I'm coming back with a shooter,' he shouted as he backed through the door. I was puzzled. Was I that scary?

Linda and Tony had a bit of a tempestuous relationship, and eventually she left the band and split from him. This left us needing a new member and John was quite keen to get Roger Glynn to rejoin the band instead of getting a replacement keyboard player. I had found Roger hard to work with at times and thought that direction we had taken with the current line up was much better, so I held out against this. We did a few gigs as a five piece but, in the end, I decided I would quit. It was a big wrench for me, quitting the band, and I was not sure what I wanted to do next. I was still running the PA with John and we had quite a few clients including *The Higsons*, the band that Charlie Higson, later to go on to be of 'Fast Show' fame, was fronting. The old building that housed Albert's rehearsal rooms and the *Elephant Recording Studio* was being pulled down, and Graham had found some space in the basement of *Metropolitan Wharf* in Wapping. He was going to move the studio there, but that would involve actually building a studio from scratch. All there was there was a big empty space so he had to put up walls as well as installing a studio. I was one of the people he employed to do this work. John Trelawney took over the space next to the studio and set up a rehearsal studio – called 'Sleazy's', with the tag line 'Damp, dirty, noisy and nasty'. We called the PA system 'Sleazy Hire' with the tagline 'beautifully tatty gear that gives your band that authentic look'.

This was working very well. We had regular gigs with *Cayenne, Rio and The Robots* and a bunch of other bands. The money was not wonderful but it kept us fed and paid the rent. It was also teaching me a lot about sound and how to mix. I had come into this completely cold. A few lessons from Pete Murdoch and I was up and running a sound system on my own. It was all a bit primitive. There were two 4560 type bass bins, a pair of homemade mid cabs and some horns, all passively crossed over in the cabs themselves and driven by a single stereo H&H S500D amplifier. This amp was built on a design by the MOD and the idea behind it was to drive the motors on missile launchers; put in a small current and get out a large one. This is the principle most amplifiers worked on but these were designed to handle DC as well. One slight malfunction and the amp would put out a high DC voltage, which was lethal to speakers – they would literally catch fire! Most amps these days have DC protection circuits to stop this. The mixing desk was an H&H 12 channel, fairly primitive but it worked - no Graphic EQ, so we had to do everything from the desk. It taught me an awful lot about equalisation. We added to this basic setup by getting two 'Voice of the Theatre' bass bins which came from an old cinema, some proper wedge monitors and another couple of amps.

One of the bands I had being doing sound for was *The Last Post*. Steve Bensusan, lead guitarist for that band asked me if I would get up and sing with them. I was not too keen. The whole *Dogwatch* thing was a bit raw and I did not want to jump back into that again so quickly. I was also a lot keener to write songs than to perform other peoples' work. In the end I agreed we should do a few rehearsals and write a couple of songs together. As a result I found myself on stage in a pub called the *White Hart* in Woodford Green doing a short set with the *Last Post*. This all went down much better than I had anticipated, and we decided to join forces and become *Roy Weard and Last Post*.

Work was progressing on rebuilding the *Elephant Recording Studio*; the walls were up and the soundproofing was all in place. We went back to the old studio to start dismantling it and transporting it to its new home in Wapping. When we arrived with the desk, tape machines and racks to go in the completed control room, Graham gathered us all together. He said he had run out of money and he could pay us till the end of the week, and then he would have to finish it on his own. There was still a lot to do. The control room was ready to have all the gear put in, but we still had to get all the soundproofing up in the main studio and vocal booth. There was a lot of wiring to be done and still a lot of painting and general decorating. It was clear this would be a long job alone and he would still have to pay rent on the property with no actual income coming in until it was finished. I offered to carry on working and be paid in studio time. A couple of the others were also willing to do the same and we carried on and finished the job. The studio time I accumulated would form the basis of the recording for the *Last Post* album.

The *Last Post* carried forward the tradition of dressing up and being generally 'out there'. I had a chain saw that I used as a percussion instrument, and lots of props. We also had rather a good road crew who would turn up and smooth out many of the bumps along the way. As a band it lacked the downright quirkiness and melodic swing of *Dogwatch*, but made up for it by really rocking. Steve was, and still is, a superb guitar player and when he is in the right place he can outplay the best of them. When I met him again after 26 years had passed I was surprised that, although he was still playing, he had never made it into a band that really justified his talents. I suppose some of it is down to how much you want something, how much you are willing to give up to do it. Standing on the right square metre of this planet when an opportunity opens in front of you is another factor. Throughout my life I have worked with everyone from the artistically bereft to the hugely gifted, and there has never been any correlation between talent and achievement. Herds of people will trample all over a creative artist to get to the banal repeater of worn out clichés. It is down to the creative artist to keep that spirit alive within themselves and not sink into the ordinary. Well, that is how I see it anyway.

Val and I were finally offered a council flat, somewhere near the Blackwall Tunnel and began decorating it while still living over the health food shop. We moved in at the end of 1980 and my son, Tim, was born in 1981. I was in the studio again when the contractions started but, this time, I was able to get to the hospital and was there for the birth.

I was trying hard to resist the temptations of some of our female fans and be a 'good boy'. The band was doing quite well by this time with a regular gig at the *Horseshoes Hotel* in Tottenham Court Road, which was always packed out. The PA system was also doing quite well but there were some pitfalls to avoid. Around this time there were a lot of skinhead bands around. I refused to hire the system out to any of these, on both political and sensible grounds. I wanted nothing to do with right wing racist zealots, and I also knew that many of these gigs led to big fights and things getting broken. We were called up by a couple called Ron and Nanda who ran monthly gigs at *The 100 Club*. I asked about the kind of music they promoted and, in the end, he came clean it was the kind of music I normally avoided.. I usually worked this by giving a silly quote that got turned down, but Ron and Nanda took me up on it. I told them I would have no truck with racism and I would pull the plug if anything like that went down. I also said that if anything was damaged they would have to pay for it, and they agreed. We did four or five gigs for them and, on the whole, the 'Oi' bands were good natured and friendly. Some of the audience were less so, but they did not bother us too much. It was a bit more difficult because I did a lot of these shows with my black friend Peter Victor. Peter was a pretty good engineer and later a really good bass player. He went on to become the news editor of *The Independent On Sunday*. One of these evenings coincided with a Peter Hammill gig I wanted to see, so I set the PA up and left Peter in charge, and went off to the gig. When I got back there was a stand-off going on. The band had launched into shouting 'There is a black bastard over there' and thing were looking nasty. We got out of there and that was the last gig we ever did for them, despite many requests.

Roy Weard and Last Post released its debut album, 'Fallout' on our own label. Recorded at the *Elephant Recording Studio* using time I had accumulated by building the studio. The man on the desk, and the person who did all of the production for us, was Simon Tassano, who went on to be Richard Thompson's tour manager, sound engineer and right hand man for over 20 years. This sold well at gigs, and we were writing a new batch of songs for the next album.

The 'Post' had a song called 'The Room' that they used to close the set with. The lyrics, by Ronnie Raymond, referred to an incident when they were at a gig and his bass amp broke down. He called a friend who said he could borrow his, but he would have to collect it so Ronnie borrowed someone's car and drove over there. On the way he got stopped by the police and could not prove he had the car with the owner's permission. They took him to the station, words were exchanged and he got roughed up a bit. The song's lyrics went like this:

'I was alone in a room by myself
When in came a policeman and somebody else
They accused me of something I didn't do
They beat me blue
They said I fell off a stool
I was alone in a room by myself – now I'm dead!'

The chorus was even better:

'I want to see every policeman in hell,
because of what they done to me, down in the cells'

We had a spell being managed by a guy called James Campbell and he got us a few gigs in odd places. One of these was *Wandsworth Prison*. As you can imagine, we decided against doing that song in the set.

It did stay as part of the set for a long time though, and even though it was not really the kind of thing I would write myself, I did enjoy the hammy stage act I did with it. I had a jacket with arrows on it, some make-up bruises and I would go and sit in the audience. Del Deacon was originally a regular member of the audience, but he took to dressing up as a spaceman and coming onstage during 'Invaders'. He also dressed as a policeman and used to come and get me from the audience and throw me on stage. I would then slit his throat during the closing chorus, and he would do the blood capsule bit.

In 1982 John Trelawney had formed a record label and management company with a guy called Mike Stockdale. He had picked up an unknown band called *The Blow Monkeys* and paid for some studio time for them to record a single. I played him some of the stuff we wanted to do in the studio and he came in and played trumpet on two of these for us. He also offered to release a couple of tracks from these sessions as a single. Once this was in place he booked the *Embassy Club* in London for a showcase. I went down early to put the PA and lighting in. My old van had died the week before, so I borrowed a van from a friend and we set off for the show.

The van was a wreck. The timing was out and it kept backfiring. It was also beginning to overheat by the time we pulled up outside the club. Wisps of steam were coming from under the bonnet as we unloaded the gear and wheeled it into the venue. The staff at the *Embassy Club* was, almost exclusively, fey young men in pale grey jogging trousers. When I started to set the PA a woman came up to me and said, 'Is that your van outside? It is on fire.'

'It is OK,' I replied, 'It is just overheating.'

She went away and then came back a short time later.

'No,' she insisted, 'it really is on fire. I have called the Fire Brigade.'

I followed her out to the street and saw she was right. I opened the engine compartment and saw that the carburettor had backfired petrol into the air intake and the air filter was burning. Not only that, but a lot of the wiring had melted and was beginning to short out. I undid the battery and was dealing with the fire when the Fire Brigade arrived. One of the young boys ran out with a fire extinguisher which did not go off.

'That's no good,' simpered one of the others. 'They are all empty, we play with them.'

I had put the fire out by then and the firemen did an inspection and wrote a report as best they could with all those young boys almost fainting over them. The gig itself was a bit of a disaster. We played well, but the PA went wrong during the changeover and *The Blow Monkeys* accused us of sabotaging it so their gig was blown. I tried to point out it was my PA and I was fixing it but they were a bit of an arrogant bunch back then. They later stitched John up when they got a better offer from a big company. Our single 'Triangle/Monopoly' was released on *Parasol Records*. Things were not easy in the band though, and even though we had *Arista Records* coming to gigs and the new single out, Steve and Ronnie Raymond decided to leave to form another band. That was it for me. I decided I would not carry on in a band. I had high hopes for *Roy Weard and Last Post* but they were not to be. I went back to being a sound engineer and another door opened, well two doors really.

Roy Weard and Last Post -Steve Bensusan, Ronnie Raymond, me 1980

CHAPTER 16

Do You Wanna Be In My Gang?

Somewhere In Europe

Both of these doors were opened for me by John Trelawney. He had talked to Manfred about me and I got a call from him to pop round to his house for a chat. He said he was putting together a tour to promote his new album 'Somewhere in Africa' and that John had mentioned my stage act. Manfred's son had been along to see us and also said it was extraordinary, so Manfred asked me if I had any ideas which I could not use in a pub or small club, something he might use for his show. I had one idea which was 'the exploding speaker cabinet'.

The idea behind this was that you took a standard 4 x 12 cab, removed the speakers and filled it with lights. This was to be the bottom part of the guitarist's stack. At a point in the show you could blast the front off the speaker, kill the house lights and hit the lights in the cab leaving the guitarist backlit for the solo. Manfred liked the idea and asked me to put a prototype together. I decided to use cut down scaffold pipes with a maroon in them to blow the front off. I assembled this and took it down to *The Workhouse*. I was so confident that it would work that I did not even try it out. We took it into a room and I demonstrated it. Well, it was somewhat similar to 'The Italian Job'. The maroons blew the front off OK and also took out some of the lights I had put inside it. The noise, in that small space, left Manfred's ears ringing for a week – but he liked the idea and we used it on the tour. Not only that, but he had a couple of other ideas, and asked me if I would come on tour and be the actor for them.

Before this tour kicked off, John had another job for me. Linda Kelsey, the *Dogwatch* keyboard player had been playing for a band he was managing, and they were going to go on a Christmas tour – supporting Gary Glitter. I had done sound for them a bit so they asked me if I would go on the tour. The first gig was in Brighton. We missed their soundcheck but set our stuff up and did ours. As they were doing the soundcheck, I noticed people putting crash barriers up across the front of the stage. I had previously questioned the point of buying on to a Gary Glitter tour in 1982 when I thought he was long washed up. I turned to Ian Pogson, who was running the PA and said, 'Crash barriers? Who are they kidding?'

'Just you wait,' he replied.

I was taken aback when I saw GG's set. The audience, well over a 1,000 people, were completely into it, singing along and chanting 'Leader, Leader'. I was amazed that he was able to be so much in control of the crowd.

'It's always like this,' Ian told me.

The tour rolled on until we got to Liverpool. During the changeover between the bands it became obvious that the local crew were paralytic. Each venue is usually asked to provide a local crew to help the band's crew rig the PA and lighting, and load and unload the truck. I went to Ian and told him and suggested that he sack the local guys, and my band and crew would stay behind and do the job so that nothing got broken. We did this. The next day Ian said I should pop in to the office in Lotts Road, Chelsea after the tour and he would have some work for me. I did this and started working for *Mike Allen Rental Services*.

Before that, though, there was the Manfred tour to do. The band consisted of John Lingwood on drums, Matt Irving on bass, Steve Waller on guitar and vocals, Chris Thompson on vocals and guitar, and Manfred Mann on keyboards. There were some other staging ideas for this tour and Manfred had a few more jobs for me to do. He always liked to put on a big show in those days and this tour was no exception. There were some good back projected cartoon films and a full on light show. Down on the stage there was a long riser with a series of fibre glass heads, each with lights in them. Stage right of this riser was a manikin of a standing robot. And on stage left a robot seated at a table with an old fashioned radio on it. These were used in a similar, if not so separated version, for the cover of the 'Somewhere in Africa' album. There was also a follow spot pointed down at Manfred. One of the stage ideas was for me to take the place of the standing robot and cue the follow spot for 'Blinded By The Light'. To this end Manfred decided I should take some mime classes from a guy from the *Ballet Rambert*. I went along and was met by a very camp dance teacher. He was already briefed by Manfred as to what he wanted, so we did a couple of lessons on movement to imitate a mechanical man. I do remember he made me walk away from him doing this movement and heard him say, 'hmmm, nice buttock action'. We played around with many ways of running the robot from one side of the stage to the other and came up with the high tech concept of a little trolley on wheels, being pulled over two pulleys by a rope. We had also embellished the exploding speaker cab routine. Steve Waller did the lead vocals and guitar on Manfred's version of the Sting song 'Demolition Man'. He would do most of the set in a top hat but, for this song I would go on and hand him a hard hat that had been painted silver. When he got to the solo he would turn the guitar down and stride confidently towards the audience, hit a chord - and nothing would happen. I would go out and play with the leads and make them squeak, give him an OK signal and he would repeat the actions, still with the guitar turned down. I would go out and play with the leads again, give him another OK signal and off we would go again. On the third time

Clip for a German newspaper showing me setting up the robots. One of those heads is still in my loft here as I write this

MMEB Tour Poster 1983

John Lingwood, Matt Irving, Manfred Mann and Steve Waller 1983

Steve Waller at *Munich Olympiahalle* 1983

David 'Wad' Wadsworth 1983

Can Can Manfred 1983

Colin Barton – with the injury he picked up skiing

Kremmen of the Bus Corps 1983

Steve Hill and Pete Reyal – PA stage right 1983

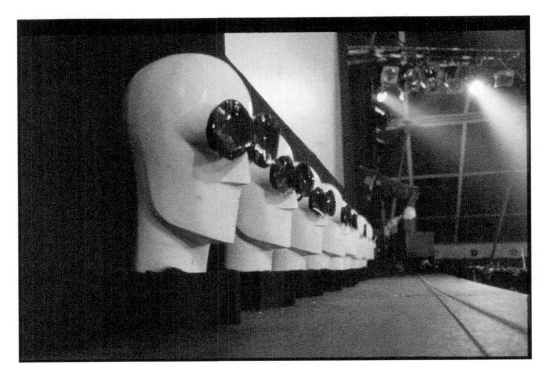

The robot heads MMEB 1983

I would pull the cable from his guitar, hold it up to his face, buzz it, give him the finger and walk off angrily. Waller would then turn on the guitar, hit the chord and the cab would explode! We did this in the full production rehearsals on a sound stage in Wembley for a few days, practising it to get the timing right for the lighting crew. As we drove away from the last of the rehearsals Dave Ed, the New Zealand monitor engineer, called over to me 'Hey Roy, is that fucking guitar going to go wrong in that song every night?' He had not realised that we had intended that to happen or, indeed, that it was part of the show.

The tour kicked off in France on 13th February and moved through Brussels, Luxembourg and up into Scandinavia. I was probably a bit wet behind the ears for this crew. They were friendly enough, but much more experienced in the real world of pro-touring than I was. Since I could not just be hired as an actor I had responsibility for setting out the stage set and then, during the show, I would look after Matt Irving and Steve Waller – not much of a task because neither of them needed a lot of looking after. Putting the stage set up was more of a task because I had to assemble a whole bunch of risers, bolt them together and build a set of cases behind the backdrop so we could get up onto the riser. I was not the only person to use the riser. Chris Thompson used to go up there to sing the Bob Marley-penned, 'Redemption Song', so it had to be sturdy and safe. I would set out all the heads in a row and put up the robots, as well as putting up the dolly that was to take me across the stage when I was in 'robot mode'. After a few shows the dolly system showed its flaws. It was OK to start with but the wheels began to move out of alignment which meant that, on a couple of occasions it would veer close to the edge of the riser, usually just over the head of John Lingwood, the drummer. The production manager had the task of hauling the rope, which dragged me across the stage and back so he had to also keep an eye on where the riser was in relation to the stage. I solved the problem by building a little monorail system across the top of the risers with a groove cut in the dolly so it would run straight. This did mean that I had to line all the rails up exactly to make sure the dolly did not get stuck from riser to riser.

There was one more drawback to the robot act. What would happen was this. I would go backstage during 'Don't Kill It Carol' (a Mike Heron song) and change into white boiler suit, gloves and rubber robot head mask. I would then go up onto the riser at the back of the curtain and wait until Manfred did his solo spot in that song. All stage lights went down and Manfred was in a spotlight. At this point I would whip off the robot manikin and take its place on the dolly to wait to be pulled along. I could only see forward when I was wearing the mask – through a grille of small holes. Just to add to the problems I had an arrangement with Matt. I had known Matt for a bit because he had also played with Boltz in a band called *Zaine Griff* and, at the start of the tour, he came up to me and handed me a large lump of dope.

'I don't play in two parts of the set,' he said. 'Can you roll a couple of spliffs for me so I can come over and have a puff?'

I would do that and we would share a couple of joints during the show. We would often have a quick meal and a drink before the show and Steve Hill, who was the PA rigger for the tour, would also rack out the odd line of speed. It was with this combination of substances in me that I would try to stand still all through the end of 'Don't Kill It Carol' until the band launched into a piece of music which was a prelude to 'Blinded By The Light'. Although this was not a long time, anyone who has tried to stand still will know that it is not that easy. The more you try to stand still the more you wobble – especially when you have little visual frame of reference. I also did not know when the dolly would start to move so it all became a bit erratic. Once the dolly was moving I had to do a series of arm movements culminating in my pointing at the follow spot at the end of the riser. This would come on and bathe Manfred in light and he would launch into 'Blinded'. The dolly would then be pulled back to the original position and I would have to wait until the final chorus of 'Blinded by the Light' when the flares went off, and I could nip off and replace the original manikin.

My other acting part, that of the roadie who could not fix the guitar, was much easier and more spectacular in its effect. By the time we had pretended that the guitar would not work for the second time the audience were usually all looking at Steve and getting restless. When the cab exploded into light there was always a massive cheer. Steve, however, was nothing if not a little confused. I would often go out for a second time for him to ask:

'Is this the second time we have done this or the third?'

One night I handed him his hard hat and he put his hand through the strap of his guitar to take it so he could not get the hand and hat back through the gap. On one song, 'I Came For You' (another Springsteen song) he used to pick up his guitar slide and play two notes. One night, in one of the larger venues, he turned to me at the side of the stage and shrugged. I went to the edge and mouthed, 'What?' He shrugged again. I crept out onto the stage thinking there was something wrong. 'I don't know why I have to play that,' he whispered in my ear.

We got to Copenhagen and we had a day off. There were three of us on the backline crew. Colin Barton, whom I knew from back in the *Bridge House* days, looked after Manfred and Chris Thompson, David 'Wad' Wadsworth, looked after John Lingwood on the drums and I, as I said, did the other two. When the bus rolled up to the hotel in the main square in Copenhagen we found that our rooms were not ready yet. It was only 11:30 am and there were people still in the process of leaving. We dropped off our bags at reception and went into town for lunch; for Colin and Wad that meant a liquid lunch. Copenhagen is the home of the *Carlsberg* brewery and its main entrance is flanked by two life sized statues of elephants. They make a beer called 'Elephant Beer', which has been described as being 'as strong as an elephant in both flavour and alcohol content'.

I had seen this first hand back in 1976 when I had toured with *Nazareth*. The Scots lighting designer on that tour had not been here before and started to drink Elephant Beer with great gusto. We did warn him about it, but he insisted that, being from Glasgow, he could handle it. The following day he arrived at the gig with no front teeth. We were told by his roommate, the front of house engineer, that he had fallen over in the shower, but I was later told that that was a face-saving (but not tooth-saving) exercise. It seems that he had come back drunk and jumped on his roommate who was asleep in bed face down. He reacted by swinging a punch over his shoulder and knocked out the guy's front teeth.

Colin and Wad threw themselves into a vat of Elephant Beer and got wrecked during the afternoon so we practically had to carry them back to the hotel and put them to bed. We all arranged to meet up and go out for an evening meal that night and when we gathered in the lobby at 7pm it was obvious that Colin and Wad were still out for the count. We went into the town, had a meal and found a bar. In the morning we got up and boarded the bus to go to the gig. Colin and Wad were not there. It seems that they had woken up about 10pm and couldn't contact anyone, because we were all out. They had gone out themselves and wound up in a strip club till 6am. They staggered back to the hotel and went to bed, so our waking them at 9am to go to the gig did not go down too well. They said they would get a taxi there later so we left.

It got to 3pm and they had not shown up. The stage and set were all up, my part of the backline was up, but no drums and no keyboards and no roadies to do them. We made an attempt to get some of the stuff set up for them and I tuned Chris' guitars. Finally, at 6pm they arrived at the gig – still drunk. Wad marched up to the tour manager, Chris 'the mushroom' Reynolds and threw his itinerary in the air.

'This,' he slurred, 'is a worthless pile of shit.'

It seems that they had not sold enough tickets for the larger venue we were due to play and so we had moved into the *Falkoner Theatre*, the venue I had done with *Black Sabbath* a few years back. The itinerary still showed the other gig so they took a taxi there, got out and found it empty, walked to a bar, had a drink and then tried to find out where they were supposed to be. The band were due at 7pm for a soundcheck so we helped them get the stuff up, and poured hot coffee down their necks to try to sober them up. We thought we had done OK, but Chris and Manfred could see immediately they were both still pissed.

During the gig Colin came over to my side of the stage.

'He's playing like a cunt tonight,' he hissed into my ear. 'I have got to go and tell him.'

Before I could stop him he marched across the stage, threw his arm around Manfred's shoulder and began talking to him. Manfred finished the song with Colin still attached and drew the microphone over to his mouth. Very calmly he announced:

'Ladies and Gentlemen, Mr Colin Barton.'

And Dave Ed led him off the stage.

I thought this would be the end of Colin's tour but Manfred came over after the show and said 'He's good value, Colin. But tell him, only once on a tour eh?' and walked off.

I liked Manfred. I thought he had a strong sense of fairness about him, and he always enjoyed the odd stage prank. During one song, 'You Angel, You', Steve Waller would do a chorus of 'If this is love then give me more, and more, and more, and more....' and then launch into a boogie style solo. At this point the whole crew, apart from the front of house lighting and sound engineers would can-can in a row across the stage with our trouser legs rolled up. During 'Redemption Song' there would be a section of African chanting using the words 'No Kwazulus'. During the course of the tour the *per diem* payments that the crew received (pocket money, really) became renamed 'Kwazulus'. There was also a section called 'Tribal Statistics' in which Manfred would take the microphone and shout 'Who are you? Give detail!' a few times over. On the last gig Dave Ed rigged a microphone back to Wad behind the drum riser and routed it to Manfred and Chris Thompson's monitors only. Just as Manfred launched into his shout, Wad, in a broad northern accent said, 'All the way from Osnabruck and no Kwazulus'. He cracked up but managed to finish the section.

On 10th March the tour came to Bremen. I was walking backstage from front of house and there was a girl walking in the opposite direction. She saw me before I saw her and the first I knew was a cry of, 'Roy?' It was Andrea. We had lost touch over the last couple of years while I was moving houses and bringing up two children. There it was again though, that familiar skip of the heart that I always got when I saw her. She was looking really good too. A lot more grown up than the last time I saw her six years before. She was with the drummer from *Vitesse*, Herman van Boeyen, and they were the support act for the European tour. We went backstage and sat talking for an hour, much to Herman's annoyance. There had been a bit of needle between the Manfred crew and Herman, who seemed more used to being a star than a support act. He had complained that we set the stage too far forward and it did not leave them enough room. We tried to explain that we had back projections and that we needed the extra stretch of stage in order to set the projector up. His problem was that he had a motorised drum kit – yes you read that right. At some point in their set the drum kit would drive forward as he played it. There was a point where a couple of Manfred's crew thought that they might crawl underneath and wire it to go forward off the stage, but decided that would be a prank too far.

It was good to sit and talk to Andrea though. I think we could both tell that there was something strong still there between us and there was an attraction that felt like it should have been visible. Of course, John Lingwood, ever the imp, immediately asked who she was and I told him. Next day Andrea came into the backstage area on roller skates dressed in clothes that accentuated her figure. John and I were sitting together and he was saying, 'Been there, done that, been there, done that.'

Always the stirrer was John Lingwood. Andrea and I continued to talk, and Herman was less and less impressed by it. I also realised that this was dangerous. I was not being the 'good boy' I had planned to be when I left on this tour. The problem for me was that I was becoming more and more re-attracted by Andrea, and all those old emotions were washing over me again. I was unsure how I could handle them. There was, somehow, a distinction between sleeping with the odd woman while on tour, and being in love with them. When Andrea suggested we met up in Hamburg on our day off, when Herman's band had another gig in another town, I chickened out and turned her down. I was trying to turn down the heat on something which was already boiling over. We did meet a few more times during the course of that tour and I tried to keep myself in check.

The bus driver, who had been christened 'Kremmen of the Bus Corps' by Dave Ed (after the Kenney Everett space captain) was a total speed freak and had a huge bag of amphetamine sulphate. It was not my favourite drug in the world, but we did indulge a bit on that tour. Kremmen was hardly ever seen without a tube up his nose. One night, after the show we went back to the bus and got our clean clothes and shower stuff, and went back into the gig to get cleaned up. When we came out the bus was not there and Dave Ed exploded with a cry of:

'Christ, Kemmen's snorted the bus!' (he had, in fact just moved it round to where the trucks were to fill up the water tank).

Kremmen did sell a few grams of speed to us and Steve Hill, who rigged the PA, was one of his most avid customers. Steve used to sit on my side of the stage and when the show started he would rack out a couple of lines of speed – and fall asleep! This behaviour became noticed by the other members of the crew and they set up a prank. We put a small flash bomb under the PA amps on our side and waited till he was asleep. We then used his intercom to call Alan Bradshaw, who did the sound out front. Alan then called back just as we woke Steve and set off the flash bomb. Alan shouted down the intercom that the top cabs of the PA on the left had stopped working and all that Steve saw was a flash as he woke up and a cloud of smoke. In a blind panic he climbed up the PA stack only to find it was all working.

We went to Zurich on 17th March 1983 and there was a day off. We were checked into a good hotel there and the bus was going off to have its brakes serviced. We had been told this in advance and knew that it would not be back until the following day so, when we arrived early that morning after the short drive from Wurzburg, we gathered all our bags and checked in. Everyone except Wad, that is. Once again he was not keen on waking up and told the three people that called him to 'fuck off' – so we did. No one told the bus driver. When Wad woke up he crawled out of his bunk and gathered his shower stuff and went off in search of catering. This was the default action for a gig day. Get out of bed, go into the gig, find the catering room and have breakfast then shower. Wad wandered around asking people where 'catering' was. They had no idea. He was in a garage not a gig. After he had worked that out he then remembered that he had thrown his itinerary at the tour manager in Copenhagen so he also had no idea what hotel we were in. It took a while before he found us again. At some point during the tour Wad also had a bit of an accident. During a bout of energetic sex with a rather large woman they had fallen out of the bed. She had landed on top of him and cracked two of his ribs. He finished the tour in some discomfort.

I had stayed in this hotel a few times when on tour so I knew it quite well. It was a businessman's haunt, as were many of the hotels that the bigger bands used in those days. There was a certain irony on the fact that the suited community would happily check in and pay these inflated prices for food, drink and accommodation on their expense account jaunts. They would sit there all smug and superior, sipping drinks in their tawdry luxury bar, and then in would march a loud, dirty sweaty road crew, fresh from loading a couple of trucks. I loved the look on their faces whenever we did that, especially when they were posing it up to some women, and even more when the women were more interested in knowing what band we were with than in examining the size of their wads.

Andrea 1982

I also knew that this hotel was the haunt of a few hookers who would set up shop in the bar, trying to ensnare said businessmen. So it was, fired up with a few lines of Kremmen's speed I went downstairs for a quick drink before leaving to go out. I was sitting in the bar alone when I was approached by a lovely looking woman. I guessed that she was working, but we chatted and I bought her a drink. She was quite nice so I tried to explain, gently, that I was not buying. She did not deny anything but stayed anyway. The bar was pretty empty. I got talking about towns and places I had been to and said I liked Zurich but I had never found any good clubs to go to. She disagreed and said there were some good places. I said that I had been there a few times now and never found any. She stood up and said, 'Come on then, I am taking you out.'

She was as good as her word. We got in a taxi and went into the town centre. We went to a couple of bars down side streets and then to a nightclub that played some good music. Finally, both of us a bit drunk, we went back to the hotel where, in the midst of some energetic sex, she fell off the bed and cracked her head on the bedside table. She kissed me goodbye and left in the morning with a large lump on her head. I did leave her a ticket for the gig on the door, but she did not show up.

It was on the Manfred tour that I also first found out about the German promoters penchant for hookers. On one of the nights off the band were invited out to a brothel. This would seem to have been standard practice in those days and Germany has very liberal laws about how brothels should be run. It was one of the few areas where they actually live up to their stereotypical image of efficiency and cool logic. We were all going off to a bar as the band were leaving on this jaunt. An hour or so later one of the band members came and found us – I won't say who it was. He said, 'We all went into this big room with a bar in it. There were women going down on men all over the place and I said to the promoter 'is it all right to watch?'. He said, 'They will all be watching you in a moment' and laughed and I chickened out and came to join you boys'. I was to get a closer view of this later in my touring career, but I was never 100% comfortable with the idea of just 'using a woman'. There is, however, something intriguing, something fascinating about it all though. Always the thought that these professional women might know some tricks that other women don't, or unlock some new ecstasy, and this idea always drew me toward the sleazier side of life. They didn't of course. Most of the time they want the money and a quick turnaround and I had better experiences with the casual women on the road.

There were a group of women who had been employed as drivers for a big gig in Hannover the year before– known by the crew as the 'Blow Orchestra', more for their liking for cocaine than for their sexual preferences. Someone from the crew gave them a call, and they came along to the hotel when we arrived in Hannover and went out with a few of us for the evening. I spent a lot of it with a woman called Varena and she said she would come along and see me again. Dave Ed was with us too and I got the impression that he had not interacted too much with the 'ladies of the road' as Bob Fripp from *King Crimson* used to call them (before he got religion and started appearing on 'Songs of Praise' that is). When we got back to the hotel he kept saying, 'We were peaking tonight, eh, Roy? Fucking peaking.'

Varena came to stay with me on a couple of other days off on that tour, including the two days spent in Munich. What you can see on the table is the *Intercontinental*'s Easter Breakfast, much of which, the cream and the honey at least, wound up in our bed. Luckily there are two beds in an Intercontinental so we slept in the clean one.

We had been offered two options for the days off after the Munich show. We could either stay on in Munich or go to Switzerland and go skiing. Colin Barton opted for the latter and came back from it with a large gash across his nose where he had walked into a chair lift. After Munich we headed down to Budapest in Hungary for three shows, all of which were filmed. The film came out as a video called *Budapest* and a live album of the same name.

After the first show we went out for the evening en masse. Budapest was still very much part of the communist bloc in 1983 so it was all a little bit police controlled. We found ourselves, towards the end of the evening, in a disco. They would play music for an hour or so and then stop and show Tom and Jerry cartoons for a while, resuming the music later. Quite late in the night there was a sudden flurry of activity and all the lights went up. A squad of police with the regulation guns and batons entered the room and started demanding ID papers. We walked up to them and I said 'English, *Manfred Mann's Earthband*. We are leaving.' To my astonishment, they parted the line and let us out. It was bluster and bravado more than anything else, but it worked. We walked back to the hotel and Steve Hill decided to relieve himself against a statue – in the Parliament square! Luckily we were not spotted because I doubt he would have got away with that. This hotel, *The Intercontinental*, Budapest, was also full of working girls and they were all keen to talk to these mad English guys rather than the businessmen that may have paid their wages. This caused a lot of problems with the pimps who, being far more Eastern Bloc than their counterparts in the west, made their displeasure known somewhat openly. We were warned not to talk to them. On the second night there we were invited out for a meal by the promoter and filmmaker.

Budapest is a city of two parts. Buda, on one side of the Danube, and Pest on the other. These were the twin fortresses of Bulgaria way back around 1000AD - and that is about it for the history lesson. The restaurant, to which we were invited, was the oldest one in the country, situated up in the hills in the big fortress that overlooks the main city. We all went up there on the coach after the gig, and were seated in a round building with the tables going round in a circle on its periphery.

When we arrived we all sat down and were served vodka cocktails. All very nice - so far. After a while there were more vodka cocktails and then some more. Someone got some of the band and crew to do the knotted handkerchief on the head bit with the serviettes, a la Monty Python. And then we all did it, including Manfred. A whisper went round the table to take them off and did not include Manfred so John Lingwood was able to stand up and point to him and say:

'There's always one, isn't there?'

So far, so childish. After the next set of vodka cocktails we were all getting a little hungry and a lot drunk. They brought bread rolls and then a man came in with a violin and started to play.

He lasted two minutes, despatched with a hail of bread rolls. The meal sort of went downhill from then. Food flew around the room and, pretty soon, we were leaving. As we went down to the bus we saw there was a very staid looking disco under the restaurant and went in there. Lots of very straight looking people in suits dancing to some very ordinary music. One of the guys joined in and dropped his trousers and pants – dancing around with his tadger hanging out. We hustled him out of the room after that and went back to the hotel.

Drunkenness continued beer hand grenades were being launched down the corridors as the lighting crew and sound crew battled it out (these are similar to the beer fight I had in Hamburg. Shake the can, pull the ring pull and throw it). Colin decided to invade someone's room and, drunk as he was, climbed out of one balcony across onto another – thirteen floors up. After that night we were banned from that hotel and everyone got told off by the tour manager.

In the three days that we spent in Budapest a lot of the boys had been out shopping and bought bottles of Stolichnaya – the premium eastern bloc vodka. These were stashed in the flight cases to take home with us. We went from Budapest to Austria to do one last show in a sports hall. After this show it was an overnight drive to the UK. The show went pretty much as usual until just before the end when I looked across the stage and saw Colin, stark naked, dancing on the monitor desk. He had launched into his stash of Stolly and was raging. Luckily he did not invade the stage in this condition and, although we could not find his clothes someone had found him a pair of underpants to put on for the load out. There he was dressed only in some borrowed underwear putting the gear away – still very drunk. He had a big road trunk with a tray in the top filled with small components. Valves, resistors, wires, tape all sorts of stuff. He was just lifting this to put it back in the trunk when Gaby, the catering girl walked past. He spun round crying,

'Gaby, this is our last night, come back to the bus with me,' and dropped the tray, upside down on the stage. He then got on his hands and knees and began shovelling the stuff back into the tray. Dave Ed and I decided to take him back to the bus for his own good. When we got there Kremmen had just finished cleaning the bus ready for the journey home. We put Colin in his bunk, but he wouldn't stay there. He sat in a seat and said:

'I'm going to throw up.'

Kremmen produced a plastic bag and held it under his chin.

'I have just cleaned the whole bus, get him out of here.'

Colin looked up with a devilish smile.

'No I'm not.......I'm going to piss myself.' And he did.

Kremmen went mad.

On the way back we got stopped by French customs who woke us all up and made us get off the bus. They insisted that we got all our luggage out and they then searched it, then searched us. When they opened my overnight bag they came across my washing bag. The shower in Austria had been one of those big communal things and there was water everywhere. This washing bag had filled with water and I had emptied it out but, since it was the last show, not bothered to clean it. It was full of small hotel soaps. The customs guys were being very stroppy in that typically French official way. The guy that was searching me pulled out my wash bag and looked me in the eye as he opened it and put his hand in. The look of superiority changed to one of disgust as he pulled out his hand dripping with semi-dissolved soaps.

'Now, if you had worked hard and passed your exams at school you wouldn't have to be standing there with a hand full of shit,' I said. He just threw it down and walked away.

We were now back in London and finishing the tour at the *Dominion Theatre* in Tottenham Court Road. A couple of the guys from *Vitesse* had come over to party with the band for the gig and with them came Andrea. I was still trying to avoid getting too involved but Val, my partner, and Jemima and Tim's mum, could clearly see there was something between us. When Manfred launched into 'The Mighty Quinn' at the end of the set *Vitesse* joined them onstage. Waller had unplugged his guitar and allowed the guitarist from *Vitesse* to plug the guitar he had with him into his amp and play with the Manfred. When it got to the final chorus of 'C'mon without, c'mon within, you ain't seen nothing like the Mighty Quinn', Waller stood singing with his hands outstretched, guitar clutched in one of them.

Steve Hill came up to me and the exchange went like this:

'Take his guitar.'

'Why?'

'He wants you to take his guitar off him.'

'No he doesn't. He is just posing.'

'Take his guitar.'

'Leave him alone, if he wants me to take it he will look at me. He will need it for the last song.'

'Fuck you!' Steve said and marched onstage and grabbed Waller's guitar.

The audience at the Dominion that night were treated to the sight of Steve Hill and Steve Waller fighting over his guitar, while we all cracked up laughing in the wings.

The set closed with 'Davy's on the Road Again', followed, as always on the tour, by a cartoon video of the band waving goodbye from a departing tour bus to the strains of 'Land of Hope

Varena in Munich

and Glory' and then the stage lights came up and Monty Python's 'Sit on my Face and Tell Me That You Love Me' blasted through the PA as we struck the stage - for one last time. What a wonderful tour.

Polly, Wad's girlfriend, came round to our flat a week or so later and mentioned Wad's fractured ribs.

'You know how he did it?' she said.

I tried to frame a suitable response, not sure what he had told her.

'He was fucking some fat old boiler and she fell on him,' she said.

Ah, rock and roll. The Manfred tour had finished, and I was left a bit high and dry, aching for another chance to get out on the road. I was back in touch with Andrea and we wrote to each other a bit, and there was *Mike Allen Rental Systems* but I was all fired up by the idea of touring now. I had itchy feet and I wanted more. As became usual for my music career, I was promised a US tour with Manfred later that year, but it did not happen. I was to have this problem with US tours all through my career.

CHAPTER 17

Is There Life with MARS?

S o the Manfred tour was over. There is always a sense of loss at the end of a tour, and whether you want to admit it or not, most major tours leave you a bit institutionalised. There is that routine. You get up, have breakfast, set up the gear, soundcheck, eat, show time, pack down, load the trucks, shower and unwind. In the early days of touring, before the advent of the sleeper bus and the on-tour catering, there were a few more elements of danger and adventure. You may go back to a hotel and go out for a drink in a club in a strange town. Stay awake too long, get too drunk and still have to drive long kilometres the next day. Even with these tours there is the '7 o'clock element'. That time when the doors open to the punters and you vacate the hall and then the show time high. Whenever I got home from a longish tour I always found myself at 9 or 9:30 thinking I should be standing at a desk waiting for the 'go' signal. If you liked the band (and I tried as much as I could to only tour with bands whose music I enjoyed) and toured with them a lot you could almost hear those opening bars in your head. *Grope*'s old singer, Al Haines, talked to me about Bowlby's 'attachment theory'. The theory that children deprived of the affection of their mother or father would seek other forms of attachment and that may explain the tight social groupings you find in bands and road crews. The odd misfits who somehow all fit together as a coherent whole and function as a single unit. I think there is also a degree of tribalism in there too. We tend to want to be a crowd of people in a loosely hierarchical structure with a common goal. I don't know what it is, but the best crews I have worked with have all had a bond of some sort and, when the bus drops you off at the pre-arranged spot, or the plane lands in a UK airport, there is often a tug of the collective heartstrings that we are all too macho to show – well there was for me.

Back in Greenwich I was at a loose end. The PA had gone down to Sleazies and I had a bit of work from my usual bands, but not much. I went round to the office of *Mike Allen Rental Systems* to renew that acquaintance. The company was based in Lott's Road, Chelsea, at the back of the *Zenith Lighting* warehouse. They did not have much on, but they gave me some gigs for Capital Radio. We used to do 'The Greatest Disco In Town' at the *Lyceum* in The Strand. This involved slinging a large PA into the venue, connecting a couple of decks and then going off to a back room and doing some drugs. I worked out that it usually cost me more than I got paid for the gig, but it was fun in a masochistic kind of way. We had to run the multicore to the desk across the boxes at the top of the venue. One of these was 'The Royal Box'. The *Lyceum* was long past its prime of life and I doubt that even Fergie would be seen in the building itself, let alone the Royal Box, but it was still kept locked which meant that we had to climb from the adjacent box, round the ornate mouldings, in order to hand down the multicore. This was some twenty feet up in the air and, one night, as I was dropping the cable a huge chunk of moulding came off in my hand. I did that classic James Bond bit of hanging on with one hand and trying to get another grip to stop myself falling and then thought, 'sod this' and swung into the Royal Box, dropped the cable to the waiting crew, and kicked the door open to get out.

I did some shows with Chris Thompson's band round London and a bit of work for Manfred himself. Manfred was very honest about this. He called me to his house one day and said, 'Roy. I don't have enough work to employ a roadie full time but can we agree an hourly rate, and I will call you up from time to time to do things? I want you to charge me for every hour you are busy for me, even charge for this discussion, so I know that if you say you cannot do it that is not because you think you won't get paid.'

He was true to that. I would list the tasks and time taken and when it got to be a reasonable sum take him the list and he would immediately write a cheque.

MARS did have a short UK tour going out and I was offered that. It was a band called *Set The Tone* featuring Kenney Hyslop, the drummer from the Scots boy band *Slik*. They were a kind of electro dance band, very reliant on sequencers. Production rehearsals for the tour were in Glasgow at the Celtic football ground social club. Their manager at the time was George 'upsidoon head'. He had been named that by Billy Connolly when he was his tour manager because he had a bald head and a beard. Mick Sturgeon was doing the monitors and I was rigging the front of house for Howard Menzies. Our part of the crew was completed by Baz Ward, an old-school roadie of the first degree. He had been roadie for *The Nice*, Keith Emerson's first big band, and used to have the job of propping up the Hammond organ while Keith threw knives into the keyboard.

Howard was very funny. He had a lot of attitude back then and had toured with quite a few large bands. The band had a guy of their own too, who was very much of the 'fetch and carry' variety. After the first night in Glasgow we went back to our hotel. I could see this was going to be a cheap tour. They had booked us into a hotel that was due to close the following month and so they were not restocking anything. When the bulb went in the bathroom the porter took one from the hall and gave it to me. Howard and I went out for a drink, but Mick stayed behind to write down all the rigging for the PA – in case 'something happened to him'. When we came back, at 2am, I asked the porter if there was another key for our room. He responded by calling the room and said, 'Open yer door. Yer mate's outside'.

Baz Ward and the Y shaped Spliff

Gruppenfuhrer Manzies *Set The Tone* 1983

Behind the desk riser in Hungary 1983

The Stage in Hungary 1983

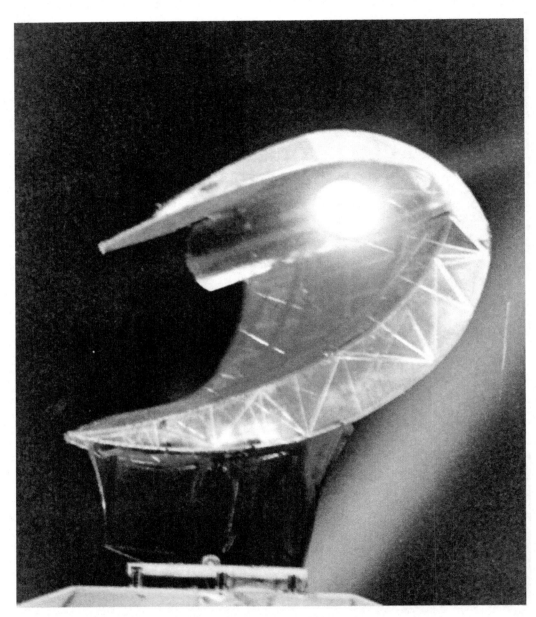

The 'bird head' - Hungary

The 'bird' breathes fire.

Toto Coele

Set The Tone – on stage in Hungary

I had been trying not to wake Mick up.

I was not completely convinced by the band. The recorded stuff sounded OK but there was just not enough going on the stage. There was a lot of attitude but not nearly enough music. Sequencers are all very well but when it comes to it, they are just a backing track and it seemed to me the musical ideas were a bit staid and ordinary too. But then I was never a fan of dance music of any kind. We set off for the tour after a couple of days of rehearsal. Howard was amusing from the start. I think he was getting up Mick's nose a bit but I was enjoying his tour managing – even if his driving was a mite erratic. Baz, because he hailed from the old days of rock and roll, was not really used to the kind of keyboards the band were using. A couple of them needed tuning every day and he had no real tuner to do it with. I showed him that the Moog had an A440 oscillator that he could use to tune the other keyboards to. I must say I regretted doing that because that 440 Hz oscillator really began to get on everyone's nerves after a while. Mick was quite into rolling trick spliffs. Long ones, and branched ones, and all sorts. We took to having competitions in the hotel rooms at night to see who could roll the most unlikely looking joint that would still smoke.

We had taken to calling Howard 'Gruppenfuhrer Menzies', and a couple of days into the tour, we found a German officer's tunic in a junk shop. We bought this and gave it to him as a tour jacket. It fitted too! He had this wonderful way of addressing the local crew when we arrived at a gig. He would gather them all together and say, 'Right then. These are the pilots,' gesturing to us, 'And you are the ground crew. Now, we don't see the pilot pushing his plane out onto the tarmac do we? The truck is over there so you guys unload it while we have a cup of tea.'

We also used to cue up a track from Zappa's 'Man From Utopia' CD so that when the ignition was turned on it would play 'Chop a Line Now', the opening words of 'Cocaine Decisions'.

We played some pretty awful places on that tour. The club in Aberdeen stands out as being one of the most drab, and - towards the end of the night - physically violent of them. One place, somewhere north of Edinburgh was right out in the open with no other buildings around it. Our hotel was only a mile up the road so we all went back there for a meal. Mick, Baz and I went to the restaurant and ordered the set meal. Luckily they had a veggie option on the set meal too. Howard came in as we were eating and sat at the next table. We were served by a very pleasant young lady who proceeded to take Howard's order. As we were eating, a tall thin man, with a passing resemblance to John Cleese, entered the room. He picked up the coffee jug which was sitting on top of the coffee machine and shouted, 'Janet!' When she emerged he continued, 'How many more times do I have to tell you not to put the jug on top of the machine?' He then put it down and stormed out. Odd, we thought.

Our desert was homemade apple pie and clotted cream. Howard saw this as he was eating his meal, thought it looked nice, so when Janet re-appeared he asked if he could order one.

'That is usually only with the set meal,' she said. 'I will ask the chef.'

Moments after that the tall man marched back into the room.

'I hear one of you has refused to pay for their meal,' he asserted.

We were at a loss because we had not even had a bill and, anyway, it was all going on the rooms to be paid the next day. We tried to explain this and he snorted and walked out. As he was leaving Janet came back in through the kitchen door. She went up to Howard and said, 'If you want the apple pie you will have to pay the full set meal price, I'm afraid.'

Howard said he thought that was a bit too expensive and not to worry, but seconds later the tall man was back.

'So, you have refused to pay for your meal,' he shouted, eyes gleaming maniacally.

'No,' Howard replied. 'I just said it was a bit expensive to pay for a three course meal just to get an apple pie and cream.'

'We can do without scum like you in here – get out – now!'

One thing outsiders cannot do to a road crew is to order them around. The hackles rise and the spurs dig in.

'We have not finished yet.'

He bristled at this, and I was looking around the room for the hidden cameras. This was so like an episode from *Fawlty Towers* it was untrue.

We stretched out the coffee for ages while the tall man tutted, huffed, puffed and generally got more and more annoyed. As we filed past him I said, 'Must be a lack of oxygen up there I suppose.'

We got all the way out to the lift before he exploded, 'Who said that?'

'Said what?' So much time had elapsed that I genuinely did not connect my comment with his rage.

Janet had joined us now, standing behind the reception desk.

'About the oxygen..... oh, out of my way Janet, I'm going to resign.'

And he threw back the flap of the desk and disappeared into the back office. We just burst into laughter and got into the lift. This was quite an old fashioned hotel, probably little changed since the '50s, and it had one of those radio speakers in every room that you could switch from station to station. I had fiddled with ours before going down to eat, and when I walked into the room, it was playing the theme from Monty Python!

The following morning the manager said:

'I hear you encountered our Mr James yesterday. I am sorry about that. He goes off on one every few months. The dinner is on us.'

The tour finished in Glasgow, Kenny's home town. Their backline man (whose name I have forgotten so I will call him Jimmy) was not averse to the odd drink. When we had finished the show we went back to the hotel for an after show drink. This was an old and rather drab hotel with the kind of bar that might easily have been the model for one of Ian Rankin's *Rebus* novels. As the night wore on more drink was consumed (as well as a bit of cocaine). Jimmy staggered out of the bar, turned and picked up a fire extinguisher, and set it off. Unfortunately it was a powder extinguisher which filled the entire room with a white mist. When the mist settled everything was covered in white dust and people were coughing and spluttering. That cost the band quite a bit because they had to have the whole bar cleaned. Probably the only time it had been cleaned in years.

Although the tour finished at this point, there was another gig to do. There had been a film a year before called *Grizzly*. One of those 'nature strikes back' type yawn fests. It was just an excuse for a few scantily clad women to scream, and some fake blood to spurt, really. Director Andre Szots, decided to make a sequel called *Grizzly II – The Predator* and the plot was that poachers had killed a brood of bear cubs and the mother goes on a rampage. Why am I telling you all this? Well the bear is supposed to go on the rampage at the rock festival in the National Park. In order to keep costs down they decided to film the concert sequence in Hungary and they put on a big gig to get the crowd scenes. This gig featured *Nazareth*, *Toto Coelo* and *Set The Tone*! Since I was only the PA rigger I did not expect to get the call to go so I was surprised when I received a ticket and details about flying out to Budapest.

The festival in Hungary was a strange affair to say the least. The site was huge, put together in an area that had been used by filmmakers before for making westerns. The stage, PA and lighting rigs were all right up there at the top of the technology tree at the time. It was designed to look like a giant fire-breathing bird. Two ranks of lights down each side were the wings and there were two 'feet' on legs that protruded from the front of the stage and had lights in them which could swivel to shine back on the stage. Mounted on top of the stage was a large head which shot jets of fire. Since this was supposed to be a festival in the USA they got a load of American trucks together and then started to give away *Grateful Dead* and other t-shirts to the Hungarian crew and some of the punters. It was a huge affair and according to some reports the largest gathering of Hungarian people since the uprising in 1965. By far the oddest thing about all this was the fact that the headline act was not a band at all. The last act on were actors, miming to a backing track because they were part of the film. I found out later that George Clooney and Charlie Sheen had parts in this film, but they were not famous then and I don't think I ever saw them while we were there. I am not sure if there were any local acts playing but the only people I actually saw performing were the three western ones. *Nazareth*, in 1983, were only doing small scale gigs around Europe, *Toto Coelo* had one hit in Europe but had not really been able to follow it up, and *Set The Tone* were unknown outside the UK dance scene. How bizarre to find all three of them on a huge stage in front of thousands of people. It was even odder for me because I had no real job to do. No one quite knew why I was there. I was along for the ride it would seem. We spent four days out there doing camera rehearsals, sound checks and various other things. The weather was sunny and we had a good time, but at the end of it the film did not get finished. I believe there are some patched together videos available, but the film never made it onto release. After the film I flew back to London and the next week popped into the *MARS* office to see what else was happening.

CHAPTER 18

All That Glitters

The talk at the *MARS* office was of the Gary Glitter tour that would be coming up just after Christmas. Ian, who had done front of house for the last couple of tours, had been offered something else to do so he asked me if I would take it on. I was happy to do that so I went along to meet Alan Gee who was managing Glitter at the time.

What can you say about Gary Glitter? There is a kind of general condemnation that he evokes these days after the porn/child sex/prison revelations, but that, as always in these cases, is an oversimplification. There is always a man under all of this.

I did a few tours with him over the years and he never came across to me as a monster. He was fairly simple in some ways, easily led but, nevertheless I always got on with him OK and I never saw any of the things for which he is reviled. The management did keep him away from us, moving him to other hotels which they said was to keep him from buying everyone drinks and running up big bills. He did hint at things at times, but I always got the impression that he was a child himself. A big, slightly spoiled, child who was living as this mad fantasy alter ego and had lived with it for far longer than was good for him. It is hard to know people in everyday life let alone in the manic contorted world of entertainment.

We all see these stars, these larger than life characters, with all their charisma and charm and foibles and we forget the simple truth that, when you strip all that away there is often a frightened, insecure person hiding underneath. God knows what was under all of Glitter's pancake and bravado. As I write this now all of the revelations about Jimmy Savile are blaring away in the press and I can see it will not be long before there are other names up there too, and people in court. No-one has an excuse to abuse any other person, least of all children or adolescents who are struck dumb by the attentions of a big star and stardom. Back in those mad days of the '60s and '70s stardom was much more mesmerising and overwhelming than it is today. People will always take advantage of their fame and position to get what they want, especially if they are used to having their own way with no questions asked. "Power tends to corrupt, and absolute power corrupts absolutely. "Great men are almost always bad men" to quote John Dalberg-Acton. That also applies to not so great men as well.

July 1983 saw Laurie Latham's late night sessions with Paul Young come to fruition. The single 'Wherever I Lay My Hat' hit No1 in the UK and Paul and his band were catapulted into stardom. Laurie became one of the most sought after producers and Pino Paladino the bass player everyone wanted on their record. Paul began to do some large gigs and, as is the way when people shift gears like this, he had no tried and tested crew to take out with him. After a few gigs with monitor engineers that were not really up to the task he was pointed in the direction of Mick Sturgeon from *MARS* and Mick went off to do a long tour with him.

Let's swing off from the history here and talk about sound engineers. In the '80s equipment had progressed quite a lot. There were all sorts of toys you could plug in to a system to improve the sound. Compressors, gates, graphic equalisers, multi effects units, and more. There was a burgeoning industry springing up to design and build these things too. There were also some pretty big sound and lighting companies. There was, however, no career path to become an engineer. You had to get a foot in the door and work your way up. I mentioned touring's hierarchical structure before and the pecking order would be tour manager, production manager, front of house engineer, lighting designer, monitor engineer and then the backline crew. That is how the structure of importance usually ran. You had to have a good front sound man because he controlled the sound that the audience were listening to, he was the key interface between what the band did and what the punters heard. Engineers who were not accepted yet as good front of house men would often be put on the monitor desk.

There is a vast difference between the two tasks. A front of house engineer is there to make the gig sound the best it can sound in whatever acoustic circumstances the band happen to be playing in. That job is exacting and has a set of challenges that require both skill and experience to deal with. The monitor engineer has to provide the band with a sound that they can work with. They have to be able to let the musicians on stage hear exactly what they want to hear to make playing the music possible. A front of house engineer will have two basic output channels, left and right. He may also have delay towers for really big rigs or flying systems or sub bass bin, but the basic mix he does is to left and right. These two main sets of speakers are right here in front of him and he can hear them so everything he does is instantly relayed back to him.

A monitor engineer has multiple mixes, typically, for the bigger gigs, one for each musician. The sound comes out of small wedge monitors, or drum / side fills (today there are more and more in ear monitors, but that is another story). Each of those mixes will probably be different and will be affected by whatever sound is near them. Although the monitor engineer has a 'listen wedge' beside him he can only hear what is being sent to the mix he chooses to listen to and he cannot hear what the man on the stage is hearing, because the man on the stage is surrounded by all sorts of other noise. To add to the problems the monitor is usually pointing straight at a microphone which will not only feedback if pushed too far but will also pick up all the sound around it and squirt that back into the mix. So this poor individual is trying to juggle eight or so mixes that he cannot hear and pay attention to the musicians on the stage who tell him want they want – all the time. And they give this job to the least experienced engineer!

Sometimes an engineer will specialise in doing monitors, and when they do they usually become very good and are worth their weight in gold, and Mick was one of those. Once you find a monitor man that does exactly the right job you hang on to him and Mick clicked with Paul Young. This caused a problem with the Glitter tour because we had no other monitor man to go out on the tour. I think that there were also some financial problems between Glitter's management and *MARS* but the end result was that *MARS* lost the tour. Alan and the band still wanted me to do it though. They got an offer from a company in Luton who were the hire side of *RSD Studiomaster*. They wanted to put their own engineer out doing front of house and they asked me to do the monitors. At the time I did not know anything about the stuff I wrote above. I thought, 'How hard can that be?' and accepted.

I went along to RSD's factory unit just outside Luton to meet Dave South, who ran the company and Rob Douglas, who was going to be doing the front of house. They ran through the wiring and set up for the monitors. It was all a bit more complex than I had first thought but I still thought I could handle it. Glitter's touring at the time was a bit of a mixture. He was more at home in the colleges and universities, but there were a few 'soup in a basket' venues dotted around. On one of these nights there was a long catwalk which he ran down completely failing to stop at the end. He shot off the stage and landed on a table, in the middle of someone's dinner. He climbed back onto the stage with as much dignity as he could muster and stood there, picking bits of lettuce and other salad from his rear, and looked straight at the audience, 'I can see its going to be one of *those* nights,' he said, before turning to flounce back up the stage and carry on.

The Glitter band at the time consisted of Gerry Shepherd on guitar, John Springate on bass, Tony Leonard on drums, Eddy Spence on keyboards, and Brian Jones on sax. Brian was the funniest of the lot. He was a Liverpudlian who had played sax for just about everyone, and was total unfazed by anything. He had two sets of false teeth, one for everyday use and one for playing the sax. The latter were slightly curved to fit round the mouthpiece. He used to come up to the monitor desk as they were playing the line from 'I Love, You Love' and, like Alien, allow his teeth to come out of his mouth still clamped around the sax mouthpiece. He was also prone to blowing the odd raspberry down the sax that would be picked up as an echoing fart noise by his sax microphone. The band had been playing this stuff so long they could do it in their sleep.

At the first gig it became evident to Rob that I had not done monitors before, and he helped me through setting them up and the all important business of ringing them out. This is where you turn up the microphone to see what will feed back and then reduce the levels of those frequencies on the graphic equalisers until the microphone is quite loud, but does not squeal. Of course you have to be careful to make sure it still sounds OK as well. It is a process of juggling. In order to help me out he got a spectrum analyser and rigged it onto the listen wedge feed. A spectrum analyser gives a visual readout of the sound spectrum being fed into it. Feedback shows up as a sharp spike and you can see what frequency that is and adjust it. I will always be grateful to Rob for that. By the end of the tour I could hear a sound and recognise the frequency immediately. I had trained my ears to be able to do that almost without thinking, and that was an invaluable tool for a monitor engineer to have.

The tours with Glitter did have a strange atmosphere to them. There was a great deal of practical joking going on and the band had been around the block so many times that they were all a little world weary. Tony Leonard used to stand up to go onstage and say, 'Oh well, time to build a few sheds then.'

Tony Slee was an inveterate practical joker. One night a member of the entourage had managed to get a woman to come back to the hotel. Tony Slee picked up the guy's room key and nipped up there first. He opened up a pack of mustard he had grabbed from the restaurant and smeared it in the bed like a big skid mark. He then went down and replaced his key. Apparently when he got her to his room she pulled back the covers, saw the mark and shouted, 'You dirty bastard' and walked out.

Glitter was usually on his own backstage. He had a separate room from the band and you could often hear him yodelling and doing what I suppose he thought were vocal warm ups. I took to dropping in just before the show started to see if he was OK, and if it was all OK on stage. There would always be a mirror on the table with a pile of speed and a pile of coke on it. It got a bit embarrassing because he used to say 'Help yourself' and I did not want it to seem I was just popping in for a line. He seemed very isolated from the rest of the band who would all be in the next room laughing and drinking. I asked him, one evening as he was walking off stage after the soundcheck, if it was alright and if he could hear himself. 'I don't know,' he said. 'I'm not him. I'll be OK when I am him,' and he wandered off.

Tony Slee told me that on a previous tour they had a tunic with a big eagle on it in LED lights. This was attached to a radio device and his dresser would press buttons in a sequence to make the lights flash and make it look like the eagles wings were flapping. Gaz would appear on stage in a blackout and the tunic would light up and go through its sequence just before he started singing. One evening the dresser had food poisoning and was not at the gig, and Alan Gee asked Tony if he could run the lights on the eagle. He handed him the remote control. Tony was in the band's room before the show talking and drinking while absent-mindedly tapping the buttons on the box. In the next room Gaz was all fired up on coke and speed, and suddenly the eagle lit up. He freaked and started tearing at it saying, 'The suit's come alive! It's taking over. Get me out of it!'

We were booked for three days in a nightclub in Birmingham during this tour and we checked into a hotel not far from the city centre. On the second night it was John Springate's birthday so we got the hotel to provide a side room for us all to have a drink. We gathered there after the show, band and crew, and waited for Gaz to arrive. There was a single rule on the Glitter tours and that was: *If the wig comes off it is light blackout, towel over his head and get him off the stage.*

We were not supposed to talk about the wigs, but it was fairly obvious after a few minutes of his being onstage. The real hair at the back was drenched in sweat but the wig stayed upright and perky.

Brian had produced a tour itinerary for Gaz at the start of the tour it went like the is:

1st Wigan
2nd Haresfield
3rd Rugby
4th Baldock

And so on.

You get the picture. When Gaz entered the room there we were all sitting round the table, 'Ah my knights of the round table,' he exclaimed.

'And here he is, Sir Rugalot,' was Brian's immediate response.

We all sat down to have food and drink and, after eating, then retired to the other end of the room where there were sofas and armchairs. After a while we were joined by Gareth Hunt and Paul Squire who were both appearing in 'Jack and The Beanstalk' at the *Birmingham Hippodrome*. They were accompanied by a couple of the women from the show. They were all a little drunk (well Paul Squire was a very little drunk) and sat there chatting with Gaz and the band.

Brian was in there straight away as soon as Gareth Hunt introduced himself, 'I'm Gareth Hunt,' he said.

'I knew your brother Worrak.' was Brian's swift reply.

There were a few spliffs going round, but somehow Gareth Hunt always managed to get the roach end. He complained about this, but I think that only made everyone arrange it so he continued to get the cardboard. He came over to us, 'Have you got any toot?' We shook our heads – and sniffed.

'I'm a bit drunk. Just a little line, to sober me up a bit.'

After that we all started to wind him up, going off to the toilet in twos and coming back sniffing and wiping our noses. He was getting very wound up about it. Jaggy and I were sharing a room and we decided it was time to abandon the party. Jaggy went over to say goodnight and fell, head first into Gareth Hunt's lap. After he struggled to his feet again we said goodnight and left. In the lift Jaggy collapsed into howls of laughter.

'What's so funny?' I asked.

'I've nicked his key,' Jaggy replied.

The next morning we found Gareth Hunt in the reception. He had his arm in a sling.

'What happened to you', I asked.

'I was pretty drunk last night and I lost my room key. I have been in all these films where you just barge into the door and it flies open so I did that – and dislocated my shoulder. The worst thing is I then kicked the bottom panel of the door in and crawled in through that. Cost me £200 for a new door.'

I felt quite sorry for him really, and a little bit guilty for not taking the key back to him. A few months later I checked into another hotel on another tour and turned on the TV. There was an old episode of *The New Avengers* with Gareth Hunt and Joanna Lumley. Gareth Hunt barged the door and it flew open.

'How did you do that?' Joanna Lumley purred.

'It's a knack,' came the reply, and I collapsed in laughter.

When the tour finished we came home for a week or so and then we went up to Scotland to do a short tour there. We took the train up to Dundee and picked up a hire car for the tour. We then drove up to the hotel and checked in. The next day we went to *Dundee University* to do the first gig. Everything was going smoothly until we finished and began to pack down. When they opened the big doors at the back of the gig we saw the car park was under a couple of feet of snow and it was still falling. We loaded out and went back to the hotel. We sat in the bar of the hotel for several hours. The night porter seemed happy enough to have the bar open and to sit and drink with us. Alan Gee went off to get a weather forecast and came back and announced that the roads further north were all closed. Our next gig was Aberdeen, followed by Inverness. Tony Slee and I started to have a chat with Gaz. The conversation went like this:

'You know the roads are all closed, Gaz.'

'Yes, what can we do?'

'I think we should get a helicopter. Let's call the army and get them to fly us to the next gig.

'You can't let your people down. You have to do the gig.' And so on for a while.

I could see Alan looking at us from across the bar, and when we had Gaz primed up and ready we sent Glitter over to talk to Alan. An intense conversation followed with Gaz repeating all the stuff about calling the army and getting a helicopter to take us up there, and I could see Alan looking daggers at Tony and I sitting smiling on the other side of the bar.

The following morning the snow lay even deeper and the cold had smashed the window of the hire car. The tour was cancelled and we all headed back to the station for the train home – but

Glitter in full swing 1983

Brian Jones
Gerry Shepherd (opposite)

Jaggy Mick
John Springate (Opposite)

Eddy Spence
Brian and Gaz - snowball fight (opposite)

Tony Leonard - snowball fight

Tony Slee - snowball fight

Gerry Shepherd

Mike Munroe

Alan Gee

Andy McCoy - Backstage at the Alabamahalle -Hanoi Rocks.

Razzle - Backstage at the Alabamahalle - Hanoi Rocks

not before having a snowball fight in hotel car park.

Glitter had a few more gigs after this and one of them was at *Rock City* in Nottingham. This was one of the few non-university or college gigs on the tour and is a dedicated venue for loud music. It is staffed by Hell's Angels who are a very together and helpful bunch of people. When we had the whole stage set up, Jaggy noticed that the stairway down the centre was pretty close to the ceiling. We got into a discussion about the possibility of Glitter emerging onto the platform catching the wig in the ceiling somewhere and charging off down the stairs leaving the rug hanging in mid-air like an executed hamster. The local crew were quite sympathetic about this and came up onto the platform to have a look. They removed a few of the ceiling tiles and we could then see it was a suspended roof and that the real roof was a lot higher. I thought this was an adequate solution, but the crew wanted to go one step further. One of them casually went back up the ladder and sawed out the centre struts leaving a long gap in the ceiling.

We got to the part in the show where Gary comes back on for the second set and as he was standing there singing 'Did you miss me?......' his eyes alighted on the edge of the roof in front of him. Never one to resist a pose he leaned forward and rested his hand on the edge and then leaned on it. As he did so the whole of the ceiling moved, because a suspended ceiling like that is only hung from a few points and they are not a very rigid structure. He was at the top of the stairs and toppled forward, correcting his stumble into a run to the front of the stage.

The most interesting thing, however, was what was going on behind him. When the ceiling moved it dislodged the last two rows of tiles, which came crashing down onto the band. Cymbal stands went flying, drums toppled over and chaos broke out. Gerry, Brian and John, who were at the front of the stage, carried on, but the drums all but stopped and Eddy was trying to get the tiles off his keyboards so he could carry on. Jaggy and I jumped up on the stage and began to clear the debris but Glitter was still out front, singing away. As we were doing this there was a crack and the two fluorescent tubes that were attached to the ceiling at the back came loose and swung down like scythes, almost decapitating Tony on the drums. Glitter never noticed a thing.

There were a few arguments after the show, but we were exonerated from blame because we had not asked them to cut great chunks from the ceiling. That was their idea. The following day *Judas Priest* was due to play the same venue and they were delayed by several hours while repairs were made. What I could not work out was how *Judas Priest* managed to fly their big eagle, which was part of that tour's stage show, in there. Not from that false ceiling that was for sure.

There was another little interlude after this tour that was probably one of the most chaotic I have ever been involved with. I had met Richard Bishop from *Rockmasters Agency* a while ago when I was doing a gig with *Rio and the Robots* and he had asked me to drive a minibus for a gig in Nottingham with *Hanoi Rocks*. I just had to pick up the band and take them to the gig and back. There was no just in it. This band was pretty wild. Going up there was not too bad, but on the way home they were passing me beer bottles to open while I was driving back down the motorway. When we got into London I was trying to get directions to their various flats which was not easy. One had only just moved and could not remember where he had moved to so we wound up driving up and down the road looking for his flat. Having dropped them off I set off to drive home and I was part way there when Razzle, the drummer, suddenly appeared from under a seat, where he had been sleeping. The others had just left him there and got out. I drove back to his place and then he realised he had left his jacket, which had his keys in it, at the gig. I dropped him at the flat of one of the others and went home.

Richard called me and asked me if I would do a short European tour with them in April that year and, for some mad reason, I agreed. I met up with them at John Henry's studios and we set off for the ferry in Sheerness. I don't think that there is a ferry from that port any more, but the one that we were getting was the overnight trip from Sheerness to Vlissingen. While we were in the queue for the ferry Mick Staplehurst, their soundman, suggested I drove the van with the gear in it, and he would drive the band. I thought that would be an easier task so I agreed.

'Have you got the carnet then?' I asked.

'No, we don't have one,' he answered.

'I don't think you will get very far without one,' I replied.

This was proved to be the case when we disembarked and tried to go through customs. I knew the score by now, having been through all that hassle with the French Customs on the *Santana* tour. I was, predictably, turned back and told to get a carnet processed. The band said they would cancel the first two shows and head off to Frankfurt and meet me there in a couple of days. I took the ferry back, and as soon as I disembarked, I unloaded the van and made a note of all the equipment and serial numbers. I then called a friend called Dave Cockburn, who ran a small trucking and minibus hire company. I gave him all the details of the equipment and got him to start a carnet going as I drove back to London. The following day I drove over to him and then went to collect the carnet from the London Chamber of Commerce. Armed with the correct documents I set off back to Europe to meet the band. We played a gig in the 'Batschkapp' in Frankfurt that night. The backstage area of this venue was a mass of graffiti and my favourite was this. The first line written in a gothic script read:

'I fucked your mother'

Underneath someone else had written:

'Go home dad, you're drunk'

Brilliant!

We went from there to Munich and did a show in a small concrete bunker called the 'Alabamahalle'. Only 87 people were in the audience that night and, after the show, I spoke to

Richard. The band were all pretty much on heroin at the time and he said he was sending them home by train the next morning because they could not get any and were becoming ill. And that was that – end of a very short tour. I cannot say I was disappointed by it. I have seldom been involved in anything as random and spaced out as that attempt at a tour. Mick, the sound man, said that he had a method of dealing with them on tour. If they went out for the night he would roll up the sleeve of their right arm and write the hotel name, address and room number on it. That way, when they got in a cab, drunk or out of it, they only had to roll up their sleeves for the cab driver and point at it. He also said he used to stay up and walk round the corridors in the early hours to check they had not passed out while trying to get the key in the door. Every morning he would go round again and push a note under the door which would read something like:

'Good Morning
Today you are in Frankfurt.
We will leave at midday and go to Munich'

Razzle was killed later that year in a car crash whilst travelling to a liquor store in California in a car driven by *Motley Crue's* singer Vince Neil. They were both drunk and speeding at the time.

Gordon Waters

Geoff Whithorn 1984

CHAPTER 19
Everybody's On The Shortlist

In the spring of 1984 I was at the RSD warehouse prepping some gear for a Caribbean festival and carnival we were doing in Leeds. A guy came in and asked us if we knew any backline technicians who would be available for a few gigs in the summer with Roger Chapman. I gave him my number and said that I was not a guitar tech as such, but I could tune them and set amps up. If they were really stuck I would be happy to do it. I always liked Roger's music right from the days of seeing *Family* play *Middle Earth* way back in the '60s. The next day I got a call from Chris Youle, Roger's manager at the time and he asked me to come and see him in Bromley. He was also meeting another guy who was up for the job. After a fairly short conversation we were both hired.

The other guy was called Gordon Waters, and we divided the stage up between us. He would do the drums and the keyboards and I would look after the guitars and saxophone. We went along to *101 Studios* in the Holloway Road to meet everyone and go over the gear. There were quite a few people crammed into that small room. The band consisted of Sam Kelly on drums, Geoff Whitehorn on guitar and vocals, Nick Pentelow on sax and keyboards, Brian Johnson on keyboards, and Tony Stevens on bass – with Roger on vocals of course! There was also Wilf Wittingham (tour manager and part time Fagin lookalike – it was he who came to RSD that day), Brian Gallivan, who seemed to have no particular function except to drive Roger to the studio and back, 'H' Griffiths, front of house engineer, and Ray Salter who did the monitors. Gordon and I had the job of driving the transit van to the gigs as well as looking after the gear. That was the beginning of a long friendship between the two of us. I think, in the five years that I toured with Roger, we never argued once.

Geoff's guitar set up was interesting. It was the first time I had come across those clamps that lock the strings in place once they are tuned. I also had to apply solder to the windings around the ball of the strings to stop them unravelling when he went savage on the whammy bar. I told him that I was not the kind of tech that would be able to take his guitar or amp apart and fix it, and said that he should show me exactly how he wanted it all set up and I would do it that way for him. This seemed to work. After an hour or so I pretty much understood how he wanted me to set the guitars up.

The gigs were a series of festivals in Germany and a few gigs in the Eastern Bloc. Roger had given a few tracks to an East German record company and they released an album. This meant that Roger was one of the few western acts to be allowed to play in East Germany. This also meant we had to get all sorts of documents and visa sorted out. Neither Gordon nor I had been in East Germany before – apart from the brief trip through the corridor to West Berlin, and my unmeaning excursion to the Polish border with *Pink Floyd*. When we had loaded the van with the back line we went to Chris Youle's house to get the money for the trip, and the information about which border post we were to go to, to cross into the east. Then Gordon and I set off to drive to Rostock, the first port of call.

East Germany was a stark place in the 1980s. Uniformly grey, as if it was the only colour that was allowed in this land. Buildings were either very old and crumbling, shored up with bad concrete patches or brand new square blocks with an austere uniformity to them. It seemed odd to cross from the jangle of colour that was the prosperous West Germany into this dark land. In later winter tours of East Germany I noticed the fog that would shroud most East German towns, but even that would stop when it got to the border. Even the fog could not escape that totalitarian regime. It was a shock for travellers used to more western delights. The food was mediocre to bad and, even the good hotels had a miasmic smell about them, sort of stale and unwashed. One thing that struck me was that all through the time I was in East Germany every single toilet had the same pungent smell. There is a book that is well worth looking up if you don't know it. It is called *The Meaning of Liff* by Douglas Adams. It is very funny. I won't go into details, but the idea behind it was that there were things and experiences that had no names for them and lots of names doing nothing useful except hanging around on signposts pointing at places. Douglas Adams put the experiences and things together with the place names. It is a great book and I used to carry a copy around with me in my briefcase. I remembered a family holiday when we rented a house on the beach at Worthing, and a summer's storm dragged in acres of seaweed and deposited it on the beach to rot. That was the smell that seemed to hang around the East German toilets, and I called it Worthing.

Whatever the country lacked in food and amenities it made up for in enthusiasm for the music. The band went down an absolute storm and we marched on through this short tour. Weimar was a lovely little town. It is famous for its cultural associations with Goethe and many other people. We stayed in the *Hotel Elephant*, whose booklet proudly trumpets a list of people who have stayed there, Bach, Liszt, Wagner, Thomas Mann and Tolstoy. It does not mention another famous guest. Adolf Hitler was pictured standing on the balcony addressing the crowd below. The room that lies behind that balcony is now the manager's office and not a suite, as it was back in the '30s when the photo was taken. Roger tried to get the manager to allow him to have his photo taken there, but was steadfastly refused. I have no doubt that it was a question he got asked a lot.

After the brief set of gigs in East Germany we went on to Yugoslavia and then to Bratislava

Roger Chapman 1984

Sam Kelly 1984

★★★ Hotel Elephant

Weimar

Pit stop in Austria 1984

The stage in Bad Ragaz

Hotel Bad Ragaz - seen from the gig

Osnabruck Poster

Backstage Pass

Chappo onstage - Giessen 1984

Nick Pentelow

Brian Gallivan

for the *Lyra Song Festival*. The *Lyra Song Festival* is the 'Commievision Song Contest' – their version of Eurovision. It takes place in a large TV studio and, not speaking any of the languages used, I had absolutely no idea what was going on most of the time. We set up Roger's gear on a rolling riser which would be pushed out into the main stage area when it was his turn to perform. Roger had a pretty big hit with the Mike Oldfield song 'Shadow on the Wall'. It was No.1 in Germany all over Christmas in 1983, and in most of Europe too. That was the song he was going to perform here.

While I was setting up for the show I was approached by a lovely woman. I thought I knew her from somewhere and when she introduced herself as Dana Gillespie I felt a little foolish for not recognising her before. I can remember the cover of hers for 'Weren't Born a Man' (a song that hints at a lesbian dalliance). She asked me if Roger was around and said they had done some recording together a while back and she hadn't seen him for ages. I was just replying that he was back at the hotel and would be along soon when Wilf yelled at me from the other end of the corridor, 'Oi, stop chatting up the tarts and get the gear ready, we are on in 20 minutes.'

Dana looked back at him.

'I think you should hold your tongue until you know who you are talking about,' she said, 'and I have not been called a tart for a long time.'

'Friend of Roger's – Dana Gillespie,' I said to Wilf as I walked past him.

So, after this, we were off to the festivals in Germany, but there were two more odd gigs to do and the first of these was in Bad Ragaz, a small town in Switzerland. We were playing a small festival right on top of a large hill. The festival site was in the ruins of what looked to be an old fort. This was one of those quirky gigs that Roger often seemed to get. One minute we would be doing some high profile gig and the next playing in a cowshed on a hillside. In many ways I liked that. Already I could see that working with Roger was going to be interesting and the music was wonderful every night. In order to get to the gig from the hotel, we had to drive along a dirt track on a long slope winding up through trees. It was even more interesting getting back after the show – after a few spliffs and glasses of wine. The stage was a ramshackle wooden thing built onto part of a turret from the fort and you could stand on the edge of the field and see the hotel way down below. We arrived there the night before the show and checked into the hotel. At least the food here was edible and the drinks were a bit better than they had been in the Eastern Bloc. During the early hours of the morning the farmer brought his cows down from the hillside to be milked. A low bovine procession of mooing wound past the hotel, to the accompaniment of jangling cow bells. Roger always used a cowbell on stage and during the set the next day he stuck it onto a drumstick and rattled it about.

'Fooking Switzerland. That is all you hear here in the morning,' he told the crowd. Seems the cows had woke him up too.

After this we went to a festival in a big fort in Belfort in France. This was a much more professional affair with a proper stage and facilities. It was typically French though with lots of world music and far less of the kind of big international acts that German festivals booked. This festival was held in the 'Chateau Belmont', which was also an old fort, but in a much better state of repair than the one in Switzerland. The main stage was set in a courtyard but there were other smaller stages dotted around the area and these could be accessed by going through a series of tunnels or arches in the fort. People were cooking stuff all over the place so there was a pall of smoke being blown around and some of the punters had taken to fancy dress and face paint – not too sure why that was. At one point, while I was walking around I came across a group wearing white face paint and long waistcoats. Together with the smoke blowing across the scene it reminded me of the camp from some long forgotten battle.

We moved on from this to Osnabruck. There seemed to be a few problems at the gig in Osnabruck. It was not running on time and the preparations were not quite in place. It appeared it was the first time they had tried to organise a festival in this particular place and when we arrived we were greeted by a poster, and a very serious faced German. The poster read:

> *To the Bands .*
> *Thanks for Coming!*
> *Excuse for Little mistakes.*
> *It is for everybody (nearly) a first time.*
> *We try to do our best*
> *Ask for Everything you need'*

The 'you need' was crammed up vertically in the bottom right corner because they had run out of space and the notice was haphazardly taped to the door. Just about summed it up really.

Then it was onto Freiburg, where the heavens had opened and deposited a vast amount of water on the site. As with many festivals this provided an excuse for drunken punters to roll around in mud. Standard festival fare really. Giessen was a bit more together, much more of a professional set up than the others. It was a much stronger bill with Joe Cocker topping it, and then *Marillion*, Roger and others. It was well attended, the weather was good and the show went really well. When it was all over we packed down and went back to the hotel. All the bands stayed in the same hotel in Geissen and, although it was of a reasonable quality, it was somewhat lacking in the flexibility that the bigger hotel chains have when it comes to late night partying. The bar room was quite large, and the bar itself was a circular thing in the centre. It was tended by a rather grumpy German who was not used to having so many people to serve so late at night.

When Gordon and I walked in it was already pretty full with bands and crew. Roger was sitting with Joe Cocker and Fish from *Marillion*. I went over to their table for a while. They were talking about touring and Roger and Joe were telling Fish he should not let them work him too hard.

'It will fuck up your throat,' Roger said. 'I won't do more than three shows without a day off to recover. Managers want to work you every day. Get as much as they can out of you and in

Wilf Whittingham - H Griffthis 1984

the end it will really mess you up.'

I left at that point and went over to the bar. Fish came up and joined me and we were talking about gigs a few years back when we used to play the same venues. I got on to my abiding hatred of the *Lynyrd Skynyrd* song 'Free Bird'. One venue that we both played in was the *Greyhound* in Chadwell Heath. The gig went on until the early hours of the morning and we would go onstage around 11pm. We were off and packed up ready to load out by 1am and our fans would hang around a while chatting, and then go home. By 1:30 am the place was empty apart from the band and crew, the DJ however never seemed to notice this and carried on playing music. We were not allowed to open the doors and load out until the music stopped and the last song he played every time was that bloody interminable 'Free Bird'. Every time I hear that song I think back to being trapped in that venue knowing that, when it finished, I still had half an hour's work with the crew, loading the van, and then had to drive home.

While we were talking, an argument began on the other side of the circular bar. The barman had decided to close the bar and Chris Youle, Roger, and a couple of others were arguing with him, saying he should keep it open and that there were at least 30 people there still drinking. Fish turned to me and said, 'Do you have a bag with you?'

I nodded and pointed to the bag on the floor. He promptly reached up over the bar to the shelf where all the spirits were kept and took down four bottles.

'Shall we go?' he said.

We went back to the room and poured some drinks. The plan went a bit wrong because the hotel found the missing bottles outside Fish's window and charged him for them. After this we went back to the UK. Chris told us he had a winter tour booked for Roger, and asked us if we would like to do that. We jumped at the chance.

CHAPTER 20

Busted Loose

The album was called 'The Shadow Knows' but the tour was called *Busted Loose* and it felt like that. We set off after a short burst of rehearsals in *Brixton Academy*. All the gear was loaded onto a truck and we flew out to Germany to start the tour. We were picked up by Alex Koerver and Petra Ostendorf. Petra had been married to Ossy Ostendorf, who ran a minibus and backline hire company, but at some point during the summer festivals she hooked up with Alex, and they were now an item. The whole thing was made a little more difficult because we had hired the tour bus from Ossy, and Petra was supposed to be the driver and merchandiser.. It did not help that, by her own admission, she needed 12 hours sleep a night so we wound up driving the bus more than she did.

A lot of this tour would be in Germany with a few gigs in Austria and Switzerland and then off into East Germany for a week at the end of it. The band were in fine form and the crew had been augmented by Gary Flemming – known as 'Goom', and Billy who were rigging and running the lights. Chappo had his own lighting rig for a while now and we were using that. He had also bought a PA system from John Henry and we were taking that out for the first time. This consisted of a new Soundcraft F.O.H. board with RSD amplifiers and the old Martin system of Y-Bins, Phillishaves and Horns. They had bought a Peavey monitor desk which was not a good choice but it was the desk that Ray had got a really good sound on in East Germany earlier that year. It became quite clear during the first few weeks of the tour, however, that Ray was not really on the case with the monitors. There was a bit of feedback going on and he was having trouble getting it sorted. Roger was not one to take incompetence by the crew easily; he was prone to throwing stuff if he felt that people were not paying attention to the job at hand.

There is (or at least there was back then) an unwritten rule that says that you can smoke a bit of dope, drink, do a few lines, whatever, so long as you do the gig you are out there to do. It makes sense, after all it is hard to be replaced at short notice and we really did all have to be as on the case as possible. Ray began to have problems from the start. On one gig I could hear a low end rumble going on and I looked over the stage to see one of the set lists, which had been taped to the side fill, was standing out at 45 degree. There was that much air being moved by the bass feedback from those speakers. This was all to come to a head much later in the tour.

For the most part, though, the tour went well. Audiences were large and loud, and the band and crew were having fun. Billy, who was from Glasgow and had never been out of the country before let alone on a rock and roll tour, was completely puzzled by it all. 'This isnae work,' he told us one day.

He was sitting backstage having a beer after having been fed. He was used to working on the roads and grafting all day. Somehow it felt wrong to him to be drinking when he was being paid. He was talking to us about being a body builder and he certainly did have that kind of physique. His hero was 'Arnie' and he had to go off somewhere each day to find something heavy to lift up and down. He said he was the person people would call on when they wanted someone brought into line. They would send Billy round for a 'chat' and usually the person would cooperate. We asked him what would scare him then.

'If I hit someone and they didn't fall over,' he answered.

Suddenly I realised why the boxer from the *Upper Cut* had looked so bemused and worried when he hit me in *Middle Earth* and why the guy in the *City Arms* had backed out of the door. I didn't fall down and they thought I should have done.

After a few gigs a guy turned up from a drum factory and offered to supply Sam Kelly with the kit of his choosing for the duration of the tour. Sam was pleased with this and they decided that he should come to the factory to choose a kit when we played in the adjacent town. Sam asked if he could travel with us that day because we were leaving in the morning and he would have more time to look at drums. I told him we were leaving pretty early because it was a long drive, and that if he was not there at 6:30 am, we would not wait for him. He agreed. The next morning I got up and went down to the bus. It was, as usual, littered with empty beer bottles so I gathered them up and put them in the bin. In among the detritus of the previous night's gigging there was an empty vodka bottle. I had an idea and so I took that into the hotel, washed it out and then half filled it with water. I told the crew about this. Sam arrived and we piled into the bus. I was taking first stint at driving. When everyone was sitting down I picked up the vodka bottle and said:

'This bottle has no lid, it's going to fall over and go everywhere. Let's finish it off.'

I took a great big swig of the water in the bottle and passed it on. It went round the bus until it got to Sam, but by then it was empty – as planned. Sam looked at us in astonishment. Gordon was rolling a spliff in the passenger seat and Gary was chopping out a few lines.

'I suppose I had better join you,' he said and pulled out a bottle of Jack Daniels and downed a huge swig of that. Gordon passed the spliff to him and within minutes of setting off he was asleep. He did not wake until we arrived at the gig.

After the soundcheck we sat down to eat, and he said to the band:

'These guys are amazing, they wake up at 6am, get in the bus, drink half a bottle of vodka, have a spliff and then drive 400km without batting an eyelid.'

I did not tell him it was water in the vodka bottle until the tour was over. We met up again in 2013 when I popped in to see 'The Chuck Farleys', a band he plays with.

'I still have not forgotten that trick with the vodka bottle,' he told me.

We went on through to Austria. It was here I learned about a tradition that the Austrian promoter, Wolfgang Klinger, had. He would put in a day off and take everyone somewhere unusual to get drunk. On this tour it was a schnapps factory on a mountain. I say 'factory', it was really a cottage industry, but they did make their own schnapps there and we were invited to sample it for free. I was never too keen on sledgehammer spirits (except tequila) so I only had a couple, but everyone else was going for it. We were sitting in a small hunting lodge type bar, decorated with animal heads and ice picks; someone suggested to Wilf that he got his hair cut and then Chris Youle bet him a week's wages that he would not have his hair cut and beard shaven off there and then. He said he would and so Chris got the guy at the bar to call for a hairdresser to come up and do it. When the hairdresser arrived she was dressed in leather trousers, and was very good looking. She proceeded to give Wilf a haircut and shave in the middle of the room. He did make a drunken attempt to get her to come to the hotel later but she never showed up.

The gigs had not been going too well for Ray. You can get into a spiral of things going wrong on a tour. Everyone has one or two bad days, but get a run of them and you can start to doubt you own ability to do the job. For a monitor engineer the worst thing that can happen is that you start to think that you are doing it wrong and then you overcompensate and it all goes downhill. You can't hear what is happening on the stage as I said before and once you get to the stage of having pulled large swathes of frequencies out of a mix all you have is a quiet mix that sounds odd. By the time we got to Austria, Ray was well along that route. His confidence was slipping and he was drinking a bit too much; a recipe for disaster in anyone's book.

We turned up at one gig in Matrei in Austria to find we were playing in a small village. Not only that, but we were actually doing the gig in a large shed that was usually used to train horses. Sawdust on the floor and a general smell of animals. It all went wrong right at the start when Martin the truck driver tried to back into the courtyard. In the process he slipped the fifth wheel, which for those of you unfamiliar with trucking terms, is the bit at the back of the cab of an articulated truck that actually latches onto the body of the box trailer. It took a bit of manoeuvring and a tractor to get the thing flat and ready to be unloaded. While all this was going on we were looking at the gig. It did not look that promising to me. The stage was big enough, but when I looked at the power box I could see it would not have enough amps to drive the PA and lights. I mentioned this to Wilf who seemed to not really know what I meant so I gathered H and Gary round the power distro. I pointed out that the lights were usually run for a 63 amp three phase box and the sound from a single 32 amp phase. This box only has a three phase 32 amp supply. They seemed to think it would be OK so we loaded the gear in. We got ready to do the soundcheck and decided we would run the soundcheck with the PA blasting and the lights all on full in order to test the system. I did not really think it was an adequate test, but I was the last person to want to pull a gig so I went with it. The soundcheck passed without incident and they all said that I was being overcautious, but I was not so sure.

When we came back after eating, the hall was alive with beer stands, Gluhwein vendors and various purveyors of pretzels and hot, meat-based, food. All of these were hooked into the hall's power supply. They may not be hooked into the actual 3 phase box that we were, but they were all drawing on the same supply somewhere and this was a small town. I could not see where all these people had come from. There were not enough houses there for them all to live in.

The show kicked off and, four numbers in, the power went off. We switched off the PA, reset the breakers and, after a quick discussion decided to continue with half the lighting. The band came back on and played from the note they had stopped at before. Very impressive. The power tripped again – and came straight back on and went straight off and came straight back on, accompanied each time by a loud thud as the amps kicked in. I rushed round to the power box to find the caretaker resetting the breakers each time they went out. I stopped him from doing that but it was too late. He had already blown some of the horns in the PA. That was it for the night. The promoter took to the stage to explain and we struck the stage. Disaster didn't stop there though. We had a free night. We were out and finished by 9pm and the promoter invited us along to his bar for a drink.

We went off to his bar after that and stayed there drinking for a while. He came over to us and said, 'Let's have a party.'

'Where?' I asked.

He took us outside and pointed at a light across the valley on the slope of an adjacent mountain.

'That is my house, we can party there.'

The gig the next day was in Graz, which is not so far away from where we were, but involves driving through some fairly narrow and winding mountain roads. Apart from that we knew we would have to repair some of the horns so we had decided we would leave early the next morning. We all decided not to go off to the guy's house. All, that is, except Ray. When he told us he was going to go I reminded him about the leave time.

'We are leaving the hotel at 7am tomorrow. If you are not on the bus by then you had better start looking for a job here.'

Ray went off with the promoter and a group of his friends and we went back to the bar for one last drink. The hotel we were staying in was the 'Sport Hotel Tyrol'. The whole basis of the hotel was to cater for the people who came up to this region in the summer to go horse riding, trekking, and all those other things that you can really only do when the sun is out. It was not in the skiing area so it was usually closed in the winter time. This meant that there was no staff at the hotel. Earlier in the evening Nick Pentelow, the band's sax player, had to operate the switchboard so he could make a call, and when we got back there was no one there to book a wake-up call with. We did have alarm clocks in the rooms so we set these and went to bed.

I got up the following morning, took a shower, and set off to go downstairs to see if there was any way to get coffee and breakfast. When the lift doors opened I was greeted by a strong smell of secondhand alcohol and the prone figure of Ray. He was asleep in the lift.

'Ray!' I cried (always the perspicacious one) and he woke up. He looked around and waved his arm.

'Come in,' he slurred.

'This is not your room, it is the lift!'

He waved a key and key fob at me.

'The key won't fit,' he stated, trying hard to focus his eyes.

'That is from the previous hotel,' I told him. 'You are in room 19. You have 40 minutes to get yourself together and we are leaving.'

He dragged himself to his feet and rushed off, unsteadily down the corridor.

Downstairs Gordon had found the coffee machine and some cups, and had got some coffee going. There was no one there to make any breakfast and not much food around so we gave up on that and just had some coffee, deciding to grab breakfast down the road a bit. We assembled at the bus, and to my amazement, Ray arrived with his bags, and we set off for Graz. There was a kind of bunk over the driver's section of the mini bus and Ray crawled into that and went to sleep. We drove to Graz and began the load in. H and I checked out the speakers and found the ones which had been damaged by the previous night's power problems and began to repair them. Once that was done we began to set the gear up. We all tried to wake Ray up and get him to come into the gig, but he stayed in the bus. Finally, with all the lights, PA and backline up H and I went to the bus and shouted at him that he had an hour and a half before soundcheck and we were not going to put the monitors together for him. That did it and he came in and started setting the gear up. He was hung over and a bit of a mess and the gig went very badly for him.

After the show, when we were all packed down, we went back to the hotel and sat up in our room having a drink and a smoke. We had got into the habit of brewing our own Gluhwein using one of those little coil heaters you can get for making tea, and the herb packets that we bought in one of the markets. When we ran out of red wine we experimented with Gluhvodka but that did not really work. Ray sat in the corner looking depressed.

'I have lost it,' he told me, 'I am not sure I can do this anymore.'

I tried to reassure him and said he needed a good night's sleep and to lay off the alcohol a bit, but he was not having any of that.

'Come for a walk with me, I need some air.'

For some reason we had been put in a hotel which was in the main red light district of Graz. The street outside was lined with leggy hookers in scanty clothing – and it is not warm in Austria in November. Ray and I left the hotel and walked through these women. Something about the mad set of Ray's face warned them off from offering their services. We walked past peep shows and strip joints and came to a bar/brothel. Ray walked straight in and I followed. The interior was so typical of the classical brothels scene from '60s films. It had red flock wallpaper and little booths with tables in them. It was dingy and almost empty. In one corner booth there was a woman in a basque talking to a middle-aged man. In the centre of the room a chubby man in a dinner jacket and bow tie sat playing sub Jacques Lousier jazz on a grand piano and, on our right, was a bar. The woman behind the bar was topless and well past her prime. She had her breasts laid out on the bar and was talking to a man seated drinking in front of her. Ray seemed quite at home in this place.

'Play some fucking rock and roll!' he slurred at the piano player. The man smiled and carried on.

Ray repeated his request louder, but got no response from the musician. Right then the woman in the booth must have concluded negotiations with the middle-aged man and stood up and walked, with a very pronounced limp, to the bar to hand over the money to the other woman. We watched as she then limped back to the table and escorted the man through some bead curtains into the back room. As she went through the curtains she broke into a hacking, consumptive, cough.

Ray stood up and bellowed:

'Have her now mate, while she is still warm!'

With visions of burly bouncers with machetes or baseball bats emerging from the back to deal with unruly drunken Englishmen, I hustled Ray out of the bar and back to the hotel.

After the Austrian leg of the tour we went back to Germany for the second part of the German tour. On the second of these gigs Alex Koerver had got very drunk, and as we drove back to the hotel, had thrown up into the waste bin in the bus. We emptied it, washed it out and wrote 'Hullo Alex' in the bottom of it, ready for the next time. We did a show in Darmstadt called

ROGER CHAPMAN
& THE SHORTLIST

BUSTED LOOSE

TOUR'84

ABOVE: The Jolly Joker in Braunschweig 1984
BELOW: Inside the hunting lodge

Chris Youle and Sam Kelly at the Hunting lodge.

Ray on the desk (opposite)
Backing into Matei Chappo 1984
The gig as seen from the stage (opposite)

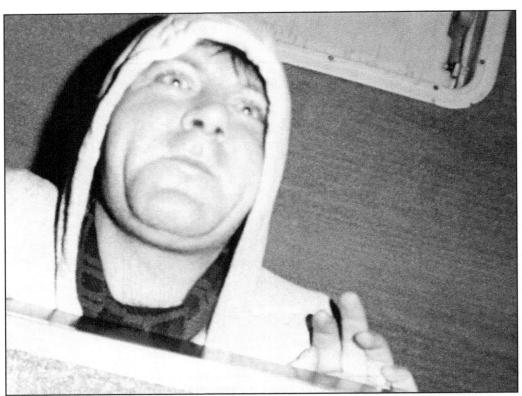

8381379 prk d

wuerden sie bitte dieses telex an mr. r. salter weiterleiten,
zu gast in ihrem hause mit roger chapman:

attn: mr. r. salter

re: urgent message

dear busted loose crew,

sorry about delay, everything is o.k, see you tomorrow
at 10.00 . for load in.

kind regards
peter rieger konzertagentur
alex + petra

622214 nofue d
8381379 prk d

TELEX ANDREAS DUMPROFF

40 minutes to soundcheck (opposite above)
H, Gary Billy and Martin backstage at the Lopsos Werkstadt (opposite below)
Telex from Alex (above)
Circus Krone (below)

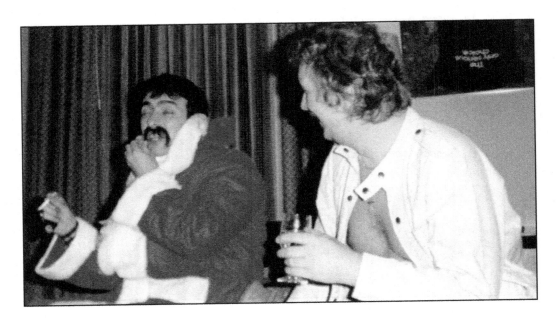

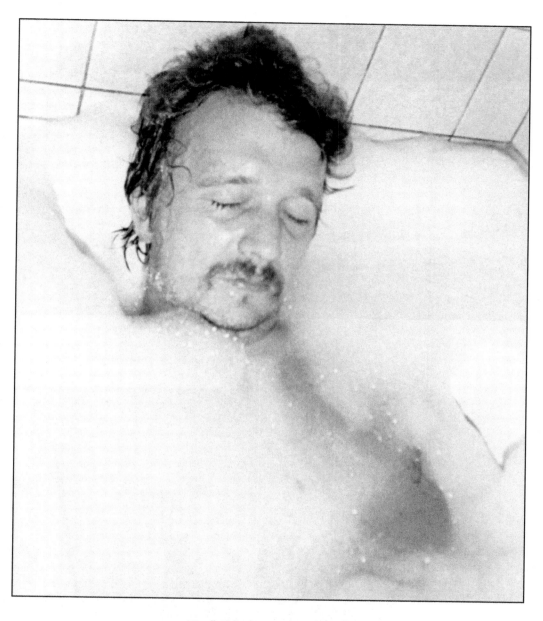

Youletide (opposite above)
East German Dirt (opposite below)
H asleep in the bath after the Berlin shows (above)

East German pipes (opposite above)
Geoff Whitehorn, Brian Gallivan, Gordon Waters and H Griffiths outside the hotel in
Karl Marx Stadt (opposite below)
Wilf Wittingham and Geoff Whitehorn (this page)

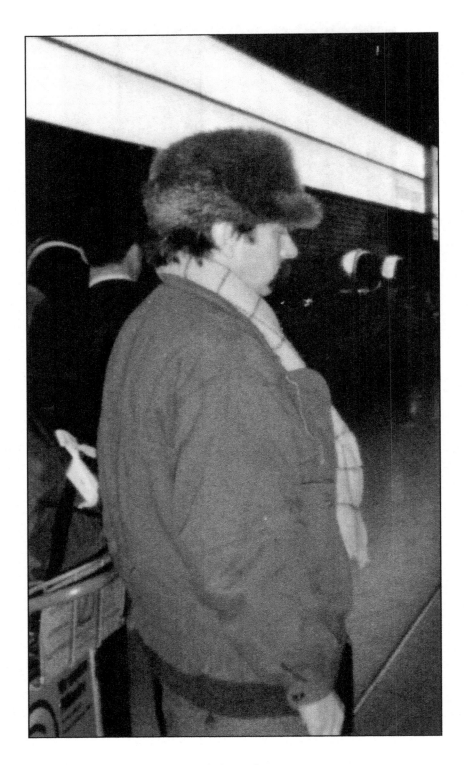

Chris Youle

H - 'that's all folks'

Busted Loose Stage 1984

the Lopos Werkstadt. I met a couple of interesting women before the show and got them to hang around afterwards. As soon and we had finished the gig and packed the backline down I went over and started talking to them again. The gig had a bar that stayed open for a while so they were able to stay, but when that closed I took them backstage. The band had all left, apart from Nick Pentelow, and I introduced the girls to him and we sat for a while having a drink. I went out to the hall to check on the progress of loading and found our crew on one side of the room and the local crew on the other. There was no loading going on. The local crew were Turkish or Iranian and there was some dispute over the load out. I asked H what was happening. He said they were refusing to load the truck. I picked out the one who looked like he was the ringleader and went up to him.

'The only reason you are here is to help us load the truck. Either you get on with that or you go home and I will make sure you don't get paid.' I told him. I shouted for Alex, who was supposed to be organising all of this, but he was upstairs drinking with the promoter and had not seen it.

After a few more words they reluctantly resumed work and we got the truck loaded. When Gordon and I had all the backline trunks on and the PA, I returned to the dressing room to make sure Nick had not made off with the women. H came up to me.

'You were brave,' he said.

'Why?'

'That guy you shouted at. He was the one with the knife.'

I had not known anything about a knife being produced so it was not hard to be brave really.

When Alex heard about this he got angry with them. He was already very drunk, and just as we were leaving; he went into their crew room and sprayed on the wall, 'Remember Auschwitz? This time I pay for the gas,' in German. This was a pretty bad thing to do on all levels, but we did not find out about it until much later. He went off into a complete rampage that night and threw all of the furniture from his room out of the window. We decided we had taken enough of this and changed the wake-up call in the morning so we could leave without him and Petra. When we got to the next gig we had a telex from Alex which read:

> *Dear busted Loose crew*
> *Sorry about delay, everything is ok.*
> *See you tomorrow at 10.00 for load in Alex and Petra*

We had a day off before the last part of the German tour and we went to Regensburg and stayed in the hotel there. The German catering girls were there already and I wound up hooking up with Ute that night. We spent all evening in my room and part way through it I decided to get dressed and go downstairs to get us some drinks. I walked into the bar to find a party in full swing. The rest of the crew, the band and the other two caterers were all down there. As I walked past Chris he produced a little packet and said, 'Do you want a toot?'

I said I did, but as he did this, the waiter walked past us. He was a fairly straight looking, late middle-aged German, wearing the traditional Bavarian waiter's outfit. He looked straight at us as Chris held out a small spoonful of coke for me to snort. Chris looked back at him.

'I suppose you want some too, do you?' I was not sure how he would take that, but to my surprise he said, 'Ja!' and took a hit. I went back upstairs to Ute with some drinks, and a couple of lines of hoot.

In Munich we played a gig called the *Cirkus Krone*. This was, in fact, a circus and functioned as such for most of the year. It was founded in 1905 by a guy called Carl Krone – hence the name – and has been run by the same family all that time. Although this is a somewhat magnificent setting for a gig it does have one serious setback. It is used, on a daily basis, in fact they live in a yard just at the back of the auditorium. My database of gigs notes 'eat where the elephants shit', which just about sums it up. We had our meals on tables set in a room with sawdust for flooring. Well, at least it was fresh sawdust. After the meal I got bored. The gig is in the middle of nowhere so I sat at the wooden trestle table, having a spliff. I drew a cartoon of the lighting truss with Gary up in it hitting it with a hammer and shouting 'Fook it, Fook it, Fook it'. The others egged me on and I expanded the cartoon to include the rest of the crew in their favourite positions and pastimes. This took me right up till show time and I had managed to fill most of the table by then. I am no great artist you understand, and that table was more the Chappo's Cistern than the *Sistine Chapel*. After the show Alex Koerver told me the promoter went wild about my defacing his table so Alex bought it. Seems he took it home with him after the tour and varnished it, and it became his kitchen table.

Christmas was fast approaching, which in Germany means a whole mass of town square markets spring up selling Gluhwein and the like, and we availed ourselves of these whenever we were near enough to get out from the gigs or had a day off. Somehow or other Chris Youle managed to acquire a Santa Claus costume and decided to invade people's rooms. He had quite a deep voice and his, 'Ho Ho Ho little boy, and what do you want for Christmas then?' was quite convincing. Youletide indeed. After two months on the road together it was turning into a rolling party.

We were getting near to the end of the tour but the German promoter had another trick to pull on us. We had played *The Metropol* in West Berlin on the 19th October, right at the start of the tour, and sold it out. They decided they would put a second show in there since we were heading to East Germany anyway. The original tour took us from Sindelfingen, which is down in the south, past Stuttgart, to Aachen, which is on the Belgian border. We had decided the best way to make sure we were there on time would be to drive overnight from the gig because part of the route took us through the 'Ruhrgebiet', that tangled mess of industrial towns and autobahns in the east part of central Germany. Going through there in the early hours of the morning would avoid the traffic jams. It was only when we were in Aachen that Chris told us we would have to overnight to Berlin after that show to get in to do the extra gig. So that was two nights without sleeping then. We got to Berlin and put the gear in. *The Metropol* is a tall building and the gig is in the top of it. There is a lift, but it is not very big so a lot of the gear has to go up the stairs making the load in a very slow affair.

Bombshell number two was dropped on us after the soundcheck for that gig. The next show was also in *The Metropol* - but in East Berlin – a stone's throw from the gig we were in, but we had a matinée to do so we would have to go straight there after the gig. We loaded out of the West German *Metropol* and drove straight to Checkpoint Charlie to go through the usual checks and questions before being granted visas and other papers and passed through to the East. The East German counterpart to *The Metropol* was very different. The West German one was pretty punk in its way. It was an old theatre but had been ripped apart and turned into a rock venue and late night disco. The East German one was a hall unchanged from its roots back in the days of music hall.

We did the gig and were taken off for a meal and thence to check into the hotel. I had almost forgotten what one of those looked like. No time for much more than a wash though because it was back to the theatre for the evening show. These three gigs were recorded live and released on an EP called 'Shadow Cross The Wall – Live in Berlin' a couple of years later. They were are also added to the extended version of 'The Shadow Knows' when that album was released on CD.

At the end of that marathon we went back to the hotel to take some welcome, and much needed, baths and showers. It had been an early gig so we were back by 10pm, which was a bonus. We were just relaxing and contemplating going to bed early when Brian knocked on our door.

'C'mon boys, we're going to a disco,' he lilted at us, so we dutifully followed him to the band's bus, and went off to an East Berlin disco.

I was pretty tired by then, but I threw myself into the spirit of things and bought a bottle of ludicrously cheap Sekt. We were joined by a bevy of scantily clad young ladies who were eager to talk to westerners. The bubbly flowed and I wound up with one of these women on my lap. I had a glass of Sekt in my hand and fell asleep – pouring the drink straight down her cleavage. I woke up when she slapped me and stormed off. It was then I realised that the band had left and I was struggling to recall the name of the hotel I was in. It was one of the few moments in my life when I cannot recall how I got back, but I woke up in my bed - in the right hotel as well.

We continued on into East Germany. One thing that continually puzzled me as we drove through the bleak fields and grey towns of the East was the continual prescience of large pipes by the roadside. These pipes seemed to go for miles and sometime reared up and went, like a bridge, across the road to continue on the other side. I kept asking people what the pipes were for and the response was usually, 'Pipes? What pipes?'

I was beginning to wonder if this was some East German secret weapon that no one was supposed to mention, and it was not until later I found out that the factories would convert any excess heat they produced as a result of the manufacturing process into hot air and then pump this into the people's homes to heat them in the winter. A good by product of the communist ideal, but there was not a lot of evidence that communism was giving them any other benefits. The shops were all pretty empty and the few goods that were in them were similar to the kind of product we had in the '50s and early '60s. The only things that were of any quality were the low tech ones, glassware and the like. Back in the summer, when we had been here last, Chris had got us to drive the van to a toy shop in the town. We marched in and in the centre of the room was a large train layout on a board, with stations, houses, little trees and people. Chris went up to the counter and announced, 'I want to buy that' and pointed at the layout. The man nodded and started getting the boxed trains down from the shelf.

'No,' Chris explained, 'not those. That!'

The man in the shop was stunned. There was a convoluted conversation for a few minutes in which Chris explained that he did not want new trains and track in boxes, he wanted the ready built layout. After a while money changed hands and Gordon and I carried the whole thing out of the shop with Chris walking along beside us, twirling the end of his moustache and saying, 'Conspicuous consumption. That's what we want. Let's show them some western excess.'

The thing was that we were being paid for the gigs in East German marks and this was a 'soft currency'. There was no way you could exchange the money for western money because there was no official exchange rate. Apart from that it was illegal to take the money out of the country. They would actually ask you to open your wallet at the borders to show you did not have any notes in there. Roger had an East German bank account because he was also being paid for the albums that he sold over there, but the rest of us were struggling to find a way to spend the money. There was really nothing to spend it on. When Chris flew back from East Germany they asked if he had any East marks. He said, 'I don't know.'

They made him open his wallet and there were a lot of East German banknotes in there. Chris removed them from his wallet and gave them to the border guard, 'Here you are, you can have them.'

The guard said he could not accept money and that Chris would have to open a bank account and put them in there. They went across the airport to the bank and started going through the process of opening an account. Chris looked round and saw a Red Cross collection box.

'Pass me that,' he said, and proceeded to cram the notes into the box. There was more money there than some of these people would have earned in a month.

'There you go,' he said, 'Now you'll have to break your fucking leg to get any of it.'

After one of the gigs in East Germany, H and I went off for a drink with the stage crew. We found ourselves in a local bar drinking vodka from cracked glasses. After a few drinks we headed back to the hotel and went into the bar. Chris and a few of the band and crew were sitting there drinking. There were two women sitting at the bar.

'Those two are for you,' Chris waved his arm at them.

'OK,' I said and we went over to talk to them. A little while later they invited us back to their place. We went off with them expecting a short journey and found ourselves travelling back to another town. Their apartment was none too luxurious. I went to the toilet and there was a hole in the roof and you could see the stars through it. I had a bit of coke on me and suggested we had a line. She did not really understand what I meant so I explained.

'There is no cocaine in East Germany,' she said.

'Oh yes there is,' I said as I chopped it out.

Dangerous really, given what we thought then, and had confirmed after the fall of the wall, about the way that the Eastern Bloc spied on and controlled its people and visitors to the country. There is an element of the Teflon coating of being on tour. You always think it won't touch you. You won't get arrested, attacked, or anything like that. You always expect the tour manager or the promoter to sort it out, but it can go very wrong. Luckily in this case it didn't.

We finished the last gig a week before Christmas and drove the bus back towards West Germany to hand it over to Petra at *Hannover Airport*. On the way back Billy, driving on an icy and untreated road, failed to stop quickly enough and whacked into one of those cardboard Trebants that were everywhere in East Germany, 'Oh fook. I've hit a dinky toy,' he exclaimed, as it spun off the road.

Luckily the ice, and the fact that a cardboard car with a lawnmower engine in it did not present much inertia, ensured that little damage was done. We continued on to *Hannover Airport* and flew home, all wearing obligatory fur hats.

Glitter Newspaper report (above)
Mr Birmingham 85 (below)

CHAPTER 21

A Bit More Glitter And Chappo
And A Spell With John Cale

There was another Glitter tour that was not due to go out until a bit later in 1985, but there was also a Fresher's Ball in Cambridge that he was booked to do so I went up to do front of house for that. I met up with the other members of the crew; Gordon from the Chappo tour was the backline man, tasked with assembling the various risers and stairs as well as doing the backline, and Tony Slee was the lighting guy. Tony was given to spot on impersonations of the 'Glitter stare' and had done his lights for some time. Lance drove the truck. Lance's nickname was 'Thermic' because, on a previous Mezzoforte tour the tail lift of the truck had seized and, instead of calling out for a repair service, he hired a thermic lance and cut it off. We also had two drummers back for the tour. Pete Phipps, one of the original drummers, was back in the band.

When we had finished the soundcheck for the gig in Cambridge we retired to the crew room to have a bit to eat and drink. Tony Slee had managed to get the students to bring us a couple of bottles of champagne so we were sitting there having a spliff, and drinking bubbly. Very nice too. This was very much a 'hoorays night out'. The gig was in a tent on the university's lawn and the patrons were exclusively in dinner jackets and ball gowns. We had contemplated getting a few DJs from a junk shop and painting crew on the back (something I did do for a different gig a bit later on). The gig had been organised by Prince Edward who was the Social Secretary for the college that year. Just before show time Tony rolled a long spliff to have at the start of the show and we walked out to the desks.

The tent was full of people eating food from the buffet and drinking champagne. The two desks were on a riser and, beside them was a round table with a follow spot on it. Lance, the truck driver, was going to do the follow spot. We took our places and got the signal to start. Cue the intro tape and off we went. The band appeared onstage, and Tony lit the spliff.

Suddenly, standing behind us on the riser was Prince Edward and his two bodyguards. We shrugged and carried on smoking the spliff. To our right Lance was getting into trouble. As Glitter launched into his first number the hoorays started to look for somewhere to ditch their plates and glasses, and found the table that Lance was standing on to be just the thing. Lance started off polite, 'Er, excuse me, please don't.....can you not....'

He was gradually being engulfed by a sea of plates of half-eaten food and discarded drinks, so much so that he soon could barely move his feet. And more was coming.

'Please don't put the plates here ....Can you?.....er...please.'

In the end the patience snapped, 'Fuck off you ignorant bunch of cunts!' he bellowed and started kicking all the plates and assorted food detritus over hoorays. I looked round and saw Edward's chin move even closer to his Adam's apple. He wobbled a moment and then got down from the riser and left.

A short while later we were joined on the riser by the guy who was organising the gig.

'It is too loud,' he said.

'No it isn't,' I replied.

'I have control of the sound,' he insisted.

'But I have my hands on the faders, are you going to try to take them off?'

The conversation carried on for a while like this until I got fed up and said, 'Look, I work for the band's manager. Go and get him, and if he says it is too loud I will turn it down.'

He trotted off to find Alan Gee, who came a while later. Alan climbed onto the riser and said, 'It sounds OK to me. I tell you what, let's have a chat for a while then you can pretend to argue with me and I will go away.'

We did that and he turned to the other guy, shrugged his shoulders and got down from the riser.

The guy climbed back up and continued to try to get me to turn it down. The show ended in the middle of one of these arguments and I said, 'Oh, OK then,' and brought the faders down, 'Quiet enough now?'

This whole thing made the papers and the *Daily Mail* had a whole section saying how the gig was full of drunken people laying on the floor, and how it had got complaints about the noise and that they had refused to pay Glitter for the show. Alan said he would have to sue Edward then, and it all got sorted out. They did not think I had done anything wrong though, and realised that it had to be that volume for the show to work. Subtle mood music it wasn't.

On the tour that followed we used the PA that Chris Youle had bought for Chappo, so H came out and did the front while I went back onto the monitors. The tour started in Hull and so we drove up from London the day before. They had hired a mini bus for us, and mini it certainly was. It was one of those really small Hyundai things. To add insult to injury we had to pick the caterers up on the way. Crammed into this little thing we drove up the M1 to Hull. By the time we got there it was pretty late and we arrived at the hotel to find it all shut up. We rang the bell and a woman appeared in a dressing gown.

She immediately started to berate us about how late it was and especially looked askance at Tony Slee's hair which was spiky and multicoloured. Her husband came downstairs and took over booking us in. We explained that we did not know it was a small hotel and we were used to being booked into hotels that at least had a night porter. He was OK about it. We asked what time breakfast was and were told 6:30. We asked if we could have it a bit later and his wife shouted from up the stairs, 'Can I hear someone interfering with my breakfast arrangements?'

It seems that her husband had to do the breakfasts before going off to work. I don't think that man had a very good life. We decided to not stay there the following night. The stupid thing was that the following night was in London – where we had just come from. This was because the first few dates had been cancelled and re-booked.

I cornered Alan at the soundcheck and suggested that he gave us a gram of coke, and we would cancel the hotel and drive straight down to London. He agreed with that so we piled into the silly mini-mini bus and rocked on back to London straight after. Tony Slee left the tour part way through it to do something else and a guy called Pete, who had already been rigging the lights, took over the lighting desk. Pete and H got on very well and on the second show they announced that they had a betting syndicate. We all slung a couple of pounds in each day and they would pick some horses in that day's races. Any money earned – which was usually quite reasonable – went into a kitty to buy dope and coke with. This was a party tour!

The band had been given green tartan suits to wear onstage a while back and they put these on for the Hammersmith show. Brian told me that they had them at a gig a few tour tours back when Glitter had a 'coke moment'. The show would always run in the same way with Gaz going off halfway through to change costume and the band doing three songs without him, the two Glitter Band hits. Gaz had got ready to come out on the stage for the second part of the set which normally started with 'Hello, Hello, I'm Back'. The band would then turn and face the back of the stage, play a fanfare, and he would appear at the top of the stairs and launch into 'Did you miss me, yeah, while I was away, did you hang my picture on your wall?'

That night he appeared, but froze and just stood there. After a while he snapped out of it and carried on.

After the show they asked him what happened. He said, 'I was out of my body. Suddenly I was sitting in the audience looking back at the band playing. It was really odd.' He was clearly spooked by what had happened.

'So you could see the band on stage then?' asked Brian.

'Yes, it was weird; I was looking straight at you all.'

'What did me suit look loike then?' Brian enquired.

When we did the gig at *Queen Mary College* in London they got to the middle spot of the set and the band turned round to do the usual fanfare, and no Gaz appeared. They turned and looked at me but I had no idea. I certainly did not have a fader on my desk that would make him appear. Gerry suggested they did it again and so they went through the fanfare once more. Still nothing. After a third time Alan Gee appeared beside me.

'He won't come on,' he said.

'Why?'

'He says he's twisted his ankle on the stairs, but I think he wants another gram of coke. I have given him four already, I can't give him any more. It will kill him one day. I know he has one taped to his head under the wig for emergencies. Can you go on and tell them it is over?'

'You do it, you are the manager – manage.'

He shrugged, walked on stage and said something in Gerry's ear.

Gerry swung round and said into the microphone.

'That's it. That's yer lot!' and walked off.

There was a near riot in the hall and they began to throw chairs at the stage. In the end the band came back on and ran through a few more songs, but it was a tense evening.

Alan then told us we were off to Bahrain. We had a week in the *Holiday Inn* in Bahrain with only two shows to do. This tour was back under RSD but Rob was off on a different tour so his place was taken by John Blackburn. I had seen John around in the warehouse and in the pub with Dave South and Rob and I assumed he was one of the regular engineers and a friend of theirs. They certainly didn't tell me any different. We flew out to Bahrain on *Gulf Air*, the company who were also promoting the gig. When we landed and disembarked we were greeted by a large gay guy who flounced over to us and said, 'Is Paul there?'

'Paul?'

'You know, Paul, Paul Gadd.' he said.

Brian looked him up and down and said to me,

'Fat Cunt.' From that moment we called him 'FC'.

At first they told us we could eat and drink as much as we wanted, but soon realised we had a strong appetite for both food and drink, and cut that down to three meals and pay for your own drinks. We spent the first day at the pool side doing very little. Eventually the container with the gear in it arrived and we were able to unload. RSD had sold the PA system to the venue and Pete's lighting company had done the same with the lighting. The stage was a crude wooden structure with a walkway. Pete and I stood on the walkway and shook our heads. The Indian stage manager came over.

'What s wrong?' he asked.

'It's this walkway. You can't leave it here. Glitter will walk out on it. I can't light him and he will cause problems with the PA.'

The guy looked crestfallen.

'And where is the white grand piano?' Pete was warming to his wind up now.

'I will sort it,' the man said and scuttled off.

A while later a man appeared on stage with a saw. He knelt down on the walkway, getting ready to saw through it. We stopped him and told him it was a joke. We then went off to find the stage manager and tell him. We found him about to get some of his men to paint the hotel's grand piano white.

After two days of doing nothing I was getting to the stage where I would be quite happy to leave. We had been invited to a party in one of the ex-pat's houses and we went along, but I found myself getting more and more irritated by the way they treated people. It was a real 'us and them' culture and they abused the 'servants' really badly. I was very uncomfortable being there and left early.

With all the gear set up we were ready to do the two shows. These were pretty uneventful and tame affairs. Without an audience howling 'Leader' at him, Glitter did not really rise to the occasion. The guy who had met us at the airport was running the show and he was around every day and was greeted by the crew with cries of 'Morning FC'.

In fact, every time we addressed him, we called him 'FC' and he looked a little puzzled by it. A friend of his came up to me one day and asked why we all called him that. I was on the spot a bit and had to do some quick thinking. I came up with an answer. I said, 'Well, we abbreviate everything in this business. Master of ceremonies is an MC, musical director, MD, FOH is front of house, lighting designer, LD, you know the kind of thing.'

He nodded.

'Well, when we have an open air show it is usually a festival of some kind and the person who is in charge of that is the festival coordinator – FC.'

'Oh, I see,' he replied, 'I will tell him that. He was worried you were slagging him off.'

'Us – never.'

From them on he would go up to people and say:

'I am the FC.'

And we would all reply:

'Yeah, we know.'

After the first show Gaz invited us to his suite for a drink. We were joined by a few of the air hostesses that were staying in the hotel. During the party there was an incident when John bit one of the women on the backside quite badly. I jokingly suggested she did it back to him and next thing I knew he had her up against the wall by the hair. I separated them and tried to sort it out. I had been talking to one of the airhostesses, and suggested we went back to my room. No sooner had we got into bed than the door opened. It was John. He had got a spare key from reception.

'I'm going to beat you up!' he was shouting flailing his fists around. I was naked but pushed him back and told him I was not going to fight with him. He was pretty insistent, but I bundled him out of the room and into the arms of the security guards that the woman had called. I went back into the room and called Alan. Then I got dressed and went back outside. The security guards wanted to take him off to the police, but Alan and I stopped them, telling that he was just drunk and they should take him to his room. John then decided to try to kick me in the crotch. At that point I gave up being peaceful, and without looking at him, my arm shot out and my fist connected with his nose. He began to bleed, and burst into tears.

'I want to go home,' he sobbed. 'He's hit me, and he's hit me,' indicating me and the guard.

'Just take him to his room please,' I said.

When he had left with the guard I spoke to Alan.

'No need to let anyone else know about this, is there? Let's keep it between us and have a word with him in the morning, when he sobers up.' I went back to bed and my airhostess.

The next morning we went to John's room. He had a sore mouth and nose where I had hit him and his wrist was bandaged up.

'What happened to that?' I asked.

'I did it hitting you,' he replied.

I didn't have a mark on me though. We suggested he told everyone he was drunk and fell over, and we would not mention the incident again. We shook hands on it and left him to it.

A few weeks later I was in the RSD office with Dave and his secretary. She said something and I joked 'Right, I am going to have to sort you out,' and made to come round her desk.

'I am not tangling with you,' she said, 'you know Kung Fu. John told us.'

'Yes,' Dave chipped in, 'He said you beat him up in Bahrain.'

'I only hit him once and he started crying,' was my answer.

'About time someone hit the little fucker. He is always picking on people.'

It seems he did this regularly. He would choose someone he thought he could beat up and attack them. It also seems that none of them there liked him at all.

Pete came up to me on the day of the second show and asked if I had spoken with the guy who had bought all the gear. I said no I hadn't. It seems that, on the day off, after the shows had finished, he wanted us to teach his people how to set it all up and run it – as if you could learn that in a day. We told him we would do it but he had to pay us because it was our day off. He refused to pay us and the argument continued for the rest of that day. If he had made us an offer we would probably have backed down from the £200 each we asked for, but he just said no. At the end of the show I unplugged everything, packed it all up and then left it where it was.

The next day we met up at breakfast. He still wanted us to show him what to do but still would not pay. Pete produced a wad of notes.

'Here you are then,' he said. 'I have written down everything about how to wire it all up.'

He looked pleased, and I was a bit surprised because he seemed so adamant he was not going to do it. The guy took the notes and looked pleased. Pete stood up, 'Oh, by the way, I have made three deliberate mistakes in there, and if it you wire it up that way it will all blow up. If you give us the £200 each I will tell you where they are.'

He walked away. The guy was crestfallen. He never gave us the money and another friend of mine, who went out there a while later, said all the gear was in a big pile in the corner of the main ballroom and he had bought a load more.

The last Glitter gig I did was at the *Hammersmith Palais*. It was a 'Glam Rock Night' with *Mud* performing just before Gaz. There were some other acts on but I don't really recall who they were. When *Mud* were about to come on Les Grey walked onto the side of the stage where the monitor desk was wearing the customary dark glasses and *Blues Brothers* attire. He said to his Roadie, 'Is the mike stand where it usually is?' The man replied in the affirmative and the band went on and started to play. I walked over to the roadie.

'If he had asked me that,' I said, 'I would have said, "Yes, in the back of the van".'

When Glitter came on they were all attired in their glittery jackets. After a few songs Gerry took his jacket off and laid it behind his amp. There was a guy standing not far from me swaying around and looking a bit pissed. No sooner had Gerry laid the jacket down than he reached over to grab it. I came round the monitor desk to stop him, and as I did he fell sideways, gashing his head against one of the dimmer racks. He got to his feet, unsteadily, and looked round blearily, still clutching the jacket. At that moment Gaz looked round and saw him.

'Ladies and Gentlemen,' he announced grandly. 'Mr Mike Leander, the man who wrote my hits with me. Come on Mike, come up on stage and play a bit of piano with us.'

The drunk Mike Leander wandered on, blood trickling down his forehead, and instead of playing piano picked up the star-shaped guitar and began to strum out some of tune chords. (The star-shaped guitar, as seen in many of the Glitter Band videos, is all 'E' strings. The whole thing is one big 'E' so playing a normal chord is not possible) The band were doing their best to cover it over, and Gerry reached down and turned the guitar off. Shortly after that Alan Gee came round, and led him off the stage.

We went out and did a few more festivals with Chappo during the summer months. These were mostly drive out at the weekend, do two shows and drive back. On one of these we arrived quite early on the Friday night. A couple turned up at the hotel and said they were part of the team that organised it and they would take us to a disco for the night. They had a mini bus and took us over to a large factory unit that had been converted into a disco. We were in there for a while, but it was all pretty tame. We asked them if they could get any dope or coke because we did not have any, but they said they didn't know. Ray went for a walk and came back to say there was a bar round the corner and we should go there. We all trooped off, out of the disco and down to this bar. This turned out to be part of the town's red light district. All of the waitresses were topless and they were showing porn movies on all four walls. Gordon spied a woman in thigh length boots and went off with her into the back room. The young couple who had brought us out were looking very uncomfortable at being there, and when Gordon got back we left.

'How was it?' H asked.

'She wanted 50 marks extra to keep the boots on,' he said, and we all laughed.

The next day, when we arrived at the gig, we found out why the couple were so super uncomfortable. The gig had been arranged by the local Christian Youth Movement and they were part of its leadership. Going out for the night with drug taking sex fiends must have set their redemption back years.

Germans have a very serious attitude to sex shows it seems. We went along to a live show in Cuxhaven while on a day off during a tour and the male participant lost his erection. I find that to be not an unsurprising event really, especially in the days before the invention of Viagra. I doubt if many people could hold it together trying to perform sex acts on a dais being watched by 20 or 30 Germans, with a beer in one hand and a cigar in the other. He was doing his best and he knew he had a 20 minute slot (so to speak) so he was trying to hide it and pretend it was still up there, but it patently wasn't. They started booing him, which was not really going to help in any way at all, and, in the end, he had to leave. I was almost expecting them to hold up placards with a score on it like in figure skating. Curiosity often got the better of me in these places. But I digress.

One of the other festivals we did with Roger that year was the big 'Out in the Green' shows with *Deep Purple*. This took us back to the *Zepplinfeld* in Nuremburg. The German town authorities had been trying to reclaim this place for the use of the town, but there was still that WW2 legacy in the minds of the American army who occupied it. Back in the '70s we had done a festival there with *Santana* and that had taken up the whole field with the stage backed onto the podium that Hitler had stood on. The Americans had built a softball pitch on it now so we were very squeezed for backstage space. The whole thing had been rotated now and the people swarmed all over that famous Third Reich edifice making it look even more bizarre. These were the last shows that Wilf Whittingham did with us as production manager. As a crew we pretty much ran ourselves and there was no need for a production manager at all. During these festivals he managed to get himself renown for being the only person on a tour to set fire to his hotel room while he was not in it. We checked into the *Intercontinental* in Hannover and he turned on his TV – and went to the bar. While he was down there the TV blew up and set fire to the room. When we did a festival down in Austria we came back to the hotel to find there was nightclub underneath it. Of course we all wound up down there drinking. The band were due to fly home the next day and had an early flight booked. At 6am while we were all still drinking a gentleman in traditional Austrian hotel uniform came into the bar, looked around, and walked straight up to Wilf.

'Mr Whittingham,' he announced., 'This is your early morning call.'

He was the only person I have ever known to get a wake up call in a nightclub.

Rob and I put a rig into *The Brighton Centre* that summer. It was for a 'Club 18 30 Reunion Night'. All the people who threw up on each other during sex in some sunny foreign place were getting together for a night in Brighton. The line up was Edwin Starr on Friday night, *The Boomtown Rats* (with Bob Geldof in pre-'Give us yore fooking monay' days) and *Black Lace* on Sunday. The whole thing was a fiasco from start to finish with very little organisation. We set the rig up and did a soundcheck for Edwin Starr on Friday. Edwin does not like to have his voice in any of the monitors on stage which I thought was a bit off, but if that is what he wants who am I to dispute it? After the soundcheck we went for something to eat and came back to the venue. Rob came up on stage with a tray containing five glasses of cider, his favourite drink, and asked me what time they were on. I said I did not know. I set off to go to the dressing room to find out and he said he would go up to the main desk, which was on the balcony. When I got to the back of the stage I met the band coming up. Rob had left the stage and was on the way to the desk so I said they should give him a few minutes to get there.

They took to the stage and started playing and I could hear the PA was not on. I was trying to see the desk but it was not visible from the monitor board. When Edwin came on and started singing a few minutes later I could tell there was no PA because his mouth was opening and shutting and there was no sound. Shortly after this, the rig kicked into life and the gig went OK. After the show Rob told me he had gone along a corridor and through a door, which closed behind him. This was a fire door, which only opened from the other side. He found himself in a closed and locked restaurant. He could see the foyer of the gig, but that door was locked too. He was banging on the door trying to get someone to let him in when he heard the band start up in the venue. He did not get onto the desk until the second song, but luckily the security guy knew what the mutes on the desk did, and took them out so the desk was live but unattended for two songs.

We were staying in the *Old Ship Hotel* on the seafront. The next day I was sitting in the reception area when I saw it had one of those boards with letters that slotted in so they could put welcome signs up. I went over to it and removed the 't' from 'Hotel' and put the 'l' in its place I then removed the 'p' from 'Ship' and put the 'T' there. The sign now read 'The Old Shit Hole'. I went and sat down again. People came in, saw the sign and either laughed or tutted. After a while the receptionist went round to see and got very cross.

The Boomtown Rats gig went off OK with no mishaps and the following day we were back to do *Black Lace*. At this juncture in their career they were a two piece with a reel to reel tape player in the middle of the stage providing the backing track. Soundcheck was quick and we said to the stage manager we were going to the pub behind the gig for lunch and to send someone to get us when they wanted us. We went back into the gig after lunch to hear the last few moments of *Black Lace*'s set. Apparently they had gone onstage to a big announcement and a cloud of smoke and when the smoke cleared they were standing there with no noise coming out, no one on either desk, and both muted. I went backstage to apologise, and they just laughed and said it was the funniest thing that had happened in ages.

Next up after the festivals was a short tour of Europe with John Cale. This was one of those moments where I chose the less lucrative tour on offer because I thought I would enjoy the music, and the tour more. We were a three man crew with myself on monitors, Peter Kirkman doing the lighting and Chris rigging the PA. There was no backline guy and we had been offered extra cash to split the backline tasks between us. I was looking after John and Ollie Halsall the guitarist, Chris looked after the bass and the drums (played by Kevin Tooley) during the show but Peter set the kit up before the gig. Phil was front of Hhuse engineer and tour manager. The system we took out was a new one, on loan to RSD by the French company *Nexo* with RSD monitors and desks. RSD desks were a bit of an anomaly at times. The hire company was associated with the manufacturing side but not directly linked to it. We would often get new kit to try out and many of us would write reports on the kit which were sent back with the desk. We would suggest ways to make the desks easier to use and then they add features - that kind of thing. We never heard anything back about this and our suggestions were never taken up.

One year RSD held a Christmas party, and the hire side were asked to put a small system in for it. Rob Douglas was approached by an Indian man.

'Ah, that is what these are used for,' he commented.

Rob showed him how it was all set up and how it was used.

'Do you work in the factory?' he asked.

'Yes.'

'So what do you do?' Rob had expected him to be in management or something like that.

'I design these things,' came the reply.

'And you don't know what they do?'

'Oh they give us the specifications and I design the circuits and layout.'

'When we try these out we send notes back with suggestions on them. Do you ever see these?'

'Yes. They told us to ignore them. They said the hire department does not know what it is talking about.' That explained a lot.

The first gig with John Cale was on the 18th October 1985 at *The Paradiso* in Amsterdam – one of my favourite gigs. It was a large old church that had been turned into a hippy haven in the sixties and seventies. It was very reminiscent of the *Roundhouse* back in the sixties and had much of the same atmosphere. For a church it had a good sound too. We were visited by one of the local dealers who supplied some coke – dope was easily available in the cafés nearby. When the band hit the stage, the place was heaving and it seemed to be a good show. John's Mesa Boogie amplifier was screamingly loud and, since it sat in front of the kick drum, bled back into the drum microphones so my first task was to rush out onto the stage and move it over. John looked at me curiously because we had not actually met by then. Ollie broke a string during the show and I quickly nipped up and grabbed the guitar when he put it down to change it. It was then that I noticed that spare guitar, owned by bass player, Dave Young, was strung right-handed whereas Ollie was left-handed and his guitar was strung that way. I looked at him standing there playing the song with no problem - with the guitar upside down! He was a true guitar virtuoso. An amazing player, who could just flip a guitar over and play just as well with the strings either way up. I changed the strings and returned the guitar to the stage. He asked if it was in tune and I told him it was. This seemed to surprise him. He looked even more surprised to find it was. As they left the stage when the show finished, I heard Ollie say:

'John, can we play some of the songs we rehearsed at the next gig?'

After the show he came over and thanked me for changing the string. He asked where the broken string was and I told him it was on the floor behind the monitor desk. He then went round and retrieved it.

'Why do you want that?' I asked.

'I tie knots in them and put them back on again'. I looked at his guitar and saw that was exactly what he did. The strings were all uniformly black, except the one I had just changed.

'They have given me 10 sets of strings for you,' I said.

'Try not to use them and I will take them home after the tour. They will last me years,' he said.

Phil came on stage and said John would like a word with me in the dressing room. I went down and asked him if everything had been OK with the monitors. John said yes it was all fine and he had been very happy with it. He then asked:

'Do you want a line?'

'Yes, thanks,' I said.

He produced a packet from his pocket and opened it.

'Did you buy any of that coke from the dealer?' he asked.

'Yes.'

'What is yours like?'

'It's up on stage, in my case. I will go and get it.'

I went upstairs, collected the packet and came back down to the dressing room. John's packet had disappeared by this time. I opened mine, showed him the contents and closed it again. We sat there and spoke for a while, but he made no move to repeat his offer of a line.

'I had better crack on and get the stage packed down,' I said and went back upstairs. I got the feeling I was being tested. I always got the impression with John that he could not take people sucking up to him. As with so many famous people, there are always those who want to come up and talk to them, and because they have absolutely no point of contact with them, they have nothing to say and so all they can do is heap platitudes and praise on them in the 'My God, you are wonderful, a genius.... (insert superfluous hyperbole here)'

The opening act for the first few Dutch shows was a then little known, Suzanne Vega. I did not get on too well with her or her band. We changed the stage around to get their gear on and the female drummer was already up on stage playing her drums while I was trying to set up the microphones. Ask any sound man what he hates the most and a good number of responses will be drummers who bash the kit while you are setting up. I can understand wanting to get the kit right, but when they sit there and bash away right by your ears it does get annoying. I suggested that she went off for a moment while I finished mic'ing the kit, but she just shrugged and carried on. I was trying to get the snare drum set on the desk and it suddenly produced a sharp 4KHz spike of feedback.

'Ow,'she squeaked, 'Don't do that!'

'If you get up, off the kit for a moment. I will sort it out.'

'I need to be here.'

'Then I can only turn it down,' I replied. I was getting a bit cheesed off with this fussy bunch. When it came to Suzanne she stood at the microphone and said to the guy on the desk, who I think was her partner at the time, 'Can you turn my voice up in the monitor?'

I turned it up a bit and said, 'How's that?'

She continued to talk to the man at the main desk.

'Can you put a bit more top on it?'

I waved to her and called over, 'I am over here!'

It was not a big stage. I could not see why she would not talk to me if she wanted something else done. After a while I stopped trying. As she left the stage and walked past the monitor desk I said, 'You know, if you talk to the monitor engineer, the monitor sound changes.'

She gave me a frosty glare and walked off. When she came on to start her set the hall was well over half full and there was a lot of chatter going on. The band walked onstage the lights went down and nothing happened. She stood still for two minutes and the chatter, which had died a little bit, began to rise up again. I wondered what she was doing and because I had never heard of her before and did not know any of her songs. I had no idea she was waiting for hushed reverence before launching into 'Tom's Diner', an a cappella number. The audience did not know who she was either and were there for John Cale's more raucous music. After a few attempts at 'shhhh' she launched into the song anyway. She went down well in the end, but it was a dumb way for an unknown support act to open a show.

A few gigs later Ollie ate a lump of hash and went into meltdown. The band were being driven around in a big American Chrysler 'multi person vehicle' by the tour manager from the local promoter. Ollie saw an American army base and began to get agitated telling them they had to pull over and go in there because the back axle was going and they would have a spare. We arrived at the hotel in Eindhoven just after the band did. We checked in and found an agitated Ollie in the foyer trying to work out where his bags were, and where his room was. He was on the same floor as us so we took him upstairs. His bags were standing outside his room.

'They came up here on their own, wow,' was all he could say. A bit later we looked out of the window to see Ollie jumping up and down beside John who was standing by the lake outside the hotel. John was threatening to throw his guitar in the lake.

The truck driver for this tour had brought his nephew along with him. They were a very rock and roll family and he wanted to introduce the boy to life on the road. He turned 18 when we had a day off in Hamburg so he decided he would take him round the fleshpots of the Reepherbahn. Chris and I came along too. We took him through the Herbertstrasse, the street where hookers present their wares in the traditional way, sitting in shop windows and beckoning to passersby, and from there we went on to a backstreet bar. I had my doubts about Chris. He sometimes seemed to be on a bit of a knife edge ready to explode at any moment. He made light of it by wandering round the gig giving status reports in the style of *Star Trek*.

'Wobble level five and rising,' and such like. I still thought he would go off at some point.

We entered the bar, ordered some drinks and were immediately surrounded by a group of women. They ushered us over to a table and we sat down with them. We were talking for a few minutes and I began to have my suspicions about them. Although quite convincingly made up and revealingly dressed I realised they were not women at all. The one I had been talking to said to me, 'I tell you, but I do not tell the others. We are all transvestites in this bar. I think you knew that, no?'

I agreed that I had already guessed that. I looked at the others. They were all chatting away and the one that was with Chris had her hand on his thigh and was looking in his eyes. I was not too sure how he would react if he went into the back room and copped a handful of the 'meat and two veg'. She did have very convincing breasts but I was not sure, or even too interested in finding out, how far the transformation had gone. I decided we should leave. I turned to the woman I was talking to and told him I thought I should get the others to go now before anything happened. She agreed, so I turned back and addressed the others:

'I think we should move on guys'

Chris seemed put out.

'Let's stay here.' he protested.

I could see that the truck driver had come to the same conclusion as I had and was not anxious to land his nephew in too dodgy a situation so we all stood up, said goodbye and left. When we got into the street Chris rounded on me, 'Why did you do that, I was getting on all right

'Thremic' at the follow spot

Glitter on stage at Hammersmith Odeon – as was

The Stage in Bahrain

Gordon within tent

Brian Jones in Bahrain (above)
The Zepplinfeld (below)

Kevin Tooly - John Cale 1985

Ollie Halsall - John Cale 1985

Typical setlist for the John Cale Tour

1. **Satellite Walk**
2. **Dead Or Alive**
3. Piano Improvisation
4. **Dr. Mudd**
5. Yellow Submarine
6. **Model Beirut Recital**
7. **Streets Of Laredo**
8. **Leaving It Up To You**
9. **Chinese Envoy**
10. **Dying On The Vine**
11. **Fear Is A Man's Best Friend**
12. **I'm Waiting For The Man**
13. **Villa Albani**
14. **Evidence**
15. **Everytime The Dogs Bark**
16. **Mercenaries (Ready For War)**
17. Guitar Improvisation
18. Pablo Picasso
19. **(I Keep A) Close Watch**

John Cale (above)
Ollie by the lake in Eindhoven that almost claimed his guitar (below)

Pete Kirkman, in the hotel room after the Berlin accident – looking like he has fallen
from a great height John Cale 1985
Rob and Dave South of *RSD Hire* at the Leeds *Carrinean Festival* (opposite)

there?'

'They were all men,' I replied.

'No they weren't, she was definitely a woman.'

I explained that the woman I was talking to had already told me, and the truck driver said he had worked it out too, but Chris would not believe us. He came with us to the next bar and then we lost him. I always wondered if he went back to the other bar.

We decided that best way to initiate the birthday boy was to take him to the *Eros Centre*. This is the sort of place that can only exist in a country like Germany. The one on the Reeperbahn is like an underground car park but it has no cars in it. It is lit by 'black light', the UV lighting that makes all of the flecks of dandruff on your shoulders fluoresce. In this case all of the hookers who stand around down there are wearing white underwear or basques and nothing else. It is these that the black light is designed to highlight. The whole scene is very surreal if you have not been in one of these before, and no first time visitor I have ever taken down there has ever managed to make it through the room without going upstairs with one of the girls. They come straight up to you and are always very nice, inviting you to go with them. Of course that is their stock in trade, that siren-like appeal to the male ego that always wants to be flattered into the belief that these women, who have seen hundreds of men pass through those doors, have singled them out as their choice of partner.

I talked to a few of these women and most see it as a way of making a pile of money in a short space of time. They are mostly young and usually very pretty. They are tested on a regular basis for sexual diseases, never have any kind of sex without a condom, and are thrown out of the *Eros Centre* if caught using any kind of drugs. There are also heavies on tap if anything gets violent. Many of them see it as a way to get money together to start a business or something similar. Once they have their victim they take them up into the room they rent above the car park for as little sex as they can get away with. We found one that looked nice and explained it was the boy's first time, paid her and let her take him away. Most people I have dropped in that situation have lasted around twenty minutes from when they are led away to rejoining us outside. Considering you have to climb the stairs, pay the money, get undressed and then get dressed afterwards and go back down the stairs that leaves a scant five to ten minutes for the actual act. The lad was in there for about forty minutes so I think she must have been kind to him. We didn't ask.

In Berlin I found myself, once more, in the *Metropol*. When you load in and out of this gig they put a wide set of stairs against the stage which is around 5m tall. During the load out for the gig someone moved the stairs to one side and Peter Kirkman (who has been working for *The Scorpions* for absolutely ages, I believe), who had been walking backwards, carrying a lighting truss, fell from the stage onto the floor. He hurt his back quite badly. A few gigs later on we were in a kind of hippie commune in Vienna. Peter had almost recovered from that injury and then accepted a lift back to the hotel from two girls. They were on a motorbike and Peter was transported, over the cobbled streets of the old part of Vienna, in the sidecar. By the time he got back to the hotel he could barely move again.

We did another show in Austria in a much smaller town. This was held in a tent some way out of town. We rolled up and were greeted by the 'promoter's wimp' as they are known in the business. He showed us the stage and then led us to a caravan out the back.

'Here is your rider,' he announced.

We looked at it. There were a couple of crates of beer, spirits, wine, food, fruit and all sorts of stuff.

'I think this is the band's rider,' I said.

'Oh no,' came the response, 'They have the same, look.'

And he led us to another caravan which was a bit bigger but had the same stuff in it. I asked him if he was sure about that, but he said he was so I took all the spirits and put them in our bus and then we got on with setting up the stage. After the soundcheck he told us there was no food at the venue so he would take us to a restaurant in town. When we settled down on a table at the restaurant and began to look at the menu John enquired about the way the promoter was settling the bill, 'You are paying for the food and we buy our own drinks, right?'

'Oh no, all drinks are included.'

'Do we have a limit?'

'No.'

John ordered a bottle of wine that cost around £150.

When we were all packed up after the show we were saying goodbye to everyone. The promoters wimp came up to me and said, 'I think I made a big mistake tonight.'

'With the riders and the drinks in the restaurant, I take it?'

'Yes, you were right. It should have been just the band and you should have bought your own drinks.'

'I thought so.' I felt sorry for him, 'We have not opened the bottles of spirits and some of the beers in the bus. You can have them back if you want.'

He straightened up, 'No, this was my mistake. It will cost me a lot of money but it was my mistake. You keep them,' he said.

I never saw him on any other gig again though.

The last gig I did with John was in the *Town and Country Club* in London. During the afternoon John asked if there was any toot around. I told him I would make a few calls and he said he did not want to get much. I had a friend who was a painter and decorator by trade, but he often liked a bit of a smoke and a line. He would often buy more than he needed for himself and sell it on. He was also massively into music. I called him and he came down, getting there just as John finished the soundcheck. The three of us went back up the stairs in the backstage area of the T&C looking for an empty room. As we ascended the stairs Nico, who was the support act that day, came down.

'Ah John,' she said airily, 'I have not seen you for ages. We must have dinner together.'

'You will have to sort your fucking act out first,' was John's reply.

John was a bit extreme in some ways but I really enjoyed doing gigs with him, and the music was different every night. Rob Douglas had told me that on a previous tour he came up to him just as the band were going on and said:

'Take all the cymbals off the kit.'

The drummer complained about this, but he said, 'You hit the cymbals too much. I pay you to play the drums.'

He did the gig that night with no cymbals and hi-hats and apparently kept hitting out for things that were not there. The next night he asked if he could have hi-hats at least and John agreed so he put two 24" ride cymbals on the hi-hat stand. Rob said they also had a tour manager who used to be production manager for *10cc*. They were sitting in the dressing room one night and he was telling them that the band used to like him to come on an announce them in a funny way; something like, 'Ladies and Gentlemen. Tonight on stage we have a bunch old guys who have run out of Moet and fuel for their rollers so they are up here to bash out a few of their old hits....*10cc*!'

John asked him how he would introduce him. The guy said there was one intro he was never allowed to use. 'Ladies and Gentlemen. Last night, during the show, a member of the audience got up and hit the piano player..........and that was the first time a fan has ever hit the shit.'

According to Rob, John just looked at him.

After this tour I did a short, but uneventful, tour with *Wishbone Ash* and 1985 drew to a close.

CHAPTER 22

A Dip In An Austrian Lake
And A Fight In A Bar In Norway

At the start of 1986 Manfred asked me to pop down to the *Workhouse Studio*. He had by this time, leased the main studio to *Stock, Aitken and Waterman* but was still using the 2nd studio to record in the back for his own stuff as well as for other people's projects. Upstairs at the *Workhouse* there were a number of rooms which had been offices at some point. *Blackhill Enterprises*, the people who managed many of the bigger acts of the '70s and '80s had an office there for a while. Most of these rooms were now just used for storage and one of them was crammed full of tapes. This was not the official tape store, which was housed in another part of the building. It was just a bunch of old tapes dating back to the start of the studio. Manfred wanted to use the room and asked me to spend a week listing the tapes and then trying to contact the owners to get them collected. Any tapes not collected by the end of the month would go in a skip.

I agreed and started sorting the tapes out. Some of it was unknown stuff with very few notes on the boxes. Some was easy to place and a few owners came along to pick the stuff up or just said to scrap it. At the back of the room there was a big pile of 2" tapes which turned out to be the multitracks for some of Roy Harper's albums. I managed to locate Peter Jenner, of *Blackhill Enterprises*, who were managing Harper at the time, and he gave me Roy's number. I called him up and he said he would be down the next day. Sure enough he turned up the following day and we loaded the tapes into his car.

'I'll buy you a drink,' he said, so we went to the local pub which, being the Old Kent Road was none too luxurious.

'I have been fighting *EMI* for possession of these tapes for over two years,' he told me. 'It is obvious they had no idea where they were. Thanks for taking the trouble to sort this out.' Sometime after this he began to release remixed versions of the old albums. I would like to think it was because I gave him back his old tapes. I met Nick Harper, his son, when he performed recently in a local Brighton gig called 'The Greys'. He has all his father's flair and manic stage presence and is, if anything, a better guitarist than his father. I told him this story and he shook my hand and said, 'Thank you. That is my heritage you gave to him.'

Among the other items I found was a 1" tape box multi-marked 'Captain Beefheart – Live'. We tracked down a 1" machine in the *Workhouse Studio* and threaded the tape up but it was just too old and started to come apart. I don't know what was on it or what happened to it after that. A lost gem maybe? Gone forever now though.

Chappo released a new album in 1986 and a tour was set up to promote it. There had been a few changes to both band and crew. Ray Salter was no longer doing the monitors and was replaced by Gavin. We had an extra backline guy, Dave Saunders, who had been Geoff's guitar tech before I took over, and Alec Nisic was running the lights. Alec had been Roger's lighting man on some of his previous tours but had been away with the *Psychedelic Furs*. Goom was still with us though. On the band front we had a new drummer, Henry Spinnetti (brother of Victor Spinnetti, the actor), a female backing vocalist, Dachelle Rae and a new keyboard player, Tim Hinkley. Tim had also been with Roger before and had a long pedigree, working with many different bands after fronting his own band, *Jody Grind*, in the late '60s and running a series of gigs with a rotating retinue of musicians under the title *Hinkley's Heroes*. The other major change was that the crew were now in a sleeper bus. I had mixed feelings about this. On the one hand it was nice to be able to go into the bus after the show and not have to hunt out a hotel, and on the other it took away all the opportunities for going out to bars and finding loose women. I also missed the driving. Absurd as it seems I quite liked those long journeys behind the wheel. It was tiring when we had to drive ourselves from place to place, going to bed late and getting up early but it was also extraordinarily stimulating and challenging. In a sleeper bus you get in the bus after a show and wake up the next day outside the next show, a rolling conveyer belt of venues. You don't see any towns and, although the bus may be loaded with drink and drugs, you are still only with the same people each night. Road crews can be a tight little family, as I have mentioned before, but I enjoyed all the other stuff that went on when I was on the road, and this does not happen when you have a tour bus.

When we got to Austria we had a few days off. We were in a small town called Wels and there really was not a lot there. Gavin's wife was going to fly out for a couple of days and H was going round saying we should keep all the hard drinking, drugs and dodgy women quiet because Gavin's wife was a friend of his wife, and he didn't want her to think he was involved in any of it in case she gave him a hard time when he got back. Naturally, being the caring and sensitive people we all were, we told him to bugger off. On the first day on the break Gavin and Tim decided to have a drinking contest to see which of them could drink a bottle of Jack Daniels first. Tim won and was not in too bad a condition, but Gavin was very out of it. To cap it all he carried on drinking. I was out in the town with a couple of girls I had met in a bar the night we arrived, so I did not see any of this happening. We came back to the hotel in the late afternoon to find all three of them; H, Gavin and Tim quite drunk. Looking out of my hotel room window I could see Gavin sitting on a child's rocking seat, a kind of duck thing mounted on a spring. He looked up and waved drunkenly – just as H emptied a wastepaper bin full of water all over him from the window below mine.

We went down to the bar in the hotel and I stood talking to Graham, the bus driver. A few moments later a woman walked into the bar looked around and then, spotting a *Chappo* T-shirt on Graham, came up to us. She introduced herself as Gavin's wife. We bought a drink and stood chatting for a moment. After a while she said, 'It is nice standing here having a drink with you two, but I did come to see my husband, have you any idea where he is?'

I glossed over the 'drunk' part – she would find that out later – and said I saw him earlier. At that moment, though, a dishevelled, soaked and drunk figure opened the door of the bar, stood there for a moment, saw his wife and screamed, 'Aaaarg!' and ran out again.

She was a bit put out by this and was about to follow him to find out what was going on when H entered the bar. She turned to him to ask him what was going on, but he was pretty clearly drunk as well. In the corner nearest to us there was a table with a group of very serious looking young Austrian men and women sitting chatting and politely sipping their drinks. H walked straight over to their table,, and for some reason he could not afterwards explain, dropped his jogging bottoms, flopped his manhood out onto the table in front of them with the words:

'Do you want to see a man's cock?'

I went over and apologised to them and took him away. Gavin's wife went off to look for Gavin.

The next day we were told Gavin was, not unsurprisingly, ill. He was seen by a local doctor and then taken off with acute alcoholic poisoning. There was no hospital in that town, but there was a nunnery so they took him there. He stayed there for five days with his wife staying there too. Her long weekend by the Austrian Alps turned into a week in a convent.

In Austria we had a caterer who had no idea of what a vegetarian might eat. I tried to make it easy for him and suggested that he just gave me the vegetables from the other meals, but he was not hot on vegetables at all. One day I got a plate of potatoes and nothing else. I suggested a few meals he could make that would be easy to do. He pondered on this and came up with a cauliflower cheese the next day. I have had cauliflower cheese in many different ways in my 44 years as a vegetarian, but no one has ever cooked it this way. He took the entire cauliflower, cooked it whole and poured cheese sauce over it. It came out looking like monkey brains. Tasted OK though.

In spite of thism the promoter, Wolfgang Klinger, arranged the usual day off to get drunk. We were staying in a hotel called *The Seehotel*, in Rust, a small town on the western shore of Lake Neusiedl near the border with Hungary. On the day off the plan was for the band and crew to go to a 'wine tasting' at a vineyard nearby. This all seemed a bit tame and far too civilised to me – it wasn't. We went there in the band's coach and when we disembarked we were all seated in a courtyard. There was some food provided, bread and black sausage, not much for a vegetarian, and then we were issued with glass mugs and shown into a long room lined with vats of wine. The host climbed onto one of the barrels and, using a long glass tube with a bowl at one end, sucked up some wine from the vats and began to fill our mugs with wine. Fill, I said, not just a small dribble but a generous helping This continued for a while and the band and crew wandered in an out of the shed, going outside to get some food and returning for a refill. After a while we were all getting a bit drunk. We had lost track of what wines were which and just referred to them by number. I remember a conversation with Geoff at one point along the lines of:

'12's OK , quite nice, have you had that one?'

'I have no idea, what one is that?'

'I don't know any more.'

After a few hours of this we were all the worse for wear. Chris bet the truck driver, who was called 'Animal' (for obvious reasons – just have a look at his photo), that he could not eat all of the large bratwurst sausages that had just been plonked down on the table for us. Animal duly ate the whole thing and Chris had to pay up. We set off back to the hotel. In Austria they have a lot of tall poles on the streets which are topped by small Christmas trees. I have no idea why. While we were stopped at a traffic light, Chris Youle tried to get his money back from Animal by betting him he could not climb the pole. We parked the bus and Animal duly climbed the pole to the top. When he got down, though, his thighs were completely bruised and battered. That was not the only time that Animal got bruised and battered on this tour. Somehow or other he managed to get in a fight in a bar. We had all been drinking in that bar that night but he stayed behind and a couple of locals picked a fight with him. He arrived back at the bus 'bloodied but unbowed' as they say.

I don't know who spotted the fact that there were rowing boats at the jetty outside the hotel, but someone suggested we all hired them. Being drunkenly gullible we did just that and were soon rowing around on the lake. Again, I don't recall who was first in the water, but pretty soon a gentle row on the lake turned into a game of pirates. I remember Dave swimming over to our boat and capsizing it, and very soon we were all in the water. We got out and made our sodden way back to the hotel. In reception I found Dave, in his underpants with his soaked clothes under his arm, shouting at a terrified looking receptionist, 'What do you mean by hiring me a boat? Couldn't you see I was drunk?' Irrefutable logic, but unfair all the same. Gordon and I went back to our room, had a spliff and both fell asleep.

We were woken a bit later by Brian banging on our door.

'C'mon on boys, we've been invited to the gig for the evening.'

The gig that we were going to play the following day was in an old mill house. It had been extensively rebuilt and renovated and was the centre of the town's social life. I had not eaten since breakfast, but there was not much there to eat. Instead, we started drinking again. Towards the end of the evening I decided it was time to go back to the hotel to sleep it all off. I went to the entrance and said to the woman in the box office.

'Can you call me a taxi?' She asked where I was going and I told her.

'The hotel is just around the corner,' she told me, 'so you don't need a taxi.'

I tried to persuade her to just call a taxi for me, but she declined so I set off. A few minutes later I was back at the gig. I must have walked around the block without noticing. I tried to convince her again.

'No, look, I do need a taxi.' She took me outside and pointed at a light.

'Do you see that light? Head for that and the hotel's right there,' she explained, patiently.

I set off once more. A few minutes passed and I noticed I was walking across a ploughed field with no idea where I was. I was about to give up when I met the band's sax player, Nick Pentelow, walking drunkenly across the same field. He was also looking for the hotel. Half an hour and a lot of walking later we found it.

I took over doing the monitors for a while and Gavin came back to join the tour when we got into Germany. I had brought a copy of the *Spinal Tap* video with me when I came out on the tour and one night Geoff came with us on our bus. We showed him the movie. He started off laughing and then said; 'Oops, I've said that' a few times. Nothing to worry about really because Geoff really did go to 11. He borrowed the video and showed it to the band. Tim Hinkley really got into it and started saying, 'Hello Cleveland!', when he walked on stage, which puzzled the German audiences a lot. When we got to Berlin it was Tim's birthday so we got Animal to make him a small Stonehenge model and hung it from the truss. The first encore in the show that night was 'Everybody's on the Shortlist' and they start this by getting Tim to come on and play some stuff on the piano and gradually morph it into a 12 bar, and as he got into the first bars of the song the band would all walk on and start playing. We told them about the Stonehenge and they all stayed off the stage. Tim walked on, started playing and we slowly lowered the model down until it was sitting on his piano. He never noticed until he looked up from the keys to see where the band had got to.

After the *Chappo* tour rolled to a halt I went out with a band called *5TA*. They were doing a support slot on the *It Bites*, 'Big Lad In The Windmill' tour. That tour had, as part of its stage set, two large vanes which hung from the back truss and were made to look like part of a windmill. There was a constant cry of, 'Ow, fuck that windmill', as crew members ducked under the black drape at the back of the stage and cracked their skulls on the vanes. *5TA* were a bit unremarkable, but their backing singer went on to much bigger things. I ran into her a year later at John Henry's rehearsal studios, and while we were chatting I asked whose band she was there with. She said 'Mine' and it was only then that I connected Julia the backing vocalist with the Julia Fordham all the music press had been lauding that year. Her and the other backing vocalist had been great fun on that tour, sticking their hands up their T-shirts and doing 'Alien' impersonations when they were not singing.

Shortly after this I got involved in one of the odder tours of my career. Steve Hill, who had been PA rigger for the Manfred tour in '83, was now running a minibus hire company in Hammersmith. He had got involved with a band called *i-Level* who had a minor disco hit in 1984 called 'Dance Together In A Minefield'. They were pretty much a studio band but Steve had convinced them to go on tour. He hired the PA from the same company that Manfred had used on the tour and had Alan Bradshaw doing front of house. He asked me if I would help with the backline, and since I had not much else on at the start of the summer I accepted. The crew was completed by Hugh 'Hugo' Richards on monitors and Lazlo on lighting. A very professional crew with a truckload of pro equipment – the trouble is we were, on the whole, playing venues that would have been overloaded by a third of that amount of gear. Steve, Lazlo and I drove in the truck, and Mr. B and Hugo used a car. The band had a tour manager who was not at all used to dealing with people like us and they also had their own travelling coke dealer, known as 'The Pope'. The whole thing was a recipe for mayhem really.

It started coming off the rails right from the start when we had serious trouble getting the equipment through the door of the first gig, and one of the people who had been hired as local crew would not do anything because he 'had his best shoes on and didn't want to scuff them.' We dragged all this equipment in and out of small discos up and down England to the amazement of many of the promoters. There was a lot of coke going down – or rather up. Lazlo was a decent chap and, more often than not, would turn down a toot saying:

'I do like it but I don't want to buy any so I won't take any of yours. I will feel obliged to reciprocate.'

He also had a great line on US tours. On one trip we were talking about touring the States and I told him I had never managed to get over to America. He said, 'When I started in this business I met a guy who had done a US tour and I thought "You're the man!". Then I met someone who had done three US tours and I thought, "No, You're the man." But as I went along and spent more and more time in this business I got disenchanted and I met a man who had turned down a US tour. I knew then he was the man!' A bit of rock and roll philosophy for you there.

When we were in Manchester we went up to the band's singer's room and The Pope had a large circular mirror. He laid out lines around the mirror like spokes and it was passed round the room. When it got to Lazlo he turned it down. The Pope said, 'Go on, it is a present from the band' so he went for it. He was sitting beside the wife of one of the band members and he turned straight to her and said, 'I'll give you £20 for a sniff of your knickers.'

Now we knew why he usually turned down the coke.

When we got to Leicester we were staying in the *Holiday Inn* and the band told us they were having a party in their room after the show. When we had loaded out and got cleaned up we went up there. The room was in darkness with the band smooching with some women to slow disco music. It was a bit like a teenage party and we quickly decided we did not really want to stay there. We went back down in one of our rooms and sat there having a smoke and a drink. The phone rang. Alan answered, and it was The Pope.

'Someone has passed out in the band's room.'

'So?'

'Can you come and deal with it?'

'Do what about it?'

'Get him out of the room so the band aren't involved.'

'Give us a couple of grams and we will.'

'OK.'

So we trooped off to the band's room where we found a prone young man. We collected the toot and then carried him out of the room to the fire stairs. As we were carrying him down the stairs Alan said, 'I don't think he is drunk. I think he is on the disco biscuits.' He leant down to the man. 'What have you taken?' he asked. His friend, who had come with us, said, 'Nothing. He hasn't taken nothing.' Alan was not convinced.

We got him down to the street and laid him on the pavement. Alan leant down again, 'Have you had any pills?' he asked.

The man stirred, 'Yes.'

'How many?' demanded Alan.

'Two bottles,' came the reply.

At first Alan looked worried. Two bottles of pills? That could be bad. Then it dawned on him that he meant Pils and not pills. He had drunk two bottles of lager and passed out! Alan straightened up in disgust.

'Fucking lightweight,' he exclaimed and we left him and his friend on the pavement.

Back up in the room we looked out of the window in time to see his friend trying to help him to his feet just as a police car pulled up beside them.

We played a gig in Brighton and the original intention was to return home to London that night and come back to a gig in a rugby club in Surrey. Steve and I decided we would get a hotel instead and, after making a few calls found one near Hickstead that had a room free at a good price. When we turned up there we found it was a country house hotel. Very nice and quite elegant. We got there around 2am and they had left the keys out for us. We went along to the room down the quiet corridors – well they were quiet. Steve Hill had a metal briefcase with a pair of handcuffs attached to them. They clanked and clattered all the way along the corridor. When we got into the room Steve set up his stereo and put some *Motörhead* on. I suggested he turned it down, but he was not keen. Pretty soon someone hammered on the wall and asked us to turn the music down. Steve refused and began a dialog with the guy. In the end I managed to get him to turn it off and we went to sleep. In the morning I was leaving the room for breakfast just as the man next door was leaving his. I apologised for the noise. He was Belgian and was working as a chef in the hotel. As we walked down the corridor he told me that he was a karate teacher and that the people who ran the hotel were all karate experts. They had at a big conference of teachers of the sport and the owners had invited him to work for them that summer.

'Your friend is lucky you were there, because I was going to come in and hit him. I had to be up at 5am to start the breakfast going.'

With only three gigs to go on the tour we rolled into Rayleigh, in Essex. I was joined there by my friend, and old *Wooden Lion* roadie, Steve Wollington, who lived up the road in Basildon. The local crew for this venue took the prize for being the stupidest I have ever met. We got them to unload the truck and then to help us unpack the cases. Most flight cases are locked using what is known as a butterfly catch. This is a hook which is mounted on an eccentric spindle rotated by kind of key. To close the case you engage the hook with the flange on the other part of the case and rotate the key. To open it you do the reverse. After a while one of the local crew came over and said, 'I know you showed us how to open these catches but we have forgotten. Can you show us again?'

We then asked them to put all the empty cases back in the truck. They came back a bit later saying, 'They don't fit.'

'But you just took them all out of the truck and a lot of the gear is in here. Has it shrunk?'

Steve and I went outside to look. They were right. They didn't fit – well not if you just wheeled them up the ramp and pushed them in randomly. We stood a couple of cases on end and a look of amazement came over their faces.

'We never thought of that,' one of them whispered.

Steve came with us to the next gig, which was in the *Lyceum* in London. The promoter was the same as for the Rayleigh gig and he had hired the same crew so we had to deal with them all over again.

The last show was down in Devon and it was in a very small club. After the show we went

Tony Stevens, Henry Spinetti and Tim Hinkley

Gavin

An Austrian cauliflower cheese

Animal

Dave Saunders

The renovated mill – Ceselly Muehle in Oslip

Animal and Stonehenge

Stonehenge coming in with Tim at the piano.

Seehotel Rust

Julia Fordham

Lazlo

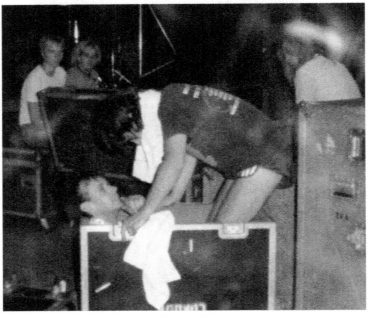

Mr B and Hugo

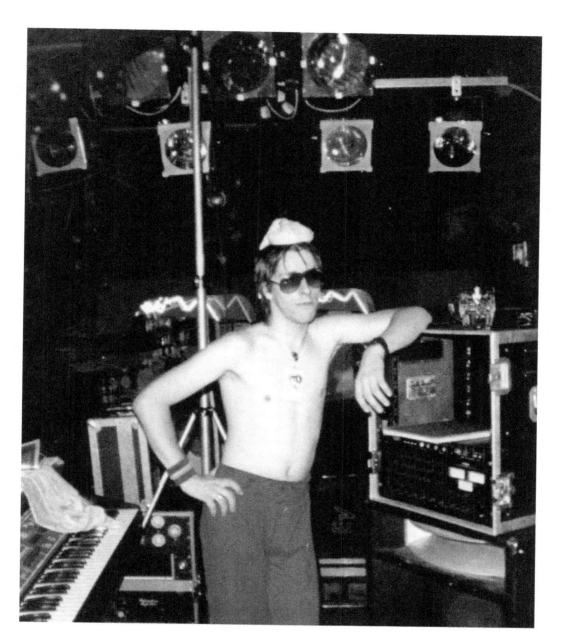

Steve Hill nursing a hangover

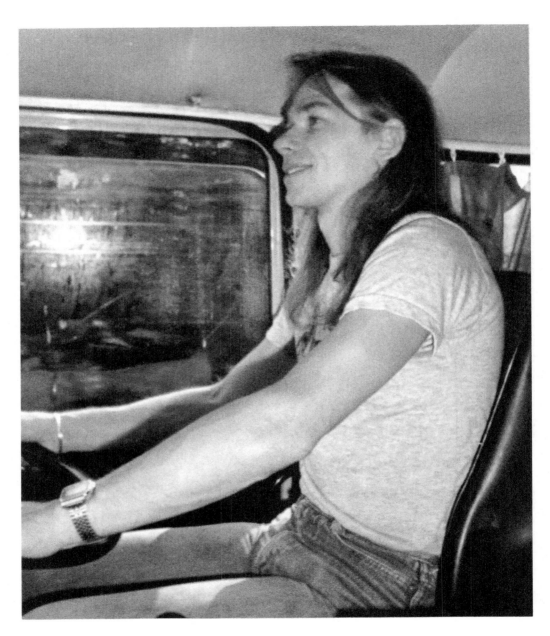

Driving the truck

Mezzoforte - From left – Frissi, Lance, Johnan, Eyþór,Gulli, Me, Chris, Noel and the two bus drivers

Fuck The Hotel

Fuck The Hotel

Rolling through Norway

Vibor 2

Vibor - This way your highness....

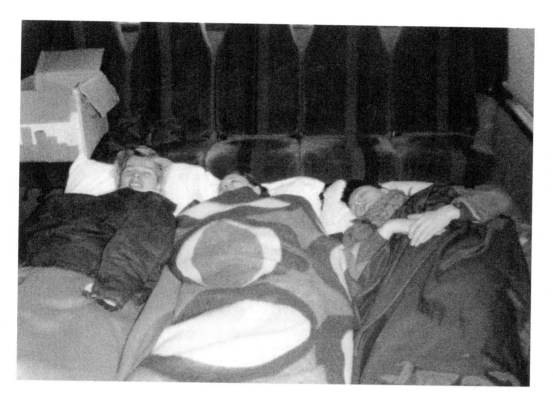

After Cocktail Hour

back to the hotel and began to go in and out of each other's rooms having a drink and saying goodbye, the usual end of tour stuff. Suddenly, there was a man standing in the corridor in a dressing gown.

'What are you all doing?' he demanded.

'Just having a drink,' someone said.

'It is after midnight. Go to bed,' he shouted. There was a general feeling of amusement at this at first, but he was getting very insistent. It was rather like having your dad come down stairs and tell you to be quiet because you were waking your mother up. He threw Steve Wollington out of the hotel because he was not booked in so he had to sleep in the cab of the truck. Luckily there was a sleeper bed in the truck and a sleeping bag so he was OK. The next morning we got up and, after breakfast, congregated in the bar to say goodbye. The irate man marched over to us again.

'I want you all out of my hotel,' he began, 'Dirty bunch of hippies.'

We said we were finishing our coffee and would go when we had and he stormed off. As he did so Hugo made a retching noise, and as he spun round, Alan moved his bag. The man went into the office and came back a few moments later.

'I have called Mr. George,' he announced. 'If I have any trouble with you he will sort you out. Which one of you threw up?'

'No one did.'

'I heard you – and he put his bag over it,' he pointed at Alan.

Alan picked up the bag.

'Look. Do you think I would put my bag in a puddle of vomit?'

Mr George duly turned up. He was a large, middle-aged man, but his largeness was confined to his stomach – and the red bulbous nose that squatted in the middle his face. He tried to glare at us menacingly but we all smiled back at him. After a while we had finished our coffee all shook hands and headed off to the cars and trucks to head home. 'Mr George' followed us out, still trying to look menacing, and got into a Reliant three-wheeled van, the kind of vehicle that that Del and Rodney drove in *Only Fools and Horses*. This made us all laugh, and because the car park was pretty big and empty we all formed a circle and began driving round and round his car so he couldn't get out. Childish, I know, but we enjoyed it.

I finished the year with a tour with *Mezzoforte*. The jazz-rock band from Iceland had recruited Noel McCalla on vocals but most of their set was instrumental so he only had to come on for the last few numbers. They also had David O'Higgins on sax. David was reasonably well known at the time, but did not yet have the jazz pedigree that he has today. The band themselves were Eyþór Gunnarsson on keyboards, Jóhann Ásmundsson on bass, Gunnlaugur Briem (Gulli) on drums and Friðrik Karlsson (Frissi) on guitar. They had to be one of the most accomplished and adept bands I have ever worked with. Lance was with the band doing the backline, I did the monitors and Chris Mount was tour manager and front of house engineer. The band spent a bit of time, and money, on the telephone, speaking to their wives and after a few days, Chris instigated the 'ET phone home award'. The band had to present Chris with the phone bill from the hotel. The person with the highest bill had to wear a small model of ET on a string around their neck for the day. We were all travelling on the same bus using house PA systems and carrying the backline under the bus.

Being a jazz band, as opposed to a full on rock band, the backline was quite small and fitted under the bus quite easily. The band had a whole box of videos to watch on the bus, but most of these had come from the band's manager who was also Icelandic. They were all in English with Icelandic subtitles, but the band, who all spoke fluent English, preferred to be able to hear the dialogue. The problem with this was that when they do the subtitling they often reduce the volume on the voice soundtrack whilst leaving the music and sound effects up. As a consequence the sound from the videos was deafening and the voices were usually lost in 'background' music and sound effects.

We kicked off the tour in Switzerland, and a couple of gigs in we were playing in St Gallen. This gig was a small concert hall with the dressing rooms under the stage. The gig seemed to be going quite well until we got close to the end. The band announced Noel onto the stage to sing, but Noel was not there. On the previous few gigs he had joined me at the monitor desk well before he was due to perform. Now there was a bit of quiet I could hear a thumping noise and a muffled shout. It seems Noel was in the toilet when the band went on and Chris had locked the dressing room. Noel had been banging on the door trying to attract someone's attention, but was unable to do so over the noise of the band.

After one gig, Gulli was interviewed by a German magazine and the following day he was sitting on the bus writing something. I looked over his shoulder as I passed and saw it was a kind of musical notation.

'What are you doing?' I asked him.

'I was interviewed yesterday,' he replied, 'And they asked me to write down my drum solo from the gig.'

I was incredulous.

'You can remember your drum solo?'

'Oh yes.' Gulli seemed surprised that I did not think he could.

One of the things I had to do for Gulli was to nip out during the solo and sit behind the drums.

Gulli's kit was a standard set of acoustic drums with triggers on them that linked to a drum simulator. Gulli would give me the nod and I would change the patch on the simulator changing the drum sounds it produced. This made for a very interesting solo so I am not surprised he attracted so much attention over it.

One of the favourite videos on the bus was *Blazing Saddles* and the part where the Clevedon Little character, Bart, rides into town to be the new sheriff was becoming a favourite of Lance's. The welcoming committee announces:

'We extend a laurel and hearty welcome to our new' and he turns to see that the new sheriff is black, 'Ni...'

Lance took to saying, 'it's our Ni', whenever Noel appeared but this was not meant, or taken, in a bad way. Noel did not seem bothered by it and dished out as much abuse back, but it did become a bit of a bus saying. This came into its own later when we got to Scandinavia.

In Hamburg I showed David round the red light district after we had finished the show at the *Grosse Freiheit*. He seemed rather bemused about the girls.

'So, these are all girls from poor families, are they?'

'No,' I replied, 'They probably earned a lot more than you did tonight.'

He could not quite get his head round that. As I said he was new to touring, and the fleshpots of the world.

We went on to Denmark and to a play a festival. Not the best of choices to run a festival that late in the year and when we rolled up in the bus you could see that the audience had thought so too. The fields were deep in mud and there were very few people there. We arrived just as Kate and Anna McGarrigle were leaving the stage and I ran into my old friend Simon Tessano who was doing front of house for them. The promoters greeted us, and did not look too happy.

'Looks like this is a bit of a disaster,' Lance observed.

The promoter shook his head.

'We have put our houses up as surety for this, we will lose everything.'

'Wanna buy a gun?' quipped Lance.

It didn't go down too well.

The common image of Scandinavia is of a clean and ordered country. There are, however, other aspects of it which lurk beneath that civilised veneer. In Vibor we checked into a hotel which was not quite finished. I felt a bit like that description of the Queen. The one where people say that she thinks the world smells of fresh paint because a few hundred yards ahead of the party there is always someone frantically painting walls. In this hotel everywhere I went there was a workman putting up a light fitting or, in the case of the foyer, frantically trying to fix the glass roof in a welter of rain and wind. The locals were less than impressed with the intrusion of this hotel into their lives as can be seen from the sign in the picture, which, given that this was in Denmark, was rather surprisingly couched in English.

Denmark is, however, a lot more of a European country than its other Scandinavian counterparts. We headed north into Norway, up through the frozen snowline. Norway can be a very beautiful country to travel through and its people are all friendly, until they start drinking. Alcohol in Norway is prohibitively expensive – taxed to the hilt, but even so, there is a certain fraction of Norwegians that do like to get drunk, and having reached that state, to behave in very unpredictable ways.

It was Sunday when we got to Maarstad and we checked into one of the country's 'temperance hotels'. If you refer to 'The Prohibition' most people will immediately think of the 1920s era gangsters of American history, but it is not widely known that many other countries tried to ban alcohol. Norway was one of these countries and they banned the sale of distilled drinks in 1916. They further banned wine and beer a few years later. There was a strong temperance movement in Norway and many of these Christian zealots built the temperance hotels you can still see, and stay in, today. They carried on the tradition of having no alcohol on the premises. We stayed in one of these on a cold, grey, Sunday night. Noel and I decided we would go for a walk into the small town and see if we could find a bar. It was all looking rather forlorn when we chanced upon a small nightclub that was open. When we went inside we found that we were the only patrons.

We sat at the bar and ordered a couple of drinks. After a while a couple of guys came and sat down at the bar beside us. The one sitting beside me banged on my arm and I turned to look at him. He held a crooked roll up in one hand and said, in a thick accent, 'Fire'. I shook my head.

'I'm afraid not,' I said, and turned back to Noel. He repeated the arm banging and request, 'Fire,' he grunted.

'Sorry,' I replied, 'I don't smoke.'

'I don't believe you,' came the response. My general reaction to brutishness is to ratchet my aloofness level up a couple of notches and go into '1950s Englishman' mode.

'That, my dear fellow, is your prerogative.'

I turned once more towards Noel, but I was watching his movements out of the corner of my eye. He had picked up an ice bucket that rested on the counter and began to lift it over my head. Just as it was above my head I reached up and tipped it backwards, spilling the ice and icy water all over my protagonist. He reached out and grabbed the back of my hair. We were both sitting on high barstools so I put my feet on the ground reached back and under his arm so that my left hand rested under his chin. Then, using his arm as a lever, I jerked his head backwards. This caused him to unbalance and, still seated, he toppled backwards to land, on his back, on the ground with all of the wind knocked out of him. Behaving far more casually than I felt at this point, I swivelled off my own stool, put one foot on his chest, grabbed his coat lapels, and said, 'I think I need to explain something to you....'

The man's companion came around us and decided to pick on Noel. Noel is not a tall person, but he is well built and was not to be cowed by this behaviour. The man poked him in the chest and said.

'Hey nigger, are you trying to start trouble?'

Noel drew himself up to all the height he could muster and replied:

'No one calls me a nigger....' he pointed at me, 'except him and his mate.'

At this juncture we both looked at each other and burst into laughter. The doorman and bartender, who had seen the thing kick off, came over and escorted the two Scando-drunks off the premises.

We went up to Trondheim, way up on the western coast of Norway, for the last gig of the Scandinavian leg of the tour. After the show, I went off with a couple of Norwegian girls for a drink and did not get back to the hotel until 4:30 am. We were due to leave that morning at 6:00 am, to drive down to Oslo to catch the ferry to Germany, so I did not bother going to bed. There was another bus tradition on this tour and that was 'cocktail hour'. Every day, when we left for the next town we would have cocktails on the bus. We took it in turn to make the cocktails, and today it was my turn. I decided to make 'White Russians'. I had the vodka, Kahlua and cream. I got a big jug from the bar and made crushed ice with the ice making machine in the hotel corridor. I filled the whole jug with the cocktail, and as the band stumbled, bleary eyed, onto the bus at 6 am, presented them with a glass of it. They were all asleep by the time we left the town and Chris said it was the quietest journey he had ever had with the band.

The ferry from Oslo to Kiel in Germany is an overnight journey on one of those large floating hotels, complete with swimming pool, sauna, restaurants and several bars. It leaves Oslo in the afternoon and travels sedately along a fjord for a few hours before hitting open sea. We all had cabins booked and, given the rigors of the night before, I decided to go and have a sauna and a meal before joining the rest of them in the bar. This process took me a while and I was feeling pleasantly refreshed when I made my way along the corridors to the bar. There are two factors to be considered about this journey. The first is the disparity between Norwegian alcohol prices and German ones. As soon as the ferry had left the dock in Oslo, the bars opened and drink was sold at German prices. For Scandinavian passengers this prompted a rush to the bar to sample the cheap booze. The second factor is the voyage itself. As I said before, the ship sails serenely down the fjord from Oslo for a few hours – and then emerges into that bit where the North Sea surges into the Skaggarak, the strait between Norway and the tip of Denmark, and thence into the Baltic Sea. This bit of sea can get quite interesting at times and this was definitely one of those times.

I joined the band at a table in the bar. There was a circular dance floor in the centre of the bar bounded by a low rail, about thigh height. The dance floor, when I arrived, was packed with drunken people dancing and whooping it up. I had barely settled down with a drink when the ship came out of the fjord. Moments later the disco began to rock and roll - literally. Cast your mind back to that seminal TV series *Voyage To The Bottom Of The Sea*. Do you recall all those bits where the ship was being attacked and the crew would shuffle from side to side? That is what went on here. The ship rolled to the left and the mass of drunken dancers all moved to the left with the outer ones hitting the rail and often toppling over onto the floor or one of the tables that surrounded the area. Then the ship rolled to the right and the dancers moved in that direction with a similar result. Pretty soon the dance floor had emptied of dancers, most of which were now were now lying on the floor or sprawled across tables. The one remaining occupant of the dance floor was a man in a wheelchair. He was also drunk, but had the front two wheels up in the air and was still dancing to the music. Many of the passengers on that ferry never made it to their cabins. The boat continued to heave and pitch, and as I made my way back to my cabin, I had to pick my way through the people sprawled on the floor in little puddles of vomit.

The final gig on this tour was in a TV studio near Baden Baden. It had a similar format to the Jools Holland show on UK TV in that the bands would play on stages set around the room, but the audience sat at tables in the centre. When we arrived they had already set out the tables and chairs which made it difficult to load in. I moved the furniture to one side so I could get the gear to the stage and the TV crew complained.. I told them that 'unless I learned the art of levitation' there was no way I could get the gear onto the stage without moving them. Once the stage was set up they came on and set the microphones up. I watched in amazement. The small microphone stands around the drum kit were placed with the long arms sticking out and up. When they had finished the kit resembled a porcupine. They were about to leave the stage when I asked them to stay for a moment.

'I'll show you how to do it right shall I?'

The stands had telescopic boom arms so I collapsed the arms in and adjusted the positions of the stands. When I had finished the microphones were in the same place, but the boom arms were all neatly retracted.

'If you had left them like that the singer would have knocked half of them over during the first number.'

We went off to get some food. In the queue, at the TV station's canteen, were *Womack and Womack* and their retinue of family, band members, babysitter and grandmother. This was the first time I had met them, but I was later to do a very short (very short!) tour with them. As I got closer to the food I could see it was not very good, quite expensive and that they had nothing vegetarian. The Womacks were also vegetarian and just accepted it, but I had a right rant about it. Chris and the producer came in just as I hit mid rant. Chris took me to one side and I suddenly realised that he had been up in the control room all the while I was having a go at the TV crew. I was expecting a dressing down.

'Come on,' he said, 'I will buy you lunch,' and we went to the front of the building and took a cab into town.

'I am sorry if I embarrassed you earlier,' I started, 'I forgot you were up in the control room with the producer.'

Chris laughed.

'That's OK. You just said everything I have wanted to say to a TV crew in my whole career - in one morning. Great stuff. That is why I am buying you lunch.'

CHAPTER 23

Stumped and facing a pistol in Vienna
(means nothing to me)

At the start of 1987 I was doing a bit of work for Chris Thompson, singer for *Manfred Mann's Earthband*. We did a few gigs around London and I helped out with some of his equipment. He had a studio in his house in Wembley which he said had been paid for on the proceeds of an advert he did for *Kelloggs*. One of the things we did was to replace some of the microphones and equipment in this studio, and because he did not want people to come round to his house to buy them, he got me to advertise them for him. Amongst the items he had for sale were a pair of Yamaha Graphic EQs, and these were duly advertised. I got a call pretty quickly about these items and I arranged with the potential buyers to meet me at a studio in Islington where I was working, so I could show them working.

Two guys showed up to have a look at them and I set them up plugged between a small desk and an amp. I turned the amp right up so they could hear there was no extra noise on the unit and then showed that all of the frequencies were working. As I moved the various faders up and down and the sound of the microphone changed, one of the two said, 'So, that is what it does.'

I was puzzled.

'If you don't know what to use this on how did you know you wanted to have one?' I asked.

It turned out that they owned the PA that was installed in the *Electric Ballroom* in Camden and the last person that had used it was upset that they had no graphics on the front of house. They asked me if I would come along and have a look at the PA and give them some advice and that was how I met Chris Mounser and got involved with *Encore PA*. More of that later.

I was doing a small gig in a university in London and I ran into Richard Bishop again. He came up to me after the band had finished and complimented me on the sound I got for them. We chatted for a while and he said I should give him a call in his office the following week and that he had a gig for me. I called him up and he said I should come in and have a chat.

I went in the next day and he gave me an album called 'Quirk Out' by a band called *Stump*. I had never heard of them before and I remembered the chaos of the *Hanoi Rocks* shows and wondered if this was going to be similar. Richard said he had wanted me to do front of house sound for them, but they had already chosen an engineer. Would I consider doing monitors? I had nothing else to do so I agreed. The next week I went along to a rehearsal room in South London to meet the band. They were a four piece. Rob McKahey on drums, Chris Salmon on guitar, Kev Hopper on bass and Mick Lynch on vocals. I had not, by this time, had a chance to play the album, and I was completely amazed at the sounds I heard. Rhythmic, yes, but odd, convoluted, and bewitching. I drove home from the studio wondering if they had intended it to sound like that or were bluffing. The whole thing sounded like they meant it, but it was not until we had done a few more rehearsals that I knew that this was meticulously planned and absolutely brilliant.

As soon as we started gigging, though, I realised that brilliant was not a word I could use to describe their choice of sound engineer. Ivan was a stick thin New Zealander with red hair. He had one of those horrible high-pitched whiney voices that some New Zealanders have and he had absolutely no idea of what he was doing. He had some ideas about sound, but none of them were very well thought out and often led him into a lot of trouble. We did a few gigs – it would be over-egging it to say it was a tour – in March, driving up to Manchester and back for a one off, a gig in London, and then a three day run; two gigs in Wales, one in Exeter and then back home. We had hired a splitter bus from *Crossbow Trucking* for these gigs. The splitter bus was not one of Dave Cockburn's finest vehicles. It was a dirty, yellow long-wheel base transit van which had a partition about half way along its length. In the back we stored the backline and the luggage, and the front had two rows of aircraft seats. I drove from Cardiff down to Exeter in the morning and I had agreed with Ivan he would drive home to London after the show. While we were eating we discussed how to get back to London from Exeter and I said the best way was to take the M5 up to the Severn Bridge and then pick up the M4 back into London. Ivan had the map out.

'That is the long way round though, eh...'

'It is longer, but it is all motorway so it will be quicker and we can stop for coffee if we need it. The other route is all single carriage roads,' I explained.

Ivan spoke to some of the locals and when we were ready to leave the gig he announced that he would take the cross country route. I told him I didn't care, but I thought it would be better to go via the motorway. We set off and pretty soon everyone in the van was asleep. I was sitting in the front and I had also nodded off but I was awakened by Ivan's voice.

'Hey. Look. It's snowing eh?'

I opened my eyes, and sure enough it was chucking buckets of snow at us and the whole landscape was completely white. We were somewhere southwest of Salisbury Plain, and the snow was everywhere. I got the impression that Ivan had never seen snow before, let alone driven on it so I suggested he eased off the gas. He ignored the advice and we pressed on. We came to a stretch of dual carriageway and the right hand side of that had been cleared by a snowplough. Ivan switched to driving on that side of the road. The band had, by now, woken up and began asking him to get back onto the left carriageway and not to drive on the wrong side of the road. He reluctantly agreed to do that and we veered across the centre back onto the left hand carriageway. We now came to a slight hill, and still travelling at an unreasonable speed, began to go up it. Ahead of us there was a truck which was not going anywhere. The band began to ask Ivan to be careful and pointed out the vehicle ahead of us, which was stationary with its drive wheels spinning in the snow.

'Can't slow down, eh?' was Ivan's response and the gap between us closed even more. Ivan attempted to overtake the vehicle, but because of the snow, he had no idea where the central reservation was. As a result the van's offside wheels mounted the slope of the reservation and also because of the snow, did not stay there. The van lurched sideways and slammed into the side of the truck. Undeterred by the collision, Ivan heaved the wheel to the right and tried again, same result and another collision with the truck. He made two more attempts, and on the last one shot past the cab of the truck and the white-faced driver looking on in horror. We carried on and shot over the brow of the hill, and down the other side.

By this time the band we all shouting at Ivan to stop the van, and he reluctantly pulled into the nearest lay by. There was a huge gouge down the side of the van and the head of Kev's bass guitar was protruding through the hole – undamaged.

When we got back to London, Ivan said to me:

'You can take the van back, eh?'

I told him in no uncertain terms that the task of returning the van was down to him.

I enjoyed working with *Stump*. They were unusual and the music could be quite stunning at times. Rob was a great drummer with an almost clockwork precision. Kev's bass lines snaked and spluttered their way through the songs as a perfect counterpoint to Chris' spiky guitar lines. All the while, over the top of this, there was Mick's Irish lilting voice. It was an unlikely combination of musicians and styles but it was quite wonderful and unique. No one had sounded like that before – or since. Best of all was that they were all intelligent and interesting in their own right. The one fly in the ointment for me was trying to cope with Ivan. With the awful sound he got from the band, the constant feedback and his complete incompetence in all forms of his task. A tour manager is supposed to be awake first in the morning, getting the trip organised and sorting out the day, not lying in bed waiting for the band to wake him up! A classic Ivan cock up happened when Rob wanted to change his snare drum. He had a deal with a company based in Bath and he wanted to return a snare drum, and collect a new one. Ivan came round and picked him up from his flat in South London and they set off for Bath. They were going through Hammersmith when Ivan suddenly said, 'Oh, I have forgotten the snare drum! Eh.'

Changing the drum was the whole purpose of the journey, so they turned around and drove back to Ivan's flat to get it, and set off again. Rob fell asleep and was woken by Ivan a couple of hours later, 'Have you got any change for the toll, eh.'

He had driven all the way down the M4 and was about to go over the Severn Bridge to Wales. If there had been no toll there I wonder if he would have been on a ferry to Ireland. He clearly had no idea where Bath was. Useless does not even come close.

I went along to the *Electric Ballroom* to have a look at *Encore*'s PA system and help set up the graphic EQs they had bought. It was a ramshackle affair, but it seemed to work. Chris Mounser was clearly the driving force – I can't even recall the name of his partner at the time. The story was that the other guy had owned the system in the first place and Chris had been running a electrical shop round the corner from the *Electric Ballroom*. The guy used to come in and buy odd electrical spares, plugs, tape and that kind of thing. One day he came in and said that the system had gone wrong, and he did not have enough money to fix it. Chris had offered to help and they became partners. From that moment Chris was in the driving seat. I set up the system for him and agreed to do a few gigs as sound engineer. Chris, however, had empire-building dreams. He wanted to make *Encore* bigger and do more with it, and he saw me as a conduit to better things.

There were, however, a few more *Chappo* gigs to do before we got into any of that. We had the usual round of festivals to do, and this had now become pretty much a routine for Gordon and I. We would go round to the various people's houses and pick up the backline and the last port of call would be Chris Youle to get the float and any last minute instructions. One of these jaunts stands out though. We got to Chris' house mid-evening, hoping to catch a night ferry and then to drive down to Sindlefingen, which is just south of Stuttgart. When we got there and asked for the float Chris said, 'I haven't got any money. I bet the float on a horse and it lost.'

We told him we did not have much money on us either and neither of us had a credit card. This was in the days before ATMs so he could not just go to a bank machine and draw some cash. He scrabbled around a bit and came up with some money, but nowhere near enough to get us to Germany. He then gave us his American Express card, 'Use this,' he said.

So we set off to drive to Sindlefingen. The van was full of fuel but it was a Luton transit and they just drank fuel so we knew we would have to stop and fill up several times. The first mistake we made was to decide to drive across France. Looking at the map it made more sense to go directly from the Calais ferry through Rheims to the German border at Saarbrucken. What we did not take into account was the fact that, even though it is a major route, everything shut down at midnight. We drove merrily on through the night, and when we got down near Rheims, began looking for a fuel station – only to find they were all shut. Pretty soon we were running on vapour and not at Rheims yet. The van did come with European breakdown cover so we stopped and explained, in halting French, that we had run out of fuel. About an hour and a half later a van appeared with a couple of gallons of fuel and poured them into the tank. The problem was that not only did they want us to pay for the fuel, but also for the callout charge. They said we could claim it back later, but that did not help our financial situation. Still we had some fuel and set off again towards Rheims. We did find a couple of garages there but none of them would take an American Express card. We topped up with what little money we could muster and carried on. As dawn broke we were still in France, running low on fuel again and still could not find any garages to take the card. In desperation we stopped at a small garage and did a deal with the guy on the pumps to buy a few litres of fuel in exchange for Gordon's duty free cigarettes, and a bottle of brandy we had bought on the boat. The next thing we saw was a toll booth. I had forgotten about those. France makes you pay for your journeys. Again there was a scrabble for change and we just dumped all the French coins we had on the counter. It was not quite enough but they let us through and the German border beckoned us. Once we were through the border we again tried to get someone to take the card but to no avail. Nobody wanted to take American Express. Finally we gave up, parked in an autobahn services and called the band's hotel with the last few deutschemarks we had left between us. Nothing was left for coffee or breakfast. It was mid-day by then. We explained what had happened, and they sent out a local promoter with money. A couple of hours later he arrived and we got fuelled up to drive the last one hundred kilometres to the gig.

We finally got there at six in the evening after travelling for twenty four hours. We unloaded and set up ready to do a soundcheck. Chris came over to me, 'You're doing monitors as well tonight,' he said casually.

'What!?'

'We sacked Gavin at the airport. He was drunk when he turned up this morning.' I was not bothered about doing the monitors as such, but I also had to look after Geoff's guitars during the show and I had no idea what they usually wanted to hear in their monitors. I went into the band's dressing room and said that I was going to put their own vocals and a bit of backing vocal in the wedges, a bit of piano in Roger's, along with that and kick snare and hat in the side fills. I also thought I would head off any potential conflict and said, 'I have been thrown in the deep end here and I don't have a lot of time to sort it out, so you will have to be a bit patient if it is not quite how you want it. If I get any flak or anything thrown at me, I will switch it all off and pull out all the plugs and go home.'

As it was, the gig went pretty well and they said the stage sound was clearer than they have ever heard it before. Once we had loaded up I asked Chris where the hotel was.

'Ah, well, it's like this. We have a couple of extra gigs that came in last night. A band pulled out of a couple of festivals so we are doing two extra shows.'

'OK,' I replied cautiously.

'Trouble is,' he went on, 'Tomorrow's show is in Bremen and we are on stage at mid-day. You will have to leave now.'

If you don't know your German geography, Bremen is up on the North Sea coast – about as far away from Sindlefingen as you can get on that side of the country. Still, we acquired a gram of 'stay awake' juice, and set off.

We drove all night and got to the gig around 8 am. Time for a quick spot of breakfast and a shower, and then we put the gear up. I ran into Manfred after the show because the 'Earthband' were next up after Roger. After we had finished playing and the gear was put away I went down and found Chris.

'Where is the hotel?' I asked.

'Munich,' was his response.

'Munich!'

'Yes, the next gig is in Munich – here are the details. You had better leave soon. You are booked into the *Holiday Inn* there.'

Off we went again, and by the time we got down to Munich we were only managing half an hour of driving each before we began to get sleepy. We turned up at the hotel, unloaded our bags and went up to reception. The man behind the jump was small and effeminately gay. We told him who we were and he said:

'I am not sure. The rooms are not booked till tomorrow we may have a.....'

He stopped short, seeing the look of growing impatience and rage on our faces.

'Give us a room now or we will come over there and take one!'

Without taking his eyes off us he reached behind him grabbed a key and said:

'We'll sort it out in the morning.'

And, for the first time in three days, we got to sleep. This was getting to be a habit. The next day we did the show in Munich, and we were standing backstage having just loaded up.

'Do you want to go back to the hotel tonight?' I asked Gordon.

Chris Thompson's Band 1987

Inside the *Stump* Bus - Ivan, Mick, Kev & Chris

Chris Youle

The Splitter Bus after the Crash

Charley, Rick and Geoff – backstage at the Munich gig - Rick ran the local crew for Munich and I have known him since the *Pink Floyd* tour in 1977

Geoff Whithorn in full flow 1987

Load in *Chappo* 1988

Soundcheck - Bob, Boz, Stevie and Roger - *Chappo* 1988

Load in 2 *Chappo* 1988

Setting the stage at a Sports Hall 1988

Bob Priddon

Stevie Simpson

Stevie Simpson and Tim Hinkley

Boz Burrell

Roger

Poli Palmer

Pinky

Gordon – eating the chocolate and a table full of Kinder egg toys.

Tim Hinkley - *Chappo* 1987

'Not really,' he said so we picked up our bags and drove straight back to England.

We had an open air show in Luxembourg, which also featured Joe Cocker headlining and had Herbert Groenemeyer just below Roger on the bill. It was a bright, sunny afternoon and we sat around backstage relaxing while the other bands played. Joe suggested that, as an encore, he would do a basic 12 bar and Roger could come on and sing the second verse, with Herbert joining them for the last verse. They all thought this would be a good idea so it was agreed. When Joe was on I went out to the front of house desk. Sure enough, when the encore started Joe played the 12 bar and Roger, accompanied by Geoff Whitehorn, joined them onstage for the second verse. I wondered if Geoff might need a guitar so I went backstage to check just as Herbert stepped onto the stage and made his way to the other microphone. One of Joe's road crew spotted him just as he reached the mic, and before he could sing a note grabbed him by the collar and gave him the bum's rush off the stage.

He was wearing a suit, and no one had told the crew this was going to happen so I can see that the guy must have thought that maybe one of the execs or German promoters had decided to go up on stage and join in. Roger and Geoff looked the part and the crew probably knew them anyway, but Herbert was not given a chance. I arrived behind the stage as Joe's tour manager was trying to calm Herbert down.

'I am the number one fucking star in Germany,' he was yelling, 'and that man has just pulled me offstage in front of 10,000 people. This is outrageous. Where is he? I will kick his ass back to England.'

Most of us were trying hard not to look amused by all of this, and it had been a big mistake to make. The tour manager had got the guy to go and stay in the bus and was trying to apologise, but Herbert was rightly furious. Even back at the hotel he was not happy at all, and there was no sign of Joe's backline guy. He, rather sensibly, stayed out of the way. Bruised egos tend to heal far slower than any other wounds.

We did a festival towards the end of the summer and Roger ran into a guy called Bob Pridden. He had been the original roadie for *The Who* when they started out and was still their monitor engineer. During the course of a drink at the hotel, Bob got hired to do monitors for the forthcoming tour. Although I was not unhappy to relinquish the role of monitor engineer, I was a bit put out by the fact that he was travelling with the band and I was expected to set the monitors up for him each day. I was also sure, from the showing on the festival, that he could not do the job. I said that I would set them up every day, but I would neither EQ them or do the mixes. That was what he was being paid for.

The band Roger used for the tour was going to be Geoff on guitar and vocals, Henry on drums, Tim on keyboards and Nick on sax. There were three new members. Steve Simpson on violin, guitar and vocals, Boz Burrell on bass and vocals, and Poli Palmer on vibes. This was one of the best line-ups that Roger had used since I started touring with him. We kicked off in Germany at the *Metropol* in Berlin, but within a few shows Bob was already having problems. Henry came up to H and I and asked us if we could check out the drum fill because it sounded wrong. The following day, after we had set up we had a listen and it sounded awful. If you hit the bass drum it sounded like someone slapping a kipper onto a sheet of plasterboard. I punched out the EQ and it sounded much better so I knew it was something to do with the graphic. I waited till Bob came in. We led him to the monitor desk and got him to check the drum fill. H sat behind the kit and hit the bass drum.

'Listen to that,' I said, 'There is no bottom end on that at all.'

He went to adjust the channel EQ on the desk, but I stopped him. I put the graphic into bypass. 'That sounds much better', H exclaimed.

Bob looked puzzled. On the Yamaha Graphic EQs there is a low pass filter (marked 'LPF'). This will set the frequency at which the bass, or bottom end, starts to fade off and the filter on the drum fill was set to 200Hz – as high as it would go. I pointed this out to him.

'Now listen,' I said, and as H hit the bass drum I lowered the filter and gradually bottom end came back into the fill.

'What is LPF?' he asked.

'Low Pass Filter,' I replied.

'What is that?'

'The thing that turns the bass off,' I answered – but he did not look any the wiser.

Bob's other big problem was with the desk. On a front of house board you have a fader that adjusts the level of the channel that is being sent to the master faders, and thence to the PA. On a monitor desk, because it has many different mixes to control, there is not usually a fader. Its place is taken by a row of knobs, each of which controls the sound to a separate mix. The desk we were using had both, and the fader controlled the level that went to all of the mixes. Once you knew this it was relatively simple to set all the faders at '0' and run the mixes from the knobs. Simple to anyone who understood it that is. Roger would ask for a bit more piano so Bob would go to the piano channel and push the fader up. The piano would get louder in everyone's mix. Some of the others would say turn the piano down so he would go to the piano fader and pull it down a bit, and it would get quieter in everyone's mix. The whole stage balance would see-saw around all over the place. I tried to explain this to him, but every day he would do exactly the same thing. One gig, Poli got so angry about the mix changing all the time he pulled out the plug and turned the thing over onto its face. I was also standing beside Bob one night when Boz turned to him and said, 'A bit more kick drum please, Bob, not that much you cunt!' all in one breath.

The other problem with running the mixes this way was feedback. Every time he pushed a vocal microphone it got louder across the stage and somewhere it would start to feedback. Instead of trying to pull the fader back, he would try to EQ the feedback away. That would be

OK if you knew which mix was feeding back, but because he had turned them all up, he had no idea which one was screaming. It was all getting a bit chaotic and I wondered how he had kept his job with *The Who* for so long.

We made two signs. One of these we put on the front of the monitor desk just before the show started. It read:

'Welcome to Bob's Whine Bar.'

The other sign was hung from the truss and lowered down over his head. That read:

'Have a Hoot And A Howl At Bob's.'

He never saw these signs because we used to take them away at the end of each gig, but the band saw them and some of them looked over and smiled. Bob thought they were all smiling at him, so he smiled and waved back.

He was constantly talking about *The Who* and Pete Townshend, who was apparently known as 'Captain Beaky' (I wonder why?). We had a megaphone in one of the flight cases and would sometimes go up into a dark or high place in the gig and call through it:

'Telephone call for Mr. Bob Pridden, Telephone call for Mr. Bob Pridden.'

His immediate response was to drop everything and rush off saying:

'That will be Captain Beaky wanting me.'

It never once occurred to him to wonder why the fake tannoy call was always in English, with a very English accent when we were in Germany. It also never occurred to him to wonder why it was the same voice in every gig – or why he never found a telephone. I must confess we were all a little cruel to him, but he had a combination of things that are guaranteed to make a crew not like you. He was useless at his job and expected us to carry him, he was pompous, and he was pathetically gullible.

When you set a system up you have a stack of speakers and amps and then the monitor desk will go behind them and the backline will go across the stage. At one gig I had very little room, and the monitor desk was hard up against the PA. To make things worse the backline was hard against the monitor desk so, when he was checking out the wedges, he had to walk all the way around the backline, test the mic and then walk back again, adjust the desk and repeat until he had it how he wanted it. I was tuning the guitars at the time and I could hear him cursing at this. The next day we had a big stage, but I set it up just the same and again he cursed at it – but never said anything to me. I carried on doing it and still he never said a word directly. After a while I said:

'Bob, how would it be if I set the monitor desk up a bit back from PA so you could walk between the desk and the PA onto the stage?'

'That would be great, can you do that?'

'No, I just wondered how it would be,' I said, and walked off. I carried on setting the desk up that way. Looking back, I think we treated him rather badly, but he brought it on himself with his attitude. He was also getting a hard time from the band about the monitors, so I was not surprised when he said he had something else to do for the second part of the tour.

After the tour I was talking to Rob Douglas who said he went to Wembley to help rig the big gig that *The Who* did there in the '80s. He was standing by the monitor desk when the band were playing 'Behind Blue Eyes' and the monitors were feeding back. He said, 'Bob, the front wedges are feeding back.'

'They always do in this song,' was Bob's answer.

I was told that Townshend kept a can of freeze spray on his amp, so that when he gashed his hands by doing the windmill guitar stuff he could freeze the wound and stop the bleeding. He used to call Bob out onto the stage and point at his monitor. When Bob bent down to check it he would freeze the top of his head and slap it. Seems we were not the only ones who gave him a hard time. I realised, though, that what would happen would be that he would turn up with a famous band, and the crew that ran the system would fall over backwards to make sure it was all set up right and working. He would come along and mess it up, and they would try to fix it as it went along. That way he never learned anything and did not get the sack. Wrong really, but I have fallen into the same trap myself as I will relate when we come to the George Clinton/*Parliament*/*Funkadelic* gig – but that comes later.

One of the caterers on this tour was 'Pinky', one of the two 'Ute's' from the first *Chappo* tour. It was, in fact, her own company, one that she set up that year. They were good fun those girls and I did have a bit of a thing for 'Pinky'. After breakfast each day they would sit down and write a shopping list for that day's food and drink, and I would sneak it away and add stuff like 10 grams cocaine and 1 kilo of hash, to it. Just for a joke, one day, they gave us all Kinder eggs for desert and we turned this into a game. We would all unwrap the eggs, but not eat the chocolate. We would then get the toys that come inside the eggs and have to be built. If you got an aeroplane you had to eat all of the chocolate on the table. If you got a car you could chose someone to eat all the chocolate. If you got a model that did not need to be built you had to be Bob's friend for the day, and if you got a ship you had to blank him. There were some other rules, but I forget them now. This was all just within the crew, and although the band usually ate with us, they never knew what was going on or could ever work out why there was such hilarity. Boz asked why the band did not get any Kinder eggs so the next night Pinky got them some. I got to Boz's egg first. I carefully unwrapped it and cut the chocolate apart. I took the toy out and replaced it with some cigarette papers, tobacco, a piece of cardboard and a small amount of dope. In other words, a Kinder 'spliff kit'. He was much amazed when he opened the yellow plastic container to find that inside. .

We had a pretty big show in Vienna and needed to put the lighting in early because there was a square box truss that had to be flown over the stage. I volunteered to get up early with the light crew and drive them to the gig in a mini bus. I was then going to come back to the hotel and bring the sound and backline crew in a couple of hours later. I was driving back, looking for the turnoff that led to the hotel, and going quite slowly, when I noticed a white Ford behind me. The road was quite wide but the central section was raised and had the tram tracks on it. There were cars parked on the right hand side so he could not overtake easily. I could see the car going from side to side behind me trying to find a way to get past. It was one of those 'boy racer specials' with all the extra lights on the front, venetian blind on the back window and the spoiler on the boot. Finally the parked cars had a gap and I moved over enough to let him through. As he overtook he swerved the car at me. I thought, 'Silly bugger, this is a hire bus, I don't care,' so I swung the bus back at him. He panicked and hauled the wheel away, bouncing onto the tram tracks and almost over to the other side of the road. He came back, pulled alongside the bus and pulled a revolver from inside his coat, waving it at me. Again I remember thinking, 'He is going have to shoot a hole in his car if he wants to shoot me, and if he starts to wind the window down I will run him off the road,' so I blew him a kiss and waved. It was only later, when I applied a bit more thought to it that I realised he could easily have shot me. Back to that business of feeling invincible when you are on the road.

When we got to Bonn we had a couple of days off, and Pinky and I went out to eat. We found a nice Italian restaurant and were presented with a menu. When it came time to order we found out that the waiter did not speak English, German or, in fact, Italian. He was French and would only take the order in that language. This reminded me of the time when I was in Frankfurt in the '70s. We were staying in one of the *Marriott* hotels and asked the doorman which way to go to get to the centre of town. He came outside with us and, when we climbed into the taxi he instructed the driver where to go. The driver turned to us and said, 'What the fuck's he saying?'

Seems the driver was an American ex-serviceman who had stayed on in Germany, but never learned to speak the language. How can you be a taxi driver and not be able to speak to your passengers?

The best crew pranks to play on bands are the ones which go almost unnoticed by the people that you play them on just make them a bit puzzled or distracted. One of the ones we pulled on the *Chappo* tour concerned a large bottle of pickled onions that H had brought with him from England. When all the onions had been consumed we were left with a bottle of vinegar. We were about to throw this out, but someone (I cannot recall who it was) had an idea. We took it up on stage and taped the jar to a broomstick. During one of the slow songs we opened the jar and pushed it out under Tim Hinkley's piano stool. When the song finished we took it away. We did this every night in the same song. After a week of this we were sitting in the catering and he said:

'I think I am going tour crazy. Every time we play that song I can smell pickled onions.' I am not sure if we ever told him what we did. Another trick that we played on him involved a little paper packet and some fishing line. Gordon said to Tim just before the show that he had lost a gram of coke somewhere. He said, 'I had it just as I was checking the stage, but I can't find it now – or I would have given you a line.'

Tim walked onstage and sat down and there was the little white packet lying by his keyboards. We were watching and he looked down at it and tried to reach it with his foot. It was, of course, just out of reach. When the song finished he moved his stool a bit, but we had pulled the packet over a bit and he still could not reach it. He moved the stool again between songs and we moved the packet, but he caught on and turned round and caught us laughing.

We came home for Christmas, but went back out again straight after to do a few more dates in northern Germany. They were pretty uneventful, but there was one thing that puzzled me. I would spend months away in a smoky, draughty bus and in gigs that were a fog of cigarette smoke and humidity, and be perfectly OK. When I got home each time I would come down with bronchitis. As soon as I was back out on the road again I was OK again. I was to work this out later, but going back out for a last week with Roger cleared my chest and set me up for the next year, and that was to be pretty much taken up with a couple of tours with *Stump*.

Mick and Kev - *Stump*

Mick Lets off Steam- *Stump*

CHAPTER 24

A Stump. A Wombat and A Burdon.

tump had a few gigs lined up for the early part of 1988. The first of these were on a short tour of Scotland. I enjoyed touring with *Stump* on many levels. I had done so much touring with bands that had been around the block for so long they were dizzy, that I had forgotten that fresh approach that a new touring band can have. Working with people like Roger was good on the level that they were all a bit more relaxed about the tour, but touring with *Stump* had a freshness about it.

We travelled up to Scotland in a 'splitter' mini bus with the band's fairly minimal backline in the back. The band had decided to buy their own bus and fitted it out. After much discussion among themselves, they decided the best colour to have it sprayed was – pink! Only a band like *Stump* could have made that decision. When we came into the upland area the band wanted to stop and climb around on the rocks. The pictures on this page were taken then and show the playfulness that they had. I must admit my photographic eye did not see some of the background flaws that a more experienced photographer would have seen, but they made for funnier pictures, which were, I feel, more in keeping with *Stump's* innate quirkiness. They were always such a unique-sounding band and had a commanding stage presence that was mesmerising. Once they were on stage it was hard to take your eyes off Mick's gyrating lankiness while your ears were continually assaulted by Chris' jagged guitar lines and Kev's virtuoso bass. All of this was held together by Rob's wonderful drumming. Do I sound like a fan? Well I was. One of the great things in the music business, well for me at least, was that I got to work alongside people whose music I liked, and the *Stump* tours were fun on so many levels. I think it was only Ivan's multi level-incompetence that got me annoyed and spoilt things a bit.. I always felt that it was like sitting on your foot for a few hours and then trying to run for a bus, dragging a numb and unresponsive limb around with you.

One of the first gigs on the tour featured a support band which made *Stump* look normal. I cannot recall what they were called, but they were a duo with one guitarist and a banjo player who had a guitar pickup mounted upside down over the banjo's strings. He also had an array of effects pedals, one of which was a distortion box, which he used to great effect playing a very Hendrix-style solo during one of the songs. They both wore heavy duty work boots which they used to create the rhythm tracks. One song remains stuck in my head to this day had these memorable lines. One would sing:

'There's a train comin''

And the other reply:

'Ay Jimmy, but it's nae stopping here'

Repeated, over and over again. It quite took me back to the '60s and the original *Soft Machine* song 'We did it Again'.

We finished this section of touring off with a gig in the *University of London* and the band went off to get their new album, 'A Fierce Pancake' ready for release.

In the gap I went to do a bit of work for *Encore*. The PA that was installed in *The Electric Ballroom* was a bit of a mess, as I found out when one of the amp racks tripped out. Instead of it being a section of the speakers not working it was a patchwork of them. Seems they had the idea that if one rack went down it would not be the whole of one side that was not working. We completely rewired it after that to get it to run a bit better. Chris Mounser was trying hard to build up the stock of equipment and to move into other areas. He was trying to get me to come and work for him, but I did not want to tie myself to a company. I was quite happy being a freelance engineer so I could pick who I worked with. When you work for a company they often choose for you, and even if they don't, you often can't go off and do a tour for someone using a rival company. Of course *Encore* had no touring PA, so the other factor would be that I would be tied to working in London and I was rather more interested in touring. Still, even though I resisted the offers to join *Encore*, I was happy to do some one-off shows for them.

We did a show at the *Electric Ballroom* with *The Red Hot Chilli Peppers*. They were not very well known at the time so the place was not exactly packed solid. There had been some complaints about the sound levels for some of the gigs at this venue. A lot of it had been down to the hollow stage under the stage left PA wing. This also made the whole sound very bass reverberant, and prone to low end feedback. The venue had closed for a short time while they did some soundproofing work and, among the restrictions placed on it when it reopened was that they installed a Db cut off. There were a set of 'traffic lights' at the back of the stage. If the sound got too loud it would move through amber, and if it stayed on red for more than 30 seconds it cut the power to the stage. I was looking after the front of house, but they had their own sound man so I was basically there in case anything went wrong. I told the guy about the Db meter when we did the soundcheck, but he said it would be no problem. When the band hit the stage at the start of the show they pulled the power within the first couple minutes! It took two more attempts before they achieved a level that would not trip the meter. Their sound man was not very happy about this, but there was nothing we could do about it. I think this was also the first gig they did in the UK, and the first time an English audience caught the spectacle of a band coming onstage naked apart from a sock attached to their private parts!

Stump, meanwhile were in rehearsal for the next tour. This was to be their first tour with a full PA and lighting rig. I hoped that having the same PA every night, and one which was plenty loud enough for all the gigs we were doing, might be what Ivan needed to get the sound right, but I was to be proved wrong. My old friend Steve Wollington joined us to rig the backline for the tour leaving me free to concentrate on the monitors. Lighting was by Derek Watson who proved to be exceptionally entertaining during the tour as well. We did a short production rehearsal in London and stayed overnight in *The Columbia Hotel* so we could get an early start in the morning. I realised then that I was the only person on the crew who could drive, so I was going to have to be behind the wheel for the entire trip. Ivan was driving the band in a separate mini bus. The hotel was one of those rock and roll hotels that everyone stays in unless they have a bit of money to spare. Not exactly luxurious, but certain to turn a blind eye to excess and to keep the bar open as long as it took to fully anaesthetise the last band or crew member standing. We ran into Alex Koerver and a couple of German promoters I knew who were staying there. Steve also met up with Peter Howard from *Skan PA*, and the whole lot of us made our way to the bar where we were joined by the crew from *All About Eve*. I said it was a rock and roll hotel. After a few drinks I realised I was going to have to bail out early so I would be up and ready to drive to the first gig which was at *The College of Art and Technology* in Cambridge. I was sharing a room with Steve and I woke when he came in, several hours later. He stood there staring intently at the two beds in the room. After a few minutes of deliberation he threw himself confidently – onto the floor between them, which he hit with a resounding thud. Rather than attempt to summon the energy and co-ordination required to make the herculean task of regaining his feet he decided the best thing to do was to reach up for the pillows and duvet and just sleep there. In the morning he was clearly the worse for the previous night's experience. I asked him why he had thrown himself on the floor.

'I came into the room and I could see three beds and I thought it has to be the middle one, but I was wrong,' was his answer. Logical I suppose, but only if your sense of logic had, that night, drowned in a vat of alcohol and other substances. We went downstairs, had breakfast and set off for the gig. Just outside London I stopped for fuel. It was still quite early in the morning, the sun was shining, the birds were singing and a little Asian man was polishing the petrol pumps when I pulled up and filled the tank. I had just finished and replaced the nozzle when the passenger side door of the bus opened. Steve leaned out and splattered his breakfast and some of the previous night's alcohol over the pump.

'That's better,' he belched, and shut the door.

The Asian guy looked horrified by this.

'He's not a well man,' I commented and went off to pay. As we drove off, the man was still staring at the pebble dashed pump in disbelief.

As the gigs progressed Ivan's confusion became more and more obvious. I was rigging the whole system. The only thing he had to do when he got there was to rig up the second tape machine. He had two cassette machines there and one was used to record the gig while the other was for the intro tape. The sole task he had at the end of the night was to take the tape player away again and after the second gig he forgot it. We gave it back to him the next day and he forgot it again. After a couple of times of doing this we decided to leave it in our bus and wait till he asked for it. He didn't, so it stayed on the bus. After a few days Derek said to him, as the show started:

'What happened to the super two tape system then Ivan?'

'Someone nicked it at a gig a while back, eh?' was his answer.

At the end of the tour I returned the bus to him, with the tape player sitting prominently on the back seat. A couple of weeks later he asked me to move some gear in the bus and it was still there. I put it in my house and then did not get around to mentioning it again until I saw Rob. I told him about Ivan forgetting it and how we tried to give it back, and he never noticed.

'That's my tape player!' he said, 'Ivan told me it had been nicked.'

I dropped it in to him the next day. At one point on the tour, Ivan's girlfriend turned up. Steve said she looked like someone had just poured a bucket of water over her. The pair of them sat in the restaurant of the hotel, and Rob and I decided they were a 'Dual Cabbageway'.

The second gig on the tour was in Brighton, and it took a while to get down there from Cambridge so we went straight to the gig at the 'Pavilion'. When the gig finished we went to the hotel only to find it closed. We rang the bell and got a very irate response from the landlady who said we were too late and that she was not going to come down and book us in. We decided to go back down to the hotels on the seafront and see if we could get a deal for a couple of rooms since it was now nearly 2am. Derek cut a deal with the *Queen's Hotel* and we got a cheap rate. We were pleasantly surprised to find the bar was still open so we went there for a nightcap. There were four other punters in the bar; two men and two women. The men were both wearing suits and the one standing at the bar was smoking a cigar and talking to the barmaid. They seemed to be playing truth or dare, and the woman on the left lost and had to take a dare. Next thing we knew she was on her knees giving him a blow job while he tried to put the other woman's hand into his trousers. He carried on talking to the barmaid through this. The bar in the *Queen's Hotel* has large windows which open to the road, and being Brighton, there were still people wandering up and down the streets and looking in. We watched this little tableaux for a while, but the long drive the following day meant I had to take my leave and go off to bed. Apparently when she was finished she wiped her mouth on a serviette and came over to chat with Steve and Derek, but the man she was with hustled her away. The following morning the same barmaid was on duty at reception.

'Interesting night last night wasn't it?' I remarked.

'Yes,' she replied, 'That woman should have kept her mouth shut.'

'Wouldn't have been as much fun for him if she had,' I replied.

At that point she realised what she had said and blushed deeply.

I had another part to play on this tour. As well as doing the monitors, I had a keyboard and a sampler by the desk and I would play in various sound effects and noises. The best one was the 'frog chorus' which formed the rhythm track for 'Charlton Heston'. When the band performed this there was just bass, guitar, bodhran, and vocals. Every night there was a lot of feedback and, when asked about it, Ivan would reply:

'It's the monitors, eh.'

I got fed up with this so, one gig, I decided to prove it was not me. I waited till 'Charlton Heston' was happening, and then muted all the monitors for a few seconds. The band looked round in surprise, and I shouted over to them:

'All the monitors are off – it is still feeding back,' and then I turned them back on again.

Everyone gets a bit of feedback sometimes, it is inevitable. A microphone will get turned towards a speaker or get just that bit too high in the mix. All sorts of things can cause it. The skill is to get on top of it quickly and stop it. Blatantly blaming the other engineer all the time is not the way to try to get away with it though. It just pisses off your colleagues.

The support act for a lot of this tour was the eccentric Ed Barton. Ed was an unlikely looking performer. Dressed in a tweedy looking jacket, and sporting a beard and ragged haircut he looks more likely to be shouting, 'Gerrof my land,' and waving a shotgun than standing on a stage with an acoustic guitar, singing. He made up for that by singing oblique, odd songs and playing his guitar with a penny because, 'All plectrums are too soft.'

'Did you kill my Brother' was one of my favourites, but nothing beat the moment in the set where he undid his jacket to reveal that his white shirt had been cut away revealing his stomach. He would move the guitar microphone over his exposed flesh and sing 'I'm Slapping my Belly' whilst – erm – slapping his belly. He was a man of unique oddness. He was also rather naive. We did a few gigs with him before, when we were hauling the backline about in the pink minibus. When we pulled up beside him as he walked towards a gig and offered him a lift he stood and studied the van for a moment before asking, 'Have you got all that gear in there?'

Quite how he expected us to be able to get a lighting rig, 32 channel mixing desk, two stacks of speakers and a monitor system in the back of a minibus I have no idea.

Derek had a great line in ranting. At one gig we encountered another local crew who were collectively useless. At first they all left because we were smoking a spliff, and then at the end of the night, they were taking in the lighting multicore. Now the same person had helped Derek earlier in the day when he put the multicore out so it should have been obvious what he had to do, but it seems not. I was packing up the stage when Derek said 'Look at that.'

The lighting multi was quite thick and heavy in those days and was on a large reel in a flight case. This flight case and reel were on the stage. The guy from the crew was trying to wind the cable in over his arm, and with each loop of cable it was getting heavier. We watched him as he struggled to the stage, onto which Derek had pushed the flight case.

'And what do we think we are going to do with that then?' he asked. 'Throw it onto the reel maybe? Cast you mind back to earlier today. How did we get that cable out? We rolled it off the reel didn't we? So now you are going to have to go all the way back to the end of the hall and then we can wind it back in again. What do you do for a living? I bet you don't do anything. I bet you are unemployed, Why do I think that? Because you are a useless waste of space that is why.'

This whole diatribe was delivered in a perfect public school accent, made all the more incongruous by the fact it was coming from a tall man with a ragged beard, long black hair and besmirched with the usual grime that lighting guys get on them when packing up after a gig. The guy had stood there, wilting under the weight of the cable during this rant, and then meekly wandered back to the end of the hall.

Local crews can be absolutely superb and many of them are pretty professional in their approach to the task, but some of them are so incompetent it hurts. On this tour I had a set of small stage monitor wedges. I wanted to have these in a case and there was no case for them. After a hunt round John Henry's warehouse, I found a case that they would all fit in, but only if you put them into it in a certain way. We were touring universities at the time and I got into a little game each day. I would choose a member of the crew and ask them to take the speakers on and put them on the stage. At the end of the night I would find the same person to collect them and put them away. Nine times out of ten they would ask if that was the right case and say they did not all fit into it. I would usually say, 'But you took them all out of it this morning didn't you?'

One guy was particularly insistent they would not fit. I put them in the case and closed it.

'What are you studying then?'

'Engineering,' he replied.

'I won't be going over any bridges that you design then,' was my response to him.

Only one place stood out. *Rock City* in Nottingham was staffed by bikers. The local crew there were all Hell's Angels. I did exactly the same with them, and the guy put them all back in the case in one go.

We were back home for a couple of weeks after the UK tour and *Encore* were, by this time, putting a lot of pressure on me to join the company. Chris had taken over maintenance for the PA system in *Dingwalls* and sacked his original partner after an argument over his commitment to the company. He had an office and small warehouse just over the road from *Dingwalls*, on the ground floor of the new building, in the one-way system.

Mobile phones had just started to be generally available, albeit at a high price, and Chris had done a deal with the local wheeler dealer phone salesman to get one for him. He finally came up with the offer of a phone with all the bills paid, co-directorship of the company and a monthly retainer, and I caved in and went for it. Phones, in those days, were not the tiny pocket devices we have now, neither were they free with a contract. These phones were £800 each with calls costing £1.50 a minute. They were also the size of a house brick with a battery life of four or five hours and a talk time measured in minutes. As a result we all carried handbags with the phone and two or three spare batteries in them. I got mine when I went in to prepare a system to go into *Dingwalls*. It was quite a hot day so I was in T-shirt and shorts and I had come in by train from Greenwich. The train journey from Greenwich to Camden was first overland to London Bridge, and then underground on the Northern Line to Camden. The overground part from London Bridge back to Greenwich in the evening tended to be mostly full of suited 'City Types' and, whenever I made my way back from *Encore* I was often regarded as an interloper. On the way home that day I was splattered with black paint from redoing some of the speakers and I had my new mobile phone in a small bag. I settled down in the carriage and it rang for the first time. I answered it and it was Chris, 'Say "Two hundred thousand dollars",' he said.

I repeated it.

'Now say "New York, Monday morning then back to Paris and on to Tokyo".'

I repeated that too.

'Now say, "Make sure it is a suite and there is champagne on ice when I check in".'

I did that.

'Are you embarrassed yet?'

'No, but there are a whole bunch of straight guys in suits with briefcases looking at me wondering why they have not got one of these toys, and how come an oik with paint all over him has got one.'

I did a gig at the *Electric Ballroom* in the gap between the end of the *Stump* UK tour and their European leg. This was for *Art Blakey and the Jazz Messengers*. The band arrived to set up and I was accosted by a large Texan in a cowboy hat who was their tour manager. His first words were: 'Hi, I'm the tour manager. Have you got anything for my nose?'

I told him that I did not have anything on me, but I could make a couple of calls and get some for later. He thought that would be OK so I called my painter and decorator friend and asked him if he wanted to come to the gig, and could he bring a bit of toot. He did.

Art Blakey himself did not turn up for the soundcheck so the first sight I had of him was when he walked onto the stage that night. The band were all young black guys and they were followed onto the stand by an old guy looking very frail and walking somewhat unsteadily. As soon as he was seated at the kit, however, he was sharp as a nail. The first few moments of most gigs are a bit frantic, a few tweaks of the sound now that the audience was in and the temperature was up a bit. I was doing this when the Texan jumped up on the riser.

'Is your man here yet?' he demanded.

'Yes he is down there,' I replied.

'Take me to him.'

I protested that I had to mix the gig and he should give me a few minutes to get it all right, but he was clearly impatient so I caught my friend's eye, and beckoned him over onto the riser. He went off with the Texan and I got on with the show.

The *Electric Ballroom* does not have dressing rooms in the venue itself. They can only be reached by going out into the yard and then back in through another door. Since it was a house rig all I had to do after the show was to pack down the mikes, cables and stands. I was therefore, finished quite quickly and the only place to wash your hands there was in the dressing room block. I went out of the building and there was the pick of the crop of British jazz, all waiting at the dressing room door. The Texan was saying to them, 'Sorry guys you will have to wait, he is doing an interview.' He caught sight of me and said, 'You are OK, you can come in.'

I squeezed through the throng and crept quietly down the stairs to the toilet to wash. The dressing room door was open and there was Art Blakey – with my friend! He was racking out a few lines and Art had all these photos out on the table, 'This is my great granddaughter. She lives in N'Oleans, and this is my cousin......' I was quite amazed. Courtney Pine and all the other jazz stars all waiting upstairs and there he was talking to a house painter, and making them wait! I put out my hand and said, 'It has been a pleasure mixing the sound for you tonight, great gig.' He had obviously just bought a bit of my friend's toot and he had a fiver in his hand. He thrust it at me, and said, 'Thar' you go boy, buy yourel' a cup of coffee.'

Encore, at the time, consisted of Chris, Danny (an Argentinean Israeli who did a lot of the electronic repairs and set up the systems), Barbara Reidling (the company secretary) and a couple of other people who made up cables and did other tasks. Barbara's husband, Pete, was just finishing a course in sound engineering and was also doing some work for us. They did make-up headed notepaper with my name on it as a director, but this was never registered at Companies House. I naively believed it was all done, although I knew Chris wanted me in for the contacts I had as well as my engineering expertise. Danny had a thick Argentinean accent and kept making small English mistakes which I pounced on ruthlessly. We had acquired one of the early office computers at the time, BTs 'One Per Desk' system which used the PSION database system. I knew all about this because I had a Sinclair QL at home and that was the database supplied with it. I made up a database of engineers details. On my entry Danny added the comment, 'You cannna talka to Thees man'. One day he came into the office and said, 'I just bought some toilet paper. It said 250 sheets. How they know how much I use?' He had finally mastered the art of the pun (you have to say it in a South American accent). He had been born in Israel, but moved to Argentina when he was quite young so he had dual nationality. He used to say, 'When I fly I am Argentinean and when I land I am Israeli.' He later got UK citizenship to add to his passport collection.

I had got quite friendly with Boz during the last *Chappo* tour and I did a few gigs with him and Tim Hinkley in this period too. Boz had a jazz band with a guy called Tam White and I went up to Edinburgh to do a few gigs with them. We did a big 'Live Earth' festival in July, up in Fife, Scotland and stayed in the hotel on the St Andrews Golf Course. Van Morrison and Phil Manzanera topped a bill, which also featured John Martyn on the day Tam and Boz played. It had bucketed down with rain the day before and the site was a mess. They had nowhere near enough punters and it was, in the end, a financial disaster. We had a good time and it was nice to see John Martyn again after so many years. He played up a storm and we all had a party side stage during Phil Manzanera's set, but then Van Morrison (or Van Mental as John renamed him) came on and insisted that everyone except his own crew was chucked off the stage – even Tim Hinkley who had been Van's musical director for a few years.

'Mr Happy is always like that,' he said philosophically.

I also had a few gigs with *Roadside Picnic*, a band that David O'Higgins from *Mezzoforte* played sax for. There were a jazz outfit consisting of Mike Bradley on drums, Mario Castronari on double bass, John G Smith on keyboards and David on saxes. One of the main reasons that I went out and did sound for them was that they wanted more of a rock and roll sound than the muted jazz feel they got usually. They got a week's residency at *Ronnie Scott's Jazz Club* in Soho, supporting *Loose Tubes*. On the first night we were halfway through the set when Ronnie Scott came up to the desk.

'I can hear the bass drum;' he hissed at me.

'That's good.'

'No it isn't, I don't want to hear the bass drum.'

'Well I suggest you go up there and tell him to stop kicking it then.'

'It will blow the peas off people's plates,' he continued.

'Well use more gravy then. Look, my job, as a sound engineer, is to make sure the sounds they make get heard. If they are using the kick drum it is obvious they want the punters to hear it, or, otherwise why bother to lug the damn thing around.'

He was clearly not happy with this reply, but he was so obviously not getting anywhere that he walked off. In the interval he got up on the mike. He was well known for his corny jokes and audience insults between act. Things like, 'That is a nice jacket you have on there, sir. Somewhere there is a Ford Cortina with no seat covers.'

When he got up after *Roadside Picnic* he said, 'Tonight we have the best sound engineer in the country. In the town he's ....'

I knew that joke and I was still standing at the desk so I muted him. He was furious and banned me from coming back there. You would think that, after all those years, he would have known better than to insult the sound man while he was on the desk.

Stump were off to Ireland and then to Europe in April of 1988. Once again it was just the band, Ivan and myself with Steve joining us to do the backline. Ireland was all quite rustic in the kind of way only Ireland could be. Dublin was probably the most together of the few gigs we did there, and the Waterford gig was in a social club in the middle of nowhere so I was quite surprised to see an audience there at all. There seemed to be a mild surprise that we expected there to be any equipment for us to use at that gig. We were back for a day or so, and then off to Holland.

I had been staying in touch with Andrea since the Manfred tour and she had married Herman, the drummer from *Vitesse* and moved to Amsterdam.

She had also had a daughter the year before, so I felt safe to tell her I was coming to Holland and arrange for us to meet. The band had a date at a radio station to do an interview, and were then going to hang around in Amsterdam for the day before leaving to go to a hotel in Nymegen, ready for the first gig the following day. I was planning to meet Andrea for lunch so I told them I would take a train to the town after lunch. Andrea came and met me at the radio station and, as I left them, Steve said, 'See you at the gig tomorrow.'

'I will take the train to the hotel later,' I said.

'Bet you don't,' he replied.

Andrea and I, with baby Joey in tow, went off to have lunch and she told me that Herman had gone off with another woman a month or so before. After lunch we walked a bit and then went back to her flat. Steve was right. I did not make it to that hotel. I stayed with Andrea, and we fell in love all over again.

Rob, Mick, Kev and Chris - *Stump*

Mick - *Stump*

Soundcheck in Scotland - *Stump* 1988

Steve – Tossing the bass amp. - *Stump* 1988.

Load in - Derek on the desk - *Stump* 1988.

Monitor City - with samp-ler and keyboard - *Stump* 1988.

Chris - *Stump* 1988.

Ed Barton - slapping his belly - *Stump* 1988.
OPPOSITE: *Stump* onstage 1988.

Rob - *Stump* 1988.

Chris and Danny, when he got his UK citizenship

Barbara Reidling in the *Encore* Office.

Pete Reidling - *Encore.*

Chris Mounser - *Encore* 1988.

Roadside Picnic.

Watching a movie on the road - Front Ivan and Rob Back Mick, Kev and Chris -
Stump 1988.

Kev Hopper at a Hotel Window in Gent - *Stump* 1988.

Rob in Third Policeman mode - Backstage at the *Electric Ballroom* - my last gig
with them - *Stump* 1988.

Trev's Briefcase - Eric Burdon 1988.

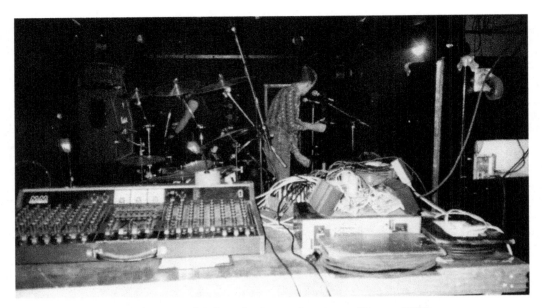

Not the most high tech rig on the tour - *Stump* 1988.

Eric Burdon Band 1988.

Andy Giddings - Eric Burdon 1988.

Jamie Moses and Steve Stroud - Eric Burdon 1988.

OPPOSITE: The only way the band could get into
the dressing room at the gig in Munich.

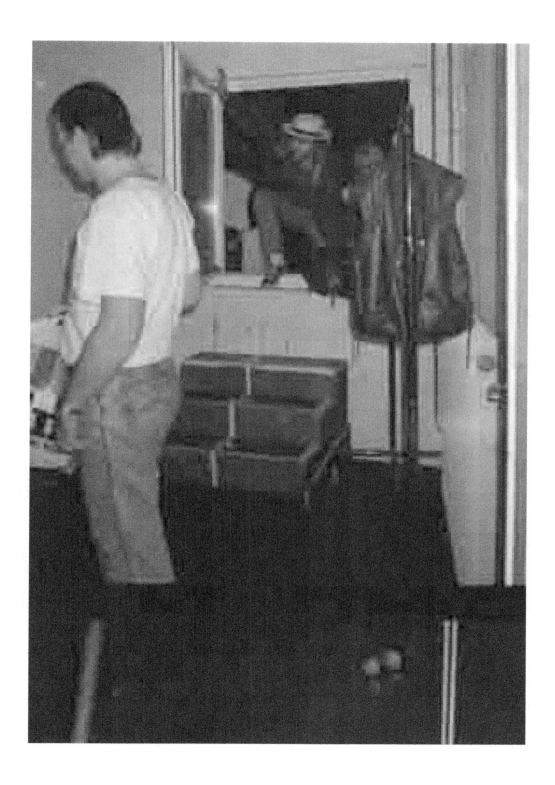

The only way the band could get into the dressing room at the gig in Munich.

The Catering crew pulling a prank on the last night.

Backstage toilet in Bad Salzuflen, Germany .

One of the videos we watched on the bus was *Young Frankenstein*, the Mel Brooks comedy. It had long been one of my favourite films, but some of the guys from *Stump* had never seen it before. Steve and I were wisecracking all the time – a habit I have never been able to break, even in the most dire of circumstances. Kev said one day, 'What I like about you two is that you make a hundred jokes each day, and so does Steve, and every now and then one or two of them are funny.'

We were watching *Young Frankenstein* as we went along the road and it got to the bit where his fiancée turns up just after he has copped off with the young German woman, Inger (played by Teri Garr). Those two and Eyegor (Marty Feldman) are all standing on the steps of the castle when the carriage pulls up with his fiancée in it. She gets out, wearing a round red hat and the coachman unloads a lot of luggage and Gene Wilder says 'Eyegore, give me a hand with the bags.'

'OK,' he replies, 'You have the blonde and I'll have the one in the turban.'

Rob burst into uncontrollable laughter.

'A roadie joke,' he gasped. 'A roadie joke in a movie. Classic.'

Various incidents during that tour made the band realise that Ivan had to go. In Den Haag we all decided to go for a drink after the show, but Ivan wanted to go back and check into the hotel. We all asked him if he would put our bags at reception for us, but when we got back to the hotel a few hours later we found someone had smashed the window and stolen the TV and video player. Ivan had not put our bags in the hotel and they had emptied all the bags onto the floor of the minibus and then stolen all the cameras, walkmans and other devices. I had about £1000 worth of cameras and lenses there, and they all went. We woke Ivan to ask what had happened and his only reply was, 'Hey, it was just some poor people, eh?'

To which Steve's reply was to haul him off the ground by his lapels and shout:

'Well, let's go up to your room and get your stuff and then we can find some poor people to give that to!'

The final straw came on the last day when we were back to do the Melkweg in Amsterdam. I had spoken with Andrea a few days before and she said that the day we were arriving was 'Queen's Day' which is a big national holiday in Holland. She asked where we were staying and said it would be hard to drive into Amsterdam that day. I asked Ivan and he said, 'Oh we can just get a hotel when we get there, eh?'

I passed on the information and told him Andrea said it would be hard to get a hotel. He did not seem to think that this was important, and did nothing about it. When we got there it was as Andrea predicted, the place was packed and Ivan went off to find a hotel while we sat in a bar. He came back and said, 'Two of us can stay in that hotel and another one in a hotel round the corner and....'

That was as far as he got. I told him that was nonsense and that we would never all get to meet up for the gig. Andrea and I took over and made some calls, but the only place we could find to stay was the *Holiday Inn* by the airport, miles out of the town, and that finally put the nail in Ivan's coffin.

A little while after this Danny was running the PA for the evening in *Dingwalls*, and Chris and I were sitting in the *Encore* office. Danny came in and sat down. We asked him why he was there and he said Ivan was doing sound for one of the bands and, 'I can't stay in there with Mr Feedback.'

I took over doing the front sound for *Stump* after this and we went back to *The Leadmill* in Sheffield to play there again. After the show the promoter came into the dressing room and said, 'Last time you were here you had all that PA and it sounded dreadful. Tonight you used our shitty little house rig and it sounded great. Why?'

Mick just pointed at me.

It was not that I was that good, you understand. Just that Ivan wasn't.

It was clear that things were not running too smoothly in the *Stump* camp, but I had other things pressing on my time. The last show I did with them was at the *Electric Ballroom*. We stayed in touch a bit after that – even after they broke apart. They were another band I really loved working with and I was kind of sad that I did not get the chance to make them sound as wonderful as they should have done. I had too few gigs on the front desk to undo what Ivan had done. They introduced me to Flan O'Brien and I gave them Viv Stanshall's *Sir Henry at Rawlinsons End* and *Young Frankenstein*. They were funny and clever and should have gone on to better things.

We did a few odd gigs with Boz and Tam and then Tim Hinkley called me up and asked me to do stage sound for *Womack and Womack*. He was musical director for a short tour they were putting together, and he wanted me on board for that. We flew up to Edinburgh for the first show in the *Tron Theatre* there. We put out four main vocal microphones even though there were only the two vocalists, Linda and Cecil Womack. Two of these were radio mikes for when they wanted to walk around and two were wired microphones for when they were sitting. Of course they used the radio mikes when sitting down and tried to walk around with the wired mikes. Obvious really. The band consisted of three keyboards, bass, and drums – played by Ted McKenna of the *Sensational Alex Harvey Band*. The entourage for the tour was the same as I had seen when they did the radio show in Germany. Cecil and Linda, the grandmother (not sure whose grandmother it was), some children and a babysitter. After the first soundcheck Tim said, as they were leaving to go to the hotel, 'You can tune guitars can't you, Roy? Can you do Cecil's guitars for him?'

I agreed, and they left. He had a main guitar and two spares. I got the spares out of the case and started to tune them. They were miles out but I knew that Americans always loosened the string on guitars when they flew with them, so I tuned them up. When I got to the one he had played I realised that was also miles out and a thought occurred to me. What if he has an odd tuning? When they came back for the show I said, 'Cecil, how do you tune your guitars?' His reply was illuminating:

'Tim, how do I tune my guitars?'

After some puzzling out we worked out they were all tuned a whole tone flat and one had a G string in place of a B string. I put them back to that and they did the show. Tim said later it was the first time the guitars had stayed in tune, but that was because it was also the first time they had even been taken up to the correct tension.

After that show we flew back to London to do the *Watermans Arts Centre* in Brentford. When we got to the airport in London we were picked up, with all the backline, in a stretch Limo. When the band arrived they had a minibus – another cock up. After the show in London we had a couple of days off before heading off to Brussels for a festival. Tim had another gig with Boz and Tam so I was in the *Encore* office, putting a small rig together to do that when my phone rang. It was Linda Womack.

'We are leaving this afternoon,' she told me.

'I have a gig tonight,' I replied, 'I will meet you at the festival tomorrow.'

'Oh no,' she said, 'we all have to travel there together this afternoon.'

I told her that Tim was doing the gig tonight with me and that we would go in his car. It was only Belgium after all. A few minutes later Tim called me to say we had both been sacked.

We later found out that they hired a guitarist to take Tim's place as MD and they all set off to drive to Belgium. They got across the ferry and then broke down just over the Belgian border. Apparently the entourage, kids and granny as well, spent four hours waiting for a rescue service in which time the new guitarist sat in the bus, smoked crack and watched porn on the video. That made me smile. About two months later they played *Dingwalls*. Tim had taken them to the Musician's Union for breach of contract, and I went over to see them. They said hello and I handed them an envelope with a writ from Tim in it.

In the summer there were a number of gigs with Roger Chapman. These were more of the usual festival format. Gordon and I would gather the backline and drive out on a Thursday or Friday, depending on when and where the first gig was, and then get back on the following Monday. The most interesting of these events was to take place in a small village in northern Germany called Hartenholm. There was a disused airfield there and that was to be the venue for a race between a motorbike and a car. The whole thing was a result of the German magazine/comic strip *Werner*. *Werner* started life when Brösel (Rötger Feldmann) started drawing his friends in the local village bar in the late 1970s. He made up comic strips involving them and a local paper offered to print them. This went on to become syndicated in larger and larger papers and, eventually, had its own comic book series. This has been the most successful German comic creation and led to films as well as making its author extremely rich. The main character in the magazine is obsessed with motorbikes and beer. At some point in 1988 the author bet someone that his bike could beat the other person's Porsche. This made its way into the magazine and became a race that would happen in reality. The loser was to be stood up against a wall and pelted with cat shit from a tennis ball serving machine. You can imply the level this was operating on. Roger was booked to headline the Saturday night, 3rd September.

Gordon and I set off on the Friday afternoon and got there that evening. There was no hotel booked for that day, but we had a caravan backstage for us to sleep in. The festival was expected to be well attended, with crowds estimated to be around 25,000. We woke in the morning and found that it was my friend Pinky who was doing the catering for the event. We had little to do until the band turned up that evening so we hung around the site, but news began to trickle in that there were a few problems. Instead of 25,000 people there were now around 300,000. All the local roads had been blocked and the German Hell's Angels were setting up impromptu road tolls. They were demanding money from people to be allowed through, and pushing cars off the road if they would not pay. The whole thing was out of hand. To make matters worse, the people on the site could not get off and the bands could not get on. Pinky came over to me and asked if I would like to come with her to go shopping. I said I would, but all the roads are blocked.

'That is OK,' she said, 'We have a hubpschrauber' (helicopter)

So I climbed into the helicopter with her and a couple of others, and we flew off over the site to the local supermarket. The site was huge with people everywhere and, as we went, I could see all the roads backed up with traffic. The local police had given up trying to sort it out – it was only a village after all and quite unused to this level of invasion. Police from the larger cities were still struggling to get through to it. We landed in the car park of the supermarket and went shopping. I wound up standing outside the supermarket with five shopping trolleys full of spirits and wine. Local Germans, who were also unused to such activity, just stared at me as they came out of the supermarket with their weekly shop.

'Just a small party round my house,' I commented as they filed past. Not that they would have necessarily understood me, being German, but I did not know how to say it in that language. We then went back to the helicopter and flew back to the site with bottles and food stuffed into every possible space in the small airplane.

The band was all flown in by helicopter as well. When the concert started it was riotous. The crowd were all going mad for the band, and Roger was on top form. As I stood there at the monitor desk a camera man began to inch his way onto the stage. I grabbed him and hauled him back. I explained that Roger hated anyone other than the band being on the stage unless they really had to be.

'It is my job,' he declared.

'Well he will hit you with a tambourine or, if you are lucky, a mic stand,' I warned him.

He was determined to go on so I let him get on with it. As soon as he was on the stage Roger tried to shoo him off. He clouted him with tambourines, and generally gave him a hard time to the extent of going right up to the camera and giving it the finger. What none of us found out till after, was that the camera was linked to a large screen over the stage and, at that point, all the audience could see was Roger's face and finger with him shouting 'Fuck off!' at the cameraman.

The crowd loved that too.

Gordon and I slept in the caravan overnight that night too because it was easier than trying to get back through the crowds, and in the morning, we set off to the next gig. When we got there we found a ramshackle wooden stage and an audience in the hundreds – one extreme to the other. We left a note on the band's dressing room door saying:

'Cancel the rollers boys. All back to normal,' and set off to find the local hotel so we could check in and get some sleep.

While I was away with this, Chris Mounser had struck up a friendship with Dave Martin, founder of *Martin Audio*, one of the companies that helped revolutionise the audio business. The Martin Audio system that comprised of Y-Bins, Phillyshaves and Horns had become a standard for many PA companies and beat most of the other systems hands down. He had been working on a new system to replace these, and had come up with a smaller system called the F1. This was quite good, although still quite bulky, with one of two drawbacks and he said that Chris could have the prototype system to use. This gave *Encore* its first step towards some real hire stock. This, together with a couple of Soundcraft desks, and some better outboard gear, made it viable to tout for work. We were doing some gigs here and there and pushing the PA around the various agencies that booked bands to go on tour, but before anything could really come to fruition Chris Youle asked us to go off and do a few weeks with Eric Burdon.

We were left to field a crew for the Eric Burdon tour of Germany The tour was due to end in Zwingenburg with a concert which would feature Eric and Roger Chapman. After that date we would carry on and do a short tour with Roger. Gordon was not available so we took on Steve Wollington, and new backline guy called Shaun to do both Eric's and *Chapp*o's backline. H was not around for the Eric Burdon stuff so I brought in Trevor Cronin to do the front of house. Trevor had done a few gigs for *Encore* and seemed competent enough – if a little wet. He was another Antipodean and was, I found out, not used to touring. Trevor made himself the target of some ridicule when, on the second gig, he asked a member of the stage crew to go to the bus with him and carry his briefcase into the gig for him. The briefcase had already been the target of some pranks while he was at *Encore*. He had noticed that some of the engineers who worked there had briefcases with them. Mine contained a set of tools for quick repairs. Paper and pens for noting down desk settings and making mike lists, a few office bits like a mini stapler and hole punch and my PSION Organiser II. (One of the reasons I have such good information on the dates is that I made a database on the PSION and noted down every gig I did with stage sizes, clearance, power, get in etc). Most of the rest of us had similar stuff in their cases. Trevor wanted to be like us and began to come in with a briefcase. We wondered what was in it so we opened it when he was not there one day. It contained a bottle opener, a pen and a newspaper. Nothing else. So we added to it. We found the heaviest mike stand base that we had and put that in there, closed it up and put it back where it was. That night he got up to leave, picked up the case and left. We had all been sitting there anticipating him saying, it was unusually heavy but there was no reaction. He came in the next day, complete with briefcase and sat down.

'How's the briefcase?' I asked.

'OK.'

'Anything different about it?'

'No.'

'It didn't seem a bit heavier than usual?' I enquired.

'What have you guys done...' He opened the case. 'Jeez, I wondered why it felt heavy.'

He had carried it all the way home and back again without even opening it. That kind of set the course for the tour to follow. He was always leaving the case somewhere, in the middle of the table after breakfast, in a corridor, all over the place. One day, when he had finished breakfast and left the case on the table, the catering girls complained about it so we climbed up and put it on a ledge above the table. It stayed there all day while he wandered around and looked for it. We finally pointed it out to him at dinner that night. This did not make him more careful and he left it behind the next day, so we took it and put it on top of the PA stack. When the show started the follow spot operator picked it out with the beam.

Andy Giddings was the keyboard player for Eric and he called the band *International Rescue* because Eric would sometimes jump over verses or miss lines out and they had to lurch from one part of a song to the next and keep it all going smoothly. His keyboards were usually right next to my monitor desk and he would often turn to me and put both hands to his mouth with a mock frightened expression on his face. By the end of each show Eric would have not played 'House of the Rising Sun'. This was a deliberate thing and as he would make to leave the stage at the end of the encore Jamie Moses, the guitarist, would playing the opening arpeggio. Eric would spin round, march to the microphone, and shout, 'I hate that fucking song. That song has been a millstone round my neck since I was seventeen and do you know why I hate that fucking song so much? It is because every time I play that fucking song some arse in England gets paid for it.'

He was referring to Alan Price who was the keyboard player for *The Animals* at the time that he had originally recorded it, and, although the song was a traditional folk song, registered *The Animals* arrangement when they first recorded it back in 1964 – before it became such a massive hit.

Andy told me that there was one song in the set in which Eric had to be able to hear the piano clearly in his monitor so he could pitch properly. I, accordingly, turned up the piano for that song and then turned it down at the end. Two weeks into the tour Eric came over to my monitor desk.

'D'you know that song where you turn the piano up at the start?' he asked.

'Yes.'

'Can you turn it back down again as soon as I start singing, it is a bit distracting?'

'Oh, OK. You should have told me earlier.' I replied.

'This is the first soundcheck I can remember coming to,' he responded. (We had soundchecked every day on the tour). He started to walk away and then turned back, 'You have to remember I gave twenty five years of my brain to acid research,' he said with a smile, and went back to the microphone.

The gig at Bonn's 'Bisquitehalle' was billed as a 'Blues Festival' and I thought that would mean I did not have to rig the PA. Quite the reverse. We not only had to rig the PA, but do the sound for all the bands. We soundchecked Eric and then moved on to the other acts. Luther Allison was OK, and then we came to Albert King. Albert King is no small person and he strode onto the stage as if he owned it. When they were all set up Trevor spoke through the monitors, 'Kick Drum'. The drummer began to hit the drum and Albert King came over to me. 'Too loud,' he said. I turned it down.

'Still too loud,' I turned it down again.

'Still too loud,' I turned it off.

'Still too loud.'

'It is off on the stage,' I said. 'You can hear the front of house.'

We repeated the process for every drum and I just switched them all off. He did not seem to care what the drummer wanted to hear, just himself. Having got through the kit and the bass guitar, Trevor called through the monitors, 'Guitar.'

'You have a lot to learn, boy!' Albert King snarled back at him.

The process of doing this soundcheck had been very slow and we were running behind schedule by the time *Taj Mahal*, another six foot black guy smoking a pipe, took to the stage. They were just about ready to go when the promoter Rainer, walked onto the stage. He said they need to open the door soon and could we hurry the soundcheck along.

'You've got one pissed off nigger on your hands already. D'you want another one?' was his reply.

Rainer retreated and left him too it. After *Taj Mahal* there were two local blues bands to do. I heard enough blues that day to last a lifetime. During Albert King's performance he said, 'This is supposed to be the Blues – if it don't sound like the blues it is because of that man out there!' and he pointed at Trevor. If that had been me I would have switched him off there and then. There is no call for that behaviour in my book. I mentioned it to Trev later and he said he didn't hear it. Was he not listening? Was the voice too low?

We got on the bus one evening and Steve took off his glasses to clean them, and promptly snapped them in half.

'Ha,' he exclaimed. 'That is why I always take a spare pair of glasses on tour with me.'

A couple of days later we were loading out one of the gigs on the tour and the place was strewn with discarded water bottles. Jojo, who was one of the catering crew, was walking along just in front of me 'Look,' I said and pointed to a coin on the floor. As he bent to retrieve it I flipped one of the water bottles over his head so it landed in front of him and splashed him with a small amount of water. A childish, but otherwise harmless, prank. What followed next was unexpected. Shaun, who had seen this from on the stage, picked up one of the large water bottles that the band had used. It was still quite full and he hurled it across the room. As my eyes took in the trajectory I could see it would hit Steve on the head, so I shouted a warning, but by then it was too late. As he turned the bottle struck him on the side of his head, smashing his second pair of glasses.

'Fuck it,' he roared and kicked the door. Unfortunately, this was a steel fire door and the next thing we knew he was doubled up in pain on the floor clutching his leg. Luckily we had a hotel that night, but he was in a lot of pain and could not walk. He also could not see. The following day we went along to an optician who sorted out a new pair of glasses for him, but when he limped onto the stage during the soundcheck the band struck up with a chorus of 'No Eyes and Legless'.

We finished the Eric Burdon tour with a gig in Zwingenburg, which also featured Roger Chapman. The gig was packed, but it was a bit of a financial disaster. The promoter was also running another show later in December, but the band had pulled out. He had used the ticket money from the gig we were doing to pay the advance money to the other band, and was having trouble getting it back. This meant that we did not get paid much from it. One of the perils of being a promoter is that success or failure are both an option. The whole thing hangs on so many different factors. If one link in the chain unravels then the whole thing can come crashing to the ground. There were a lot of grim faces and heavy discussions going on and Rainer, from the German agency, took over running the door so we at least got the walk up ticket sales. He was even more pissed off because he managed to run his own briefcase over in the car park that day. Not the best of things to happen to him.

Trevor left us after that go off and do a couple of shows in Greece with Eric. His parting shot came when he was sitting backstage with the band. He came up with the immortal line, 'I have really enjoyed this tour, I feel like the sixth member of the band.'

Everyone looked at him in disbelief. He tried hard, and he was a good engineer, but he left the toilet door open too often and had the piss taken out of him in so many ways. I was usually up first in the morning, but one day I got out of my bunk to find Trevor sitting there with a cup of coffee. There was a gleam in his eye.

'Ah, I am up first today. I can make fun of you now.'

'If you think that your powers of wit and repartee are up to a bit of mental sparring with me at this hour of the morning you are welcome to engage in the fray, but I would predict that you are doomed to an ignoble defeat,' I can recall replying. He really had nothing to say after that. A short *Chappo* tour took over at that point and we were off again.

It was my 40th Birthday on the day we did the *Glasshaus* in Bad Salzuflen – coincidentally I had also had my 39th birthday there the previous year. In the backstage toilet area the lights had fused and no one had got around to fixing them. There seemed to be a problem with the wiring and there were wires hanging out of the wall. I said, as a joke, to Nicky Bell, 'Can you go and sort out the lights in the toilet before the band get here.' A while later I went back there and found he had taken me at my word and put two PAR cans in there, one each side of the bowl. The toilet unit itself was on a kind of plinth – sort of a 'toilet riser' and was tastefully lit by the two purplish lamps. It was also quite warm in there because of the lights. I have this photo in a frame in my own toilet.

At the end of that short tour the crew came back to the UK, but I went to stay with Andrea for a while. I came back to England via the ferry from the Hook of Holland which docked at Harwich. I then got on a train which took me into London. It was while I was sitting on this train I noticed a very odd picture on the front page of the paper the man opposite me was reading. I bought a paper of my own when I changed trains at Liverpool St. Station and it was then that I learned about the Lockerbie air crash – the photo had been that iconic image of the plane's cabin lying on its side in a field. It was not until I spoke to Steve Harley the following year that I learned that Paul Jeffries, who played bass with the original *Cockney Rebel* and later with Paul Balance's *Warm Jets*, had been on that plane.

Andrea came over to stay with her friend Jo that Christmas and we met in London a few times, going to one of Steve Waller's gigs with his blues band in South London or just meeting up. It was while we stood outside *Hammersmith Odeon*, with her about to go off to stay with Jo, and me going back to Greenwich, that we decided we were madly in love. At that point it became clear that things had to change, but I was at a loss to know how to change them. We lived in two different cities on two different land masses, but we wanted to find a way somehow.

In my absence I found that Chris Mounser had taken on partnership with another PA company called 'Peak Audio'. They were based in Perivale, in Middlesex and had a reasonable sized PA system. Paul Kellet, who ran that system, became another director of *Encore* (on paper at least – this was a clever trick that Chris Mounser used a few times) and the other engineers who already worked with them became absorbed into the *Encore* retinue. Chris had done a deal to put both systems together to go out to do a *Motörhead* post-Christmas tour in Germany so I went out on that. I was basically in charge of the monitor system – although *Motörhead* had their own engineer. There were another four bands on that short excursion, but none of them went on to make any mark on the music world. I sat in the *Motörhead* bus and had a chat with Lemmy one day. The last time I had seen him was when I did the *5TA* tour a while back, and *Motörhead* were playing in Edinburgh on our day off there.

They were renown for the amount of speed they usually had and I recall their tour manager, when asked if they could spare some for our guys, holding up a big bag of white powder and saying, 'This is all we have and it has to last until we get to Hammersmith in two days.'

It reminded me of when *Hawkwind* played the *Sundown Theatre* in Edmonton back in the '70s. Alan, from *Wooden Lion*, was playing synth with them that night at Lemmy's request and we were there in the afternoon. Lemmy asked if I had my car and then got me to drive him right across to West London in order to score some more speed. He missed the sound check that night. It was clear, while talking to Lemmy on the tour bus, that he knew that he had known me for years, but could not quite recall why, or where from.

One of the support acts on this mini tour was from the States and had a fierce female manager. One evening one of the *Peak Audio* engineers who was looking after the front of house sound for the support acts, came up to the monitor board before the show. He was swigging from a Jack Daniels bottle and was clearly drunk already.

'Have a good show,' he slurred and went off to the desk.

During the show the band kept looking at me in a puzzled way. I checked the monitors but all seemed in order so I went to the edge of the stage. I could hear why they were looking strained. The sound was wavering, with various parts going up and down in some sort of random way. I could not work out what was happening until I went out front to see the engineer swaying back and forth, almost unable to stand. He was clutching at the desk for support pulling or pushing the faders as he did. As this was going on he was being beaten about the head and body by the band's diminutive, but fierce manager. We got someone else to take over the board and sent him off to the bus to recover.

Andrea met us when we set off to go out on the *Motörhead* jaunt and came over to Dusseldorf in the coach before travelling back to Amsterdam. And that was the end of 1988.

CHAPTER 25

Come Up and See me – buy me Sake

At the start of 1989 I went in to the office at *Encore* to see what was happening for the next year. There were a few things planned, but nothing of any great length. It looked like it would be a lean year with Roger not planning anything much. There was a whiteboard on the wall used as a running diary and one item on the board took my eye. It lasted three days and read 'Steve Harley – production rehearsals – *Electric Ballroom*'. Steve was preparing for a few gigs and wanted to do some rehearsals there. I said I would be happy to look after that. I had always liked Harley's stuff – especially the album 'Love's a Prima Donna' so I was happy to look after them for a few days. I had expected him to have a sound and lighting engineer in tow and a full backline crew. As it was there was just me, and I was mixing it. That was fine by me. The band consisted of Stuart Elliot (*Cockney Rebel's* original drummer), Rick Driscoll on guitars and vocals, Barry Wickens on violin, acoustic guitar and vocals, Kevin Powell on bass and Ian Nice on keyboards. Steve was, of course, singing and playing acoustic and electric guitars. The lighting guy, Clive Davies, turned up on the second day, but there was no backline crew in sight. At the end of the rehearsals Steve asked me if I would do a gig for him at the *Albany Empire* in Deptford and maybe come on tour in Scandinavia with them. So, on the 22nd February 1989 I found myself doing the sound for Steve Harley's first real gig in eight years.

I ran into Dave from *Zenith Lighting* just before this and told him I was off on tour with Steve. 'You don't want to do that,' he said. 'The man's an arse,' but I never found him to be so on the tour. In fact he seemed pretty good. Clive and I were the only two crew members and we helped the band set their gear up before the gig and take it down afterwards. It was all very civilised – too civilised really. After four years with *Chappo* I was used to a much more rough and ready approach to touring.

After the Scandinavian tour we went to Greece to do two nights in the *Rodon Club* in Athens; in reality it was more an old cinema and pretty big for a club, but that was what they called it. It was all going pretty well. The band were absolutely tight as a drum. Every one of them was a professional player and they played and sang well. It was a joy to be mixing them.

We went to Holland to do a few more gigs and I took Andrea along to the first of these – a venue in Maastricht in Holland. When we arrived I was walking round the venue and I noticed pictures of a concert orchestra playing on this stage and saw that they had draped the walls with big padded blankets. As soon as I had fired up the PA system I realised why that was. This venue made a swimming pool sound dead. Sound-wise the gig was a complete disaster. Without the soundproofing panels there was nothing anyone could do to make it sound nice. I thought that Andrea must have got a very bad impression of my abilities as an engineer from that. Luckily, two nights later, we played the *Paradiso* and it sounded absolutely fine. I learned later that the venue in Maastricht had been demolished because it was completely unusable.

After that we came back for a few shows in UK and I took an *Encore* PA out for that. We used the *Martin* F1 rig for this tour and I was pretty impressed with it. Shame it never made it into production. I thought it had a good warm sound and the coverage was better than the later F2 rig. For this tour we also had Peter Reidling doing the monitors, and a backline guy, Dave Thomas, for the first time. This was the first UK tour I had done for a while because most of the stuff with Roger was in Germany. It was interesting to see how much less organised the UK venues were. Most of the European ones had proper 'C-Form' three phase mains connectors for the power distribution – even the disaster of a gig in Austria had proper connectors. Here in the UK, we had to connect the bare wires into the distribution boxes and this was something that many people baulked at. Somehow electricity is still a bit of a black art for many people. The US comedian Steven Wright said, in his stage act, 'I got my electricity bill today. I sent it back with a note saying "I have not seen any all month."'

Even though you have to turn the isolator switch to the 'OFF' position before you can open the box they seem to think it is waiting just beyond the last wire. Waiting poised to reach out and spark them to death. I do recall going into the old *Hammersmith Palais* though and starting to put the mains in only to find it was still live, but that was because the guy in the power room had said I should take the house PA 'tails' out first and pointed at the box. I opened it and got one out before touching the next one across to the earth strap with the screwdriver. The tool flew out of my hand and embedded itself in the wall. I stepped back and looked at it and realised I was taking out the 128 amp feel to the whole system. Not a fuse between me and the substation!

We did the *International II* in Manchester at the start of this tour and I was able to invite my friend Erica Wright (the woman I met at the *Pink Floyd* show back in the *Bingley Hall* in 1976) along to the gig with her daughter Jade. (Jade is now a presenter for TV and Radio in Manchester – amazing to think I had known her since she was first born).

By the time we had finished that tour I was put in charge of the production for the next one later that year and firmly part of the entourage. Steve Mather, who was managing Steve Harley at the time through the *John Lennard Enterprises Agency*, was already working on the next two tours, one starting in May in the UK and the other going to Scandinavia and Europe in August. Before they took off, though, there were a few more shows to do with *Chappo*.

Some Festivals and a short East German tour were in the diary.

It was coming back from one of these festivals that I had the first of many run in with UK customs. I went to stay with Andrea in Amsterdam on the way back from one of the festivals and stayed there for a few days. When I flew back from *Schipol Airport* I walked out through the 'nothing to declare' zone. A customs officer pulled me over and opened my bag. He pulled out my can of shaving foam and shook it.

'What is in here?' he asked.

'Judging by the label I would say it was shaving foam. That was what came out of it when I had a shave this morning.'

He shook it again.

'Does not sound like shaving foam to me.' he said.

'What does shaving foam sound like, then?' I asked him. I was intrigued.

'I am going to have to open it up,' he declared.

'Are you going to buy me some more shaving foam then?'

He did not seem too impressed by this, scowled at me and marched off, ordering me to stay where I was. Ten minutes later came back.

'What was in there?' I asked him innocently.

'Shaving foam!' he snapped back, closing my case.

'Stands to reason,' I said and left.

The following week I flew back to the UK from another festival and got pulled over by the same customs guy. As he beckoned me over I began reaching behind my back and looking over my shoulder.

'What are you doing?' he snapped at me.

'I thought I had taken that target off my back, but it must still be there,' was my reply.

'Didn't I pull you up last week?' he asked.

'Mmmm, shaving foam,' was all I said.

'Fuck off,' was the answer and he waved me away, laughing.

On another occasion I had made a slight mistake. I had a small tin which I used to keep my dope in. It was a little round brass tin, with Chinese writing on the top, that I had bought in the *Paradiso* years ago. I would usually put it into my toolbox when I flew back, but on this particular trip, I forgot and left it in my briefcase. I was stopped at customs and the inspector picked up the tin and opened it. It was empty, of course, but he sniffed it and examined it closely. Then he said, 'This smells like it has had cannabis in it.'

'Yep,' I replied.

'I will have to test it.'

'Why?'

'To see if it has had cannabis in it.'

'I just told you that it did.'

'You might be lying.'

I could not work out what he was on about. Why would I lie about it that way. I might lie about it and say it had not have cannabis in it but not that it had. Anyhow, he went away with the tin and returned a few minutes later.

'This tin has had cannabis in it,' he announced, triumphantly. This was all getting a little surreal.

'I know that it had cannabis in it. I told you that. I put it there. Then I took it out and smoked it so it is not there anymore. I don't see what you think you can do about it. I don't have any on me now but you are welcome to look. Can you arrest me for having a tin that smells like it has had cannabis in it?'

He paused and gave it some thought.

'No.' He said and gave me back the tin.

'Off you go.'

Chappo's East German tour started in April in Jena, home of the *Karl Zeiss* optical factory and a bit of an industrial heartland – if such a thing existed in East Germany. As I mentioned before, the Russian rulers of this section of Germany had put very little into it since the war and most of its industry was pretty much still operating as it did back in the '40s. It was all coal fired, steam driven and technology free. The *Karl Zeiss* factory was probably the jewel in the crown of East Germany's industry. It was already a respected producer of lenses and cameras before the war and was one of the few companies that exported its products to the west. Practika cameras and Zeiss binoculars and telescopes could be found in many shops in western cities and were the better option if you could not afford an expensive *Nikon* or other camera. I had one of these myself and was planning to buy a couple of lenses with my East German marks while I was there, but I found out that the top of the range stuff that I had was only ever exported and not sold in the country in which it was made. Anyhow, geography lesson over – let's get back to the music.

The first odd thing about the tour was the visa situation. Normally, when we had travelled to East Germany in the past, there was a very strict set of instructions about what border crossing to take. This time it was a little vague. Still we travelled to Jena in the usual van loaded with gear. When we got to the border the guards were not as officious as usual, stamped the passports and carnet and let us through. H was away on tour with David Essex so I was on the front board which I enjoyed immensely. The band was a little different this time around. Geoff had quit at the end of the last tour so, Steve Simpson was joined on guitar and backing vocals by Bobby Tench, a former *Streetwalkers* member. John Lingwood, from Manfred's band, was on drums and Ian Curtis had taken over the keyboard role from Tim Hinkley. The PA was provided by an East German company so it was all pretty relaxed.

The second show in was in Dresden and we had a day off afterwards. We all went along to the motor museum there which had some really stunning examples of old German cars. When you consider that the streets were filled with Trabants (a car made of cardboard with a lawnmower engine in it) and it was only the richer people who could afford the better cars – Skodas – the walk through the museum was quite surreal. As we left and walked out into the grey East German streets John said, 'This is the only place I have ever been to where the cars in the museum are better than the ones on the streets.'

He had a point.

We also went to the railway station. This looked like it had come straight out of a black and white '50's film. At any moment I expected to see Robert Mitchum or Jack Hawkins stagger up to me in a trench coat, with a knife sticking out of his back, clutching a piece of paper saying, 'Get this to Londonnnnn....' before collapsing onto the floor as the police whistles sound and .... well. you get the picture.

As with all East German tours we were given an 'interpreter' to travel with us. In reality it was someone to watch us to make sure we did not interact too much with locals, and report back to the STASI. In this case it was a guy called Karl. The morning after I went along to the station with my camera to take some photos and I ran into Karl. He invited me to breakfast so we went along to the station café and sat down. I had been pretty impressed with the old parts of the town I had seen, those that still remained, anyway.

'This must have a beautiful town before we bombed the shit out of it,' I said casually.

'It was,' he replied.

'I always think that it is so one sided after a war. The winner gets to put the loser on trial for all the things they did wrong, but no one really questions the winner. In my view Dresden, Hamburg and the other towns the British firebombed were also war crimes. If you want to claim the moral high ground you have to behave responsibly too,' was my reply. Something I have long held to be true.

'Ah,' he responded, leaning forward.

'So now you see that Adolf Hitler was not so bad aft.......'

That was as far as he got. Just like in a movie he could see by the expression on my face that I was not applauding the long dead tyrant, but expressing my disapproval at the actions of my own government in that regard.

On one of the earlier tours the 'interpreter' had been a woman called Steffie. She travelled with us all through the first tour. We had a large bottle of white wine in the bus that we had got in Austria but which tasted awful. Every now and then someone would drink a bit and go 'yeech' and put it back. Steffie took a drink and loved it. We decided that you were allowed to have taste buds in East Germany, but not allowed to use them. Steffie turned up on this little tour too, and came along to the hotel for a drink. She was not the most beautiful woman I have ever seen and no one on the crew had shown much interest in her, but she was a good person and we all had a good time together. Steve wound up sleeping with her after one of the gigs. When we got on the bus the next day Roger said, 'Steve, you didn't, did you?'

Steve nodded in the affirmative.

'She said it was either fight or fuck and I thought I would get less bruised that way' - always ready with a quick quip.

When we got to Karl Marx Stadt (which has now reverted to its previous name of Chemnitz) we also had a bit of time off. On a previous tour I had bought an alto sax with my East marks and a friend of mine said he would happily buy one off me if I got it for him. With that in mind I took advantage of the day off in Karl Marx Stadt and went along to a music shop and bought an alto saxophone. Since I had quite a few East German marks on me I also decided to buy a trumpet and sell that when I got home too. When I came back to the hotel I ran into Brian Gallivan in reception.

'What have you got there then,' he asked.

I explained about taking them back and selling them and he was very interested. When he was not on tour he worked part time in the Brixton 'Buy, Sell Exchange' shop.

'Show me where this shop is,' was his reaction, and, after leaving my purchases in my room, we went back there.

Brian was one of those people who don't believe that anyone in the world has ever not learned some English and never made any attempt to speak any words in any other language. He marched into the shop, and in his lilting Welsh voice, trilled,

'Have you got any more saxophones then?'

East Germany was a poor society. Its shops were often quite large but had very little in them, rather like supermarkets when there has been a scare or strike on and everyone has bought and stockpiled stuff except that the crisis had been going on since the wall went up and there was nothing there to buy in the first place. She had only had one alto sax in the shop and I had bought that earlier. Brian looked around, desperate to buy something.

'Trumpets. Have you got any trumpets then?' was his next question.

The woman produced three trumpets from the back room and opened the cases on that counter.

'I'll have them, then,' Brian said. The woman was trying to ask which one but Brian wanted all three. I managed to explain this to her and she looked amazed. Brian, however, was not finished. He was looking around to see what else he could buy. His gaze fell upon a display of harmonicas. He pointed at these and the woman got out a box of harmonicas from under the table. Brian bought the whole box! All around the walls of the shop were pictures of the people who worked there and one bore one of those 'employee of the month' type badges. Having sold two saxophones, four trumpets and about thirty harmonicas in one morning I am willing to bet she would be sporting that same badge that month.

The next day we moved on to a small town called Suhl. We were staying in a hotel just off the town square and the gig was the other side of the square so we decided to leave the minibus at the hotel and walk over to the gig. While the lighting was going up, Steve and I went off for a walk and found another music shop. I was getting a bit carried away by it all by this time so I bought a bass recorder, a couple of ordinary recorders, a banjo and a wooden glockenspiel. Steve bough a Hawaiian guitar – yes, you heard me correctly, a Hawaiian guitar in that grey desolate East German town. We took all this back to the gig and that inspired a couple of other guys to go and buy stuff. This meant that, when the show had finished, we had a whole bunch of stuff to carry back to the hotel. I decided to go and get the minibus.

The town was a typical East German hamlet, with that omnipresent grey fog clogging the streets. It had not changed since the end of the war and the streets were all narrow and winding and it was not as easy as I had thought to get back to the rear of the venue. After a few wrong turns and U turns I swung the bus into a yard only to find it was not the entrance to the gig. I spun round the empty car park and was confronted by a couple of East German police in a Trabant. They got out and came over. In situations like this, in foreign towns, it was best to pretend that I did not even have the small amount of German that I did possess. I feigned ignorance, but it was not much of a feign, because, apart from driving into the wrong yard (and I could now see that the gig was just the other side of the fence) I had no idea what I could have done wrong.

The police produced an East German Highway Code, and pointed at a sign – the universal one for a one-way street. It seems I had driven the wrong way down one of these in order to get to the yard. One of the police had a little English, 'Driving licence,' he barked.

I produced my English driving licence. That flimsy green paper thing that always used to puzzle so many foreign hire car companies and police. They turned it over in their hands and looked in vain for a photograph.

'Passport!' was the next request.

'In the hotel,' I responded. East German hotels would always collect and hold onto your passport until you left. They debated the issue between themselves in staccato German. They then turned to me, 'Dollars' they requested, rubbing their thumb and first two fingers together in that other universal symbol that accompanies a request for money.

I shook my head, 'No dollars,' I said.

'Deutschmarks,' was the next choice.

'East marks,' I offered pulling some money from my pocket.

It was their turn to shake their heads at this offer. Even the people who lived there did not want their own currency. I was getting bored by this and decided it was time to end it. Impulsively I reached out and shook them both by the hand in turn.

'Well it has been nice chatting to you chaps,' I said in my best BBC English, 'but I have to get on. Things to do you know. Have a good life,' and I got back into the bus and drove off. I was watching them in the mirror as they stood there in that empty car park, wondering if they would try to chase me in their 'Trabby' or pull out their guns and start firing, but they were still standing there watching me disappear into the fog. I came to the conclusion that these people were so used to people being scared of them and doing exactly what they say that they had no idea what to do when they were ignored. Of course this only worked with people at the bottom of authority's food chain. Higher up, where the power sizzles like electricity through their veins, I do not think I would have tried the same stunt.

The last show was in Leipzig, and in an attempt to shed a bunch of East marks, Chris Youle took us all for a Japanese meal. Band and crew piled into a restaurant in the centre of town. I found myself sitting beside Roger and we immediately order a couple of flasks of sake.

'Gotta drink it while it's hot. Tastes horrid when it gets cold,' he said, so we downed the first couple of flasks – and ordered two more. This went on through the meal and most of the flasks seemed to be coming to our table. At the end of the meal Chris called for the bill.

Steve Harley and Cockney Rebel - L to R Barry Wickens, Peter Reidling, Kevin Powell, Steve with his son, Me, Ian Nice, Stuart Elliot, Rick Driscoll and Clive Davies - UK 1989.

On the desk for Steve Harley - note the huge Mobile phone.

Erica and Jade Wright at the Manchester International - Steve Harley 1989.

Bobby Tench - *Chappo* 1989.

ABOVE: Ian Curtis - *Chappo* 1989.
BELOW: Trabants in Dresden.

ABOVE: Dresden Motor Museum.
BELOW: Dresden Station.

Steve Wolling and Shaun at one of the few shops in E. Germany with any stock –
the vodka shop..

The Fabrik - Hamburg - Steve Harley 1989.

Brian and Shaun at the Japanese Meal.

Last Mayday in Madgeburg.

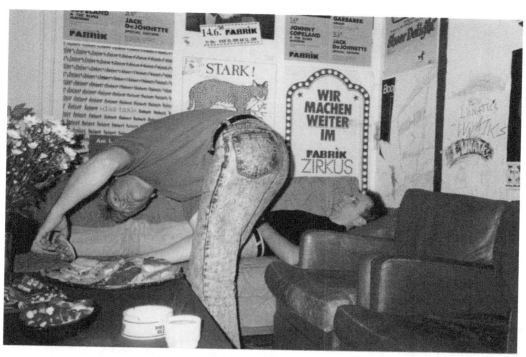

Backstage at the *Fabrik* – Stuart Elliot sleeps while Kevin examines the catering - Steve Harley 1989.

Soundcheck l-r Barry Wickens, Tom Scott, Kevin Powell, Rick Driscoll, Ian Nice - Steve Harley 1989.

Pete Hopkins aka Sooty.

Steve Harley.

Barry Wickens and Rick Driscoll - Steve Harley 1989.

OPPOSITE: Barry Wickens.

'What's this?' he exclaimed when he looked at it. 'Eighty-seven flasks of sake?'

I thought he was going to come after us to pay for the excessive amount we had drunk that night, but then he said.

'I am not leaving here until we have drunk the other thirteen!' which he duly ordered and we happily consumed. I told this story to a backline guy on another tour I did, and the next time we happened to be out on the road together I heard him re-telling it as if it had happened to him. He had clearly forgotten that it was me that told him about it in the first place.

When we got back to the hotel we found there was no bar and we sat around chatting in the reception area. Chris obviously still had a big pile of East marks and went over to the portly concierge who was almost cartoonlike in his suited, moustachioed, stereotypicality.

'I'll buy you all hookers,' Chris shouted back to us, and then, turning to the man, 'Get me twelve hookers.'

'There are no prostitutes in East Germany,' he replied in a flat tone.

'Of course there are,' Chris replied, but the man was having none of this. Even if he knew where to get a bunch of hookers he was clearly not going to allow this bunch of drunk English people to get their hands on them.

I stopped off at Andrea's flat in Amsterdam for a couple of days before going back to the UK and then flew back in to Heathrow. As I was going through the 'Nothing to Declare' zone I was again pulled over. He pointed to the pile of instruments on my trolley, and the conversation went like this:

'What are these?'

'Musical instruments.'

'They look new.'

'Well they are.'

'Where did you buy them?'

''Karl Marx Stadt, East Germany.'

'This is the 'Nothing to Declare' lane. Should you not be paying duty on them?'

By this time he was opening the cases and looking at the shiny new instruments within.

'Do you have receipts?'

I produced the receipts for the items and he added the amounts up totalling a few hundred marks.

'What currency is this?'

'East German marks.'

'And what is the exchange rate?'

'There isn't one. It is a soft currency. You cannot change the East marks back into any western money. The only place you can get anything for them is *Hannover Airport* and there they give you one Deutschemark for twenty five East marks and that means these are under the value on which I have to pay duty.'

'That can't be right. Wait there.'

He went off into the back room and I waited for him to return. 'I have been here before,' I thought. After a while he came back, closed the cases, slung the receipts on top of them and, in the time honoured parlance of all disgruntled officialdom uttered a dismissive, 'Fuck off.'

I left.

We did one more East German gig with Roger that year and it was in East Berlin. It was an open air show in a sports park on a lake, and we were based in a hotel that was previously reserved for their top flight athletes. When we were leaving the UK to go to the gig I asked Chris once more about the visas and what border crossing to use. Once again they had not told us so we went to Checkpoint Charlie. The guards on the post seemed to be totally uninterested. They took a perfunctory look at our papers, stamped the carnet and waved us on. I asked about the visas and they said that they would be at the hotel and that was it. It was the same story when we left too No surprises then, when on November 9th that year I sat round at Andrea's flat in Amsterdam and we watched the Berlin Wall being breached. The heart had gone out of the Eastern Bloc that year. We stayed in a hotel in Magdeburg on the 1st May and watched the May Day procession march its way down the main street but had little idea this would be the last May Day under Russian rule and that, pretty soon, the two halves of Germany would be re-united. Not only that, but when Roger Waters played the *Pink Floyd* epic, 'The Wall', at the Brandenburg Gate I noticed, as the credits rolled at the end, that the show was partly put together by my old friend Mick Worwood who had started *Brockum* all those years ago.

1989 was proving to be a busy year. Quite apart from the festivals with Roger there were also some for *Steve Harley and Cockney Rebel*. They played *Roskilde Festival* in Denmark and a few others so I was zapping backwards and forwards from Europe and managing to find time to stay with Andrea in Amsterdam every now and then. The summer also saw Steve Harley start a UK tour. Clive was not available to do the lighting for this so we had a new lighting engineer, Peter Hopkins, and a new monitor engineer, Tom Scott. Tom's great grandfather had been the man who had designed, among other things, the iconic British telephone box. We also had a tour manager for the first time. I cannot recall the guy's real name now but he had a somewhat pronounced northern accent and was prone to stating the obvious. One day I called him 'Brain of Barnsley' which we immediately shortened to 'Bob'. From then on that was his name. We would greet him in the morning with 'Hello Bob' and he would reply:

'That's not my name,' to which we would reply:

'Yes, we know, Bob.'

Ah, that road crew cruelty again. They can be an unforgiving bunch. I don't know if he ever knew why we called him that. The name Hopkins had some connotations for me too. I knew a few people called Hopkins and they almost invariably managed to screw up in some massive way. I came to the conclusion that, as is the case with names like Thatcher, Smith or Butcher, it referred to the occupations of some long forgotten ancestor. The ancient line of Hopkins were, of course, known as 'Those who shot themselves in the foot'. One particular Hopkins I knew was known as 'Five Minute Hopkins' because that was the shortest job he ever had. Apparently, when Murray Head (famous for his *Jesus Christ Superstar* role and massive in Europe during the '70s and '80s) was touring France his monitor engineer fell ill and the call went out for a replacement engineer. This guy flew to Paris, got on a train and spent a few hours travelling down to get to the gig. When he arrived he walked into the venue and up onto the stage. At the back of the stage there was a large paper covered hoop - the sort of thing you see in circus performances.

'What cunt jumps through that then?' he asked.

'This cunt does – you're fired,' came the voice of Murray Head, who was standing right behind him.

That was it. He got back on the train and travelled into the annals of road crew history.

Steve 'Boltz' Bolton, who had been with me decorating Manfred's flat back in 1982, had been touring a lot with Paul Young. The band's management had sacked him a few times because his general style and appearance, not to mention the jerky way he moved around the stage whilst playing, took the attention away from Paul. During one of these lay-offs he got a phone call, which, he told me, went like this:

'Is that Steve Bolton?'

'Yes, who is this?'

'It's Pete Townshend here.'

'Fuck off. Who is it?'

'No it really is Pete Townshend. I would like you to play for *The Who* on a world tour.'

'No. Who is it really?.....etc.'

Steve took some convincing it really was Pete Townshend, but he went off to tour playing lead guitar for *The Who* – made all the better because they were one of his favourite bands in the world.

The other thing that was on the up in 1989 was the rise of 'rave culture'. Es and raves had been around for a while, but they were getting bigger and bigger during 1989. It was that period when the organisers would find a disused factory or, during the summer months, an accessible field and put on an all-night rave. *Encore* had got in on this from the very start and was one of the leading PA systems providers. Most weekends they would load a truck with PA and park it on the M25 waiting for a call which would tell them where the gig was going to happen. This was all made possible by the coincidental rise of the mobile phone. As soon as the venue was announced, the truck would set off to get the system rigged and the organisers would spread the word. *Encore* made a lot of money on these gigs and pretty soon had a shiny new Martin F2 rig. I could never get into this kind of thing. For me, at least, music needed something a bit more tangible behind it and the rave culture really just consisted of driving beats, electronics and dancing. I avoided doing these gigs as much as possible, mostly because there was no engineering to do, just set it up and wait till the end of the rave and take it down again. I busied myself with all the other band gigs that were going on. We put a rig into a school in Ringwood, Surrey for *Blue Peter*'s Kampuchea Appeal. Boz was there for that too playing with Andy Fairweather-Lowe (from *Amen Corner*), Nicky Hopkins and a host of other luminaries of the '70s rock scene. Bill Wyman handed out the awards. I came back from one of these gigs quite late, around 2am, and unloaded the equipment back into the warehouse in Camden. While I was there the phone rang. It was *Clink Studios* in Southwark. They had hired a bunch of small systems for an all night rave and one had stopped working. It was on my way home so I said I would call in and check it out.

Clink Studios was on the Thames, just upstream from London Bridge and it was built upon the site of the original *Clink Prison* which dated from 1144 and was one of the first prisons in England. It was from this prison that the phrase 'In the Clink', meaning to go to jail, originated. The studio itself was on several floors and all the studios had been emptied and set up as individual venues. Frankie Howard was there, trawling for young men I believe. I was led to one of the rooms, which was in silence. Our rig sat in the corner and, all around it people were laying on the floor, sleeping. Even the DJ himself was fast asleep on the floor. I checked out the amp rack and found it was not powered up so I followed the cable back to find it was unplugged. When I looked at the mains distribution I saw that there was no space for it to be plugged in which was a bit puzzling. One of the slots was occupied by a lamp so I unplugged that, inserted the amp rack power, switched it all on and put on the record on the turntable. (No CDs or MP3s on laptops then – everything was vinyl). The music kicked into life and all around me the sleepers lurched from their sleeping positions on the floor, up onto their feet and began to dance. Like some rhythmic zombie horde brought back to life by the power of the rave. The DJ too woke up and said: 'Oh, you fixed it.'

'Not really,' I replied. 'It was only unplugged. Someone unplugged the amps to plug a light in.'

A look of almost cognition crossed his face.

'Oh, that was me,' came the mumbled reply.

'Didn't you notice that when you unplugged the amp the music stopped then?'

'Oh, yeah.'

I gave up and went home. That was why I could not stand these things, they had a collective IQ in single figures.

Encore was riding the crest of the rave wave though and rave culture was beginning to edge live music out of the spotlight. I was still doing the odd stint as sound engineer at *Dingwalls* and the *Electric Ballroom* but *Encore* were not really pursuing the touring market because raves made so much more money. *Encore* also found that, as the raves got bigger and more frequent, they needed more equipment. Chris' friendship with Dave Martin had brought him the opportunity to get really good deals on the new system that they brought out that year, the Martin F2. Soon they had managed to fill the warehouse with lots of these black boxes but even that was not enough to feed the growing number of rave gigs. He began sub-hiring from a company called *Capital Sound* and they worked together to standardise the way the amps were set up to make their equipment interchangeable. In September, however, we set out on another Cockney Rebel tour, this time with a PA and lighting rig so I was able to wave goodbye to a bunch of stoned ravers and do some real work.

The Steve Harley tour kicked off in Helsingborg, Sweden, in a venue, impressively called *Caesar's Palace*, which, given that this was small town Sweden bore no resemblance to either a Roman villa or a glitzy hang out for the rich and Mafia connected in Las Vegas. We spent a week or so touring Scandinavia and then went down into Germany and came to Hamburg. We played a gig called the *Fabrik* in Hamburg - a bomb factory during the war which was a tall wooden structure with a great sound. Steve was using a track from the music Ennio Morricone composed for the film *The Mission* as an intro for the set and I was approached by a woman from the audience to ask what that track was. She was pretty and we chatted for a while. I would normally have tried to get something going but I was completely in love with Andrea and had, for the first time, arrived at a state of fidelity. I did like her, however, and I took her phone number and address so we could meet again next time I was in Hamburg. I did not realise at the time she was to prove to be a much bigger part of my life.

Being on the road with a crew in a minibus again restored some of the mayhem that usually surrounded touring. One thing that was obvious from the start was that Pete was likely to be the one at the centre of any arguments. There were long disputes between him and Dave Thomas, the backline guy, about where the centre of the stage was. He also had a degree of mischievousness about him, although it was hard to distinguish between a lack of awareness of the disruption he caused from downright cussedness. Quite apart from the arguments about stage positioning he also had a tendency to take down the lamps at the end of the show and plonk them down on top of the cables. He would leave the two lighting trees that stood behind the PA as late as possible before dismantling them - making it hard to dismantle the PA itself. The problem with crews when these things start to cause friction is how to deal with them and resolve the conflict without causing a confrontation. Unlike people in a normal job, road crews live in each other's pockets – especially small crews like ours. I was nominally the 'Production Manager' as well as being F.O.H. engineer and so it fell to me to make sure that the show was up and running each night. The interesting thing was, for all his obstructive behaviour, Pete would often respond to a direct request and did not seem to take umbrage. He was, however, more often than not pretty drunk by the time they closed the truck doors on the last piece of lighting gear. I tended to be the most sober of the crew and would usually drive the bus back to the hotel after the show. Once we arrived at the hotel there was usually a bit of scrabbling about getting bags and stuff together to take into the place that we were staying in. Again, more often than not, it would be Pete bemusedly trying to decide if he needed a bag or not, or not being able to find something or other, and me that was standing around waiting for him to do this so I could lock the bus.

One night, in a small town in Austria, I got fed up with it. He was trying to sort out his case so he could just take the minimum amount of stuff in with him but he was very drunk too. I gave him the key to the bus and said, 'There, you lock it when you have finished', and went into the hotel.

I shared a room with Dave and we sat up for a while having a bit of wine and a couple of spliffs. In the morning I was awoken by a call from reception. It seems I had inadvertently parked the bus partly blocking an entrance and I had to move it. I told the woman that the people in the other room had the keys. A few moments later she called to say that they denied having the keys. I told her that I had left the keys with Pete in the other room and I could not move the bus without them. I got up, got dressed and went downstairs to go to breakfast. In the lobby I found Tom standing there with an Austrian policeman.

'He's got my passport,' Tom said.

'More fool you for giving it to him,' I replied heading towards the restaurant. The policeman chipped in at this point.

'Were you the driver?' he asked.

'Yes.'

'You must move your bus or we will tow it away.'

'I would if I had the keys,' was my response, 'I left the keys with his roommate last night.'

'Driving licence!' he demanded. I was clearly not going to get breakfast yet. The two of them followed me up to my room where Dave was still blissfully asleep. On the bedside table was a lump of hash. I grabbed it and woke Dave, handing it to him to get it out of sight.

'Too early,' he mumbled and put it back on the table. Knowing the police were just behind me I quickly put the lamp over the dope and got my briefcase. I handed the paper driving licence to the police who looked at it with the usual incomprehension shown by foreign police when presented with an English paper licence without a photo. Out of the window I could see the tow truck attempting – and failing – to hitch up the mini bus.

'Passport,' came the next demand. I had been here before, I thought, but the Austrian police were not as easily rebuffed as the East German ones had been. I produced my passport and held it up for him to see. He reached for it and I pulled it away. He held out his hand for it and I said 'No, you cannot have it.' I opened it at the front page and read it to him:

'Her Britannic Majesty's Secretary of State Requests and Requires in the Name of Her Majesty all those whom it may concern to allow the bearer to pass freely without let or hindrance and too offer the bearer such assistance and protection as may be necessary'. He looked at me, 'Property of the UK government, mate and I can see by your uniform you are not in the UK Government.'

'We are the Austrian Police,' he said firmly.

'Yes I know, just one step away from the jackboots, you boys,' I responded, although I am not sure he appreciated the inference.

By this time the tow truck had given up trying to move the bus and had driven off. Pete has also appeared holding the keys which he had, in his drunken state, gone to bed with!

'I must fine you a thousand Schillings,' the police told me.

'Why?'

'For towing away you bus.'

'But you didn't tow it away did you? It is still there. If the plumber comes round to fix your pipes, and goes away without doing anything you don't pay him do you?'

I was, however, not in a good position because he had Tom's passport. In the end I had to pay him and went out to move the van before finally going to breakfast.

Pete always managed to get very dirty during the day. Lighting is, in general, a task which usually gets you dirtier than sound does because there is a lot of metalwork to manhandle and shift not to mention all that crawling along trusses to focus the lights once they were up, but Pete seemed to be a dirt magnet. By the end of the day he was usually pretty much filthy. In Berlin there was (and probably still is) a main street on which the most elegant street hookers I have ever seen parade their wares. These are far removed from the sleazy scruffy hookers you see on the streets in the UK or France. They are usually very well dressed – or undressed - and it always amazed me, when we drove down there, that they were working the streets. The venue that we played in Berlin was at the end of this street and, at the end of the load out, caked in dirt as usual, Pete said, 'I'll see you at the hotel, I am going for a hooker,' and marched off.

The thought of this shambling tramp-like figure going up to one of those street women was so funny that we all burst out laughing. I was tempted to follow him just to see if he got rejected.

We finished this tour in Holland and, once again, Andrea came out to visit me. Matters were coming to a head back in the UK though, and with much heart wrenching, I finally moved out of the flat in Greenwich. I went to stay with Pete Reidling and his wife who were in a very civilised squat in the *Guinness Trust* buildings round the corner from Tower Bridge. It was not an ideal situation but it gave me some respite from having to find a place of my own and decide whether I should move to Amsterdam. I did not want to move out of the country because of my two children, but I also wanted very much to be with Andrea and the two things were incompatible. This was a big problem.

In the meantime I was working with *Encore* and managed to get over to Amsterdam for a week or so in between. There were no cheap flights in those days so it was all a bit expensive. I ended the year with a short burst of German gigs with *Chappo* and a few *Cockney Rebel* UK dates. But, at the end of these I was still no closer to working out what to do. My chest problem, however, did not seem so bad this time around – that was until I spent a day at the flat in Greenwich with the children. They had guinea pigs and I helped them clean out the cages. That evening I really felt bad and the coughing returned with a vengeance. I went to the hospital and was diagnosed as being asthmatic. All those times that the doctors had told me I had bronchitis were, in fact, asthma attacks. I knew, from my work at the hospital all those years ago, that this was often a symptom of allergies and I immediately suspected the cause was the guinea pigs in the flat. That was one problem solved anyway.

One thing that had changed, by the time I was back from tour, was that *Encore* had, bacteria-like, absorbed *Capital Sound* and now the directors were, Chris Mounser, Pete Kellet and John Tinline (owner of Cap Sound). I was no longer on that list. Of course it was all nonsense. Chris had never set up any company directors at Companies House and so it was just words on paper, but it spelled out for me the fact that I was no longer needed to be one of the driving forces of Chris' growing empire.

Dave Thomas Backline Tech LKJ 1990.

CHAPTER 26

Romania, Reggae, and A Vast Upheaval

I spent the New Year period at Andrea's flat in Amsterdam and it was only the longing to see my children and the need to work that drew me back to the UK; I could easily have stayed there. Steve Mather, who was handling Steve Harley at the time, had a few other acts on his books and asked me if I would go out on tour with Lynton Kwesi Johnson. I was not a big fan of reggae but I was to be joined by Dave Thomas (backline tech for Harley) and my friend Mick Tyas doing the monitors. Mick and I were a dangerous couple and shared a dodgy, and somewhat caustic, sense of humour. You could guarantee that, if I did not say it, he would and vice versa. He was also the best monitor man I had ever worked with. A few tours with Iron Maiden had honed his ability to get the monitors screamingly loud without feedback. This was one of the first tours I ever did where the main complaint from the band was that the monitors were too loud. Once you got them too loud, of course, turning them down to comfortable was easy. Mick had come out on that tour mostly because we were friends, and he had a little time to spare. This meant he did not have to watch his Ps and Qs as much as someone who is concerned about keeping his job. As a consummate professional he always did a great job behind the desk, but that was accompanied by a very offhand attitude. The lighting designer was Pete Hopkins from the previous year's Harley tour.

Lynton's backing band was the *Dennis Bovell Dub Band*. This was a superb band in many ways. Even I, who tolerated reggae at best, was impressed by their playing and Dennis' bass playing in particular. I did quite a few gigs with reggae bands when I ran the *Sleazyhire* sound system back in the '70s and early '80s. There was one band, called *Son of Man in Roots*, who continually hired me. I used to enjoy doing all the echoes and stuff that is the icing on the cake of dub music. One night we were all sitting backstage at a gig sharing a spliff and I asked them, 'Why do you always ask for me to do your gigs? All the people here are black, apart from me. I would have thought you would have had a black engineer by now, someone more into what you do.'

I was expecting them to say that I was cheap or that I was very good at the mix, and I had been quite frank with them about how reggae was not my first choice of listening by any means.

'You is the only white man effa got us stoned, man, innit. Respec,' came the unexpected answer. I thought back and realised that they had also sampled the same temple ball that had laid *Cayenne*'s keyboard player out. Made sense I suppose.

Anyhow, Dennis' band were a severely good act, although I did have a chuckle every night when Lynton sang these words from 'Di Great Insohreckshan', about the 1980 Brixton Riots.

> 'It waz event af di year
> An I wish I ad been dere
> Wen ri run riat all owevah Brixtan'

I *was* there. Mous and I were doing a reggae and poetry gig at the social centre just up the road from the Brixton Police Station. It was a peaceful day where we were. Lots of people getting up and reading poetry and small bands performing some fairly innocuous stuff. Nothing hardcore at all, in fact I believe they were even serving tea and cakes. Mous (our lighting girl) had gone down into the high street earlier to get some ice cream because it was so warm. At the end of the gig I came out of the hall to go and get the truck to load out and was immediately confronted with wall to wall police cars and guys in riot gear. At first I thought we were about to be raided and nipped back into the club to stash my dope tin. When I came out the second time there was a tall Rasta striding insouciantly down the street.

'What's going on?' I asked him.

'Oh Dey burning Brixtan, man,' he said and carried on down the road. Event of the year?

The first gig on the Lynton tour was in Gent, Belgium. I had been staying at Andrea's place and took the train down to Gent to meet the guys only to find no one there and no hotel booked. It seemed I was a day early! I checked myself into the hotel and called *Encore*. They were laughing to think I had arrived a day early, but the smile was on my face when they turned up late next day, having been stuck for most of the night on the cross channel ferry due to high winds. They were bedraggled and wiped out whereas I, on the other hand, was fresh, breakfasted and rested. When the show was over and we had started breaking the rig down I noticed that one of the lighting trees was still up with lights on it. This was right behind the stage right PA wing so I asked Pete to take it down. When I had finished stripping the stage left PA the tree was still up. I asked him again and thought he was just being bloody minded. After a third request he got two stage hands and dragged it out of the way – still erect. These particular trees were pumped up by using compressed air and it seemed that the valve that was supposed to allow the air to escape to let the unit collapse had jammed. He climbed up a ladder and took the lights off it but, by doing so, he lightened the load and so only managed to extend the main column further. We had loaded everything into the truck by now except this one stubborn tree. We tried to lay it across the top on the gear but it was just too long to go in so we had to leave it there. When we got to the next gig there was a dressing room liberally splattered with band and crew graffiti so I added to it.

> *'Peter the heater got a stiffy in Gent*
> *It wouldn't come down, so we left it and went'*

Lynton came in as I was finishing it, looked at it for a while and said:

'Seem like dere anudder poet on der tour.'

Anyhow the tour went pretty well. Every day I had to leave the hall when Mick ran the monitors up because they were louder than the front of house PA. There was a good deal of friendly banter going on between the band and crew too. Nelson Mandela got released from prison while we were on the tour and the news reached us on the day we played the *Longhorn*, Stuttgart (rather incongruously this was a country and western style gig, all decorated with cow horns and the like – as I said before Germans seem to have a penchant for the wild west as it wasn't). Mick was reading the paper when the band arrived and he held it up for them to see when they walked into the dressing room.

'Look, they've let him go now. What are you guys gonna complain about next then?'

At the end of the tour we were all sitting in a bar at the hotel, saying our goodbyes. Dennis turned to Mick and said, 'You are the best monitor engineer I have ever worked with.'

Mick smiled, 'Yeah. I'm the best monitor engineer you could never afford. I am only here because we are friends,' he said gesturing at me.

At the last gig another two trucks turned up from *Encore*. Chris had come out a few days before and said there was a short tour of Romania coming up if we wanted to do it. This was a much bigger thing so we loaded the PA into the first of these trucks, which was already packed with extra speakers. They had already unloaded the extra lighting gear from it into the truck we were using and the LKJ lighting rig went into that. We flew back to the UK for a couple of days to get our stuff together to go out to Romania seven days later.

These were turbulent times. Not only had Nelson Mandela regained his freedom but Romania had just been through a violent revolution – one which had seen the dictator Nicolae Ceauşescu first ousted, and then summarily executed along with his wife on Christmas Day 1989. Some point shortly after that the BBC decided that this poor, run down, country still traumatised by the events of the revolution in December needed something special........Rock for Romania, three UK rock bands, and a BBC film crew!

Things began to go wrong from the outset. We all arrived at Heathrow to fly out to Romania on the same flight. The rest of the flight was mostly made up of people off for a January skiing trip – the Romanian mountains being a cheaper option to the plush resorts of Switzerland.

There was a bit of a rumpus going on at the check-in desk with people clutching skis and being told there was no room on the plane for them because the bands and BBC crew were taking up a lot of the excess baggage space. At one point, one of the disgruntled customers came up and shouted at the organisers.

'You have ruined our holiday!' only to be informed:

'Well, we are working.'

An argument, which understandably did not impress the family, who were looking at the assembled bunch of musicians with distaste.

The plane was, of course, delayed and we sat for a few hours in the airport and at the terminal gate while it was all sorted. We were led down to the plane and asked to identify our baggage before boarding. As we pointed each piece out it was removed to go into the hold. The tour manager came on the plane and asked, 'Has everyone had identified their bags?'

The bands and crews were, by this time, fuelled with a few drinks in the airport lounge and so in a boisterous mood. Someone looked out of the window and saw Anne Nightingale standing dejectedly on the tarmac.

'Can someone go down and identify Annie, please?' someone shouted to a ripple of laughter. It seemed that in all the mess at the check-in desk her luggage had already gone missing.

When we arrived at the airport in Romania we were all escorted onto a bus to take us to the hotel. I had not really been involved in too many tours where the transport that picks you up at the airport is of the luxury standard, overflowing with free drinks, hospitality and scantily clad dancing girls – and this one was no exception. In fact it leaned heavily towards the Spartan in its lack of any form of luxury and comfort. This kind of set the tone for the rest of the week. We rattled through potholed roads on a suspension that seemed to be made of concrete, on seats with the bare minimum of padding or covering, but that did not dampen the mood of the people travelling on the vehicle.

There were three UK acts participating in this venture. *Jesus Jones*, *Crazyhead* and *Skin Games*. Only the first had any real previous experience of touring away from the UK. We arrived at the hotel, which was one of those big old fashioned affairs, and, after what seemed like an age, got checked in. There were quite a few of us. A five man sound crew, five man lighting crew, three bands, technicians, a production manager and a tour manager – not to mention the BBC crew and reporters.

The shows themselves were little better. It turned out that, not only were the bands doing this for free but the 'crews' they had brought along with them were also friends rather than pro road crews and, while they all got along and were trying hard, they lacked the experience and technical ability to deal with getting a band on and off a big stage in a tight schedule. The only other person, apart from the sound and lighting crew, who was being paid was 'DJ' who was

Mick Tyas - LKJ 1990

Lynton Kwesei Johnson On stage 1990 .

Dave with the Nelson Mandela Headline - LKJ 1990.

Romania desks.

Transport from the gig Romania.

Romanian PA.

Romania Lighting Rigger running the power from the railway line.

Matt Dowden Lighting Engineer and Tony the truck driver - Steve Harley 1990.

OPPOSITE: Nick and me (Zaphod Bebblebrox Impersonation Society) Steve Harley 1990.

Steve Harley onstage 1990.

employed by Jesus Jones to program and run the sequencers used during their show. The first show, in Timisoara, was delayed by bits of equipment not working and not properly plugged in. I was in charge of the PA and mixing the sound for *Skin Games* who were a pretty good act. *Crazyhead* and *Jesus Jones* had brought engineers so I had time to get back onto the stage to help sort out some of the chaos, but some of the guys they had brought along as crew had no idea what plugged into what. Not only that, but these were big gigs, huge auditoriums which were packed with people. People fresh from a revolution and banned from listening to rock music in previous years. The journey from the front desk to the stage was not a short one.

I have to confess that I was, at this stage, a bit stretched out emotionally. The whole business with the family had left me rather stressed, and I was doing far too much cocaine. All in all I was running a bit wild, and although I could cope on a normal tour, being plunged into this mess was a bit much. Mick was also a bit over the top so we played off each other and the result was the attitude clock got ratcheted up a few notches. On the first day we discovered there was not enough power to run the lighting rig so their technician climbed out of the window at the rear of the building and broke into a power box by the side of the railway line that ran past the rear of the hall. During that gig the singer from *Crazyhead* completely trashed the mike stand. I went back to complain and to point out we were not exactly in a place where we could get more stands if he kept breaking them, but I wound up putting it far more forcefully than I intended and we had a stand up shouting match. As the four-show tour wore on it all got worse. The food was awful and usually cold. The transport uncomfortable or non-existent – at one show we were left standing at the gig after the truck was loaded and there was no transport to take us back to the hotel. Luckily there was an empty truck and we all piled into that in order to get back. The second day we were in Bucharest, capital city of Romania. We did two nights there in a huge stadium and, while I was setting up, a girl came up to me and asked a few questions about the sound system. She was amazed by how it was wired up and how large it was. She was one of the stadium's sound engineers and I had already seen how primitive the equipment was there. I gave her a guided tour of the whole system and then she took me up into the little booth at the back of the hall where their desk was. For this huge hall they had a 12 channel mixing board and a set of graphic equalisers all marked in Cyrillic writing. There were a couple of her male colleagues there and they asked if I wanted a glass of wine. I said yes and was presented with a glass of syrupy yellowish liquid that had a severe kick to it. Wine it certainly was not. Her name was Mariana Vinau and she had a young daughter. Over the next few years we wrote to each other a bit and I sent her Christmas parcels of soaps and other stuff you could not get in Romania. After a while, though, we lost contact. While I was writing this book she got back in touch via FaceBook! Amazing how the internet joins things up more and more. We got back the hotel early that night because all the gear stayed up so we went across the road to a nightclub. This building was surrounded by people in uniform. Police or army, it was hard to tell. They were allowing in the well dressed patrons and keeping out the obvious lower echelons. We shouldered our way through the line with a single word, 'English!'

The whole thing had the air of a 1950s style club. There was a cocktail singer and a magician and it all looked like we had stepped back in time. We did get thrown out a while later though when the food arrived and a couple of the guys, who were a little more drunk than Mick and I, started throwing some of it around.

The second show in Bucharest turned into a big party with all of the bands on stage singing Neil Young's 'Keep on Rockin' in the Free World'. It was all filmed for the reportage programme and shown on BBC TV. There were many emotive speeches and one of the guys from one of the bands said, over the microphone:

'This has been the best week of my life.'

If you listen carefully to the BBC recording you can just hear Mick Tyas yell from the monitor desk, 'You must have had a life like dog shit!'

At the end of that show the pack down and load out seemed to take forever. It was quite late by the time we finally closed the doors of the truck. Exhausted and underfed we made our way to the troop transport buses and took our seats to head back to the hotel. Mick and I were sitting on the front two seats, and the Asian presenter of the BBC programme was standing in the door of the bus. We sat for a while like that and then Mick said, 'Why are we not going? The bus is full.'

The presenter turned to us and said:

'I can't decide whether to wait for my translator or go back to the hotel now.'

I stood up and took him by the lapels, lifted him bodily and placed him on the ground outside the bus.

'Wrong answer,' I said, 'There will be another bus along in a few minutes,' and I shut the bus door, sat down and said to the driver.

'Hotel, please.'

We had all had enough by then and I was fed up with the amateur way this whole thing was being run.

The last show was in Brasov – deep into Dracula territory. We set the gear up and the band and managers went off to eat. We, on the other hand, were presented with a selection of sandwiches. At that point I led a revolt of the sound and lighting crews, and we demanded to be taken to the restaurant to eat. They were surprised when they saw us arrive and order food, and even more surprised when we told them they could soundcheck when we were finished eating and not before. I suppose, for the Romanians, we were just workers and the musicians and management were the higher realm. That was how their society worked; the workers got the shit and the officials the cream.

After the show we were taken back to the hotel and told we had to leave at 2am to get to the airport. Since it was, by that time, 1am we decided we may as well have a shower and stay up.

Mick and I had saved a bit of toot and some hash so sat down to imbibe. There was a knock on the door and it was DJ, from *Jesus Jones*. He walked in bearing two bottles of champagne.

'I thought I would share this with the only other professional members of this whole crew,' he said, so we racked him out a line of coke and we sat around chatting. Finally we parted and got our cases together to leave. We faced a five hour drive to the airport in what amounted to a troop transport so I decided to take the duvet from the bed. I knew I would not get it through reception so I tossed it out of the window, intending to collect it on the way to the bus. When I got there I found the singer from *Crazyhead* picking it up and taking it to the bus. When I got on the bus we had an argument about it, like two schoolchildren. We were both drunk and I was fuelled up with a load of coke so I managed to separate him from it and retreated to my seat. I recall shouting at him, 'When you are back on the dole, where you belong, I will still be on tour. Remember that!'

We later apologised to each other – but not for many years.

There were so many people on this outing that this tour was organised into teams. I was running the sound team so I had to check all of my guys were on the bus and then, when each team had reported back, the bus could leave. When we got to the airport the tour manager for *Jesus Jones* realised that DJ was not on the bus. A quick check revealed he was not on the other bus either and the main tour manager called the hotel. It was early in the morning. He asked to be put through to the room, and when the occupant answered he said, 'Look, no time to explain. You need to get to the airport. Just pack everything and leave right away, grab a taxi and get to the airport. There is only one flight so you have to be on it. If you miss it you will be stuck here and we won't be able to get you out, OK?'

He put the phone down.

As he did so DJ walked into the airport, saw us and came over to our group.

'I saw the bus leave as I was on my way down so I grabbed a taxi and got him to drive me,' he announced nonchalantly. This means that the tour manager called someone else. Someone peacefully sleeping in a hotel room in a town riddled with bullet holes, with tanks still on the streets, soldiers and guns everywhere, just after a bloody revolution that had seen many people die, and the execution of the country's leaders. Not only that but he had told that random person he had to get out immediately or he would not be allowed to leave. Bet that woke him up!

It was a relief to get home, but when I got back to London, I flew into a shit storm which was partly of my own making, however. The first thing that happened when I arrived at *Encore* to unload the PA truck was that John called me into the office and said that they were no longer going to pay for my mobile phone or give me a retainer – both things that Chris Mounsor had offered me to get me to join the company in the first place. There had been a phone in the office, which for the previous two years, had never been billed. It was an oversight somewhere, but we had a live phone which we used to make international phone calls on. I called Andrea on it several times a week, Barbara called her family in the States and Danny would call his father in Israel too. We were not the only ones making calls on it, but I suspect the bill, had it ever arrived, would have been horrendous. While I had been away BT had caught up with this phone line and began to make noises about billing us. Chris managed to sidestep that but it prompted John into looking into the way the company was run and he decided that my perks were among the ones to go. Chris had, of course, never mentioned that he had made me a director – on paper at least – so he thought I was just employed as a part-time engineer. Shortly after this the results of my antics in Romania began to filter in. I was complained about from many quarters – *Crazyhead*, the BBC and the tour managers were not exactly lining up to join my fan club. Luckily Steve Harley had a few festivals and a tour to do so I was able to make myself scarce doing those and earn some money.

By the time we set out on the UK tour with Steve Harley the band line up had changed. Apart from Ian – who was still on keyboards – everyone else was different. Robbie Gladwell played guitars, Paul Francis was on drums, and Bill Dwyer on bass. I met someone on that first gig who was to become one of my closest friends, Nick Pynn, who was playing violin and acoustic guitar. We also had Matt Dowden running the lighting and Tom Scott back on monitors.

The second gig of the tour was in the *Assembly Hall Theatre* in Tunbridge Wells and in that I had one of the more bizarre encounters I have ever had. Having set up the system I was running it up with a CD and walking around the venue making sure I had the speakers positioned correctly to get the most coverage. A woman emerged from one of the doors at the rear of the hall and came over to me.

'It is too loud,' she complained.

'I am just running it up to test it, I won't be long,' I replied.

This was not enough for her.

'I am trying to work in the office next door. Don't turn it up so loud.'

I tried to explain that the only way to get it right for the show was to run it up now while I could still change things but she was adamant.

'What do you do?' I asked her.

'I am a secretary,' she replied.

'Well, I am a sound engineer. Why don't you go back to your office and secrete and I will stay in here and engineer sound. That way we are both doing what we are supposed to aren't we?'

She flounced off in a huff and I was just about to turn the PA back on again when she shouted back across the hall, 'I don't see why you have to have it so loud when there is only you listening to it!'

She had totally failed to understand what I was doing.

The question of volume came up again a few gigs later when we played the Worthing *Assembly Halls*. The PA was set up and there was a curious gap in the seat on the right hand side. There were two rows missing from the front. It all became clear when, just before the show, the attendants wheeled in a group of people in wheelchairs. Two days later I got a complaint that the show was too loud for these people and, 'because they were disabled they could not move further back'. I am not surprised it was too loud because they were sitting right against the PA. That was where they were put. The logic of that escaped me.

We ended that short UK section at the *Hammersmith Odeon* (or *Apollo* as it is now known). Jim Cregan, guitarist with *Cockney Rebel* in the days of 'Come up and See Me, Make Me Smile' guested on guitar, and Rod Stewart popped into the dressing room so it was quite a star studded day.

There were a couple of months off before we were due to go out on the European leg of this tour and I did a few gigs here and there for *Encore*. I also took the opportunity to spend some time with my children. I was driving back from *Encore* when I got a call from Andrea. She was staying with her parents in Hamburg and was upset that I had not called her on her birthday, a couple of days before when I was out with the children. The call was to be the end of the relationship and I was left on my own, living in a squat with a rapidly diminishing income. Things were looking pretty bleak at that point.

I spent a day at the old flat with the kids and then, when Val came home, went off to visit an old friend in the next street. Things were a bit frosty between Val and I so we could not really stay in the same room together for any length of time. I was round at my friend's house till the early hours of the morning, but the day's sojourn at the flat had played havoc with my lungs. I finally got home at 2am and felt decidedly wheezy. I then realised I no longer had my inhaler. I supposed I had left it in my friend's house so I had a cup of tea and went to bed. In the morning I felt even worse. I got up and sat on the sofa trying to get my breathing under control. One by one the people who lived there got up and went to work. One of their girlfriends was the last to leave, and she could see I was not well.

'Are you OK?' she asked.

All I could manage was, 'Call me an ambulance.'

A few moments later I was being whisked off to *Guy's Hospital*. Once they had stabilised my breathing a doctor came in and announced cheerily, 'You were lucky there. Another half an hour and you would have died.'

I had always looked on the asthma as a minor inconvenience and had no idea it was life threatening.

They kept me in for a week, but I knew that the Steve Harley tour was looming so I started to hassle them to let me go. In the middle of all of this Steve Mather called me up (they allowed mobile phones in hospitals then) and asked me if I wanted to do a tour with Donovan. I jumped at the chance. I had always liked Donovan and I thought that this could be a really good tour. Time was ticking on and we were due to leave to go off on the Harley tour. I finally persuaded them to discharge me, and the tour bus picked me up from the hospital, dropped me at the flat, and waited while I packed a case, and we set off on another tour. Straight from the hospital to the first gig – that is how to do it in style.

CHAPTER 27

The Long Arm Of The Law vs Sunshine Superman

At the end of the year I was offered a couple of weeks work with 'The Legends of Motown' tour. This was an *Encore* job and consisted of a few people who had been part of some of the Motown acts of the sixties and were now touring as facsimiles of the original bands. The gigs were in the larger discos and these establishments were of the 'no jeans, no trainers' school of 'bouncering'. The band's crew were all willing to dress up in smart clothes to do the show, but I was only rigging the PA so I would go in during the day, rig it and wait until the soundcheck was over. I would then retire to the hotel until I was called back to de-rig it and put it back in the truck. The upside of this was that I was not required to actually listen to this stuff.

Just before Christmas the tour was due to go to Swansea and I decided I would pop round to pick up some dope and coke for the few days away and drop some money in to my ex-partner to get some stuff together for the children. Luckily the man with the drugs lived quite close so I could do the two things in almost one hit. I drove the truck to the street where they lived and parked it. I then walked round to my friend's house. The curtains were still drawn in the house where he lived. I walked back and went towards the flat the children lived in, but then I noticed that her car was not there so I guessed she was not in. I turned round to walk back to the truck and when I was halfway to it a police car pulled up and two police officers stepped out.

'Where are you going?' they demanded.

'To that truck over there,' I said, pointing.

'Why did you turn around and walk the other way when you saw us coming?'

'I didn't see you coming,' I said, and tried to explain but they interrupted me.

'We think you smell of cannabis' (fair point, I had sat up all the night before smoking and doing stage plans) 'and we want to search you. Do you have anything on you we should know about?'

'No,' I replied.

They proceeded to go through my pockets and then through my wallet. I watched them flick through the notes and cards, past a small packet of coke and then back through it again. Second time round they spotted the single edged razor blade tucked into the packet and pulled it from my wallet.

'What is this?'

'Oh that. That is cocaine,' I said nonchalantly.

'I thought you said you had nothing on you we should know about.'

'Well, I did not think you should know about it.'

It was the wrong thing to say, of course, but I could not resist it and the look of incomprehension on their face was priceless. They arrested me, of course.

We climbed into their car and headed off to Greenwich Police Station.

'You don't seem very worried about this,' one of them said.

'Well I am not. What is going to happen? When you open that packet you will see there is hardly anything in it, and when you finish testing it there will not be anything left to present in court. I am going to appear in court and get fined an amount of money that will not even cover the costs of your wages and petrol. It will not affect my behaviour and the whole thing is a complete waste of time and taxpayers' money.'

'But cocaine is illegal,' he persisted.

'It is not a law I really believe in,' was my answer.

'You can't just obey the laws you want to and not the laws you don't.'

'Well, the government only passes the laws it wants to. It never passes any of the laws I want.'

He looked exasperated.

Donovan – Leeds Town Hall 17-01-1991.

Donovan and Damien Maddison backstage at Leeds 1991.

Ralph McTell at the 'Antik Hotel' 1991.

Johnny Jones - Donovan 1991.
Donovan in the Castle in Gent.

En route to Hamburg - Donovan 1991.

'I can't follow that philosophy,' he said.

'That is how you can be a policeman and I can't,' I replied.

So I made a statement, got charged with possession, got bailed and went back to visit the kids and then pick up some dope and coke from my friend – as I said, it would not affect my behaviour . I had to go back to the police station every month to report as a condition of bail. The first time I went to report I was called in to the CID office and was told they had lost my statement. They asked me if I could fill it in again. I said (with barely disguised irony – that was lost on them) that, as they knew, I took drugs and could not remember what I said. They then suggested that I signed a blank statement and they would fill it in.

'I may take drugs but I am not stupid,' I said. 'You write it out and I will read it and sign it if I agree with it. I left without signing anything. A couple of months later I was due to go off for the weekend to do some gigs in Denmark. This would take me over the date I was supposed to report on so I went in and told them I would be away in Denmark.

'You are not supposed to go on holiday,' the sergeant behind the desk said.

'I am working. I will come in when I get back the day after.'

When I came back after the gigs he said.

'They didn't miss you.' I asked him what that meant and he said he went and told CID and they did not care or ask him to fix a date to see me. I then asked what I should do about it. He told me to just go home and forget about it.

'Oh, right, so you can arrest me for skipping bail I suppose?'

'No,' he nodded. 'Forget it – we have your phone number. We can arrest you on the phone if we need to.'

And that was that. The case was dropped. Phew!

I went off to tour with Donovan at the start of 1991. I had met up with his manager Pat Hehir at the end of 1990 and we did a short run of UK gigs, which was to be followed by a longer spate of European gigs. This was probably one of the most unusual tours I did because it was just the two of us, two men and a guitar for the most part. We spent more time in bars and restaurants than we did in venues, and we got on very well right from the start. I was tour manager and F.O.H. engineer for this tour, but that was really quite a simple task too.

I only used three channels from the stage, one for Don's guitar, one from the Roland JC 120 amp and the last was for his vocal. I put on my spec for this that I wanted a minimum 24 channel board mostly because I did not want to find myself sitting in front of some cheap 12 channel piece of tat and struggling to get it to sound nice. At the start of the tour I just did a bit of reverb on the vocals but there was one song in the set which was itching to have more done with it. 'Sand and Foam' was on the 1967 UK release of 'Sunshine Superman' (although it appeared on the album 'Mellow Yellow' in the US). Don starts the song with a flowing arpeggio on the guitar and narrates the story of being burnt out after his first couple of hits and needing to go off on a holiday. He and Gypsy Dave were sent to Mexico and were told to 'go to Rosie's Cantina'. When they arrived there they were taken down the river to some grass huts where they stayed and relaxed. In the words of the preamble 'down the river came the marijuana, we smoked the marijuana and I wrote this song...' In the middle of the song he always played an instrumental passage and made monkey noises. One night I had good stereo echo machine in the rack so I punched in two different repeats and faded these in and out as he was doing the monkey noises. From then on I did it every night. I never said a word about it for ages - and neither did he. One night, several gigs into the tour I mentioned it to him while we were sitting having a drink after the show.

'You know I do those echoes in 'Sand and Foam' every night? Is that all right? Are you happy with that?'

Don looked at me for a moment and said:

'That was how I always heard that song in my head, but never told anyone. When you started to do that I was really pleased, but I never said anything in case it broke the spell.'

That was typical of Don. He was a gentle kind of person and we spent ages on tour just talking about all sorts of stuff.

The support act for most of the UK gigs was a great young singer songwriter called Damien Maddison. One night, at a venue in Newcastle, he completed his set and walked confidently off the stage with well deserved applause ringing in his ears. The back of the stage was curtained off and it was all very dark. He walked through the curtains – and straight off the end of the stage. Someone had removed the stairs that had been there when he walked on. He landed badly and it became pretty clear that he had to go off to the hospital where a broken foot was diagnosed. He said he would probably have to quit the tour, but Don would not have that so we took him with is in our car – crutches and all. Damien and I are still in touch and he is doing pretty well, still performing with two albums and many live gigs under his belt. He lives in Manchester and one night, during a jokey aside at one of the hotels, I said, 'Oh yes, you come from Psychedelic Birmingham don't you?'

That has been a running joke between us for the last 20 odd years. I sent him a copy of my band's last album when it came out and addressed it to 'The Psychedelic Birmingham Tourist Board' – and it got there.

A lot of the time, especially in Europe, I had to struggle with sound systems and other people's preconceptions about what constituted a sufficient spec for a Donovan gig. So many people said, 'It's just a folk gig. He does not need anything special.'

In Landshut, a small town just north of Munich, I arrived to find the mixing desk was at the side of the stage. I asked them to move it to the front of house and they refused. This led to a stand off. I was trying to explain that I could not get a good sound unless I could hear the speakers, and they said that most of the other acts were happy with it being there. In the end I made a bet with the house sound man. I said:

'I tell you what. I will blindfold you and then you can have a shave with a cutthroat razor. If you can shave yourself without cutting yourself, whilst not seeing what you are doing, I will mix from somewhere that I cannot hear the speakers.'

He gave in and moved the desk.

On another occasion I arrived to find that the main mixing desk was made by 'Soundtraks'. In the spec that I used to send out on tours I used to put the words 'Dynacord, Mitec, Soundtraks, or other similar makes of desks are unacceptable.' in large letters. I started to run the system up to see what it sounded like but the graphic equalisers did nothing at all. When I looked round the back I found they were not even plugged in. I called the man who had rigged it and pointed this out and he said he did not know how to plug them in. I went to his leads case, found the right cables and plugged them in. The same was true for the reverb and FX units. I was beginning to get annoyed about this. I managed to get the system to sound reasonable and did the gig. After the show the soundman came over and said, 'That sounded really good – you will see us again in a couple of days.'

'I don't want to see this desk again,' I said. 'Do you not have any proper mixing desks? Soundcraft or something like that?'

'Oh, I have a 16 channel Soundcraft in the van,' he replied. 'You specified a 24 channel desk and this is the only 24 channel we had!'

Typical. When faced with a choice between a desk with fewer channels, and a crap desk they chose the latter without even asking me.

'You don't do this for a living, do you?' I asked.

He shook his head, 'No.'

'Do you know how I know you don't do this for a living? It is because you are fat. If you did this for a living you would be thin because no one would ever pay you and you would starve!'

When we went to Munich it had snowed and was pretty cold. It was not good weather to be out and about but I called my American friend Rick, who I had known since the *Pink Floyd* days back in 1977 and invited him and his friends along to the show. After the show they came backstage and suggested we all went to 'The Tomato' for a drink. I said I had to take Don back to the hotel but I may join him there later and Don said, 'I'll come.'

One thing I had found out about Don was that he was a not a heavy drinker and I remembered an incident a couple of years back, when Nicky Bell, *Chappo's* lighting man, had got seriously drunk when we had gone with Rick and his friends to that bar. In an attempt to get back to the hotel that night Nicky had fallen over and Rick tried to help him to regain his footing. In the process he had seriously restructured Rick's nose. Nick was brought back into the hotel in a wheelchair. I was hoping that we would avoid this happening again. When we got the bar I divided my time between fending off people who wanted to buy Don a drink, and drinking Tequila Slammers with Rick. Charley, a large bear of a Bavarian, arrived in the early hours of the morning. It was his birthday that day and he had been drinking since lunchtime and was, therefore, seriously impaired when he got there. He topped this up with a few tequilas and by the time we all left he was practically unable to walk in any form of a straight line. We walked out of the club and he was bouncing off walls and street furniture in an oblivious state. Just to make things harder, the snow, which had fallen in the day, was now rapidly turning to ice. We rounded the corner to the taxi rank and there was only one taxi standing there. There were eight of us. Don walked straight over to the taxi, opened the door, and ushered Charley into it. He then turned to Rick, 'Make sure the driver knows where he lives,' he said, 'It is far to cold for anyone in his condition to be out on the streets.'

Every other star of any standing that I had worked for in the past would have opened the cab door got inside and left everyone else on the street, but this completely summed Don up. He cared for the wellbeing of a drunk he had never met before that day and with whom he had probably exchanged two or three words, and was quite prepared to stand out in the cold and wait for the next cab. A thoroughly decent man.

We did part of this tour with Ralph McTell as the support act. It was really more of a double headline and Ralph would come back on stage and do a duet with Don for one of the encores. Ralph was also a really straight up guy. He always managed to see the serious side of things. Sometimes I would sit and read the newspaper in the bus and point out something I would find funny and Ralph would always find the sympathetic side of the story. He travelled with Johnny Jones as his PA Johnny was a real character and had been around the music business for many years. We went to do a gig on the German side of the Dutch border and stayed in a hotel that both Ralph and Johnny had stayed in a few times before. They knew the hotel's owner very well and he came along to the gig that night. The hotel was in two parts, a conventional, small town 'German Gasthaus' with a series of self-contained chalets at the rear, and Johnny was in one of these. Don, Ralph, our German driver / TM and I were in the main building. The hotel proprietor asked us if we wanted to go out to a bar in Holland after the show, and most of us decided to pass on this offer. This was partly because it was a pretty sleazy strip club and that did not appeal to either Don or Ralph, and also because the following day we had a long drive to get to the next show. Johnny, however, was very keen and, when we got back to the hotel, he promptly set off with the hotel owner to go to the club.

The following morning Don, Ralph and I were sitting having breakfast when we were interrupted by the hotel's maid.

'You friend, he is in the chalets. He is dead!' she exclaimed.

'Dead?'

'Yes, dead. Come quick, help!'

This was all beginning to look like an episode of *Midsomer Murders* or something like that, but we all got up from the table and followed the quaking woman out of the French windows and across the lawn to the chalet in question. The door was open, and through it we could see the front room of the suite. There, sprawled face down, fully clothed, half on and half off of the sofa was Johnny, looking, for all the world, just like a scene from one of those cheesy murder programmes. The maid would go nowhere near him but Ralph walked forward and tapped him on the shoulder. Johnny stirred, half opened an eye and muttered, 'Whaaat?'

It seems he had made it back from the club very much the worse for wear, got to his chalet but not to the bedroom. He had spent the night face down, fully dressed, almost on the sofa. It took him most of that day to recover from his night out.

After the tour with Ralph, Don and I went on to do a series of gigs in Belgium. I had spent a lot of time with Don, probably more than I had ever spent with any of the people I have worked for. Some of that time was spent in hotel bars or restaurants and Don was a mine of stories from the early days of the music business. Back in the early '60s, when he was the UK's folk poster boy, he would be out on tour with 'pop' packages which included people like *The Walker Brothers*, *The Animals*, *The Kinks* and that whole pantheon of stars. We had played a gig at the end of Worthing Pier earlier that year and he told me about playing there on one of those tours in 1965, when 'Catch The Wind' was riding high in the charts. He said they turned up in big limousines – one for each band/artist. *The Walker Brothers* were in car in front of his and he watched as the car was mobbed by young girls. A large black box on wheels was pushed through the melee and a door, in the front of this box, was opened as it approached the car so that the car's passenger door could be opened to allow the band to step into the box. The door would then be closed and the box, containing the band, would be wheeled along the pier to the theatre at the end. Don said that there were breathing holes bored into these boxes and that the girls would poke notes and fingers through them, hoping to contact their heroes.

Don also talked a lot about being in India with the Maharishi, at the same time as Mia Farrow, *The Beach Boys* and *The Beatles*. He said it was a formative period of his life and that he had a taken a lot of good lessons and experiences from that time. He still meditates and it remained, for him, one of the most important and emotional times, especially since he was only 17 at the time and the whole world was so new. The stories he told about this are for him to tell and I only mention this to give some background to the events at a castle in Ghent.

The Belgian tour was a bit unusual. Belgium is a small country and the promoter decided we would be better off staying in one hotel in Ghent and travelling out to each gig and back to the same hotel each night. On one of the days we were due to film sequence for a TV show. Neither of us had seen this TV show but it was, apparently, one of the biggest shows on Belgian TV at the time. It was also unusual in that it used puppets to interview the guests. We were due to film this in the depths of a castle in the centre of the town. Ghent had been pretty badly damaged in the fighting during the Second World War, but this castle seemed to have either escaped unscathed or been substantially rebuilt. The castle, and the surrounding buildings, seems to be a small enclave of the old town

Dirty Rick Explains

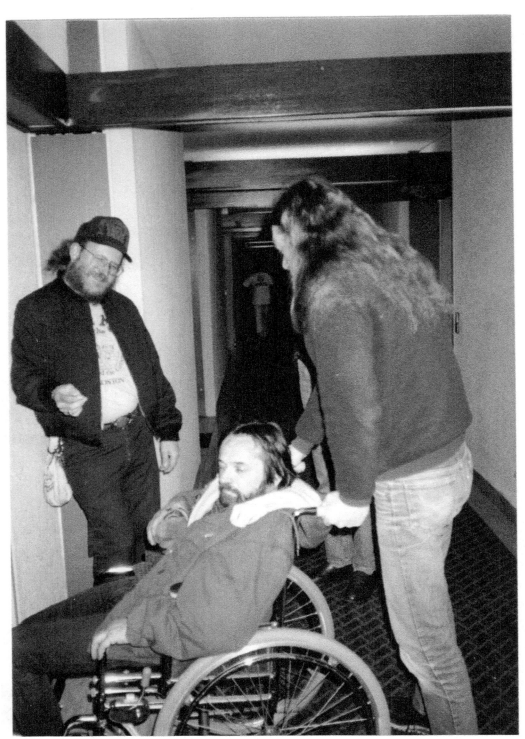
Nicky Bell in the wheelchair.

surrounded by many modern, square constructions. I had been to Ghent many times before but never seen this area until then.

We drove to the castle and met up with the TV crew. Don's first question, when he was shown the puppet that was to be his interviewer, was: 'Is this going to be a serious interview or are we going to treat it as comedy?'

He was assured by the producer that this was all serious and, although his interviewer was something that resembled a camel, all questions would be quite serious. He was asked to sit down on a stool with his guitar and the puppeteer would lie on the ground in front of him, holding the animal. It was a cold morning so Don was sitting there in his overcoat and the guy lying on the floor must have been frozen.

The interview went well at first while they spoke about his early career, and since this was about the time of the first Iraq War, about the Buffy Saint Marie song he played back in the sixties – 'The Universal Soldier'. The conversation then moved to the days in India with the Maharishi and famous friends. The puppet began to waffle on about 'Peace and Love, man. Oh Hippy, Trippy...'

Don was getting uncomfortable about this. I could see he felt that the man was not only making fun of him, but also mocking his friends and the whole Indian experience. I was standing behind the camera and he suddenly looked straight at me and swivelled his eyes to one side – the direction of the exit. I took the hint, and walked towards the side of the camera nearest to the exit. Don stood up and said, 'That's it. This is over now!'

There was a hullabaloo from the crew and producer, but I accompanied Don out of the castle and took his guitar as he walked over to the car and got in. The producer tried to remonstrate with me and suggested that I tell him to come back. I told him that I thought he had been offended by the way the interview had been conducted and we were going back to the hotel. I suggested that he called me at the hotel later that day.

Once back at the hotel Don and I went for lunch. Don reiterated his position on this.

'I am used to people making fun of me and my hippy past, but I will not have them using me to make fun of my friends or of a period of my life which was very important to me. If they had said it was not going to be serious I would have talked it through with them but they didn't do that.'

I asked what I should say to them when they called later and Don said he would think about it. We had a gig that night in Ghent itself so he suggested that we could talk to the producer there. Don went off to shower and rest, and I waited for the producer to call. When he did I got the usual claims of importance.

'This is the biggest show on Belgian TV right now,' he said. 'Yes, but it is only Belgium. Don tours the world and he feels he has been made fun of.'

In the end we agreed to meet at the gig, after the soundcheck. The producer ate some humble pie and Don conducted the interview there before the show – there was no mention of hippies.

Manfred Mann, Noel McKalla, Steve Kinch and Mick Roger onstage at Berlin.
Dave Thomas doing the backline duty - MMEB 1992.

Relaxing before the show in Copenhagen - MMEB 1992.

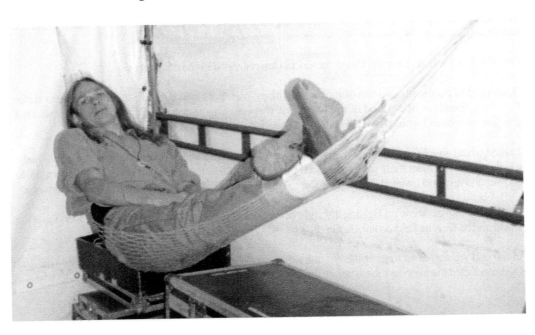

CHAPTER 28

Pool Attendants!

In 1989, after the first few gigs with Steve Harley I called Manfred. With typical caution his opening gambit was, 'What would you like me to do for you? I should say that I don't back people's projects, lend money or give out free studio time.'

I replied that I wanted to do something for him and arranged to meet him at the *Workhouse Studio*. He had not been on tour for a couple of years and I asked him if I could be considered to do the sound for him should he go out. I felt that a couple of tours with Harley, and generally good reviews for those, would stand me in enough stead to get a chance at the job. As it was he was not going on tour, but since Harley was doing the *Dominion Theatre* at the end of the next tour I invited him along anyway. He seemed favourably impressed with the sound and said he would definitely talk to me should he go on tour.

This did not happen for another year, and when the call came I was away on tour with Don. This meant that I could not do the production rehearsals or the meetings that preceded the tour. Manfred did, however, offer me the job of monitor engineer so I went off and did that.

Among the gigs we did were a series of festivals with the *Beach Boys* and *Allman Brothers*. At the bar in the hotel, after one of these festivals, Manfred was standing talking to Gregg Allman when a strange expression came over his face and he excused himself and left. He came over and joined us.

'I was just talking Gregg Allman,' he said, 'and he was saying he was much healthier now he had stopped snorting coke, freebasing and injecting heroin. I said that was good and he looked better than the last time I had seen him. He then said that he got all his drugs made up as a suppository now – and offered to make one for me!'

Manfred's singer, Chris Thompson, had left the band before this series of festivals and, on the previous tour, he had been sharing vocal duties with Noel McKalla, my old friend from the *Mezzoforte* tour. Noel had taken over all the vocals for these gigs and was sounding pretty good. I recalled that the first time I had heard Noel was when Manfred lent me of copy of an album Noel had made with his old band *Moon*. Manfred was very keen on swimming at the time and tried to get into the hotel swimming pool in the mornings if there was one. Noel liked this too. We flew to Sweden for a festival there and were met by a female tour representative. On the drive from the airport she was running over the itinerary and said that the band were staying in one hotel, and the crew in another. Noel asked if their hotel had a swimming pool and she said that it didn't. Noel said that they had to have a pool and could she change the hotel to one that did have one. After a few calls she did that and the crew were moved to the hotel the band would have stayed in, and given the band's rooms.

The drummer on that tour was Clive Bunker, former drummer of *Jethro Tull*, and the bass player was Steve Kinch. Steve was in the hotel lobby when Noel came down and asked the receptionist about the pool. The conversation went something like this:

'Hi, what time does the pool open in the morning?'

'We don't usually open the pool until 2pm, sir.'

'Oh, that is no good. I am with *Manfred Mann's Earthband* and Manfred likes to have a swim in the mornings.'

'I am afraid we don't have anyone to open it earlier, can't he have a swim in the afternoon?'

'We have to be at the soundcheck at 2pm, can't you see if it can be opened earlier just for us?'

'I will check it out for you.'

She took his name and room number and went off. After a while she came back again and said they would try to get the attendant in to open the pool at 11am. So far quite ordinary, but Steve had overheard all of this and went up to Clive's room. They decided to call Noel, and Steve put on a fake Swedish accent.

'Mr McKalla?' He started.

'Yes.'

'We have arranged for the pool to be open for you. Where shall we send the bill?'

'Bill?' said Noel, no one had mentioned a bill. 'What for?'

Clive Bunker MMEB - 1992.

Pool Closed - MMEB 1992.

'Well we had to pay the attendant to come in and there are the extra heating costs. Who shall we make it out to?'

'It won't be much will it?'

'It is about 10,000 kronor' he said.

'That is about £10 isn't it?'

'No you will find it is much more than that. There are roughly 10 kronor to the pound.'

'Oh. That is far too much. You had better cancel it.'

'It is too late to cancel it,' he said. Noel was beginning to worry now.

'We will have to charge you. Who shall we make the bill out to?'

By this time Steve was almost bursting with laughter and was having a hard time keeping up the fake accent. Clive said he should pass the phone to him. Steve did this saying 'One moment Mr McKalla, I will pass you to the hotel manager.'

Clive launched straight into the conversation in a broad cockney voice.

'Oi tosh, what's the problem 'ere. You asked for the pool to be opened and we have booked it. Are we gonna 'ave any bovver with you? Just tell me who to make the bill out to. Shall I make it out to the band?'

Noel agreed and then he hung up. Steve and Clive fell about laughing at this and then decided to call Manfred and tell him. Manfred then called up Noel and started asking him what this bill was all about. They kept him on the hook until later that evening when Steve and Clive confessed. The funny thing was that when they were leaving the hotel, there was a bill for early opening of the pool, but it was nowhere near 10,000 kronor.

The next day we all flew down to Cologne for a show there, and in the band's dressing room there was a hand basin. We got squares of black gaffa tape and stuck them to the bottom of the sink to look like tiles, made a miniature ladder and a diving board and then a small sign that said 'Pool Closed'. A few gigs later the crew were all issued with T-shirts that had been made up by the production manager. The front bore a picture of a person diving into a pool, and on the back it said 'Earthband Pool Attendants'.

CHAPTER 29

Sniffin'

The summer of 1991 was dotted with festivals for Steve Harley and Manfred along with a few odd shows with Donovan. I was jumping backwards and forwards between the UK, Scandinavia and mainland Europe. In the period after parting with Andrea I had been seeing a lot of Saskia, the woman I met in the *Fabrik* in Hamburg a couple of years ago. We had always tried to meet up whenever I had a gig in Hamburg, and what was a platonic friendship, had blossomed into something a lot stronger. We took a couple of weeks and went off to drive around England in my battered series one BMW. It was sort of like doing a tour without actually doing any gigs. We went to Liverpool and called in on my old friend and long time *Wooden Lion/Dogwatch/Last Post* roadie, Steve Wollington, who was looking after all of the instruments for the touring version of 'The Buddy Holly Story'. That summer we drove all over the UK, up to Scotland and over to Ireland when my BMW blew up as we entered Dublin, spewing oil all around. Luckily I had full RAC cover because I sometimes used the car on tour, and so I was able to get it recovered to London for repair.

The following year I set out on tour with *Sniff 'n The Tears*. I knew the name, but not the music and I had somehow got the impression that they were some sort of 'Disco' type outfit. I was pleasantly surprised to find they were not – in fact they were an excellent band. Paul Roberts, who was the lead vocalist and major songwriter had a vast back catalogue of great albums although they only had one hit, 'Driver's Seat' some years before. *Panasonic* had used this song on an advert for a car stereo and an opportunist record label had re-released it as a single again. It went back into the charts and the band went out on tour. Unfortunately the success of the single was not reflected in the number attending the gigs, and although we did some great shows there were not a lot of people there to see them. At the Bad Salzuflen gig, the one I had done so many times before with Roger Chapman and Steve Harley among others, there was the strange spectacle of the promoter apologising to Paul for the small audience, and Paul apologising back for not pulling enough people. Those who did go saw some great gigs though.

The band featured Les Davidson on guitar and vocals, Jeremy Meek on bass, Steve Jackson on drums, and Andy Giddings on keyboards.

We rolled into Cologne to play *The Live Music Hall* on the 12th February 1992. This was a great aircraft hanger of a gig – for small aircraft. All through the tour Sniff's backline guy had been waffling on about PA systems and how good Turbosound rigs were. I had not had many good experiences with them myself and was prone to saying, 'Plastic speakers in blue cardboard boxes,' to him, just to shut him up.

When we walked into the hall there were two stacks of blue Turbosound speakers, one each side of the stage.

'Oh look. Turbosound. Your favourite PA,' he shouted at me.

A tall thin man came over and said:

'Ah so you like my PA then?'

I repeated the 'Plastic speakers in blue cardboard boxes' quip at which he looked a bit crestfallen. The guy turned out to be the owner of the system and was based in Wuppertal. His name was Frank Trazkowski and we were later to become very good friends. First, however, I had to wind him up about his system. He was a very serious person, especially when working with the PA so winding him up was not too hard.

We actually had a really good gig that night and there were quite a few people there. When we had packed down and were heading to the bus to go I walked over to Frank to say goodbye. I took a few paces away and then turned back and said, 'Actually this is the best sound I have ever had from a Turbosound rig. It sounded really good – but don't tell anyone.'

As I walked to the bus Frank ran after me and said:

'Give me your number and come and do some shows for me.'

So I did. And that started something.

One thing I recalled, looking back at my photo album from this tour, was that Steve, the drummer, always managed to look really sad on every photo. It was a good tour though.

Paul Roberts, Jeremy Meek and Andy Giddins - *Sniff 'n the Tears* 1992.
Sniff 'n the Tears - Onstage - 1992.

The German Tour Manager, Les Davidson , Steve Jackson, Paul Roberts and Andy Giddings - *Sniff 'n the Tears* 1992.

Les Davidson - guitar - *Sniff 'n the Tears* 1992.

CHAPTER 30

Yes You Can Blow a Tyre

Straight after this tour we went out again with Steve Harley. I was touring with my favourite crew; Matt Dowling on the lights, Dave Thomas doing the backline and Iain Hargreaves doing the monitors. They were all really good at their jobs and great guys to tour with. Steve had released a new CD that year entitled 'Yes You Can'. It was his first album release for 8 years, and the first gig was to be the *Capitol* in Hannover. I spoke to Steve's manager when I got the itinerary and told him that the PA system in the *Capitol* was pretty bad, and that he should consider putting in a better desk and monitors for the first show on the tour. My thinking was, that if the first show went well, the rest would be easier. When I got there nothing had been done about it. If anything, the system was in a worse state than it was on the previous gig I had done there. There were channels not working on the desk, faders broken off the graphics, and the monitors had horn drivers broken. I complained about the system to Patrick, who was the tour rep from A.S.S., the company who were promoting the German tour. I was trying to explain that it was in their interest to get venues to make an effort. If I go to a gig and the sound is always bad I will not keep going there. People go to hear the music and they want it to sound as good as possible. When people say that audiences are dropping off for live music I always say that part of it is because the people who present that music seem to be just interested in getting the ticket money. Quite often this stuff is not in the band's hands.

Patrick said he did not know what I was complaining about so I took him to the desk. I put on a CD and panned it from side to side with the EQ off. There was a clear difference in the way each side of the system sounded.

'See?' I said.

'See what?' he replied, clearly puzzled.

'It sounds different doesn't it? The left side is much brighter than the right, and low mids on the right side are distorting because some of the speakers are broken.'

'Sounds OK to me,' was the response.

'Never invite me to your house to listen to your stereo then,' was all I could say.

During the show that night he came up to the desk.

'The sound is fine, I don't see why you got so upset,' he hissed into my ear.

'It only sounds this good because I am a good sound engineer and because I spent a while this afternoon tuning the system. If you put someone with less experience in it will sound completely shit and the gig will be ruined. But you can't see that can you?'

That argument coloured our relationship for a while after, and although I worked for A.S.S. a few times after I had moved to Hamburg, he was always very short with me. I don't think he ever understood that sound engineering was never really a 'job' for me; it was something I did because I enjoyed it and because I had a passion for music and the way it sounded.

The tour was going pretty well. The band were all on form and there were no tensions within the crew, which made it a nice easy trip. We were travelling in a 'split' minibus which had seats in the front and a closed off section at the rear for the backline. This was a pretty chunky, twin wheelbase vehicle, and, although it was not exactly the height of luxury, it was OK for us. It had been hired from Mark Warmsley, who was a man of many hats. He ran a rehearsal studio down by the Elephant and Castle and managed *Cardiacs* – one of my favourite bands.

We travelled through Germany and down to Switzerland. After the second show there, in Bern, I wandered into the dressing room and Billy, the band's bass player, slid a lump of hash across the table to me and said, 'Skin up.'

I dutifully rolled a spliff and was lighting it when Steve came into the room and complained at me for doing that in his dressing room. I apologised and left with Billy to smoke it somewhere else. This little incident came back to me at the end of the tour.

We worked our way back up through Germany, playing a small club called *The Musickgallerie* in Uelzen. We had played this place before and the man who ran the place was really very friendly. He wanted to take Steve off to a nightclub in his expensive sports car and came around with trays of vodka cocktails for the band and crew after the show. We were doing this with house or hired PA systems rather than taking our own with us so I had a very easy time of it in terms of physical work. It did, however, mean that I had a lot of setting up to do at some of the venues where the PA or the people who ran it were less than adequate. On this occasion, however, the crew were great and the system sounded really sweet. When they left they said, 'You will see us again next week, in Berlin,' which was a pleasing thing. Berlin was the last gig on the tour and it would be good to go out with a good sound and a nice easy

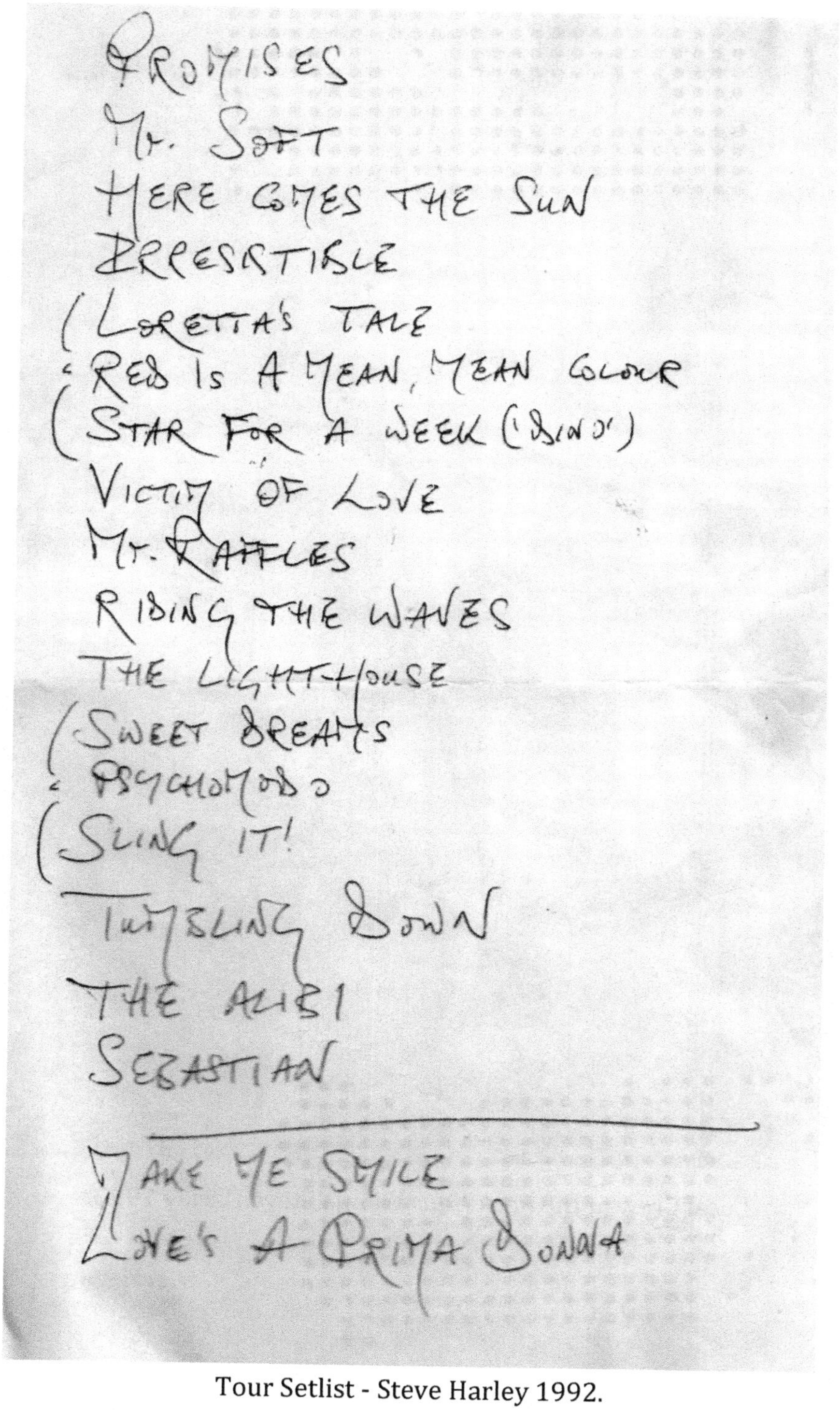

PROMISES
Mr. SOFT
HERE COMES THE SUN
IRRESISTIBLE
(LORETTA'S TALE
'RED IS A MEAN, MEAN COLOUR
(STAR FOR A WEEK ('DINO')
VICTIM OF LOVE
Mr. RAFFLES
RIDING THE WAVES
THE LIGHT-HOUSE
(SWEET DREAMS
'PSYCHOMODO
(SLING IT!
TUMBLING DOWN

THE ALIBI
SEBASTIAN

_____

MAKE ME SMILE
LOVE'S A PRIMA DONNA

Tour Setlist - Steve Harley 1992.

Local Crew at the *Rock Haus* Vienna Steve Harley 1992 .

gig – or so I thought.

We went off to Holland to do a couple of gigs there and thence to Hamburg to play the 'Grosse Freiheit' (Big Freedom) a gig right in the middle of the Reepherbahn, close to the place where the *Beatles* had played all those years ago.

It was on the way to Hamburg that we noticed a bulge beginning to appear in the nearside rear tyre. The Hamburg gig was on a Saturday, and we did not have the time to visit a tyre place to get it sorted out so we nursed the van to the gig and hoped it would last out until after Berlin, the next day.

It didn't.

On the way to Berlin the tyre blew. We were on the main Autobahn between Hamburg and Berlin and in the section which, before reunification, had been in East German hands. We pulled over and dragged out the spare tyre only to find that we did not have a jack or a wheel brace. We decided to drive to the next services and see if we could buy a wheelbrace there and we did have another wheel on that side. OK. We got there, but there was nothing there except a cheesy café and a petrol station with no means of fixing the wheel. We enquired about borrowing a wheel brace and jack, but no one wanted to do that. In the end we decided to set off slowly and see if we could get to the gig on five wheels.

To be honest, I was pretty convinced that would not work – and it didn't. We got a few miles down the road and the blown tyre began to shred. A few miles further on and the tyre, which was now a revolving mass of steel wires, lanced the good, inner tyre and the trip was over. We were stuck in the middle of a bleak East German Autobahn still a long way from Berlin. None of us had mobile phones that worked in Europe so Dave volunteered to hitch into Berlin and get the band to send something to pick us, and the backline, up. As the vehicle that Dave had managed to get a lift in disappeared into the distance we settled down for a long wait – and rolled a spliff.

We were all asleep when the PA truck hove into view closely followed by a breakdown truck. We loaded the backline into the back of the PA truck, climbed in ourselves and set off for the gig. It was already well past 7pm by this time and we did not arrive at the gig, 'The Latin Quarter', in Berlin until almost 9pm – we were due on stage at 9:30! The load in for this gig is at the side of the venue and we opened the doors to see a packed hall staring at a stage which had a PA, lighting rig and a sea of microphone stands – but absolutely no instruments. The band were glad to see us but could not understand how we could set up and do a soundcheck in a gig already packed with punters. I walked to the desk thinking exactly that too. Dave was frantically setting up the kit and the band themselves were up on stage getting their own stuff together while Matt was focussing the lights. The sound would be a bigger problem. Front of house sound can be done, at a pinch, in these conditions. I had been doing sound for these guys for five years by then so I had a pretty good idea of how to set it up, but for Ian, who had to set up eight mixes that he could not hear, it was going to be a nightmare.

I was greeted at the desk by a cheery smile from the rig's engineer, 'Hi, remember us?' he beamed.

It was the sound engineer from 'Musickgallerie' and I recalled then that he had said he would do the Berlin gig. Oh well, I thought, at least it is a decent PA. I looked down at the desk and the marking tape looked very familiar. On closer inspection I realised it was my writing.

'Is that my tape from the last gig?' I asked.

'Oh yes,' came the response.

'So have you not used this desk since then?' I was beginning to see a glimmer of hope for an easier ride here.

'Oh yes, we have used it...' Damn ..... 'But I made a note of all of your settings and put it back the way you left it.'

Boingggg! That was the sound of my hopes going through the ceiling. I looked at the desk and it did look like the sort of EQ I would do. I decided to trust this man, after all, it would be easier than kicking off with a flat desk. I have done that in the past and it is not easy at the best of times.

I went up onto the stage. Ian was standing there looking in disbelief at his board. They had done the same thing to him. We went out onto the stage and tried out the monitors and they sounded perfect. Matt was up in the lighting rig doing some focussing and Dave was still putting the drum kit together, but after a hasty discussion we all agreed that, so long as everything went OK we could kick off in 15minutes – just 20minutes after loading the back line in.

I have always mixed from the gain pots. Let me explain to the non sound tech people. At the top of the desk there is a knob called 'Gain' and that adjusts the level of the signal coming into the desk. You can adjust this so the meter reads '0' and a lot of engineers do, but I like to get the output fader at the bottom end of the desk to around -10Db. That way all of the faders on the desk are in a straight line and I feel the channel is operating at its most efficient. It is not because I like the look of it. Setting things this way gives me more 'headroom' (I can give the channel more volume when I want it – for a solo for instance) and, importantly, I always know where it should be returned to. That way I avoid the problem of everything gradually getting louder. This paid dividends here because I knew exactly where to line up the faders to get back to the mix I had in the previous gig.

I went backstage and there were some tense faces.

'What do we do?' I was asked 'can we sound check?'

'We won't need a soundcheck' I answered, 'Onstage in 15 minutes, I think.'

I went and found Steve and told him that we could go in 15 minutes but we then discovered that his acoustic guitar was still in the hotel. They hastily despatched a runner to go and get it and, once it was tuned, nerves steadied and sinews set I fired up the intro tape and the band marched onstage only 20 minutes late!

I stood back from the desk and crossed my arms – flying on blind trust. Faders at -10Db. And it worked. The band sounded pretty good. I gave the guy a big smile, and then started doing all the little tweaking things you have to do at the start of a show. Not a squeak of feedback from PA or monitors; the show went flawlessly. At the end I shook the man's hand in gratitude and went backstage. 'Come in,' said Steve, 'have a glass of wine, roll a joint.'

Switzerland was forgiven then.

That was the end of that tour. The minibus, with two new tyres on it, trundled off to England, after dropping me off in Hamburg to stay with Saskia.

Iain checks the tyre pressure - Steve Harley 1992.

Kevin Ayers - France 1992.

CHAPTER 31
Ayers and Places

S teve Harley's agent also looked after Kevin Ayers at the time and he asked me if I
would tour manage and do the sound for their European tour. Kevin's music always
had a special place in my heart. Right from the early days of *UFO* and *Middle Earth* I
had enjoyed listening to the first line up of *Soft Machine* and I can still recall listening
to them playing stuff from their first album with Kevin laconically repeating 'We Did It
Again' over and over whilst Mike Ratledge's keyboards wove around Robert Wyatt's frantic
and skilful drumming. At the time people eulogised over Ginger Baker ('Toad!', I hear you
shout) and Keith Moon, but Robert Wyatt was the first drummer that ever impressed me with
the kind of complexity and skill that could turn a beat upside down and then put it back on its
feet again.

I had also seen Kevin as a solo artist many times. At a theatre in London somewhere where the
curtains opened to find Kevin and Archie Leggett sitting on a stage playing chess with half
bananas. Kevin reached over to Archie's side of the board and ate one of his 'pieces' – and
they stood up and started playing. I could also vividly picture the gig at the *Rainbow Theatre*
where Kevin came on alone for the encore and sang 'Falling in Love Again' at the piano,
before Ollie came flying in on a rope, dressed, if I recall, in a striped jersey or shirt of some
kind that made him look like a demented bumble bee. Frantically playing the guitar solo from
'Dr Dream', he crashed into the back of the stage and then the wings before being lowered
onto the ground and somehow inflating his jacket to complete the bumble bee effect. Of
course I jumped at the chance of doing the tour.

As I started to write this chapter I heard the news that Kevin had passed away in his sleep at
the age of 68. For all the trials and tribulations of the tour I still had an incredibly soft spot for
him and his music, and it is hard not to let the fact that he has died not colour the stories that

follow but I will endeavour to tread an even path. I had suggested that Dave Thomas, Harley's backline guy, came out with us to look after the instruments. That seemed OK with the management, but Kevin vetoed it on the grounds that 'Hendrix only had one roadie' so it was just going to be me then. I decided that I was not going to get into humping the gear in and out on my own, and told the band they had to do it themselves. The band consisted of Kevin Ayers, Ollie Halsall on guitar and vocals, Claudia Payo on keyboards, guitar and vocals, Marcello Fuentes on bass guitar and Enrico Villaframe on drums. The last three were from Argentina and were all superb musicians.

One other difficulty was that I was not going to be picking up any money on the tour. All the tour fees had already been paid to the agency in London, so I was only picking up the odd bit of expenses at gigs. I was told I was not allowed to give any of this to Kevin or the band but to bring as much back as possible. We had a sleeper bus booked for the tour, but there were no hotels for the days off. It was not exactly easy to spend a day off in a car park with no shower or proper toilet, but that was how this had been set up. The bus was owned and driven by Rainer Ravelin from Hamburg. He had previously driven for one of Harley's tours so we knew each other quite well.

The first port of call was Amsterdam for a radio interview. This was just for Kevin and Ollie and was supposed to be just an interview about the album Kevin had just put out – 'Still Life with Guitar'. When we arrived at the studio the interviewer asked them if they could play a few tracks live in the studio. Kevin responded saying that this was an electric tour and they did not have any acoustic guitars. The studio offered to get some so Kevin agreed, but only if the studio took us all out for a meal that night and got us a hotel. Deal done, and a runner was despatched to get two acoustic guitars. When the runner returned he had two guitars but they were both right handed and Ollie was left handed. Ollie was unfazed by this, as usual, and just turned it upside down and played it that way. Now I had seen Ollie do this with an electric guitar on the John Cale tour a few years before, but here he was again, playing the guitar upside down in exactly the same way he played when it was the right way round and picking it with his fingers – not using a plectrum! Astonishing – how can anyone do that?

It was not to be an easy tour. We headed down to do some shows in France and there were some tensions within the band. I had been told that they had all been paid before the tour and that they knew there would be no hotels, but they were all asking for money for food and for hotel rooms on the days off. Luckily there were not too many days off and we managed to shower at the gigs at least. Food was also provided at the gigs so that staved off some of the problems. Kevin and Ollie had both been living in Spain for a long time and spoke fluent Spanish. One night, when I went to bed, I heard Kevin and Ollie having a furious argument – in Spanish – punctuated by swear words – in English! Both of them were prone to drinking too much although this only occasionally affected the gigs. The set would start with the band taking to the stage and playing a couple of chords over and over until Kevin joined them and launched into the song. One night he was a bit too wasted and just kept playing the chords. On the desk tape for that night you can clearly hear Ollie shouting,

'Play the fucking song, you cunt!' just before Kevin lurched into the right chords. The general

Marcello Fuentes, Enrico Villaframe and me - Kevin Ayers 1992.

Claudia Payo - Kevin Ayers 1992.
Marcello, Kevin and Ollie.

Dancing in Rothenburg - Kevin Ayers 1992.

Kevin Ayers onstage 1992.

drunkenness also meant that they would leave the rear lounge of the bus in a mess and Rainer was a very tidy person. Every morning he would complain bitterly about the state of his bus. He would, however, often join me on the front of house desk during the show.

'In the morning, when I clear up their mess, I fucking hate them,' he said one day as the show started, 'and then I hear music and I forgive them everything – until the next morning.'

After a few shows in France we went back to Belgium, but there was a day off between the Rennes gig and Brussels. Rainer said he could get a cheap hotel, just outside a town called Beauvoir, one that he had used on some of his non-rock and roll tours and the management agreed so we all went there. This was close to Mont St Michael – the famous monastery on an island off the French coast (the same as the one in Cornwall, the land for which was given to the French Monastery in 1067 after they gave support to William in his invasion of 1066 – bit of history for you). Rainer decided to take us all over to the island for the day.

From the distance this looks like a picturesque and stunning place, but when you get there, you find a mass of tourist tat, rubbish fast food restaurants and all the clutter of modern day-tripperism. I was quite amused by this dichotomy, but Kevin seemed embarrassed to be there and Ollie was looking decidedly glum. On the other hand, the three Argentinean musicians were happy to be there.

It was the same when Rainer had stopped off at town called Rothenburg ob der Tauber. This place was held a special importance to the Germans and especially for the Nazis because it signified a 'typical idealised German town'. They stationed troops there during the war and when the US troops were about to take the town they were ordered not to use artillery shells so as not to destroy it. It was rebuilt after the war and it certainly was a very pretty place. I found it interesting, but both Kevin and Ollie had no real wish to be there on the tourist trail. It did not help that is was a dull wet day.

The photo shows Claudia and Marcello dancing in the rain with Enrico in the background under an umbrella, and a dispirited Ollie looking on.

When we arrived in Germany, Kevin began to get more depressed. He did not really like German food, and the thought of playing a few gigs there brought him right down. I had been manipulating the band's rider and keeping the spirits hidden away till after the show, but in the first gig both Kevin and Ollie started asking for the tequila that was on their list. The promoter was in the room at the time and I said, 'Oh, he will bring it in later. It is all arranged.' I turned to him and suggested he just brought a couple of glasses right now.

He jumped in, however, and suggested they could have a bottle right now.

'We only want a couple of glasses,' Ollie replied. 'We won't drink it all before the show.'

Needless to say they did – with predictable results.

After this we got Kevin a day room to let him sleep a bit because he was beginning to look very down and tired. When Rainer went to pick him his for the show he cheerfully announced, 'I've drunk everything white in the mini-bar.'

That didn't work then.

In Holland they were supposed to be playing on a bill with five other acts in a mini indoor festival. They were due to take to the stage as headliners at midnight, but neither Kevin nor Ollie fancied that so Kevin told the promoter he was ill and really needed sleep. This prompted the guy to move them to an earlier slot. Kevin also asked for a doctor and one was duly called. What he was hoping for was a doctor with a rock and roll attitude that he could play up to in order to get a few pick me up pills. The doctor had other ideas though, and decided he had the onset of flu or a cold and gave him a B12 injection in the backside!

A friend of Kevin's did turn up later that day with a couple of grams of coke – much to Kevin and Ollie's delight. Down came the mirror from the wall and they were gleefully snorting huge lines of it when the promoter visited his 'sick' star. He took one look and turned around and slammed the door. Kevin's cover was blown then, and at the end of the night when I went in to speak to the promoter, he was very angry about the way Kevin had behaved. I really could not say a lot to placate him.

There were a couple more gigs in eastern France after that and then we were due to head up to Paris. At the last one before Paris a couple of women arrived for Kevin. At the end of the show Kevin announced he was going back to their flat to spend the night with them and he would take a train to Paris the next day. I reminded him he had a radio interview in the afternoon and gave him all the details about where to go and what time to be there. I provided him with his train fare and we headed out to Paris. Kevin did not make the interview. I was not really surprised. He did not want to do it and was far more interested in the women. Worn and frazzled as he was, he still had that beguiling attraction that drew women to him. When we arrived at the gig the French record company were seething, furious that Kevin had missed the interview.

'He is a grown man,' I told them. 'He makes his own decisions. He is not some kid who is just starting out and he knows the score. I suggest you sort it out with him.'

We did two shows in Paris and, at the first, Daevid Allen, the *Gong* alumnus, turned up. Marcello pulled me to one side, 'That Daevid Allen?' he asked. I nodded yes and he looked shocked. 'He look like my grandfather.'

We all went to a restaurant after the show for a meal. The restaurant was completely deserted apart from us, and Kevin's English manager, who had flown over to argue with them about money and hotels. While this was going on someone managed to sneak in and steal my briefcase with my DAT recorder in it. Even worse it contained mine and Kevin's passport and some money Kevin had given me to look after during the show. God knows how the thief had managed to steal the case with so many eyes about and no other punters.

We came back to the UK and the tour ended with a show in the *Shaw Theatre*, on the Euston Road, London. Despite my requests, the management had declined to put in a system and so I was forced to use the house rig which was set up for a theatre production. They did bring the desk into the auditorium, but the facilities were limited and some of the sends were patched into speakers I did not really know the location of. During the show there was some feedback – the first I had on the whole tour and Ollie, a little drunk and coked out shouted at me from the stage. After the show I went backstage and told him in no uncertain terms that I had 'put up with enough shit on this tour and that, if we ever worked together again and he repeated that behaviour I would come back down onto the stage and sort him out.' It was an annoying end to the tour. The German bus, which had carried us around for the tour was booked to go off on the UK leg of the next Steve Harley tour two days later, so Rainer had dropped the band at the venue and left to clean the bus and launder the sheets. At the end of the show I drove away from the venue in my car and I saw the band walking down the road to the hotel, carrying their instruments. The management had not even arranged transport for them! No end of tour party or anything. It was an unfitting end to it all really and I felt bad about the way it had been done, and about my own outburst at Ollie. I somehow saw Ollie and Kevin as lost children whose bodies had managed to grow into adulthood without the incumbent mental responsibility of actually growing up. I felt even worse when, one month later, on the 29th May 1992 Ollie was the victim of a massive heart attack and died. I was told that he had gone back to Spain after the tour and was freebasing when it happened.

Right now, writing this just after Kevin has also died, I realise the world has lost two very creative, if damaged, people. Ollie had the musical ability to have been a world class guitarist had he only managed to stay sober enough to make it happen. Kevin wrote and sang some amazing songs in his beautiful baritone voice, but was just never interested in fame. I have a desk tape from the Paris show which illustrates just how good they were together, but then we all touch this world in one way or another and sometimes fame and fortune rips the heart of an artist. So many people go from youthful creativity to jaded, clichéd, commerciality. The tape shows them flawed, but still glowing, and I felt they were on that stage to light a flame in people's hearts, and not to put petrol in a limousine.

Fury In The Slaughterhouse - Steve Harley 1992.

CHAPTER 31

Can You?

W hen we set out on another UK tour with Steve Harley I did not realise it was to be my last for him. Things were a little strained between the management and me after the Kevin Ayers tour. They did not blame me for the problems on the tour, but we were not on as friendly terms as we were before. There was a matter of some money, which was owed me at the end of the tour and which I could see being swept under the carpet during the current tour.

I had laid down a few ground rules for this outing, one of which concerned Dave Thomas, who was the guitar tech and backline guy. Dave was diabetic and I insisted that we had some food, tea and coffee available at every gig when we arrived. I did not want much, a few sandwiches, cans of coca cola, tea, that kind of thing because he needed the carbohydrate and sugar sometimes to stop him becoming hypoglycaemic. In the UK there was a tendency for promoters to not bother with this stuff even though it was on the 'rider' and to just offer the crew some cash to cater for themselves. I would normally not worry too much, but I knew that, given the choice between food and cash, Dave would take the cash and not eat and that was a dangerous situation. Apart from that we had a support band, a German act called *Fury In The Slaugherhouse* (a title referring to the horse hero from the American TV series *Champion the Wonderhorse* who had been renamed 'Fury' when the series was translated into German. The series - by whatever name - ran from 1955 to 1960). They were a nice bunch of guys and we got on well, but they had been promised they could put their equipment in the truck that was carrying the PA, lighting and Harley's backline. That would have been fine with us had there been enough room for it, but it was a very tight pack and we barely managed to get all our gear in it.

The PA was provided by *ESS* from Nottingham so I had no idea of the physical size of the boxes or what was being provided other than the fact that it fitted my specification. The band's manager seemed to think we were deliberately not allowing them to put their gear in the truck and complained to Steve's management and the whole thing got a bit contentious. I invited Steve's manager to come and watch a truck pack so he could see for himself how tight it was, but he never did, and instead of taking the logical step of trying to get a larger truck, just insisted I tried to get it in. The tightness of the pack meant that we had to draw 'maps' of each layer with every box having an allocated place in the scheme of things. This tightness proved to be a godsend when we played *the Manchester International II* because we had sent out the bass amplifier, but someone in the crew had conveniently hidden it - hoping to steal it later, no doubt. When it did not arrive to take its place in the jigsaw we stopped loading and went to look for it, and so uncovered the attempted theft.

Tensions rose when we drove all day to get from Edinburgh to Dublin and were told it was a 'day off'. A day off, in my opinion, is sitting by a hotel swimming pool with a cool cocktail in your hand, not slogging down roads, negotiating ferries and armed checkpoints to get to the next town! It did not help that I was still involved in a separate altercation with Steve's manager about the outstanding money from the Kevin Ayers tour earlier on that year. This was not proving to be a very happy tour.

The music, however, was really good. Steve and the band were really on top form and the PA was pretty good too. The first gig was in Nottingham, and I met Richard John, one of the owners of *ESS*, there. He turned up at the second gig, and then the third. I began to wonder if he was a Steve Harley fan so I tackled him in the hotel bar that night. He was with a small group of people I did not know, but I walked up and said, 'How come you are coming to so many gigs?'

'I am just showing the system off to some potential clients,' he replied. 'After I saw the first show I thought I would invite my potential clients along to some shows on this tour because you make my PA sound so nice.'

I was a bit taken aback by this, not a reply I had expected, but I was pleased to get the compliment. He said he was puzzled by one thing and that was why I took four of the pan control knobs off at the start of a song called 'The Alibi'. I explained that I cross-panned the violin and keyboards during that song and the pan pots were too close together on this desk. My fat fingers just would not fit!

We left Dublin to drive to Reading, catching the overnight ferry from Dun Laoghaire. Matt made a sizeable dent in the bar stock on the ferry and was quite the worse for wear by the time we trooped back to the car to complete the drive. He was, in fact, fast asleep by the time we drove off the ferry and were pulled over by the customs. The officer opened the rear door of the car to rouse him and he stared back at him, bleary eyed. He had already asked us what we were doing and where we were going , and we had told him we were Steve Harley's road crew. 'And what do you do?' he asked Matt.

'I'm a fucking lighting designer,' he snapped, 'what do you do?'

Wrong answer. The customs man hauled Matt out of the car, got him to point out his luggage

Steve Harley onstage at Weston Super Mare - 1992.
Tyred and Emotional.

and subjected him to a lengthy search.

Once we had Matt and his luggage back in the car we set off for Reading. Matt was soon asleep again, but after about an hour of driving, we burst a front tyre – at about 100mph. We slewed to a halt at the side of the road. Matt slept on. We unloaded the car, retrieved the spare wheel and jack. Matt slept on. We changed the wheel and reloaded the car. Matt slept on. We got back in and Dave rolled a spliff – Matt woke up.

'Are we there yet?' he asked.

At the end of that tour I basically moved to Hamburg full time. I had thought that I would still get work from the various people I knew in England and there were a few intimations that that would happen, but in the music business, you need to be there, buying people drinks and oiling the wheels. Saskia and I moved to a new flat in the Damtor district of Hamburg, and I became a resident of Hamburg.

CHAPTER 33

Leaving Germany

So that was, in fact, pretty much that for the kind of touring I had been doing up till then. The phone did not ring with offers of tours, and I had pretty much burned my bridges with Harley's manager. The row about the Kevin Ayers money was still going on when I met Dave Cockburn, an old friend who ran a fleet of tour busses and trucks. He had hired one of these buses out on a Harley tour and it had got damaged. The management would not pay for the repairs so he was a bit pissed off with them (which was the reason that we wound up using the minibus without a jack on the last tour).

We went out for a drink and I told him about not being paid for the Kevin Ayers gig.

'I am going to buy a can of brake fluid and pour it over the bonnet of his Range Rover,' I said (that would ruin the paintwork), 'If he does not pay me he will have to pay to get it resprayed.'

'Don't do that!' Dave exclaimed, 'Give me a call, I have loads of it in the garage, I'll come over and help you.'

As it was I did get paid, but after that I was not in the frame for the next outing. I was, however working with *LTT* (*Litch und Ton Technic*), the sound and light company that was run by Frank Trazkowsky, the man I had met when I was out with *Sniff 'n' The Tears*. They were OK, but really had no idea how it was done by the bigger companies. I explained about making looms and using one plug to connect the desk instead of 40. All the short cuts that pro systems used. They began to get more work, mostly because they worked hard and did a good job, but it was still a bit low key. It was all a bit exhausting too. I would get on a train in Hamburg and then travel down to Cologne, do a gig and get the night train back to Hamburg. We did have a few tours – several with the band *America*, who were great fun to work with, and some with Lynton Kwesi Johnson, as well as some European acts. The trouble was that all

I was doing was building the system and letting someone else mix. All the fun for me was mixing it. It was OK with *America* because Bill Crook, their engineer, was spot on every night but sometimes I was working with someone who should not be allowed to mix cement, let alone music. It was all a bit too much like work and not like the fun it was before.

We got a boost when Frank pitched for some gigs with the bands that the German wing of *EMI* were promoting. We were sitting in a café somewhere and he was on the phone to the tour manager. The guy must have asked him about the crew, and Frank mentioned me.

He then said, 'Yes, he is sitting right beside me. I will pass the phone to him,' and gave me the phone.

The tour manager turned out to be Alex Koerver, who had been with me on several *Chappo* tours, and, as a result, we got booked to do some work with these acts. I wound up working with an odd, Swiss/German band called *The Secrets Of Industrialised Noise*. They had their own sound man, but he was also trying to control a lot of the onstage effects via a long MIDI lead as well as running the samples from the desk. After a few gigs he realised that this did not work well. The MIDI lead was too long and things kept dropping out so he moved onstage and I took over the mix.

Saskia was, by this time, also pregnant with our first child. I turned down all the shows that were offered to me around the time of the forecast birth date, but the baby was stubbornly late in arriving. One act I had done a bit of work with was Marla Glenn, an androgynous female vocalist with a smoky voice and a great backing band. My old friend Dave, who had done the backline for Steve Harley, was doing backline for her too, but the sound engineer, provided by the French management team, was pretty awful. I spent most of the gigs quietly tweaking the graphic equalisers to get the sound back to 'reasonable'. When I was asked to go down to Munich with some backline for them and take over the sound duty I jumped at the chance. The gig was a good two weeks after the baby was due so I thought it had to be OK. As it was, on the day I was leaving, the child had still not been born. I drove down to Munich – a good 6 hour drive – stopping every now and then to check in. Still no baby.

I got to Munich and then found that their old sound engineer was still working for them so, for me at least, it was a wasted journey The following day I delivered the vehicle back to the hire company and took a taxi back to the hotel to pick up my bag and head off to the station and a train back to Hamburg. When I got to the hotel I got the message that Saskia was in labour. There I was 500Km away. A repeat, on a larger scale, of Jemima's birth back in 1979, and just as impossible for me to get there on time for the birth.

Shortly after Julia's birth on 4th July 1994 we decided we would move to England. I was reluctant to return to London because, after the open spaces of Hamburg, London seemed so closed and congested. We decided to try to find somewhere in Brighton and travelled there, complete with a one month old child, to look for a house. I had about 10 days between tours so we stayed at my mother's house in Bognor and drove round Brighton looking at places. Having found one we liked we returned to Hamburg and set up the process of buying it. The

Frank Trazkowsky and me. Backstage at the Dusseldorf gig .

Marla Glen.

Simon Rickman.

sale went through in early November and we packed everything up and got ready to leave. What furniture we had was shipping in a removal van and we went across in my BMW.

Our flat in Rutschbahn was over the top of a couple of basement shops, the one directly below us was an all night video rental store, and our bedroom window only looked out onto a chimney-like section which ran down from the roof to the basement. All of the furniture had gone so we were sleeping on a mattress of the floor. On one of the last nights there we went to bed and I was awoken by a sharp noise and a kind of gasp or sigh. I was not sure if I had heard it or dreamed it. The man in the flat above was quite old and I wondered if he had fallen. I lay awake for a while waiting for another noise, but none came and I drifted off back to sleep.

The following morning we were woken by the police. It seems there had been an armed robbery of the video store, and the guy who was running it had been shot dead. A good time to leave, I thought.

CHAPTER 34

Accept it – It's a Vicious Rumour

I also got a call from *Accept*. They were one of the few German bands, along with *The Scorpions* who were acknowledged outside Germany. A straight up metal band consisting of guitar, bass, drums and vocals whose most famous song seemed to be 'Balls To The Wall'. Frank suggested I mixed front of house and he did monitors, but I said that was silly. He really liked the band and I thought he should do the front sound. He was not convinced he was good enough to do it, but I talked him round and we went out to do a few gigs.

I was doing the monitors on the side of the stage on the first gig when I noticed that Udo, the band's singer, bore more than a passing resemblance to Les Dawson. I think it was the way he pursed his lips when he was not singing, but I had a lasting impression of Les Dawson doing his middle-aged housewife act, hoiking on his bra strap and singing 'I've got my balls to ze vall' – cracked me up every night.

The band liked Frank and he did a great job on the sound (as I knew he would) so we got their next tour. The support act for this was a band called *Vicious Rumours* from San Francisco. I was recording the *Accept* set on the tour on an array of ADAT machines for release as a live album (I don't know if it ever came out) and mixing the front for *Vicious Rumours*. Frank wanted a lighting designer for the tour and I suggested Simon Rickman, who had been LD for Manfred. As a result of this Simon and I wound up going on a short European tour with *Vicious Rumours*.

Their 1996 tour was to promote a new album, 'Something Burning', but the band's lead singer Carl Albert had just died in a car accident, and lead guitarist and band leader, Geoff Thorpe, had taken over vocals. I thought the band was pretty good, but for some reason, the band's fans were not willing to follow this and the tour was very under-attended. The gigs in northern Germany were OK, but as we travelled south audiences grew thinner. In Lütterwitzt we reached a real low point. This was a town that had been formerly in East Germany before the re-unification, and even though most of the former East Germany was now slowly clawing its way out of monochrome, this place had been bypassed. The gig itself was the solitary building in a sea of grey, overcast skies and ploughed fields.

It did not get any better once inside either. The toilets were rank and there was no hot water – or hot anything for that matter. The hall was dark and musty smelling and that all-pervasive East German fog seemed to creep in through walls. Soundcheck over, we sat backstage and had a bite to eat – from the cold buffet – before venturing outside to man our stations for the gig. As we approached the doors that led out into the hall we knew it was not right. The usual hubbub was not there, and when we opened the doors we could see why. There was no audience. 12 people at the most in a hall which would hold 800. Maybe they were in a bar that we had not seen before I thought, but I was not convinced. I remembered one of Harley's tour managers explaining why the hall was pretty empty about half hour before the show.

'They are all upstairs in the venue's bar,' he said, 'as soon as you start playing they'll come rushing in like flies round shit.'

Steve had not been impressed by this analogy.

That time it was true, and by the time I cranked up the intro music the hall was heaving - this time, I felt, was different. The band took to the stage and bravely did their whole set to the 12 people who stood staring, open mouthed, at a full on heavy rock band, with wall to wall amps and massive double drum kit, performing to an empty hall with all the bravado of a band playing to a packed stadium. When they finished the last number and retired to the dressing room, Simon and I just looked at each other. Two nights before, playing in a gig the size of someone's living room, with toytown desks and miniscule sound and lighting equipment we had looked at each other and said, 'What am I doing here?'

This time we knew what to do. We got down from the desks, walked over to the tiny audience, shook each of them firmly by the hand and said, 'Thank you for coming to our little show.'

They did not understand that either.

It was during this tour that my first daughter, Jemima, gave birth to my grandson, Ashley. I became a grandfather, but felt I got away with having to grow up because of it - by being on tour when it happened.

'What does granddad do?'

'He is on tour in Europe with an American Metal Band'

CHAPTER 35

And Then......

During this time we spent getting the house sorted and I had gone off for a few nondescript tours with some even more nondescript people. There were some gems in there as well, though. *The Accept* and *Vicious Rumours* tours were quite fun if not that lucrative. Touring with Julian Dawson was also fun and relaxed, and I did another tour for LTT with *America* but a lot of it was pretty awful. Saskia was stuck at home with a small child when I was away, and did not know anyone here so I decided I had to stop touring and try to find my way back into 'normal work'. One thing that all that time on the road does not give you is the ability to slip quietly back into 'normal work'. There are all sorts of reasons why that is not a viable option. On the road you have to make your own decisions and go with what you think is best. There is also the 'us against the world' attitude to most kinds of authority from outside the tour group. I did not find it easy.

I had slipped into writing a column for a computer magazine and got quite involved with software in the period in which I had lived in Hamburg, so I tried to make that work. In the late eighties and early nineties it was still all to play for in the world of computers. *Microsoft* had not managed the world domination position that it later achieved, and there were a great number of flourishing competitors. *Atari, Commodore, Acorn, Apple* and many others were still in there all with different operating systems and I was still involved with the 'Sinclair QL' side of things. MS-DOS, which was *Microsoft*'s O/S was still mostly monochrome and single tasking, whereas the others, including the 'Sinclair', were in 4 four colours and multitasking (when they had enough memory). I could see no reason why *Microsoft* should succeed over them. Shows you how much of a pundit I was.

The one good thing about running my little 'Sinclair' software company (named Q-Branch by my business partner Steve Hall because most QL software started with or contained the letter 'Q' and he was a big fan of James Bond) was that I got to do some travelling again. Short trips mostly, to Holland, Germany, Austria and France to do weekend computer shows, but I also got talked into travelling to the States. It was a bizarre trip. I got up in the morning, took a bus to Heathrow and boarded a plane to America. I was picked up at the airport and we drove for two or three hours to a motel somewhere in New England. After a meal and a few drinks I went to bed. I got up the following day and did the show. This was followed by another meal and bed again. After a swift breakfast I was transported back to the airport to fly back to England. When I stood in the concourse at Heathrow, a mere two and a half days later, it was almost as if it had not happened. At least I had broken my run of not getting over to the U.S.

I did another seven of these shows, but after the first whirlwind, in and out trip, I decided that I would extend my stay. I hooked up with one of the other traders, a German named Jochen Merz who had a passion for rollercoasters. Every time we went over after that he looked up the highest or the fastest coaster and we went there. The business of selling peripherals for niche computers was dying, though, as *Microsoft* extended its stranglehold on the computer world. After an unsuccessful attempt to run a shop, I wound up taking a real job, working for a small computer company in Hove. The first real nine to five job since the sixties.

Over the next few years I did very little music, but it was never really far from my life. Nick Pynn, Steve Harley's violin and guitar player called me up and got me to do the sound for a show he was putting on in the *Sallis Benny Theatre* in Brighton. This led to a few more local shows for Nick and other people, and this got me reconnected. *Dogwatch's* second drummer, John Mortimer, was in *Maidstone Prison* serving a longish stretch for conspiracy to import marching power so the next thing I got involved in was a charity gig at the prison featuring a mix of inmates and musicians from the outside. Tony Morley, my long time musical collaborator, put the whole thing together and among the musicians were Glen Tilbrook from *Squeeze* and Stevie Simpson from *Chappo's* band.

Q-Branch had a website which was primarily set up to sell *Sinclair QL* software and hardware, but I decided to set up a page on it that was purely dedicated to my old bands and touring. Over the course of many nights in hotels doing QL computer shows I had regaled my fellow traders with tales of rock and roll mayhem, and I thought I should put some of this up on the web.

The first person to get in touch was Roger Glynn, former guitar player with *Dogwatch* and then Alan Essex, former synth player with *Wooden Lion*. Way back in the late eighties I had cleared out Boz Burrell's lockup for him. Over the course of a few days I listed guitars, amps and keyboards, tested stuff to see if it worked and then he decided what to keep and what to throw out. In among this musical miscellany was an EMS Synthi A, the original bleeping, swooshing, screaming noise generating synthesiser as used by many bands in the seventies. Bands such as the *Pink Floyd, Roxy Music, Hawkwind* and many others, always had one of these on stage. *Wooden Lion* had one too. Alan had started with a homemade synth and then gone to the EMS unit in Wandsworth to buy one. Boz said I should throw it away so I asked if I could have it and he gave it to me, along with a bass guitar someone had made for him that was too heavy to use on stage.

When Alan came round to my house for dinner in 2005 I pulled the Synthi out and said

That Legendary Wooden Lion onstage in Brighton at the
Real Music Club April 2013.

The work room in Brighton where I wrote all this.

'Remember this?'

I leant it to him to play with, and before I knew it we were making plans to put the band back together and do a gig – just for fun. Oh dear!

So that brings us up to date. I have sat here in my office for the last year dragging all these memories out of long fried brain cells, trying to make sense of what happened when, and to whom. Over the course of that recalling I have come to remember people I thought I had forgotten, places I had been to and all manner of odd circumstances.

We did form a band, not the original one as we had intended, but an amalgam of many bands. Alan and I first tried to do something with Tony and Terry Morley, but Tony had too many irons in the fire at the time. We tried many drummers – most of which could not drum and were on the verge of giving up when Steve Bensusan, from the *Last Post*, called to say he had a drummer and bass player who were up for it, and so we became *That Legendary Wooden Lion*. In 2007 we did our first gig in a pub in Deptford called *The Quebec Curve*. They sure know how to conjure up romantic names for pubs, don't they? The set consisted of a couple of *Dogwatch* songs, a few *Last Post* songs, three songs Tony and I had written in the eighties for an album that did not happen, and a bunch of new stuff. The surprise for me was the new stuff. I was pretty amazed that I had new songs in me, but once I started writing it just poured out. As I stood at the side of the stage at that first gig, dressed in flying helmet and jacket I heard the band launch into the opening bars of 'Triangle'. I suddenly thought 'I wonder if I can remember how to do this.' Minutes later I was on stage. Seems I did.

We went on to release an album in 2011, 'Writing in a Skeleton Key' and that all dragged me back into the world I loved. Although that band fell apart at the end of 2011, I carried on and found new people to work and write with, and a new album is slowly taking shape. I also got more involved in the local music scene in Brighton, mixing sound, doing live recordings and putting on gigs with *The Real Music Club*. As a result of the *Real Music Club* connection, I also got involved with *Brighton and Hove Community Radio* and found myself sitting behind a microphone playing tracks – something I never expected to do at all. I suppose, throughout my life, I have been passionate about getting people to listen to new things, new songs, new bands and it should have been a natural step, but not one that had occurred to me before.

All in all I can say that, as I sat here typing these words over the last year, I have been reflecting on a life which has taken many twists and turns, but I would have forgone none of it. Life through the 20th Century seems to have moved at an accelerated pace in comparison of other periods, but that may just be because that was my timeline. It is inevitable that, when you look back on 65 years of life, you will see many changes. I do think that I was very lucky to be born when I was and to have lived in London through most of my youth. Our generation was the first, in so many years, that was not forced to march off to a major war, we were the beneficiaries of free medical care and social security, and we lived through some incredible scientific discoveries and innovations. I went from a community in which having a phone in your home was a novelty, to one where almost everyone you see in the street, young and old, has a mobile phone clamped to their ear.

I am also lucky to have spent most of my adolescence and early years in the sunshine period – post 'The Pill' and pre-AIDS, when the drugs we took were mostly shared around by friends and not sold by vicious gangsters and pushers, and when there was a genuine feeling that we could create an 'alternative society'. That society never really came to be a reality, but there are still seeds there, little pockets of resistance to the conventional, capitalist, repressive paradigm that has haunted and scarred the western world for so long.

And then we had the music. Every generation probably feels they had the best music, but the sixties was a take off point when, as a result of all of the above - drugs, technology, sex and the alternative culture - 'popular music' (as they called it) shook off the shackles of being a 'product' and tried to be an art form. In many ways that period lasted only a short time, but like many of the ideas from that period, it started something that still exists, and in many cases, flourishes. Here in the opening decades of the 21st Century we still have 'Boy Bands' and artists whose intellect and creative ability is tissue thin, but we also have a strong undercurrent of people who create, produce and perform music that comes from the heart and soul. Not only that, but modern technology means you don't need an expensive studio to make it in or even a record company to sell it. The computer and the Internet have delivered a power into the hands of artists that may, one day, allow them to do away with the commercial machine altogether. Life remains interesting. My father died while I was on tour with *Manfred Mann's Earthband* in 1990. The last words he said to me, when I saw him just before leaving for the tour were, 'I still feel the way I felt when I was seventeen.' I have always wondered why we deny that, and pretend to grow up.

Looking back, as I have in writing this, I cannot say that I achieved great things, but I have loved and been loved by many more wonderful women than I deserved, and tried to live my life by the principles I felt were right in the sixties. I never grew out of being a hippie at heart and I still feel there is something there, beyond the naivety, which, could the world ever get to embrace it and give up grasping for wealth and power, would make human life so much better. In writing this book I revisited and relived many happy times, mistakes, loves and passions, and if I could go back and start again, I would probably do it all the same way.

I hope I have not offended or annoyed any of the people I have written about here. For most of the time we were fellow travellers on a road of mayhem and nonsense with a bit of great music thrown in for good measure. I hope those that I am not still in touch with are happy, and in good health, and that reading all this will make them smile.

All of this happened because I completely failed to grow up in the sixties.

Roy's Musical History

1966	Mostly a solo folk musician – sometimes as a duo with Sheila Harrigan
1967	Early attempts at bands. Firstly as *Orian* (duo with another guitarist called Ian) leading to forming a band with Alan Grey called *Stranger Than Yesterday*
1968	Highlight of *Stranger than Yesterday* – supporting Pink Floyd:

1969	*Stranger than Yesterday* ends and *Grope* emerges
1971	*Wooden Lion* is formed by Roy, Johnny Lyons (former bassist in *Grope*) and Gareth Kiddier
1978	Joins *Dogwatch* as vocalist to replace Paul Ballance
1979	5th April - 'Penfriend' album released by *Bridge House Records*
1980	'Cutouts' / 'Mornington Crescent' single released by *Half Tone Records*
1981	After *Dogwatch* split joins *Last Post* as vocalist
	'Fallout' album released on *Half Tone Records*
1982	'Monopoly' / 'Triangle' single released on *Parasol Records*
1983	Performed as 'actor' for *Manfred Mann's Earthband*
	'Somewhere in Europe Tour 83'
2007	Formed *That Legendary Wooden Lion* with Steve Bensusan from *Last Post* and

	Alan Essex (The Cardinal Biggles) from *Wooden Lion*
2011	10th Jan. 'Writing In a Skeleton Key' album released by *Turquiose Road Records*
2012	'Penfriend' by *Dogwatch* and 'Fallout' by *Last Post* released on CD by *Bridge House Records* – both with unreleased bonus tracks. (http://thebridgehousee16.com/shop.html)

http://www.woodenlion.com/discography.php

Books

There is still such a
thing as alternative
Publishing

Robert Newton Calvert: Born 9
March 1945, Died 14 August 1988
after suffering a heart attack.
Contributed poetry, lyrics and
vocals to legendary space rock
band Hawkwind intermittently on
five of their most critically
acclaimed albums, including Space
Ritual (1973), Quark, Strangeness
& Charm (1977) and Hawklords
(1978). He also recorded a number
of solo albums in the mid 1970s.
CENTIGRADE 232 was Robert Cal
vert's first collection of poems.

Hype   'And now, for all you speed
ing street smarties out there, the
one you've all been waiting for, the
one that'll pierce your laid back
ears, decoke your sinuses, cut clean
thru the schlock rock,
MOR/crossover, techno flash mind
mush. It's the new Number One with
a bullet … with a bullet … It's Tom,
Supernova, Mahler with a pan galac
tic biggie …' And the Hype goes on.
And on. Hype, an amphetamine hit of
a story by Hawkwind collaborator
Robert Calvert. Who's been there
and made it back again. The
debriefing session starts here.

Rick Wakeman is the world's most
unusual rock star, a genius who has
pushed back the barriers of electronic
rock. He has had some of the world's
top orchestras perform his music, has
owned eight Rolls Royces at one time,
and has broken all the rules of com
posing and horrified his tutors at the
Royal College of Music. Yet he has
delighted his millions of fans. This
frank book, authorised by Wakeman
himself, tells the moving tale of his
larger than life career.

There are nine Henrys, pur ported to be the world's first cloned cartoon charac ter. They live in a strange lo fi domestic surrealist world peopled by talking rock buns and elephants on wobbly stilts.

They mooch around in their minimalist universe suffer ing from an existential crisis with some genetically modified humour thrown in.

Marty Wilde on Terry Dene: "Whatever happened to Terry becomes a great deal more comprehensible as you read of the callous way in which he was treated by people who should have known better many of whom, frankly, will never know better of the sad little shadows of the past who eased themselves into Terry's life, took everything they could get and, when it seemed that all was lost, quietly left him — Dan Wood ing's book tells it all."

Rick Wakeman: "There have always been certain 'careers' that have fascinated the public, newspapers, and the media in general. Such include musicians, actors, sportsmen, police, and not surprisingly, the people who give the police their employ ment: The criminal. For the man in the street, all these careers have one thing in common: they are seemingly beyond both his reach and, in many cases, understanding and as such, his only associ ation can be through the media of newspapers or tele vision. The police, however, will always require the ser vices of the grass, the squealer, the snitch, (call him what you will), in order to assist in their investiga tions and arrests; and amaz ingly, this is the area that seldom gets written about."

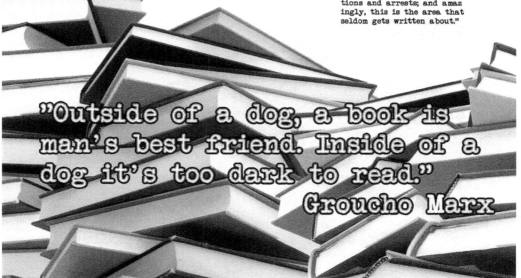

"Outside of a dog, a book is man's best friend. Inside of a dog it's too dark to read."
Groucho Marx

Bill Harkleroad joined Captain Beef heart's Magic Band at a time when they were changing from a straight ahead blues band into something completely dif ferent. Through the vision of Don Van Vliet (Captain Beefheart) they created a new form of music which many at the time considered atonal and difficult, but which over the years has continued to exert a powerful influence. Beefheart re christened Harkleroad as Zoot Horn Rollo, and they embarked on recording one of the classic rock albums of all time Trout Mask Replica - a work of unequalled daring and inventiveness.

Politics, paganism and .... Vlad the Impaler. Selected stories from CJ Stone from 2003 to the present. Meet Ivor Coles, a British Tommy killed in action in September 1915, lost, and then found again. Visit Mothers Club in Erdington, the best psyche delic music club in the UK in the '60s. Celebrate Robin Hood's Day and find out what a huckle duckle is. Travel to Stonehenge at the Summer Solstice and carouse with the hippies. Find out what a Ranter is, and why CJ Stone thinks that he's one. Take LSD with Dr Lilly, the psychedelic scientist. Meet a headless soldier or the ghost of Elvis Presley in Gabalfa, Cardiff. Journey to Whitstable, to New York, to Malta and to Transylvania, and to many other places, real and imagined, polit ical and spiritual, transcendent and mundane. As The Independent says, Chris is "The best guide to the underground since Charon ferried dead souls across the Styx."

This is is the first in the highly acclaimed vampire novels of the late Mick Farren. Victor Renquist, a surprisingly urbane and likable leader of a colony of vampires which has existed for centuries in New York is faced with both admin istrative and emotional prob lems. And when you are a vampire, administration is not a thing which one takes lightly.

"The person, be it gentleman or lady, who has not pleasure in a good novel, must be intolerably stupid."

Jane Austen

'Over thousands of years, nature has provided the resources that have helped humans survive and flourish. Now, in a time of need, we must help nature to survive. This wonderful new book highlights the magnificent wet forests of Victoria, and why it is so critical to protect them for their biodiversity, their beauty, and for all of humanity.'

Dr Jane Goodall, DBE
*Founder of the Jane Goodall Institute
and UN Messenger of Peace*

THE
GREAT
FOREST

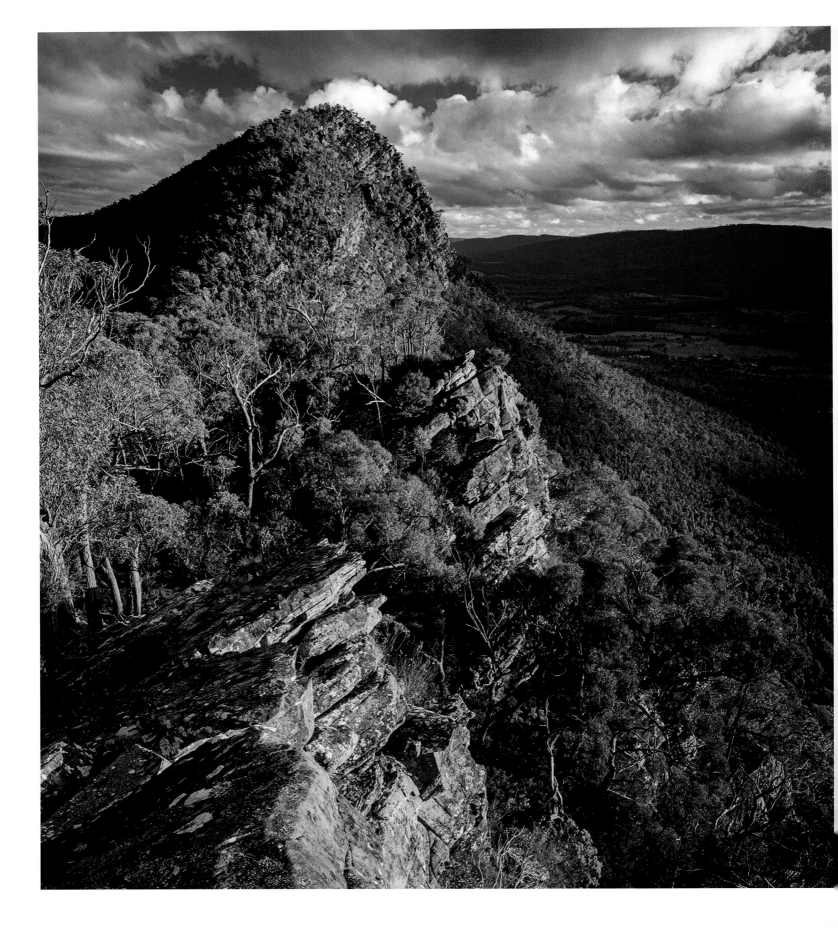

THE GREAT FOREST

THE RARE BEAUTY OF THE VICTORIAN CENTRAL HIGHLANDS

DAVID LINDENMAYER

WITH PHOTOGRAPHS BY
CHRIS TAYLOR,
SARAH REES
AND
STEVEN KUITER

ALLEN&UNWIN
SYDNEY • MELBOURNE • AUCKLAND • LONDON

To the late David Blair (1971–2019)

Father, husband, forest ecologist,
scout master, soccer player, colleague,
and friend. An extraordinary person
dedicated to conserving a most
wonderful forest.

CONTENTS

Statement of sovereignty   8

Introduction: The Central Highlands   13

1. Landscapes   27

2. Geology   45

3. Rainforest   57

4. Mountain Ash and other forests   67

5. The understorey and forest floor   87

6. Water   107

7. Fire   131

8. Wildlife   141

9. Logging   157

The future   179

About the author   182

About the photographers   183

Acknowledgements   184

Sources for Aboriginal place names   185

Index   186

STATEMENT OF SOVEREIGNTY

In October 2019, First Nations people came together to call on the Victorian Government to acknowledge our sovereignty over the forests and landscapes of the Central Highlands region. We called for an end to the destruction of these lands. The government has never sought, nor have we given, permission to log our forests. These places are homes to our totems, our ancestors and our people. Our cultural obligation is to care for Country, land and water. It is time for the Traditional Owners to be given a place at the table in decision-making about the forests, the landscapes and the water that is our Country.

Lidia Thorpe, the first Aboriginal senator for Victoria, on behalf of Elders and Traditional Owners of Gunnai, Taungurung and Wurundjeri Countries of eastern Victoria

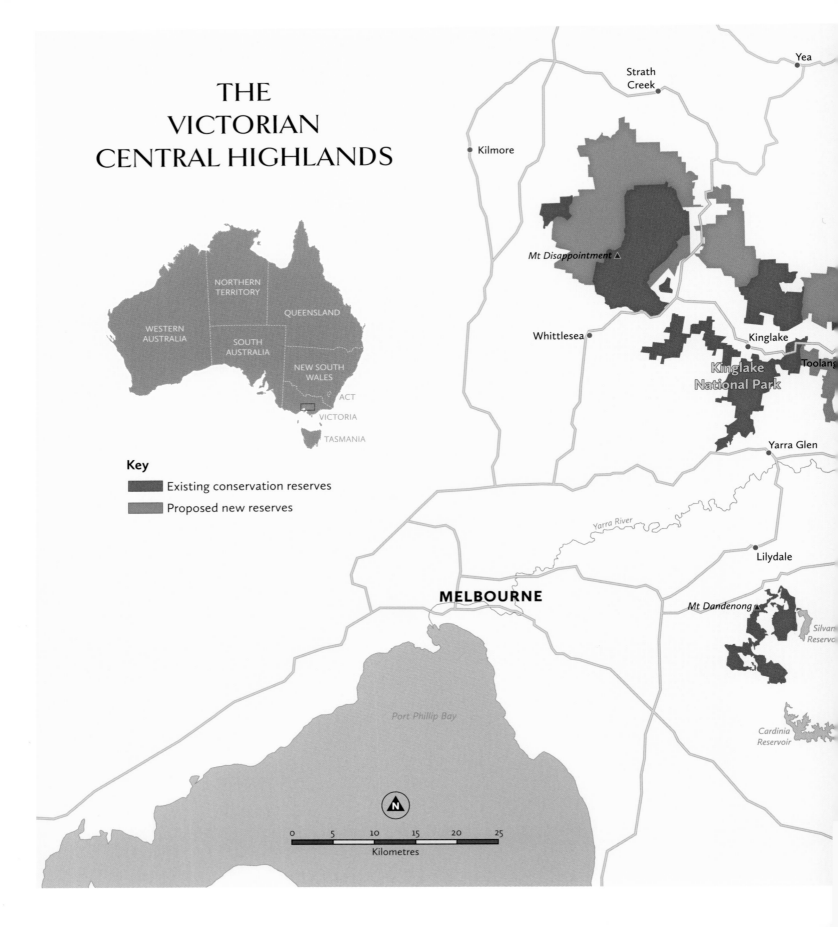

THE
VICTORIAN
CENTRAL HIGHLANDS

NORTHERN
TERRITORY

QUEENSLAND

WESTERN
AUSTRALIA

SOUTH
AUSTRALIA

NEW SOUTH
WALES

ACT

VICTORIA

TASMANIA

Key

Existing conservation reserves

Proposed new reserves

Yea

Strath
Creek

Kilmore

Mt Disappointment △

Whittlesea

Kinglake

Kinglake
National Park

Toolang

Yarra Glen

Yarra River

Lilydale

MELBOURNE

Mt Dandenong △

Silvar
Reservo

Port Phillip Bay

Cardinia
Reservoir

0   5   10   15   20   25
Kilometres

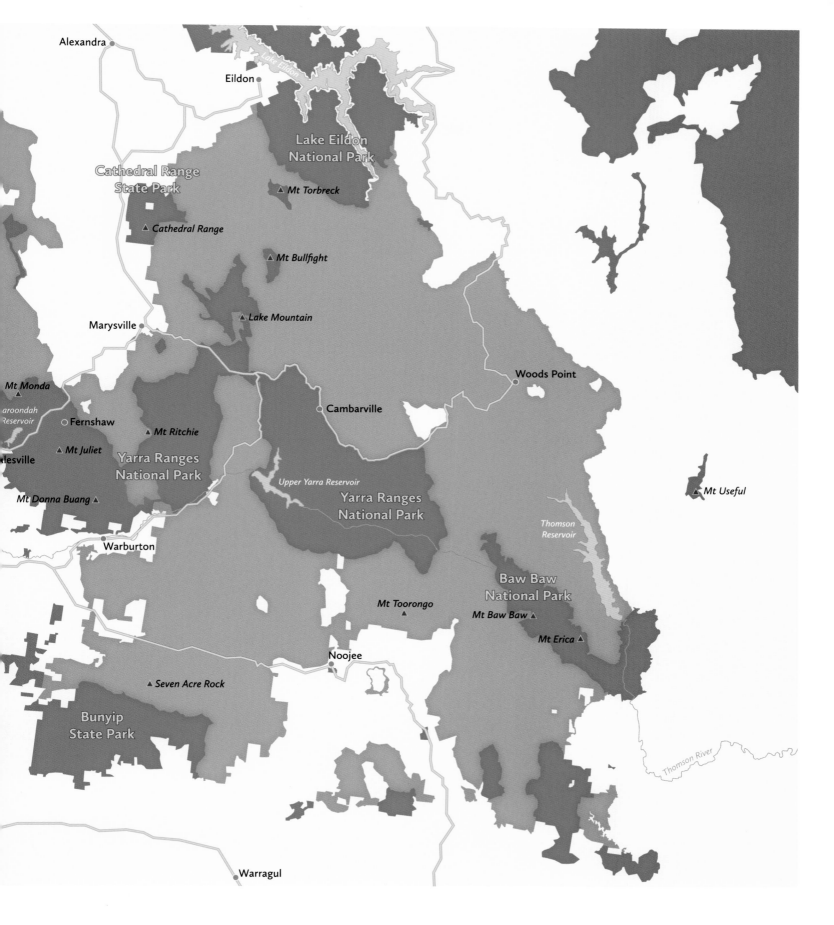

THE CENTRAL HIGHLANDS

The city of Melbourne (called Naarm in the First Nation's Kulin language) sits on a vast ancient plain with a dark blue mountainous rim to its east. As Melbourne's more than five million residents go about their daily lives, many are unaware that this backdrop of hills and peaks is more than just a geographical boundary—it is home to some of the tallest forests on Earth, which provide the city with nearly all of its drinking water. As you leave the city, the built environment gives way to a landscape of rolling pastures dominated by an impressive mountainous amphitheatre. On clear days, the haze of the forest tints the mountains a distinctive blue colour. When the weather closes in, the mountains are draped in curtains of cloud, where the water cycle commences. Beyond the rolling rural landscape is a forest 60 million years in the making. It is a forest that the Traditional Custodians, the Gunaikurnai, Taungurung and Wurundjeri Peoples, sustained for tens of thousands of years, their cultures shaping the forests while the forest shaped their culture. Many First Nations languages are now being rediscovered and are increasingly being used by Traditional Custodians. We have used First Nations words for locations in this book as well as for some of the charismatic species, such as the Leadbeater's Possum (Wollert) and the Superb Lyrebird (Buln Buln).

When you enter the forest, urban life, just kilometres away, recedes. A different world opens up—of ancient rainforests, extraordinary trees and an array of native animals. This forested region is known as the Central Highlands of Victoria. These unique and diverse forests extend from the outer urban areas north and east of Melbourne to the Baw Baw Plateau in the east, Lake Eildon in the north and the Latrobe Valley in the south. The region covers around 1.1 million hectares, of which 710,000 hectares is forest or other kinds of native vegetation. The region supports the largest intact areas of remaining Mountain Ash forests in mainland Australia. These mighty eucalypt forests once held the record for the tallest trees on Earth, with some reputed to be over 120 metres tall. Such giants are no longer standing, but there are still some individuals that exceed 90 metres, equivalent to the height of a 25-storey building.

The forests of the Central Highlands have been targeted for extensive industrial logging for over a hundred years: the tall slender trees of the Mountain Ash forests and their relatives in the Alpine Ash forests have long been sources of wood for timber and pulp

Opposite: **Dawn rays over Healesville on Wurundjeri Country** (Sarah Rees) The small town of Healesville, 50 kilometres north-east of Melbourne, is one of the gateways to the magnificent forests, landscapes and waterways of the Central Highlands.

mills. Over many decades, the impacts of clearfell logging have become more and more evident. Then, in 2009, the tragic Black Saturday wildfires, which killed 173 Victorians, burned through nearly half a million hectares of Mountain Ash and other kinds of forest. With an ever-increasing area impacted by wildfires in Victoria (and Australia more broadly), preserving the remaining unburned areas has become critically important. This book is based on the important science behind the vital need to preserve intact forests. Establishing a new national park—the Great Forest National Park—is important not just to protect the region's biodiversity and Melbourne's drinking water, but also to create valuable tourism and other job opportunities for local people.

One example of the advantages of protecting natural places is the Purnululu National Park—also known as the Bungle Bungles—in far north-western Australia. The Jaru and Gidja peoples have been the Traditional Custodians of Purnululu for tens of thousands of years, but the area was largely unseen by non-Aboriginal people until 1983. It was then protected as a national park. As well as being a haven for biodiversity, Purnululu National Park quickly became a focal point for domestic and international tourism, and an important source of direct and indirect employment for Aboriginal people.

The majestic wet forests of the Central Highlands of Victoria have the same potential for tourism and employment opportunities. Although revered and cared for by the Gunaikurnai, Taungurung and Wurundjeri Peoples for millennia, these forests have remained largely unappreciated by other Australians. But they are the equal of the forests of Tasmania, with spectacular mountains and waterfalls, and the tallest flowering plant on Earth, the Mountain Ash—not to mention luxuriant rainforest, prehistoric ferns and the world's tallest moss. They also support wonderful wildlife, with some species found nowhere else on Earth. It can be difficult to see these animals, because many are active

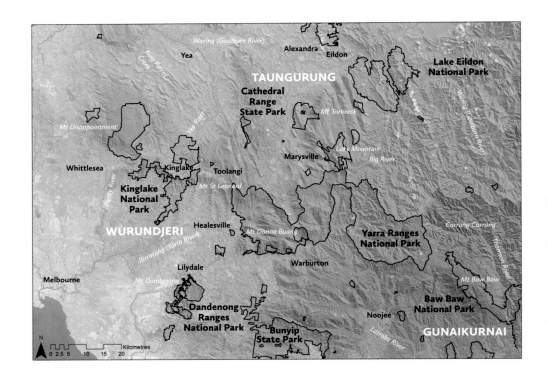

The forests of the Central Highlands of Victoria with Registered Aboriginal Party land boundaries
These are the forests of the Gunaikurnai, Taungurung and Wurundjeri Peoples. The forests and mountains of the Central Highlands form a distinctive arc around the city of Melbourne and extend into the beautiful Victorian Alps.

only at night and the forest is incredibly dense. However, it is worth the effort—they include one of Victoria's faunal emblems, the Wollert, back from the brink of extinction; a silent glider with snow-white fur; and a bright orange robin, found at the edge of the forest. Indeed, the forests of the Central Highlands are recognised as key areas of both global zoological and national botanical significance because of the extraordinary diversity of plants and animals they support.

This book takes you into the amazing forests of the Central Highlands. It follows a journey that began nearly 40 years ago when, as a professor of ecology and conservation scientist at The Australian National University, I first established long-term monitoring sites to measure changes in the structure and composition of the forest and in the populations of unique wildlife that the area supports. It was July 1983, not long after the devastating Ash Wednesday wildfires that saw thousands of hectares burned. The drought had just broken and it rained almost constantly for two months. I worked alone for much of the following year and grew to appreciate the grandeur of the forest. Thus began a lifelong passion to better understand how the forest worked—why animals occur where they do, what the links between animals and plants are, how disturbance changes the ecosystem, and how it recovers. The work is far from over. The more we learn, the more

The eastern end of the Cerberean Cauldron on Taungurung Country (Chris Taylor) Imposing tors deep in the forest are relics of the Cerberean Cauldron, formed 373 million years ago (see Chapter 2). Here, we see volcanic rock lining the ancient radial dyke of the cauldron. Much of the dyke has long since eroded except for a few hard volcanic rocks.

there is to learn. With greater understanding comes greater awareness of the need to carefully manage natural places.

The aim of this book is to bring these extraordinary forests to the attention of all Australians. To showcase a part of the world so close to Melbourne yet largely unknown to Melburnians or people elsewhere in Australia and around the world. I, and the amazing photographers who have contributed their images to this book, hope to rekindle Australians' interest in these wild places, to motivate them to go and see them for themselves, and to create employment and economic opportunities for people in regional communities. We also want to remind people that despite the devastation from fires and pandemics, the world is still a beautiful place. A place that is worth experiencing and worth conserving.

The path through this book

This book is not only a voyage through time, but also across landscapes, and from the canopy to the forest floor. Our journey into the forest begins in Chapter 1 with an overview of what we see when we first enter the Central Highlands: forest landscapes. Geology has an enormous impact on how landscapes are configured—the height of mountains, where waterfalls form, what types of forest occur where—and is covered in Chapter 2. The oldest forests in these landscapes are those dating from ancient Gondwanan times, and they are the subject of the third chapter.

The magnificent Mountain Ash and other eucalypt forests, a more recent ecological innovation, feature in Chapter 4. When we think of forests, we usually focus on trees, but the forest floor is also fascinating, and Chapter 5 touches on this vital part of the ecosystem. Geology, tall trees and forests, and the ground layer all influence where and how much water occurs in the landscape, from rivers and waterfalls to dams, and these are the topic of Chapter 6. Fire also shapes the forest, often in dramatic ways, and it is discussed in Chapter 7.

Chapter 8 is about the remarkable wildlife that inhabits the wet forests of the Central Highlands. The distribution and abundance of animals and plants are strongly influenced by all of the things explored in the preceding chapters—from the elevation of mountains and types of forest to soil conditions, water availability and past fires. The occurrence of animals is also heavily affected by human disturbance, especially logging, which is the focus of Chapter 9.

The final chapter touches on two key and intimately interrelated issues for the future—the urgent need for strengthened forest protection, and for Aboriginal people to have a greater say over the management of their lands, including identifying an appropriate First Nation's name for the area encompassing the proposed Great Forest National Park.

Opposite: **The Furmston Tree on Wurundjeri Country surrounded by admirers** (State Library Victoria)
Large old trees have always had a special place in the human psyche. They are sacred to Aboriginal people, and were often used as birthing sites. In the early 1900s, the Furmston Tree, a giant Mountain Ash, became a favourite stopping point and picnic area for people from nearby towns and villages as well as travellers making longer journeys on the Maroondah Highway (Chapter 4).

A profusion of tree ferns in wet eucalypt forests on Wurundjeri Country (Sarah Rees)
The young fronds of tree ferns were a delicacy and an important source of protein for Aboriginal people. They are also browsed by the Mountain Brushtail Possum, which is far more likely to be found in parts of the forest where tree ferns are abundant. The possums' appetite for young fronds was not lost on early European colonisers, who set snares for the animals in the tops of tree ferns. The possums' dense pelts were then shipped to London, where they fetched high prices, even exceeding those for sea otter pelts imported from North America. Fortunately, the colonial fur trappers are now long gone and the Mountain Brushtail Possum can live in wet eucalypt forests and feed on tree fern fronds without the risk of being converted into hats for the English gentry.

The Mountain Brushtail Possum (Steven Kuiter)

Most Australians are familiar with the Common Brushtail Possum, a widespread inhabitant of urban areas and a notorious raider of vegetable gardens and fruit trees. Very few people will have seen the Mountain Brushtail Possum, a large, charismatic animal found in wet forests and rainforests (see Chapter 8). The two species are easy to tell apart—the Common Brushtail Possum has a pointed face and ears resembling a fox (hence its species name, *vulpecula*, derived from the Latin name for fox, *Vulpes vulpes*). The Mountain Brushtail Possum in Victoria (and southern New South Wales) has a face resembling a dog (and its Latin name used to be *caninus*).

Moss catching water and a ray of light (Sarah Rees)
The wet forests of the Central Highlands support a wide range
of species of mosses, lichens and hornworts, including some that
are not currently formally described by scientists and appear to be
unique to wet forests. Others are well known and widely distributed,
occurring not only in Victoria but also in New Zealand, subantarctic
islands and even Antarctica. (See Chapter 5.)

Fungi among moss on Taungurung Country (Steven Kuiter)
The wet forests support an extraordinary array of fungi. They play
pivotal roles in the ecosystem, especially in breaking down dead wood
and leaf litter. (See Chapter 5.)

Montane fens on the Baw Baw Plateau on Wurundjeri Country (Chris Taylor)
The fens, or marshland, around the Carrang-Carrang/Tambo (Thomson River) on the Baw Baw Plateau support a unique assemblage of plants (Chapter 6). The surrounding forest is also home to the last populations of the Baw Baw Frog, and these forests provide habitat for colonies of the Critically Endangered Wollert (Leadbeater's Possum).

River on the Baw Baw Plateau on Gunaikurnai Country that eventually flows into the Thomson Reservoir, a key part of Melbourne's water supply (Chris Taylor)
The Baw Baw Plateau and associated escarpments receive some of the highest rainfall in Victoria. Many streams flow from the plateau, cascading down the escarpment and into the Thomson Reservoir, Melbourne's largest source of water. These rivers provide water not only for Melbourne but also for many towns north of the Great Dividing Range. The amount of water generated in a catchment area is a function of the age of the forest. (See Chapter 6.)

Logging in the Thomson catchment on Gunaikurnai Country
(Chris Taylor)
Extensive areas of wet forest have been logged in the Thomson
catchment. These logging operations have major impacts on the amount
of water that flows into reservoirs like the Thomson Reservoir in the
background. (See Chapter 9.)

CHAPTER 1

LANDSCAPES

Picture an intricate mosaic ceiling in a cathedral or the walls of an ancient mosque—stunning scenes created from hundreds or even thousands of ceramic tiles. Forest landscapes are also mosaics, assembled from many different pieces—gullies, ridges, midslopes, streams, rocky outcrops, patches of old trees, stands of young trees, different tree species, wetlands and open grassy areas. A diversity of 'patch types' is critical to the diversity of life in forest landscapes.

Aboriginal people have been reading the subtleties of these landscapes for thousands of years, knowing where to find particular plants and animals. For a forest scientist today, understanding how a landscape functions is a colossal task. This is because no two parts of a landscape are the same. Just as every human is different, so too is every tile in the mosaic that makes a landscape. Each place differs, even if only slightly, in steepness, aspect, distance from water and myriad other features, such as the time since the last disturbance (for example, logging or fire) or how many disturbances have occurred there. Even soils can vary—sometimes over a distance of just a few metres. What makes a good landscape for wildlife will also vary depending on the species and how that animal perceives its environment. A Sooty Owl and a beetle will perceive the same landscape in markedly different ways.

Acknowledging all of these complexities, since 1983 scientists from The Australian National University have been painstakingly piecing together how the configuration of the mosaic 'tiles' in wet forests influences biodiversity—part of which is identifying animals' preferred habitats. We have found that the Yellow-bellied Glider—a fluffy, social and very vocal animal—will most likely occur where the landscape is dominated by large patches of old-growth forest, or forest that has been established for 170 years or more. The Greater Glider and the Wollert (Leadbeater's Possum) are seldom found in places where much of the surrounding landscape has been logged, burned or both, while the Flame Robin is most common in areas where there has been recent fire. The Pink Robin occurs most often in cool temperate rainforest, even in patches just half a hectare in size.

Opposite: **Baw Baw Plateau on Wurundjeri Country** (Chris Taylor)
The juxtaposition of vegetation and exposed rock is very important for species such as reptiles that need to bask to warm their bodies, particularly in sub-alpine areas. The rock surfaces allow them to access sunshine, with easy shelter from predators in the nearby vegetation. Some snakes, such as the Highland Copperhead, have black scales on their heads that allow them to warm more quickly without fully exposing their bodies.

Pink Robin on Taungurung Country
(Steven Kuiter)
Cool temperate rainforests are often quiet places, with relatively few birds. An exception is the beautiful Pink Robin, whose distinctive 'chuckle' can often be heard from larger stands of rainforest.

THE LANGUAGE OF BIRDS

For almost two decades my team and I have conducted annual bird counts in the forest. Many different species of birds can be found in Mountain Ash forests, and their calls create a special ambience. Learning to identify the calls is a challenge for a number of reasons. Each species makes a range of different calls, but some also mimic others—and not just the famous Superb Lyrebird; other skilled impersonators include the tiny Brown Thornbill. In addition, males and females of the same species sometimes have different calls. The Eastern Whipbird is a classic example: the male makes the characteristic whip-crack call, whereas the female answers with a *chow-eee* call. (This is a special kind of duet—an antiphonal duet. However, the female does not want to be taken for granted and answers only intermittently.) Further, the same species in different places can have different 'dialects'—just as a person from Yorkshire speaks completely differently to a person from Cape York. Learning to identify bird calls is much like learning a language and is best achieved through repeated visits to the forest. The language of birds is as wonderful to hear as any human tongue, and the diversity of species reveals a lot about the condition of the forest.

Some species do not seem to respond to how landscapes are configured, at least not in ways that can be measured easily or accurately by ecologists. Birds such as the Grey Shrike-thrush (one of Australia's most widely distributed bird species) and the Brown Thornbill are found almost everywhere in wet eucalypt forests. There must be things that affect the distribution and abundance of even these most common of species. Indeed, while conserving rare and threatened species is a critical part of conservation science, maintaining populations of common species is also essential, as these animals do most of the 'heavy lifting' in maintaining a forest's crucial ecological processes, such as pollination, seed dispersal and litter decomposition.

How forest landscapes are configured not only affects biodiversity but can also influence disturbances (that in turn shape landscapes). Patterns of landscape cover, disturbances and biodiversity are therefore intimately interwoven. For instance, logging creates major gaps in the forest cover, with marked boundaries between the logged areas and adjacent uncut forest. These large gaps in the canopy can have dramatic effects on microclimatic conditions such as wind speeds. Landscapes with many logged areas tend to be much windier as there are fewer trees to block the movement of air. Higher wind speeds mean that trees in uncut patches are at greater risk of being blown down. This problem is particularly pronounced in very tall, wet forests where trees survive only if they win the race for light with their neighbours, meaning that growth patterns emphasise a rapid increase in height. Large old trees can be especially prone to collapse, with major effects on the animals that depend on these trees.

Rocky outcrops across the Baw Baw Plateau on Gunaikurnai and Wurundjeri Countries (Chris Taylor)
Rocky outcrops support a rich array of plants and animals, including species that are rare or even entirely absent from the rest of the landscape. In forested landscapes, rocky outcrops provide valuable basking sites for reptiles. The area shown in the background of this photograph was saved from logging and is one of the last intact large patches of wet eucalypt forest in mainland Australia.

The Carrang-Carrang/Tambo (Thomson River) and a montane fen along the Baw Baw Plateau on Wurundjeri Country (Sarah Rees)
The Carrang-Carrang/Tambo flows from the north-west edge of the Baw Baw Plateau through a series of alpine and montane fens surrounded by Snow Gum woodland and tall wet forests. The upper reaches of the river are in Wurundjeri Country, and the river flows into Gunaikurnai Country. These fens and adjacent forests have been recognised as sites of national botanical and global zoological significance, due to the unique assemblages of plants and animals in the area. Two of Victoria's most at-risk species—the Baw Baw Frog and the Wollert (Leadbeater's Possum)—can be found here.

Logging makes forests younger, and several studies have found that fires are more likely to burn at higher severity in landscapes dominated by young forest; these areas are possibly also susceptible to repeated reburning. In other words, logging begets more fire (a major problem in a warming world), leaving the forest 'trapped' as young forest and unable to 'break out' and grow to maturity before it is reburned. Again, this affects a large number of animal and plant species that are dependent on old-growth forest, or at least the remnants of old-growth forest such as very large old trees.

As we'll see in later chapters, the landscape mosaics that comprise the wet forests of the Central Highlands (and elsewhere in mainland south-eastern Australia) have changed dramatically in the 230 years since European colonisation. Once-extensive stands of old-growth forest that Aboriginal people were so familiar with have been replaced by much younger, more fire-prone, regrowth forest. These changes in forest landscapes matter: they affect biodiversity, how fire burns, how much carbon is stored, and how much water is produced. Protecting the forest is a critical measure to encourage the recovery and expansion of old-growth forest, restoring the Central Highlands landscapes and the species that depend on them.

Above: **Mount Torbreck on Taungurung Country in late spring** (Chris Taylor)
Left: **Mount Torbreck on Taungurung Country in winter** (Chris Taylor)
At 1516 metres, Mount Torbreck is the second highest mountain in the Central Highlands region (after Mount Baw Baw at 1567 metres). In spring, the forest echoes with the voices of songbirds like the Grey Shrike-thrush and the Golden Whistler. Many bird species migrate to warmer places in winter, and snow mutes the sounds of the forest.

Looking across the upper reaches of the Waring (Goulburn River) valley towards the Victorian Alps across Taungurung Country
(Chris Taylor)
The remote eastern ranges of the Central Highlands are defined by deeply dissected valleys extending far into the Victorian Alps. Rocky ridgelines and steep slopes support a diverse array of forest types and vegetation communities. A walk along one of the many high points reveals stunning views of ever-receding ridgelines as far as the eye can see. Here, the mountains feed the Waring, the Taungurung name for the Goulburn River.

Sunrise across the southern face of Mount Monda on Wurundjeri Country (Sarah Rees)
Mount Monda is on the edge of the Maroondah Catchment, most of which has been closed to logging and human access for a century. The entire town of Fernshaw was removed in the late nineteenth century to preserve water quality. In this image, trees burned in the 2009 Black Saturday fires fringe the distant ridges.

Sunset over alpine heathland at Mount Baw Baw with a backdrop of the Victorian Alps on Wurundjeri and Gunaikurnai Countries
(Chris Taylor)
The stand of alpine heathland in this image is among the last remaining areas of this type of vegetation in Victoria that has escaped being burned in the past two decades.

Above: **View of the Victorian Alps from Mount Torbreck on Taungurung Country** (Chris Taylor)
The Central Highlands is physically connected to the Victorian Alps. These regions are joined by extensive areas of intact forested landscapes which support several types of forests and very high levels of biodiversity.

Left: **Winter sunset from Mount Torbreck on Taungurung Country** (Chris Taylor)
An evening view from Mount Torbreck through fire-damaged Snow Gum woodland to the Rubicon range. More than 90 per cent of Victoria's subalpine Snow Gum woodland has been burned in the past 25 years, with many areas burned several times—this is far more frequent than would have occurred historically.

Opposite: **A spectacular view on Gunaikurnai Country from the Baw Baw Plateau across to the Victorian Alps** (Chris Taylor)
Vista from the Baw Baw Plateau to the Victorian Alps, including the iconic Bluff (top left) made famous in several movies. Careful observation enables better 'reading' of the landscape. Here, the different rounded and open versus closed pyramid shapes of the tree crowns show not only the presence of different species but also different ages of stands of trees of the same species.

View on Taungurung Country in the Victorian Alps looking towards the Central Highlands (Chris Taylor) This spectacular image shows several pieces of a landscape mosaic—flaked and broken sedimentary rocks, shrublands, patches of Snow Gum woodland (some burned, some undisturbed), and mixed-species forest in the gullies and valleys.

**Rainbow across the north-west spur of Mount Juliet on
Wurundjeri Country** (Sarah Rees)
Rainbows are a common sight over wet forests, dramatically
contrasted against the low clouds that cling to the canopies
of intact areas.

**Cloud along the southern escarpment of Mount Donna Buang
on Wurundjeri Country** (Sarah Rees)
The crowns of tall trees can spend part of the day enveloped by
cloud. Droplets of water condense on the leaves and this can add
substantially to the water budget of these forests, which are already
some of the wettest places in mainland southern Australia.

Rain falling over the foothills on Wurundjeri Country (Sarah Rees)
Forests generate rain. Some of the rain that falls in wet forests is taken up from the soil by trees and then transpired through the leaves back into the atmosphere. The high levels of moisture in the air above forests can then become part of weather systems moving through an area and then re-precipitated. A study in the Amazon forests of South America suggests that the average water droplet falls as rain and is transpired into the atmosphere several times before it flows into the ocean.

CHAPTER 2

GEOLOGY

Landscapes are shaped over many time frames. The daily cycle of night and day, and those times at the margins when it is a bit of both—dusk and dawn. The annual seasons and the run of years. Generations of plants and animals, including humans. The millions of years involved in the evolution of species. And then there are the geological cycles—from the creation of rocks, their weathering and erosion, and their reformation as new rocks. Geological time frames—constituting hundreds of millions, even billions, of years—are almost incomprehensible to the human mind; for example, if counting to a million took 89 days, counting to a billion would take 250 years.

Below the forests of the Central Highlands is a geological legacy nearly 400 million years in the making. More than 380 million years ago, much of this land was a swamp. Over millions of years, the mud and sand at the bottom of the swamp hardened and became sandstone and other sedimentary rocks. Geologist Dr Bill Birch tells us that a large magma chamber formed deep in the Earth below this swamp and it abruptly collapsed in a massive geological event at the end of the Devonian period, some 373 million years ago, forming two giant cauldrons.

The larger and perhaps more spectacular is the Cerberean Cauldron, which is approximately 30 kilometres in diameter and bounded by a radial dyke. Radial dykes are often formed when the magma chamber of a cauldron collapses and molten rock rises through ring-shaped faults along the perimeter of the collapsed chamber. The hardened sandstone of the ancient swamp fell into the cauldron, forming the stunning near-vertical slabs of Nanadhong (the Cathedral Range) that lean against the slowly eroding radial dyke. The molten rock from the collapsed chamber formed the extensive granodiorite extrusions of Lake Mountain, Mount Bullfight and Mount Torbreck. (Granodiorite is a kind of rock similar to granite but with different mineral composition.) Fault lines were created across the cauldron that now form stunning gorges and waterfalls such as Snob Creek Falls. The radial dyke can be seen from the southern ridgeline of Nanadhong.

To the south of the Cerberean Cauldron, the smaller of the two cauldrons, the Acheron, collapsed in a similar way. It is dominated by Mount Donna Buang, Mount Juliet and Mount Ritchie. The dyke surrounding this cauldron has largely eroded, and its southernmost remnants now lie below the beautiful town of Warburton.

Opposite: **The ridgeline of Nanadhong on Taungurung Country** (Chris Taylor) In this view across the Nanadhong (the Taungurung name for the Cathedral Range), tilted sandstone slabs line the western rim of the Cerberean Cauldron, which imploded 373 million years ago. The cauldron is up to 27 kilometres wide by 33 kilometres long, and the implosion would have been a massive event, likely influencing the planet's climate. The ancient sandstone slabs fell into the cauldron and the hardest rock now leans up against the remains of the cauldron dyke.

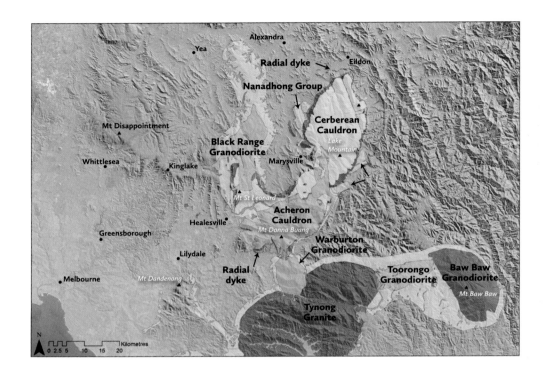

Key geological features of the Cerberean Cauldron, Acheron Cauldron, Tynong Granite, Toorongo Granodiorite and Baw Baw Plateau Granodiorite across Gunaikurnai, Taungurung and Wurundjeri Countries

In the north of the Central Highlands, the Cerberean Cauldron is the dominant geological feature. It was formed 373 million years ago when the ancient sandstone of the Devonian landscape collapsed into a large magma chamber. In the south, the Acheron Cauldron was also formed around the same time. Further to the south, the granodiorite batholith of Mount Baw Baw—the region's highest mountain—dominates. It is dissected by a unique pattern of gorges and waterways, making it a site of national geological and geomorphological significance. This map was generated from data compiled by geologist Alfons Vandenberg and his co-authors (A.H.M. Vandenberg, C.E. Willman, S. Maher et al. (2000), *The Tasman Fold Belt System in Victoria*, Geological Survey of Victoria Special Publication).

Tilted sandstone rock at Nanadhong on Taungurung Country (Chris Taylor)
The layers of sandstone lying on their side along the western periphery of the Cerberean Cauldron can be seen along the sheer cliff face on the northern flank of the 'Jawbones' at Nanadhong.

The Nanadhong ridgeline on Taungurung Country (Chris Taylor)
The curve of the western rim of the Cerberean Cauldron can be seen from
various vantage points. Here, the distinctive peaks of Nanadhong follow the
radial dyke, part of which can also be seen in the distant mountain ranges.

Further south again, a different geological history emerged, characterised by batholiths—large intrusive masses of igneous granite and granodiorite rock formed from cooled magma within the Earth's crust. Three of the largest batholiths are the Baw Baw Plateau Granodiorite, Toorongo Granodiorite and the Tynong Granite. The Baw Baw batholith is a defining feature of the Central Highlands, forming the region's highest plateau. Geologist Neville Rosengren and his colleagues tell us that the Baw Baw Plateau supports unique geological features, such as broad concave valleys, peaty flats, tors and stepped valleys. Perhaps the most remarkable feature of the Baw Baw batholith is its distinctive rectangular drainage pattern, which follows a regular pattern of joints in the granodiorite. The lack of glaciation across the batholith during the last ice age suggests a unique weathering process unfolding over millions of years. As a result, the Baw Baw batholith has been recognised as a site of national geological and geomorphological significance.

The Tynong Granite batholith is located south of the town of Warburton and is one of the largest in Victoria. After its formation more than 370 million years ago, the surrounding sedimentary rock eroded to reveal an extensive range of granite mountains. Today, the forests of the batholith surround large tors that have resisted millions of years of erosion. Some of these tors, such as Seven Acre Rock, tower above the forest canopy.

These geological legacies are fundamental to the fabric of the forest. They have created the different types of soil on which the forest grows—whether deep fertile earths or shallow, skeletal scree slopes. Soil fertility can affect the amount of nutrients in the leaves of eucalypts growing in an area and, in turn, the occurrence and breeding patterns of animals such as the Greater Glider, which feeds almost exclusively on eucalypt leaves. The leaves of trees growing on rich soils tend to be high in nutrients; in such areas, there are high densities of gliders. In less fertile areas, the leaves have fewer nutrients, there are fewer gliders and they are monogamous. So geology not only profoundly affects where animals occur, and how many of them there are, but even how they live and breed.

The highest point in the Cerberean Cauldron on Taungurung Country (Chris Taylor)
The ridge of Mount Torbreck forms the highest point in the Cerberean Cauldron. Adorned with large tors and extensive rocky outcrops, the mountain is a defining feature of the cauldron, rising from the valley floor and standing clear of surrounding mountains.

Opposite: **A dawalin (the Taungurung word for waterfall) in the Cerberean Cauldron on Taungurung Country** (Chris Taylor)
Many dawalin cascade along fault lines formed when the Cerberean Cauldron collapsed. The waterfall here is a magnificent juxtaposition of clear water, mossy rocks and luxuriant ferns in a sheltered chasm.

Left: **Seven Acre Rock on Wurundjeri Country** (Sarah Rees)

Seven Acre Rock is a prominent tor of the Tynong Granite Batholith. Rising above the Upper Bunyip Valley and towering over the surrounding Mountain Ash forest, this geological formation is one of the largest exposed rock faces of the batholith. The top of the rock provides extensive views across the Upper Bunyip Valley to Westernport Bay (which is Bunurong Country). This photo also shows the range of ages of trees in the surrounding forest—from stands that regenerated after the 1939 Black Friday fires to those that germinated after the devastating Black Saturday fires in 2009. Seven Acre Rock was the boundary of the 2009 fire, with the forest to the west and north escaping incineration.

Overleaf: **A rock pool on the Baw Baw Plateau on Wurundjeri Country** (Chris Taylor)

While rock pools occur in many rock types, they are especially common in granite outcrops. They were important as water sources for Aboriginal people. These rock pools form naturally through chemical weathering of rocks, but Aboriginal people often enlarged them by lighting fires in the dry depressions and scraping away the loosened rock. Some aquatic insects are found only in these granite rock pools.

Opposite: **Tors on the floor of the forest on Gunaikurnai Country** (Chris Taylor)

Large granodiorite tors are a key feature of the forest floor in many parts of the Baw Baw Plateau and surrounding escarpments. These 'mushroom rocks' are located in Shining Gum forest near Mount Erica. This area was a trading route for the Gunaikurnai People. It was also habitat for the Spotted-tailed Quoll, which uses rocky areas as communal latrine sites. This species is now either very rare or possibly even regionally extinct in the Central Highlands.

CHAPTER 3

RAINFOREST

Hidden deep within the eucalypt forests of the Central Highlands are cool temperate rainforests, relicts from more than 60 million years ago, when the Australian continent was still joined with New Zealand, South America and Antarctica as part of the supercontinent of Gondwana. The climate was very different then—a cool, moist environment where fire was likely to have been rare. Cool temperate rainforests were once extensive across eastern Australia, and only remnants now occur in Tasmania, Victoria and New South Wales. These forests typically sit within more recently arrived eucalypt-dominated forests that appear to have originated in South America but have become a quintessential part of Australian landscapes.

Cool temperate rainforests are dominated by trees other than eucalypts. Myrtle Beech is the primary species of tree in most patches of cool temperate rainforest in the Central Highlands. This tree can reach an impressive 50 metres in height, but it looks short in comparison to the overstorey Mountain Ash giants, which can grow to more than 90 metres. Myrtle Beech has small, deep-green leaves, although new foliage produced in spring can be a spectacular orange or even pink colour. The species' scientific name is *Nothofagus cunninghamii*; Nothofagus means 'false beech', alluding to its crude resemblance to beech trees of the Northern Hemisphere, which have the genus name Fagus. However, the two genera of trees are only very distantly related.

Another common tree species in stands of cool temperate rainforest is Sassafras. When crushed, the distinctive toothed leaves produce a strong nutmeg-like smell. Sassafras and Myrtle Beech often grow together around streams and deep wet gullies.

Rainforest trees such as Myrtle Beech can be particularly long-lived (exceeding many hundreds of years) and, like eucalypts, can develop hollows, providing a refuge for wildlife. In a detailed radio-tracking study, we found six radio-collared Mountain Brushtail Possums denning during the day in a large old Myrtle Beech. Such communal sheltering behaviour can be associated with extremely cold weather, such as heavy snowfalls, or with drought and fire. Animals have been observed moving from surrounding burned areas to rainforest refuges after wildfires, and returning to the drier forests several years later. This behaviour has greatly affected patterns of genetic variability among possums.

Opposite: **The closed canopy of cool temperate rainforest on Wurundjeri Country** (Sarah Rees)
Cool temperate rainforests are hotspots of diversity for species of mosses, liverworts, hornworts and lichens. These plants require damp environments as they dry out quickly. The trunks and branches of old rainforest trees can be covered in these plants.

Cool temperate rainforest on Wurundjeri Country (Chris Taylor)
This rainforest is on the southern slopes of Mount Donna Buang. Rainforests often support an extremely dense layer of tree ferns, some of which are over 350 years old and can even be 1000 years old. The fronds of tree ferns, like all ferns, have a very distinctive way of unfurling, with the head of the stem held erect like a horse in an equestrian event. This unique pattern—sometimes called a fiddlehead because of the resemblance to the top of a string instrument—is caused by differences in the rate of growth between the upper and lower layers of the frond as it unfurls.

Cool temperate rainforest trees are also important for the Wollert (Leadbeater's Possum). This animal likes to nest in large old eucalypts with dense vegetation, especially Myrtle Beech, close to the entrance hollow. The cover allows the possum to easily jump out of the hollow onto surrounding vegetation without having to come to the ground; this way it can leave its daytime nest site undetected by predators, and head out to find food.

Unlike tropical rainforests, which are renowned for their extraordinary diversity of birds, insects and other creatures (and the resulting cacophony of calls), cool temperate rainforests are often quiet places. They also lack the insect and bird activity of adjacent eucalypt forest, although some species, like the Pink Robin, can be common, as are some ancient invertebrate groups like springtails. These wingless animals are typically around 5 millimetres long and have a tail-like appendage that can fling them into the air to avoid predators. Trees such as Myrtle Beech don't offer the kinds of food that many animal species find attractive, such as nectar, abundant seeds, fruits and fleshy leaves. Rather, Myrtle Beech trees have small flowers (with both male and female flowers on the same tree) and a limited number of small, winged seeds.

In the Central Highlands, cool temperate rainforest is generally restricted to wetter and more sheltered areas, and is most luxuriant in gullies. It is more likely to develop in flatter places, although scattered Myrtle Beech trees can be found on steep slopes where Mountain Ash is the dominant overstorey tree. Cool temperate rainforest stands are most commonly found within old-growth wet eucalypt forests. Here they form a deep-green understorey layer in combination with other trees and tall shrubs such as wattles, Musk Daisy Bush and Hazel Pomaderris. Cool temperate rainforest is best developed in areas where there has been limited disturbance, such as logging, for 50 years or more. In places that have been logged, trees such as Myrtle Beech need 50–60 years to begin to recover.

River and rainforest on Gunaikurnai Country (Chris Taylor)
This magical place is on the Tyers River near where it cascades down the escarpment of the Baw Baw Plateau. Magnificent Myrtle Beech trees reach over the river, creating a natural cathedral-like arch. The heavily shaded sections of the river are important habitat for native frogs, fish and crayfish.

Left: **Mosses adorning Myrtle Beech trees on Wurundjeri Country** (Sarah Rees)
The trunks of rainforest trees can be covered by mosses, lichens and hornworts (collectively known as bryophytes); this moist layer of primitive plants is sometimes several centimetres deep. Different kinds of bryophytes colonise different environments—from rocks and logs to the trunks of living and dead trees. This group is very diverse in cool temperate rainforests.

Above: **Sassafras on Wurundjeri Country** (Sarah Rees)
A Wurundjeri Elder has told us that for thousands of years her people harvested the leaves of Sassafras trees to brew into a tea. It has a similar taste to nutmeg.

Opposite: **A Rainforest Site of National Significance along the boundary between Taungurung and Wurundjeri Countries** (Chris Taylor)
There is a myth long held by some foresters that if Mountain Ash is left undisturbed, it will eventually be replaced by cool temperate rainforest. This is unlikely for several reasons. First, not all parts of landscapes are suitable for rainforest trees; rainforest is most likely to develop in the wettest parts of the landscape. Second, while rainforest is a prominent part of the understorey of old-growth eucalypt forest, almost no stands of Mountain Ash exceed 550 years old (which is the maximum lifespan of these eucalypts). Mountain Ash stands are usually burned well before this time and begin the process of natural regeneration.

Above: **Rainforest and mist on Wurundjeri Country** (Sarah Rees)
The small, densely spaced, dark-green, horizontal leaves of Myrtle Beech trees mean that little light penetrates to the forest floor. In contrast, the leaves of Mountain Ash trees hang vertically, allowing light to reach the midstorey and understorey layers below.

Rainforest on Toorongo Plateau on Gunaikurnai Country (Chris Taylor)
On the Toorongo Plateau, a granodiorite batholith rock formation, cool temperate rainforest straddles ridgelines and mountain summits—a unique feature, as this forest type is found mostly in sheltered gullies and valleys.

CHAPTER 4

MOUNTAIN ASH AND OTHER FORESTS

As the Australian continent moved northwards over the past 25 million years (at about the same speed as fingernails grow each year), there was a very slow change in climate. Rainfall decreased and temperatures increased. The cool temperate rainforest retracted and a new group of tree species evolved to dominate the landscape—the eucalypts. Eucalypts originated in a part of Gondwana that is now South America and the tallest species of this hyper-diverse group (with more than 820 species) is Mountain Ash. Indeed, there is perhaps nothing more extraordinary than an old-growth Mountain Ash forest. The Mountain Ash is the tallest flowering plant in the world. For the first 50 years of its life, a Mountain Ash can grow at a staggering 1 metre per year, sometimes even faster in places with good soils and high rainfall. It can reach a top height after 120–150 years of 90–100 metres, with some individuals reportedly even taller. The girth of these giants can exceed 30 metres.

The Giant Redwoods (or Giant Sequoias) in California are taller than Mountain Ash but they are conifers, not flowering plants. They also grow much more slowly, with the oldest trees dated at about 3200 years old, whereas the oldest Mountain Ash have been estimated to be 550 years old. That is, the Mountain Ash reaches similar heights to the Giant Sequoias but in a quarter to half the time.

Large old Mountain Ash trees have some distinctive features. First, they can develop very large buttresses to prevent them from falling over, especially on sloping ground. The sheer size of these buttresses can make it difficult to accurately measure the diameter of giant trees. Secondly, large old trees often have many hollows, in the trunk and on large lateral branches. These develop where the tree has been wounded by falling branches or lightning strikes, or where lateral branches are not cleanly shed and rot begins to occur. Hollows first become large and obvious in trees that are approximately 120 years old. Significant amounts of decay often occur around a tree's crown, especially where the canopy is blown out by windstorms (and particularly after a tree has been weakened by prolonged drought). When a tree has lost its main canopy but the dead upper branches persist, it can resemble the head of antlers on a male deer, and so very large trees are sometimes called 'stags'. (Another reason for the name is that North Americans call standing

Opposite: **Old-growth Mountain Ash tree with snow and lichens on Gunaikurnai Country** (Chris Taylor)
Occasional snowfalls add to the moisture budget in wet eucalypt forests. A dense cover of mosses, lichens and hornworts grows on the persistent bark stocking around the buttresses of old-growth trees. This tree is on the south face of Mount Baw Baw, in an area known as the Mountain Monarchs.

dead trees 'snags', but this has connotations of barbecued food in Australia, so the term was exchanged for stag.)

Stands of old-growth trees shed tonnes of bark every year, producing bark streamers that provide a critical microhabitat for a rich community of species such as tree crickets and spiders, which, in turn, are prey for possums, gliders and birds. As trees mature, they direct more of their available energy away from growth and into reproduction, so large old trees produce substantially more flowers and seeds than young trees. The effect of this is also seen after a wildfire—seed germination is far higher when an old forest is burned than when young forests are burned. Old-growth trees are also more likely to support mistletoe than younger trees, as well as animals like the Mistletoebird, which feeds on mistletoe fruit. These animals are much more likely to be detected in old-growth forest than elsewhere in wet forest environments.

Large old trees have thicker bark at their base than younger trees, which means they are more resistant to the effects of fire. Although Mountain Ash is considered to be fire-sensitive (and young trees are typically killed by fire), many large living trees have fire scars at their base, indicating that they have survived past fires. Indeed, studies of the growth rings of very large trees have found that some of them have survived up to seven fires. The fire scars on Mountain Ash trees are blackened with charcoal and shaped like a church door. The pattern is caused by new tissue growing around the wounds created by the hottest parts of the fire front at the base of trees. Surprisingly, these wounds occur on the leeward side of the fire's direction and can therefore provide valuable information about fire behaviour, including how to 'read a landscape' by looking at patterns in forest stands of different ages.

The main types of forest and other kinds of vegetation in the Central Highlands region
The pale green areas on this map show the extent of the Mountain Ash (*Eucalyptus regnans*) forests in the Central Highlands, along with the similar looking Alpine Ash (*Eucalyptus delegatensis*) forests that grow at higher elevations. The Central Highlands region supports the most extensive areas of Mountain Ash remaining on mainland Australia. Mountain Ash is also found in smaller patches across the Otway Ranges in south-west Victoria and the Strzelecki Ranges in South Gippsland, as well as in East Gippsland. Some of these areas suffered intensive land clearing for agriculture following European colonisation.

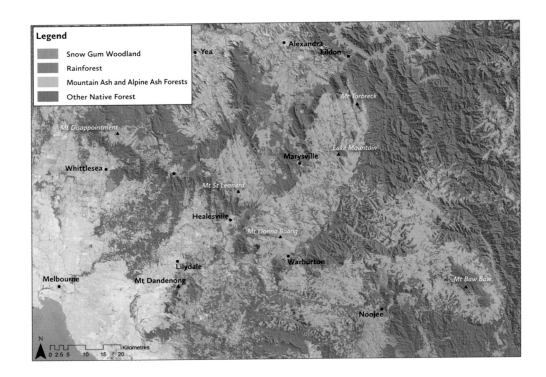

Legend
- Snow Gum Woodland
- Rainforest
- Mountain Ash and Alpine Ash Forests
- Other Native Forest

Old-growth Mountain Ash forest on Taungurung Country
(Chris Taylor)
The oldest Mountain Ash trees have been dated at 550 years old, and germinated some 300 years before British colonisers arrived in 1788. The stand of forest in this image has at least three distinct age cohorts of trees, which is typical for the few remaining areas in the Central Highlands region that are dominated by old-growth Mountain Ash. Such multi-aged forests support a very high diversity of forest birds and arboreal marsupials. In spite of this, many of these areas remain unprotected, such as this old-growth Mountain Ash forest, which is scheduled for logging.

Many people think of dead trees as useless—indeed, we often talk metaphorically of discarding 'dead wood'. In the ecological world, however, dead wood is critical: huge numbers of animals, plants and fungi depend on these structures in the forest. Some animals select them over living trees. The rotting wood inside a dead standing tree (sometimes given the charming name 'mudguts') generates an enormous amount of heat, much like a giant upright compost heap, providing a cosy winter shelter for small animals like the Wollert (Leadbeater's Possum).

Living in dead trees comes with risks, including tree collapse. Driving in the forest late one afternoon, I was forced to stop due to a large dead tree lying across the track. Before pulling a chainsaw from the back of the truck, I inspected the tree. Among the splintered wood was a nest with four Wollerts—still alive. They quickly shot into the forest, leaving behind their nest, a tightly woven ball of bark strips, which I collected and photographed. The nest was crawling with a species of flea that occurs only on the Wollert.

Even in the absence of human disturbances such as logging, it is unlikely that old-growth forests occupied all parts of forested landscapes. Old growth is more likely to occur in areas with low levels of sunlight, possibly because these areas are wetter and there is less fire. When fires do occur in old-growth forests, they are less severe than elsewhere in the landscape. Given the extent of logging and fire, the amount of old-growth forest is now severely diminished. Old-growth forest once comprised 30–60 per cent of the Mountain Ash ecosystem. Now it makes up just 1.16 per cent of these environments, much of it in patches less than a few hectares in size. Approximately 98 per cent of Mountain Ash forest across the Central Highlands is now less than 80 years old. These changes have been so profound and the forests are now so vulnerable to the effects of recurrent fire that the Mountain Ash forests of the Central Highlands region have been formally classified as Critically Endangered under the International Union for the Conservation of Nature (IUCN).

Large old Mountain Ash trees are most spectacular when they occur in extensive stands of similar-sized trees—that is, old-growth forest. Some of the most extensive areas of old-growth forest in the Central Highlands are deep within closed water catchments that have been off limits to logging and other human access for a century or longer. As shown throughout this book, old-growth forests are important for many reasons. Compared to young forests, they support the most nutrient-rich soils, store larger amounts of carbon, and generate much more water. They also support high levels of biodiversity. Old-growth forests have multiple layers—an overstorey of giant eucalypts; an understorey of wattles, Hazel Pomaderris and rainforest trees; a layer of shrubs and tree ferns; and dense ground cover. From the canopy to the ground, there are many different habitat and foraging niches for a large number of bird species, as well as gliders and bats. Old-growth trees support many more hollows than young trees and these provide critical denning and nesting sites for many species of animals.

Mountain Ash in flower on Taungurung Country (Sarah Rees)
Mountain Ash typically flower between December and May; the timing varies depending on elevation, aspect and other environmental factors. In addition, not all trees flower in a given year. Young trees allocate most of their energy to growth (to win the race for light). However, well-established old trees dedicate much of their energy and resources to flowering and seed production. Therefore, the greatest pulses of flowers are in old-growth stands, providing an important source of food for many animal species.

Following pages: **Mountain Ash and mist on Wurundjeri Country** (Sarah Rees)
Mountain Ash trees have a distinctive smooth upper trunk and a dark red-brown stocking at the base. The trees in these mountainous areas are often immersed in thick fog at the beginning of the day.

Right: **The entire village of Fernshaw assembled around the Furmston Tree on Wurundjeri Country in 1933** (State Library Victoria)

Until the early 1990s, the Furmston Tree stood at the edge of the Maroondah Catchment close to the route of the old Maroondah Highway. I was devastated when I found out that the Furmston Tree had collapsed, yet another of the once common giants lost from the forest. The dimensions of this Mountain Ash tree were incredible: 87.5 metres in height, with a girth of 19.5 metres (at 2.7 metres above the ground). Yet there were many trees even larger; the girth of the Edward VII Tree in the Upper Yarra area was almost twice that of the Furmston Tree. The Ferguson Tree in the Watts Catchment near the town of Healesville was named after the Inspector of State Forests who measured it in 1872 after it had fallen over at 132.6 metres, although some people have disputed this record.

Opposite: **Multi-aged Mountain Ash forest on Taungurung Country** (Chris Taylor)

One of the most remarkable things about giant Mountain Ash trees is the relatively small size of the crown. It is astonishing that these enormous trees can be fuelled by photosynthesis from so few leaves. As shown in this photograph, stands of old-growth trees shed tonnes of bark every year, creating bark streamers that are in turn habitat for a wide range of animals from carnivorous tree crickets to spiders.

Above: **Greater Glider on Wurundjeri Country** (Steve Kuiter)
The Greater Glider, the world's largest gliding marsupial, can be extremely abundant in old-growth Mountain Ash forests. The species feeds almost entirely on eucalypt leaves, and must consume large quantities of leaves every night to survive. I've spent many nights patiently sitting under huge old trees waiting for a glider to emerge. When an animal first leaves its hollow, it sits silently preening itself before releasing a shower of 'processed' leaves onto the forest floor (and observing biologist) far below. (The pellets are small and dry, so there are worse experiences.) These animals almost never den in the same tree as they eat but instead glide long distances into the forest to feed—possibly as a way to reduce the risk that predators will find their shelter.

Right: **A large old Mountain Ash tree in the Toolangi Forest on Taungurung Country** (Chris Taylor)
Large old trees develop buttresses to stabilise their great height and weight and reduce the risk of collapse. These buttresses also provide support for lichens and deep mats of mosses. The other side of this magnificent tree has a blackened 'church door' fire scar—evidence that it has survived wildfire. I was once measuring the circumference of a tree similar to this one only to be startled by a female White-throated Treecreeper flushed from a hollow that had developed around a fire scar no more than a metre off the ground. The White-throated Treecreeper is a relatively common bird in the Mountain Ash forest, and has a distinctive behaviour. It spirals up the trunk of a tree, probing bark in search of invertebrates while also issuing a loud *piping* call.

Alpine Ash forest on Gunaikurnai Country (Chris Taylor)
Alpine Ash forest looks similar to Mountain Ash, although it is shorter, the understorey is less dense and the trees are typically more widely spaced. It is also more geographically widespread, dominating the slopes of the Australian Alps throughout Victoria, New South Wales and the Australian Capital Territory. Alpine Ash is also found in Tasmania. One feature of these forests is especially remarkable—the smell. The faint mint-like aroma makes an Alpine Ash forest almost instantly recognisable.

Alpine Ash forest on the Torbreck Range, Taungurung Country (Chris Taylor)
This image shows a stand of Alpine Ash that regenerated after the Black Friday
fires in 1939. The trees are all the same age, as they all germinated at the same
time—soon after the catastrophic fires had passed. Like Mountain Ash, Alpine Ash
is sensitive to being burned and easily killed by high-intensity and high-severity
wildfires. Unfortunately, this forest is scheduled for logging.

Above: **Mountain Grey Gums and wattles on Taungurung Country**
(Chris Taylor)
Mountain Grey Gum is a prominent feature in the mixed-species
forests occurring at lower elevations in the Central Highlands.
The forest pictured is in the Big River Valley, one of the more remote
areas, characterised by deep forested valleys and rocky ridgelines.
Unlike Alpine Ash and Mountain Ash forests, which tend to be
dominated by just one species of eucalypt, mixed-species forests can
include several kinds of eucalypts, such as Peppermint and Manna
Gums, as well as the pictured Mountain Grey Gums.

Opposite: **Manna Gum with moss and fungi at its base
in Taungurung Country** (Sarah Rees)
Manna Gum is an incredible tree. The Wurundjeri People called
it Wurun. It is also known as White Gum in Tasmania and Ribbon
Gum in New South Wales. Manna Gum ranges from a relatively
short, stunted tree in northern inland Victoria to a forest giant
in Tasmania and Central Victoria. It is a critical tree for specialist
leaf-eating animals such as the Koala and the Greater Glider. Not
all eucalypts are created equal in the diet of such iconic Australian
animals and the leaves of Manna Gum are particularly high in
nutrients; other tree species can have far fewer nutrients as
well as large concentrations of toxic chemicals that make the
leaves unpalatable.

Opposite: **A Snow Gum standing tall on a ridgeline on Taungurung Country** (Chris Taylor)
While many Snow Gums are bent and twisted, others tower over the landscape, such as this tree high above the Waring (Goulburn River) valley.

Above: **Snow Gums on the Baw Baw Plateau on Gunaikurnai Country** (Chris Taylor)
The contorted forms of old-growth Snow Gums are one of the most stunning sights in the Australian high country, including in the subalpine woodlands of the Central Highlands region. Like most eucalypts, Snow Gums shed their bark annually. However, in Snow Gums the process of bark shedding gives rise to a beautiful mix of olive, salmon and near-white colours on their trunks. Snow Gum woodlands have been heavily affected by wildfires, with few old-growth stands remaining unburned in Victoria in the past 25 years. However, the species can recover after fire, albeit slowly.

These stands of Snow Gum have a distinct low shrub layer, which creates a well-aerated environment under the snow in winter, called subnivean space. This is a safe place for small mammals to forage in winter, sheltered from predators such as the Red Fox. The Snow Gums pictured here are on the Baw Baw Plateau and are a subspecies found only on the plateau and nearby on Mount Useful.

Snow Gums on the Baw Baw Plateau on Gunaikurnai Country
(Chris Taylor)
Almost all tree species in areas subject to heavy snowfall have a pyramid shape—narrow at the top and broader at the base, often with small lateral branches. The many species of conifers in the Northern Hemisphere are classic examples. Snow Gum is an exception to this rule, with old-growth trees characterised by large, spreading branches. Heavy piles of snow can accumulate on the trunk and branches, and frozen leaves are common in winter. The contorted branching patterns of Snow Gum give each tree a unique shape.

CHAPTER 5

THE UNDERSTOREY AND FOREST FLOOR

Although far less appreciated, the understorey and forest floor are as impressive as the trees towering above it. We often measure the age of the forest by that of the overstorey trees, yet the understorey can sometimes be much older and characterised by biological legacies centuries in the making. The tree ferns and daisy bushes that often dominate the understorey of Mountain Ash forests can survive fire, resprouting soon after a fire has passed through. This allows them to persist in a burned area even if the overstorey of eucalypt trees has been killed. In fact, tree ferns are often the first sign of green in an otherwise burned forest. They grow very quickly after a fire because the sunlight is no longer blocked by canopy trees, which have either been killed or lost their crowns. Many tree ferns have lived through a number of fires, and they can be very old. Botanists have estimated that Soft Tree Ferns in the closed water catchments (where logging is banned) such as the O'Shannassy Water Catchment are up to 350 years old and are potentially even 1000 years old.

When they fall, Mountain Ash trees become giant logs that can support deep mats of mosses and lichens and numerous ferns, which help to retain moisture in logs on the forest floor. Logs are nursery sites for the germination of other plants, such as rainforest trees. They are runways for animals such as the Mountain Brushtail Possum, and nesting sites for small mammals like the Bush Rat. They also shelter predators such as the venomous Tiger Snake and Highland Copperhead.

There are huge volumes of logs in Mountain Ash forests—over 550 tonnes per hectare. This is far more than in tropical ecosystems, where logs break down very quickly. The high wood density of eucalypts and slow rates of decay are two of the reasons why so much carbon is stored on the floor of Mountain Ash forests.

The soils in Mountain Ash forests can be extremely rich in nutrients. As discussed in the previous chapter, the highest levels of nutrients and soil moisture occur in long-undisturbed forests. Fires and logging can severely deplete nutrient levels and change the soil structure, for example making it sandier and drier.

The floor of Mountain Ash forests offers many surprises. One of these is the world's tallest moss, Dawsonia. It is perhaps apt that the world's tallest moss occurs in a forest of the world's tallest flowering trees. But Dawsonia is just one of a vast array of species

Opposite: **Mixed forests on Wurundjeri Country** (Sarah Rees)
Natural forests can sometimes be a mix of treed areas and more open places characterised by tree ferns and shrubs and fewer trees. These open patches are often important for reptiles as sunlight can penetrate closer to the forest floor. In these exposed places animals can bask on large logs in the sunlight.

A Fringed Violet on Wurundjeri Country
(Sarah Rees)
This plant species is a member of the lily group, and sometimes called a Fringed Lily. Each flower has three fringed petals and three narrower fringeless parts. Each flower lasts just one day, however the plant can produce many flowers over several months.

THE BIRDS AND THE TREES

Struggling through dense vegetation in wet forests can be noisy, which scares away many of the birds. But when you are quietly measuring plants, some bird species become curious and will venture close—before quickly moving away. The Eastern Whipbird is a good example. This relatively large bird (measuring about 30 centimetres in length) will come to scope you out, all the while calling to its mate. Some other birds will stay close by for prolonged periods. Once I was followed for 30 minutes by an Eastern Yellow Robin, waiting for me to stir up insects which it then expertly caught.

Tall Astelia on Wurundjeri Country (Chris Taylor)
There are just twelve known populations of Tall Astelia, a rare lily,
in the world; all but one of these are found in the wet forests of the
Central Highlands. The species appears to be sensitive to wildfires and
has declined dramatically since European colonisation. Tall Astelia is
also at risk from logging and disease.

Rough Tree Ferns in the Toolangi Forest on Taungurung Country (Chris Taylor)
Tree ferns are a critical part of the structure of Victoria's wet forests. Two species are prominent—the Rough Tree Fern (*Cyathea australis*) and Soft Tree Fern (*Dicksonia antarctica*). As suggested by their common names, these ferns can easily be distinguished by the texture of their trunks.

of mosses, lichens and hornworts in the Central Highlands. These plants colonise a wide range of environments, from rocky outcrops to fallen logs, tree trunks, and the stems of tree ferns and other plants. There have been few surveys of these primitive plants in Victoria's wet forests, but the limited work to date suggests there are many species that have yet to be formally described by scientists.

The cool, wet conditions that characterise these forests also make them ideal environments for fungi, including truly spectacular species such as the iridescent Ghost Fungus. Recent detailed genetic analyses of soil samples from these wet forest environments have recorded upwards of 10,000 different gene sequences for fungi.

The soil also stores seeds of many plants. Wattle seeds can lie dormant in the soil for decades, perhaps even centuries, only to germinate after a fire or soil disturbance such as logging. Wattles then become a key part of the structure of the forest, fixing nitrogen for eucalypts, and providing food such as sap, leaves and seeds for a range of species, from insects to possums, gliders and birds. Wattles also provide an interconnected set of pathways for animals like the Wollert (Leadbeater's Possum) to travel through the forest.

Other plants, such as Giant Mountain Grass, spend long periods of time unseen, persisting in the soil seed bank only to appear relatively briefly after fire, before disappearing again after just a few years until the next disturbance. When this species emerged following the 2009 wildfires, so few people recognised it as a native grass that field crews initially sprayed it, thinking it was a weed.

Eugene von Guérard, *Ferntree Gully in the Dandenong Ranges,* 1857 (National Gallery of Australia)
This painting depicts an area near Dobsons Creek in the Dandenongs that was thick with ancient tree ferns, as depicted by travelling colonial artist Eugene von Guérard. When the European colonists came to Australia, many commented that the landscape was like a 'gentleman's park'. However, as this image clearly shows, not all of the landscape was park-like. There are two lyrebirds in the foreground.

Above: **Tree ferns among multi-aged forest on Wurundjeri Country**
(Sarah Rees)

The crowns of tree ferns can act like a basket, catching seeds falling
from the trees overhead. Some rainforest tree species such as Myrtle
Beech take advantage of this by germinating in the 'basket', getting a
substantial head start on competitors that begin their growth on the
forest floor.

Right: **Senescing and dying wattles on Wurundjeri Country**
(Sarah Rees)

Wattles are part of the cycle of life in the forest. Most wattles start
to die after several decades, but their legacy lives on in the seeds
in the soil. A disturbance such as fire or the upturned root bole of a
giant eucalypt is enough to trigger the germination of a new cohort
of young wattles.

Under the tree ferns on Wurundjeri Country (Sarah Rees)
The deep litter layer under tree ferns is an ideal foraging environment
for a range of forest birds, including the Scaly or Bassian Thrush
and the Eastern Yellow Robin. The Scaly Thrush almost wallows
in litter, flicking leaves and small branches aside while hunting for
invertebrates. The Eastern Yellow Robin has an entirely different
strategy—it sits and waits on a branch or tree trunk and pounces
on its invertebrate prey when it moves.

Wattles and rainforest rising above a layer of Hardwater Ferns on Wurundjeri Country (Sarah Rees)
The wattle layer is a critical part of the architecture of wet eucalypt forests. Wattle leaves and seeds are eaten by animals such as the Mountain Brushtail Possum, and the sap is a source of carbohydrates for the Wollert (Leadbeater's Possum) and the Sugar Glider. The leaves are also eaten by insects, which are preyed on by possums, gliders and birds. The dense interconnected branches of wattles create an understorey highway, allowing animals to move through the forest without having to come to the ground.

Mosses holding water following rain on Wurundjeri Country
(Sarah Rees)
There is significantly more moss cover in old-growth forests than in younger stands. It has been estimated that it can take up to 30 years for moss to entirely cover the surface of logs. The luxuriant, species-rich moss communities that develop on very large fallen trees may be the reason why these logs stay moisture-laden, even during prolonged drought.

Young Wollert (Leadbeater's Possum) on Taungurung Country
(Steven Kuiter)
Young Wollerts are tiny versions of their parents. Adults and young
alike have a black stripe of fur on their backs. This marking is shared
with many other nocturnal possums and gliders. The reason for
the stripe is not known, although ecologists have noticed that it is
most often found on species that eat sap and gum from wattles and
eucalypts. The black strip resembles gum secretions on trees and may
provide some camouflage for animals when they are feeding—a time
when they are at risk of being taken by owls.

Opposite: **Dawsonia on Wurundjeri Country** (Sarah Rees)
Dawsonia, the world's tallest moss, has vertical stems that reach 50 centimetres in height. Unlike almost all other mosses, it has well-developed tissues that conduct water and the products of photosynthesis. It is most commonly found on the forest floor under Mountain Ash trees.

Above: **Forest lichens on Gunaikurnai Country** (Sarah Rees)
Lichens are a composite entity: an amalgam of an alga or a cyanobacterium living around the filaments of a fungus. Both organisms are changed completely in the compact—and they cannot return to what they were. The two partners live in symbiosis; that is, they mutually benefit from the association. The fungus is typically the dominant partner, even though its appearance is transformed. Lichens are highly sensitive to pollutants such as excessive amounts of nitrogen in the atmosphere and can be used as indicators of air quality.

Fungus in leaf litter on Wurundjeri Country (Sarah Rees)
Fungi are everywhere in the forest. Some occur only on dead trees. There is even a special technical name for species that depend on dead wood—saproxylic organisms. Others, like truffles, grow on the roots of trees and help to capture nutrients for the sole use of the host plant. Fungi can transform apparently lifeless areas, such as rock slabs, into micro hotspots of biodiversity.

Fungi on a tree on Wurundjeri Country (Sarah Rees)
This bracket fungi flourishes on the trunks of living trees.

Opposite: **Fungi growing on a tree trunk on Wurundjeri Country** (Sarah Rees)
I have often observed the Mountain Brushtail Possum eating the fungi shown in this image. It eats a range of kinds of mushrooms, including some reputed to have hallucinogenic effects in humans, but it is unknown whether they have the same effect on brushtail possums.

Fungi on a tree trunk on Taungurung Country (Steven Kuiter)
In Australia, fungi are especially important for helping to create hollows
in trees, because our continent lacks animals, such as woodpeckers,
that create cavities—indeed, Australia is the only vegetated land mass
on Earth without woodpeckers. While fungi (and animals like termites)
can form cavities, it is a far slower process than in the forests of other
parts of the world—what can take a few months or years in North
America can extend over decades or even centuries in Australia. The
slow process of hollow development in Australian trees is all the more
remarkable when you consider that our extraordinary continent
supports proportionately more cavity-dependent species than
anywhere else on Earth; over 300 species of mammals, birds, reptiles
and frogs, and countless thousands of invertebrates, cannot survive
without access to cavities in trees.

Left: **Fungi on leaf litter on Taungurung Country** (Steven Kuiter) Fungi are critical in the decomposition of leaf litter—an essential ecological process in all forests worldwide.

Below left: **Ghost Fungus on Taungurung Country** (Steven Kuiter) Ghost Fungi grow on the trunks of trees and glow iridescent green, creating a wonderful night-time display in the forest. It is not just fungi that are capable of biofluorescence, or absorbing and emitting light. Recent studies have shown that many frogs and salamanders in the Northern Hemisphere light up like glow sticks—they are biofluorescent under blue or ultraviolet light. It is possible that the skin, bones and even urine of some Australian frogs are also biofluorescent—although scientific studies will be needed to determine if this is the case. In an even more remarkable and recent discovery, it is now clear that many Australian mammals are also biofluorescent, including animals such as the Platypus.

Fungus on moss on Taungurung Country (Steven Kuiter)
This tiny fungus stands 0.5 to 2 cm in height and is sometimes called Pixie's Parasol. Like many species of mushrooms, it grows primarily on rotting wood.

CHAPTER 6

WATER

Almost no living thing can survive without water, including us. Water is perhaps the most important ecosystem service provided by the wet forests of the Central Highlands. Virtually all the water used by the more than five million Melburnians and many people north of the Great Dividing Range comes from these forests. Tens of thousands of businesses also depend on this source of water.

The value of the Central Highlands for water production has long been understood. From the mid-nineteenth century, water catchments surrounding Melbourne began to be closed to human access to protect water quality. This was, in part, a response to health problems in the early days of Melbourne when waterborne diseases such as typhoid were a killer. The authorities' foresight in closing the catchments meant that the Melbourne and Metropolitan Board of Works (and its predecessors) was more than 50 years ahead of planners for many other cities around the world, including large North American cities such as New York and Boston. The legacy of these decisions is that Melbourne has some of the best drinking water of any major city in the world.

Not all landscapes are equal in terms of yielding water. The condition of forest catchments makes a significant difference to how much water is produced. Decades of studies have shown that old-growth forests generate the most water—up to 12 million litres more water per hectare each year than young forests. Young trees transpire vast amounts of water through their leaves, which reduces the amount available to flow into streams and then into dams. This also leaves young, fast-growing forests much drier than old-growth forests—another possible reason why younger forests are more prone to high-severity fires, as discussed in the following chapter.

Different types of forest also vary in terms of water yields. Unsurprisingly, wet eucalypt forests produce substantially more water than dry forests. In the Thomson Catchment—the largest in the network of catchments that comprise Melbourne's water supply system—almost two-thirds of rain falls in just one-third of the area, and that part is dominated by ash-type eucalypt forests.

Early policy makers wanted the forests right across the Central Highlands and all the way east to the Baw Baw Plateau to be fully protected from timber interests to safeguard catchment values and Melbourne's water security. However, several important

Opposite: **Birrarung (Yarra River) on Wurundjeri Country** (Chris Taylor)
Vegetation close to rivers is often denser and larger than in other parts of the landscape. Trees that fall into streams and rivers provide valuable habitat for a range of aquatic animals. The leaves and twigs that find their way into watercourses eventually break down and add nutrients for the growth of other plants as well as food for a range of native animals that inhabit these environments.

catchments—including the Thomson Catchment—remained open to logging operations. A study of the Thomson Catchment has quantified the impact of logging on water yields. By 2050, continued logging will reduce the amount of water generated by the equivalent of the amount of water consumed by more than 600,000 people. The effects of logging on water yield are so substantial that they outweigh the effects of climate change under even the most extreme climate change projections.

The most likely alternative source of water that does not come from catchments is desalinisation plants. This water is, however, both energy-intensive and expensive to produce—about $1650 per megalitre more than water generated from forests. From an economic and water-security perspective, the best long-term strategy is to close catchments for the purpose of unimpeded water production, much as suggested by those far-sighted people who established Melbourne's water supply system more than a century ago. Work based on environmental and economic accounting shows that water from the forests of the Central Highlands is worth more than 25 times the commercial value of the timber.

Beyond the mechanics and economics of water catchments, the networks of rivers and streams in the Central Highlands form some of the most stunning parts of the landscapes in the region. It's in these areas that cool temperate rainforests are most likely to occur, the largest trees are most likely to be found, and glades of ferns and diverse communities of mosses and lichens are best developed and, accordingly, most luxuriant. These waterways are also home to endangered native fish, native crayfish, and well-known faunal icons like the Platypus and Rakali (the native water rat).

The Central Highlands region has numerous spectacular waterfalls. Some are very accessible, while others are hidden in rugged terrain. Many have extraordinary features, such as the evidence of a geological fault line in the Cora Lynn Falls in the Cumberland Scenic Reserve.

SPOTLIGHT IN THE FOG

Fog adds to the moisture budget in the wet forests of the Central Highlands. However, dense fog can create enormous challenges for navigation in the forest, especially at night. Long before the days of personal hand-held global positioning systems, I got thoroughly lost in the forest during a night-time spotlight survey. The fog was so thick, and all the trees so similar, that it was impossible to find my way back to the four-wheel drive. Giving up, I sat on a log for a few hours until dawn and then retraced my steps in the early morning light. Animals continue to call in the fog, and that long night was no exception, with a nearby Sugar Glider yipping like a puppy—its typical contact call—for more than half an hour.

A dawalin (the Taungurung word for waterfall) during a storm in the Toolangi Forest on Taungurung Country (Chris Taylor)
The Mountain Ash forests of the Central Highlands are among the wettest environments of south-eastern mainland Australia, with rainfall approaching two metres per year in some areas. The region supports more than twenty spectacular waterfalls, each quite different in its own special way.

Opposite: **A dawalin at Wilhelmina Falls on Taungurung Country**
(Chris Taylor)
Wilhelmina Falls features a spectacular rockface revealing the Black Range Granodiorite. It flows high above the Murrindindi Valley and extensive views can be seen along specially built viewing platforms adjacent to the falls.

Left: **Little River on Taungurung Country**
(Chris Taylor)
Little River follows a distinctive fault line in the Cerberean Cauldron. The river flows out of the cauldron and past Nanadhong (the Cathedral Range) to the Waring (Goulburn River).

Dawalin at Strath Creek on Taungurung Country (Chris Taylor)
The waterfall at Strath Creek is a defining feature of the gorge dissecting
a mountainous plateau north of Mount Disappointment. In 1862, colonial
artist Eugene von Guérard made a special journey to paint this waterfall;
his painting captures the V-shape at the head of the gorge.

Eugene von Guérard, *Waterfall*, *Strath Creek*, **1862** (Art Gallery
of New South Wales)
The notes accompanying this painting of Strath Creek Falls describe
how it is 'imbued with a sense of awe and wonder', a German
Romantic belief that art allowed insight into the divine. The waterfalls
of the Central Highland region are indeed awe-inspiring and are the
equal of many waterfalls elsewhere around Australia.

Toorongo Falls, on the boundary of Wurundjeri and Gunaikurnai Countries (Chris Taylor)
Toorongo Falls cascades down the granite rock faces associated with the Toorongo Batholith, which defines the geology of the area. This is one of the most accessible and beautiful waterfalls in the Central Highlands region.

Amphitheatre Falls on Gunaikurnai Country (Chris Taylor)
Amphitheatre Falls is on a walking circuit and is only a short distance from
the Toorongo Falls. Like the Toorongo Falls, it is characterised by the exposed
granite of the Toorongo Batholith. The circuit walk features impressive
stands of Mountain Ash, Mountain Grey Gum, Manna Gum and Blackwood.

Left: **Big River on Taungurung Country** (Chris Taylor)
Big River is one of the longest rivers in the Central Highlands region. Originating on the highest ridgelines of the Cerberean Cauldron, it cascades into remote and rugged dissected valleys and joins with the Waring (Goulburn River) at Lake Eildon.

Above: **Dawalin at Snobs Creek Falls on Taungurung Country** (Chris Taylor)
The dawalin at Snobs Creek Falls is a unique feature of the Cerberean Cauldron. The ancient rock under this waterfall was formed along one of the many fault lines that dissect the cauldron. The stream falls several hundred metres into a deeper recess of the fault line, where it continues its flow to the Waring (Goulburn River).

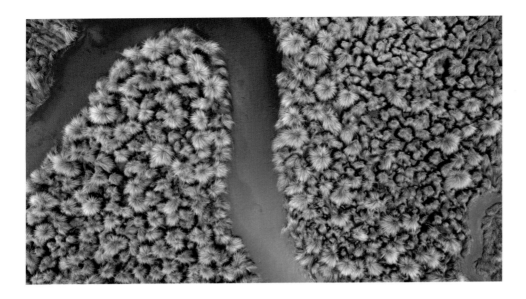

Above: **Montane fen north-west of the Baw Baw Plateau on Wurundjeri Country** (Sarah Rees)

Right: **Montane fen on Carrang-Carrang/Tambo (Thomson River) on Wurundjeri Country** (Sarah Rees)
A fen is a grassy marshland, sometimes also called a mire. Trees grow on the drier, slightly more elevated areas. Some of the most spectacularly developed fens in the Central Highlands region are those around the Carrang-Carrang/Tambo (Thomson River). Carrang-Carrang means 'brackish water': the water in the river is tea-coloured because of tannins naturally washed into streams.

Left: **Alpine fens on Gunaikurnai Country** (Chris Taylor)
Many rivers in the Central Highlands have their origins high in the mountains of the region. This small lake is located in an alpine fen atop the Baw Baw Plateau and is the starting point for the Tyers River.

Above: **The Baw Baw Frog on a bed of moss in Gunaikurnai Country** (Damian Goodall, Zoos Victoria)
The Baw Baw Frog is a Critically Endangered species: only an estimated 250 individuals remain. The frog has a highly restricted distribution confined to an area of approximately 10 square kilometres on the Baw Baw Plateau and its southern escarpments. A key part of its habitat has been protected from logging, but populations of the species have been affected by a disease called Chytrid Fungus that is likely to have been spread around the world as a result of the illegal pet trade. Chytrid Fungus is the world's worst wildlife disease and has contributed to the decline of more than 500 species of amphibians globally and the extinction of 90 species.

Cascades on the southern escarpment of the Baw Baw Plateau on Gunaikurnai Country (Chris Taylor)
The unique geology of the Baw Baw Plateau and surrounding escarpments provides for superb cascades. The large granodiorite boulders in cool streams and shaded by cool temperate rainforests are covered in mosses and lichens, some of which are rare species.

Logs across a river on the Baw Baw Plateau on Gunaikurnai Country
(Chris Taylor)
Rocks and logs are critical parts of the architecture of streams,
trapping sand and creating deep pools for fish and Platypus. Mosses
quickly begin to colonise the parts of logs and rocks exposed above
the surface of the water, showing how dynamic forest and river
ecosystems can be.

Tors along a river at Baw Baw Plateau on Gunaikurnai Country
(Chris Taylor)
Forest waterways form some of the most beautiful riverscapes
anywhere. The boulders and logs slow the water's flow and result in
a mosaic of shallow sandy areas and deeper pools, creating habitats
for a diversity of aquatic life, from Platypus to native fish and
freshwater crayfish.

The Maroondah Reservoir on Wurundjeri Country
(Sarah Rees)
The relatively small Maroondah Reservoir is one of the oldest dams
in Melbourne's domestic water supply network. The surrounding
forest catchment was closed during the Second World War to logging
and all agricultural and urban development to protect the water
supply from pollution.

The Birrarung (Yarra River) in flood on Wurundjeri Country (Sarah Rees)
From its source near the north-western escarpment of the Baw Baw
Plateau, the Birrarung or Yarra River flows from the highest points on
Wurundjeri Country into deep valleys where it feeds the Upper Yarra
Reservoir, one of Melbourne's largest reservoirs. It then flows past the
town of Warburton and descends from the mountains onto the broad
floodplains around Healesville, before making its meandering journey
to Naarm (Melbourne).

Above: **The Thomson Reservoir, Melbourne's largest water supply, on Gunaikurnai Country** (Chris Taylor)
Old-growth forests generate far more water than young forests. Part of this area has been logged, as can be seen in breaks in the tree canopy cover on the ridgelines in the background of this image where there are several clearfelled coupes. As a result, the amount of water generated is significantly less than it would have been had the catchment been left intact.

Following pages: **The Birrarung (Yarra River), bounded by Manna Gums, flowing through the Yarra Valley on Wurundjeri Country** (Chris Taylor)
The Birrarung has been central to the lives of the Wurundjeri People for thousands of years, providing a source of water and food. Since European colonisation, large areas of forest around the Birrarung have been lost due to urban development, agriculture, mining and logging. Remaining areas of forest along its banks are often dominated by Manna Gums, or Wurun, from which the Wurundjeri take their name.

CHAPTER 7

FIRE

Fire is a critical part of the ecology of almost all terrestrial ecosystems in Australia, including the Central Highlands. Australia is the most fire-prone continent on Earth, and many species can be badly affected by fires. However, the impacts of fires can be extremely difficult to study. Every fire is different: different in when it occurs, what and how fast it burns, how patchy it is, how many previous fires have occurred and how recently. It is also different depending on how much other disturbance has occurred (e.g. logging or clearing), which species of animals and plants have been affected, and myriad other factors. Further, almost all plant species respond to a fire (and the sequence of fires) in different ways. Some recover slowly, others quickly, and populations of some seem largely unaffected.

The concept of a fire regime encompasses the key aspects of fire in a particular area and ecosystem. This includes fire intensity (how much heat is produced), fire severity (how heavily the vegetation is burned), the timing of the fire (in which season it occurred), the frequency of fire, and how many fires have occurred there in the past. Effects on biodiversity and ecosystems can be particularly detrimental when fire regimes change. Altered fire regimes pose the second greatest threat to birds in Australia (after land clearing).

There is a well-established direct link between more frequent and widespread wildfires and climate change. This is because climate and weather are the key drivers of fire risk and are the primary influences on fire behaviour. There is strong evidence that fire regimes are changing—more fires are occurring more frequently and burning larger areas. The 2019–20 fires in Australia were unprecedented in terms of area burned (more than 12.3 million hectares) and the extent of biodiversity that was lost: more than three billion individual animals perished. Moreover, the extent of wildfires is increasing significantly in parts of south-eastern Australia. There have been three mega-fires (that is, exceeding 1 million hectares in size) in Victoria since 2003, whereas the previous century saw only one (the Black Friday fires of 1939). Some of the areas burned in 2019–20 had been burned two or even three times in the previous 25 years, including places that should normally burn only once every 75–150 years.

Opposite: **Burned forest close to the abandoned town of Cambarville on Wurundjeri Country** (Sarah Rees)
This stand of trees near the now ghost township of Cambarville, east of Marysville, supports a broad mix of different ages of Mountain Ash forest. Cambarville was largely abandoned when its sawmill was moved to the township of Narbethong in the 1970s. The relocated mill at Narbethong then closed—as have almost all sawmills in the Central Highland region. Some trees at Cambarville were burned severely in 2009, while others were burned less severely, with the fire failing to reach their crowns. This forest supported a large population of more than 50 Mountain Brushtail Possums at the time of the 2009 fires, and every individual survived the fire.

Detailed long-term investigations by The Australian National University in the wet forests of the Central Highlands have documented the responses of populations of animals and plants following fires in 1983 and 2009. In one of the longest running fire and disturbance studies in Australia, fire is identified as essential for the persistence of tree species like Mountain Ash; it is needed to trigger both seed fall from the canopy and their subsequent germination as seedlings. However, too-frequent fires can eliminate the species by killing young trees before they are old enough to produce viable crops of seeds. Following the 'Goldilocks principle', forests need neither too little fire nor too much, but something in between. Even in the case of drier, mixed-species forests that resprout after fire, too much burning can prevent them from recovering.

Studies following the 2009 Black Saturday fires showed a highly variable range of responses among animals. Individuals of some species persisted on burned sites, including places subject to very high intensity and very high severity wildfire. These included the Agile Antechinus (a small, mouse-sized carnivorous marsupial), Bush Rat and Mountain Brushtail Possum. These species had fully recovered to pre-fire levels within a few years. Numbers of other species, like the Flame Robin, boomed soon after the 2009 fire—possibly they were attracted from other places. Yet others, such as the Greater Glider and the Wollert (Leadbeater's Possum), continued to decline in numbers long after the fire occurred. The 2009 fire consumed many of the large old dead trees that these species use as denning and nesting sites and accelerated the collapse of many others.

The impact of fires depends upon the age of a forest when it burns. As we've seen, fires tend to burn at lower severity in old-growth forest than in young forest. Further, when old-growth forest is burned, animals are more likely to persist on burned sites and recover faster. One of the primary reasons for this difference is the types and numbers of what are termed 'biological legacies'. These are the living and dead elements of the previous stand of trees that remain in the new stand that recovers after fire. Biological legacies can include living and dead trees, logs, shrubs and other plants, eggs, seeds and

Black Spur after the 1939 Black Friday fires swept through

The Maroondah Highway winds its way through what has been called the Black Spur. The Maroondah Highway used to be called the Yarra Track and it took gold prospectors as far as Woods Point at the very eastern edge of the Central Highlands region. Parts of the Black Spur forests have been burned several times in the past century, including in 1926, 1939 and 2009. The Black Spur was the location of one of the first ever Australian studies in the discipline of ecology—it was published in 1929.

even living animals (such as Bush Rats and Mountain Brushtail Possums). Old-growth forests support more biological legacies after wildfires than do young forests, especially young forests that have been logged and then regrown.

The fact that young forests burn at higher severity than old forests means that the impacts of fire are not independent of other disturbances such as logging. Indeed, logging operations make forests more prone to high-severity fire. These effects can last for up to 40 years after an area has been logged and then regenerated. This ecological process is called a cumulative impact or an interaction chain. Disturbances such as logging that increase the likelihood of crown fires also can increase the severity of fire in surrounding, unlogged forest through promoting pyrocumulonimbus events—the formation of massive mushroom clouds that accompany major wildfires and even start their own fires through dry lightning storms.

Fire can also interact with other kinds of disturbances, such as browsing by invasive herbivores such as deer. These animals target the new green shoots that grow in burned areas, and significantly impair the recovery of vegetation after a fire. Large numbers of kangaroos and wallabies can have similar impacts on vegetation recovery in burned areas.

While much has been learnt about fire in the wet forests of Victoria, a lot remains to be discovered, and there are some puzzles still to be solved. For example, why do some Gondwanan relict rainforest trees like Myrtle Beech resprout after fire? This seems such an odd response, because fire would have been rare in the cool, wet ancient landscapes where these trees evolved. We know that Aboriginal people did use, and move through, these forests, but we don't know whether they used what is sometimes called 'igni-culture'—careful planned and repeated burning—in these landscapes. It is not possible to take the low-intensity and low-severity burns typical of traditional Aboriginal burning in other vegetation types and apply them in wet eucalypt forests and cool temperate rainforests—it is simply too wet, and repeated fire would destroy the capability of these ecosystems to recover.

Drums of petrol explode in the main street of Woods Point during the 1939 Black Friday fires

The 1939 Black Friday fire caused enormous loss of life and property, in part because there were so many people living and working as timber getters deep in the forest, including in the Central Highlands. There was no modern firefighting equipment—planes, helicopters, excavators or fire trucks. Historical film footage shows people instead trying to suppress the wildfires with rakes and hessian sacks.

Burned Mountain Ash stand at night on Wurundjeri Country (Chris Taylor)
This night-time image shows burned trees following the 2009 Black Saturday fires. At the time of the fire, this stand included both relatively young regrowth trees (on the right) and large old-growth trees (left). Large dead trees can be important nesting sites for possums and gliders in forests regenerating after fire. Indeed, some species of animals will occur in young forests only if there are remnant large trees from a previous old-growth stand.

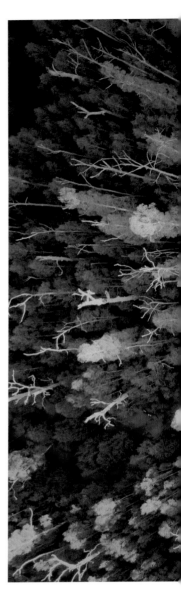

Flame Robin on Taungurung Country (Steven Kuiter)
Male and female Flame Robins almost look like different species.
The female's feathers are a dull grey-brown—probably to reduce the
risk of being detected by predators when sitting on the nest. The
brilliant orange-red flash of the male's chest makes it one of the most
stunning small birds in the wet forests of the Central Highlands.
Males respond to red and orange colours, so my field team and I do
not wear red or orange clothing during field surveys of birds to avoid
attracting Flame Robins and biasing results by over-counting this
species. The Flame Robin is the only bird species that becomes more
common in wet forests after fire.

Above: **Regenerating forest around the Murrindindi River on Taungurung Country** (Sarah Rees)
This aerial view of the forests around Murrindindi River, which were burned in the 2009 fires, highlights how rich and varied natural landscapes can be. Scattered among the huge fire-killed trees are intact living old-growth giants, young regrowth eucalypts, grey-coloured wattles and dark-green Myrtle Beech rainforest trees.

Following pages: **The 2019 Bunyip wildfires from Wurundjeri Country** (Sarah Rees)
The massive mushroom clouds created by the wildfires in the Bunyip State Park in 2019 stretched many kilometres into the atmosphere, and the smoke blanketed Melbourne and the Yarra Valley for days. These pyrocumulonimbus clouds can create their own weather, such as lightning strikes, leading to yet more fires.

CHAPTER 8

WILDLIFE

The wet forests of Central Victoria are incredibly important for biodiversity and support a wide variety of habitats for many remarkable species, including some which are Endangered or Critically Endangered. While the fauna is diverse, careful observation is often needed to see it. Many of the mammals are active only at night, while some of the birds are hard to see in the dense understorey or up in the canopy, more than 70 metres above the ground, even during the day. The few species of reptiles are even harder to see, with most species rarely observed.

Mountain Ash forests in the Central Highlands are habitat to a particularly rich assembly of possums and gliders, ranging in size from the 15-gram Feathertail Glider to the 3.5-kilogram Mountain Brushtail Possum. A lot of work has been dedicated to understanding how so many different species of possums and gliders can coexist in the forest. The answer is that they partition nesting and food resources to avoid competing. For example, the Greater Glider prefers the large old hollows in tall living or recently dead trees, while the Mountain Brushtail Possum prefers hollows in short, highly decayed trees. There are also marked differences in the various species' foraging behaviour, breeding systems, social organisation (e.g. pairs versus colonies) and many other aspects of their life history.

One of the more enigmatic arboreal marsupials, the Mountain Brushtail Possum occurs in wet forests from southern Victoria to central Queensland. Research into the animal across its distribution in the 1990s involved careful measurements of body size and the collection of genetic samples and types of parasites. The work resulted in a surprising discovery—the Mountain Brushtail Possum is not just one but two distinct species. The break between the two species seems likely to occur just south of Sydney: animals north of the city are what is now called the Short-eared Possum, while those in the south are still known as the Mountain Brushtail Possum. The southern species was given the Latin name *Trichosurus cunninghami* after Ross Cunningham, a brilliant statistician who first recognised that animals from southern Australia were different from those in northern New South Wales and Queensland. Of course, this animal had been well known to Aboriginal people for tens of thousands of years before it was 'classified' by western science. It is now time is to find the appropriate Aboriginal name for this wonderful animal.

Opposite: **King Parrot near Mount Torbreck on Taungurung Country** (Chris Taylor) The King Parrot is a stunning sight in wet eucalypt forests, and is seen most often in areas where there are very large trees. However, there are also resident populations of this species in human settlements, such as the town of Marysville. Like humans, parrots are either left-footed or right-footed; their preference can be identified through careful observation of them holding food. While most large parrots such as the Sulphur-crested Cockatoo are left-footed, almost all King Parrots are right-footed.

The wet eucalypt forests of the Central Highlands are famous for another species of arboreal marsupial. That animal is one of Victoria's faunal emblems—the Leadbeater's Possum, with the Aboriginal name of Wollert. This 'Lazarus species' was thought to be extinct until it was rediscovered in 1961. In fact, the animal was first known from fossils collected in southern New South Wales in the nineteenth century, but western scientists classified it at that time as a separate species. It was not until later that the fossils and the living animals were recognised as being the same creature. The fossil records of the Wollert show that it used to occur from south-east of Melbourne to the Wombeyan Caves south of Sydney—a distribution that is far larger than it is currently.

The wet forests of Victoria are home to approximately 70 species of birds, about half of which are common, or at least were common when The Australian National University began monitoring them around two decades ago. They range from tiny species, such as the Brown and Striated Thornbills, which weigh just a few grams, to the Superb Lyrebird and Wedge-tailed Eagle, which can weigh several kilograms.

The Superb Lyrebird (or Buln Buln in Woiwurrung language) is relatively abundant, and populations rebounded well after the 2009 wildfires. The species is famous for its songs and especially its remarkable ability to mimic other noises—not just natural sounds such as the calls of other birds, but also cameras, logging machinery, chainsaws and even the occasional *coooeee*. Beyond its extraordinary vocal ability, the Superb Lyrebird plays a critical role in the functioning of healthy ecosystems. With its enormous feet, each lyrebird turns over up to 150 tonnes of leaf litter and soil every year in search of food, speeding up the decomposition of material that might otherwise be fuel for wildfires. Superb Lyrebirds are ecosystem engineers, playing a key role in critical processes that shape forest environments.

The health of a forest is intimately connected to the health of its wildlife. Animals such as the Mountain Brushtail Possum and the Bush Rat dig up and eat fungi, including truffles that grow underground on tree roots and fix nutrients for their host trees. Fungal spores germinate only once they have passed through the gut of an animal. The interdependence between these animals, fungi and trees underpins the condition of the forest.

Over the past four decades, The Australian National University has undertaken careful monitoring to determine how populations of possums, gliders and birds have been changing over time. Almost half of the bird species have decreased, and all species of possums and gliders have declined—some catastrophically, like the Greater Glider, which is now found at approximately 80 per cent fewer sites than it was in the late 1990s. The Yellow-bellied Glider has become so rare that it is now impossible to conduct robust statistical analyses of its patterns of occurrence. Other Threatened, Endangered or even Critically Endangered species include the Wollert, the Baw Baw Frog and the Barred Galaxias (a small native fish). Like the gliders, these species are at risk from fire, logging, climate change and disease, and from the combined effects of these threats, as discussed in previous chapters. To prevent the decline and even extinction of these (and many other) beautiful animals, it is essential to increase levels of protection of the forest to ensure their habitats are conserved and extensive stands of old growth will once again distinguish the Central Highlands region.

Greater Glider on Wurundjeri Country
(Steven Kuiter)
Mountain Ash forests, like the forests of many parts of eastern Australia, support two distinct colour variants of Greater Glider—one with jet-black fur on its back and another with white fur. The second variant is less common but spectacular. Some individual gliders are a mix of the two colours, like the one in this image. The Greater Glider is what is known as a 'sentinel species'—the condition of the population tells us about the condition of the forest. The species is sensitive to land clearing, logging, fire and climate change. The catastrophic decline in populations of the Greater Glider clearly indicate that Mountain Ash forests need far better protection.

ESSENCE OF GLIDER

Some things that happen in a day's work in the forest can stay with you for a long time. Arriving in the Rubicon Valley in the northern part of the Central Highlands early one morning for a day of measuring vegetation, I found a Greater Glider on the ground—where it should not be, especially in daylight. These placid creatures are nocturnal, and if possible avoid coming to the ground, where they are easy prey for foxes, cats and dingoes. Unsure if the animal was injured, I carefully picked it up to move it to the closest large old hollow tree. The glider promptly peed on my hands, leaving an extraordinarily pungent Eucalyptus smell. This 'essence' of glider indelibly permeated the band of my wristwatch: for the next few years, every time I sweated, it would rejuvenate the glider 'perfume', reminding me of both the wonderful Mountain Ash forests and one of the stunning creatures that live there.

Several years later, I was engaged in a project that involved extensive studies of the Greater Glider, this time at Tumut, west of Canberra. Handling the animals every night, it was not uncommon to be peed on. Again the smell was long lasting. But intriguingly, the odour was subtly different—most likely because some of the tree species that form the glider's diet differ between the wet forests of Victoria and Tumut.

Opposite: **Wollert (Leadbeater's Possum) on Wurundjeri Country** (Steven Kuiter)

The Wollert was once thought to be extinct, then rediscovered. Now Critically Endangered, it is strongly associated with a Critically Endangered ecosystem—the Mountain Ash forest. The Wollert is one of Victoria's two faunal emblems (the other one—the Helmeted Honeyeater—is also Critically Endangered). More than 25 years ago, I discovered that I could mimic the Wollert's alarm calls—a repeated *zit-zit-zit*. This resulted in possums coming to within a few metres of me, and even jumping on my head. The species lives in colonies, and a rapid response to the alarm call is likely to be one way in which animals protect others in a group. However, possums will only be fooled by the 'prank' calls once or twice before they stop responding.

Above: **Feathertail Glider on Bunurong Country** (Steven Kuiter)

The Feathertail Glider is Australia's smallest gliding marsupial, weighing just 10–15 grams. The species has extraordinary adaptations to assist it in landing after gliding. A study using a scanning electron microscope showed that the footpads have tiny ridges perforated by a battery of sweat glands. Moisture from these glands creates surface tension, turning the footpads into mini suction cups. The tension is so strong that it allows the Feathertail Glider to move on even the most slippery surfaces, such as vertical panes of glass. Feathertail Gliders are seen only rarely during night-time surveys in wet eucalypt forests. Sometimes, when an animal emerges from a tree at dusk, the initial glide resembles a falling leaf spiralling towards the ground before it lands on a tree or shrub.

The loud gurgling call of the Yellow-bellied Glider is one of the most unusual calls made by any Australian animal. The sound has been likened to a cross between a frothing espresso machine and a squealing pig. Animals often call soon after leaving a den tree at dusk and will continue calling as they glide through the forest. The Yellow-bellied Glider is highly mobile, capable of a 'flight' of up to 80 metres, after which it lands heavily on a tree trunk, gripping it with its feet. Females have a special reinforced pouch to prevent their young from being injured by these high-impact landings. I have painful memories of working with the Yellow-bellied Glider. They have very sharp teeth to wound eucalypt trees and feed on the sap. Their teeth can also readily bite through a fingernail—which happened to me when I was trapping animals in the mid-1980s; more than 35 years later, my nail still has not properly healed.

Highland Copperhead snakes are relatively common in Mountain Ash forests, especially near streams where they hunt frogs. They are docile animals, although their venom could easily dispatch an adult human. The copperhead can be active when it is too cold for other snakes. I have fond memories of these snakes when radio-tracking possums on cold mornings. One radio-collared animal lived in a huge hollow tree close to a creek where a break in the canopy meant that the sun penetrated to the forest floor. On many occasions the 1.2-metre copperhead that 'owned' that patch of sun would not budge from it, even if I came within a metre.

The Barred Galaxias is one of many species of a highly diverse family of small native fish. It has a very small distribution limited to the mountainous region of the Goulburn River catchment. It is now Critically Endangered in Victoria, largely as a result of predation by introduced trout. The Barred Galaxias persists largely where trout are absent. Protection of intact catchments is likely to be important for the conservation of the Barred Galaxias, but recent logging has badly damaged stream habitats in areas of forest important to the species.

Above: **Buln Buln (Superb Lyrebird) on Wurundjeri Country** (Steven Kuiter)

The Buln Buln or Superb Lyrebird is truly one of Australia's natural wonders. Its ability to mimic the sounds of the forest is remarkable. The calls are passed from males to their offspring. Lyrebirds were introduced to Tasmania in the 1930s and 1940s because ornithologists believed that foxes would hunt them to extinction on the mainland. Introduced lyrebirds in Tasmania still mimic the calls of birds from the mainland that do not occur on the island state. I have listened to Superb Lyrebird songs on one site at Cambarville in the Central Highlands for almost 40 years, and the sequence of calls that is mimicked has stayed the same for all of that time. Lyrebirds can live for a long time—at least 30 years—and it is unclear whether the bird that I hear at that site, making the same sequence of calls, is the same bird singing now as it was in the early 1980s, or one of its descendants.

Opposite: **Gang-gang Cockatoo in a Snow Gum on Taungurung Country** (Chris Taylor)

The bright red crest of the male Gang-gang Cockatoo contrasts beautifully with the smoky grey of its body. This fairly social bird has a unique 'squeaky door' voice, and the screeching calls of small flocks are an atmospheric addition to tall eucalypt forests. Like almost all species of parrots, they nest in large old hollow trees, which are now declining rapidly in wet eucalypt forests. Populations of the Gang-gang Cockatoo are declining too, and in some places, like New South Wales, it is already listed as Vulnerable.

Early morning rain over the Maroondah Catchment on Wurundjeri Country (Sarah Rees)
Early morning is the best time to count birds in wet eucalypt forests. The dawn chorus can comprise up to 40 species, some of which call almost exclusively at this time of the day, such as the Scaly Thrush with its distinctive *foo-wee* call.

Left: **The Spotted Pardalote on Bunurong Country** (Steven Kuiter)

The diminutive and beautiful Spotted Pardalote is one of the species that begins calling in earnest when the sun starts to break through the early morning mist. It has a distinctive call that sounds like 'Paul Keating, Paul Keating' or 'Miss Piggy, Miss Piggy'. The call is extremely loud for such a small bird. Once I heard a Spotted Pardalote making its piercing call only metres away from where I was working. The bird was almost within touching distance but would not move and continued to call repeatedly. The reason then became clear—a huge Tiger Snake was basking just a metre away.

Below left: **The Crested Shrike-tit on Bunurong Country** (Steven Kuiter)

This wonderful bird is often heard before it is seen, due to the noise it makes when tearing apart the bark streamers that hang from the branches of large Mountain Ash and Alpine Ash trees. This species has been declining markedly everywhere we have been monitoring it in south-eastern Australia—not only in cool wet mountain forests but also in coastal forests and inland temperate woodlands. I have been able to summon this species by mimicking one of its calls. Like the Sulphur-crested Cockatoo, the birds raise their crests when they become agitated.

Above: **Boobook Owl on Wurundjeri Country** (Steven Kuiter)
The Boobook Owl is by far the most common species of owl in the wet ash forests of Victoria. It has a distinctive *mo-poke* call that is often heard just after dusk as the night shift of animals becomes active and the day shift has gone to bed. The Boobook Owl is the smallest species of owl in mainland Australia and hunts small vertebrates and invertebrates. On several occasions, I have witnessed amazing interactions between Boobook Owls and Sugar Gliders. Owls will fly over the marsupials when they are gliding and knock them to the ground. Research in Tasmania has shown that Sugar Gliders are major predators of birds, especially nestlings, which suggests that the owl may be trying to protect its young. Brushtail Possums are known to eat the eggs of Boobook Owls and in other cases force earlier fledging of nestlings.

Opposite: **Powerful Owl with its prey on Bunurong Country** (Steven Kuiter)
The Powerful Owl is one of the most imposing animals in the forest. It is uncommon in wet eucalypt forests, and more likely to be found in warmer, drier forests at lower elevations. However, field surveys have been detecting the Powerful Owl more often in wet forests in the past twenty years. These owls prey on possums and gliders—as seen by the fresh kill in this image. I'll never forget my first encounter in the forest with a Powerful Owl. It had just caught a young brushtail possum, and it sat in my spotlight and calmly severed the possum's head and tail before dropping them at my feet.

A male Mistletoebird on Bunurong Country (Steven Kuiter)
The bright red plumage of the male Mistletoebird is not commonly
seen in the Mountain Ash forests of Victoria. The species is rare
because mistletoe fruit is its key source of food, which is itself rare,
found mostly only high in the canopy of very old trees in old-growth
patches. The bird almost never comes close to the ground, but it can
be readily identified by its distinctive, high-pitched *tippee-tip-tip* call.

The seeds of Mistletoe plants become very sticky after they pass
through the gut of a bird and can adhere to branches. This allows
these parasitic plants to germinate and begin drawing nutrients from
a host tree. Amazingly there are no mistletoes in Tasmania, even
though suitable host trees like Mountain Ash occur there. Likewise,
Mistletoebirds are also mostly absent from Tasmania, although birds
have occasionally been blown across Bass Strait. But the seeds of
mistletoes are voided within 25 minutes of ingestion, longer than
the time it would take a Mistletoebird to get to Tasmania.

A Bundjil (Wedge-tailed Eagle) soaring high above the magnificent ash forests on Wurundjeri Country (Sarah Rees)
There is arguably nothing in the sky more majestic than a Bundjil, otherwise known as a Wedge-tailed Eagle. These birds can sometimes be seen on roads feeding on roadkill such as dead wallabies and wombats, but they also hunt live prey. During one memorable lunchbreak in a clearing on Mount Gregory at the edge of the Upper Yarra catchment, I watched as a panicked young Swamp Wallaby sprinted across the grassland within a few metres of me, being pursued by a fully grown adult Wedge-tailed Eagle. I don't know if the Swamp Wallaby survived the ordeal, but it most likely found protection in the thick undergrowth.

CHAPTER 9

LOGGING

The Mountain Ash and Alpine Ash forests of Victoria, including those in the Central Highlands region, have been logged for more than 150 years. By the 1920s there were over 240 sawmills in the Central Highlands. Now there are just six, although the region also supplies timber to a handful of mills in other parts of Victoria. In the 1920s there was as much timber being shipped from Port Melbourne as there was from Seattle in the United States, a much larger timber region than Central Victoria. The legacy of such extensive cutting is a rapidly dwindling timber supply, almost no old growth, declines of many animal populations and a more fire-prone landscape.

Logging was a largely selective operation from the late 1800s until the 1960s, in which only the straightest trees were felled. By the late 1960s, loggers switched to industrial clearfelling, also known as clearcutting. In this process, all the saleable trees are removed from a cutblock, or coupe, of 15–40 hectares. Approximately 50–60 per cent of the forest biomass is left on the forest floor—wood and other vegetation that is not wanted. This debris is left for one to two years before it is burned in a fire deliberately lit to promote the regeneration of a new stand of trees in the ash bed left after the fire. Finally, the area is seeded and a new crop of trees emerges.

Clearfelling is a highly efficient industrialised way of cutting down and then regrowing crops of trees, but it causes major damage to forest ecosystems. This form of logging typically occurs in areas with high levels of biodiversity, including many threatened forest-dependent species of animals and plants. As clearfelling results in the substantial reduction (or often the total elimination) of large old trees, it has devastating impacts on species such as possums and gliders that use cavities in trees for their nests and dens. The loss of these trees means that clearfelled and regenerated areas can remain unsuitable as habitat for these animals for up to two centuries.

Some species of plants are also severely affected, especially those that would naturally survive fire and recover by resprouting but are largely eliminated from clearfelled forest by the mechanical disturbance from heavy machinery. Tree ferns are an example: populations of these important components of wet eucalypt forests are reduced by more than 95 per cent by logging operations. Logging also affects soils, with marked losses of nutrients, reduced levels of moisture and increases in coarse materials like sand. These

Opposite: **A clearfell logging operation seen from the summit of Mount Torbreck on Taungurung Country** (Chris Taylor) The commencement of a clearfelling operation in 80-year-old Mountain Ash forest. The environmental impacts are anything but benign, and compromise the entire forest ecosystem—from losses of key soil nutrients (including carbon) below the surface to destruction of large old trees and populations of species across landscapes.

impacts can last for up to 80 years. Indeed, our recent research shows that the effects of logging on the below-ground environment can be equally as profound as they are above the ground.

Significant carbon emissions result from clearfelling, in part because of the massive amount of debris that remains in the forest after logging. The smoke from regeneration fires creates air pollution in cities and regional towns, with health implications for people, especially those with pre-existing respiratory issues. Moreover, most of the timber extracted from the forest goes to making paper or cardboard boxes, which have a short operational life before being often discarded into landfill and generating further emissions. This makes the manufacturing of forest products from logging native forests a highly ineffective way to store carbon. The best long-term secure carbon storage is an intact forest. The use of wood products can be a useful way to reduce greenhouse gas emissions if they replace steel and aluminium in buildings. However, the best source of wood products that generate the least carbon emissions is from well-managed plantations, not from native forests—especially if those plantations had been established on previously cleared agricultural land.

The impact of clearfelling on the age of forests has significant implications for water yields, as old forests generate more water. For this reason, the aim of water managers is to keep forests as old as possible. While some water catchments in the Central Highlands are closed to logging, others are available to cut. This has enormous impacts on water supply: the effects of logging on water yields exceed even the projected effects of climate change.

Logging fragments the forest landscape, creating extensive stands of young, disturbed forest surrounding small patches of undisturbed forest. These changes in landscape configuration have profound effects on how forests function. As discussed in Chapter 1, fragmentation can increase wind speeds, which in turn increase the rates of collapse of large old trees. It can also result in forests becoming unsuitable for many species, such as the Yellow-bellied Glider, because there is insufficient connected habitat for them to effectively maintain a territory and find food. Further, the vast network of roads constructed to facilitate access to cutblocks for logging operations can assist invasions

ALMOST ALL IS LOST

Deliberately lit industrial logging fires are widely used to burn the hundreds of tonnes of debris (or 'slash') left after wet forests are logged. But they often also burn the trees retained on sites to provide habitat for wildlife. Some years ago, I sat quietly on a hillside watching a burning operation for a logging coupe that contained 'islands' of forest that were to be conserved. The burn started routinely, with a vast column of flame in the centre of the cutblock. But then a retained island ignited, and every tree in it was burned in just a few seconds. All of the cutting crew's efforts to keep those trees were wasted, along with the chance that the site would eventually become habitat for wildlife that depend on big trees.

Logging in Mountain Ash forests at Mount Disappointment on Taungurung and Wurundjeri Countries in 1898 (Forests Commission RPA)

Until the 1960s, logging in Mountain Ash forests involved selective harvesting. Prior to mechanisation—the advent of chainsaws, log trucks with folding jinkers for carrying logs, and log skidders—trees were laboriously cut down with axes and crosscut saws, and the timber was removed by horses and railways built through the forest. Old steel lines and timber bogeys can still be found in the forest today. I remember a long conversation in 1990 with a couple of old-timer tree fallers—a rare husband-and-wife team who had retired but were still living in the forest. She had a good ear and used to tap trees with a tuning fork to determine whether the massive standing giants were 'sound', or suitable for logging. Her husband was then directed to fell the tree.

of predatory pest species like foxes and cats. Logged and regenerated areas also attract invasive herbivores like Sambar Deer, which browse heavily in wet forests and damage vegetation. Forest management programs are needed to control these invasive species, and nurture native wildlife.

As harmful as clearfelling is to the forest and to biodiversity, another form of logging has even greater impacts. Post-fire logging (often referred to by the logging industry as 'salvage' logging) is used to recover some of the economic value of forests after they have been burned in wildfires. The word 'salvage' is a misnomer and should not be used as nothing is really being salvaged, or saved, at all—the effects are entirely negative and substantial, recovery is impaired and the burned timber has very limited economic value. Many studies from around the world have highlighted the severe negative impacts of post-fire logging on key ecosystem processes, impairing the forest's recovery and profoundly affecting soils, plants, large old trees, birds, possums and gliders. This is most likely because post-fire logging subjects forest ecosystems to a pair of disturbances in rapid succession—initially a major natural disturbance (fire) and then a human disturbance (logging). Such intense and severe disturbances coming so close together can lead to the entire collapse of ecosystems. Extensive logging was conducted after wildfires in 1939, 1983 and 2009, and the impacts of these operations will be apparent in Victoria's wet eucalypt forests until well into the next century.

Many people consider that logging in the Mountain Ash and Alpine Ash forests is acceptable because of the economic and social benefits generated by the industry. In fact, the Victorian Government's logging company rarely makes even a small profit, and employment in the industry has been declining significantly for many years. In 2019–2020 alone, the loss on logging operations was $20 million. Environmental and economic accounting clearly shows that other natural assets like water production and carbon storage are more valuable economically than the native forest logging industry. As is tourism.

Also important is a poorly kept secret: as a result of past overcutting and recurrent wildfires, there is now very little forest that if logged will produce sawn timber. Only poor-quality trees that will be chipped for paper making are left. The bottom line is that Victoria would be financially better off without logging in Mountain Ash and Alpine Ash forests: some estimates suggest that the state would be ahead by between $110 million and $190 million annually if logging stopped today. Moreover, the Traditional Custodians of the forest have never been consulted about how the forest on their lands has been managed. This problem needs to be rectified, and the right of all Australians to enjoy the beauty of Mountain Ash and Alpine Ash forests in the Central Highlands of Victoria should be recognised.

Opposite: **Smoke rising from a clearfell logged area on Gunaikurnai Country**
(Chris Taylor)
Industrial logging burns, or regeneration burns, usually conducted in autumn or early winter, create vast amounts of smoke. These burns consume up to 450 tonnes of logging debris per hectare—more than ten times the amount combusted in hazard reduction burns. The smoke from regeneration burns is a health hazard for people in rural and regional areas living close to forests as well as the more than five million residents of Melbourne.

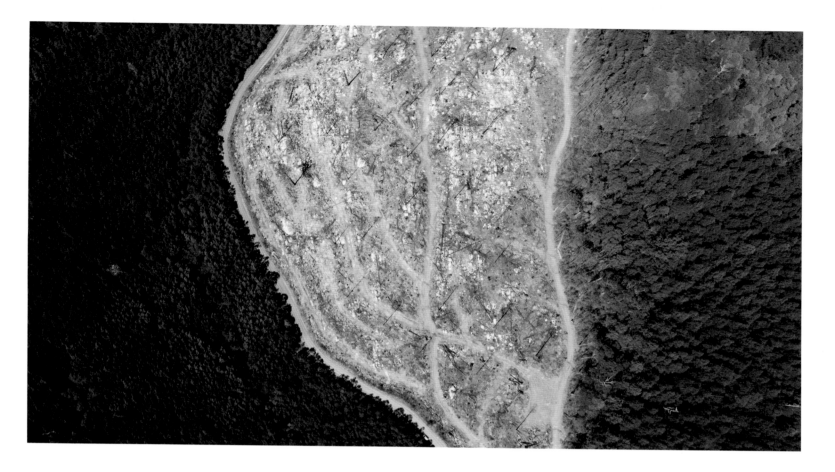

Opposite: **Industrial logging burn on Wurundjeri Country** (Chris Taylor)

At least 50 per cent of the biomass of a forest is left on the forest floor after logging. This debris consists of tree crowns, lateral branches, and understorey trees and shrubs—anything that cannot be used for pulp or sawn timber. The logging 'slash' is left for one to two years to dry out before it is consumed in a regeneration burn, whereupon a new stand of trees is grown. Although regeneration burns involve high-intensity fires, large amounts of waste timber remain partially burned on the ground, covering the floor of a newly regenerated stand of regrowth forest. This adds to the fuel load in young forests and is likely to be one of the reasons why logged and then regenerated forests are prone to high-severity fire.

Above: **Logging in Starvation Creek water supply catchment on Wurundjeri Country** (Sarah Rees)

If you look carefully at the bottom centre of this industrial logging coupe, you can see a white four-wheel-drive vehicle parked by the side of the road. This underscores the size of the area that has been logged. The area to the left of the logging coupe supports extensive stands of young logged and regenerated forest, whereas the forest to the right is older. This logged forest is within the network of catchments for Melbourne's water supply.

Opposite: **Industrial logging on a hilltop near Warburton on Wurundjeri Country** (Sarah Rees)

It can be hard to appreciate the sheer size of logging coupes in photographs such as this one without a point of reference—here, the three vehicles at the junction of the roads in this 77-hectare cutblock. After logging, the soil becomes compacted around the benches (or terraced tracks) cut into the steep slopes. Studies have estimated that tree growth is impaired in approximately 12 per cent of forest that has been cut, due to soil compaction on roads and tracks used to drag logs to landings where bark and branches are removed and loaded onto trucks.

Above: **Logging on steep slopes on Taungurung Country** (Chris Taylor)

Logging operations are subject to laws and a code of practice which stipulate that areas steeper than 30 degrees must not be cut to avoid subsequent soil runoff and erosion and the fouling of waterways. The slope in this photograph is 34 degrees—a clear breach of the law. This example is far from isolated; it is estimated that 75 per cent of cutblocks in the Upper Goulburn River water supply catchment alone breach this code of practice.

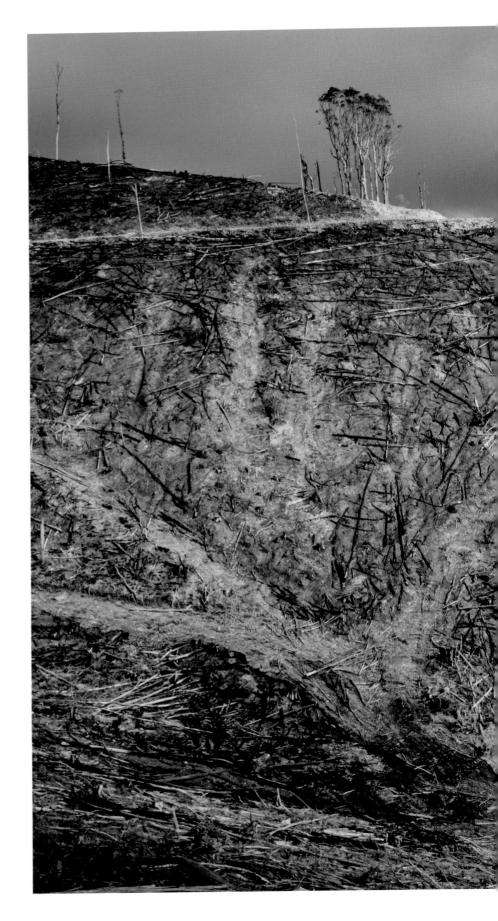

Extensive soil disturbance across a steep slope on Taungurung Country (Chris Taylor)
The slope shown in this image is so steep that logging contractors had to cut benches into the side of the hill to log it. Steep slopes are dangerous places to work, putting timber workers' lives at risk. Forests on steep slopes also produce lower volumes of timber (especially sawlogs) compared to flatter terrain, making them unprofitable to cut.

Heavily disturbed landscape on Taungurung Country (Chris Taylor)
This image illustrates the extensive disturbances that occur in wood
production landscapes. There is a cut and regenerated stand in the
foreground, a five- to ten-year post-logged area in the middle ground,
and a coupe subject to a regeneration burn in the background. Many
of these landscapes support no stands of old-growth trees, and even
isolated large old trees are extremely rare.

New kinds of logging on Gunaikurnai Country (Chris Taylor)
This cutblock has been subject to a new form of logging that is
supposedly less intensive than conventional clearfelling. However, the
retained trees and the retained 'island' (on the right of the image) have
all been severely burned in the high-intensity fire lit to promote the
regeneration of new trees after logging. Most of these 'retained' trees
have been killed in the blaze, and long-term studies show that they
will quickly fall, leaving the area with few if any of the large old trees
that are essential for wildlife.

A log dump on Taungurung Country (Chris Taylor)
Cut trees are stored in log dumps before being transported. Soil
compaction and damage around log dump areas is extensive, with
effects like nutrient loss and changes to the composition of the soil
lasting for at least 80 years (and potentially much longer). The natural
regeneration of forests is often substantially impaired on logged areas
with heavily compacted soils.

Burned young regrowth forest on Taungurung Country
(Chris Taylor)
This stand of young, logged forest had been thinned to produce
pulpwood for paper manufacturing before it burned at very high
severity in the 2009 wildfires. A series of studies has shown that the
condition of a forest before a fire can have a marked effect on the
severity of that fire. Stands regrowing after logging burn at greater
severity than mature and old-growth stands. The increased risks of
elevated fire severity last for 40 years after logging. This means that
40-year-old forests, which can be over 50 metres tall, can be subject
to fires with a flame height of 60 metres or more.

A logged and burned young stand on Taungurung Country
(Chris Taylor)
The burned forest in this photo had been logged several years
previously. There are a number of reasons why logged and burned
forests are prone to subsequent high-severity fire. These include the
amount of debris left in the forest adding to fire fuels; the loss of
wet forest plants such as tree ferns, which shade the soil; and the
dense stands of young saplings, which change the architecture of
the forest and add extra fine and medium fuel to the forest floor.
Research scientist Chris Taylor first developed the idea of analysing
the relationship between logging history and fire severity after
visiting this site in 2009.

Burning of harvesting debris, or logging slash, on Gunaikurnai Country (Chris Taylor)

Fires lit to reduce the amount of debris left after logging operations can damage or even kill trees that are retained on coupes. These trees are supposed to provide habitat for wildlife so they can recolonise regenerating forests. Lone trees in logged areas are also prone to being blown down by wind or killed by overheating through sun exposure, which can impair the movement of water inside trees.

Widespread industrial logging on Taungurung Country (Chris Taylor)
There are more than fifteen logging coupes shown in this scene, with
almost no remaining forest more than 80 years old. In fact, almost
98 per cent of the wet forest in the Central Highlands is now 80 years
old or younger. I'm often asked: 'What happens to animals when the
forest is logged?' In the case of arboreal marsupials, they simply die
on site. I was once on a field tour of the forest with a senior Victorian
State Government minister; while discussing forest management
in logging coupes, he found himself standing next to the skeleton
of a Mountain Brushtail Possum that had been killed in the logging
operation and then incinerated in the subsequent industrial
logging burn.

Growth stages in a Mountain Ash forest on Taungurung Country
(Sarah Rees)
The taller stands of trees on the right of this image are old-growth
Mountain Ash, replete with dark brown mistletoe in their canopies.
Open areas between the trees reveal the dense layer of tree ferns
shading the forest floor. The closely spaced trees on the left are
Mountain Ash trees regrowing from a previous clearfell logging
operation and have more pointed, pyramid-shaped crowns.

Wurundjeri women performing a ritual sorry dance in a recently logged area (Sarah Rees)
Local Wurundjeri women have a deep spiritual connection to their land. They perform a ritual sorry dance on areas that have been extensively disturbed by logging—a form of land management for which none of the three First Nations in the Central Highlands region has granted permission.

THE FUTURE

The images in this book clearly demonstrate the extraordinary beauty and majesty of the wet forests of the Central Highlands. As we consider the future of these forests, we must first look to the past. The forests photographed in this book are those of the Gunaikurnai, Taungurung and Wurundjeri Peoples, who have been custodians of this region for tens of thousands of years. European colonisation of the forests was brutal and catastrophic, and its damaging legacy persists to this day. Any vision of restoring the health of these forests must look to the long-held traditions and the sovereignty of Aboriginal people. A future for this region must therefore be one determined in consultation with its Traditional Custodians.

At the same time, we must not forget about the people in small towns and regional areas who make a living from logging forests. They must not be ignored as the forest industry transitions further into well-managed plantations and agroforestry, with native forests better protected and managed for their more lucrative and sustainable water, tourism, and carbon storage values. Logging contractors are highly skilled at firefighting in native forests. We must not lose these skills, but rather re-employ these timber workers as elite firefighters, protecting people and property in regional Australia during summer and applying strategic hazard reduction burns in winter. Taxpayers already fund them to fight fires in the summer, but now this complete shift to full-time firefighting needs to be formalised and become a year-round profession. These jobs will become increasingly important as the impacts of climate change become further pronounced nationwide and its influence on fire regimes are magnified, especially in south-eastern Australia.

In a carbon-constrained economy, native forests will play a crucial role in the long-term storage of large amounts of carbon. A well-marshalled regional workforce will be needed to manage these carbon stocks, protecting them from fire, revegetating key areas, and limiting the impacts of invasive animal species such as introduced deer.

As shown in this book, at the heart of Victoria's wet forests are large old trees and old-growth stands. Yet, the team at The Australian National University has documented a massive decline in the area of old growth in the past 25 years. Across all of the different ecosystems in Victoria, almost 77 per cent of the old growth that was mapped between 1996 and 2000 has now been lost. We must make enormous efforts to restore landscapes

Opposite: **Southern Sassafras on Wurundjeri Country** (Sarah Rees)
Southern Sassafras is a spectacular tree that is most common in wet temperate rainforest that occur in the coolest and most moist parts of the landscape. The species has characteristic 'teeth' on the outer edges of the leaves. I have commonly seen this tree species begin life with a two-metre head start after germinating in the basket of a tree fern. Over time the Sassafras tree will overgrow the trunk of the Tree Fern.

A rainbow over the Central Highlands of Victoria (Sarah Rees)

Opposite: **Banksia trees on Wurundjeri Country** (Sarah Rees)
The name Banksia is derived from the botanist Joseph Banks. They can be relatively common in the understorey of drier foothill forests in the Central Highlands region, such as those dominated by Red Stringybark and Messmate.

so they support more old forest and recapture the natural legacy that there once was. Recovering areas of old growth will take a long time, so it is critical that we start now. This is essential for several reasons: to ensure key water catchments for Melbourne's water security, to improve fire safety, to recover biodiversity, and to create tourism and job opportunities.

Our hope is that this book will inspire more people to respectfully visit some of the globally unique forests featured here. We encourage people to explore the natural environment, and to acknowledge the deep connections and knowledge of the Aboriginal people of this land. Government has a vital role to play in consulting with the Traditional Custodians, learning and adapting expert knowledge and cultural practices relating to forest and water management. Assets like aerial walkways and extended trails to enrich the visitor experience in this impressive landscape should become a critical part of the tourism infrastructure and will assist in rebuilding local and regional economies, while ensuring that the cultural and environmental values of the forest are carefully nurtured and maintained. The aim should be to show that this is not a contest between jobs and the environment. Rather, well-managed conservation is good for all—the environment, the economy and our society. It can generate new opportunities for current and future generations of Australians, and for the forests, and every living thing that relies on their survival.

ABOUT THE AUTHOR

Professor David Lindenmayer AO is based at the Fenner School of Environment and Society, The Australian National University. He is a world-leading expert in natural resource management, conservation science and biodiversity conservation. David has maintained some of the largest long-term environmental research programs in Australia. He currently runs seven large-scale, long-term research programs in south-eastern Australia, primarily focused on developing ways to conserve biodiversity in farmland, wood production forests, plantations and reserves. He has published widely, including over 800 peer-reviewed papers in international scientific journals, and 47 books, including many award-winning textbooks.

David held a prestigious Australian Research Council Laureate Fellowship from 2013 to 2018. He is a member of the Australian Academy of Science (elected in 2008) and a Fellow of the Ecological Society of America (elected in 2019). He was appointed an Officer of the Order of Australia (AO) in 2014.

David's biodiversity research has been recognised through numerous awards, including the Eureka Science Prize (twice), the Whitley Award for the publication of scientific books administered by the Royal Zoological Society of New South Wales (ten times), the Serventy Medal for Ornithology, and the Australian Natural History Medallion. In 2018, he was awarded the prestigious Whittaker Medal from the Ecological Society of America.

ABOUT THE PHOTOGRAPHERS

Dr Chris Taylor is a Research Fellow at the Fenner School of Environment and Society, The Australian National University. He is also a keen hiker and photographer with a passion for the unique forests of Victoria. Chris has published many studies on these forests, including key studies of fire, logging history and biodiversity, and completed his PhD on Forest Certification in 2012. He seeks to capture and share his own sublime experience of the landscape through his photography—the sense of feeling so insignificant amid the grandeur and age of this land, yet also elevated by being in the forest. He has held numerous exhibitions of his photographs.

Sarah Rees works as a consultant in media, knowledge brokering and philanthropy. She has lived and worked in the forests of Victoria for more than 25 years. Sarah specialises in drone photography and macro-photography, and is also a film-maker. Sarah has two decades of experience in the Australian environment sector, with over six years' experience on boards overseeing forest standards and fifteen years on boards of non-government environmental organisations. She has a strong presence on many key social media platforms associated with forest conservation and the protection of Australian forests and biodiversity.

Steven Kuiter is a wildlife photographer from the Mornington Peninsula in Victoria who specialises in capturing images of rare and hard-to-find animals, the majority of which are nocturnal. While many of his images are intended for research and scientific purposes, he sometimes manages to capture animals in their true beautiful form. When Steven is not spending his nights in the forest, he can be found scuba diving, modifying camera equipment or at the local wildlife shelter. He believes that the three keys to wildlife photography are learning about our flora and fauna, patience, and developing new and non-invasive ways of using camera equipment.

ACKNOWLEDGEMENTS

This project involved the help of many people. David Lindenmayer would like to thank Tabitha Boyer and Claire Shepherd for assistance with numerous editorial and other tasks that enabled this book to be completed far more smoothly than it would otherwise have been. He would also like to thank the hundreds of exceptional scientists with whom he has worked for almost four decades. This includes field staff such as Lachie McBurney, who has been working in the wet forests for nearly twenty years.

This book is dedicated to the memory of Dr Dave Blair. He was a close colleague and worked with the field research team at The Australian National University for more than a decade, primarily in the Mountain Ash forests of Victoria. It was not possible to ask for a more outstanding employee. He completed countless vegetation, bird and possum surveys while at the same time finishing his PhD on the vegetation of Mountain Ash forests. Dave died not long after being awarded his PhD in late 2019. He still had so much to contribute. His death was a massive loss not only for his wonderful partner and family and the many community organisations to which he contributed, but also to the forest that he worked so hard to protect.

Chris Taylor would like to acknowledge Ellen Taylor, Brian Taylor and Heidi Taylor for their amazing and unwavering support support of his photography. Chris would like to thank Wurundjeri and Dja Dja Wurrung Woman Stacie Piper for her guidance, advice and amazing discussions about Country. These discussions had a profound effect on the way he views and respects Country along with its Sovereign people. Chris would also like to thank Damien Schulze for his four-wheel driving skills in getting him to distant and rugged places where some of the photographs in this book were taken.

Sarah Rees would like to acknowledge her mother, from whom she has crafted a worldview that is always optimistic. She would like to thank her father for his wisdom and her children for their blossoming brilliance despite growing up knowing that they face major natural system challenges. Lastly, she thanks her partner, whose care, guidance and support have helped in so many ways.

Steven Kuiter would like to acknowledge his father, Rudie Kuiter, for his passion for conservation, love for the natural world and wealth of information about cameras and engineering, and to thank all his friends for their ongoing support and dedication to saving our amazing forests.

The author and photographers wish to acknowledge the Bunurong, Gunaikurnai, Taungurung and Wurundjeri Peoples, upon whose lands we have studied and photographed. We sincerely pay our respects to their Elders past, present and emerging, and recognise their continuing custodianship in protecting these unique forests and their living cultural legacies.

David Lindenmayer
Chris Taylor
Sarah Rees
Steven Kuiter
April 2021

SOURCES FOR ABORIGINAL PLACE NAMES

Elder Aunty Lee Healy and Taungurung Clans Aboriginal Corporation (n.d.), Taungurung Language App, Victorian Aboriginal Corporation for Languages

Sue Wesson (2001), *Aboriginal Flora and Fauna Names of Victoria: As extracted from early surveyors' reports*, Victorian Aboriginal Corporation for Languages, Melbourne

Wurundjeri Woi Wurrung Cultural Heritage Aboriginal Corporation (2020), Wurundjeri, www.wurundjeri.com.au, accessed 25 September 2020. This website supports a wide range of information about the Wurundjeri nation, including language, cultural considerations, education and other valuable material.

INDEX

Page numbers in *italics* refer to
photographs or illustrations

Acheron Cauldron *46*
Agile Antechinus 132
Alpine Ash
    Alpine Ash forest *78, 79*
    fire sensitivity 79
    geographical spread 78
    range in the Central Highlands 68
Amphitheatre Falls *115*
aquatic insects 53
Australian National University, The 15, 27,
    132, 179

Banksia *180*, 180
Barred Galaxias 142, 147, *147*
Bassian Thrush 94
batholiths 49, 64
Baw Baw Frog 22, 30, 121, *121*, 142
Baw Baw Plateau 13, *26, 27, 29, 30, 37,* 121
    cascades *122*
    fens 22–3, *30,* 118, 119, *120–1*
    geological features 46, 49, *53*
    rainfall 24
    rivers of 24, *59, 123, 124*
    rockpool *54–5*
    Snow Gums on *83, 84–5,* 189
Baw Baw Plateau Granodiorite *46,* 49
Big River *116–17,* 117
    Big River Valley *80*
biodiversity
    common species, roles of 29
    fire regimes, impact of change in 131
    forest landscapes and 27, 29, 30, 37
    fungi *see* fungi
    logging, impacts on 157, 158, 160
    loss during wildfires 131
    Mountain Ash forests *see* Mountain Ash
        forests
    national parks 14
    old-growth forests 71
biofluorescence 103
Birch, Dr Bill 45

birds
    Bassian Thrush 94
    bird calls 28, 148
    Boobook Owl 152, *152*
    Brown Thornbill 28, 29, 142
    Buln Buln (Superb Lyrebird) 13, 28, 142,
        148, *148*
    Bundjil (Wedge-tailed Eagle) 155, *155*
    counting birds 150
    Crested Shrike-tit 151, *151*
    dawn chorus 150
    decrease in species 142
    Eastern Whipbird 28, 88
    Eastern Yellow Robin 88, 94
    Flame Robin 27, 132, *136*
    Gang-gang Cockatoo 148, *149*
    Golden Whistler 31
    Grey Shrike-thrush 29, 31
    King Parrot *140,* 141
    migration 31
    Mistletoebird 68, 154, *154*
    Pink Robin 27, 28, 58
    Powerful Owl 152, *153*
    Scaly Thrush 94, 150
    Spotted Pardalote 151, *151*
    Striated Thornbill 142
    Sulphur-crested Cockatoo 141, 151
    White-throated Treecreeper 76
Birrarung (Yarra River) *107, 126–7, 128–9*
Black Range Granodiorite *111*
Black Spur 132, *132*
Blackwood 115
Boobook Owl 152, *152*
Brown Thornbill 28, 29, 142
bryophytes 61
Buln Buln (Superb Lyrebird) 13, 28, 142,
    148
Bundjil (Wedge-tailed Eagle) 155, *155*
Bunyip State Park wildfires *138–9*
Bush Rat 87, 132, 142

Cambarville 131
carbon store in forests 30, 71, 158, 179
    carbon emissions due to logging 157, 158
    Mountain Ash forests 87

Carrang-Carrang/Tambo (Thomson River)
    22–3, *30, 30*
    fens *118–19*
Cathedral Range *see* Nanadhong
    (Cathedral Range)
Central Highlands of Victoria 14
    eastern ranges *32–3*
    forests of *see* forests of Central
        Highlands of Victoria
    geology of 45, 46, *46,* 49, 114, 122
    main types of forest and vegetation 68
    map *10–11*
    Registered Aboriginal Party land
        boundaries 14
    waterfalls *see* dawalin (waterfalls)
Cerberean Cauldron 15, 44, *46,* 47, *48, 50,*
    111, 115
    dawalin (waterfalls) *51*
    formation of 45, 46
Chytrid Fungus 121
clouds
    low *40,* 41
    pyrocumulonimbus 133, 137, *138–9*
Common Brushtail Possum 19
conservation 180
    Barred Galaxias 147, *147*
    science 29
cool temperate rainforest 27, 56, 57, *58,*
    108, 122
    birds and animals 58, 59
    remaining Australian remnants 57
    trees of 57
Cora Lynn Falls 108
Crested Shrike-tit 151, *151*
Cunningham, Ross 141

dawalin (waterfalls) 108, *109*
    Amphitheatre Falls *115*
    Cerberean Cauldron *51*
    Cora Lynn Falls 108
    Strath Creek *112, 113*
    Toorongo Falls *114,* 115
    Wilhelmina Falls *110*
Dawsonia 14, 87, *98*
dead trees 70, 132, 134

deer, invasive 133, 160, 179
    Sambar deer 160

Eastern Whipbird 28, 88
Eastern Yellow Robin 88, 94
ecosystems 142
    logging, damage caused by 157, 158, 160
    Mountain Ash forest 70, 87
    rivers 123, 124
    Superb Lyrebird, role in 142
European colonisation 30, 68, 89, 91, 179

fauna 141
    coexistence of species 141
    decline in possums and gliders 142
    decrease in bird species 142
    'sentinel species' 143
    Threatened, Endangered, Critically
        Endangered 142
    threats to 142
Feathertail Glider 141, 145, *145*
fens 30, 118
    alpine 30, *120-1*
    montane fens *22-3*, 30, *118*, 119
ferns *see* tree ferns
Fernshaw 34, 74
fire 131
    1939 Black Friday 53, 79, 131, *132*, 133
    1983 Ash Wednesday 15, 132
    2009 Black Saturday 14, *34*, 53, 132, *134-5*
    2019 Bunyip State Park *138-9*
    2019-20 131
    animal responses 132
    biological legacies 132
    deaths 14
    essential for some tree species 132
    fire regime, concept 131
    forest burned 14
    frequency, increasing 131
    igniculture 133
    mega-fires 131
    Mountain Ash, burned *134-5*
    plant responses 132, 133
    severity in young/regenerated forests
        132, 163, 171, *171*, 172, *172*
firefighting 179
fish
    Barred Galaxias 142, 147, *147*
    trout, introduced 147
Flame Robin 27, 132, *136*

flowers
    Fringed Violet (Fringed Lily) *88*
    Mountain Ash 14, 67, 71
    Tall Astelia *89*
fog 108
forest floor 87
    biomass after logging 157, 163, 172
    fungi *see* fungi
    granodiorite tors 53
    light penetration 63
    litter decomposition 29, 103
    logs on 87
    plants on 87-91
    seed storage 90
    tree ferns *see* tree ferns
forests of Central Highlands of Victoria
    age 13
    biodiversity 14, 15, 27
    cool temperate *see* cool temperate
        rainforest
    decline in area 179
    extent and location 13
    forest floor *see* forest floor
    fragmentation due to logging 158
    geology of 45, 46, *46*, 49, 114, 122
    mixed-species forests 80, *86*
    monitoring, long-term 15, 142
    old-growth forests *see* old-growth
        forests
    'patch types' 27
    preservation of 14, 180
    rain, as generators of 42
    understorey *see* understorey
    wet eucalypt *see* wet eucalypt forests
    younger 30, 70, 163, 174
Fringed Violet (Fringed Lily) *88*
fungi *21*, *81*, 90, *100*, *101*, *102*, *103*
    bracket fungi 100, *100*
    Ghost Fungus 90, *103*
    leaf litter decomposition 103
    Pixie's Parasol *104-5*, 105
    role 21, 102, 103, 142

Gang-gang Cockatoo 148, *149*
Giant Mountain Grass 91
Giant Redwoods (Giant Sequoias) 67
gliders
    decline in species 142
    Feathertail Glider 141, 145, *145*
    Greater Glider 27, 49, 76, *76*, 80, 132, *143*

Sugar Glider 95, 108, 152
Yellow-bellied Glider 27, 142, *146*, 147,
    158
Golden Whistler 31
Goulburn River *see* Waring (Goulburn
    River)
granodiorite 45, 46, 49, 53, 64, 111, 122
    tors 49, *52*, 53
Great Forest National Park 14, 16
Greater Glider 27, 49, 76, *76*, 80, 132, 143,
    143
    'sentinel species', as 143
Grey Shrike-thrush 29, 31
Gunaikurnai People 13, 53, 179
    forests of, map *14*

habitat 68, 70, 74, 134
    old hollow trees, decline in 148
Hardwater Ferns 95
Hazel Pomaderris 59, 71
Healesville *12*, 74, 126
heathland, alpine 35
Highland Copperhead 27, 87, 147, *147*
hollows in trees 57, 67, 71, 102, 141, 148
hornworts 20, 57, 61, 67

igniculture 133
International Union for the Conservation
    of Nature (IUCN) 70

kangaroos and wallabies 133
King Parrot *140*, 141
Koala 80

Lake Eildon 13, 117
Lake Mountain 45
landscape mosaics 27, 30, *38*
Latrobe Valley 13
Leadbeater's Possum *see* Wollert
    (Leadbeater's Possum)
lichens 20, 57, 61, 67, 76, 99, *99*
Little River 111
liverworts 57
logging 13-14, *157*, 163, *168*, *174-5*, 179
    animals and 174
    biomass left on forest floor 157, 163, 172
    carbon emissions due to 158
    clearfell, impacts of 14, 157
    code of practice, breaches of 165
    economic and employment effects of 160

logging *continued*
    ecosystems, damage to 157
    fire severity and 30, 163, 171, *171*, 172, *172*
    fragmentation of forests 158
    history of in Central Highlands 157, 159
    industrial logging fires 158, *161*, *162*, 169, 173, *173*
    invasive species, attracting 133, 160
    log dumps *170*
    Mountain Ash forests *159*
    new form of 169, *169*
    post-fire logging 160
    road creation 158, 165
    soil compaction 165, 170
    soil erosion 165
    soil nutrients, loss 157
    steep slopes, on 165, *165*, 166, *166-7*
    tree ferns, effect on 157
    water flows, impact on 25
    water yield, impact on 25, 108, 158
    wind speeds, effect on 29, 158
logs 87
    forest floor, on 87
    moss growth on 96

Manna Gums (Wurun) 80, 81, *81*, 115, *128-9*, 129
Maroondah Catchment 34, 74, *150*
Maroondah Highway 16, 74, 132, *132*
Maroondah Reservoir *125*
Marysville 131
Melbourne (Naarm) 13, 126
    drinking water source 13, 14, 24, 107, 125
Mistletoe plants 154, *176*
Mistletoebird 68
mosses 20, *20*, 57, *60-1*, 67, 76, *81*, 96
    Dawsonia 14, 87, 98
Mount Baw Baw 31, 46, *67*
    alpine heathland *35*
Mount Bullfight 45
Mount Disappointment 112, *159*
Mount Donna Buang *41*, 45, *58*
Mount Erica 53
Mount Gregory 155
Mount Juliet *40*, 45
Mount Monda 34, *34*
Mount Ritchie 45
Mount Torbreck *31*, *36-7*, 45, *50*, *157*
Mount Useful 83

Mountain Ash 13, 57, 59, *67*, 67-8, *71*, *72*, *73*, 115
    see also Mountain Ash forests
    2009 Black Saturday wildfires 14, *134-5*
    buttresses 67, *76-7*
    canopy size 67-8, 74
    Edward VII Tree 74
    fire scars 68
    flowering plant 14, 67, 71
    food source, as 71
    the Ferguson Tree 74
    the Furmston Tree *16*, 74
    growth rates 67
    habitat, as 68, 71, 74
    lifespan 63, 67, 69
    old-growth forests 70, 71
Mountain Ash forests 13, *69*
    burning of 63, 68, 131
    carbon store 71, 87
    Critically Endangered ecosystem 70, 145
    decay, slow rates of 87
    ecosystem 87
    forest floor 63, 87, 90
    growth stages of *176*
    logging 69, *157*, *159*
    logs on forest floor 87
    multi-aged forests 69, *75*
    range in the Central Highlands *68*
    soil nutrients 49, 71, 87
Mountain Brushtail Possum 18, *19*, 57, 87, 95, 100, 132, 141, 142
Mountain Grey Gums *80*, 115
Mountain Monarchs 67
Murrindindi River *137*, *137*
    Murrindindi Valley 111
    regenerating forest *137*
Musk Daisy Bush 59
Myrtle Beech 57, 58, *59*, 59, *60-1*, 63, 92, 133

Nanadhong (Cathedral Range) *44*, 45, *47*, *48*, 111
Narbethong 131

old-growth forests 30, 70, 71
    carbon stores in 71
    clearfelling, impact on 157
    decline in area 30, 174, 179
    fires in 70, 132, 133, 171
    layers of 71
    logging of 69, 70, 174

    moss cover in 98
    Mountain Ash forests 70, 71
    nutrient-rich soil in 71
    replacement with younger 30, 70, 174
    water producers, as 107, 127, 158
O'Shannassy Water Catchment 87

Peppermint Gums 80
Pink Robin 27, *28*, 58
Platypus 103, 108, 123, 124
pollination 29
possums
    Common Brushtail Possum 19
    decline in species 142
    eggs as food source 152
    Mountain Brushtail Possum 18, *19*, 57, 87, 95, 100, 132, 141
    Short-eared Possum 141
    Wollert *see* Wollert (Leadbeater's Possum)
Powerful Owl 152, *153*
Purnululu National Park (Bungle Bungles) 14

radio-tracking studies 57
rain *42-3*
rainbows 40, *180*
rainforest 63, *63*
    A Rainforest Site of National Significance *63*
    cool temperate *see* cool temperate rainforest
    range in the Central Highlands *68*
    tropical 58, 87
Rakali (Water Rat) 108
Red Fox 83
reptiles 27, 29
rock, exposed 27, 29
rock pools 53, *54-5*
    rivers, in 123, 124
Rosengren, Neville 49
Rubicon Valley 143

Sassafras 57, 61
    Southern Sassafras *178*
Scaly Thrush 94, 150
seed dispersal 29
Seven Acre Rock 49, *53*
Shining Gum 53
Short-eared Possum 141

Snob Creek Falls 45, 117, *117*
Snow Gums 30, *38*, *82*, *83*, *84*, *84–5*, 189, *190-1*
 fire damage 37, 83
 range in the Central Highlands *68*
soil
 compaction 165, 170
 fertility 49, 87
 logging and loss of nutrients 157, 165
 old-growth forests, in 71, 87
 seed bank, as 90, 91, 92
 variation 27
Sooty Owl 27
Spotted Pardalote 151, *151*
Spotted-tail Quoll 53
springtails 58
Starvation Creek water catchment *163*
Strath Creek *112*, *113*
Striated Thornbill 142
Strzelecki Ranges 68
Sugar Glider 95, 108, 152
Sulphur-crested Cockatoo 141, 151
Superb Lyrebird *see* Buln Buln (Superb Lyrebird)

Tall Astelia *89*
Tasmania 14, 57, 78, 80, 148
Taungurung People 13, 179
 forests of, map *14*
Taylor, Chris 172
Thomson Catchment 107, 108
Thomson Reservoir 24, *25*, *127*
Thomson River *see* Carrang-Carrang/Tambo (Thomson River)
Thorpe, Lidia 8
Tiger Snake 87
Toolangi Forest 76, *109*
Toorongo Falls *114*, 115
Toorongo Granodiorite *46*, 49, 114, 115
Toorongo Plateau *64–5*
Torbreck Range *79*
Traditional Custodians/Owners 8, 13, 160, 177, 179, 180
tree collapse 29, 70, 158
tree crickets 68
tree ferns *18*, 58, *58*, 87, 92, *94*, 176
 food source, as 18
 germination in basket by other plants 92, 179
 litter layer under 94

logging, impact on 157, 172
 Rough Tree Fern 90, *90*
 Soft Tree Fern 87, 90
Tyers River 59, 121
Tynong Granite *46*, 49, 53

understorey 59, 63, 78, 87
 fungi 90
 plants 71, 87–90, 95, 180
 seed bank, as 90, 91

Vandenburg, Alfons
 The Tasman Fold Belt System in Victoria 46
Victorian Alps 32, 35, *36–7*, *37*, *38*
von Guérard, Eugene
 Ferntree Gully in the Dandenong Ranges 91
 Waterfall, Strath Creek 112, *113*

Warburton 45, 49, *164*
Waring (Goulburn River) 111, 117
 Waring valley *32–3*, 83
water cycle 13, 42
water production
 forest as generator 13, 14, 24, 71, 107
 old-growth as major producer 107, 127, 158
water supply
 closed water catchments 34, 87, 107, 108, 125, 158
 desalination 108
 forest as generator 13, 14, 24, 71, 107, 158
 logging, impact on 25, 108, 158
 quality, preservation of 34
waterfalls *see* dawalin (waterfalls)
Water Rat *see* Rakali (Water Rat)
wattles 71, 90, 92, *92–3*, 95
Watts Catchment 74
Wedge-tailed Eagle *see* Bundjil (Wedge-tailed Eagle)
wet eucalypt forests 14, *18*, 29, 59, 107
 see also forests of the Central Highlands of Victoria; wet forests
 biodiversity 142, *143*, 145
 birds 29, 150, 152
 logging *see* logging
 old hollow trees, decline in 148
 rainforest *see* cool temperate rainforest

tree ferns *18*, 90, 157, 172
water production 107
wattle layer 95
wet forests 14, 25, 29, 107
 see also forests of the Central Highlands of Victoria; wet eucalypt forests
 animals 19, 136, *141–2*
 biodiversity 27, 141
 logging *see* logging
 plants 20, 21, 89, 90, 95
 water production 107
White-throated Treecreeper 76
Wilhelmina Falls *110*
Wollert (Leadbeater's Possum) 13, 15, 22, 27, 58, 90, 95, *97*, 132, *144*
 Critically Endangered classification 30, 142, 145
 fossil records 142
 habitat 70, 132
Woods Point 132, *133*
Wurundjeri People 13, 61, 179
 Birrarung and 129
 forests of, map *14*
 ritual sorry dance *177*

Yarra River *see* Birrarung (Yarra River)
Yellow-bellied Glider 27, 142, *146*, 147, 158

Following pages: **Snow Gum on the Baw Baw Plateau, Gunaikurnai Country** (Chris Taylor) The twisted forms of multi-stemmed Snow Gum woodland are a stark contrast to the towering single-stemmed Mountain Ash and Alpine Ash forests. Woodlands such as these will often show signs of repeated fires, with trees regrowing from the base after they have been burned, giving them a mallee-like form with several trunks.

Allen & Unwin
83 Alexander Street
Crows Nest NSW 2065
Australia
Phone: (61 2) 8425 0100
Email: info@allenandunwin.com
Web: www.allenandunwin.com

A catalogue record for this
book is available from the
National Library of Australia

ISBN 978 1 76087 982 2

Internal design by Philip Campbell Design
Front endpaper: Photograph of montane fens by Sarah Rees
p. 2: Photograph of Mount Cathedral at Nanadhong (Cathedral Range)
by Chris Taylor
pp. 4–5: Photograph of Clematis flower by Sarah Rees
p. 6: Photograph of wattles and ferns by Sarah Rees
p. 9: Photograph of ridgeline tors at Mount Torbreck by Chris Taylor
pp. 10–11: Map by Guy Holt
pp. 14, 46 and 68: Figures by Chris Taylor
Back endpaper: Photograph of wattle understorey by Sarah Rees
Printed in China by 1010 Printing Limited

10 9 8 7 6 5 4 3 2 1

THIS IS YOUR WAY SIR

Jonathan Riddell and Nicolette Tomkinson

Capital Transport

The Gateway to the North, Anonymous, 1923–1939
St Pancras and Euston were only two of London's gateways to the north, but of course the LMS would not mention the rival LNER's services from nearby King's Cross station.

ISBN 978-1-85414-343-3

Published by
Capital Transport Publishing
www.capitaltransport.com

Printed by
1010 Printing International Ltd.

Acknowledgements:
The posters are from the collections of the National Railway Museum, copyright Science & Society Picture Library, and Christies. The smaller publicity items are from the collections of Stan Friedman and Peter Mitchell.

Introduction

In 1923 the many railway companies which operated throughout Britain were formed into just four large concerns. One of these new ones was the London Midland & Scottish Railway which was created out of a large number of disparate operations. Although at first there were some difficulties and tensions between these old companies which now formed the LMS, the new company soon began to create its own identity.

The first LMS posters retained the style of those issued by its former constituents such as the Caledonian Railway with only the company name on the poster being changed to inform passengers that a new company had taken over. In March 1923 the Midland Railway's former Superintendent of Advertising, T C Jeffrey, was appointed to the post of Superintendent of Advertising and Publicity. This led to the LMS's publicity adopting the Midland Railway's style. It was not until 1924 that the LMS really began to establish its own corporate identity through its posters. The LMS approached Norman Wilkinson to design three posters (he was eventually to design over 100 for the LMS and, more than any other man, shaped the direction and style of LMS posters) and also to advise the LMS on ways it could improve its publicity, which was already beginning to be compared unfavourably with the LNER's. His proposal to commission members of the Royal Academy to design a series of posters was quickly adopted. Wilkinson believed that this unusual step of attempting to mix fine art and commercial art was worth the risk. Although scarcely any of the Royal Academicians had designed a poster before, Wilkinson considered that the resultant publicity would be highly beneficial for the company even if some of the posters did not meet with critical acclaim. Of the eighteen artists approached by Wilkinson, only Brangwyn, who was already working for the LNER, declined. Wilkinson chose the subjects, but it was left to the artists how they approached the work. These posters began to appear from early 1924 and featured a wide range of subjects from castles to landscapes. Three of the posters set a new trend by featuring industry whilst others illustrated the operational side of the railway which the passenger would not usually see. Wilkinson rightly believed that passengers were interested in how the railway was run. Not all of the royal academicians' works received critical acclaim. Percy Bradshaw wrote in *Art in Advertising* that a poster of Carlisle by Maurice Greiffenhagen was the only good design. His view must have been popular as this poster became one of the best selling LMS posters in its day, particularly in America. It is interesting how tastes change, as today it is no longer considered to be amongst the best of the LMS posters.

One critic wrote that most of the academicians did not realise "that a good picture is not necessarily a good poster".

Wilkinson's scheme was a success with a large amount of generally favourable publicity for the LMS. Exhibitions of the original paintings were shown in Britain and America. The posters sold well and a calendar and booklet were produced. The style of this first series under the guiding eye of Wilkinson set the tone for the LMS, which marketed itself on its quality of service. No doubt the rather more conventional and perhaps even staid style of many of its posters was felt to be more in keeping with the taste of most of its passengers. Even though the LNER and other railway companies did sometimes produce the more traditional landscape painting as a poster, the LMS managed to retain its own easily recognisable distinctive style and this worked to the company's benefit. On the whole an artist employed by one of the four railway companies did not usually work for another, although nearly all also worked for the London Underground.

It was also said at the time that although the LMS posters advertised travel throughout the country, they did not sufficiently promote rail, as opposed to motor, travel. This criticism was no doubt based on the fact that whilst they showed beautiful landscapes, the posters did not explain the advantages of rail as opposed to the motor car or coach. In short there was no hard sell.

The LMS like the other railways had a relatively short life from 1923 to 1947 when it was nationalised, but it was a period that covered the golden years of the poster in Britain. The outbreak of the war in 1939 put an effective end for a while to the pictorial poster as such, as none of the railway companies could advertise non-essential leisure travel for holidays. And after the war neither the economy nor the LMS was in any fit state to restart the widespread advertising campaigns it had done before. Rationing was still in force and the railways needed to rebuild themselves from the effects of wartime damages and deprivations. A few posters were issued in the two years after the war finished but these tended to show aspects of the railway itself.

It can be claimed that with the formation of British Railways on 1st January 1948, the LMS poster eventually went through a form of revival, as several of its posters were re-issued by British Railways to advertise their own services with only the wording changed to reflect the new organisation. This no doubt reflected the timeless images used by the LMS, whereas the more fashionable and artistically acclaimed designs used by the other companies were quickly to look dated before they were to become fashionable again.

Holiday booklets

Holiday travel was important for all the railways and the LMS issued its own series of booklets advertising "Holidays by LMS". At the time the train was the only practical option for most people wishing to take a holiday. These booklets, full of practical information for the tourist, were priced at 6d and complemented the numerous free leaflets that the LMS also issued to advertise specific locations and parts of the country, not just the seaside. From these examples shown it would appear that the company knew precisely its intended audience and the type of holiday that its passengers would like to take. All show a seaside scene and all but one shows a young woman wearing a swimsuit, the odd one out showing a small girl atop a sandcastle. A separate series of regional booklets was also issued by the LMS for the Lake District, Lancashire Coast and Scottish Resorts, each priced 3d.

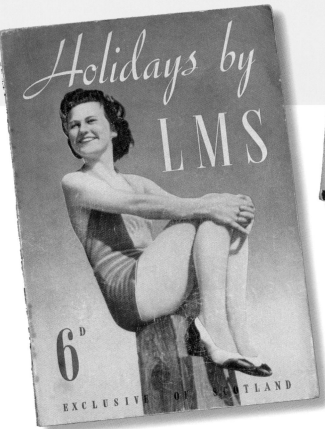

6

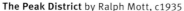

The Peak District by Ralph Mott, c1935
The Peak District was ideally situated for both days out and longer holidays, surrounded as it is by many of the north's large industrial towns and well served by railways.

See the Peak District by S R Wyatt, 1932
This poster shows an LMS passenger train crossing the Monsal viaduct. When it opened in 1863 there was much criticism from those who felt it destroyed the beauty of the Wye valley. The railway closed in 1968, and the bridge is now used as a cycleway and footpath and is a site of architectural and historical interest. In 1951 the Peak District became England's first national park.

Peak District
The exact location of the illustration shown on the cover of this brochure dating from 1935 is unknown, but it could well be of a view of Miller's Dale, the well known beauty spot which was served by an LMS station of the same name.

Peak District
This 1938 brochure is clearly aimed at the modern young person keen to enjoy a day's walking in the Peak District. Exploring the countryside was increasingly popular with young people who were aided and abetted by the formation and sudden growth of the Youth Hostel Association in the 1930s, which provided the opportunity for them to have a cheap holiday in the countryside. The signpost on the cover points not just to three popular tourist spots, but they are also the LMS's main stations in the Peak District. Dovedale is arguably the prettiest valley in the Peak District and it is certainly one of the most popular. In recent years there have been various proposals to reopen the complete route from Buxton to Matlock via Bakewell. Dovedale was served by the romantically named Thorpe Cloud station, which closed to regular passenger services as early as 1954 and is now part of a long distance trail.

Rhyl by Jackson Burton, c1930s
The six miles of golden sands between Rhyl and Prestatyn would have drawn the family holidaymaker to this popular destination in North Wales which was easily reached by the LMS's trains. Children were a popular subject for the poster artist and Jackson Burton's poster promoting Sunny Rhyl as 'The children's paradise' is particularly successful. Interestingly the simple formula of sand and sea for a successful family holiday was promoted by advertisers in 1930 in the same way as it would be today. So popular was this area that in 1939 the LMS together with Thomas Cook built a holiday camp at Prestatyn. It was later sold to Pontins before closing in the 1980s.

New Brighton & Wallasey by Septimus E Scott, c1934
The Lancashire resorts competed to outdo each other with newer and bigger attractions. This poster from 1934 shows the newly opened pool which was claimed at the time to be the finest and largest aquatic stadium in the world. Within a week over 100,000 people had paid to visit the pool and within four months nearly one million people had tried out its facilities. Damage by hurricane force winds in 1990 led to its demolition.

Southport by Fortunino Matania, 1925
Whilst many of the LMS posters promote travel in the summer, this image is particularly interesting as it is promoting the cultural attractions of 'Southport in wintertime', this time by an Italian artist, Fortunino Matania. Matania regularly exhibited at the Royal Academy and was another example of an important artist secured for commercial work by the LMS. The image of the theatregoers leaving the Garrick immaculately dressed in the finest fashion of the day was one of the most glamorous seen to promote the LMS. Southport remains one of the most popular resorts in the UK although the magnificent Garrick theatre, a listed building on tree lined Lord Street, is now home to a bingo emporium.

Saltcoats by Tom Gilfillan, 1935

Saltcoats is located on the North Ayrshire coast opposite the Isle of Arran and was a popular resort for holidaymakers from Glasgow. The development of the beach pavilion in the 1920s and the swimming pool in the 1930s enabled the resort to promote itself as a healthy destination on 'The Finest Tidal Lake on the Firth of Clyde'. It was certainly the largest tidal pool in Scotland at that time. This sun drenched image is artistic licence at its best as the tanned, attractive holiday makers are cooling down in the water in a resort with an average summer temperature of only 18 degrees.

13

Lytham St Annes for Sea Breezes and Sunshine by W Smithson Broadhead (from a photograph by Mendel Saidman), 1923–1947
This poster by W Smithson Broadhead is unusual in that not just the artist but also the photographer is credited. It is not known how many other posters were based on photographs but it is unlikely that all of the artists would have visited the locations they portrayed.

Lytham St Annes by Charles Pears, c1926
Lytham St Annes was a popular resort to the south of Blackpool and regarded as being more select.

GREAT YARMOUTH &
GORLESTON–ON–SEA

FREE ILLUSTRATED GUIDE FROM PUBLICITY MANAGER GREAT YARMOUTH OR ANY LMS OR L·N·E·R STATION

TRAVEL BY RAIL

Great Yarmouth & Gorleston-on-Sea by Charles Pears, 1923–1939
The railway seaside poster tended to keep its own style as the railway companies worked jointly with the resorts on their publicity, with only the LNER retaining the right to an artistic veto. One well known poster designer at the time described the traditional railway poster thus: "The ingredients vary but little, golden sands, blue water, brilliant sunshine, parasols, deck chairs, a bandstand, pretty flappers in pretty clothes or perhaps a supply of eligible young men, children with bare brown feet, building sandcastles … The whole is brilliantly coloured, quite outshining the rainbow." There was certainly an element of truth in this but some at least of the LMS's seaside posters showed more imagination. This poster issued jointly by the LMS and LNER does not quite conform to this description, though it does have the ubiquitous woman in a bathing costume even if the sea is not blue and there are clouds in the sky.

THE NEW LUXURY SWIMMING POOL

MORECAMBE AND HEYSHAM

BRITAIN'S MOST MODERN AND PROGRESSIVE RESORT

EXPRESS SERVICES AND CHEAP TICKETS BY L M S

OFFICIAL HOLIDAY GUIDE FROM ADVERTISING MANAGER, TOWN HALL. MORECAMBE.

Morecambe and Heysham by Frank Sherwin, c1936
In contrast to Blackpool, which attracted holiday-makers from the Lancashire Mill towns, Morecambe attracted more holiday-makers from Yorkshire and Scotland. In the 1920s and 1930s it was a thriving and stylish seaside resort and could justify its claim to be "Britain's most modern and progressive resort". The poster shows Morecambe's new pool which opened on 27 July 1936. At 110 yards long the pool claimed to be the largest open-air pool in Europe, able to hold up to 1,200 bathers and 3,000 spectators. It was a fine example of the new modernist style of architecture and was situated next to the newly refurbished Midland Hotel which was owned by the LMS.

Bournemouth, The Centre of Health & Pleasure
by Leonard Richmond, c1930s

Weston-super-Mare
by Claude Buckle, 1946

The LMS network just managed to reach the south coast via the former Somerset and Dorset Line which ran from Bath to Bournemouth. The service on this line was operated jointly by the LMS and Southern Railways. Of particular importance to the LMS on this lightly used line was the Summer Saturday traffic, as large numbers of holidaymakers would travel from their northern towns for their week or fortnight on the south coast. This explains why the LMS issued posters promoting Bournemouth – a resort well outside its usual territory. With their main purpose to convey passengers from the north, these holiday trains often ran non-stop from south of Bath.

Lancashire with its many large industrial towns such as Liverpool, Manchester, Oldham and Bury was one of the most heavily populated counties in England, and its coastal resorts were popular holiday destinations for the inhabitants of those towns. The advent of the railways saw the growth of these resorts from former fishing villages, which as holiday resorts were almost totally dependent on the railway for their holiday trade.

GLENEAGLES HOTEL
PERTHSHIRE
A PALACE AT THE GATE OF THE HIGHLANDS
AN LMS HOTEL
ARTHUR TOWLE · CONTROLLER · LMS HOTEL SERVICES

Gleneagles Hotel Anonymous, 1924
This poster was issued to commemorate the opening of the Gleneagles Hotel on 3rd June 1924. Situated on the threshold of the Perthshire Highlands and on the main line of the West Coast railway, the hotel was opened by Arthur Towle, the controller of all LMS hotels in the inter-war period. The poster describes the hotel as 'A Palace at the Gate of the Highlands'. Today the hotel is famous as much for its international conferences as for its golf. As part of the opening night celebrations, the first ever radio outside broadcast in Scotland took place from the hotel.

Midland Hotel, Morecambe Anonymous, 1933

Morecambe is located in Lancashire on the north west coast of England with views across to the Lake District. The Midland Hotel replaced an earlier Victorian hotel latterly of the same name but originally known as the North Western Hotel, reflecting its original ownership. The new 40 room Midland Hotel was designed for the LMS by the architect Oliver Hill in 1932 in an iconic art deco style. Integral to the design were the works of art by several of the leading artists and designers of the day such as Eric Gill, Eric Ravilious and Marion Dorn. In its glamorous heyday it was regularly visited by Coco Chanel and Laurence Olivier and in 1989, it was used in the filming of episodes of television's 'Poirot'. It was taken over by the government for the duration of the Second World War, but remained in railway ownership only until 1952. The post-war years saw it gradually decline until it was finally refurbished and re-opened in 2008 with the ground floor of the hotel restored as closely as possible to the original. It is now a Grade 2 listed building and is held in such high regard locally that it has its own 'Friends of the Midland Hotel' group who campaign to raise the awareness of the architectural importance of the building.

Turnberry Anonymous, 1923–1939
On its formation in 1923 the LMS took over 40 hotels, including four in Ireland, to become the owner of Europe's largest hotel business. These hotels were a profitable asset for the LMS with many located next to the company's stations. They were famous for their high standards. The LMS owned three golf courses adjacent to Scottish hotels and a holiday camp at Prestatyn, the latter in partnership with Thomas Cook & Sons. In 1939 many of the hotels were requisitioned for war service. Afterwards many of them struggled to return to their former glory.

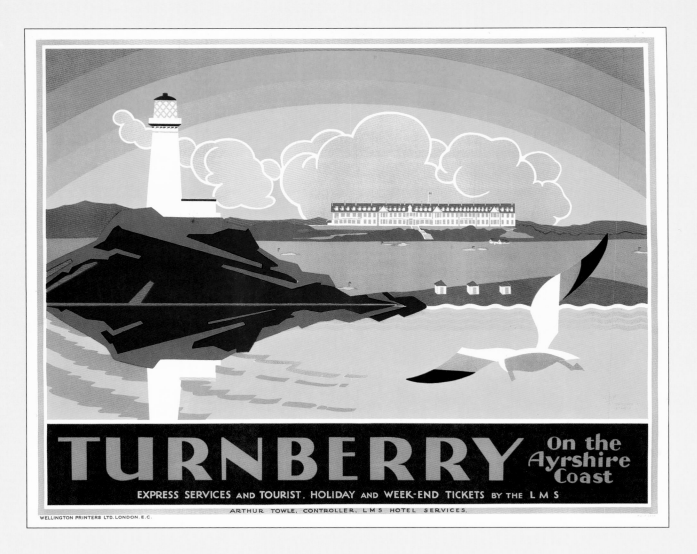

Turnberry Anonymous, 1923–1939

Turnberry on the Ayrshire coast is renowned for its famous lighthouse and golf as highlighted in this art deco poster for the resort. The hotel featured in the poster was built on an 800 acre site in the style of an opulent country house in 1900 using a distinctive combination of white plasterwork and a red roof. When it opened in 1906 it offered unrivalled luxury such as electric lighting, central heating, hot and cold running water, and saltwater plunge baths. The first formal golf course was constructed in 1901 and the famous hotel is now a year-round destination favoured by royalty and celebrities alike. The lighthouse that predates the hotel was built to warn vessels to keep away from Brest Rocks.

The English Lakes by Welsh, 1923–1939
Unlike today, the Lake District was well served by railways in the 1920s and 1930s. Windermere, shown here, is the largest lake in England. The boat shown heading along the lake was probably operated by the LMS, as it took over the ferries previously run by the Furness Railway which linked Lakeside Station to Ambleside. In 1936 the LMS introduced two new motor boats. The village of Birthwaite was renamed Windermere after the lake. It grew rapidly in size following the opening of the railway in 1847.

The Lake District – for rest and quiet imaginings by S J Lamorna Birch, 1924–1939
Birch was a very prolific artist, best known for his paintings of northern England and of Cornwall where he eventually lived. This peaceful
view is typical of his style.

English Lakes for Holidays
by Clodagh Sparrow, c1935
The quotation on this poster "Infinite riches in a little room" was taken from Christopher Marlowe's play *The Jew of Malta*, but in this context, no doubt refers to the wide variety of scenery to be found in the Lake District, which as mountain regions go, due to its relative compactness, could be considered as a "little room". Clodgah Sparrow also designed several leaflets advertising the many holiday regions served by the LMS.

Two leaflets advertising the Lake District as a holiday destination. Each was part of an annual series covering the main holiday areas covered by the LMS network.

Grange over Sands by Frank Ball, 1923–1939

Grange over Sands is located seven miles from Windermere on the shores of Morecambe Bay on the edge of the Lake District and has one of the mildest climates in the north of England. The arrival of the Furness Railway transformed the small fishing village of Grange over Sands into a fashionable resort. The wealthy industrialists of Lancashire and Yorkshire were frequent visitors attracted by the wildlife, parks and ornamental gardens. Frank Ball's attractive poster, though still portraying two elegant ladies in swimming costumes, manages to capture the more peaceful and genteel nature of the resort in contrast to the busier seaside towns advertised in many of the LMS's other posters.

TRAVEL TO IRELAND BY
THE SHORT SEA ROUTE
STRANRAER-LARNE

MAGNIFICENT NEW TURBINE STEAMERS
'PRINCESS MAUD' AND 'PRINCESS MARGARET'

GREATLY ACCELERATED SERVICES

PARTICULARS OF TRAIN AND STEAMER TIMES FROM
ANY LMS STATION

Firth of Clyde Cruises by Norman Wilkinson, c1934
The Firth of Clyde was the major area for coastal cruising in the UK and the railway's shipping services served both holidaymakers and locals alike to the resorts and islands in the Firth as well as those just wanting to take a cruise on the ships. The *Caledonia* and *Mercury* entered service on 1st March 1934 which was a Glasgow holiday weekend. They then settled into a regular programme sailing from Gourock and Wemyss Bay to Dunoon, Rothesay, and beyond. Although it cannot be seen clearly in this poster, surprisingly these new ships were both paddle steamers, by then almost outdated technology. Although sister ship *Caledonia* was owned by the Caledonian Steam Packet Company, this was itself a wholly-owned subsidiary of the LMS. Due to a quirk in legislation this allowed it to operate over a wider area of the Clyde than ships owned directly by the LMS. The *Caledonia* replaced an earlier paddle ship of the same name, dating from 1889. Renamed *Goatfell* she served in the Second World War as minesweeper but regained her old name after the war. From 1969 to 1980 she served as a floating pub on the Thames Embankment in London until she was destroyed by fire. Her engines are preserved at Hollycombe in Hampshire.

Stranraer-Larne by Norman Wilkinson, c 1934
On its formation in 1923 the LMS inherited a large shipping empire from its various constituent companies. There had been strong competition between the companies on the profitable route to Northern Ireland, but all of these northern ferry routes became part of the LMS. The *Princess Maud*, the first turbine-driven ship, was launched in 1931 and the *Princess Margaret* in 1934, both to serve the Stranraer to Larne route. The administration in Northern Ireland preferred the Stranraer route and the Post Office permitted a first class sleeping car to be attached to the down West Coast Postal train.

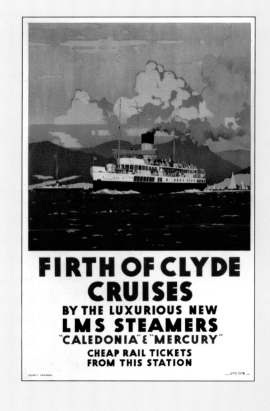

FIRTH OF CLYDE CRUISES
BY THE LUXURIOUS NEW
LMS STEAMERS
"CALEDONIA" & "MERCURY"
CHEAP RAIL TICKETS
FROM THIS STATION

HEYSHAM BOAT IN
MORECAMBE BAY
by Norman Wilkinson

Heysham Boat in Morecambe Bay by Norman Wilkinson, 1935

It would be wrong to consider the LMS as just a railway company. It was the largest hotel group in Europe and also had extensive shipping interests mainly operating across the Irish Sea. Fortunately Norman Wilkinson, the man responsible for advising and also designing many of the LMS posters, was a noted marine artist ideally suited to the task. The harbour at Heysham had been built by the Midland Railway so that it could compete on the profitable routes to Northern Ireland, but with the formation of the LMS in 1923 it was to become just one of the LMS's many routes to Ireland. In 1928 the LMS acquired three new large ferries to operate out of Heysham, allowing the company to close the route from Fleetwood to Belfast. The new ships received the traditional Fleetwood "Duke" names of *Duke of Argyll, Duke of Lancaster* and *Duke of Rothesay*. In 1935 a fourth ship the *Duke of York* was added to the LMS's Heysham to Belfast Service. It is this ship which is shown in the poster.

Holiday traffic was important for the LMS, with many families taking the traditional one or two week break. With few people owning cars, the train was almost the only option. Whilst the colourful pictorial posters caught the eye, pamphlets and leaflets contained the information necessary for prospective passengers. Even in the 1920s and 30s a whole week's unlimited travel for 10/- (50p) was a real bargain.

Most of the LMS's publicity was not dated. The exceptions to the rule were timetables and Cheap Fares leaflets. The covers of these two booklets both depict a stylised return ticket. Buying a return ticket rather than two singles was almost always cheaper and was one of the easiest ways to save money.

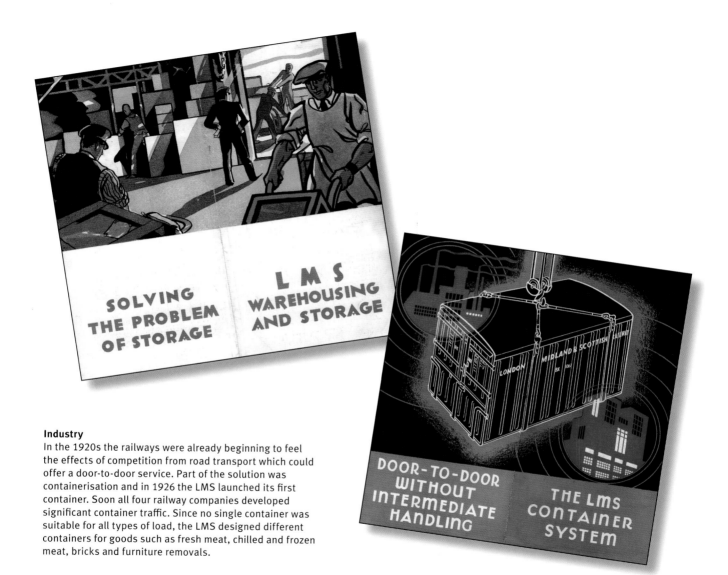

SOLVING THE PROBLEM OF STORAGE

L M S WAREHOUSING AND STORAGE

DOOR-TO-DOOR WITHOUT INTERMEDIATE HANDLING

THE LMS CONTAINER SYSTEM

Industry

In the 1920s the railways were already beginning to feel the effects of competition from road transport which could offer a door-to-door service. Part of the solution was containerisation and in 1926 the LMS launched its first container. Soon all four railway companies developed significant container traffic. Since no single container was suitable for all types of load, the LMS designed different containers for goods such as fresh meat, chilled and frozen meat, bricks and furniture removals.

The LMS was keen to be seen as the solution to all of industry's transportation needs. The modern style of this attractive leaflet advertising that the LMS could carry "exceptional loads" clearly reinforces the message that the LMS could provide "Modern Transportation Methods".

Rock of Cashel by Norman Wilkinson, c1930s
Prior to the Norman invasion the Rock of Cashel was the traditional seat of the Kings of Munster. It is one of the most visited heritage sites in Ireland and is located at Cashel, South Tipperary. This spectacular group of medieval buildings shown in silhouette in Wilkinson's poster contains one of the finest collections of Celtic art anywhere in Europe.

Donegal for Holidays
by Norman Wilkinson, 1923–1947
Wilkinson portrays a gentle view of
Donegal, looking across Sheephaven Bay
and the patchwork of fields to a distant
Errigal Mountain.

SHEEPHAVEN
By NORMAN WILKINSON R.I.

DONEGAL
FOR HOLIDAYS

LONDON MIDLAND AND SCOTTISH RAILWAY

LMS

WICKLOW

IRELAND
for HOLIDAYS

PAUL HENRY

Illustrated folder from any London Midland & Scottish Railway Station or Agency

Wicklow – Ireland for Holidays
by Paul Henry, c1926
Paul Henry is considered one of Ireland's most important landscape painters of the 20th century and it was almost certainly quite a coup for the LMS to have him working for it. In 1929 Henry settled in Kilmaconogue in County Wicklow, now one of the most popular film-making locations in Ireland and an area also popular with both Dubliners and foreign visitors. Henry's poster design involved a deceptively simple composition which emphasised the rolling hills and mountains and an absence of people. His style defined a view of the Irish landscape and his original paintings now command the highest prices internationally. It is therefore no surprise to learn that Paul Henry's posters sold the most copies when the LMS made them available for sale in the 1920s.

LMS NORTHERN IRELAND
by Hesketh Hubbard V-P.R.B.A.,R.O.I.

Northern Ireland by Hesketh Hubbard, 1944
The LMS was also the only one of the Big Four to operate rail services in Northern Ireland. Posters depicting the beauties of Northern Ireland countryside and coastline were aimed at the English market in the hope of encouraging tourism. Other posters advertised the LMS shipping services across the Irish Sea.

The Face of Scotland by Brian Cook, 1935

Brian Cook was in the envious position of being able to design a poster to advertise a book containing his own illustrations. The book was very popular and went through several editions from 1933 to 1947. The poster is unusual in that although at first glance it appears to be advertising Scotland by LMS and LNER, the secondary text is very heavily slanted to promoting the book with only one line given over to promoting the "frequent restaurant and sleeping car expresses" operated by the two railways to Scotland.

Galloway by Norman Wilkinson, 1927

Galloway in the Southern Highlands of Scotland was well known for horses, cattle rearing and milk and beef production. Much of the employment in the local area is still in agriculture and forestry. Tourism therefore makes a significant contribution to the local economy. The tourist can explore the mountainous region of outstanding natural beauty and Wilkinson's serene landscape certainly captures this feeling of space and tranquillity to be found in abundance in these Southern Highlands.

LMS — GALLOWAY — THE SOUTHERN HIGHLANDS OF SCOTLAND. BY NORMAN WILKINSON.

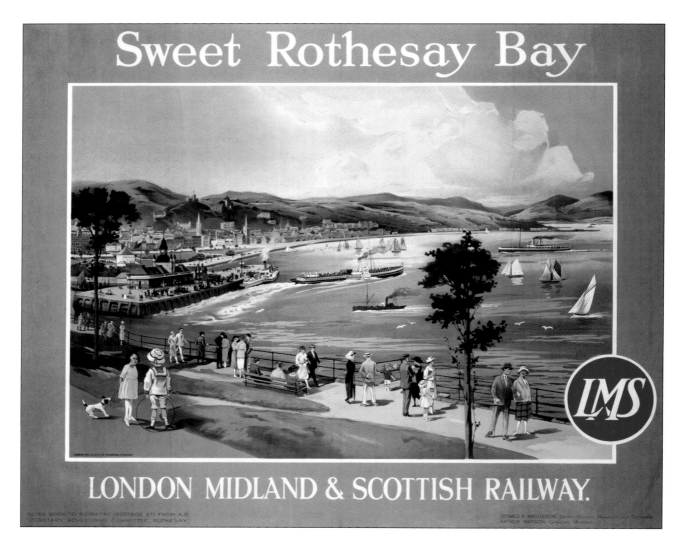

Sweet Rothesay Bay Anonymous, c1923
This style of poster was inherited directly from the Caledonian Railway by the LMS on its formation in 1923. It was only with the appointment of Norman Wilkinson in 1924 that the LMS was to adopt its own distinctive poster style. Rothesay is the principal town on the Isle of Bute and can be reached by ferry from Wemyss Bay, which offers an onward rail link to Glasgow.

Anglesey, by Norman Wilkinson 1923–1939

Anglesey is situated off the North Wales coast near Snowdonia and separated from the mainland by the Menai Strait. It was easily reached by LMS trains as Holyhead was an important port for the company's connecting ferries to Ireland. The tourist to Anglesey could enjoy the very best fishing harbours, bracing sea air on the beaches, rugged coastline, castles and ancient sites. Wilkinson's poster singles out the port of Amlwch for a visit, due to its important place in Welsh industrial history, and in particular its connection to copper mining. Of equal interest is Bull Bay, the most northerly golf course in Wales. This headland golf course offered views of the Isle of Man and the Lake District.

Snowdonia by Charles H Baker, c1933

The area of Snowdonia was designated a National Park in 1955 and the region's name is derived from Snowdon, the highest mountain in Wales. This poster though shows Tryfan, which is one of the more dramatic looking peaks in North Wales. Snowdonia was well served by railways including, of course, the Snowdon Mountain Railway up Snowdon, which opened in 1896 and was based on the best Swiss mountain railway engineering known at the time. The nearest stations by road to Tryfan would have been either Bethesda or Betws-y-Coed, the latter still open on the line to Blaenau Ffestiniog. The landscape painter Charles H Baker's poster successfully captures the breathtaking scenery and peace and solitude to be found in the region in a style very similar to Norman Wilkinson's.

THE PASS OF ABERGLASLYN

by Norman Wilkinson

NORTH WALES

The Pass of Aberglaslyn, North Wales by Norman Wilkinson, 1945 Since Victorian times the village of Beddgelert and the neighbouring Aberglaslyn Pass have both been popular with tourists. From 1923 to 1937 the narrow gauge Welsh Highland Railway ran services from an interchange with LMS services at Dinas through the pass to Portmadoc but by the time this poster was issued at the end of the war there were no longer train services to the village and through the pass. Any LMS passengers wishing to see the area would have arrived via local bus services from Caernarfon. Since 2010 the Welsh Highland Railway has reopened through the pass allowing more tourists to see this beautiful part of North Wales from the comfort of a train.

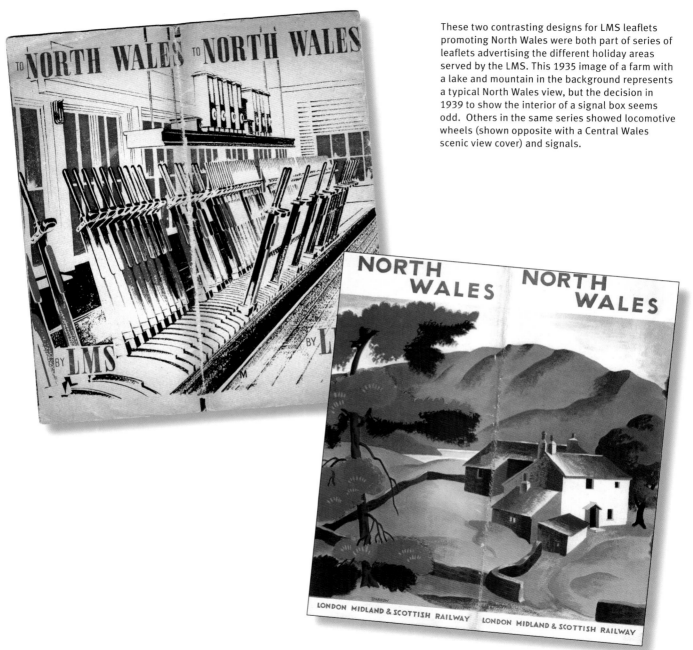

These two contrasting designs for LMS leaflets promoting North Wales were both part of series of leaflets advertising the different holiday areas served by the LMS. This 1935 image of a farm with a lake and mountain in the background represents a typical North Wales view, but the decision in 1939 to show the interior of a signal box seems odd. Others in the same series showed locomotive wheels (shown opposite with a Central Wales scenic view cover) and signals.

Colwyn Bay by George Ayling, c1930s
This colourful poster shows the relatively genteel seaside
resort of Colwyn Bay on the edge of Snowdonia. Linked at one
time to Llandudno both by tram as well as railway, it was well
served by LMS trains from London and the northwest. North
Wales was fortunate in having both rugged mountains as well
as miles of beautiful sandy beaches, and this poster makes
claim to both by depicting a colourful town with its sandy beach
and seaside pier yet describing itself as "The Gateway to the
Welsh Rockies".

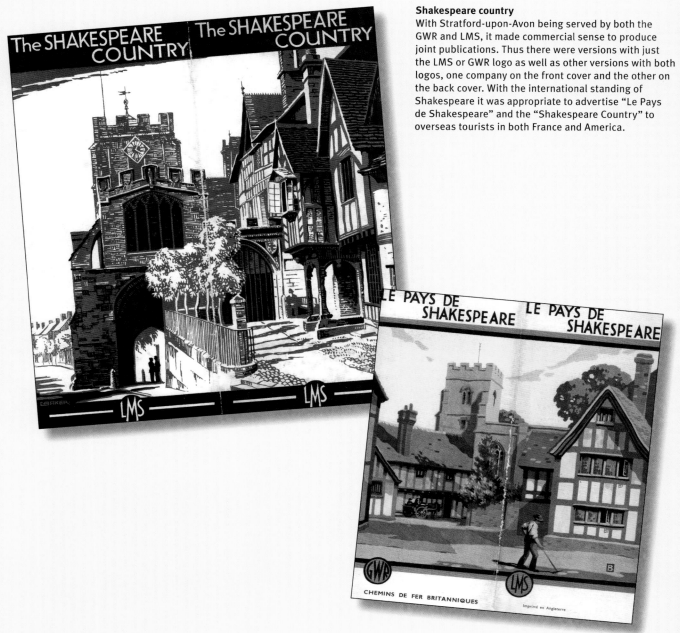

Shakespeare country
With Stratford-upon-Avon being served by both the GWR and LMS, it made commercial sense to produce joint publications. Thus there were versions with just the LMS or GWR logo as well as other versions with both logos, one company on the front cover and the other on the back cover. With the international standing of Shakespeare it was appropriate to advertise "Le Pays de Shakespeare" and the "Shakespeare Country" to overseas tourists in both France and America.

SHAKESPEARE COUNTRY

THE SHAKESPEARE WASHINGTON & FRANKLIN COUNTRIES

LONDON MIDLAND AND SCOTTISH RAILWAY

The leaflet linking Shakespeare with George Washington and Benjamin Franklin was aimed at the American market. These three great figures, it was felt, would appeal to Americans. George Washington's ancestors came from England although he himself never lived here, whilst Franklin, although never a president, was a key founder in the establishment of the United States, and lived for many years in England.

LMS LONDON BY LMS
PICCADILLY CIRCUS BY NIGHT
MAURICE GREIFFENHAGEN, R. A.

London by LMS, Piccadilly Circus by Night by Maurice Greiffenhagen, 1926
The many attractions of central London by night are brought to life and portray Piccadilly Circus as a fashionable destination in this colourful poster. Iconic red London buses, combined with elegantly dressed theatre goers, the London bobby, the flower seller and the paper boy successfully draw the country dweller to the bright lights. The London bus enthusiast will have observed that the 163 bus never served Piccadilly Circus but ran between Upton Park and Creekmouth in 1926.

LONDON: St. James's Palace

By Christopher Clark, R.I.

In 1530, King Henry VIII, tiring of Kennington, built himself a "goodly manor" at St. James's as a country seat. Formerly there had been a religious house there, founded "before the time of man's memory." To-day, St. James's Palace is the official residence of H.R.H. the Prince of Wales, and here, according to ancient practice, the Changing of the King's Guard of His Majesty's Foot Guards, accompanied by one of their magnificent bands, is made at 10.45 a.m. (on Sundays at 9.45 a.m.); though during recent years, when His Majesty is in London, the actual ceremony of Changing the Guard is in the Courtyard of Buckingham Palace and a detachment of the King's Guard is mounted at St. James's Palace.

LMS

E.R.O. 55361

PRINTED IN GREAT BRITAIN BY McCORQUODALE & CO. LIMITED, GLASGOW AND LONDON.

London St James's Palace by Christopher Clark, 1923–1939
Christopher Clark was well connected within the military and became primarily known as a historical painter and illustrator. He was made a member of the Royal Institute in 1905 and was commissioned by the LMS to depict many military and state occasions with posters titled 'British Army Ceremonial' and 'Trooping The Colour'. His effective use of bold strong colours is particularly successful in this image of St James's Palace and conveys a real sense of occasion. This poster was re-issued in a British Railways' version in the 1950s.

LMS SPORT ON THE LMS
YACHTING.
NORMAN WILKINSON.R.I.

Sport on the LMS by Norman Wilkinson, 1924
The LMS issued a series of posters advertising "Sport on the LMS". This busy view of racing yachts was an ideal subject for Norman Wilkinson, who was a noted marine artist. The LMS must have intended this attractive poster to appeal to a much wider public than just those who could afford to participate in the sport as otherwise it would have had a very limited appeal.

GOLF IN NORTHERN IRELAND
THE 8TH GREEN AT PORTRUSH
by
NORMAN WILKINSON, R.I.

LMS

Golf in Northern Ireland – The 8th Green at Portrush by Norman Wilkinson, 1923–1939
The attractions of Northern Ireland provided great inspiration to the LMS poster artists and popular spots such as The Giant's Causeway, 15th century Dunluce Castle, Portstewart and Portrush all featured. The seaside town of Portrush in County Antrim flourished as a holiday resort following the development of the railways in the 19th century. The major part of the old town was built on a mile long peninsula, Ramore Head, which extends into the Atlantic Ocean on the north coast. The town is well known for three sandy beaches – White Rocks, West Strand and East Strand. Royal Portrush Golf Club as featured in Wilkinson's poster is located next to the East Strand. The club was opened in 1888 and became known as Royal Portrush in 1895. The course affords views of Donegal to the west and the Isle of Islay and Southern Hebrides in the north.

 THE DAY BEGINS

The Day Begins by Terence Cuneo, 1946
After the war the LMS, like the other railway companies, needed to rebuild its network before it could start promoting holiday and leisure travel again. Of the posters issued, many concentrated on the behind the scenes work of the railway. This early poster by Cuneo shows the locomotive 'City of Hereford' on a turntable surrounded by engines at the company's Willesden depot in London. Cuneo, who studied at the Chelsea and Slade Art Schools, soon made his name designing railway posters for British Railways.

LMS PASSENGER EXPRESS
THE SYMBOL OF COMFORTABLE TRAVEL
NORMAN WILKINSON, R.I.

Passenger Express by Norman Wilkinson, 1930s
It has been claimed by critics that the LMS pictorial posters advertised the countryside but not specifically travel by rail. This poster does the exact opposite, advertising the means but not the destination. The train and in particular the locomotive dominate the poster, whilst the subtitle reinforces the message that the train is "The symbol of comfortable travel."

YOUR FRIENDS ON THE LMS

Your Friends on the LMS by Septimus E Scott, 1946

Typical of the postwar poster, this one depicts the many vital roles played by staff on the LMS. From the guard to the chef, to the signalman, ticket collector and porter – all but two of these vital roles were undertaken by men. After the Second World War many more of the women who joined the railways remained working for them. This was not the case after the First World War when they were made to leave to make way for the men coming back from the Front to their old jobs.

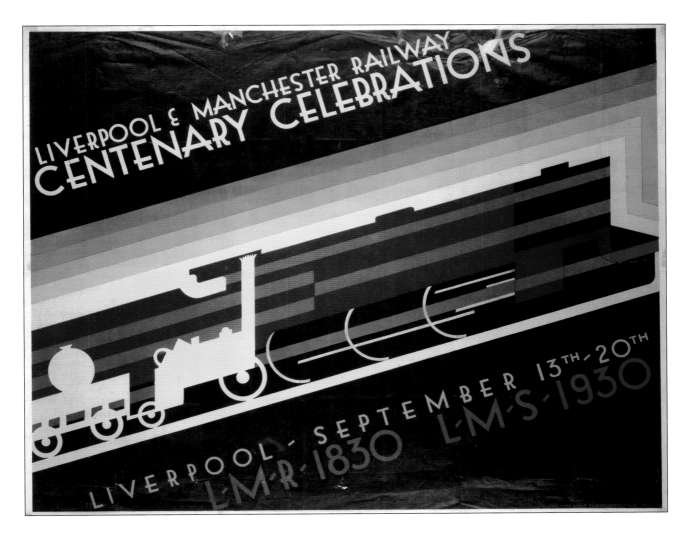

Liverpool & Manchester Railway Centenary Celebrations by P Irwin Brown, 1930
The LMS's centenary celebrations, which were held in Liverpool from 13th to 20th September 1930, included a railway exhibition at St George's Hall, a railway display pageant with fireworks at Wavertree Playground and a banquet in honour of the American Ambassador given by the Lord Mayor of Liverpool, at the Town Hall. This modernist poster by P Irwin Brown not only gives an impression of speed but clearly contrasts the difference in size between the original locomotives and that of the LMS's latest designs.

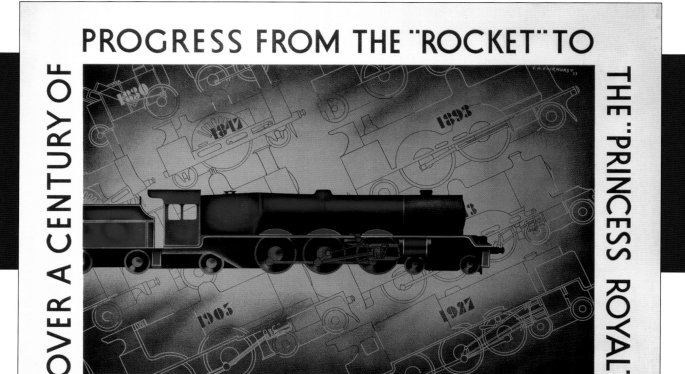

Over a Century of Progress by E H Fairhurst, 1933
This poster, issued just three years after the LMS centenary celebrations, highlighted the technical progress in locomotive design and marks the introduction of the LMS's Princess Royal class of locomotive which was introduced in that year for express passenger services.

LMS **CREWE WORKS**
BUILDING "CORONATION" CLASS ENGINES

Crewe Works by Lili Rethi, 1937
The Crewe Locomotive Works were originally founded in 1840, when the Grand Junction Company bought the Chester & Crewe Railway and large areas of land around the town. For over 150 years around one locomotive a week was produced at Crewe. This poster by the Austrian artist Lili Rethi, depicts workers at Crewe building a 'Coronation' class engine in the foreground while others are seen painting the bodywork of another locomotive in the background. Only five locomotives were streamlined and painted Caledonian Railway blue with silver horizontal lines to match the Coronation Scot train they were designed to pull. Stanier, the designer of the locomotives, believed that the added weight of the streamlining outweighed the advantages gained at high speed.

British Industries – Coal by George Clausen, 1924
Freight accounted for approximately two-thirds of LMS revenue and this may explain why the LMS issued a series of posters in recognition of its important role. The Royal Academicians such as Clausen who were selected to design a poster were given a subject but were then left to interpret it in their own way. Here Clausen has emphasised the importance of the workforce by depicting miners walking home in the centre of his poster, with the railway sidings in the middle ground and the mines themselves in the background.

LMS

BRITISH INDUSTRIES
STEEL
BY RICHARD JACK, R.A.

British Industries – Steel by Richard Jack, 1924
Steel was another heavy industry served by the LMS. In this dramatic image the sky itself above the works seems almost to be alight with red flames. Rather than concentrate on the process taking place inside the works Richard Jack's image shows the works with what could be the main line in the foreground with a solitary locomotive on a siding in the distance.

Rugby School by Norman Wilkinson, 1937

This famous public school is housed in a series of imposing buildings in the middle of the town of Rugby in Warwickshire. The school was founded in 1567 and Wilkinson's dramatic poster features the School Close where in 1823 William Webb ran with the ball and invented the game of rugby football. Old Rugbeians include Prime Minister Neville Chamberlain and authors Lewis Carroll and Salman Rushdie. All of the posters in the LMS Public School series followed the same format with a text panel detailing the history of the school featured. Rugby is one of the oldest independent schools, which was maybe why it was considered worthy of a quad royal format.

RUGBY SCHOOL
by Norman Wilkinson, P.R.I.

Rugby School was founded in 1567 by Lawrence Sheriff of London, a native of Rugby or Brownsover. The School was moved to its present site in 1750, and the buildings shown above date from the beginning of the Nineteenth Century. The view is taken from the School Close, where, as is recorded on the stone tablet shown in the picture, "William Webb Ellis, with a fine disregard for the rules of football as played in his time, first took the ball in his arms and ran with it, thus originating the distinctive feature of the Rugby game, A.D. 1823."

Famous Public Schools on the LMS